The Saturn Game

Volume Three

The Collected Short Works of Poul Anderson

Edited by Rick Katze

NESFA Press

Post Office Box 809
Framingham, MA 01701
www.nesfa.org/press
2010

© 2010 by the Trigonier Trust

"The Eternal Conversation" © 2010 by Tom Easton

"Editor's Introduction" © 2010 by Rick Katze

Dust jacket illustration © 2010 by Bob Eggleton

Dust jacket design © 2010 by Alice N. S. Lewis

ALL RIGHTS RESERVED.
NO PART OF THIS BOOK MAY BE REPRODUCED IN ANY FORM OR BY ANY ELECTRONIC, MAGICAL OR MECHANICAL MEANS, INCLUDING INFORMATION STORAGE AND RETRIEVAL, WITHOUT PERMISSION IN WRITING FROM THE PUBLISHER, EXCEPT BY A REVIEWER, WHO MAY QUOTE BRIEF PASSAGES IN A REVIEW.

FIRST EDITION, July 2010

ISBN-10: 1-886778-89-2
ISBN-13: 978-1-886778-89-4

Publication History

Editor's Introduction is original to this volume.

"The Eternal Conversation" by Tom Easton is original to this volume.

"The Saturn Game" first appeared in *Analog Science Fiction / Science Fact*, February 1981.

"No Truce with Kings" first appeared in *The Magazine of Fantasy & Science Fiction*, June 1963.

"Operation Salamander" first appeared in *The Magazine of Fantasy & Science Fiction*, January 1957.

"Sam Hall" first appeared in *Astounding Science Fiction*, August 1953.

"Robin Hood's Barn" first appeared in *Astounding Science Fiction*, January 1959.

"The Only Game in Town" first appeared in *The Magazine of Fantasy & Science Fiction*, January 1960.

"Supernova" appeared in *Analog Science Fiction / Science Fact*, January 1967.

"Sunjammer" writing as Winston P. Sanders first appeared in *Analog Science Fiction / Science Fact*, April 1964.

"Arsenal Port" first appeared in *The Magazine of Fantasy & Science Fiction*, April 1965.

"Hiding Place" first appeared in *Analog Science Fact–Fiction*, March 1961.

"A Tragedy of Errors" first appeared in first appeared in *Galaxy Science Fiction*, February 1968.

"What'll You Give" by Winston P. Sanders first appeared in *Analog Science Fiction / Science Fact*, April 1963.

"A Sun Invisible" first appeared in *Analog Science Fiction / Science Fact*, April 1966.

"Mustn't Touch" appeared in *Analog Science Fiction / Science Fact*, June 1964.

"Elementary Mistake" writing as Winston P. Sanders first appeared in *Analog Science Fiction / Science Fact*, February 1967.

"Peek, I See You" first appeared in *Analog Science Fiction / Science Fact*, February 1968.

"Eve Times Four" first appeared in *Fantastic Science Fiction Stories*, April 1960.

"Hunter's Moon" first appeared in *Analog Science Fiction / Science Fact*, November 1978.

Untitled Limericks and Songs appeared in *Hombrew*, NESFA Press, February 1976.

Contents

Editor's Introduction 6
The Eternal Conversation by Tom Easton 7
The Saturn Game 10
No Truce with Kings 51
Limerick 95
Operation Salamander 96
Limerick 116
Sam Hall 117
Robin Hood's Barn 141
Limerick 164
The Only Game in Town 165
Untitled Song 187
Supernova 188
Untitled Song 220
Sunjammer 221
Arsenal Port 244
Limerick 289
Hiding Place 290
A Tragedy of Errors 319
What'll You Give? 363
Limerick 381
A Sun Invisible 382
Musn't Touch 408
Elementary Mistake 420
Peek, I see You 432
Limerick 454
Eve Times Four 455
Hunter's Moon 481
Limerick 510
Acknowledgments 511

The Saturn Game

Editor's Introduction

This is volume 3 in a series collecting Poul Anderson's short fiction. When concluded, I expect that there will be between 6 and 8 volumes encompassing about 1.5 million to 2 million words of the approximate 4 million words of short fiction that he wrote during his career.

Some stories are a piece of a larger history. Some are stand-alone. Excepting the first volume which contained the three "Wing Alak" short stories, these volumes are not intended to include complete series. Nor are they published in any internal chronological order. For the most part, except for a few changes in the words used by Poul Anderson in later versions of the stories, I have selected the original magazine version.

The reader will notice that in "Operation Salamander", "Chevvy" is used instead of the usual "Chevy." I checked several sources to verify that this was not a proofreading error. This spelling is used in different editions and in different stories about these characters.

As such, you will find stories of time travel, fantasy, the near future, and the far future.

Manse Everard, David Falkyn, and Nicholas van Rijn are represented. I hope to have a Dominic Flandry story in a later volume.

Poul Anderson was a devoted fan of Sherlock Holmes. Previous volumes had included Sherlockian stories, such as "The Martian Crown Jewels" and "The Queen of Air and Darkness" which used a character with many of the traits of Sherlock Holmes. This volume also contains a Sherlockian story (No, I do not intend to name it) which is far less obvious until the finale.

Sit back, open the book, and read. And enjoy reading stories by a master craftsman who gave us so many good stories.

Rick Katze
Framingham, MA
May 2010

THE ETERNAL CONVERSATION
by Tom Easton

When I was invited to write the introduction to this volume of Poul Anderson's collected short stories, my first thought was, "Why me?" My closest connection to the man was first as a reader and later as a reviewer. But perhaps that is enough, for I read Anderson's stories over the course of many years. He was always one of my favorite writers, not least because I often felt that he was speaking to me almost as if we were facing each other across a table with drinks in our hands. His style, though it could wax poetic as in "The Saturn Game" (1981), was always easy, conversational, and accessible, and it dealt with topics dear to the heart of every science fiction fan. In fact, he introduced us to some of those topics.

Many of the ideas he introduced were later picked up by other writers, but that is no surprise. One of the remarkable things about science fiction is the way its writers are in continuous conversation with each other, their readers, and the general—but especially the science-technology-engineering—culture.

I was reminded of this recently when I saw *Avatar* (which some say closely resembles Poul Anderson's 1957 story, "Call Me Joe"). There have been a great many SF stories in which the driving force behind the plot was the search for and rapacious efforts to obtain some difficult-to-find raw material. Engineers have used the term "unobtainium" (with "handwavium," "buzzwordium," "wishalloy," and others as rough synonyms) to refer to such materials since at least the 1950s, and "unobtainium" has appeared in previous films (e.g., *The Core*, 2003). It has also appeared in a disparaging sense, as a way of saying "Oh, c'mon now! You'd have to make that out of unobtainium!" It has even been trademarked.

So it's a good example of the conversation, where an idea bounces from one realm to another over the years. If we restrict our focus to science fiction alone, the field has long accepted that any writer who comes up with a nifty idea or gizmo will see others use it too. Blasters, anyone? Positronic brains? Warp drives? Hyperspace? Time travel?

The conversation also deals with more abstract topics, as when Tom Godwin's "The Cold Equations" (1954) used the conflict between the laws of physics and sentiment to say that of course the cute stowaway would have to be tossed out the airlock. The basic idea had been used before, but the story was still instantly controversial—we would, after all, prefer to have the universe bow to our wishes—and spawned a number of literary ripostes, including Poul Anderson's "What'll You Give" (1963), which says that sometimes we just have to follow the dictates of sentiment, and doing so may even pay off in a very practical, engineering sort of way.

Anderson's "The Saturn Game" represents another kind of conversation, less between writers than between one writer and his surrounding culture. Precursors of today's massively multiplayer online roleplaying games (MMORPGs) existed at the time, but the general public was more familiar with the term "psychodrama." As the story hints, the precursor games were largely text-based; if a player had an avatar, it was not an on-screen image; it existed in the player's head. Like psychodrama, those games could serve to explore one's own psyche, as well as the psyches of fellow players. Some people claimed that, again like psychodrama, they could be therapeutic. But those games, like today's, could be totally absorbing to the point of distraction.

To Anderson, the game is an aspect of reality, a way of revealing his characters, a way of playing science fiction and fantasy against each other, and a way both of commenting on a fascinating world and—via distraction—of helping to build the crisis at the heart of the story. The conversation also deals with the way people crave to deny harsh realities (compare with "The Cold Equations" and "What'll You Give"). It is thus a multi-leveled and even recursive conversation, and thus intriguingly complex. But Anderson, for all that he wrote "scifi," a genre often vilified as simple-minded, was rarely a simple-minded writer. He could be direct and tightly focused on a single idea, but a great deal of his work rewards careful reading.

At times, sometimes after a couple of drinks, any conversation turns reflective. This happens with SF writers too. A number of renowned members of the clan have, in their later years, chosen to link all the tales they ever wrote, either by creating a connecting thread to tie everything into a single future history or by calling all the tales alternate visions or worlds and creating a bridge to let them mingle.

Poul Anderson takes a third approach to building a capstone for a career in *The Boat of a Million Years* (1990). Very briefly, it is as if he said to himself, "Let's see…I've written about all these ages of the world, in all these styles, about all these types of characters. Men and women, whores and merchants, leaders and followers. Romans and robots. Oxcarts and spaceships. Fantasies and historicals and science fiction. I wonder…Can I find a way to use it all? Not repeating myself, no. A new story, something that needs all I have ever learned to do, something that unifies all the many things I have been concerned with over the years."

Introduction

The result is an astonishing display of virtuosity. Anderson posits that very, very occasionally an immortal is born. Meet Hanno the Phoenician, Rufus the Gaul, Deathless the Amerindian shaman, Aliyat of Syria, Svoboda of the steppes, others. Each draws attention by failing to age and must, to survive, cut and run, time and again, losing homes, loves, wealths. Endlessly, they must adapt and cope in whatever ways they can, though they may find professional niches—prostitute, bureaucrat—that permit both stability and relative invisibility. Yet they are lonely, and they yearn for others like themselves. Occasionally, they meet. Sometimes those meetings produce enduring partnerships, conversations as enduring as the one science fiction conducts with fantasy, history, science, and technology. The tale begins in Phoenician times and ends in the era of space travel and of listening posts that detect the conversations of distant sentients.

The conversation never ends!

Tom Easton
Dedham, MA
April 2010

The Saturn Game

-1-

If we would understand what happened, which is vital if we would avoid repeated and worse tragedies in the future, we must begin by dismissing all accusations. Nobody was negligent; no action was foolish. For who could have predicted the eventuality, or recognized its nature, until too late? Rather should we appreciate the spirit with which those people struggled against disaster, inward and outward, after they knew. The fact is that thresholds exist throughout reality, and that things on their far sides are altogether different from things on their hither sides. The *Chronos* crossed more than an abyss, it crossed a threshold of human experience.

—Francis L. Minamoto,
Death Under Saturn: A Dissenting View
(Apollo University Communications, Leyburg, Luna, 2057)

"The City of Ice is now on my horizon," *Kendrick says. Its towers gleam blue.* "My griffin spreads his wings to glide." *Wind whistles among those great, rainbow-shimmering pinions. His cloak blows back from his shoulders; the air strikes through his ring-mail and sheathes him in cold.* "I lean over and peer after you." *The spear in his left hand counterbalances him. Its head flickers palely with the moonlight that Wayland Smith hammered into the steel.*

"Yes, I see the griffin," *Ricia tells him,* "high and far, like a comet above the courtyard walls. I run out from under the portico for a better look. A guard tries to stop me, grabs my sleeve, but I tear the spider-silk apart and dash forth into the open." *The elven castle wavers as if its sculptured ice were turning to smoke. Passionately, she cries,* "Is it in truth you, my darling?"

"Hold, there!" *warns Alvarlan from his cave of arcana ten thousand leagues away.* "I send your mind the message that if the King suspects this is Sir Kendrick of the Isles, he will raise a dragon against him, or spirit you off beyond any chance of rescue. Go back, Princess of Maranoa. Pretend you decide that it is only an eagle. I will cast a belief-spell on your words."

"I stay far aloft," *Kendrick says.* "Save he use a scrying stone, the Elf King will not be aware this beast has a rider. From here I'll spy out city and castle." *And* then—? He knows not. He knows simply that he must set her free or die in the quest. How long will it take him, how many more nights will she lie in the King's embrace?

"I thought you were supposed to spy out Iapetus," Mark Danzig interrupted.

His dry tone startled the three others into alertness. Jean Broberg flushed with embarrassment, Colin Scobie with irritation; Luis Garcilaso shrugged, grinned, and turned his gaze to the pilot console before which he sat harnessed. For a moment silence filled the cabin, and shadows, and radiance from the universe.

To help observation, all lights were out except a few dim glows at instruments. The sunward ports were lidded. Elsewhere thronged stars, so many and so brilliant that they well-nigh drowned the blackness which held them. The Milky Way was a torrent of silver. One port framed Saturn at half phase, dayside pale gold and rich bands amidst the jewelry of its rings, nightside wanly ashimmer with starlight and moonlight upon clouds, as big to the sight as Earth over Luna.

Forward was Iapetus. The spacecraft rotated while orbiting the moon, to maintain a steady optical field. It had crossed the dawn line, presently at the middle of the inward-facing hemisphere. Thus it had left bare, crater-pocked land behind it in the dark, and was passing above sunlit glacier country. Whiteness dazzled, glittered in sparks and shards of color, reached fantastic shapes heavenward; cirques, crevasses, caverns brimmed with blue.

"I'm sorry," Jean Broberg whispered. "It's too beautiful, unbelievably beautiful, and...almost like the place where our game had brought us—Took us by surprise—"

"Huh!" Mark Danzig said. "You had a pretty good idea of what to expect, therefore you made your play go in the direction of something that resembled it. Don't tell me any different. I've watched these acts for eight years."

Colin Scobie made a savage gesture. Spin and gravity were too slight to give noticeable weight. His movement sent him through the air, across the crowded cabin, until he checked himself by a handhold just short of the chemist. "Are you calling Jean a liar?" he growled.

Most times he was cheerful, in a bluff fashion. Perhaps because of that, he suddenly appeared menacing. He was a big, sandy-haired man in his mid-thirties; a coverall did not disguise the muscles beneath, and the scowl on his face brought forth its ruggedness.

"Please!" Broberg exclaimed. "Not a quarrel, Colin."

The geologist glanced back at her. She was slender and fine-featured. At her age of forty-two, despite longevity treatment, the reddish-brown hair that fell to her shoulders was becoming streaked with white, and lines were engraved around large gray eyes. "Mark is right," she sighed. "We're here to do science, not daydream." She reached forth to touch Scobie's arm, smiled shyly. "You're still full of your Kendrick persona, aren't you? Gallant, protective—" She stopped. Her voice had quickened with more than a hint of Ricia. She covered her lips and flushed again. A tear broke free and sparkled off on air currents. She forced a laugh. "But I'm just physicist Broberg, wife of astronomer Tom, mother of Johnnie and Billy."

Her glance went Saturnward, as if seeking the ship where her family waited. She might have spied it, too, as a star that moved among stars, by the solar sail.

However, that was now furled, and naked vision could not find even such huge hulls as *Chronos* possessed, across millions of kilometers.

Luis Garcilaso asked from his pilot's chair: "What harm if we carry on our little *commedia dell' arte*?" His Arizona drawl soothed the ear. "We won't be landin' for a while yet, and everything's on automatic till then." He was small, swart, deft, still in his twenties.

Danzig twisted the leather of his countenance into a frown. At sixty, thanks to his habits as well as to longevity, he kept springiness in a lank frame; he could joke about wrinkles and encroaching baldness. In this hour, he set humor aside.

"Do you mean you don't know what's the matter?" His beak of a nose pecked at a scanner screen which magnified the moonscape. "Almighty God! That's a new world we're about to touch down on—tiny, but a world, and strange in ways we can't guess. Nothing's been here before us except one unmanned flyby and one unmanned lander that soon quit sending. We can't rely on meters and cameras alone. We've got to use our eyes and brains." He addressed Scobie. "You should realize that in your bones, Colin, if nobody else aboard does. You've worked on Luna as well as Earth. In spite of all the settlements, in spite of all the study that's been done, did you never hit any nasty surprises?"

The burly man had recovered his temper. Into his own voice came a softness that recalled the serenity of the Idaho mountains whence he hailed. "True," he admitted. "There's no such thing as having too much information when you're off Earth, or enough information, for that matter." He paused. "Nevertheless, timidity can be as dangerous as rashness—not that you're timid, Mark," he added in haste. "Why, you and Rachel could've been in a nice O'Neill on a nice pension—"

Danzig relaxed and smiled. "This was a challenge, if I may sound pompous. Just the same, we want to get home when we're finished here. We should be in time for the Bar Mitzvah of a great-grandson or two. Which requires staying alive."

"My point is, if you let yourself get buffaloed, you may end up in a worse bind than—Oh, never mind. You're probably right, and we should not have begun fantasizing. The spectacle sort of grabbed us. It won't happen again."

Yet when Scobie's eyes looked anew on the glacier, they had not quite the dispassion of a scientist in them. Nor did Broberg's or Garcilaso's. Danzig slammed fist into palm. "The game, the damned childish game," he muttered, too low for his companions to hear. "Was nothing saner possible for them?"

-2-

Was nothing saner possible for them? Perhaps not.

If we are to answer the question, we should first review some history. When early industrial operations in space offered the hope of rescuing civilization, and Earth, from ruin, then greater knowledge of sister planets, prior to their development, became a clear necessity. The effort must start with Mars, the least hostile. No natural law forbade sending small manned spacecraft yonder. What did was the absurdity of as much fuel, time, and effort as were required, in order that three or four persons might spend a few days in a single locality.

Construction of the *J. Peter Vajk* took longer and cost more, but paid off when it, virtually a colony, spread its immense solar sail and took a thousand people to their goal in half a year and in comparative comfort. The payoff grew overwhelming when they, from orbit, launched Earthward the beneficiated minerals of Phobos that they did not need for their own purposes. Those purposes, of course, turned on the truly thorough, long-term study of Mars, and included landings of auxiliary craft, for ever lengthier stays, all over the surface.

Sufficient to remind you of this much; no need to detail the triumphs of the same basic concept throughout the inner Solar System, as far as Jupiter. The tragedy of the *Vladimir* became a reason to try again for Mercury...and, in a left-handed, political way, pushed the Britannic-American consortium into its *Chronos* project.

They named the ship better than they knew. Sailing time to Saturn was eight years.

Not only the scientists must be healthy, lively-minded people. Crewfolk, technicians, medics, constables, teachers, clergy, entertainers, every element of an entire community must be. Each must command more than a single skill, for emergency backup, and keep those skills alive by regular, tedious rehearsal. The environment was limited and austere; communication with home was soon a matter of beamcasts; cosmopolitans found themselves in what amounted to an isolated village. What were they to *do*?

Assigned tasks. Civic projects, especially work on improving the interior of the vessel. Research, or writing a book, or the study of a subject, or sports, or hobby clubs, or service and handicraft enterprises, or more private interactions, or—There was a wide choice of television tapes, but Central Control made sets usable for only three hours in twenty-four. You dared not get into the habit of passivity.

Individuals grumbled, squabbled, formed and dissolved cliques, formed and dissolved marriages or less explicit relationships, begot and raised occasional children, worshipped, mocked, learned, yearned, and for the most part found reasonable satisfaction in life. But for some, including a large proportion of the gifted, what made the difference between this and misery was their psychodramas.

—Minamoto

Dawn crept past the ice, out onto the rock. It was a light both dim and harsh, yet sufficient to give Garcilaso the last data he wanted for descent.

The hiss of the motor died away, a thump shivered through the hull, landing jacks leveled it, stillness fell. The crew did not speak for a while. They were staring out at Iapetus.

Immediately around them was desolation like that which reigns in much of the Solar System. A darkling plain curved visibly away to a horizon that, at man-height, was a bare three kilometers distant; higher up in the cabin, you saw farther, but that only sharpened the sense of being on a minute ball awhirl among the stars. The ground was thinly covered with cosmic dust and gravel; here and there a minor crater or an upthrust mass lifted out of the regolith to cast long, knife-edged, utterly black shadows. Light reflections lessened the number of visible stars, turning heaven into a bowlful of night. Halfway between the zenith and the south, half-Saturn and its rings made the vista beautiful.

Likewise did the glacier—or the glaciers? Nobody was sure. The sole knowledge was that, seen from afar, Iapetus gleamed bright at the western end of its orbit and grew dull at the eastern end, because one side was covered with whitish material while the other side was not; the dividing line passed nearly beneath the planet which it eternally faced. The probes from *Chronos* had reported the layer was thick, with puzzling spectra that varied from place to place, and little more about it.

In this hour, four humans gazed across pitted emptiness and saw wonder rear over the world-rim. From north to south went ramparts, battlements, spires, depths, peaks, cliffs, their shapes and shadings an infinity of fantasies. On the right Saturn cast soft amber, but that was nearly lost in the glare from the east, where a sun dwarfed almost to stellar size nonetheless blazed too fierce to look at, just above the summit. There the silvery sheen exploded in brilliance, diamond-glitter of shattered light, chill blues and greens; dazzled to tears, eyes saw the vision glimmer and waver, as if it bordered on dreamland, or on Faerie. But despite all delicate intricacies, underneath was a sense of chill and of brutal mass; here dwelt also the Frost Giants.

Broberg was the first to breathe forth a word. "The City of Ice."

"Magic," said Garcilaso as low. "My spirit could lose itself forever, wanderin' yonder. I'm not sure I'd mind. My cave is nothin' like this, nothin'—"

"Wait a minute!" snapped Danzig in alarm. "Oh, yes. Curb the imagination, please." Though Scobie was quick to utter sobrieties, they sounded drier than needful. "We know from probe transmissions the scarp is, well, Grand Canyon-like. Sure, it's more spectacular than we realized, which I suppose makes it still more of a mystery." He turned to Broberg. "I've never seen ice or snow as sculptured as this. Have you, Jean? You've mentioned visiting a lot of mountain and winter scenery when you were a girl in Canada,"

The physicist shook her head. "No. Never. It doesn't seem possible. What could have done it? There's no weather here…is there?"

"Perhaps the same phenomenon is responsible that laid a hemisphere bare," Danzig suggested.

"Or that covered a hemisphere," Scobie said. "An object seventeen hundred kilometers across shouldn't have gases, frozen or otherwise. Unless it's a ball of such stuff clear through, like a comet. Which we know it's not." As if to demonstrate, he unclipped a pair of pliers from a nearby tool rack, tossed it, and caught it on its slow way down. His own ninety kilos of mass weighed about seven. For that, the satellite must be essentially rocky.

Garcilaso registered impatience. "Let's stop tradin' facts and theories we already know about, and start findin' answers."

Rapture welled in Broberg. "Yes, let's get out. Over *there*."

"Hold on," protested Danzig as Garcilaso and Scobie nodded eagerly. "You can't be serious. Caution, step-by-step advance—"

"No, it's too wonderful for that." Broberg's tone shivered.

"Yeah, to hell with fiddlin' around," Garcilaso said. "We need at least a preliminary scout right away."

The furrows deepened in Danzig's visage. "You mean you too, Luis? But you're our pilot!"

"On the ground I'm general assistant, chief cook, and bottle washer to you scientists. Do you imagine I want to sit idle, with somethin' like that to explore?" Garcilaso calmed his voice. "Besides, if I should come to grief, any of you can fly back, given a bit of radio talk from *Chronos* and a final approach under remote control."

"It's quite reasonable, Mark," Scobie argued. "Contrary to doctrine, true; but doctrine was made for us, not vice versa. A short distance, low gravity, and we'll be on the lookout for hazards. The point is, until we have some notion of what that ice is like, we don't know what the devil to pay attention to in this vicinity, either. No, we'll take a quick jaunt. When we return, then we'll plan."

Danzig stiffened. "May I remind you, if anything goes wrong, help is at least a hundred hours away? An auxiliary like this can't boost any higher if it's to get back, and it'd take longer than that to disengage the big boats from Saturn and Titan."

Scobie reddened at the implied insult. "And may I remind you, on the ground I am the captain? I say an immediate reconnaissance is safe and desirable. Stay behind if you want—In fact, yes, you must. Doctrine is right in saying the vessel mustn't be deserted."

Danzig studied him for several seconds before murmuring, "Luis goes, however, is that it?"

"Yes!" cried Garcilaso so that the cabin rang.

Broberg patted Danzig's limp hand. "It's okay, Mark," she said gently. "We'll bring back samples for you to study. After that, I wouldn't be surprised but what the best ideas about procedure will be yours."

He shook his head. Suddenly he looked very tired. "No," he replied in a monotone, "that won't happen. You see, I'm only a hardnosed industrial chemist who saw this expedition as a chance to do interesting research. The whole way through space, I kept myself busy with ordinary affairs, including, you remember, a couple of inventions I'd wanted leisure to develop. You three, you're younger, you're romantics—"

"Aw, come off it, Mark." Scobie tried to laugh. "Maybe Jean and Luis are, a little, but me, I'm about as other-worldly as a plate of haggis."

"You played the game, year after year, until at last the game started playing you. That's what's going on this minute, no matter how you rationalize your motives." Danzig's gaze on the geologist, who was his friend, lost the defiance that had been in it and turned wistful. "You might try recalling Delia Ames."

Scobie bristled. "What about her? The business was hers and mine, nobody else's."

"Except afterward she cried on Rachel's shoulder, and Rachel doesn't keep secrets from me. Don't worry, I'm not about to blab. Anyhow, Delia got over it. But if you'd recollect objectively, you'd see what had happened to you, already three years ago."

Scobie set his jaw. Danzig smiled in the left corner of his mouth. "No, I suppose you can't," he went on. "I admit I'd no idea either, till now, how far the process had gone. At least keep your fantasies in the background while you're outside, will you? Can you?"

In half a decade of travel, Scobie's apartment had become idiosyncratically his—perhaps more so than was usual, since he remained a bachelor who seldom had women visitors for longer than a few nightwatches at a time. Much of the furniture he had made himself; the agrosections of *Chronos* produced wood, hide, fiber as well as food and fresh air. His handiwork ran to massiveness and archaic carved decorations. Most of what he wanted to read he screened from the data banks, of course, but a shelf held a few old books, Childe's border ballads, an eighteenth-century family Bible (despite his agnosticism), a copy of *The Machinery of Freedom* which had nearly disintegrated but displayed the signature of the author, and other valued miscellany. Above them stood a model of a sailboat in which he had cruised Northern European waters, and a trophy he had won in handball aboard this ship. On the bulkheads hung his fencing sabers and numerous pictures—of parents and siblings, of wilderness areas he had tramped on Earth, of castles and mountains and heaths in Scotland where he had often been too, of his geological team on Luna, of Thomas Jefferson and, imagined, Robert the Bruce.

On a certain evenwatch he had, though, been seated before his telescreen. Lights were turned low in order that he might fully savor the image. Auxiliary craft were out in a joint exercise, and a couple of their personnel used the opportunity to beam back views of what they saw.

That was splendor. Starful space made a chalice for *Chronos*. The two huge, majestically counter-rotating cylinders, the entire complex of linkages, ports, locks, shields, collectors, transmitters, docks, all became Japanesely exquisite at a distance of several hundred kilometers. It was the solar sail which filled most of the screen, like a turning golden sun-wheel; yet remote vision could also appreciate its spiderweb intricacy, soaring and subtle curvatures, even the less-than-gossamer thinness. A mightier work than the Pyramids, a finer work than a refashioned chromosome, the ship moved on toward a Saturn which had become the second brightest beacon in the firmament.

The door chime hauled Scobie out of his exaltation. As he started across the deck, he stubbed his toe on a table leg. Coriolis force caused that. It was slight, when a hull this size spun to give a full gee of weight, and a thing to which he had long since adapted; but now and then he got so interested in something that Terrestrial habits returned. He swore at his absent-mindedness, good-naturedly, since he anticipated a pleasurable time.

When he opened the door, Delia Ames entered in a single stride. At once she closed it behind her and stood braced against it. She was a tall blonde woman who did electronics maintenance and kept up a number of outside activities. "Hey!" Scobie said. "What's wrong? You look like—" he tried for levity— "something my cat wouldn't've dragged in, if we had any mice or beached fish aboard."

She drew a ragged breath. Her Australian accent thickened till he had trouble understanding: "I...today...I happened to be at the same cafeteria table as George Harding—"

Unease tingled through Scobie. Harding worked in Ames' department but had much more in common with him. In the same group to which they both belonged, Harding likewise took a vaguely ancestral role, N'Kuma the Lionslayer. "What happened?" Scobie asked. Woe stared back at him. "He mentioned...you and he and the rest...you'd be taking your next holiday together...to carry on your, your bloody act uninterrupted."

"Well, yes. Work at the new park over in Starboard Hull will be suspended till enough metal's been recycled for the water pipes. The area will be vacant, and my gang has arranged to spend a week's worth of days—"

"But you and I were going to Lake Armstrong!"

"Uh, wait, that was just a notion we talked about, no definite plan yet, and this is such an unusual chance—Later, sweetheart. I'm sorry." He took her hands. They felt cold. He essayed a smile. "Now, c'mon, we were going to cook a festive dinner together and afterward spend a, shall we say, quiet evening at home. But for a start, this absolutely gorgeous presentation on the screen—"

She jerked free of him. The gesture seemed to calm her. "No, thanks," she said, flat-voiced. "Not when you'd rather be with that Broberg woman. I only came by to tell you in person I'm getting out of the way of you two."

"*Huh?*" He stepped back. "What the flaming hell do you mean?"

"You know jolly well."

"I don't! She, I, she's happily married, got two kids, she's older than me, we're friends, sure, but there's never been a thing between us that wasn't in the open and on the level—" Scobie swallowed. "You suppose maybe I'm in love with her?"

Ames looked away. Her fingers writhed together. "I'm not about to go on being a mere convenience to you, Colin. You have plenty of those. Myself, I'd hoped— But I was wrong, and I'm going to cut my losses before they get worse."

"But...Dee, I swear I haven't fallen for anybody else, and I, I swear you're more than a body to me, you're a fine person—" She stood mute and withdrawn. Scobie gnawed his lip before he could tell her: "Okay, I admit it, a main reason

I volunteered for this trip was I'd lost out in a love affair on Earth. Not that the project doesn't interest me, but I've come to realize what a big chunk out of my life it is. You, more than any other woman, Dee, you've gotten me to feel better about the situation."

She grimaced. "But not as much as your psycho-drama has, right?"

"Hey, you must think I'm obsessed with the game. I'm not. It's fun and—oh, maybe 'fun' is too weak a word—but anyhow, it's just little bunches of people getting together fairly regularly to play. Like my fencing, or a chess club, or, or anything."

She squared her shoulders. "Well, then," she asked, "will you cancel the date you've made and spend your holiday with me?"

"I, uh, I can't do that. Not at this stage. Kendrick isn't off on the periphery of current events, he's closely involved with everybody else. If I didn't show, it'd spoil things for the rest."

Her glance steadied upon him. "Very well. A promise is a promise, or so I imagined. But afterward—Don't be afraid. I'm not trying to trap you. That would be no good, would it? However, if I maintain this liaison of ours, will you phase out of your game?"

"I can't—" Anger seized him. "No, God damn it!" he roared.

"Then goodbye, Colin," she said, and departed. He stared for minutes at the door she had shut behind her.

Unlike the large Titan and Saturn-vicinity explorers, landers on the airless moons were simply modified Luna-to-space shuttles, reliable but with limited capabilities. When the blocky shape had dropped below the horizon, Garcilaso said into his radio: "We've lost sight of the boat, Mark. I must say it improves the view." One of the relay micro-satellites which had been sown in orbit passed his words on.

"Better start blazing your trail, then," Danzig reminded. "My, my, you *are* a fussbudget, aren't you?"

Nevertheless Garcilaso unholstered the squirt gun at his hip and splashed a vividly fluorescent circle of paint on the ground. He would do it at eyeball intervals until his party reached the glacier. Except where dust lay thick over the regolith, footprints were faint, under the feeble gravity, and absent when a walker crossed continuous rock.

Walker? No, leaper. The three bounded exultant, little hindered by space suits, life support units, tool and ration packs. The naked land fled from their haste, and even higher, ever more clear and glorious to see, loomed the ice ahead of them.

There was no describing it, not really. You could speak of lower slopes and palisades above, to a mean height of perhaps a hundred meters, with spires towering farther still. You could speak of gracefully curved tiers going up those braes, of lacy parapets and fluted crags and arched openings to caves filled with wonders, of mysterious blues in the depths and greens where light streamed through translucencies, of gem-sparkle across whiteness where radiance and shadow wove mandalas—and none of it would convey anything more than Scobie's earlier, altogether inadequate comparison to the Grand Canyon.

"Stop," he said for the dozenth time. "I want to take a few pictures."

"Will anybody understand them who hasn't been here?" whispered Broberg.

"Probably not," said Garcilaso in the same hushed tone. "Maybe no one but us ever will."

"What do you mean by that?" demanded Danzig's voice.

"Never mind," snapped Scobie.

"I…think…I…know," the chemist said. "Yes, it is a great piece of scenery, but you're letting it hypnotize you."

"If you don't cut out that drivel," Scobie warned, "we'll cut you out of the circuit. Damn it, we've got work to do. Get off our backs."

Danzig gusted a sigh. "Sorry. Uh, are you finding any clues to the nature of that—that thing?"

Scobie focused his camera. "Well," he said, partly mollified, "the different shades and textures, and no doubt the different shapes, seem to confirm what the reflection spectra from the flyby suggested. The composition is a mixture, or a jumble, or both, of several materials, and varies from place to place. Water ice is obvious, but I feel sure of carbon dioxide too, and I'd bet on ammonia, methane, and presumably lesser amounts of other stuff."

"Methane? Could they stay solid at ambient temperature, in a vacuum?"

"We'll have to find out for sure. However, I'd guess that most of the time it's cold enough, at least for methane strata that occur down inside where there's pressure on them."

Within the vitryl globe of her helmet, Broberg's features showed delight. "Wait!" she cried. "I have an idea—about what happened to the probe that landed." She drew breath. "It came down almost at the foot of the glacier, you recall. Our view of the site from space seemed to indicate that an avalanche buried it, but we couldn't understand how that might have been triggered. Well, suppose a methane layer at exactly the wrong location melted. Heat radiation from the jets may have warmed it, and later the radar beam used to map contours added the last few degrees necessary. The stratum flowed, and down came everything that had rested on top of it."

"Plausible," Scobie said. "Congratulations, Jean."

"Nobody thought of the possibility in advance?" Garcilaso scoffed. "What kind of scientists have we got along?"

"The kind who were being overwhelmed by work after we reached Saturn, and still more by data input," Scobie answered. "The universe is bigger than you or anybody can realize, hotshot."

"Oh. Sure. No offense." Garcilaso's glance returned to the ice. "Yes, we'll never run out of mysteries, will we?"

"Never." Broberg's eyes glowed enormous. "At the heart of things will always be magic. The Elf King rules—"

Scobie returned his camera to its pouch. "Stow the gab and move on," he ordered curtly.

His gaze locked for an instant with Broberg's. In the weird, mingled light, it could be seen that she went pale, then red, before she sprang off beside him.

Ricia had gone alone into Moonwood on Midsummer Eve. The King found her there and took her unto him as she had hoped. Ecstasy became terror when he afterward bore her off; yet her captivity in the City of Ice brought her many more such hours, and beauties and marvels unknown among mortals. Alvarlan, her mentor, sent his spirit in quest of her, and was himself beguiled by what he found. It was an effort of will for him to tell Sir Kendrick of the Isles where she was, albeit he pledged his help in freeing her.

N'Kuma the Lionslayer, Bela of Eastmarch, Karina of the Far West, Lady Aurelia, Olav Harp-master had none of them been present when this happened.

The glacier (a wrong name for something that might have no counterpart in the Solar System) lifted off the plain abruptly as a wall. Standing there, the three could no longer see the heights. They could, though, see that the slope which curved steeply upward to a filigree-topped edge was not smooth. Shadows lay blue in countless small craters. The sun had climbed just sufficiently high to beget them; a Iapetan day is more than seventy-nine of Earth's.

Danzig's question crackled in earphones; "Now are you satisfied? Will you come back before a fresh landslide catches you?"

"It won't," Scobie replied. "We aren't a vehicle, and the local configuration has clearly been stable for centuries or better. Besides, what's the point of a manned expedition if nobody investigates anything?"

"I'll see if I can climb," Garcilaso offered.

"No, wait," Scobie commanded. "I've had experience with mountains and snowpacks, for whatever that may be worth. Let me study out a route for us first."

"You're going onto that stuff, the whole gaggle of you?" exploded Danzig. "Have you completely lost your minds?"

Scobie's brow and lips tightened. "Mark, I warn you again, if you don't get your emotions under control we'll cut you off. We'll hike on a ways if I decide it's safe."

He paced, in floating low-weight fashion, back and forth while he surveyed the jökull. Layers and blocks of distinct substances were plain to see, like separate ashlars laid by an elvish mason...where they were not so huge that a giant must have been at work...The craterlets might be sentry posts on this lowest embankment of the City's defenses...

Garcilaso, most vivacious of men, stood motionless and let his vision lose itself in the sight. Broberg knelt down to examine the ground, but her own gaze kept wandering aloft.

Finally she beckoned. "Colin, come over here, please," she said. "I believe I've made a discovery."

Scobie joined her. As she rose, she scooped a handful of fine black particles off the shards on which she stood and let it trickle from her glove. "I suspect this is the reason the boundary of the ice is sharp," she told him.

"What is?" Danzig inquired from afar. He got no answer.

"I noticed more and more dust as we went along," Broberg continued. "If it fell on patches and lumps of frozen stuff, isolated from the main mass, and covered them, it would absorb solar heat till they melted or, likelier, sublimed. Even water molecules would escape to space, in this weak gravity. The main mass was too big for that; square-cube law. Dust grains there would simply melt their way down a short distance, then be covered as surrounding material collapsed on them, and the process would stop."

"H'm." Scobie raised a hand to stroke his chin, encountered his helmet, and sketched a grin at himself. "Sounds reasonable. But where did so much dust come from—and the ice, for that matter?"

"I think—" Her voice dropped until he could barely hear, and her look went the way of Garcilaso's. His remained upon her face, profiled against stars. "I think this bears out your comet hypothesis, Colin. A comet struck Iapetus. It came from the direction it did because of getting so near Saturn that it was forced to swing in a hairpin bend around the planet. It was enormous; the ice of it covered almost a hemisphere, in spite of much more being vaporized and lost. The dust is partly from it, partly generated by the impact."

He clasped her armored shoulder. "*Your* theory. Jean. I was not the first to propose a comet, but you're the first to corroborate with details."

She didn't appear to notice, except that she murmured further: "Dust can account for the erosion that made those lovely formations, too. It caused differential melting and sublimation on the surface, according to the patterns it happened to fall in and the mixes of ices it clung to, until it was washed away or encysted. The craters, these small ones and the major ones we've observed from above, they have a separate but similar origin. Meteorites—"

"Whoa, there," he objected. "Any sizeable meteorite would release enough energy to steam off most of the entire field."

"I know. Which shows the comet collision was recent, less than a thousand years ago, or we wouldn't be seeing this miracle today. Nothing big has since happened to strike, yet. I'm thinking of little stones, cosmic sand, in prograde orbits around Saturn so that they hit with low relative speed. Most simply make dimples in the ice. Lying there, however, they collect solar heat because of being dark, and re-radiate it to melt away their surroundings, till they sink beneath. The concavities they leave reflect incident radiation from side to side, and thus continue to grow. The pothole effect. And again, because the different ices have different properties, you don't get perfectly smooth craters, but those fantastic bowls we saw before we landed."

"By God!" Scobie hugged her. "You're a genius."

Helmet against helmet, she smiled and said, "No. It's obvious, once you've seen for yourself." She was quiet for a bit while still they held each other. "Scientific intuition is a funny thing, I admit," she went on at last. "Considering the problem, I was hardly aware of my logical mind. What I thought was—the City of Ice, made with starstones out of that which a god called down from heaven—"

"Jesus Maria!" Garcilaso spun about to stare at them. Scobie released the woman. "We'll go after confirmation," he said unsteadily. "To the large crater you'll remember we spotted a few klicks inward. The surface appears quite safe to walk on."

"I called that crater the Elf King's Dance Hall," Broberg mused, as if a dream were coming back to her.

"Have a care." Garcilaso's laugh rattled. "Heap big medicine yonder. The King is only an inheritor; it was giants who built these walls, for the gods."

"Well, I've got to find a way in, don't I?" Scobie responded.

"Indeed," *Alvarlan says*. "I cannot guide you from this point. My spirit can only see through mortal eyes. I can but lend you my counsel, until we have neared the gates."

"Are you sleepwalking in that fairytale of yours?" Danzig yelled. "Come back before you get yourselves killed!"

"Will you dry up?" Scobie snarled. "It's nothing but a style of talk we've got between us. If you can't understand that, you've got less use of your brain than we do."

"Listen, won't you? I didn't say you're crazy. You don't have delusions or anything like that. I do say you've steered your fantasies toward this kind of place, and now the reality has reinforced them till you're under a compulsion you don't recognize. Would you go ahead so recklessly anywhere else in the universe? Think!"

"That does it. We'll resume contact after you've had time to improve your manners." Scobie snapped off his main radio switch. The circuits that stayed active served for close-by communication but had no power to reach an orbital relay. His companions did likewise.

The three faced the awesomeness before them. "You can help me find the Princess when we are inside, Alvarlan," *Kendrick says*.

"That I can and will," *the sorcerer vows*.

"I wait for you, most steadfast of my lovers," *Ricia croons*.

Alone in the spacecraft, Danzig well-nigh sobbed, "Oh, damn that game forever!" The sound fell away into emptiness.

-3-

>To condemn psychodrama, even in its enhanced form, would be to condemn human nature.
>
>It begins in childhood. Play is necessary to an immature mammal, a means of learning to handle the body, the perceptions, and the outside world. The young human plays, must play, with its brain too. The more intelligent the child, the more its imagination needs exercise. There are degrees of activity, from the passive watching of a show on a screen, onward through reading, daydreaming, storytelling, and psychodrama... for which the child has no such fancy name.

We cannot give this behavior any single description, for the shape and course it takes depend on endlessly many variables. Sex, age, culture, and companions are only the most obvious. For example, in pre-electronic North America little girls would often play "house" while little boys played "cowboys and Indians" or "cops and robbers," whereas nowadays a mixed group of their descendants might play "dolphins" or "astronauts and aliens." In essence, a small band forms; each individual makes up a character to portray, or borrows one from fiction; simple props may be employed, such as toy weapons, or any chance object such as a stick may be declared something else, such as a metal detector, or a thing may be quite imaginary, as the scenery almost always is. The children then act out a drama which they compose as they go along. When they cannot physically perform a certain action, they describe it. ("I jump real high, like you can do on Mars, an' come out over the edge o' that ol' Valles Marineris, an' take that bandit by surprise.") A large cast of characters, especially villains, frequently comes into existence by fiat.

The most imaginative member of the troupe dominates the game and the evolution of the story line, though in a rather subtle fashion, through offering the most vivid possibilities. The rest, however, are brighter than average; psychodrama in this highly developed form does not appeal to everybody.

For those to whom it does, the effects are beneficial and lifelong. Besides increasing their creativity through use, it lets them try out a play version of different adult roles and experiences. Thereby they begin to acquire insight into adulthood.

Such playacting ends when adolescence commences, if not earlier—but only in that form, and not necessarily forever in it. Grown-ups have many dream-games. This is plain to see in lodges, for example, with their titles, costumes, and ceremonies; but does it not likewise animate all pageantry, every ritual? To what extent are our heroisms, sacrifices, and self-aggrandizements the acting out of personae that we maintain? Some thinkers have attempted to trace this element through every aspect of society.

Here, though, we are concerned with overt psychodrama among adults. In Western civilization it first appeared on a noticeable scale during the middle twentieth century. Psychiatrists found it a powerful diagnostic and therapeutic technique. Among ordinary folk, war and fantasy games, many of which involved identification with imaginary or historical characters, became increasingly popular. In part this was doubtless a retreat from the restrictions and menaces of that unhappy period, but likely in larger part it was a revolt of the mind against the inactive entertainment, notably television, which had come to dominate recreation.

The Chaos ended those activities. Everybody knows about their revival in recent times—for healthier reasons, one hopes. By projecting three-dimensional scenes and appropriate sounds from a data bank—or, better yet, by having a computer produce them to order—players gained a sense of reality that intensified their mental and emotional commitment. Yet in those games that went on for episode after episode, year after real-time year, whenever two or more members of a group could get together to play, they found themselves less and less dependent on such appurtenances. It seemed that, through practice, they had regained the vivid imaginations of their childhoods, and could make anything, or airy nothing itself, into the objects and the worlds they desired.

I have deemed it necessary thus to repeat the obvious in order that we may see it in perspective. The news beamed from Saturn has brought widespread revulsion. (Why? What buried fears have been touched? This is subject matter for potentially important research.) Overnight, adult psychodrama has become unpopular; it may become extinct. That would, in many ways, be a worse tragedy than what has occurred yonder. There is no reason to suppose that the game ever harmed any mentally sound person on Earth; on the contrary. Beyond doubt, it has helped astronauts stay sane and alert on long, difficult missions. If it has no more medical use, that is because psychotherapy has become a branch of applied biochemistry.

And this last fact, the modern world's dearth of experience with madness, is at the root of what happened. Although he could not have foreseen the exact outcome, a twentieth-century psychiatrist might have warned against spending eight years, an unprecedented stretch of time, in as strange an environment as the *Chronos*. Strange it certainly has been, despite all efforts—limited, totally man-controlled, devoid of countless cues for which our evolution on Earth has fashioned us. Extraterrestrial colonists have, thus far, had available to them any number of simulations and compensations, of which close, full contact with home and frequent opportunities to visit there are probably the most significant. Sailing time to Jupiter was long, but half of that to Saturn. Moreover, because they were earlier, scientists in the *Zeus* had much research to occupy them en route, which it would be pointless for later travelers to duplicate; by then, the interplanetary medium between the two giants held few surprises.

Contemporary psychologists were aware of this. They understood that the persons most adversely affected would be the most intelligent, imaginative, and dynamic—those who were supposed to make the very discoveries at Saturn which were the purpose of the undertaking. Being less familiar than their predecessors with the labyrinth that lies, Minotaur-haunted, beneath every human consciousness, the psychologists expected purely benign consequences of whatever psychodramas the crew engendered.

—Minamoto

Assignments to teams had not been made in advance of departure. It was sensible to let professional capabilities reveal themselves and grow on the voyage, while personal relationships did the same. Eventually such factors would help in deciding what individuals should train for what tasks. Long-term participation in a group of players normally forged bonds of friendship that were desirable, if the members were otherwise qualified.

In real life, Scobie always observed strict propriety toward Broberg. She was attractive, but she was monogamous, and he had no wish to alienate her. Besides, he liked her husband. (Tom did not partake of the game. As an astronomer, he had plenty to keep his attention happily engaged.) They had played for a couple of years, their bunch had acquired as many as it could accommodate in a narrative whose milieu and people were becoming complex, before Scobie and Broberg spoke of anything intimate.

By then, the story they enacted was doing so, and maybe it was not altogether by chance that they met when both had several idle hours. This was in the weightless recreation area at the spin axis. They tumbled through aerobatics, shouting and laughing, until they were pleasantly tired, went to the clubhouse, turned in their wingsuits, and showered. They had not seen each other nude before; neither commented, but he did not hide his enjoyment of the sight, while she colored and averted her glance as tactfully as she was able. Afterward, their clothes resumed, they decided on a drink before they went home, and sought the lounge.

Since evenwatch was approaching nightwatch, they had the place to themselves. At the bar, he thumbed a chit for Scotch, she for pinot chardonnay. The machine obliged them and they carried their refreshments out onto the balcony. Seated at a table, they looked across immensity. The clubhouse was built into the support frame on a Lunar gravity level. Above them they saw the sky wherein they had been as birds; its reach did not seem any more hemmed in by far-spaced, spidery girders than it was by a few drifting clouds. Beyond, and straight ahead, decks opposite were a commingling of masses and shapes which the scant illumination at this hour turned into mystery. Among those shadows the humans made out woods, brooks, pools, turned hoar or agleam by the light of stars which filled the skyview strips. Right and left, the hull stretched off beyond sight, a dark in which such lamps as there were appeared lost.

Air was cool, slightly jasmine-scented, drenched with silence. Underneath and throughout, subliminal, throbbed the myriad pulses of the ship.

"Magnificent," Broberg said low, gazing outward. "What a surprise."

"Eh?" asked Scobie.

"I've only been here before in daywatch. I didn't anticipate a simple rotation of the reflectors would make it wonderful."

"Oh, I wouldn't sneer at the daytime view. Mighty impressive."

"Yes, but—but then you see too plainly that everything is manmade, nothing is wild or unknown or free. The sun blots out the stars; it's as though no universe existed beyond this shell we're in. Tonight is like being in Maranoa," the kingdom of which Ricia is Princess, a kingdom of ancient things and ways, wildernesses, enchantments.

"H'm, yeah, sometimes I feel trapped myself," Scobie admitted. "I believed I had a journey's worth of geological data to study, but my project isn't going anywhere very interesting."

"Same for me." Broberg straightened where she sat, turned to him, and smiled a trifle. The dusk softened her features, made them look young. "Not that we're entitled to self-pity. Here we are, safe and comfortable till we reach Saturn. After that we should never lack for excitement, or for material to work with on the way home."

"True." Scobie raised his glass. "Well, skoal. Hope I'm not mispronouncing that."

"How should I know?" she laughed. "My maiden name was Almyer."

"That's right, you've adopted Tom's surname. I wasn't thinking. Though that is rather unusual these days, hey?"

She spread her hands. "My family was well-to-do, but they were—are—Jerusalem Catholics. Strict about certain things; archaistic, you might say." She lifted her wine and sipped. "Oh, yes, I've left the Church, but in several ways the Church will never leave me."

"I see. Not to pry, but, uh, this does account for some traits of yours I couldn't help wondering about."

She regarded him over the rim of her glass. "Like what?"

"Well, you've got a lot of life in you, vigor, sense of fun, but you're also—what's the word?—uncommonly domestic. You've told me you were a quiet faculty member of Yukon University till you married Tom." Scobie grinned. "Since you two kindly invited me to your last anniversary party, and I know your present age, I deduced that you were thirty then." Unmentioned was the likelihood that she had still been a virgin. "Nevertheless—oh, forget it. I said I don't want to pry."

"Go ahead, Colin," she urged. "That line from Burns sticks in my mind, since you introduced me to his poetry. 'To see oursels as others see us!' Since it looks as if we may visit the same moon—"

Scobie took a hefty dollop of Scotch. "Aw, nothing much," he said, unwontedly diffident. "If you must know, well, I have the impression that being in love wasn't the single good reason you had for marrying Tom. He'd already been accepted for this expedition, and given your personal qualifications, that would get you in too. In short, you'd grown tired of routine respectability and here was how you could kick over the traces. Am I right?"

"Yes." Her gaze dwelt on him. "You're more perceptive than I supposed."

"No, not really. A roughneck rockhound. But Ricia's made it plain to see, you're more than a demure wife, mother, and scientist—" She parted her lips. He raised a palm. "No, please, let me finish. I know it's bad manners to claim somebody's persona is a wish fulfillment, and I'm not doing that. Of course you don't want to be a free-roving, free-loving female scamp, any more than I want to ride around cutting down assorted enemies. Still, if you'd been born and raised in the world of our game, I feel sure you'd be a lot like Ricia. And that potential is part of you, Jean." He tossed off his drink. "If I've said too much, please excuse me. Want a refill?"

"I'd better not, but don't let me stop you."

"You won't." He rose and bounded off.

When he returned, he saw that she had been observing him through the vitryl door. As he sat down, she smiled, leaned a bit across the table, and told him softly: "I'm glad you said what you did. Now I can declare what a complicated man Kendrick reveals you to be."

"What?" Scobie asked in honest surprise. "Come on! He's a sword-and-shield tramp, a fellow who likes to travel, same as me; and in my teens I was a brawler, same as him."

"He may lack polish, but he's a chivalrous knight, a compassionate overlord, a knower of sagas and traditions, an appreciator of poetry and music, a bit of a bard...Ricia misses him. When will he get back from his latest quest?"

"I'm bound home this minute. N'Kuma and I gave those pirates the slip and landed at Haverness two days ago. After we buried the swag, he wanted to visit Bela and Karina and join them in whatever they've been up to, so we bade goodbye for the time being." Scobie and Harding had lately taken a few hours to conclude that adventure of theirs. The rest of the group had been mundanely occupied for some while.

Broberg's eyes widened. "From Haverness to the Isles? But I'm in Castle Devaranda, right in between."

"I hoped you'd be."

"I can't wait to hear your story."

"I'm pushing on after dark. The moon is bright and I've got a pair of remounts I bought with a few gold pieces from the loot." *The dust rolls white beneath drumming hoofs. Where a horseshoe strikes a flint pebble, sparks fly ardent. Kendrick scowls.* "You aren't with...what's his name?...Joran the Red? I don't like him."

"I sent him packing a month ago. He got the idea that sharing my bed gave him authority over me. It was never anything but a romp. I stand alone on the Gerfalcon Tower, looking south over moonlit fields, and wonder how you fare. The road flows toward me like a gray river. Do I see a rider come at a gallop, far and far away?"

After many months of play, no image on a screen was necessary. *Pennons on the night wind stream athwart the stars.* "I arrive. I sound my horn to rouse the gatekeepers."

"How I do remember those merry notes—"

That same night, Kendrick and Ricia become lovers. Experienced in the game and careful of its etiquette, Scobie and Broberg uttered no details about the union; they did not touch each other and maintained only fleeting eye contact; the ultimate goodnights were very decorous. After all, this was a story they composed about two fictitious characters in a world that never was.

The lower slopes of the jökull rose in tiers which were themselves deeply concave; the humans walked around their rims and admired the extravagant formations beneath. Names sprang onto lips, the Frost Garden, the Ghost Bridge, the Snow Queen's Throne, *while Kendrick advances into the City, and Ricia awaits him at the Dance Hall, and the spirit of Alvarlan carries word between them so that it is as if already she too travels beside her knight.* Nevertheless they proceeded warily, vigilant for signs of danger, especially whenever a change of texture or hue or anything else in the surface underfoot betokened a change in its nature.

Above the highest ledge reared a cliff too sheer to scale, Iapetan gravity or no, *the fortress wall.* However, from orbit the crew had spied a gouge in the vicinity, forming a pass, doubtless plowed by a small meteorite *in the war between the gods and the magicians, when stones chanted down from the sky wrought havoc so accursed that none dared afterward rebuild.* That was an eerie climb, hemmed in by heights which glimmered in the blue twilight they cast, heaven narrowed to a belt between them where stars seemed to blaze doubly brilliant.

"There must be guards at the opening," *Kendrick says.*

"A single guard," *answers the mind-whisper of Alvarlan,* "but he is a dragon. If you did battle with him, the noise and flame would bring every warrior here upon you. Fear not. I'll slip into his burnin' brain and weave him such a dream that he'll never see you."

"The King might sense the spell," *says Ricia through him.* "Since you'll be parted from us anyway while you ride the soul of that beast, Atvarlan, I'll seek him out and distract him."

Kendrick grimaces, knowing full well what means are hers to do that. She has told him how she longs for freedom and her knight; she has also hinted that elven lovemaking transcends the human. Does she wish for a final time before her rescue?... Well, Ricia and Kendrick have neither plighted nor practiced single troth. Assuredly Colin Scobie had not. He jerked forth a grin and continued through the silence that had fallen on all three.

They came out on top of the glacial mass and looked around them. Scobie whistled. Garcilaso stammered, "J-J-Jesus Christ!" Broberg smote her hands together.

Below them the precipice fell to the ledges, whose sculpturing took on a wholly new, eldritch aspect, gleam and shadow, until it ended at the plain. Seen from here aloft, the curvature of the moon made toes strain downward in boots, as if to cling fast and not be spun off among the stars which surrounded, rather than shone above, its ball. The spacecraft stood minute on dark, pocked stone, like a cenotaph raised to loneliness.

Eastward the ice reached beyond an edge of sight which was much closer. ("Yonder could be the rim of the world," Garcilaso said, *and Ricia replies,* "Yes, the City is nigh to there.") Bowls of different sizes, hillocks, crags, no two of them eroded the same way, turned its otherwise level stretch into a surreal maze. An arabesque openwork ridge which stood at the explorers' goal overtopped the horizon. Everything that was illuminated lay gently aglow. Radiant though the sun was, it cast the light of only, perhaps, five thousand full Lunas upon Earth. Southward, Saturn's great semidisc gave about one-half more Lunar shining; but in that direction, the wilderness sheened pale amber.

Scobie shook himself. "Well, shall we go?" His prosaic question jarred the others; Garcilaso frowned and Broberg winced.

She recovered. "Yes, hasten," *Ricia says.* "I am by myself once more. Are you out of the dragon, Alvaran?"

"Aye," *the wizard informs her.* "Kendrick is safely behind a ruined palace. Tell us how best to reach you."

"You are at the time-gnawed Crown House. Before you lies the Street of the Shieldsmiths—"

Scobie's brows knitted. "It is noonday, when elves do not fare abroad," *Kendrick says remindingly, commandingly.* "I do not wish to encounter any of them. No fights, no complications. We are going to fetch you and escape, without further trouble."

Broberg and Garcilaso showed disappointment, but understood him. A game broke down when a person refused to accept something that a fellow player tried to put in. Often the narrative threads were not mended and picked up for many days. Broberg sighed.

"Follow the street to its end at a forum where a snow fountain springs," *Ricia directs.* "Cross, and continue on Aleph Zain Boulevard, You will know it by a gateway in the form of a skull with open jaws. If anywhere you see a rainbow flicker in the air, stand motionless until it has gone by, for it will be an auroral wolf…"

At a low-gravity lope, the distance took some thirty minutes to cover. In the later part, the three were forced to detour by great banks of an ice so fine-grained that it slid about under their bootsoles and tried to swallow them. Several of these lay at irregular intervals around their destination.

There the travelers stood again for a time in the grip of awe.

The bowl at their feet must reach down almost to bedrock, a hundred meters, and was twice as wide. On this rim lifted the wall they had seen from the cliff, an arc fifty meters long and high, nowhere thicker than five meters, pierced by intricate scrollwork, greenly agleam where it was not translucent. It was the uppermost edge of a stratum which made serrations down the crater. Other outcrops and ravines were more dreamlike yet…was that a unicorn's head, was that a colonnade of caryatids, was that an icicle bower…? The depths were a lake of cold blue shadow.

"You have come, Kendrick, beloved!" *cries Ricia, and casts herself into his arms.*

"Quiet," *warns the sending of Alvarlan the wise.* "Rouse not our immortal enemies."

"Yes, we must get back." Scobie blinked. "Judas priest, what possessed us? Fun is fun, but we sure have come a lot farther and faster than was smart, haven't we?"

"Let us stay for a little while," Broberg pleaded. "This is such a miracle—the Elf King's Dance Hall, which the Lord of the Dance built for him—"

"Remember, if we stay we'll be caught, and your captivity may be forever." Scobie thumbed his main radio switch. "Hello, Mark? Do you read me?"

Neither Broberg nor Garcilaso made that move. They did not hear Danzig's voice: "Oh, yes! I've been hunkered over the set gnawing my knuckles. How are you?"

"All right. We're at the big hole and will be heading back as soon as I've gotten a few pictures."

"They haven't made words to tell how relieved I am. From a scientific standpoint, was it worth the risk?"

Scobie gasped. He stared before him.

"Colin?" Danzig called. "You still there?"

"Yes. Yes."

"I asked what observations of any importance you made."

"I don't know," Scobie mumbled. "I can't remember. None of it after we started climbing seems real."

"Better you return right away," Danzig said grimly. "Forget about photographs."

"Correct." Scobie addressed his companions: "Forward march."

"I can't," *Alvarlan answers*. "A wanderin' spell has caught my spirit in tendrils of smoke."

"I know where a fire dagger is kept," *Ricia says*. "I'll try to steal it."

Broberg moved ahead, as though to descend into the crater. Tiny ice grains trickled over the verge from beneath her boots. She could easily lose her footing and slide down.

"No, wait," *Kendrick shouts to her*. "No need. My spearhead is of moon alloy. It can cut—"

The glacier shuddered. The ridge cracked asunder and fell in shards. The area on which the humans stood split free and toppled into the bowl. An avalanche poured after. High-flung crystals caught sunlight, glittered prismatic in challenge to the stars, descended slowly and lay quiet.

Except for shock waves through solids, everything had happened in the absolute silence of space.

Heartbeat by heartbeat, Scobie crawled back to his senses. He found himself held down, immobilized, in darkness and pain. His armor had saved, was still saving his life; he had been stunned but escaped a real concussion. Yet every breath hurt abominably. A rib or two on the left side seemed broken; a monstrous impact must have dented metal. And he was buried under more weight than he could move.

"Hello," he coughed. "Does anybody read me?" The single reply was the throb of his blood. If his radio still worked—which it should, being built into the suit—the mass around him screened him off.

It also sucked heat at an unknown but appalling rate. He felt no cold because the electrical system drew energy from his fuel cell as fast as needed to keep him warm and to recycle his air chemically. As a normal thing, when he lost heat through the slow process of radiation—and, a trifle, through kerofoam-lined bootsoles—the latter demand was much the greater. Now conduction was at work on every square centimeter. He had a spare unit in the equipment on his back, but no means of getting at it.

Unless—He barked forth a chuckle. Straining, he felt the stuff that entombed him yield the least bit under the pressure of arms and legs. And his helmet rang slightly with noise, a rustle, a gurgle. This wasn't water ice that imprisoned him, but stuff with a much lower freezing point. He was melting it, subliming it, making room for himself.

If he lay passive, he would sink, while frozenness above slid down to keep him in his grave. He might evoke superb new formations, but he would not see them. Instead, he must use the small capability given him to work his way upward, scrabble, get a purchase on matter that was not yet aflow, burrow to the stars.

He began.

Agony soon racked him, breath rasped in and out of lungs aflame, strength drained away and trembling took its place, he could not tell whether he ascended or slipped back. Blind, half suffocated, Scobie made mole-claws of his hands and dug.

It was too much to endure. He fled from it—

His strong enchantments failing, the Elf King brought down his towers of fear in wreck. If the spirit of Alvarlan returned to its body, the wizard would brood upon things he had seen, and understand what they meant, and such knowledge would give mortals a terrible power against Faerie. Waking from sleep, the King scryed Kendrick about to release that fetch. There was no time to do more than break the spell which upheld the Dance Hall. It was largely built of mist and starshine, but enough blocks quarried from the cold side of Ginnungagap were in it that when they crashed they should kill the knight. Ricia would perish too, and in his quicksilver intellect the King regretted that. Nevertheless he spoke the necessary word.

He did not comprehend how much abuse flesh and bone can bear. Sir Kendrick fights his way clear of the ruins, to seek and save his lady. While he does, he heartens himself with thoughts of adventures past and future—

—and suddenly the blindness broke apart and Saturn stood lambent within rings.

Scobie belly-flopped onto the surface and lay shuddering.

He must rise, no matter how his injuries screamed, lest he melt himself a new burial place. He lurched to his feet and glared around.

Little but outcroppings and scars was left of the sculpture. For the most part, the crater had become a smooth-sided whiteness under heaven. Scarcity of shadows made distances hard to gauge, but Scobie guessed the new depth as about seventy-five meters. And empty, empty.

"Mark, do you hear?" he cried.

"That you, Colin?" rang in his earpieces. "Name of mercy, what's happened? I heard you call out, and saw a cloud rise and sink…then nothing for more than an hour. Are you okay?"

"I am, sort of. I don't see Jean or Luis. A landslide took us by surprise and buried us. Hold on while I search."

When he stood upright, Scobie's ribs hurt less. He could move about rather handily if he took care. The two types of standard analgesic in his kit were alike useless, one too weak to give noticeable relief, one so strong that it would turn him sluggish. Casting to and fro, he soon found what he expected, a concavity in the tumbled snowlike material, slightly aboil.

Also a standard part of his gear was a trenching tool. Scobie set pain aside and dug. A helmet appeared. Broberg's head was within it. She too had been tunneling out.

"Jean!"—"Kendrick!" She crept free and they embraced, suit to suit. "Oh, Colin."

"How are you?" rattled from him.

"Alive," she answered. "No serious harm done, I think. A lot to be said for low gravity...You? Luis?" Blood was clotted in a streak beneath her nose, and a bruise on her forehead was turning purple, but she stood firmly and spoke clearly.

"I'm functional. Haven't found Luis yet. Help me look. First, though, we'd better check out our equipment."

She hugged arms around chest, as if that would do any good here. "I'm chilled," she admitted.

Scobie pointed at a telltale. "No wonder. Your fuel cell's down to its last couple of ergs. Mine isn't in a lot better shape. Let's change."

They didn't waste time removing their backpacks, but reached into each other's. Tossing the spent units to the ground, where vapors and holes immediately appeared and then froze, they plugged the fresh ones into their suits. "Turn your thermostat down," Scobie advised. "We won't find shelter soon. Physical activity will help us keep warm."

"And require faster air recycling," Broberg reminded.

"Yeah. But for the moment, at least, we can conserve the energy in the cells. Okay, next let's check for strains, potential leaks, any kind of damage or loss. Hurry. Luis is still down underneath."

Inspection was a routine made automatic by years of drill. While her fingers searched across the man's spacesuit, Broberg let her eyes wander. "The Dance Hall is gone," *Ricia murmurs*. "I think the King smashed it to prevent our escape."

"Me too. If he finds out we're alive, and seeking for Alvarlan's soul—Hey, wait! None of that!"

Danzig's voice quavered. "How're you doing?"

"We're in fair shape, seems like," Scobie replied. "My corselet took a beating but didn't split or anything. Now to find Luis...Jean, suppose you spiral right, I left, across the crater floor."

It took a while, for the seething which marked Garcilaso's burial was minuscule. Scobie started to dig. Broberg watched how he moved, heard how he breathed, and said, "Give me that tool. Just where are you bunged up, anyway?"

He admitted his condition and stepped back. Crusty chunks flew from her toil. She progressed fast, since whatever kind of ice lay at this point was, luckily, friable, and under Iapetan gravity she could cut a hole with almost vertical sides.

"I'll make myself useful," Scobie said, "namely, find us a way out."

When he started up the nearest slope, it shivered. All at once he was borne back in a tide that made rustly noises through his armor, while a fog of dry white motes blinded him. Painfully, he scratched himself free at the bottom and tried elsewhere. In the end he could report to Danzig: "I'm afraid there is no easy route. When the rim collapsed where we stood, it did more than produce a shock which wrecked the delicate formations throughout the crater. It let tons of stuff pour down from the surface—a particular sort of ice that, under local conditions, is like fine sand. The walls are covered by it. Most places, it lies meters deep over more stable material. We'd slide faster than we could climb, where the layer is thin; where it's thick, we'd sink."

Danzig sighed. "I guess I get to take a nice, healthy hike."

"I assume you've called for help."

"Of course. They'll have two boats here in about a hundred hours. The best they can manage. You knew that already."

"Uh-huh. And our fuel cells are good for perhaps fifty hours."

"Oh, well, not to worry about that. I'll bring extras and toss them to you, if you're stuck till the rescue party arrives. M-m-m...maybe I'd better rig a slingshot or something first."

"You might have a problem locating us. This isn't a true crater, it's a glorified pothole, the lip of it flush with the top of the glacier. The landmark we guided ourselves by, that fancy ridge, is gone."

"No big deal. I've got a bearing on you from the directional antenna, remember. A magnetic compass may be no use here, but I can keep myself oriented by the heavens. Saturn scarcely moves in this sky, and the sun and the stars don't move fast."

"Damn! You're right. I wasn't thinking. Got Luis on my mind, if nothing else." Scobie looked across bleakness toward Broberg. Perforce she was taking a short rest, stoop-shouldered above her excavation. His earpieces brought him the harsh sound in her windpipe.

He must maintain what strength was left him, against later need. He sipped from his water nipple, pushed a bite of food through his chow-lock, pretended an appetite. "I may as well try reconstructing what happened," he said. "Okay, Mark, you were right, we got crazy reckless. The game—Eight years was too long to play the game, in an environment that gave us too few reminders of reality. But who could have foreseen it? My God, warn *Chronos*! I happen to know that one of the Titan teams started playing an expedition to the merfolk under the Crimson Ocean—on account of the red mists—deliberately, like us, before they set off..."

Scobie gulped. "Well," he slogged on, "I don't suppose we'll ever know exactly what went wrong here. But plain to see, the configuration was only metastable. On Earth, too, avalanches can be fatally easy to touch off. I'd guess at a methane layer underneath the surface. It turned a little slushy when temperatures rose after dawn, but that didn't matter in low gravity and vacuum...till we came along. Heat, vibration—Anyhow, the stratum slid out from under us, which triggered a general collapse. Does that guess seem reasonable?"

"Yes, to an amateur like me," Danzig said. "I admire how you can stay academic under these circumstances."

"I'm being practical," Scobie retorted. "Luis may need medical attention earlier than those boats can come for him. If so, how do we get him to ours?"

Danzig's voice turned stark. "Any ideas?"

"I'm fumbling my way toward that. Look, the bowl still has the same basic form. The whole shebang didn't cave in. That implies hard material, water ice and actual rock. In fact, I see a few remaining promontories, jutting out above the sandlike stuff. As for what *it* is—maybe an ammonia-carbon dioxide combination, maybe more exotic—that'll be for you to discover later. Right now…my geological instruments should help me trace where the solid masses are least deeply covered. We all carry trenching tools, of course. We can try to shovel a path clear, along a zigzag of least effort. Sure, that may well often bring more garbage slipping down on us from above, but that in turn may expedite our progress. Where the uncovered shelves are too steep or slippery to climb, we can chip footholds. Slow and tough work; and we may run into a bluff higher than we can jump, or something like that."

"I can help," Danzig proposed. "While I waited to hear from you, I inventoried our stock of spare cable, cord, equipment I can cannibalize for wire, clothes and bedding I can cut into strips, whatever might be knotted together to make a rope. We won't need much tensile strength. Well, I estimate I can get about forty meters. According to your description, that's about half the slope length of that trap you're in. If you can climb halfway up while I trek there, I can haul you the rest of the way."

"Thanks," Scobie said, "although—"

"Luis!" shrieked in his helmet. "Colin, come fast, help me, this is dreadful!"

Regardless of pain, except for a curse or two, Scobie sped to Broberg's aid.

Garcilaso was not quite unconscious. In that lay much of the horror. They heard him mumble, "—Hell, the King threw my soul into Hell, I can't find my way out, I'm lost, if only Hell weren't so cold—" They could not see his face; the inside of his helmet was crusted with frost. Deeper and longer buried than the others, badly hurt in addition, he would have died shortly after his fuel cell was exhausted. Broberg had uncovered him barely in time, if that.

Crouched in the shaft she had dug, she rolled him over onto his belly. His limbs flopped about and he babbled, "A demon attacks me, I'm blind here but I feel the wind of its wings," in a blurred monotone. She unplugged the energy unit and tossed it aloft, saying, "We should return this to the ship if we can." Not uncommonly do trivial details serve as crutches.

Above, Scobie gave the object a morbid stare. It didn't even retain the warmth to make a little vapor, like his and hers, but lay quite inert. Its case was a metal box, thirty centimeters by fifteen by six, featureless except for two plug-in prongs on one of the broad sides. Controls built into the spacesuit circuits allowed you to start and stop the chemical reactions within and regulate their rate manually; but as a rule you left that chore to your thermostat and aerostat. Now those reactions had run their course. Until it was recharged, the cell was merely a lump.

Scobie leaned over to watch Broberg, some ten meters below him. She had extracted the reserve unit from Garcilaso's gear, inserted it properly at the small of his back, and secured it by clips on the bottom of his packframe. "Let's have your contribution, Colin," she said. Scobie dropped the meter of heavy-gauge insulated wire which was standard issue on extravehicular missions, in case you needed to make a special electrical connection or a repair. She joined it by Western Union splices to the two she already had, made a loop at the end and, awkwardly reaching over her left shoulder, secured the opposite end by a hitch to the top of her packframe. The triple strand hobbled above her like an antenna.

Stooping, she gathered Garcilaso in her arms. The Iapetan weight of him and his apparatus was under ten kilos, of her and hers about the same. Theoretically she could jump straight out of the hole with her burden. In practice, her spacesuit was too hampering; constant-volume joints allowed considerable freedom of movement, but not as much as bare skin, especially when circum-Saturnian temperatures required extra insulation. Besides, if she could have reached the top, she could not have stayed. Soft ice would have crumbled beneath her fingers and she would have tumbled back down.

"Here goes," she said. "This had better be right the first time, Colin. I don't think Luis can take much jouncing."

"Kendrick, Ricia, where are you?" Garcilaso moaned. "Are you in Hell too?"

Scobie dug heels into the ground near the edge and crouched ready. The loop in the wire rose to view. His right hand grabbed hold. He threw himself backward, lest he slide forward, and felt the mass he had captured slam to a halt. Anguish exploded in his rib cage. Somehow he dragged his burden to safety before he fainted.

He came out of that in a minute. "I'm okay," he rasped at the anxious voices of Broberg and Danzig. "Only lemme rest a while."

The physicist nodded and knelt to minister to the pilot. She stripped his packframe in order that he might lie flat on it, head and legs supported by the packs themselves. That would prevent significant heat loss by convection and cut loss by conduction. Still, his fuel cell would be drained faster than if he were on his feet, and first it had a terrible energy deficit to make up.

"The ice is clearing away inside his helmet," she reported. "Merciful Mary, the blood! Seems to be from the scalp, though; it isn't running any more. His occiput must have been slammed against the vitryl. We ought to wear padded caps in these rigs. Yes, I know accidents like this haven't happened before, but—" She unclipped the flashlight at her waist, stooped, and shone it downward. "His eyes are open. The pupils—yes, a severe concussion, and likely a skull fracture, which may be hemorrhaging into the brain. I'm surprised he isn't vomiting. Did the cold prevent that? Will he start soon? He could choke on his own vomit, in there where nobody can lay a hand on him."

Scobie's pain had subsided to a bearable intensity. He rose, went over to look, whistled, and said, "I judge he's doomed unless we get him to the boat and give him proper care almighty soon. Which isn't possible."

"Oh, Luis." Tears ran silently down Broberg's cheeks.

"You think he can't last till I bring my rope and we carry him back?" Danzig asked.

"'Fraid not," Scobie replied. "I've taken paramedical courses, and in fact I've seen a case like this before. How come you know the symptoms, Jean?"

"I read a lot," she said dully.

"They weep, the dead children weep," Garcilaso muttered.

Danzig sighed. "Okay, then. I'll fly over to you."

"*Huh?*" burst from Scobie, and from Broberg: "Have you also gone insane?"

"No, listen," Danzig said fast. "I'm no skilled pilot, but I have the same basic training in this type of craft that everybody does who might ride in one. It's expendable; the rescue vessels can bring us back. There'd be no significant gain if I landed close to the glacier—I'd still have to make that rope and so forth—and we know from what happened to the probe that there would be a real hazard. Better I make straight for your crater."

"Coming down on a surface that the jets will vaporize out from under you?" Scobie snorted. "I bet Luis would consider that a hairy stunt. You, my friend, would crack up."

"Nu?" They could almost see the shrug. "A crash from low altitude, in this gravity, shouldn't do more than rattle my teeth. The blast will cut a hole clear to bedrock. True, then surrounding ice will collapse in around the hull and trap it. You may need to dig to reach the airlock, though I suspect thermal radiation from the cabin will keep the upper parts of the structure free. Even if the craft topples and strikes sidewise—in which case, it'll sink down into a deflating cushion— even if it did that on bare rock, it shouldn't be seriously damaged. It's designed to withstand heavier impacts." Danzig hesitated. "Of course, could be this would endanger you. I'm confident I won't fry you with the jets, assuming I descend near the middle and you're as far offside as you can get. Maybe, though, maybe I'd cause a…an ice quake that'll kill you. No sense in losing two more lives."

"Or three, Mark," Broberg said low. "In spite of your brave words, you could come to grief yourself."

"Oh, well, I'm an oldish man. I'm fond of living, yes, but you guys have a whole lot more years due you. Look, suppose the worst, suppose I don't just make a messy landing but wreck the boat utterly. Then Luis dies, but he would anyway. You two, however, you should have access to the stores aboard, including those extra fuel cells. I'm willing to run what I consider to be a small risk of my own neck, for the sake of giving Luis a chance at survival."

"Um-m-m," went Scobie, deep in his throat. A hand strayed in search of his chin, while his gaze roved around the glimmer of the bowl.

"I repeat," Danzig proceeded, "if you think this might jeopardize you in any way, we scrub it. No heroics, please. Luis would surely agree, better three people safe and one dead than four stuck with a high probability of death."

"Let me think." Scobie was mute for minutes before he said: "No, I don't believe we'd get in too much trouble here. As I remarked earlier, the vicinity has had its avalanche and must be in a reasonably stable configuration. True, ice will volatilize. In the case of deposits with low boiling points, that could happen explosively and cause tremors. But the vapor will carry heat away so fast that only material in your immediate area should change state. I daresay that the finegrained stuff will get shaken down the slopes, but it's got too low a density to do serious harm; for the most part, it should simply act like a brief snowstorm. The floor will make adjustments, of course, which may be rather violent. However, we can be above it—do you see that shelf of rock over yonder, Jean, at jumping height? It has to be part of a buried hill; solid. That's our place to wait…Okay, Mark, it's go as far as we're concerned. I can't be absolutely certain, but who ever is about anything? It seems like a good bet."

"What are we overlooking?" Broberg wondered. She glanced down to him who lay at her feet. "While we considered all the possibilities, Luis would die. Yes, fly if you want to, Mark, and God bless you."

—But when she and Scobie had brought Garcilaso to the ledge, she gestured from Saturn to Polaris and: "I will sing a spell, I will cast what small magic is mine, in aid of the Dragon Lord, that he may deliver Alvarlan's soul from Hell," *says Ricia.*

-4-

No reasonable person will blame any interplanetary explorer for miscalculations about the actual environment, especially when some decision has to be made, in haste and under stress. Occasional errors are inevitable. If we knew exactly what to expect throughout the Solar System, we would have no reason to explore it.

—Minamoto

The boat lifted. Cosmic dust smoked away from its jets. A hundred and fifty meters aloft, thrust lessened and it stood still on a pillar of fire.

Within the cabin was little noise, a low hiss and a bone-deep but nearly inaudible rumble. Sweat studded Danzig's features, clung glistening to his beard stubble, soaked his coverall and made it reek. He was about to undertake a maneuver as difficult as rendezvous, and without guidance.

Gingerly, he advanced a vernier. A side jet woke. The boat lurched toward a nosedive. Danzig's hands jerked across the console. He must adjust the forces that held his vessel on high and those that pushed it horizontally, to get a resultant that would carry him eastward at a slow, steady pace. The vectors would change instant by instant, as they do when a human walks. The control computer, linked to the sensors, handled much of the balancing act, but not the crucial part. He must tell it what he wanted it to do.

His handling was inexpert. He had realized it would be. More altitude would have given him more margin for error, but deprived him of cues that his eyes found on the terrain beneath and the horizon ahead. Besides, when he reached the glacier he would perforce fly low, to find his goal. He would be too busy for the precise celestial navigation he could have practiced afoot.

Seeking to correct his error, he overcompensated, and the boat pitched in a different direction. He punched for "hold steady" and the computer took over. Motionless again, he took a minute to catch his breath, regain his nerve, rehearse in his mind. Biting his lip, he tried afresh. This time he did not quite approach disaster. Jets aflicker, the boat staggered drunkenly over the moonscape.

The ice cliff loomed nearer and nearer. He saw its fragile loveliness and regretted that he must cut a swathe of ruin. Yet what did any natural wonder mean unless a conscious mind was there to know it? He passed the lowest slope. It vanished in billows of steam.

Onward. Beyond the boiling, right and left and ahead, the Faerie architecture crumbled. He crossed the palisade. Now he was a bare fifty meters above surface, and the clouds reached vengefully close before they disappeared into vacuum. He squinted through the port and made the scanner sweep a magnified overview across its screen, a search for his destination.

A white volcano erupted. The outburst engulfed him. Suddenly he was flying blind. Shocks belled through the hull when upflung stones hit. Frost sheathed the craft; the scanner screen went as blank as the ports. Danzig should have ordered ascent, but he was inexperienced. A human in danger has less of an instinct to jump than to run. He tried to scuttle sideways. Without exterior vision to aid him, he sent the vessel tumbling end over end. By the time he saw his mistake, less than a second, it was too late. He was out of control. The computer might have retrieved the situation after a while, but the glacier was too close. The boat crashed.

"Hello, Mark?" Scobie cried. "Mark, do you read me? Where are you, for Christ's sake?"

Silence replied. He gave Broberg a look which lingered. "Everything seemed to be in order," he said, "till we heard a shout, and a lot of racket, and nothing. He should've reached us by now. Instead, he's run into trouble. I hope it wasn't lethal."

"What can we do?" she asked as redundantly. They needed talk, any talk, for Garcilaso lay beside them and his delirious voice was dwindling fast.

"If we don't get fresh fuel cells within the next forty or fifty hours, we'll be at the end of our particular trail. The boat should be someplace near. We'll have to get out of this hole under our own power, seems like. Wait here with Luis and I'll scratch around for a possible route."

Scobie started downward. Broberg crouched by the pilot.

"—alone forever in the dark—" she heard.

"No, Alvarlan." She embraced him. Most likely he could not feel that, but she could. "Alvarlan, hearken to me. This is Ricia. I hear in my mind how your spirit calls. Let me help, let me lead you back to the light."

"Have a care," advised Scobie. "We're too damn close to rehypnotizing ourselves as is."

"But I might, I just might get through to Luis and...comfort him...Alvarlan, Kendrick and I escaped. He's seeking a way home for us. I'm seeking you. Alvarlan, here is my hand, come take it."

On the crater floor, Scobie shook his head, clicked his tongue, and unlimbered his equipment. Binoculars would help him locate the most promising areas. Devices that ranged from a metal rod to a portable geosonar would give him a more exact idea of what sort of footing lay buried under what depth of unclimbable sand-ice. Admittedly the scope of such probes was very limited. He did not have time to shovel tons of material aside in order that he could mount higher and test further. He would simply have to get some preliminary results, make an educated guess at which path up the side of the bowl would prove negotiable, and trust he was right.

He shut Broberg and Garcilaso out of his consciousness as much as he was able, and commenced work.

An hour later, he was ignoring pain while clearing a strip across a layer of rock. He thought a berg of good, hard frozen water lay ahead, but wanted to make sure.

"Jean! Colin! Do you read?"

Scobie straightened and stood rigid. Dimly he heard Broberg: "If I can't do anything else, Alvarlan, let me pray for your soul's repose."

"Mark!" ripped from Scobie. "You okay? What the hell happened?"

"Yeah, I wasn't too badly knocked around," Danzig said, "and the boat's habitable, though I'm afraid it'll never fly again. How are you? Luis?"

"Sinking fast. All right, let's hear the news."

Danzig described his misfortune. "I wobbled off in an unknown direction for an unknown distance. It can't have been extremely far, since the time was short before I hit. Evidently I plowed into a large, um, snowbank, which softened the impact but blocked radio transmission. It's evaporated from the cabin area now. I see tumbled whiteness around, and formations in the offing...I'm not sure what damage the jacks and the stern jets suffered. The boat's on its side at about a forty-five degree angle, presumably with rock beneath. But the after part is still buried in less whiffable stuff—water and CO_2 ices, I think—that's reached temperature equilibrium. The jets must be clogged with it. If I tried to blast, I'd destroy the whole works."

Scobie nodded. "You would, for sure."

Danzig's voice broke. "Oh, God, Colin! What have I done? I wanted to help Luis, but I may have killed you and Jean."

Scobie's lips tightened. "Let's not start crying before we're hurt. True, this has been quite a run of bad luck. But neither you nor I nor anybody could have known that you'd touch off a bomb underneath yourself."

"What was it? Have you any notion? Nothing of the sort ever occurred at rendezvous with a comet. And you believe the glacier is a wrecked comet, don't you?"

"Uh-huh, except that conditions have obviously modified it. The impact produced heat, shock, turbulence. Molecules got scrambled. Plasmas must have been momentarily present. Mixtures, compounds, clathrates, alloys—stuff formed that never existed in free space. We can learn a lot of chemistry here."

"That's why I came along... Well, then, I crossed a deposit of some substance or substances that the jets caused to sublime with tremendous force. A certain kind of vapor refroze when it encountered the hull. I had to defrost the ports from inside after the snow had cooked off them."

"Where are you in relation to us?"

"I told you, I don't know. And I'm not sure I can determine it. The crash crumpled the direction-finding antenna. Let me go outside for a better look."

"Do that," Scobie said. "I'll keep busy meanwhile."

He did, until a ghastly rattling noise and Broberg's wail brought him at full speed back to the rock.

Scobie switched off Garcilaso's fuel cell. "This may make the difference that carries us through," he said low. "Think of it as a gift. Thanks, Luis."

Broberg let go of the pilot and rose from her knees. She straightened the limbs that had threshed about in the death struggle and crossed his hands on his breast. There was nothing she could do about the fallen jaw or the eyes that glared at heaven. Taking him out of his suit, here, would have worsened his appearance. Nor could she wipe tears off her own face. She could merely try to stop their flow. "Goodbye, Luis," she whispered.

Turning to Scobie, she asked, "Can you give me a new job? Please."

"Come along," he directed. "I'll explain what I have in mind about making our way to the surface."

They were midway across the bowl when Danzig called. He had not let his comrade's dying slow his efforts, nor said much while it happened. Once, most softly, he had offered Kaddish.

"No luck," he reported like a machine. "I've traversed the largest circle I could while keeping the boat in sight, and found only weird, frozen shapes. I can't be a huge distance from you, or I'd see an identifiably different sky, on this miserable little ball. You're probably within a twenty or thirty kilometer radius of me. But that covers a bunch of territory."

"Right," Scobie said. "Chances are you can't find us in the time we've got. Return to the boat."

"Hey, wait," Danzig protested. "I can spiral onward, marking my trail. I might come across you."

"It'll be more useful if you return," Scobie told him. "Assuming we climb out, we should be able to hike to you, but we'll need a beacon. What occurs to me is the ice itself. A small energy release, if it's concentrated, should release a large plume of methane or something similarly volatile. The gas will cool as it expands, recondense around dust particles that have been carried along—it'll steam—and the cloud ought to get high enough, before it evaporates again, to be visible from here."

"Gotcha!" A tinge of excitement livened Danzig's words. "I'll go straight to it. Make tests, find a spot where I can get the showiest result, and...how about I rig a thermite bomb?...No, that might be too hot. Well, I'll develop a gadget."

"Keep us posted."

"But I, I don't think we'll care to chatter idly," Broberg ventured.

"No, we'll be working our tails off, you and I," Scobie agreed.

"Uh, wait," said Danzig. "What if you find you can't get clear to the top? You implied that's a distinct possibility."

"Well, then it'll be time for more radical procedures, whatever they turn out to be," Scobie responded. "Frankly, at this moment my head is too full of...of Luis, and of choosing an optimum escape route...for much thought about anything else."

"M-m, yeah, I guess we've got an ample supply of trouble without borrowing more. Tell you what, though. After my beacon's ready to fire off, I'll make that rope we talked of. You might find you prefer having it to clean clothes and sheets when you arrive." Danzig was silent for seconds before he ended: "God damn it, you *will* arrive."

Scobie chose a point on the north side for his and Broberg's attempt. Two rock shelves jutted forth, near the floor and several meters higher, indicating that stone reached at least that far. Beyond, in a staggered pattern, were similar outcrops of hard ices. Between them, and onward from the uppermost, which was scarcely more than halfway to the rim, was nothing but the featureless, footingless slope of powder crystals. Its angle of repose gave a steepness that made the surface doubly treacherous. The question, unanswerable save by experience, was how deeply it covered layers on which humans could climb, and whether such layers extended the entire distance aloft.

At the spot, Scobie signaled a halt. "Take it easy, Jean," he said. "I'll go ahead and commence digging."

"Why don't we together? I have my own tool, you know."

"Because I can't tell how so large a bank of that pseudo-quicksand will behave. It might react to the disturbance by a gigantic slide."

She bridled. Her haggard countenance registered mutiny. "Why not me first, then? Do you suppose I always wait passive for Kendrick to save me?"

"As a matter of fact," he rapped, "I'll bargain because my rib is giving me billy hell, which is eating away what strength I've got left. If we run into trouble, you can better come to my help than I to yours."

Broberg bent her neck. "Oh. I'm sorry. I must be in a fairly bad state myself, if I let false pride interfere with our business." Her look went toward Saturn, around which *Chronos* orbited, bearing her husband and children.

"You're forgiven." Scobie bunched his legs and sprang the five meters to the lower ledge. The next one was slightly too far for such a jump, when he had no room for a running start.

Stooping, he scraped his trenching tool against the bottom of the declivity that sparkled before him, and shoveled. Grains poured from above, a billionfold, to cover what he cleared. He worked like a robot possessed. Each spadeful was nearly weightless, but the number of spadefuls was nearly endless. He did not bring the entire bowlside down on himself as he had half feared, half hoped. (If that didn't kill him, it would save a lot of toil.) A dry torrent went right and left over his ankles. Yet at last somewhat more of the underlying rock began to show.

From beneath, Broberg listened to him breathe. It sounded rough, often broken by a gasp or a curse. In his spacesuit, in the raw, wan sunshine, he resembled a knight who, in despite of wounds, did battle against a monster.

"All right," he called at last. "I think I've learned what to expect and how we should operate. It'll take the two of us."

"Yes...oh, yes, my Kendrick."

The hours passed. Ever so slowly, the sun climbed and the stars wheeled and Saturn waned.

Most places, the humans labored side by side. They did not require more than the narrowest of lanes—but unless they cut it wide to begin with, the banks to right and left would promptly slip down and bury it. Sometimes the conformation underneath allowed a single person at a time to work. Then the other could rest. Soon it was Scobie who must oftenest take advantage of that. Sometimes they both stopped briefly, for food and drink and reclining on their packs.

Rock yielded to water ice. Where this rose very sharply, the couple knew it, because the sand-ice that they undercut would come down in a mass. After the first such incident, when they were nearly swept away, Scobie always drove his geologist's hammer into each new stratum. At any sign of danger, he would seize its handle and Broberg would cast an arm around his waist. Their other hands clutched their trenching tools. Anchored, but forced to strain every muscle, they would stand while the flood poured around them, knee-high, once even chest-high, seeking to bury them irretrievably deep in its quasi-fluid substance. Afterward they would confront a bare stretch. It was generally too steep to climb unaided, and they chipped footholds.

Weariness was another tide to which they dared not yield. At best, their progress was dismayingly slow. They needed little heat input to keep warm, except when they took a rest, but their lungs put a furious demand on air recyclers. Garcilaso's fuel cell, which they had brought along, could give a single person extra hours of life, though depleted as it was after coping with his hypothermia, the time would be insufficient for rescue by the teams from *Chronos*. Unspoken was the idea of taking turns with it. That would put them in wretched shape, chilled and stifling, but at least they would leave the universe together.

Thus it was hardly a surprise that their minds fled from pain, soreness, exhaustion, stench, despair. Without that respite, they could not have gone on as long as they did.

At ease for a few minutes, their backs against a blue-shimmering parapet which they must scale, they gazed across the bowl, where Garcilaso's suited body gleamed like a remote pyre, and up the curve opposite to Saturn. The planet shone lambent amber, softly banded, the rings a coronet which a shadow band across their arc seemed to make all the brighter. That radiance overcame sight of most nearby stars, but elsewhere they arrayed themselves multitudinous, in splendor, around the silver road which the galaxy clove between them.

"How right a tomb for Alvarlan," *Ricia says in a dreamer's murmur.*

"Has he died, then?" *Kendrick asks.*

"You do not know?"

"I have been too busied. After we won free of the ruins and I left you to recover while I went scouting, I encountered a troop of warriors. I escaped, but must needs return to you by devious, hidden ways." *Kendrick strokes Ricia's sunny hair.* "Besides, dearest dear, it has ever been you, not I, who had the gift of hearing spirits."

"Brave darling...Yes, it is a glory to me that I was able to call his soul out of Hell. It sought his body, but that was old and frail and could not survive the knowledge it now had. Yet Alvarlan passed peacefully, and before he did, for his last magic he made himself a tomb from whose ceiling starlight will eternally shine."

"May he sleep well. But for us there is no sleep. Not yet. We have far to travel."

"Aye. But already we have left the wreckage behind. Look! Everywhere around in this meadow, anemones peep through the grass. A lark sings above."

"These lands are not always calm. We may well have more adventures ahead of us. But we shall meet them with high hearts."

Kendrick and Ricia rise to continue their journey.

Cramped on a meager ledge, Scobie and Broberg shoveled for an hour without broadening it much. The sand-ice slid from above as fast as they could cast it down. "We'd better quit this as a bad job," the man finally decided. "The best we've done is flatten the slope ahead of us a tiny bit. No telling how far inward the shelf goes before there's a solid layer on top. Maybe there isn't any."

"What shall we do instead?" Broberg asked in the same worn tone.

He jerked a thumb. "Scramble back to the level beneath and try a different direction. But first we absolutely require a break."

They spread kerofoam pads and sat. After a while during which they merely stared, stunned by fatigue, Broberg spoke.

"I go to the brook," *Ricia relates.* "It chimes under arches of green boughs. Light falls between them to sparkle on it. I kneel and drink. The water is cold, pure, sweet. When I raise my eyes, I see the figure of a young woman, naked, her tresses the color of leaves. A wood nymph. She smiles."

"Yes, I see her too," *Kendrick joins in.* "I approach carefully, not to frighten her off. She asks our names and errands. We explain that we are lost. She tells us how to find an oracle which may give us counsel."

They depart to find it.

Flesh could no longer stave off sleep. "Give us a yell in an hour, will you, Mark?" Scobie requested.

"Sure," Danzig said, "but will that be enough?"

"It's the most we can afford, after the setbacks we've had. We've come less than a third of the way."

"If I haven't talked to you," Danzig said slowly, "it's not because I've been hard at work, though I have been. It's that I figured you two were having a plenty bad time without me nagging you. However—Do you think it's wise to fantasize the way you have been?"

A flush crept across Broberg's cheeks and down toward her bosom. "You listened, Mark?"

"Well, yes, of course. You might have an urgent word for me at any minute—"

"Why? What could you do? A game is a personal affair."

"Uh, yes, yes—"

Ricia and Kendrick have made love whenever they can. The accounts were never explicit, but the words were often passionate.

"We'll keep you tuned in when we need you, like for an alarm clock," Broberg clipped. "Otherwise we'll cut the circuit."

"But—Look, I never meant to—"

"I know," Scobie sighed. "You're a nice guy and I daresay we're overreacting. Still, that's the way it's got to be. Call us when I told you."

Deep within the grotto, the Pythoness sways on her throne, in the ebb and flow of her oracular dream. As nearly as Ricia and Kendrick can understand what she chants, she tells them to fare westward on the Stag Path until they met a one-eyed graybeard who will give them further guidance; but they must be wary in his presence, for he is easily angered. They make obeisance and depart. On their way out, they pass the offering they brought. Since they have little with them other than garments and his weapons, the Princess gave the shrine her golden hair. The knight insists that, close-cropped, she remains beautiful.

"Hey, whoops, we've cleared us an easy twenty meters!" Scobie said, albeit in a voice which weariness had hammered flat. *At first the journey, through the land of Narce, is a delight.*

His oath afterward had no more life in it. "Another blind alley, seems like." *The old man in the blue cloak and wide-brimmed hat was indeed wrathful when Ricia refused him her favors and Kendrick's spear struck his own aside. Cunningly, he has pretended to make peace and told them what road they should take next. But at the end of it are trolls. The wayfarers elude them and double back.*

"My brain's stumbling around in a swamp, a fog," Scobie groaned. "My busted rib isn't exactly helping, either. If I don't get another nap I'll keep on making misjudgments till we run out of time."

"By all means, Colin," Broberg said. "I'll stand watch and rouse you in an hour."

"What?" he asked in dim surprise. "Why not join me and have Mark call us as he did before?"

She grimaced. "No need to bother him. I'm tired, yes, but not sleepy."

He lacked wit or strength to argue. "Okay," he said, stretched his insulating pad on the ice, and toppled out of awareness.

Broberg settled herself next to him. They were halfway to the heights, but they had been struggling, with occasional breaks, for worse than twenty hours, and progress grew more hard and tricky even as they themselves grew more weak and stupefied. If ever they reached the top and spied Danzig's signal, they would have something like a couple of hours' stiff travel to shelter.

Saturn, sun, stars shone through vitryl. Broberg smiled down at Scobie's face. He was no Greek god, and sweat, grime, unshavenness, the manifold marks of exhaustion were upon him, but—For that matter, she was scarcely an image of glamour herself.

Princess Ricia sits by her knight, where he slumbers in the dwarf's cottage, and strums a harp the dwarf lent her before he went off to his mine, and sings a lullaby to sweeten the dreams of Kendrick. When it is done, she passes her lips lightly across his, and drifts into the same gentle sleep.

Scobie woke a piece at a time. "Ricia, beloved," *Kendrick whispers, and feels after her. He will summon her up with kisses—*

He scrambled to his feet. "Judas priest!" She lay unmoving. He heard her breath in his earplugs, before the roaring of his pulse drowned it. The sun glared farther aloft, he could see it had moved, and Saturn's crescent had thinned more, forming sharp horns at its ends. He forced his eyes toward the watch on his left wrist.

"Ten hours," he choked.

He knelt and shook his companion. "Come, for Christ's sake!" Her lashes fluttered. When she saw the horror on his visage, drowsiness fled from her.

"Oh, no," she said. "Please, no."

Scobie climbed stiffly erect and flicked his main radio switch. "Mark, do you receive?"

"Colin!" Danzig chattered. "Thank God! I was going out of my head from worry."

"You're not off that hook, my friend. We just finished a ten hour snooze."

"What? How far did you get first?"

"To about forty meters' elevation. The going looks tougher ahead than in back. I'm afraid we won't make it."

"Don't say that, Colin," Danzig begged.

"My fault," Broberg declared. She stood rigid, fists doubled, features a mask. Her tone was steady. "He was worn out, had to have a nap. I offered to wake him, but fell asleep myself."

"Not your fault, Jean," Scobie began.

She interrupted: "Yes. Mine. Perhaps I can make it good. Take my fuel cell. I'll still have deprived you of my help, of course, but you might survive and reach the boat anyway."

He seized her hands. They did not unclench. "If you imagine I, I could do that—"

"If you don't, we're both finished," she said unbendingly. "I'd rather go out with a clear conscience."

"And what about my conscience?" he shouted. Checking himself, he wet his lips and said fast: "Besides, you're not to blame. Sleep slugged you. If I'd been thinking, I'd have realized it was bound to do so, and contacted Mark. The fact that you didn't either shows how far gone you were yourself. And…you've got Tom and the kids waiting for you. Take my cell." He paused. "And my blessing."

"Shall Ricia forsake her true knight?"

"Wait, hold on, listen," Danzig called. "Look, this is terrible, but—oh, hell, excuse me, but I've got to remind you that dramatics only clutter the action. From what descriptions you've sent, I don't see how either of you can possibly proceed solo. Together, you might yet. At least you're rested—sore in the muscles, no doubt, but clearer in the head. The climb before you may prove easier than you think. Try!"

Scobie and Broberg regarded each other for a whole minute. A thawing went through her, and warmed him. Finally they smiled and embraced. "Yeah, right," he growled. "We're off. But first a bite to eat. I'm plain, old-fashioned hungry. Aren't you?" She nodded.

"That's the spirit," Danzig encouraged them. "Uh, may I make another suggestion? I am just a spectator, which is pretty hellish but does give me an overall view. Drop that game of yours."

Scobie and Broberg tautened.

"It's the real culprit," Danzig pleaded. "Weariness alone wouldn't have clouded your judgment. You'd never have cut me off, and—But weariness and shock and grief did lower your defenses to the point where the damned game took you over. You weren't yourselves when you fell asleep. You were those dream-world characters. They had no reason not to cork off!"

Broberg shook her head violently. "Mark," said Scobie, "you are correct about being a spectator. That means there are some things you don't understand. Why subject you to the torture of listening in, hour after hour? We'll call you back from time to time, naturally. Take care." He broke the circuit.

"He's wrong," Broberg insisted.

Scobie shrugged. "Right or wrong, what difference? We won't pass out again in the time we have left. The game didn't handicap us as we traveled. In fact, it helped, by making the situation feel less gruesome."

"Aye. Let us break our fast and set forth anew on our pilgrimage."

The struggle grew stiffer. "Belike the White Witch has cast a spell on this road," *says Ricia*.

"She shall not daunt us," *vows Kendrick*.

"No, never while we fare side by side, you and I, noblest of men."

A slide overcame them and swept them back a dozen meters. They lodged against a crag. After the flow had passed by, they lifted their bruised bodies and limped in search of a different approach. The place where the geologist's hammer remained was no longer accessible.

"*What shattered the bridge?*" *asks Ricia.*

"*A giant,*" *answers Kendrick.* "*I saw him as I fell into the river. He lunged at me, and we fought in the shallows until he fled. He bore away my sword in his thigh.*"

"*You have your spear that Wayland forged,*" *Ricia says,* "*and always you have my heart.*"

They stopped on the last small outcrop they uncovered. It proved to be not a shelf but a pinnacle of water ice. Around it glittered sand-ice, again quiescent. Ahead was a slope thirty meters in length, and then the rim, and stars. The distance might as well have been thirty light-years. Whoever tried to cross would immediately sink to an unknown depth.

There was no point in crawling back down the bared side of the pinnacle. Broberg had clung to it for an hour while she chipped niches to climb by with her knife. Scobie's condition had not allowed him to help. If they sought to return, they could easily slip, fall, and be engulfed. If they avoided that, they would never find a new path. Less than two hours' worth of energy abode in their fuel cells. Attempting to push onward while swapping Garcilaso's back and forth would be an exercise in futility.

They settled themselves, legs dangling over the abyss, and held hands and looked at Saturn and at one another.

"*I do not think the orcs can burst the iron door of this tower,*" *Kendrick says,* "*but they will besiege us until we starve to death.*"

"*You never yielded up your hope erenow, my knight.*" *replies Ricia, and kisses his temple.* "*Shall we search about? These walls are unutterably ancient. Who knows what relics of wizardry lie forgotten within? A pair of phoenix-feather cloaks, that will bear us laughing through the sky to our home—?*"

"*I fear not, my darling. Our weird is upon us.*" *Kendrick touches the spear that leans agleam against the battlement.* "*Sad and gray will the world be without you. We can but meet our doom bravely.*"

"*Happily, since we are together.*" *Ricia's gamin smile breaks forth.* "*I did notice that a certain room holds a bed. Shall we try it?*"

Kendrick frowns. "*Rather should we seek to set our minds and souls in order.*"

She tugs his elbow. "*Later, yes. Besides—who knows?—when we dust off the blanket, we may find it is a Tarnkappe that will take us invisible through the enemy.*"

"*You dream.*"

Fear stirs behind her eyes. "*What if I do?*" *Her words tremble.* "*I can dream us free if you will help.*"

Scobie's fist smote the ice. "No!" he croaked. "I'll die in the world that is."

Ricia shrinks from him. He sees terror invade her. "You, you rave, beloved," *she stammers.*

He twisted about and caught her by the arms. "Don't you want to remember Tom and your boys?"

"Who—?"

Kendrick slumps. "I don't know. I have forgotten too."

She leans against him, there on the windy height. A hawk circles above. "The residuum of an evil enchantment, surely. Oh, my heart, my life, cast it from you! Help me find the means to save us." *Yet her entreaty is uneven, and through it speaks dread.*

Kendrick straightens. He lays hand on Wayland's spear, and it is though strength flows thence, into him. "A spell in truth," *he says. His tone gathers force.* "I will not abide in its darkness, nor suffer it to blind and deafen you, my lady in domnei." *His gaze takes hold of hers, which cannot break away.* "There is but a single road to our freedom. It goes through the gates of death."

She waits, mute and shuddering.

"Whatever we do, we must die, Ricia. Let us fare hence as our own folk."

"I—no—I won't—I will—"

"You see before you the means of your deliverance. It is sharp, I am strong, you will feel no pain."

She bares her bosom. "Then quickly, Kendrick, before I am lost!"

He drives the weapon home. "I love you," *he says. She sinks at his feet.* "I follow you, my darling," *he says, withdraws the steel, braces shaft against stone, lunges forward, falls beside her.* "Now we are free."

"That was…a nightmare." Broberg sounded barely awake.

Scobie's voice shook. "Necessary, I think, for both of us." He gazed straight before him, letting Saturn fill his eyes with dazzle. "Else we'd have stayed…insane? Maybe not, by definition. But we'd not have been in reality either."

"It would have been easier," she mumbled.

"We'd never have known we were dying."

"Would you have preferred that?"

Broberg shivered. The slackness in her countenance gave place to the same tension that was in his. "Oh, no," she said, quite softly but in the manner of full consciousness. "No, you were right, of course. Thank you for your courage."

"You've always had as much guts as anybody, Jean. You just have more imagination than me." Scobie's hand chopped empty space, a gesture of dismissal. "Okay, we should call poor Mark and let him know. But first—" His words lost the cadence he had laid on them. "First—"

Her glove clasped his. "What, Colin?"

"Let's decide about that third unit, Luis's," he said with difficulty, still confronting the great ringed planet. "Your decision, actually, though we can discuss the matter if you want. I will not hog it for the sake of a few more hours. Nor will I share it; that would be a nasty way for us both to go out. However, I suggest you use it."

"To sit beside your frozen corpse?" she replied. "No. I wouldn't even feel the warmth, not in my bones—"

She turned toward him so fast that she nearly fell off the pinnacle. He caught her. *"Warmth!"* she screamed, shrill as the cry of a hawk on the wing. "Colin, we'll take our bones home!"

"In point of fact," said Danzig, "I've climbed onto the hull. That's high enough for me to see over those ridges and needles. I've got a view of the entire horizon."

"Good," grunted Scobie. "Be prepared to survey a complete circle quick. This depends on a lot of factors we can't predict. The beacon will certainly not be anything like as big as what you had arranged. It may be thin and short-lived. And, of course, it may rise too low for sighting at your distance." He cleared his throat. "In that case, we two have bought the farm. But we'll have made a hell of a try, which feels great by itself."

He hefted the fuel cell, Garcilaso's gift. A piece of heavy wire, insulation stripped off, joined the prongs. Without a regulator, the unit poured its maximum power through the short circuit. Already the strand glowed.

"Are you sure you don't want me to do it, Colin?" Broberg asked. "Your rib—" He made a lopsided grin. "I'm nonetheless better designed by nature for throwing things," he said. "Allow me that much male arrogance. The bright idea was yours."

"It should have been obvious from the first," she said. "I think it would have been, if we weren't bewildered in our dream."

"M-m, often the simple answers are the hardest to find. Besides, we had to get this far or it wouldn't have worked, and the game helped mightily...Are you set, Mark? Heave ho!"

Scobie cast the cell as if it were a baseball, hard and far through the Iapetan gravity field. Spinning, its incandescent wire wove a sorcerous web across vision. It landed somewhere beyond the rim, on the glacier's back.

Frozen gases vaporized, whirled aloft, briefly recondensed before they were lost. A geyser stood white against the stars.

"I see you! Danzig yelped. "I see your beacon, I've got my bearing, I'll be on my way! With rope and extra energy units and everything!"

Scobie sagged to the ground and clutched at his left side. Broberg knelt and held him, as if either of them could lay hand on his pain. No large matter. He would not hurt much longer.

"How high would you guess the plume goes?" Danzig inquired, calmer.

"About a hundred meters," Broberg replied after study.

"Uh, damn, these gloves do make it awkward punching the calculator...Well, to judge by what I observe of it, I'm between ten and fifteen klicks off. Give me an hour or a tad more to get there and find your exact location. Okay?"

Broberg checked gauges. "Yes, by a hair. We'll turn our thermostats down and sit very quiet to reduce oxygen demand. We'll get cold, but we'll survive."

"I may be quicker," Danzig said. "That was a worst case estimate. All right, I'm off. No more conversation till we meet. I won't take any foolish chances, but I will need my wind for making speed."

Faintly, those who waited heard him breathe, heard his hastening footfalls. The geyser died.

They sat, arms around waists, and regarded the glory which encompassed them. After a silence, the man said: "Well, I suppose this means the end of the game. For everybody."

"It must certainly be brought under strict control," the woman answered. "I wonder, though, if they will abandon it altogether—out here."

"If they must, they can."

"Yes. We did, you and I, didn't we?"

They turned face to face, beneath that star-beswarmed, Saturn-ruled sky. Nothing tempered the sunlight that revealed them to each other, she a middle-aged wife, he a man ordinary except for his aloneness. They would never play again. They could not.

A puzzled compassion was in her smile. "Dear Friend—" she began.

His uplifted palm warded her from further speech. "Best we don't talk unless it's essential," he said. "That'll save a little oxygen, and we can stay a little warmer. Shall we try if we can sleep?"

Her eyes widened and darkened. "I dare not," she confessed. "Not till enough time has gone past. Now, I might dream."

No Truce With Kings

"Song, Charlie! Give's a song!"

"Yay, Charlie!"

The whole mess was drunk, and the junior officers at the far end of the table were only somewhat noisier than their seniors near the colonel. Rugs and hangings could not much muffle the racket, shouts, stamping boots, thump of fists on oak and clash of cups raised aloft, that rang from wall to stony wall. High up among shadows that hid the rafters they hung from, the regimental banners stirred in a draft, as if to join the chaos. Below, the light of bracketed lanterns and bellowing fireplace winked on trophies and weapons.

Autumn comes early on Echo Summit, and it was storming outside, wind-hoot past the watchtowers and rain-rush in the courtyards, an undertone that walked through the buildings and down all corridors, as if the story were true that the unit's dead came out of the cemetery each September Nineteenth night and tried to join the celebration but had forgotten how. No one let it bother him, here or in the enlisted barracks, except maybe the hex major. The Third Division, the Catamounts, was known as the most riotous gang in the Army of the Pacific States of America, and of its regiments the Rolling Stones who held Fort Nakamura were the wildest.

"Go on, boy! Lead off. You've got the closest thing to a voice in the whole goddamn Sierra," Colonel Mackenzie called. He loosened the collar of his black dress tunic and lounged back, legs asprawl, pipe in one hand and beaker of whisky in the other: a thickset man with blue wrinkle-meshed eyes in a battered face, his cropped hair turned gray but his mustache still arrogantly red.

"Charlie is my darlin', my darlin', my darlin'," sang Captain Hulse. He stopped as the noise abated a little. Young Lieutenant Amadeo got up, grinned, and launched into one they well knew.

> *I am a Catamountain, I guard a border pass.*
> *And every time I venture out, the cold will freeze m—*

"Colonel, sir. Begging your pardon."

Mackenzie twisted around and looked into the face of Sergeant Irwin. The man's expression shocked him. "Yes?"

I am a bloody hero, a decorated vet:
The Order of the Purple Shaft, with pineapple clusters yet!

"Message just come in, sir. Major Speyer asks to see you right away."

Speyer, who didn't like being drunk, had volunteered for duty tonight; otherwise men drew lots for it on a holiday. Remembering the last word from San Francisco, Mackenzie grew chill.

The mess bawled forth the chorus, not noticing when the colonel knocked out his pipe and rose.

The guns go boom! Hey, tiddley boom!
The rockets vroom, the arrows zoom.
From slug to slug is damn small room.
Get me out of here and back to the good old womb!
(Hey, doodle dee day!)

All right-thinking Catamounts maintained that they could operate better with the booze sloshing up to their eardrums than any other outfit cold sober. Mackenzie ignored the tingle in his veins; forgot it. He walked a straight line to the door, automatically taking his sidearm off the rack as he passed by. The song pursued him into the hall.

For maggots in the rations, we hardly ever lack.
You bite into a sandwich and the sandwich bites right back.
The coffee is the finest grade of Sacramento mud.
The ketchup's good in combat, though, for simulating blood.
(Cho-orus!)
  The drums go bump! Ah-tumpty-tump!
  The bugles make like Gabri'l's trump—

Lanterns were far apart in the passage. Portraits of former commanders watched the colonel and the sergeant from eyes that were hidden in grotesque darknesses. Footfalls clattered too loudly here.

I've got an arrow in my rump.
Right about and rearward, heroes, on the jump!
(Hey, doodle dee day!)

Mackenzie went between a pair of fieldpieces flanking a stairway—they had been captured at Rock Springs during the Wyoming War, a generation ago—and upward. There was more distance between places in this keep than his legs liked at their present age. But it was old, had been added to decade by decade; and it needed to be massive, chiseled and mortared from Sierra granite, for it guarded a key to the nation. More than one army had broken against its revetments, before the Nevada marches were pacified, and more young men than Mackenzie wished to think about had gone from this base to die among angry strangers.

But she's never been attacked from the west. God, or whatever you are, you can spare her that, can't you?

The command office was lonesome at this hour. The room where Sergeant Irwin had his desk lay so silent: no clerks pushing pens, no messengers going in or out, no wives making a splash of color with their dresses as they waited to see the colonel about some problem down in the Village. When he opened the door to the inner room, though, Mackenzie heard the wind shriek around the angle of the wall. Rain slashed at the black windowpane and ran down in streams which the lanterns turned molten.

"Here the colonel is, sir," Irwin said in an uneven voice. He gulped and closed the door behind Mackenzie.

Speyer stood by the commander's desk. It was a beat-up old object with little upon it: an inkwell, a letter basket, an interphone, a photograph of Nora, faded in these dozen years since her death. The major was a tall and gaunt man, hooknosed, going bald on top. His uniform always looked unpressed, somehow. But he had the sharpest brain in the Cats, Mackenzie thought; and Christ, how could any man read as many books as Phil did! Officially he was the adjutant, in practice the chief adviser.

"Well?" Mackenzie said. The alcohol did not seem to numb him, rather make him too acutely aware of things: how the lanterns smelled hot (when would they get a big enough generator to run electric lights?), and the floor was hard under his feet, and a crack went through the plaster of the north wall, and the stove wasn't driving out much of the chill. He forced bravado, stuck thumbs in belt and rocked back on his heels. "Well, Phil, what's wrong now?"

"Wire from Frisco," Speyer said. He had been folding and unfolding a piece of paper, which he handed over.

"Huh? Why not a radio call?"

"Telegram's less likely to be intercepted. This one's in code, at that. Irwin decoded it for me."

"What the hell kind of nonsense is this?"

"Have a look, Jimbo, and you'll find out. It's for you, anyway. Direct from GHQ."

Mackenzie focused on Irwin's scrawl. The usual formalities of an order; then:

> *You are hereby notified that the Pacific States Senate has passed a bill of impeachment against Owen Brodsky, formerly Judge of the Pacific States of America, and deprived him of office. As of 2000 hours this date, former Vice Humphrey Fallon is Judge of the PSA in accordance with the Law of Succession. The existence of dissident elements constituting a public danger has made it necessary for Judge Fallon to put the entire nation under martial*

law, effective at 2100 hours this date. You are therefore issued the following instructions:

1. The above intelligence is to be held strictly confidential until an official proclamation is made. No person who has received knowledge in the course of transmitting this message shall divulge same to any other person whatsoever. Violators of this section and anyone thereby receiving information shall be placed immediately in solitary confinement to await court-martial.

2. You will sequestrate all arms and ammunition except for ten percent of available stock, and keep same under heavy guard.

3. You will keep all men in the Fort Nakamura area until you are relieved. Your relief is Colonel Simon Hollis, who will start from San Francisco tomorrow morning with one battalion. They are expected to arrive at Fort Nakamura in five days, at which time you will surrender your command to him. Colonel Hollis will designate those officers and enlisted men who are to be replaced by members of his battalion, which will be integrated into the regiment. You will lead the men replaced back to San Francisco and report to Brigadier General Mendoza at New Fort Baker. To avoid provocations, these men will be disarmed except for officers' sidearms.

4. For your private information, Captain Thomas Danielis has been appointed senior aide to Colonel Hollis.

5. You are again reminded that the Pacific States of America are under martial law because of a national emergency. Complete loyalty to the legal government is required. Any mutinous talk must be severely punished. Anyone giving aid or comfort to the Brodsky faction is guilty of treason and will be dealt with accordingly.

Gerald O'Donnell, Gen. APSA, CINC

Thunder went off in the mountains like artillery. It was a while before Mackenzie stirred, and then merely to lay the paper on his desk. He could only summon feeling slowly, up into a hollowness that filled his skin.

"They dared," Speyer said without tone. "They really did."

"Huh?" Mackenzie swiveled eyes around to the major's face. Speyer didn't meet that stare. He was concentrating his own gaze on his hands, which were now rolling a cigarette. But the words jerked from him, harsh and quick:

"I can guess what happened. The warhawks have been hollering for impeachment ever since Brodsky compromised the border dispute with West Canada. And Fallon, yeah, he's got ambitions of his own. But his partisans are a minority and he knows it. Electing him Vice helped soothe the warhawks some, but he'd never make Judge the regular way, because Brodsky isn't going to die of old age before Fallon does, and anyhow more than fifty percent of the Senate are sober, satisfied bossmen who don't agree that the PSA has a divine mandate to reunify the continent. I don't see how an impeachment could get through an honestly convened Senate. More likely they'd vote out Fallon."

"But a Senate had been called," Mackenzie said. The words sounded to him like someone else talking. "The newscasts told us."

"Sure. Called for yesterday 'to debate ratification of the treaty with West Canada.' But the bossmen are scattered up and down the country, each at his own Station. They have to *get* to San Francisco. A couple of arranged delays—hell, if a bridge just happened to be blown on the Boise railroad, a round dozen of Brodsky's staunchest supporters wouldn't arrive on time—so the Senate has a quorum, all right, but every one of Fallon's supporters are there, and so many of the rest are missing that the warhawks have a clear majority. Then they meet on a holiday, when no cityman is paying attention. Presto, impeachment and a new Judge!" Speyer finished his cigarette and stuck it between his lips while he fumbled for a match. A muscle twitched in his jaw.

"You sure?" Mackenzie mumbled. He thought dimly that this moment was like one time he'd visited Puget City and been invited for a sail on the Guardian's yacht, and a fog had closed in. Everything was cold and blind, with nothing you could catch in your hands.

"Of course I'm not sure!" Speyer snarled. "Nobody will be sure till it's too late." The matchbox shook in his grasp.

"They, uh, they got a new Cinc too, I noticed."

"Uh-huh. They'd want to replace everybody they can't trust, as fast as possible, and De Barros was a Brodsky appointee." The match flared with a hellish *scrit*. Speyer inhaled till his cheeks collapsed. "You and me included, naturally. The regiment reduced to minimum armament so that nobody will get ideas about resistance when the new colonel arrives. You'll note he's coming with a battalion at his heels just the same, just in case. Otherwise he could take a plane and be here tomorrow."

"Why not a train?" Mackenzie caught a whiff of smoke and felt for his pipe. The bowl was hot in his tunic pocket.

"Probably all rolling stock has to head north. Get troops among the boss men there to forestall a revolt. The valleys are safe enough, peaceful ranchers and Esper colonies. None of them'll pot-shot Fallonite soldiers marching to garrison Echo and Donner outposts." A dreadful scorn weighted Speyer's words.

"What are we going to do?"

"I assume Fallon's take-over followed legal forms; that there was a quorum," Speyer said. "Nobody will ever agree whether it was really Constitutional...I've been reading this damned message over and over since Irwin decoded it. There's a lot between the lines. I think Brodsky's at large, for instance. If he were under arrest this would've said as much, and there'd have been less worry about rebellion. Maybe some of his household troops smuggled him away in time. He'll be hunted like a jackrabbit, of course."

Mackenzie took out his pipe but forgot he had done so. "Tom's coming with our replacements," he said thinly.

"Yeah. Your son-in-law. That was a smart touch, wasn't it? A kind of hostage for your good behavior, but also a backhand promise that you and yours won't suffer if you report in as ordered. Tom's a good kid. He'll stand by his own."

"This is his regiment too," Mackenzie said. He squared his shoulders. "He wanted to fight West Canada, sure. Young and...and a lot of Pacificans did get killed in the Idaho Panhandle during the skirmishes. Women and kids among 'em."

"Well," Speyer said, "you're the colonel, Jimbo. What should we do?"

"Oh, Jesus, I don't know. I'm nothing but a soldier." The pipestem broke in Mackenzie's fingers. "But we're not some bossman's personal militia here. We swore to support the Constitution."

"*I* can't see where Brodsky's yielding some of our claims in Idaho is grounds for impeachment. I think he was right."

"Well—"

"A *coup d'état* by any other name would stink as bad. You may not be much of a student of current events, Jimbo, but you know as well as I do what Fallon's Judgeship will mean. War with West Canada is almost the least of it. Fallon also stands for a strong central government. He'll find ways to grind down the old bossman families. A lot of their heads and scions will die in the front lines; that stunt goes back to David and Uriah. Others will be accused of collusion with the Brodsky people—not altogether falsely—and impoverished by fines. Esper communities will get nice big land grants, so their economic competition can bankrupt still other estates. Later wars will keep bossmen away for years at a time, unable to supervise their own affairs, which will therefore go to the devil. And thus we march toward the glorious goal of Reunification."

"If Esper Central favors him, what can we do? I've heard enough about psi blasts. I can't ask my men to face them."

"You could ask your men to face the Hellbomb itself, Jimbo, and they would. A Mackenzie has commanded the Rolling Stones for over fifty years."

"Yes. I thought Tom, someday—"

"We've watched this brewing for a long time. Remember the talk we had about it last week?"

"Uh-huh."

"I might also remind you that the Constitution was written explicitly 'to confirm the separate regions in their ancient liberties.'"

"Let me alone!" Mackenzie shouted. "I don't know what's right or wrong, I tell you! Let me alone!"

Speyer fell silent, watching him through a screen of foul smoke. Mackenzie walked back and forth a while, boots slamming the floor like drumbeats. Finally he threw the broken pipe across the room so it shattered.

"Okay." He must ram each word past the tension in his throat. "Irwin's a good man who can keep his lip buttoned. Send him out to cut the telegraph line a few miles downhill. Make it look as if the storm did it. The wire breaks often enough, heaven knows. Officially, then, we never got GHQ's message. That gives us a few days to contact Sierra Command HQ. I won't go against General Cruikshank…but I'm pretty sure which way he'll go if he sees a chance. Tomorrow we prepare for action. It'll be no trick to throw back Hollis' battalion, and they'll need a while to bring some real strength against us. Before then the first snow should be along, and we'll be shut off for the winter. Only we can use skis and snowshoes, ourselves, to keep in touch with the other units and organize something. By spring—we'll see what happens."

"Thanks, Jimbo." The wind almost drowned Speyer's words. "I'd...I'd better go tell Laura."

"Yeah." Speyer squeezed Mackenzie's shoulder. There were tears in the major's eyes.

Mackenzie went out with parade-ground steps, ignoring Irwin: down the hall, down a stairway at its other end, past guarded doors where he returned salutes without really noticing, and so to his own quarters in the south wing.

His daughter had gone to sleep already. He took a lantern off its hook in his bleak little parlor, and entered her room. She had come back here while her husband was in San Francisco.

For a moment Mackenzie couldn't quite remember why he had sent Tom there. He passed a hand over his stubbly scalp, as if to squeeze something out... oh, yes, ostensibly to arrange for a new issue of uniforms; actually to get the boy out of the way until the political crisis had blown over. Tom was too honest for his own good, an admirer of Fallon and the Esper movement. His outspokenness had led to friction with his brother officers. They were mostly of bossman stock or from well-to-do protectee families. The existing social order had been good to them. But Tom Danielis began as a fisher lad in a poverty-stricken village on the Mendocino coast. In spare moments he'd learned the three R's from a local Esper; once literate, he joined the Army and earned a commission by sheer guts and brains. He had never forgotten that the Espers helped the poor and that Fallon promised to help the Espers...Then, too, battle, glory, Reunification, Federal Democracy, those were heady dreams when you were young.

Laura's room was little changed since she left it to get married last year. And she had only been seventeen then. Objects survived which had belonged to a small person with pigtails and starched frocks—a teddy bear loved to shapelessness, a doll house her father had built, her mother's picture drawn by a corporal who stopped a bullet at Salt Lake. Oh, God, how much she had come to look like her mother.

Dark hair streamed over a pillow turned gold by the light. Mackenzie shook her as gently as he was able. She awoke instantly, and he saw the terror within her.

"Dad! Anything about Tom?"

"He's okay." Mackenzie set the lantern on the floor and himself on the edge of the bed. Her fingers were cold where they caught at his hand.

"He isn't," she said. "I know you too well."

"He's not been hurt yet. I hope he won't be." Mackenzie braced himself. Because she was a soldier's daughter, he told her the truth in a few words; but he was not strong enough to look at her while he did. When he had finished, he sat dully listening to the rain.

"You're going to revolt," she whispered.

"'I'm going to consult with SCHQ and follow my commanding officer's orders," Mackenzie said.

"You know what they'll be...once he knows you'll back him."

Mackenzie shrugged. His head had begun to ache. Hangover started already? He'd need a good deal more booze before he could sleep tonight. No, no time for sleep—yes, there would be. Tomorrow would do to assemble the regiment in the courtyard and address them from the breech of Black Hepzibah, as a Mackenzie of the Rolling Stones always addressed his men, and—He found himself ludicrously recalling a day when he and Nora and this girl here had gone rowing on Lake Tahoe. The water was the color of Nora's eyes, green and blue and with sunlight glimmering across the surface, but so clear you could see the rocks on the bottom; and Laura's own little bottom had stuck straight in the air as she trailed her hands astern.

She sat thinking for a space before saying flatly: "I suppose you can't be talked out of it." He shook his head. "Well, can I leave tomorrow early, then?"

"Yes. I'll get you a coach."

"T-t-to hell with that. I'm better in the saddle than you are."

"Okay. A couple of men to escort you, though." Mackenzie drew a long breath. "Maybe you can persuade Tom—"

"No. I can't. Please don't ask me to, Dad."

He gave her the last gift he could: "I wouldn't want you to stay. That'd be shirking your own duty. Tell Tom I still think he's the right man for you. Goodnight, duck." It came out too fast, but he dared not delay. When she began to cry he must unfold her arms from his neck and depart the room.

"But I had not expected so much killing!"

"Nor I...at this stage of things. There will be more yet, I am afraid, before the immediate purpose is achieved."

"You told me—"

"I told you our hopes, Mwyr. You know as well as I that the Great Science is only exact on the broadest scale of history. Individual events are subject to statistical fluctuation."

"That is an easy way, is it not, to describe sentient beings dying in the mud?"

"You are new here. Theory is one thing, adjustment to practical necessities is another. Do you think it does not hurt me to see that happen which I myself have helped plan?"

"Oh, I know, I know. Which makes it no easier to live with my guilt."

"To live with your responsibilities, you mean."

"Your phrase."

"No, this is not semantic trickery. The distinction is real. You have read reports and seen films, but I was here with the first expedition. And here I have been for more than two centuries. Their agony is no abstraction to me."

"But it was different when we first discovered them. The aftermath of their nuclear wars was still so horribly present. That was when they needed us—the poor starveling anarchs—and we, we did nothing but observe."

"Now you are hysterical. Could we come in blindly, ignorant of every last fact about them, and expect to be anything but one more disruptive element? An element

whose effects we ourselves would not have been able to predict. That would have been criminal indeed, like a surgeon who started to operate as soon as he met the patient, without so much as taking a case history. We had to let them go their own way while we studied in secret. You have no idea how desperately hard we worked to gain information and understanding. That work goes on. It was only seventy years ago that we felt enough assurance to introduce the first new factor into this one selected society. As we continue to learn more, the plan will be adjusted. It may take us a thousand years to complete our mission."

"But meanwhile they have pulled themselves back out of the wreckage. They are finding their own answers to their problems. What right have we to—"

"I begin to wonder, Mwyr, what right you have to claim even the title of apprentice psychodynamician. Consider what their 'answers' actually amount to. Most of the planet is still in a state of barbarism. This continent has come farthest toward recovery, because of having the widest distribution of technical skills and equipment before the destruction. But what social structure has evolved? A jumble of quarrelsome successor states. A feudalism where the balance of political, military, and economic power lies with a landed aristocracy, of all archaic things. A score of languages and subcultures developing along their own incompatible lines. A blind technology worship inherited from the ancestral society that, unchecked, will lead them in the end back to a machine civilization as demoniac as the one that tore itself apart three centuries ago. Are you distressed that a few hundred men have been killed because our agents promoted a revolution which did not come off quite so smoothly as we hoped? Well, you have the word of the Great Science itself that, without our guidance, the totaled misery of this race through the next five thousand years would outweigh by three orders of magnitude whatever pain we are forced to inflict."

"—Yes. Of course. I realize I am being emotional. It is difficult not to be at first, I suppose."

"You should be thankful that your initial exposure to the hard necessities of the plan was so mild. There is worse to come."

"So I have been told."

"In abstract terms. But consider the reality. A government ambitious to restore the old nation will act aggressively, thus embroiling itself in prolonged wars with powerful neighbors. Both directly and indirectly, through the operation of economic factors they are too naive to control, the aristocrats and freeholders will be eroded away by those wars. Anomic democracy will replace their system, first dominated by a corrupt capitalism and later by sheer force of whoever holds the central government. But there will be no place for the vast displaced proletariat, the one-time landowners and the foreigners incorporated by conquest. They will offer fertile soil to any demagogue. The empire will undergo endless upheaval, civil strife, despotism, decay, and outside invasion. Oh, we will have much to answer for before we are done!"

"Do you think…when we see the final result…will the blood wash off us?"

"No. We pay the heaviest price of all."

Spring in the high Sierra is cold, wet, snowbanks melting away from forest floor and giant rocks, rivers in spate until their canyons clang, a breeze ruffling puddles in the road. The first green breath across the aspen seems infinitely tender against pine and spruce, which gloom into a brilliant sky. A raven swoops low, gruk, gruk, look out for that damn hawk! But then you cross timber line and the world becomes tumbled blue-gray immensity, with the sun ablaze on what snows remain and the wind sounding hollow in your ears.

Captain Thomas Danielis, Field Artillery, Loyalist Army of the Pacific States, turned his horse aside. He was a dark young man, slender and snub-nosed. Behind him a squad slipped and cursed, dripping mud from feet to helmets, trying to get a gun carrier unstuck. Its alcohol motor was too feeble to do more than spin the wheels. The infantry squelched on past, stoop-shouldered, worn down by altitude and a wet bivouac and pounds of mire on each boot. Their line snaked from around a prowlike crag, up the twisted road and over the ridge ahead. A gust brought the smell of sweat to Danielis.

But they were good joes, he thought. Dirty, dogged, they did their profane best. His own company, at least, was going to get hot food tonight, if he had to cook the quartermaster sergeant.

The horse's hoofs banged on a block of ancient concrete jutting from the muck. If this had been the old days...but wishes weren't bullets. Beyond this part of the range lay lands mostly desert, claimed by the Saints, who were no longer a menace but with whom there was scant commerce. So the mountain highways had never been considered worth repaving, and the railroad ended at Hangtown. Therefore the expeditionary force to the Tahoe area must slog through unpeopled forests and icy uplands, God help the poor bastards.

God help them in Nakamura, too, Danielis thought. His mouth drew taut, he slapped his hands together and spurred the horse with needless violence. Sparks shot from iron shoes as the beast clattered off the road toward the highest point of the ridge. The man's saber banged his leg.

Reining in, he unlimbered his field glasses. From here he could look across a jumbled sweep of mountainscape, where cloud shadows sailed over cliffs and boulders, down into the gloom of a canyon and across to the other side. A few tufts of grass thrust out beneath him, mummy brown, and a marmot wakened early from winter sleep whistled somewhere in the stone confusion. He still couldn't see the castle. Nor had he expected to, as yet. He knew this country... how well he did!

There might be a glimpse of hostile activity, though. It had been eerie to march this far with no sign of the enemy, of anyone else whatsoever; to send out patrols in search of rebel units that could not be found; to ride with shoulder muscles tense against the sniper's arrow that never came. Old Jimbo Mackenzie was not one to sit passive behind walls, and the Rolling Stones had not been given their nickname in jest.

If Jimbo is alive. How do I know he is? That buzzard yonder may be the very one which hacked out his eyes.

Danielis bit his lip and made himself look steadily through the glasses. Don't think about Mackenzie, how he outroared and outdrank and outlaughed you and you never minded, how he sat knotting his brows over the chessboard where you could mop him up ten times out of ten and *he* never cared, how proud and happy he stood at the wedding...Nor think about Laura, who tried to keep you from knowing how often she wept at night, who now bore a grandchild beneath her heart and woke alone in the San Francisco house from the evil dreams of pregnancy. One of those dogfaces plodding toward the castle which has killed every army ever sent against it—every one of them has somebody at home and hell rejoices at how many have somebody on the rebel side. Better look for hostile spoor and let it go at that.

Wait! Danielis stiffened. A rider—He focused. *One of our own.* Fallon's army added a blue band to the uniform. *Returning scout.* A tingle went along his spine. He decided to hear the report firsthand. But the fellow was still a mile off, perforce riding slowly over the hugger-mugger terrain. There was no hurry about intercepting him. Danielis continued to survey the land.

A reconnaissance plane appeared, an ungainly dragonfly with sunlight flashing off a propeller head. Its drone bumbled among rock walls, where echoes threw the noise back and forth. Doubtless an auxiliary to the scouts, employing two-way radio communication. Later the plane would work as a spotter for artillery. There was no use making a bomber of it; Fort Nakamura was proof against anything that today's puny aircraft could drop, and might well shoot the thing down.

A shoe scraped behind Danielis. Horse and man whirled as one. His pistol jumped into his hand.

It lowered. "Oh. Excuse me, Philosopher."

The man in the blue robe nodded. A smile softened his stern face. He must be around sixty years old, hair white and skin lined, but he walked these heights like a wild goat. The Yang and Yin symbol burned gold on his breast.

"You're needlessly on edge, son," he said. A trace of Texas accent stretched out his words. The Espers obeyed the laws wherever they lived, but acknowledged no country their own: nothing less than mankind, perhaps ultimately all life through the space-time universe. Nevertheless, the Pacific States had gained enormously in prestige and influence when the Order's unenterable Central was established in San Francisco at the time when the city was being rebuilt in earnest. There had been no objection—on the contrary—to the Grand Seeker's desire that Philosopher Woodworth accompany the expedition as an observer. Not even from the chaplains; the churches had finally gotten it straight that the Esper teachings were neutral with respect to religion.

Danielis managed a grin. "Can you blame me?"

"No blame. But advice. Your attitude isn't useful. Does nothin' but wear you out. You've been fightin' a battle for weeks before it began."

Danielis remembered the apostle who had visited his home in San Francisco—by invitation, in the hope that Laura might learn some peace. His simile had been still homelier: "You only need to wash one dish at a time." The memory brought a smart to Danielis' eyes, so that he said roughly:

"I might relax if you'd use your powers to tell me what's waiting for us."

"'I'm no adept, son. Too much in the material world, I'm afraid. Somebody's got to do the practical work of the Order, and someday I'll get the chance to retire and explore the frontier inside me. But you need to start early, and stick to it a lifetime, to develop your full powers." Woodworth looked across the peaks, seemed almost to merge himself with their loneliness.

Danielis hesitated to break into that meditation. He wondered what practical purpose the Philosopher was serving on this trip. To bring back a report, more accurate than untrained senses and undisciplined emotions could prepare? Yes, that must be it. The Espers might yet decide to take a hand in this war. However reluctantly, Central had allowed the awesome psi powers to be released now and again, when the Order was seriously threatened; and Judge Fallon was a better friend to them than Brodsky or the earlier Senate of Bossmen and House of People's Deputies had been.

The horse stamped and blew out its breath in a snort. Woodworth glanced back at the rider. "If you ask me, though," he said, "I don't reckon you'll find much doin' around here. I was in the Rangers myself, back home, before I saw the Way. This country feels empty."

"If we could know!" Danielis exploded. "They've had the whole winter to do what they liked in the mountains, while the snow kept us out. What scouts we could get in reported a beehive—as late as two weeks ago. What have they planned?"

Woodworth made no reply.

It flooded from Danielis, he couldn't stop, he had to cover the recollection of Laura bidding him good-by on his second expedition against her father, six months after the first one came home in bloody fragments:

"If we had the resources! A few wretched little railroads and motor cars; a handful of aircraft; most of our supply trains drawn by mules—what kind of mobility does that give us? And what really drives me crazy...we know how to make what they had in the old days. We've got the books, the information. More, maybe, than the ancestors. I've watched the electrosmith at Fort Nakamura turn out transistor units with enough bandwidth to carry television, no bigger than my fist. I've seen the scientific journals, the research labs, biology, chemistry, astronomy, mathematics. And all useless!"

"Not so," Woodworth answered mildly. "Like my own Order, the community of scholarship's becomin' supranational. Printin' presses, radiophones, telescribes—"

"I say useless. Useless to stop men killing each other because there's no authority strong enough to make them behave. Useless to take a farmer's hands off a horse-drawn plow and put them on the wheel of a tractor. We've got the knowledge, but we can't apply it."

"You do apply it, son, where too much power and industrial plant isn't required. Remember, the world's a lot poorer in natural resources than it was before the Hellbombs. I've seen the Black Lands myself, where the firestorm passed over the Texas oilfields." Woodworth's serenity cracked a little. He turned his eyes back to the peaks.

"There's oil elsewhere," Danielis insisted. "And coal, iron, uranium, everything we need. But the world hasn't got the organization to get at it. Not in any quantity. So we fill the Central Valley with crops that'll yield alcohol, to keep a few motors turning; and we import a dribble of other stuff along an unbelievably inefficient chain of middlemen; and most of it's eaten by the armies." He jerked his head toward that part of the sky which the handmade airplane had crossed. "That's one reason we've got to have Reunification. So we can rebuild."

"And the other?" Woodworth asked softly.

"Democracy—universal suffrage—" Danielis swallowed. "And so fathers and sons won't have to fight each other again."

"Those are better reasons," Woodworth said. "Good enough for the Espers to support. But as for that machinery you want—" He shook his head. "No, you're wrong there. That's no way for men to live."

"Maybe not," Danielis said. "Though my own father wouldn't have been crippled by overwork if he'd had some machines to help him…Oh, I don't know. First things first. Let's get this war over with and argue later." He remembered the scout, now gone from view. "Pardon me, Philosopher, I've got an errand."

The Esper raised his hand in token of peace. Danielis cantered off.

Splashing along the roadside, he saw the man he wanted, halted by Major Jacobsen. The latter, who must have sent him out, sat mounted near the infantry line. The scout was a Klamath Indian, stocky in buckskins, a bow on his shoulder. Arrows were favored over guns by many of the men from the northern districts: cheaper than bullets, no noise, less range but as much firepower as a bolt-action rifle. In the bad old days before the Pacific States had formed their union, archers along forest trails had saved many a town from conquest; they still helped keep that union loose.

"Ah, Captain Danielis," Jacobsen hailed. "You're just in time. Lieutenant Smith was about to report what his detachment found out."

"And the plane," said Smith imperturbably. 'What the pilot told us he'd seen from the air gave us the guts to go there and check for ourselves."

"Well?"

"Nobody around."

"What?"

"Fort's been evacuated. So's the settlement. Not a soul."

"But—but—" Jacobsen collected himself. "Go on."

"We studied the signs as best's we could. Looks like noncombatants left some time ago. By sledge and ski, I'd guess, maybe north to some strong point. I suppose the men shifted their own stuff at the same time, gradual-like, what they couldn't carry with 'em at the last. Because the regiment and its support units, even field artillery, pulled out just three-four days ago. Ground's all tore up. They headed downslope, sort of west by northwest, far's we could tell from what we saw."

Jacobsen choked. "Where are they bound?"

A flaw of wind struck Danielis in the face and ruffled the horses' manes. At his back he heard the slow plop and squish of boots, groan of wheels, chuff of motors, rattle of wood and metal, yells and whipcracks of muleskinners. But it seemed very remote. A map grew before him, blotting out the world.

The Loyalist Army had had savage fighting the whole winter, from the Trinity Alps to Puget Sound—for Brodsky had managed to reach Mount Rainier, whose lord had furnished broadcasting facilities, and Rainier was too well fortified to take at once. The bossmen and the autonomous tribes rose in arms, persuaded that a usurper threatened their damned little local privileges. Their protectees fought beside them, if only because no rustic had been taught any higher loyalty than to his patron. West Canada, fearful of what Fallon might do when he got the chance, lent the rebels aid that was scarcely even clandestine.

Nonetheless, the national army was stronger: more matériel, better organization, above everything an ideal of the future. Cinc O'Donnell had outlined a strategy—concentrate the loyal forces at a few points, overwhelm resistance, restore order and establish bases in the region, then proceed to the next place—which worked. The government now controlled the entire coast, with naval units to keep an eye on the Canadians in Vancouver and guard the important Hawaii trade routes; the northern half of Washington almost to the Idaho line; the Columbia Valley; central California as far north as Redding. The remaining rebellious Stations and towns were isolated from each other in mountains, forests, deserts. Bossdom after bossdom fell as the loyalists pressed on, defeating the enemy in detail, cutting him off from supplies and hope. The only real worry had been Cruikshank's Sierra Command, an army in its own right rather than a levy of yokels and citymen, big and tough and expertly led. This expedition against Fort Nakamura was only a small part of what had looked like a difficult campaign.

But now the Rolling Stones had pulled out. Offered no fight whatsoever. Which meant that their brother Catamounts must also have evacuated. You don't give up one anchor of a line you intend to hold. So?

"Down into the valleys," Danielis said; and there sounded in his ears, crazily, the voice of Laura as she used to sing. *Down in the valley, valley so low.*

"Judas!" the major exclaimed. Even the Indian grunted as if he had taken a belly blow. "No, they couldn't. We'd have known."

Hang your head over, hear the wind blow. It hooted across cold rocks.

"There are plenty of forest trails," Danielis said. "Infantry and cavalry could use them, if they're accustomed to such country. And the Cats are. Vehicles, wagons, big guns, that's slower and harder. But they only need to outflank us, then they can get back onto Forty and Fifty—and cut us to pieces if we attempt pursuit. I'm afraid they've got us boxed."

"The eastern slope—" said Jacobsen helplessly.

"What for? Want to occupy a lot of sagebrush? No, we're trapped here till they deploy in the flatlands." Danielis closed a hand on his saddlehorn so that the knuckles went bloodless. "I miss my guess if this isn't Colonel Mackenzie's idea. It's his style, for sure."

"But then they're between us and Frisco! With damn near our whole strength in the north—"

Between me and Laura, Danielis thought.

He said aloud: "I suggest, Major, we get hold of the C.O. at once. And then we better get on the radio." From some well he drew the power to raise his head. The wind lashed his eyes. "This needn't be a disaster. They'll be easier to beat out in the open, actually, once we come to grips."

Roses love sunshine, violets love dew,
Angels in heaven know I love you.

The rains which fill the winter of the California lowlands were about ended. Northward along a highway whose pavement clopped under hoofs, Mackenzie rode through a tremendous greenness. Eucalyptus and live oak, flanking the road, exploded with new leaves. Beyond them on either side stretched a checkerboard of fields and vineyards, intricately hued, until the distant hills on the right and the higher, nearer ones on the left made walls. The freeholder houses that had been scattered across the land a ways back were no longer to be seen. This end of the Napa Valley belonged to the Esper community at St. Helena. Clouds banked like white mountains over the western ridge. The breeze bore to Mackenzie a smell of growth and turned earth.

Behind him it rumbled with men. The Rolling Stones were on the move. The regiment proper kept to the highway, three thousand boots slamming down at once with an earthquake noise, and so did the guns and wagons. There was no immediate danger of attack. But the cavalrymen attached to the force must needs spread out. The sun flashed off their helmets and lance heads.

Mackenzie's attention was directed forward. Amber walls and red tile roofs could be seen among plum trees that were a surf of pink and white blossoms. The community was big, several thousand people. The muscles tightened in his abdomen. "Think we can trust them?" he asked, not for the first time. "We've only got a radio agreement to a parley."

Speyer, riding beside him, nodded. "I expect they'll be honest. Particularly with our boys right outside. Espers believe in non-violence anyway."

"Yeah, but if it did come to fighting—I know there aren't very many adepts so far. The Order hasn't been around long enough for that. But when you get this many Espers together, there's bound to be a few who've gotten somewhere with their damned psionics. I don't want my men blasted, or lifted in the air and dropped, or any such nasty thing."

Speyer threw him a sidelong glance. "Are you scared of them, Jimbo?" he murmured.

"Hell, no!" Mackenzie wondered if he was a liar or not. "But I don't like 'em."

"They do a lot of good. Among the poor, especially."

"Sure, sure. Though any decent bossman looks after his own protectees, and we've got things like churches and hospices as well. I don't see where just being charitable—and they can afford it, with the profits they make on their holdings—I don't see where that gives any right to raise the orphans and pauper kids they take in, the way they do: so's to make the poor tikes unfit for life anywhere outside."

"The object of that, as you well know, is to orient them toward the so-called interior frontier. Which American civilization as a whole is not much interested in. Frankly, quite apart from the remarkable powers some Espers have developed, I often envy them."

"You, Phil?" Mackenzie goggled at his friend.

The lines drew deep in Speyer's face. "This winter I've helped shoot a lot of my fellow countrymen," he said low. "My mother and wife and kids are crowded with the rest of the Village in the Mount Lassen fort, and when we said good-by we knew it was quite possibly permanent. And in the past I've helped shoot a lot of other men who never did me any personal harm." He sighed. "I've often wondered what it's like to know peace, inside as well as outside."

Mackenzie sent Laura and Tom out of his head.

"Of course," Speyer went on, "the fundamental reason you—and I, for that matter—distrust the Espers is that they do represent something alien to us. Something that may eventually choke out the whole concept of life that we grew up with. You know, a couple weeks back in Sacramento I dropped in at the University research lab to see what was going on. Incredible! The ordinary soldier would swear it was witchwork. It was certainly more weird than…than simply reading minds or moving objects by thinking at them. But to you or me it's a shiny new marvel. We'll wallow in it.

"Now why's that? Because the lab is scientific. Those men work with chemicals, electronics, subviral particles. That fits into the educated American's worldview. But the mystic unity of creation…no, not our cup of tea. The only way we can hope to achieve Oneness is to renounce everything we've ever believed in. At your age or mine, Jimbo, a man is seldom ready to tear down his whole life and start from scratch."

"Maybe so." Mackenzie lost interest. The settlement was quite near now.

He turned around to Captain Hulse, riding a few paces behind. "Here we go," he said. "Give my compliments to Lieutenant Colonel Yamaguchi and tell him he's in charge till we get back. If anything seems suspicious, he's to act at his own discretion."

"Yes, sir." Hulse saluted and wheeled smartly about. There had been no practical need for Mackenzie to repeat what had long been agreed on; but he knew the value of ritual. He clicked his big sorrel gelding into a trot. At his back he heard bugles sound orders and sergeants howl at their platoons.

Speyer kept pace. Mackenzie had insisted on bringing an extra man to the discussion. His own wits were probably no match for a high-level Esper, but Phil's might be.

Not that there's any question of diplomacy or whatever. I hope. To ease himself, he concentrated on what was real and present—hoofbeats, the rise and fall of the saddle beneath him, the horse's muscles rippling between his thighs, the creak and jingle of his saber belt, the clean odor of the animal—and suddenly remembered this was the sort of trick the Espers recommended.

None of their communities was walled, as most towns and every bossman's Station was. The officers turned off the highway and went down a street between colonnaded buildings. Side streets ran off in both directions. The settlement covered no great area, though, being composed of groups that lived together, sodalities or super-families or whatever you wanted to call them. Some hostility toward the Order and a great many dirty jokes stemmed from that practice. But Speyer, who should know, said there was no more sexual swapping around than in the outside world. The idea was simply to get away from possessiveness, thee versus me, and to raise children as part of a whole rather than an insular clan.

The kids were out, staring round-eyed from the porticoes, hundreds of them. They looked healthy and, underneath a natural fear of the invaders, happy enough. But pretty solemn, Mackenzie thought; and all in the same blue garb. Adults stood among them, expressionless. Everybody had come in from the fields as the regiment neared. The silence was like barricades. Mackenzie felt sweat begin to trickle down his ribs. When he emerged on the central square, he let out his breath in a near gasp.

A fountain, the basin carved into a lotus, tinkled in the middle of the plaza. Flowering trees stood around it. The square was defined on three sides by massive buildings that must be for storage. On the fourth side rose a smaller temple-like structure with a graceful cupola, obviously headquarters and meeting house. On its lowest step were ranked half a dozen blue-robed men, five of them husky youths. The sixth was middle-aged, the Yang and Yin on his breast. His features, ordinary in themselves, held an implacable calm.

Mackenzie and Speyer drew rein. The colonel flipped a soft salute. "Philosopher Gaines? I'm Mackenzie, here's Major Speyer." He swore at himself for being so awkward about it and wondered what to do with his hands. The young fellows he understood, more or less; they watched him with badly concealed hostility. But he had some trouble meeting Gaines' eyes.

The settlement leader inclined his head. "Welcome, gentlemen. Won't you come in?"

Mackenzie dismounted, hitched his horse to a post and removed his helmet. His worn reddish-brown uniform felt shabbier yet in these surroundings. "Thanks. Uh, I'll have to make this quick."

"To be sure. Follow me, please."

Stiff-backed, the young men trailed after their elders, through an entry chamber and down a short hall. Speyer looked around at the mosaics. "Why, this is lovely," he murmured.

"Thank you," said Gaines. "Here's my office." He opened a door of superbly grained walnut and gestured the visitors through. When he closed it behind himself the acolytes waited outside.

The room was austere, whitewashed walls enclosing little more than a desk, a shelf of books, and some backless chairs. A window opened on a garden. Gaines sat down. Mackenzie and Speyer followed suit, uncomfortable on this furniture.

"We'd better get right to business," the colonel blurted.

Gaines said nothing. At last Mackenzie must plow ahead:

"Here's the situation. Our force is to occupy Calistoga, with detachments on either side of the hills. That way we'll control both the Napa Valley and the Valley of the Moon...from the northern ends, at least. The best place to station our eastern wing is here. We plan to establish a fortified camp in the field yonder. I'm sorry about the damage to your crops, but you'll be compensated once the proper government has been restored. And food, medicine—you understand this army has to requisition such items, but we won't let anybody suffer undue hardship and we'll give receipts. Uh, as a precaution we'll need to quarter a few men in this community, to sort of keep an eye on things. They'll interfere as little as possible. Okay?"

"The charter of the Order guarantees exemption from military requirements," Gaines answered evenly. "In fact, no armed man is supposed to cross the boundary of any land held by an Esper settlement. I cannot be party to a violation of the law, Colonel."

"If you want to split legal hairs, Philosopher," Speyer said, "then I'll remind you that both Fallon and Judge Brodsky have declared martial law. Ordinary rules are suspended."

Gaines smiled. "Since only one government can be legitimate," he said, "the proclamations of the other are necessarily null and void. To a disinterested observer, it would appear that Judge Fallon's title is the stronger, especially when his side controls a large continuous area rather than some scattered bossdoms."

"Not any more, it doesn't," Mackenzie snapped.

Speyer gestured him back. "Perhaps you haven't followed the developments of the last few weeks, Philosopher," he said. "Allow me to recapitulate. The Sierra Command stole a march on the Fallonites and came down out of the mountains. There was almost nothing left in the middle part of California to oppose us, so we took over rapidly. By occupying Sacramento, we control river and rail traffic. Our bases extend south below Bakersfield, with Yosemite and King's Canyon not far away to provide sites for extremely strong positions. When we've consolidated this northern end of our gains, the Fallonite forces around Redding will be trapped between us and the powerful bossmen who still hold out in the Trinity, Shasta, and Lassen regions. The very fact of our being here has forced the enemy to evacuate the Columbia Valley, so that San Francisco may be defended. It's an open question which side today has the last word in the larger territory."

"What about the army that went into the Sierra against you?" Gaines inquired shrewdly. "Have you contained them?"

Mackenzie scowled. "No. That's no secret. They got out through the Mother Lode country and went around us. They're down in Los Angeles and San Diego now."

"A formidable host. Do you expect to stand them off indefinitely?"

"We're going to make a hell of a good try," Mackenzie said. "Where we are, we've got the advantage of interior communications. And most of the freeholders are glad to slip us word about whatever they observe. We can concentrate at any point the enemy starts to attack."

"Pity that this rich land must also be torn apart by war."

"Yeah. Isn't it?"

"Our strategic objective is obvious enough," Speyer said. "We have cut enemy communications across the middle, except by sea, which is not very satisfactory for troops operating far inland. We deny him access to a good part of his food and manufactured supplies, and most especially to the bulk of his fuel alcohol. The backbone of our own side is the bossdoms, which are almost self-contained economic and social units. Before long they'll be in better shape than the rootless army they face. I think Judge Brodsky will be back in San Francisco before fall."

"If your plans succeed," Gaines said.

"That's our worry." Mackenzie leaned forward, one fist doubled on his knee. "Okay, Philosopher. I know you'd rather see Fallon come out on top, but I expect you've got more sense than to sign up in a lost cause. Will you cooperate with us?"

"The Order takes no part in political affairs, Colonel, except when its own existence is endangered."

"Oh, pipe down. By 'cooperate' I don't mean anything but keeping out from under our feet."

"I am afraid that would still count as cooperation. We cannot have military establishments on our lands."

Mackenzie stared at Gaines' face, which had set into granite lines, and wondered if he had heard aright. "Are you ordering us off?" a stranger asked with his voice.

"Yes," the Philosopher said.

"With our artillery zeroed in on your town?"

"Would you really shell women and children, Colonel?"

O Nora—"We don't need to. Our men can walk right in."

"Against psi blasts? I beg you not to have those poor boys destroyed." Gaines paused, then: "I might also point out that by losing your regiment you imperil your whole cause. You are free to march around our holdings and proceed to Calistoga."

Leaving a Fallonite nest at my back, spang across my communications southward. The teeth grated together in Mackenzie's mouth.

Gaines rose. "The discussion is at an end, gentlemen," he said. "You have one hour to get off our lands."

Mackenzie and Speyer stood up too. "We're not done yet," the major said. Sweat studded his forehead and the long nose. "I want to make some further explanations.

Gaines crossed the room and opened the door. "Show these gentlemen out," he said to the five acolytes.

"No, by God!" Mackenzie shouted. He clapped a hand to his sidearm.

"Inform the adepts," Gaines said.

One of the young men turned. Mackenzie heard the slap-slap of his sandals, running down the hall. Gaines nodded. "I think you had better go," he said.

Speyer grew rigid. His eyes shut. They flew open and he breathed, "*Inform the adepts?*"

Mackenzie saw the stiffness break in Gaines' countenance. There was no time for more than a second's bewilderment. His body acted for him. The gun clanked from his holster simultaneously with Speyer's.

"Get that messenger, Jimbo," the major rapped. "I'll keep these birds covered."

As he plunged forward, Mackenzie found himself worrying about the regimental honor. Was it right to open hostilities when you had come on a parley? But Gaines had cut the talk off himself—

"Stop him!" Gaines yelled.

The four remaining acolytes sprang into motion. Two of them barred the doorway, the other two moved in on either side. "Hold it or I'll shoot!" Speyer cried, and was ignored.

Mackenzie couldn't bring himself to fire on unarmed men. He gave the youngster before him the pistol barrel in his teeth. Bloody-faced, the Esper lurched back. Mackenzie stiff-armed the one coming in from the left. The third tried to fill the doorway. Mackenzie put a foot behind his ankles and pushed. As he went down, Mackenzie kicked him in the temple, hard enough to stun, and jumped over him.

The fourth was on his back. Mackenzie writhed about to face the man. Those arms that hugged him, pinioning his gun, were bear strong. Mackenzie put the butt of his free left hand under the fellow's nose, and pushed. The acolyte must let go. Mackenzie gave him a knee in the stomach, whirled, and ran.

There was not much further commotion behind him. Phil must have them under control. Mackenzie pelted along the hall, into the entry chamber. Where had that goddamn runner gone? He looked out the open entrance, onto the square. Sunlight hurt his eyes. His breath came in painful gulps, there was a stitch in his side, yeah, he was getting old.

Blue robes fluttered from a street. Mackenzie recognized the messenger. The youth pointed at this building. A gabble of his words drifted faintly through Mackenzie's pulse. There were seven or eight men with him—older men, nothing to mark their clothes...but Mackenzie knew a high-ranking officer when he saw one. The acolyte was dismissed. Those whom he had summoned crossed the square with long strides.

Terror knotted Mackenzie's bowels. He put it down. A Catamount didn't stampede, even from somebody who could turn him inside out with a look. He could do nothing about the wretchedness that followed, though. *If they clobber me, so much the better, I won't lie awake nights wondering how Laura is.*

The adepts were almost to the steps. Mackenzie trod forth. He swept his revolver in an arc. "Halt!" His voice sounded tiny in the stillness that brooded over the town.

They jarred to a stop and stood there in a group. He saw them enforce a cat-like relaxation, and their faces became blank visors. None spoke. Finally Mackenzie was unable to keep silent.

"This place is hereby occupied under the laws of war," he said. "Go back to your quarters."

"What have you done with our leader?" asked a tall man. His voice was even but deeply resonant.

"Read my mind and find out," Mackenzie gibed. *No, you're being childish.* "He's okay, long's he keeps his nose clean. You too. Beat it."

"We do not wish to pervert psionics to violence," said the tall man. "Please do not force us."

"Your chief sent for you before we'd done anything," Mackenzie retorted. "Looks like violence was what he had in mind. On your way."

The Espers exchanged glances. The tall man nodded. His companions walked slowly off. "I would like to see Philosopher Gaines," the tall man said.

"You will pretty soon."

"Am I to understand that he is being held a prisoner?"

"Understand what you like." The other Espers were rounding the corner of the building. "I don't want to shoot. Go on back before I have to."

"An impasse of sorts," the tall man said. "Neither of us wishes to injure one whom he considers defenseless. Allow me to conduct you off these grounds."

Mackenzie wet his lips. Weather had chapped them rough. "If you can put a hex on me, go ahead," he challenged. "Otherwise scram."

"Well, I shall not hinder you from rejoining your men. It seems the easiest way of getting you to leave. But I most solemnly warn that any armed force which tries to enter will be annihilated."

Guess I had better go get the boys, at that. Phil can't mount guard on those guys forever.

The tall man went over to the hitching post. "Which of these horses is yours?" he asked blandly.

Almighty eager to get rid of me, isn't he—Holy hellfire! There must be a rear door!

Mackenzie spun on his heel. The Esper shouted. Mackenzie dashed back through the entry chamber. His boots threw echoes at him. No, not to the left, there's only the office that way. Right...around this corner—

A long hall stretched before him. A stairway curved from the middle. The other Espers were already on it.

"Halt!" Mackenzie called. "Stop or I'll shoot!"

The two men in the lead sped onward. The rest turned and headed down again, toward him.

He fired with care, to disable rather than kill. The hall reverberated with the explosions. One after another they dropped, a bullet in leg or hip or shoulder. With such small targets, Mackenzie missed some shots. As the tall man, the last of them, closed in from behind, the hammer clicked on an empty chamber.

Mackenzie drew his saber and gave him the flat of it alongside the head. The Esper lurched. Mackenzie got past and bounded up the stair. It wound like something in a nightmare. He thought his heart was going to go to pieces.

At the end, an iron door opened on a landing. One man was fumbling with the lock. The other blue-robe attacked.

Mackenzie stuck his sword between the Esper's legs. As his opponent stumbled, the colonel threw a left hook to the jaw. The man sagged against the wall.

Mackenzie grabbed the robe of the other and hurled him to the floor. "Get out," he rattled.

They pulled themselves together and glared at him. He thrust air with his blade. "From now on I aim to kill," he said.

"Get help, Dave," said the one who had been opening the door. "I'll watch him." The other went unevenly down the stairs. The first man stood out of saber reach. "Do you want to be destroyed?" he asked.

Mackenzie turned the knob at his back but the door was still locked. "I don't think you can do it," he said. "Not without what's here."

The Esper struggled for self-control. They waited through minutes that stretched. Then a noise began below. The Esper pointed. "We have nothing but agricultural implements," he said, "but you have only that blade. Will you surrender?"

Mackenzie spat on the floor. The Esper went on down.

Presently the attackers came into view. There might be a hundred, judging from the hubbub behind them, but because of the curve Mackenzie could see no more than ten or fifteen—burly fieldhands, their robes tucked high and sharp tools aloft. The landing was too wide for defense. He advanced to the stairway, where they could only come at him two at a time.

A couple of sawtoothed hay knives led the assault. Mackenzie parried one blow and chopped. His edge went into meat and struck bone. Blood ran impossibly red, even in the dim light here. The man fell to all fours with a shriek. Mackenzie dodged a cut from the companion. Metal clashed on metal. The weapons locked. Mackenzie's arm was forced back. He looked into a broad suntanned face. The side of his hand smote the young man's larynx. The Esper fell against the one behind and they went down together. It took a while to clear the tangle and resume action.

A pitchfork thrust for the colonel's belly. He managed to grab it with his left hand, divert the tines, and chop at the fingers on the shaft. A scythe gashed his right side. He saw his own blood but wasn't aware of pain. A flesh wound, no more. He swept his saber back and forth. The forefront retreated from its whistling menace. *But God, my knees are like rubber, I can't hold out another five minutes.*

A bugle sounded. There was a spatter of gunfire. The mob on the staircase congealed. Someone screamed.

Hoofs banged across the ground floor. A voice rasped: "Hold everything, there! Drop those weapons and come on down. First man tries anything gets shot."

Mackenzie leaned on his saber and fought for air. He hardly noticed the Espers melt away.

When he felt a little better, he went to one of the small windows and looked out. Horsemen were in the plaza. Not yet in sight, but nearing, he heard infantry.

Speyer arrived, followed by a sergeant of engineers and several privates. The major hurried to Mackenzie. "You okay, Jimbo? You been hurt!"

"A scratch," Mackenzie said. He was getting back his strength, though no sense of victory accompanied it, only the knowledge of aloneness. The injury began to sting. "Not worth a fuss. Look."

"Yes, I suppose you'll live. Okay, men, get that door open."

The engineers took forth their tools and assailed the lock with a vigor that must spring half from fear. "How'd you guys show up so soon?" Mackenzie asked.

"I thought there'd be trouble," Speyer said, "so when I heard shots I jumped through the window and ran around to my horse. That was just before those clodhoppers attacked you; I saw them gathering as I rode out. Our cavalry got in almost at once, of course, and the dogfaces weren't far behind."

"Any resistance?"

"No, not after we fired a few rounds in the air." Speyer glanced outside. "We're in full possession now."

Mackenzie regarded the door. "Well," he said, "I feel better about our having pulled guns on them in the office. Looks like their adepts really depend on plain old weapons, huh? And Esper communities aren't supposed to have arms. Their charters say so...That was a damn good guess of yours, Phil. How'd you do it?"

"I sort of wondered why the chief had to send a runner to fetch guys that claim to be telepaths. There we go!"

The lock jingled apart. The sergeant opened the door. Mackenzie and Speyer went into the great room under the dome.

They walked around for a long time, wordless, among shapes of metal and less identifiable substances. Nothing was familiar. Mackenzie paused at last before a helix which projected from a transparent cube. Formless darknesses swirled within the box, sparked as if with tiny stars.

"I figured maybe the Espers had found a cache of oldtime stuff, from just before the Hellbombs," he said in a muffled voice. "Ultra-secret weapons that never got a chance to be used. But this doesn't look like it. Think so?"

"No," Speyer said. "It doesn't look to me as if these things were made by human beings at all."

"But do you not understand? They occupied a settlement! That proves to the world that Espers are not invulnerable. And to complete the catastrophe, they seized its arsenal."

"Have no fears about that. No untrained person can activate those instruments. The circuits are locked except in the presence of certain encephalic rhythms which result from conditioning. That same conditioning makes it impossible for the so-called adepts to reveal any of their knowledge to the uninitiated, no matter what may be done to them."

"Yes, I know that much. But it is not what I had in mind. What frightens me is the fact that the revelation will spread. Everyone will know the Esper adepts do not plumb unknown depths of the psyche after all, but merely have access to an advanced physical science. Not only will this lift rebel spirits, but worse, it will cause many, perhaps most of the Order's members to break away in disillusionment."

"Not at once. News travels slowly under present conditions. Also, Mwyr, you underestimate the ability of the human mind to ignore data which conflict with cherished beliefs."

"But—"

"Well, let us assume the worst. Let us suppose that faith is lost and the Order disintegrates. That will be a serious setback to the plan, but not a fatal one. Psionics was merely one bit of folklore we found potent enough to serve as the motivator of a new orientation toward life. There are others, for example the widespread belief in magic among the less educated classes. We can begin again on a different basis, if we must. The exact form of the creed is not important. It is only scaffolding for the real structure: a communal, anti-materialistic social group, to which more and more people will turn for sheer lack of anything else, as the coming empire breaks up. In the end, the new culture can and will discard whatever superstitions gave it the initial impetus."

"A hundred-year setback, at least."

"True. It would be much more difficult to introduce a radical alien element now, when the autochthonous society has developed strong institutions of its own, than it was in the past. I merely wish to reassure you that the task is not impossible. I do not actually propose to let matters go that far. The Espers can be salvaged."

"How?"

"We must intervene directly."

"Has that been computed as being unavoidable?"

"Yes. The matrix yields an unambiguous answer. I do not like it any better than you. But direct action occurs oftener than we tell neophytes in the schools. The most elegant procedure would of course be to establish such initial conditions in a society that its evolution along desired lines becomes automatic. Furthermore, that would let us close our minds to the distressing fact of our own blood guilt. Unfortunately, the Great Science does not extend down to the details of day-to-day practicality.

"In the present instance, we shall help to smash the reactionaries. The government will then proceed so harshly against its conquered opponents that many of those who accept the story about what was found at St. Helena will not live to spread the tale. The rest...well, they will be discredited by their own defeat. Admittedly, the story will linger for lifetimes, whispered here and there. But what of that? Those who believe in the Way will, as a rule, simply be strengthened in their faith, by the very process of denying such ugly rumors. As more and more persons, common citizens as well as Espers, reject materialism, the legend will seem more and more fantastic. It will seem obvious that certain ancients invented the tale to account for a fact that they in their ignorance were unable to comprehend."

"I see..."

"You are not happy here, are you, Mwyr?"

"I cannot quite say. Everything is so distorted."

"Be glad you were not sent to one of the really alien planets."

"I might almost prefer that. There would be a hostile environment to think about. One could forget how far it is to home."

"Three years travel."

"You say that so glibly. As if three shipboard years were not equal to fifty in cosmic time. As if we could expect a relief vessel daily, not once in a century. And...as if the region that our ships have explored amounts to one chip out of this one galaxy!"

"That region will grow until someday it engulfs the galaxy."

"Yes, yes, yes. I know. Why do you think I chose to become a psychodynamician? Why am I here, learning how to meddle with the destiny of a world where I do not belong? 'To create the union of sentient beings, each member species a step toward life's mastery of the universe.' Brave slogan! But in practice, it seems, only a chosen few races are to be allowed the freedom of that universe."

"Not so, Mwyr. Consider these ones with whom we are, as you say, meddling. Consider what use they made of nuclear energy when they had it. At the rate they are going, they will have it again within a century or two. Not long after that they will be building spaceships. Even granted that time lag attenuates the effects of interstellar contact, those effects are cumulative. So do you wish such a band of carnivores turned loose on the galaxy?

"No, let them become inwardly civilized first; then we shall see if they can be trusted. If not, they will at least be happy on their own planet, in a mode of life designed for them by the Great Science. Remember, they have an immemorial aspiration toward peace on earth; but that is something they will never achieve by themselves. I do not pretend to be a very good person, Mwyr. Yet this work that we are doing makes me feel not altogether useless in the cosmos."

Promotion was fast that year, casualties being so high. Captain Thomas Danielis was raised to major for his conspicuous part in putting down the revolt of the Los Angeles citymen. Soon after occurred the Battle of Maricopa, when the loyalists failed bloodily to break the stranglehold of the Sierran rebels on the San Joaquin Valley, and he was brevetted lieutenant colonel. The army was ordered northward and moved warily under the coast ranges, half expecting attack from the east. But the Brodskyites seemed too busy consolidating their latest gains. The trouble came from guerrillas and the hedgehog resistance of bossman Stations. After one particularly stiff clash, they stopped near Pinnacles for a breather.

Danielis made his way through camp, where tents stood in tight rows between the guns and men lay about dozing, talking, gambling, staring at the blank blue sky. The air was hot, pungent with cookfire smoke, horses, mules, dung, sweat, boot oil; the green of the hills that lifted around the site was dulling toward summer brown. He was idle until time for the conference the general had called, but restlessness drove him. *By now I'm a father*, he thought, *and I've never seen my kid.*

At that, I'm lucky, he reminded himself. *I've got my life and limbs.* He remembered Jacobsen dying in his arms at Maricopa. You wouldn't have thought the human body could hold so much blood. Though maybe one was no longer human, when the pain was so great that one could do nothing but shriek until the darkness came.

And I used to think war was glamorous. Hunger, thirst, exhaustion, terror, mutilation, death, and forever the sameness, boredom grinding you down to an ox...I've had it. I'm going into business after the war. Economic integration, as the bossman system breaks up, yes, there'll be a lot of ways for a man to get ahead, but decently, without a weapon in his hand—Danielis realized he was repeating thoughts that were months old. What the hell else was there to think about, though?

The large tent where prisoners were interrogated lay near his path. A couple of privates were conducting a man inside. The fellow was blond, burly, and sullen. He wore a sergeant's stripes, but otherwise his only item of uniform was the badge of Warden Echevarry, bossman in this part of the coastal mountains. A lumberjack in peacetime, Danielis guessed from the look of him; a soldier in a private army whenever the interests of Echevarry were threatened; captured in yesterday's engagement.

On impulse, Danielis followed. He got into the tent as Captain Lambert, chubby behind a portable desk, finished the preliminaries, and blinked in the sudden gloom.

"Oh." The intelligence officer started to rise. "Yes, sir?"

"At ease," Danielis said. "Just thought I'd listen in."

"Well, I'll try to put on a good show for you." Lambert reseated himself and looked at the prisoner, who stood with hunched shoulders and widespread legs between his guards. "Now, sergeant, we'd like to know a few things."

"I don't have to say nothing except name, rank, and home town," the man growled. "You got those."

"Um-m-m, that's questionable. You aren't a foreign soldier, you're in rebellion against the government of your own country."

"The hell I am! I'm an Echevarry man."

"So what?"

"So my Judge is whoever Echevarry says. He says Brodsky. That makes you the rebel."

"The law's been changed."

"Your mucking Fallon got no right to change any laws. Especially part of the Constitution. I'm no hillrunner, Captain. I went to school some. And every year our Warden reads his people the Constitution."

"Times have changed since it was drawn," Lambert said. His tone sharpened. "But I'm not going to argue with you. How many riflemen and how many archers in your Company?"

Silence.

"We can make things a lot easier for you," Lambert said. "I'm not asking you to do anything treasonable. All I want is to confirm some information I've already got."

The man shook his head angrily.

Lambert gestured. One of the privates stepped behind the captive, took his arm, and twisted a little.

"Echevarry wouldn't do that to me," he said through white lips.

"Of course not," Lambert said. "You're his man."

"Think I wanna be just a number on some list in Frisco? Damn right I'm my bossman's man!"

Lambert gestured again. The private twisted harder. "Hold on, there," Danielis barked. "Stop that!"

The private let go, looking surprised. The prisoner drew a sobbing breath.

"I'm amazed at you, Captain Lambert," Danielis said. He felt his own face reddening. "If this has been your usual practice, there's going to be a court-martial."

"No, sir," Lambert said in a small voice. "Honest. Only…they don't talk. Hardly any of them. What'm I supposed to do?"

"Follow the rules of war."

"With rebels?"

"Take that man away," Danielis ordered. The privates made haste to do so.

"Sorry, sir," Lambert muttered. "I guess…I guess I've lost too many buddies. I hate to lose more, simply for lack of information."

"Me too." A compassion rose in Danielis. He sat down on the table edge and began to roll a cigarette. "But you see, we aren't in a regular war. And so, by a curious paradox, we have to follow the conventions more carefully than ever before."

"I don't quite understand, sir."

Danielis finished the cigarette and gave it to Lambert: olive branch or something. He started another for himself. "The rebels aren't rebels by their own lights," he said. "They're being loyal to a tradition that we're trying to curb, eventually to destroy. Let's face it, the average bossman is a fairly good leader. He may be descended from some thug who grabbed power by strong-arm methods during the chaos, but by now his family's integrated itself with the region he rules. He knows it, and its people, inside out. He's there in the flesh, a symbol of the community and its achievements, its folkways and essential independence. If you're in trouble, you don't have to work through some impersonal bureaucracy, you go direct to your bossman. His duties are as clearly defined as your own, and a good deal more demanding, to balance his privileges. He leads you in battle and in the ceremonies that give color and meaning to life. Your fathers and his have worked and played together for two or three hundred years. The land is alive with the memories of them. You and he *belong*.

"Well, that has to be swept away, so we can go on to a higher level. But we won't reach that level by alienating everyone. We're not a conquering army; we're more like the Householder Guard putting down a riot in some city. The opposition is part and parcel of our own society."

Lambert struck a match for him. He inhaled and finished: "On a practical plane, I might also remind you, Captain, that the federal armed forces, Fallonite and Brodskyite together, are none too large. Little more than a cadre, in fact. We're a bunch of younger sons, countrymen who failed, poor citymen, adventurers, people who look to their regiment for that sense of wholeness they've grown up to expect and can't find in civilian life."

"You're too deep for me, sir, I'm afraid," Lambert said.

"Never mind," Danielis sighed. "Just bear in mind, there are a good many more fighting men outside the opposing armies than in. If the bossmen could establish a unified command, that'd be the end of the Fallon government. Luckily, there's too much provincial pride and too much geography between them for this to happen—unless we outrage them beyond endurance. What we want the ordinary freeholder, and even the ordinary bossman, to think, is: 'Well, those Fallonites aren't such bad guys, and if I keep on the right side of them I don't stand to lose much, and should even be able to gain something at the expense of those who fight them to a finish.' You see?"

"Y-yes. I guess so."

"You're a smart fellow, Lambert. You don't have to beat information out of prisoners. Trick it out."

"I'll try, sir."

"Good." Danielis glanced at the watch that had been given him as per tradition, together with a sidearm, when he was first commissioned. (Such items were much too expensive for the common man. They had not been so in the age of mass production; and perhaps in the coming age—) "I have to go. See you around."

He left the tent feeling somewhat more cheerful than before. *No doubt I am a natural-born preacher,* he admitted, *and I never could quite join in the horseplay at mess, and a lot of jokes go completely by me; but if I can get even a few ideas across where they count, that's pleasure enough.* A strain of music came to him, some men and a banjo under a tree, and he found himself whistling along. It was good that this much morale remained, after Maricopa and a northward march whose purpose had not been divulged to anybody.

The conference tent was big enough to be called a pavilion. Two sentries stood at the entrance. Danielis was nearly the last to arrive, and found himself at the end of the table, opposite Brigadier General Perez. Smoke hazed the air and there was a muted buzz of conversation, but faces were taut.

When the blue-robed figure with a Yang and Yin on the breast entered, silence fell like a curtain. Danielis was astonished to recognize Philosopher Woodworth. He'd last seen the man in Los Angeles, and assumed he would stay at the Esper center there. Must have come here by special conveyance, under special orders...

Perez introduced him. Both remained standing, under the eyes of the officers. "I have some important news for you, gentlemen," Perez said most quietly. "You may consider it an honor to be here. It means that in my judgment you can be trusted, first, to keep absolute silence about what you are going to hear, and second, to execute a vital operation of extreme difficulty." Danielis was made shockingly aware that several men were not present whose rank indicated they should be.

"I repeat," Perez said, "any breach of secrecy and the whole plan is ruined. In that case, the war will drag on for months or years. You know how bad our position is. You also know it will grow still worse as our stocks of those supplies the enemy now denies us are consumed. We could even be beaten. I'm not defeatist to say that, only realistic. We could lose the war.

"On the other hand, if this new scheme pans out, we may break the enemy's back this very month."

He paused to let that sink in before continuing:

"The plan was worked out by GHQ in conjunction with Esper Central in San Francisco some weeks ago. It's the reason we are headed north—" He let the gasp subside that ran through the stifling air. "Yes, you know that the Esper Order is neutral in political disputes. But you also know that it defends itself when attacked. And you probably know that an attack was made on it by the rebels. They seized the Napa Valley settlement and have been spreading malicious rumors about the Order since then. Would you like to comment on that, Philosopher Woodworth?"

The man in blue nodded and said coolly: "We've our own ways of findin' out things—intelligence service, you might say—so I can give y'all a report of the facts. St. Helena was assaulted at a time when most of its adepts were away, helpin' a new community get started out in Montana." *How did they travel so fast?* Daniels wondered. *Teleport, or what?* "I don't know, myself, if the enemy knew about that or were just lucky. Anyhow, when the two or three adepts that were left came and warned them off, fightin' broke out and the adepts were killed before they could act." He smiled. "We don't claim to be immortal, except the way every livin' thing is immortal. Nor infallible, either. So now St. Helena's occupied. We don't figure to take any immediate steps about that, because a lot of people in the community might get hurt.

"As for the yarns the enemy command's been handin' out; well, I reckon I'd do the same, if I had a chance like that. Everybody knows an adept can do things that nobody else can. Troops that realize they've done wrong to the Order are goin' to be scared of supernatural revenge. You're educated men here, and know there's nothin' supernatural involved, just a way to use the powers latent in most of us. You also know the Order doesn't believe in revenge. But the ordinary foot soldier doesn't think your way. His officers have got to restore his spirit somehow. So they fake some equipment and tell him that's what the adepts were really usin'—an advanced technology, sure, but only a set of machines that can be put out of action if you're brave, same as any other machine. That's what happened.

"Still, it is a threat to the Order; and we can't let an attack on our people go unpunished, either. So Esper Central has decided to help out your side. The sooner this war's over, the better for everybody."

A sigh gusted around the table, and a few exultant oaths. The hair stirred on Danielis' neck. Perez lifted a hand.

"Not too fast, please," the general said. "The adepts are not going to go around blasting your opponents for you. It was one hell of a tough decision for them to do as much as they agreed to. I, uh, understand that the, uh, personal development of every Esper will be set back many years by this much violence. They're making a big sacrifice.

"By their charter, they can use psionics to defend an establishment against attack. Okay…an assault on San Francisco will be construed as one on Central, their world headquarters."

The realization of what was to come was blinding to Danielis. He scarcely heard Perez' carefully dry continuation:

"Let's review the strategic picture. By now the enemy holds more than half of California, all of Oregon and Idaho, and a good deal of Washington. We, this army, we're using the last land access to San Francisco that we've got. The enemy hasn't tried to pinch that off yet, because the troops we pulled out of the north—those that aren't in the field at present—make a strong city garrison that'd sally out. He's collecting too much profit elsewhere to accept the cost.

"Nor can he invest the city with any hope of success. We still hold Puget Sound and the southern California ports. Our ships bring in ample food and munitions. His own sea power is much inferior to ours: chiefly schooners donated by coastal bossmen, operating out of Portland. He might overwhelm an occasional convoy, but he hasn't tried that so far because it isn't worth his trouble; there would be others, more heavily escorted. And of course he can't enter the Bay, with artillery and rocket emplacements on both sides of the Golden Gate. No, about all he can do is maintain some water communication with Hawaii and Alaska.

"Nevertheless, his ultimate object is San Francisco. It has to be—the seat of government and industry, the heart of the nation.

"Well, then, here's the plan. Our army is to engage the Sierra Command and its militia auxiliaries again, striking out of San Jose. That's a perfectly logical maneuver. Successful, it would cut his California forces in two. We know, in fact, that he is already concentrating men in anticipation of precisely such an attempt.

"We aren't going to succeed. We'll give him a good stiff battle and be thrown back. That's the hardest part: to feign a serious defeat, even convincing our own troops, and still maintain good order. We'll have a lot of details to thresh out about that.

"We'll retreat northward, up the Peninsula toward Frisco. The enemy is bound to pursue. It will look like a God-given chance to destroy us and get to the city walls.

"When he is well into the Peninsula, with the ocean on his left and the Bay on his right, we will outflank him and attack from the rear. The Esper adepts will be there to help. Suddenly he'll be caught, between us and the capital's land defenses. What the adepts don't wipe out, we will. Nothing will remain of the Sierra Command but a few garrisons. The rest of the war will be a mopping-up operation.

"It's a brilliant piece of strategy. Like all such, it's damn difficult to execute. Are you prepared to do the job?"

Danielis didn't raise his voice with the others. He was thinking too hard of Laura.

Northward and to the right there was some fighting. Cannon spoke occasionally, or a drumfire of rifles; smoke lay thin over the grass and the wind-gnarled live oaks which covered those hills. But down along the seacoast was only surf, blowing air, a hiss of sand across the dunes.

Mackenzie rode on the beach, where the footing was easiest and the view widest. Most of his regiment were inland. But that was a wilderness: rough ground, woods, the snags of ancient homes, making travel slow and hard. Once this area had been densely peopled, but the firestorm after the Hellbomb scrubbed it clean and today's reduced population could not make a go on such infertile soil. There didn't even seem to be any foemen near this left wing of the army.

The Rolling Stones had certainly not been given it for that reason. They could have borne the brunt at the center as well as those outfits which actually were there, driving the enemy back toward San Francisco. They had been blooded often enough in this war, when they operated out of Calistoga to help expel the Fallonites from northern California. So thoroughly had that job been done that now only a skeleton force need remain in charge. Nearly the whole Sierra Command had gathered at Modesto, met the northward-moving opposition army that struck at them out of San Jose, and sent it in a shooting retreat. Another day or so, and the white city should appear before their eyes.

And there the enemy will be sure to make a stand, Mackenzie thought, *with the garrison to reinforce him. And his positions will have to be shelled; maybe we'll have to take the place street by street. Laura, kid, will you be alive at the end?*

Of course, maybe it won't happen that way. Maybe my scheme'll work and we'll win easy—What a horrible word "maybe" is! He slapped his hands together with a pistol sound.

Speyer threw him a glance. The major's people were safe; he'd even been able to visit them at Mount Lassen, after the northern campaign was over. "Rough," he said.

"Rough on everybody," Mackenzie said with a thick anger. "This is a filthy war."

Speyer shrugged. "No different from most, except that this time Pacificans are on the receiving as well as the giving end."

"You know damn well I never liked the business, anyplace."

"What man in his right mind does?"

"When I want a sermon I'll ask for one."

"Sorry," said Speyer, and meant it.

"I'm sorry too," said Mackenzie, instantly contrite. "Nerves on edge. Damnation! I could almost wish for some action."

"Wouldn't be surprised if we got some. This whole affair smells wrong to me."

Mackenzie looked around him. On the right the horizon was bounded by hills, beyond which the low but massive San Bruno range lifted. Here and there he spied one of his own squads, afoot or ahorse. Overhead sputtered a plane. But there was plenty of concealment for a redoubt. Hell could erupt at any minute… though necessarily a small hell, quickly reduced by howitzer or bayonet, casualties light. (Huh! Every one of those light casualties was a man dead, with women and children to weep for him, or a man staring at the fragment of his arm, or a man with eyes and face gone in a burst of shot, and what kind of unsoldierly thoughts were these?)

Seeking comfort, Mackenzie glanced left. The ocean rolled greenish-gray, glittering far out, rising and breaking in a roar of white combers closer to land. He smelled salt and kelp. A few gulls mewed above dazzling sands. There was no sail or smoke-puff—only emptiness. The convoys from Puget Sound to San Francisco and the lean swift ships of the coastal bossmen were miles beyond the curve of the world.

Which was as it should be. Maybe things were working out okay on the high waters. One could only try, and hope. And...it had been his suggestion, James Mackenzie speaking at the conference General Cruikshank held between the battles of Mariposa and San Jose; the same James Mackenzie who had first proposed that the Sierra Command come down out of the mountains, and who had exposed the gigantic fraud of Esperdom, and succeeded in playing down for his men the fact that behind the fraud lay a mystery one hardly dared think about. He would endure in the chronicles, that colonel, they would sing ballads about him for half a thousand years.

Only it didn't feel that way. James Mackenzie knew he was not much more than average bright under the best of conditions, now dull-minded with weariness and terrified of his daughter's fate. For himself he was haunted by the fear of certain crippling wounds. Often he had to drink himself to sleep. He was shaved, because an officer must maintain appearances, but realized very well that if he hadn't had an orderly to do the job for him he would be as shaggy as any buck private. His uniform was faded and threadbare, his body stank and itched, his mouth yearned for tobacco but there had been some trouble in the commissariat and they were lucky to eat. His achievements amounted to patchwork jobs carried out in utter confusion, or to slogging like this and wishing only for an end to the whole mess. One day, win or lose, his body would give out on him—he could feel the machinery wearing to pieces, arthritic twinges, shortness of breath, dozing off in the middle of things—and the termination of himself would be as undignified and lonely as that of every other human slob. Hero? What an all-time laugh!

He yanked his mind back to the immediate situation. Behind him a core of the regiment accompanied the artillery along the beach, a thousand men with motorized gun carriages, caissons, mule-drawn wagons, a few trucks, one precious armored car. They were a dun mass topped with helmets, in loose formation, rifles or bows to hand. The sand deadened their footfalls, so that only the surf and the wind could be heard. But whenever the wind sank, Mackenzie caught the tune of the hex corps: a dozen leathery older men, mostly Indians, carrying the wands of power and whistling together the Song Against Witches. He took no stock in magic himself, yet when that sound came to him the skin crawled along his backbone.

Everything's in good order, he insisted. *We're doing fine.*

Then: *But Phil's right. This is a screwball business. The enemy should have fought through to a southward line of retreat, not let themselves be boxed.*

Captain Hulse galloped close. Sand spurted when he checked his horse. "Patrol report, sir."

"Well?" Mackenzie realized he had almost shouted. "Go ahead."

"Considerable activity observed about five miles northeast. Looks like a troop headed our way."

Mackenzie stiffened. "Haven't you anything more definite than that?"

"Not so far, with the ground so broken."

"Get some aerial reconnaissance there, for Pete's sake!"

"Yes, sir. I'll throw out more scouts, too."

"Carry on here, Phil." Mackenzie headed toward the radio truck. He carried a minicom in his saddlebag, of course, but San Francisco had been continuously jamming on all bands and you needed a powerful set to punch a signal even a few miles. Patrols must communicate by messenger.

He noticed that the firing inland had slacked off. There were decent roads in the interior Peninsula a ways further north, where some resettlement had taken place. The enemy, still in possession of that area, could use them to effect rapid movements.

If they withdrew their center and hit our flanks, where we're weakest—

A voice from field HQ, barely audible through the squeals and buzzes, took his report and gave back what had been seen elsewhere. Large maneuvers right and left, yes, it did seem as if the Fallonites were going to try a breakthrough. Could be a feint, though. The main body of the Sierrans must remain where it was until the situation became clearer. The Rolling Stones must hold out a while on their own.

"Will do." Mackenzie returned to the head of his columns. Speyer nodded grimly at the word.

"Better get prepared, hadn't we?"

"Uh-huh." Mackenzie lost himself in a welter of commands, as officer after officer rode to him. The outlying sections were to be pulled in. The beach was to be defended, with the high ground immediately above.

Men scurried, horses neighed, guns trundled about. The scout plane returned, flying low enough to get a transmission through: yes, definitely an attack on the way; hard to tell how big a force, through the damned tree cover and down in the damned arroyos, but it might well be at brigade strength.

Mackenzie established himself on a hilltop with his staff and runners. A line of artillery stretched beneath him, across the strand. Cavalry waited behind them, lances agleam, an infantry company for support. Otherwise the foot soldiers had faded into the landscape. The sea boomed its own cannonade, and gulls began to gather as if they knew there would be meat before long.

"Think we can hold them?" Speyer asked.

"Sure," Mackenzie said. "If they come down the beach, we'll enfilade them, as well as shooting up their front. If they come higher, well, that's a textbook example of defensible terrain. 'Course, if another troop punches through the lines further inland, we'll be cut off, but that isn't our worry right now."

"They must hope to get around our army and attack our rear."

"Guess so. Not too smart of them, though. We can approach Frisco just as easily fighting backwards as forwards."

"Unless the city garrison makes a sally."

"Even then. Total numerical strengths are about equal, and we've got more ammo and alky. Also a lot of bossman militia for auxiliaries, who're used to disorganized warfare in hilly ground."

"If we do whip them—" Speyer shut his lips together.

"Go on," Mackenzie said.

"Nothing."

"The hell it is. You were about to remind me of the next step: how do we take the city without too high a cost to both sides? Well I happen to know we've got a hole card to play there, which might help."

Speyer turned pitying eyes away from Mackenzie. Silence fell on the hilltop.

It was an unconscionably long time before the enemy came in view, first a few outriders far down the dunes, then the body of him, pouring from the ridges and gullies and woods. Reports flickered about Mackenzie—a powerful force, nearly twice as big as ours, but with little artillery; by now badly short of fuel, they must depend far more than we on animals to move their equipment. They were evidently going to charge, accept losses in order to get sabers and bayonets among the Rolling Stones' cannon. Mackenzie issued his directions accordingly.

The hostiles formed up, a mile or so distant. Through his field glasses Mackenzie recognized them, red sashes of the Madera Horse, green and gold pennon of the Dagos, fluttering in the iodine wind. He'd campaigned with both outfits in the past. It was treacherous to remember that Ives favored a blunt wedge formation and use the fact against him...One enemy armored car and some field-pieces, light horse-drawn ones, gleamed wickedly in the sunlight.

Bugles blew shrill. The Fallonite cavalry laid lance in rest and started trotting. They gathered speed as they went, a canter, a gallop, until the earth trembled with them. Then their infantry got going, flanked by its guns. The car rolled along between the first and second line of foot. Oddly, it had no rocket launcher on top or repeater barrels thrust from the fire slits. Those were good troops, Mackenzie thought, advancing in close order with that ripple down the ranks which bespoke veterans. He hated what must happen.

His defense waited immobile on the sand. Fire crackled from the hillsides, where mortar squads and riflemen crouched. A rider toppled, a dogface clutched his belly and went to his knees, their companions behind moved forward to close the lines again. Mackenzie looked to his howitzers. Men stood tensed at sights and lanyards. Let the foe get well in range—There! Yamaguchi, mounted just rearward of the gunners, drew his saber and flashed the blade downward. Cannon bellowed. Fire spurted through smoke, sand gouted up, shrapnel sleeted over the charging force. At once the gun crews fell into the rhythm of reloading, relaying, refiring, the steady three rounds per minute which conserved barrels and broke armies. Horses screamed in their own tangled red guts. But not many had been hit. The Madera cavalry continued in full gallop. Their lead was so close now that Mackenzie's glasses picked out a face, red, freckled, a ranch boy turned trooper, his mouth stretched out of shape as he yelled.

The archers behind the defending cannon let go. Arrows whistled skyward, flight after flight, curved past the gulls and down again. Flame and smoke ran ragged in the wiry hill grass, out of the ragged-leaved live oak copses. Men pitched to the sand, many still hideously astir, like insects that had been stepped on. The fieldpieces on the enemy left flank halted, swiveled about, and spat return fire. Futile...but God, their officer had courage! Mackenzie saw the advancing lines waver. An attack by his own horse and foot, down the beach, ought to crumple them. "Get ready to move," he said into his minicom. He saw his men poise. The cannon belched anew.

The oncoming armored car slowed to a halt. Something within it chattered, loud enough to hear through the explosions.

A blue-white sheet ran over the nearest hill. Mackenzie shut half-blinded eyes. When he opened them again, he saw a grass fire through the crazy patterns of afterimage. A Rolling Stone burst from cover, howling, his clothes ablaze. The man hit the sand and rolled over. That part of the beach lifted in one monster wave, crested twenty feet high, and smashed across the hill. The burning soldier vanished in the avalanche that buried his comrades.

"*Psi blast!*" someone screamed, thin and horrible, through chaos and ground-shudder. "The Espers—"

Unbelievably, a bugle sounded and the Sierran cavalry lunged forward. Past their own guns, on against the scattering opposition...and horses and riders rose into the air, tumbled in a giant's invisible whirligig, crashed bonebreakingly to earth again. The second rank of lancers broke. Mounts reared, pawed the air, wheeled and fled in every direction.

A terrible deep hum filled the sky. Mackenzie saw the world as if through a haze, as if his brain were being dashed back and forth between the walls of his skull. Another glare ran across the hills, higher this time, burning men alive.

"They'll wipe us out," Speyer called, a dim voice that rose and fell on the air tides. "They'll re-form as we stampede—"

"No!" Mackenzie shouted. "The adepts must be in that car. Come on!"

Most of his horse had recoiled on their own artillery, one squealing, trampling wreck. The infantry stood rigid, but about to bolt. A glance thrown to his right showed Mackenzie how the enemy themselves were in confusion, this had been a terrifying surprise to them too, but as soon as they got over the shock they'd advance and there'd be nothing left to stop them...It was as if another man spurred his mount. The animal fought, foam-flecked with panic. He slugged its head around, brutally, and dug in spurs. They rushed down the hill toward the guns.

He needed all his strength to halt the gelding before the cannon mouths. A man slumped dead by his piece, though there was no mark on him. Mackenzie jumped to the ground. His steed bolted.

He hadn't time to worry about that. Where was help? "Come here!" His yell was lost in the riot. But suddenly another man was beside him, Speyer, snatching up a shell and slamming it into the breach. Mackenzie squinted through the telescope, took a bearing by guess and feel. He could see the Esper car where it squatted among dead and hurt. At this distance it looked too small to have blackened acres.

Speyer helped him lay the howitzer. He jerked the lanyard. The gun roared and sprang. The shell burst a few yards short of target, sand spurted and metal fragments whined.

Speyer had the next one loaded. Mackenzie aimed and fired. Overshot this time, but not by much. The car rocked. Concussion might have hurt the Espers inside; at least, the psi blasts had stopped. But it was necessary to strike before the foe got organized again.

He ran toward his own regimental car. The door gaped, the crew had fled. He threw himself into the driver's seat. Speyer clanged the door shut and stuck his face in the hood of the rocket-launcher periscope. Mackenzie raced the machine forward. The banner on its rooftop snapped in the wind.

Speyer aimed the launcher and pressed the firing button. The missile burned across intervening yards and exploded. The other car lurched on its wheels. A hole opened in its side.

If the boys will only rally and advance—Well, if they don't, I'm done for anyway. Mackenzie squealed to a stop, flung open the door and leaped out. Curled, blackened metal framed his entry. He wriggled through, into murk and stenches.

Two Espers lay there. The driver was dead, a chunk of steel through his breast. The other one, the adept, whimpered among his unhuman instruments. His face was hidden by blood. Mackenzie pitched the corpse on its side and pulled off the robe. He snatched a curving tube of metal and tumbled back out.

Speyer was still in the undamaged car, firing repeaters at those hostiles who ventured near. Mackenzie jumped onto the ladder of the disabled machine, climbed to its roof and stood erect. He waved the blue robe in one hand and the weapon he did not understand in the other. "Come on, you sons!" he shouted, tiny against the sea wind. We've knocked 'em out for you! Want your breakfast in bed too?"

One bullet buzzed past his ear. Nothing else. Most of the enemy, horse and foot, stayed frozen. In that immense stillness he could not tell if he heard surf or the blood in his own veins.

Then a bugle called. The hex corps whistled; triumphantly; their tomtoms thuttered. A ragged line of his infantry began to move toward him. More followed. The cavalry joined them, man by man and unit by unit, on their flanks. Soldiers ran down the smoking hillsides.

Mackenzie sprang to sand again and into his car. "Let's get back," he told Speyer. We got a battle to finish."

"Shut up!" Tom Danielis said.

Philosopher Woodworth stared at him. Fog swirled and dropped in the forest, hiding the land and the brigade, gray nothingness through which came a muffled noise of men and horses and wheels, an isolated and infinitely weary sound. The air was cold, and clothing hung heavy on the skin.

"Sir," protested Major Lescarbault. The eyes were wide and shocked in his gaunted face.

"I dare tell a ranking Esper to stop quacking about a subject of which he's totally ignorant?" Danielis answered. "Well, it's past time that somebody did."

Woodworth recovered his poise. "All I said, son, was that we should consolidate our adepts and strike the Brodskyite center," he reproved. "What's wrong with that?"

Danielis clenched his fists. "Nothing," he said, "except it invites a worse disaster than you've brought on us yet."

"A setback or two," Lescarbault argued. "They did rout us on the west, but we turned their flank here by the Bay."

"With the net result that their main body pivoted, attacked, and split us in half," Danielis snapped. "The Espers have been scant use since then…now the rebels know they need vehicles to transport their weapons, and can be killed. Artillery zeroes in on their positions, or bands of woodsmen hit and run, leaving them dead, or the enemy simply goes around any spot where they're known to be. We haven't got enough adepts!"

"That's why I proposed gettin' them in one group, too big to withstand," Woodworth said.

"And too cumbersome to be of any value," Danielis replied. He felt more than a little sickened, knowing how the Order had cheated him his whole life; yes, he thought, that was the real bitterness, not the fact that the adepts had failed to defeat the rebels—by failing, essentially, to break their spirit—but the fact that the adepts were only someone else's cat's paws and every gentle, earnest soul in every Esper community was only someone's dupe.

Wildly he wanted to return to Laura—there'd been no chance thus far to see her—Laura and the kid, the last honest reality this fog-world had left him. He mastered himself and went on more evenly:

"The adepts, what few of them survive, will of course be helpful in defending San Francisco. An army free to move around in the field can deal with them, one way or another, but your…your weapons can repel an assault on the city walls. So that's where I'm going to take them."

Probably the best he could do. There was no word from the northern half of the loyalist army. Doubtless they'd withdrawn to the capital, suffering heavy losses en route. Radio jamming continued, hampering friendly and hostile communications alike. He had to take action, either retreat southward or fight his way through to the city. The latter course seemed wisest. He didn't believe that Laura had much to do with his choice.

"I'm no adept myself," Woodworth said. "I can't call them mind to mind."

"You mean you can't use their equivalent of radio," Danielis said brutally. "Well, you've got an adept in attendance. Have him pass the word."

Woodworth flinched. "I hope," he said, "I hope you understand this came as a surprise to me too."

"Oh, yes, certainly, Philosopher," Lescarbault said unbidden.

Woodworth swallowed. "I still hold with the Way and the Order," he said harshly. "There's nothin' else I can do. Is there? The Grand Seeker has promised a full explanation when this is over." He shook his head. "Okay, son, I'll do what I can."

A certain compassion touched Danielis as the blue robe disappeared into the fog. He rapped his orders the more severely.

Slowly his command got going. He was with the Second Brigade; the rest were strewn over the Peninsula in the fragments into which the rebels had knocked them. He hoped the equally scattered adepts, joining him on his march through the San Bruno range, would guide some of those units to him. But most, wandering demoralized, were sure to surrender to the first rebels they came upon.

He rode near the front, on a muddy road that snaked over the highlands. His helmet was a monstrous weight. The horse stumbled beneath him, exhausted by—how many days?—of march, countermarch, battle, skirmish, thin rations or none, heat and cold and fear, in an empty land. Poor beast, he'd see that it got proper treatment when they reached the city. That all those poor beasts behind him did, after trudging and fighting and trudging again until their eyes were filmed with fatigue.

There'll be chance enough for rest in San Francisco. We're impregnable there, walls and cannon and the Esper machines to landward, the sea that feeds us at our backs. We can recover our strength, regroup our forces, bring fresh troops down from Washington and up from the south by water. The war isn't decided yet...God help us.

I wonder if it will ever be.

And then, will Jimbo Mackenzie come to see us, sit by the fire and swap yarns about what we did? Or talk about something else, anything else? If not, that's too high a price for victory.

Maybe not too high a price for what we've learned, though. Strangers on this planet...what else could have forged those weapons? The adepts will talk if I myself have to torture them till they do. But Danielis remembered tales muttered in the fisher huts of his boyhood, after dark, when ghosts walked in old men's minds. Before the holocaust there had been legends about the stars, and the legends lived on. He didn't know if he would be able to look again at the night sky without a shiver.

This damned fog—

Hoofs thudded. Danielis half drew his sidearm. But the rider was a scout of his own, who raised a drenched sleeve in salute. "Colonel, an enemy force about ten miles ahead by road. Big."

So we'll have to fight now. "Do they seem aware of us?"

"No, sir. They're proceeding east along the ridge there."

"Probably figure to occupy the Candlestick Park ruins," Danielis murmured. His body was too tired for excitement. "Good stronghold, that. Very well, Corporal." He turned to Lescarbault and issued instructions.

The brigade formed itself in the formlessness. Patrols went out. Information began to flow back, and Danielis sketched a plan that ought to work. He didn't want to try for a decisive engagement, only brush the enemy aside and discourage them from pursuit. His men must be spared, as many as possible, for the city defense and the eventual counteroffensive.

Lescarbault came back. "Sir! The radio jamming's ended!"

"What?" Danielis blinked, not quite comprehending.

"Yes, sir. I've been using a minicom—" Lescarbault lifted the wrist on which his tiny transceiver was strapped—"for very short-range work, passing the battalion commanders their orders. The interference stopped a couple of minutes ago. Clear as daylight."

Danielis pulled the wrist toward his own mouth. "Hello, hello, radio wagon, this is the C.O. You read me?"

"Yes, sir," said the voice.

"They turned off the jammer in the city for a reason. Get me the open military band."

"Yes, sir." Pause, while men mumbled and water runneled unseen in the arroyos. A wraith smoked past Danielis' eyes. Drops coursed off his helmet and down his collar. The horse's mane hung sodden.

Like the scream of an insect:

"—here at once! Every unit in the field, get to San Francisco at once! We're under attack by sea!"

Danielis let go Lescarbault's arm. He stared into emptiness while the voice wailed on and forever on.

"—bombarding Potrero Point. Decks jammed with troops. They must figure to make a landing there—"

Danielis' mind raced ahead of the words. It was as if Esp were no lie, as if he scanned the beloved city himself and felt her wounds in his own flesh. There was no fog around the Gate, of course, or so detailed a description could not have been given. Well, probably some streamers of it rolled in under the rusted remnants of the bridge, themselves like snowbanks against blue-green water and brilliant sky. But most of the Bay stood open to the sun. On the opposite shore lifted the Eastbay hills, green with gardens and agleam with villas; and Marin shouldered heavenward across the strait, looking to the roofs and walls and heights that were San Francisco. The convoy had gone between the coast defenses that could have smashed it, an unusually large convoy and not on time: but still the familiar big-bellied hulls, white sails, occasional fuming stacks, that kept the city fed. There had been an explanation about trouble with commerce raiders; and the fleet was passed on into the Bay, where San Francisco had no walls. Then the gun covers were taken off and the holds vomited armed men.

Yes, they did seize a convoy, those piratical schooners. Used radio jamming of their own; together with ours, that choked off any cry of warning. They threw our supplies overboard and embarked the bossman militia. Some spy or traitor gave them the recognition signals. Now the capital lies open to them, her garrison stripped, hardly an adept left in Esper Central, the Sierrans thrusting against her southern gates, and Laura without me.

"We're coming!" Danielis yelled. His brigade groaned into speed behind him. They struck with a desperate ferocity that carried them deep into enemy positions and then stranded them in separated groups. It became knife and saber in the fog. But Danielis, because he led the charge, had already taken a grenade on his breast.

East and south, in the harbor district and at the wreck of the Peninsula wall, there was still some fighting. As he rode higher, Mackenzie saw how those parts were dimmed by smoke, which the wind scattered to show rubble that had been houses. The sound of firing drifted to him. But otherwise the city shone untouched, roofs and white walls in a web of streets, church spires raking the sky like masts, Federal House on Nob Hill and the Watchtower on Telegraph Hill as he remembered them from childhood visits. The Bay glittered insolently beautiful.

But he had no time for admiring the view, nor for wondering where Laura huddled. The attack on Twin Peaks must be swift, for surely Esper Central would defend itself.

On the avenue climbing the opposite side of those great humps, Speyer led half the Rolling Stones. (Yamaguchi lay dead on a pockmarked beach.) Mackenzie himself was taking this side. Horses clopped along Portola, between blankly shuttered mansions; guns trundled and creaked, boots knocked on pavement, moccasins slithered, weapons rattled, men breathed heavily and the hex corps whistled against unknown demons. But silence overwhelmed the noise, echoes trapped it and let it die. Mackenzie recollected nightmares when he fled down a corridor which had no end. *Even if they don't cut loose at us*, he thought bleakly, *we've got to seize their place before our nerve gives out.*

Twin Peaks Boulevard turned off Portola and wound steeply to the right. The houses ended; wild grasses alone covered the quasi-sacred hills, up to the tops where stood the buildings forbidden to all but adepts. Those two soaring, iridescent, fountainlike skyscrapers had been raised by night, within a matter of weeks. Something like a moan stirred at Mackenzie's back.

"Bugler, sound the advance. On the double!"

A child's jeering, the notes lifted and were lost. Sweat stung Mackenzie's eyes. If he failed and was killed, that didn't matter too much…after everything which had happened…but the regiment, the regiment—

Flame shot across the street, the color of hell. There went a hiss and a roar. The pavement lay trenched, molten, smoking and reeking. Mackenzie wrestled his horse to a standstill. *A warning only. But if they had enough adepts to handle us, would they bother trying to scare us off?* "Artillery, open fire!"

The field guns bellowed together, not only howitzers but motorized 75s taken along from Alemany Gate's emplacements. Shells went overhead with a locomotive sound. They burst on the walls above and the racket thundered back down the wind.

Mackenzie tensed himself for an Esper blast, but none came. Had they knocked out the final defensive post in their own first barrage? Smoke cleared from the heights and he saw that the colors which played in the tower were dead and that wounds gaped across loveliness, showing unbelievably thin framework. It was like seeing the bones of a woman murdered by his hand.

Quick, though! He issued a string of commands and led the horse and foot on. The battery stayed where it was, firing and firing with hysterical fury. The dry brown grass started to burn, as red-hot fragments scattered across the slope. Through mushroom bursts, Mackenzie saw the building crumble. Whole sheets of facing broke and fell to earth. The skeleton vibrated, took a direct hit and sang in metal agony, slumped and twisted apart.

What was that which stood within?

There were no separate rooms, no floors, nothing but girders, enigmatic machines, here and there a globe still aglow like a minor sun. The structure had enclosed something nearly as tall as itself, a finned and shining column, almost like a rocket shell but impossibly huge and fair.

Their spaceship, Mackenzie thought in the clamor. *Yes, of course, the ancients had begun making spaceships, and we always figured we would again someday. This, though—!*

The archers lifted a tribal screech. The riflemen and cavalry took it up, crazy, jubilant, the howl of a beast of prey. By Satan, we've whipped the stars themselves! As they burst onto the hillcrest, the shelling stopped, and their yells overrode the wind. Smoke was acrid as blood smell in their nostrils.

A few dead blue-robes could be seen in the debris. Some half-dozen survivors milled toward the ship. A bowman let fly. His arrow glanced off the landing gear but brought the Espers to a halt. Troopers poured over the shards to capture them.

Mackenzie reined in. Something that was not human lay crushed near a machine. Its blood was deep violet color. *When the people have seen this, that's the end of the Order.* He felt no triumph. At St. Helena he had come to appreciate how fundamentally good the believers were.

But this was no moment for regret, or for wondering how harsh the future would be with man taken entirely off the leash. The building on the other peak was still intact. He had to consolidate his position here, then help Phil if need be.

However, the minicom said, "Come on and join me, Jimbo. The fracas is over," before he had completed his task. As he rode alone toward Speyer's place, he saw a Pacific States flag flutter up the mast on that skyscraper's top.

Guards stood awed and nervous at the portal. Mackenzie dismounted and walked inside. The entry chamber was a soaring, shimmering fantasy of colors and arches, through which men moved troll-like. A corporal led him down a hall. Evidently this building had been used for quarters, offices, storage, and less understandable purposes…There was a room whose door had been blown down with dynamite. The fluid abstract murals were stilled, scarred, and sooted. Four ragged troopers pointed guns at the two beings whom Speyer was questioning.

One slumped at something that might answer to a desk. The avian face was buried in seven-fingered hands and the rudimentary wings quivered with sobs.

Are they able to cry, then? Mackenzie thought, astonished, and had a sudden wish to take the being in his arms and offer what comfort he was able.

The other one stood erect in a robe of woven metal. Great topaz eyes met Speyer's from a seven-foot height, and the voice turned accented English into music.

"—a G-type star some fifty light-years hence. It is barely visible to the naked eye, though not in this hemisphere."

The major's fleshless, bristly countenance jutted forward as if to peck. "When do you expect reinforcements?"

"There will be no other ship for almost a century, and it will only bring personnel. We are isolated by space and time; few can come to work here, to seek to build a bridge of minds across that gulf—"

"Yeah," Speyer nodded prosaically. "The light-speed limit. I thought so. If you're telling the truth."

The being shuddered. "Nothing is left for us but to speak truth, and pray that you will understand and help. Revenge, conquest, any form of mass violence is impossible when so much space and time lies between. Our labor has been done in the mind and heart. It is not too late, even now. The most crucial facts can still be kept hidden—oh, listen to me, for the sake of your unborn!"

Speyer nodded to Mackenzie. "Everything okay?" he said. "We got us a full bag here. About twenty left alive, this fellow the bossman. Seems like they're the only ones on Earth."

"We guessed there couldn't be many," the colonel said. His tone and his feelings were alike ashen. "When we talked it over, you and me, and tried to figure what our clues meant. They'd have to be few, or they'd've operated more openly."

"Listen, listen," the being pleaded. "We came in love. Our dream was to lead you—to make you lead yourselves—toward peace, fulfillment...Oh, yes, we would also gain, gain yet another race with whom we could someday converse as brothers. But there are many races in the universe. It was chiefly for your own tortured sakes that we wished to guide your future."

"That controlled history notion isn't original with you," Speyer grunted. "We've invented it for ourselves now and then on Earth. The last time it led to the Hellbombs. No, thanks!"

"But we *know*! The Great Science predicts with absolute certainty—"

"Predicted this?" Speyer waved a hand at the blackened room.

"There are fluctuations. We are too few to control so many savages in every detail. But do you not wish an end to war, to all your ancient sufferings? I offer you that for your help today."

"You succeeded in starting a pretty nasty war yourselves," Speyer said.

The being twisted its fingers together. "That was an error. The plan remains, the only way to lead your people toward peace. I, who have traveled between suns, will get down before your boots and beg you—"

"Stay put!" Speyer flung back. "If you'd come openly, like honest folk, you'd have found some to listen to you. Maybe enough, even. But no, your do-gooding had to be subtle and crafty. You knew what was right for us. We weren't entitled to any say in the matter. God in heaven, I've never heard anything so arrogant!"

The being lifted its head. "Do you tell children the whole truth?"

"As much as they're ready for."

"Your child-culture is not ready to hear these truths."

"Who qualified you to call us children—besides yourselves?"

"How do you know you are adult?"

"By trying adult jobs and finding out if I can handle them. Sure, we make some ghastly blunders, we humans. But they're our own. And we learn from them. You're the ones who won't learn, you and that damned psychological science you were bragging about, that wants to fit every living mind into the one frame it can understand.

"You wanted to re-establish the centralized state, didn't you? Did you ever stop to think that maybe feudalism is what suits man? Some one place to call our own, and belong to, and be part of; a community with traditions and honor; a chance for the individual to make decisions that count; a bulwark for liberty against the central overlords, who'll always want more and more power; a thousand different ways to live. We've always built supercountries, here on Earth, and we've always knocked them apart again. I think maybe the whole idea is wrong. And maybe this time we'll try something better. Why not a world of little states, too well rooted to dissolve in a nation, too small to do much harm—slowly rising above petty jealousies and spite, but keeping their identities—a thousand separate approaches to our problems. Maybe then we can solve a few of them...for ourselves!"

"You will never do so," the being said. "You will be torn in pieces all over again."

"That's what you think. I think otherwise. But whichever is right—and I bet this is too big a universe for either of us to predict—we'll have made a free choice on Earth. I'd rather be dead than domesticated.

"The people are going to learn about you as soon as Judge Brodsky's been reinstated. No, sooner. The regiment will hear today, the city tomorrow, just to make sure no one gets ideas about suppressing the truth again. By the time your next spaceship comes, we'll be ready for it: in our own way, whatever that is."

The being drew a fold of robe about its head. Speyer turned to Mackenzie. His face was wet. "Anything...you want to say...Jimbo?"

"No," Mackenzie mumbled. "Can't think of anything. Let's get our command organized here. I don't expect we'll have to fight any more, though. It seems to be about ended down there."

"Sure." Speyer drew an uneven breath. "The enemy troops elsewhere are bound to capitulate. They've got nothing left to fight for. We can start patching up pretty soon."

There was a house with a patio whose wall was covered by roses. The street outside had not yet come back to life, so that silence dwelt here under the yellow sunset. A maidservant showed Mackenzie through the back door and departed.

He walked toward Laura, who sat on a bench beneath a willow. She watched him approach but did not rise. One hand rested on a cradle.

He stopped and knew not what to say. How thin she was!

Presently she told him, so low he could scarcely hear: "Tom's dead."

"Oh, no." Darkness came and went before his eyes.

"I learned the day before yesterday, when a few of his men struggled home. He was killed in the San Bruno."

Mackenzie did not dare join her, but his legs would not upbear him. He sat down on the flagstones and saw curious patterns in their arrangement. There was nothing else to look at.

Her voice ran on above him, toneless: "Was it worth it? Not only Tom, but so many others, killed for a point of politics?"

"More than that was at stake," he said.

"Yes, I heard on the radio. I still can't understand how it was worth it. I've tried very hard, but I can't."

He had no strength left to defend himself. "Maybe you're right, duck. I wouldn't know."

"I'm not sorry for myself," she said. "I still have Jimmy. But Tom was cheated out of so much."

He realized all at once that there was a baby, and he ought to take his grandchild to him and think thoughts about life going on into the future. But he was too empty.

"Tom wanted him named after you," she said.

Did you, Laura? he wondered. Aloud: "What are you going to do now?"

"I'll find something."

He made himself glance at her. The sunset burned on the willow leaves above and on her face, which was now turned toward the infant he could not see. "Come back to Nakamura," he said.

"No. Anywhere else."

"You always loved the mountains," he groped. "We—"

"No." She met his eyes. "It isn't you, Dad. Never you. But Jimmy is not going to grow up a soldier." She hesitated. "I'm sure some of the Espers will keep going, on a new basis, but with the same goals. I think we should join them. He ought to believe in something different from what killed his father, and work for it to become real. Don't you agree?"

Mackenzie climbed to his feet against Earth's hard pull. "I don't know," he said. "Never was a thinker…Can I see him?"

"Oh, Dad—"

He went over and looked down at the small sleeping form. "If you marry again," he said, "and have a daughter, would you call her for her mother?" He saw Laura's head bend downward and her hands clench. Quickly he said, "I'll go now. I'd like to visit you some more, tomorrow or sometime, if you'll have me."

Then she came to his arms and wept. He stroked her hair and murmured, as he had done when she was a child. "You do want to return to the mountains, don't you? They're your country too, your people, where you belong."

"Y-you'll never know how much I want to."

"Then why not?" he cried.

His daughter straightened herself. "I can't," she said. "Your war is ended. Mine has just begun."

Because he had trained that will, he could only say, "I hope you win it."

"Perhaps in a thousand years—" She could not continue.

Night had fallen when he left her. Power was still out in the city, so the street lamps were dark and the stars stood forth above all roofs. The squad that waited to accompany their colonel to barracks looked wolfish by lantern light. They saluted him and rode at his back, rifles ready for trouble; but there was only the iron sound of horseshoes.

UNTITLED LIMERICK

A foolish young chemist named Kroll
heated fulminate up in a bowl.
  Without distillation
  he got separation,
i.e., of his body and soul.

Operation Salamander

The sky was full of broomsticks and the police were going nuts trying to handle the traffic. The Homecoming game always attracts an overflow crowd, also an overflow of high spirits. These I did not share. I edged my battered prewar Chevy past a huge 200-dragonpower Lincoln with sky-blue handle, polyethylene straw, and blatting radio. It sneered at me, but I got to the vacant rack first. Dismounting, I pocketed the runekey and mooched glumly through the mob.

The Weather Bureau kachinas are obliging about game nights. There was a cool crisp tang to the air, and dry leaves scrittled across the sidewalks. A harvest moon was rising like a big yellow pumpkin over darkened campus buildings. I thought of Midwestern fields and woods, damp earthy smells and streaming mists, out beyond the city, and the wolf part of me wanted to be off and away after jackrabbits. But with proper training a were can control his reflexes, and polarized light doesn't have to cause more than a primitive tingle along his nerves.

For me, the impulse was soon lost in bleaker thoughts. Ginny, my darling! She should have been walking beside me, face lifted to the wind and long hair crackling in the thin frost; but the only consolation was an illegal hip-flask. Why the hell was I attending the game anyhow?

Passing Teth Caph Sameth frat house, I found myself on the campus proper. Trismegistus was founded after the advent of modern science, and its layout reflects that fact. The largest edifice houses the Language Department, because exotic tongues are necessary for the more powerful spells—which is why so many African and Asian students come here to learn American slang; but there are two English halls, one for the arts college and one for Engineering Poetics. Nearby is the Therianthropology Building, which always has interesting displays of foreign technique: this month it was Eskimo, in honor of the visiting agekok, Dr. Ayingalak. A ways off is Zoology, carefully isolated inside its pentagonal fence, for some of those long-legged beasties are not pleasant neighbors. The medical school has a shiny new research center, courtesy of the Rockefeller Foundation, from which has already come such stunning advances as the polaroid filter-lenses that make it possible for those afflicted with the Evil Eye to lead normal lives.

Only the law school is unaffected. Their work has always been of the other world.

Crossing the Mall, I went by the grimy little Physical Sciences Building just in time for Dr. Griswold to hail me. He came puttering down the steps, a small wizened fellow with goatee and merry blue eyes. Somewhere behind their twinkle lay a look of hurt bafflement, as of a child who could never quite understand why no one else was really interested in his toys.

"Ah, Mr. Matuchek," he said. "Are you attending the game?"

I nodded, not especially wanting company, but he tagged along and I had to be sociable. Not that I was apple-polishing—I was in his chemistry and physics classes, but they were snaps. I simply didn't have the heart to rebuff a nice, lonely old geezer.

"Me too," he went on. "I understand the cheerleaders have planned something spectacular between halves."

"Yeh?"

He cocked his head and gave me a birdlike glance. "If you're having any difficulty, Mr. Matuchek…if I can help you…it's what I'm here for, you know."

"It's OK," I lied. "Thanks anyway, sir.'

"It can't be easy for a mature man, a combat veteran and a famous actor, to start in with a lot of giggling freshmen," he said. "I remember how you helped me in that…ah…unfortunate incident last month. Believe me, Mr. Matuchek, I am grateful."

"Oh, hell, that was nothing. I came here to get an education." *And to be with Virginia Graylock—but that's impossible now.*

I saw no reason to load the details on him. It was simple enough. After we beat the kaftans off the Caliphate, I returned to Metro-Goldwyn-Merlin and resumed werewolfing for them. But the same exploit which introduced me to Ginny had left me bobtailed, and a brush piece is a nuisance. I had medals, sure, but war heroes were a dime a coven—not that I claim an undue share of courage, events had merely flogged me into doing what I did. I couldn't get real conviction into my role in *Abbott and Costello Meet Paracelsus*; I don't look down on pure entertainment, but I discovered a new-born wish to do something more significant.

Ginny could get me into the Arcane Agency of which she was head witch, and I could work on that control of paranatural forces on which the whole world now depends. To be precise, I shared the common dream of taming Fire and Air enough to hitch them to a ship and reach the planets. But first I needed professional training. So Stephen Matuchek and MGM parted company with noises of mutual esteem, and I went to college on my savings and my G.I.

Ginny herself wanted a Ph.D.—she already had an M.A. from Congo—and Trismegistus offered her an instructorship while she took an extended leave of absence from the agency. Same school…we'd be together all our free hours, and I could probably talk her into an early marriage. Wonderful setup.

Like hell.

Griswold sighed, perhaps understanding my withdrawal. "There are times when I feel altogether useless," he said.

"Not in the least, sir," I answered with careful heartiness. "How on Middle Earth would—oh, say alchemy—be practical without a grounding in chemistry and nuclear physics? You'd produce poisonous compounds, or blow up half a county."

"Of course, of course. You understand. You know something of the world—more than I, in all truth. But the students…well, I suppose it's only natural. They want to speak a few words, make a few passes, and get what they desire, just like that, without bothering to learn the Sanskrit grammar or the periodic table. They haven't realized that you never get something for nothing."

"They will. They'll grow up."

"Even the administration…this University simply doesn't appreciate the need for physical science. Now at California, they're getting a billion-volt Philosopher's Stone, but here—" Griswold shrugged. "Excuse me. I despise self-pity."

We came to the stadium, and I handed over my ticket but declined the night-seeing spectacles. They'd given me witch-sight in basic training. My seat was on the thirty-yard line, between a fresh-faced coed and an Old Grad already hollering himself raw. An animated tray went by, and I bought a hot dog and rented a crystal ball. But that wasn't to follow the details of play. I muttered over the globe and peered into it and saw Ginny.

She was seated on the fifty, opposite side, the black cat Svartalf on her lap, her hair a shout of red against the human drabness around. That witchcraft peculiarly hers was something more old and strong than the Art in which she was so adept. Even across the field and through the cheap glass gazer, she made my heart stumble.

The problem was simply this: Trismegistus' President Malzius was a pompous mediocrity whose chief accomplishment had been to make the trustees his yes-men. What he said, went. And it was his arrogant idea to insist that all personnel take a geas to obey every University regulation while their contracts were in force. He had still corralled a pretty good faculty for the salaries were good and the rules the ordinary ones. Ginny had signed her contract a month before I enrolled and not felt the kicker till too late.

Students and faculty members, right down to the instructor level, were not permitted to date each other.

Naturally I had stormed my way into Malzius' office and demanded an exception. No use. He wasn't going to revise the book for me—"bad precedent, Mr. Matuchek, bad precedent"—and I agreed sulkily that it was, indeed, a bad precedent. The rule would have had to be stricken completely, as the geas didn't allow special dispensations. Nor did it allow for the case of a student from another school, so it was pointless for me to transfer. The only solution, till Ginny's contract expired in June, would have been for me to drop entirely, and with that cold-iron determination of hers she wouldn't hear of that. Lose a whole year? What was I, a wolf or a mouse? We had quite a quarrel about it, right out in public. And when you can only meet at official functions, it just isn't easy to kiss and make up.

Oh, sure, we were still engaged and still saw each other at smokers, teas… really living it up. Meanwhile, as she pointed out with that icy logic I knew was defensive but never could break past, we were human. From time to time, she would be going out with some bachelor colleague, wishing he were me, and I'd squire an occasional girl around...

Tonight she was with Dr. Alan Abercrombie, Assistant Professor of Comparative Nigromancy, sleek, blond, handsome, the lion of the tiffins. He'd been paying her a lot of attention while I smoldered alone.

Quite alone. I think Svartalf considers my morals no better than his. I had every intention of fidelity, but when you've parked your broomstick in a moonlit lane and a cute bit of fluff is snuggled against you...those round yellow eyes glowing from a nearby tree are remarkably style-cramping. I soon gave up and spent my evenings studying or drinking beer.

Heigh-ho. I drew my coat tighter about me and shivered in the wind. There was a smell of wrongness to the air...probably only my bad mood, I thought, but I'd sniffed trouble up in the future before now.

The Old Grad blasted my ears off as the teams trotted out into the moonlight, Trismegistus' Gryphons and the Albertus Magnus Wyverns. The very old grads say they can't get used to so many four-eyed runts wearing letters—apparently a football team was composed of dinosaurs back before the Thaumaturgic Age. But of course the Art is essentially intellectual and has given its own tone to sports.

This game had its interesting points. The Wyverns levitated off and their skinny little quarterback turned out to be a werepelican. Dushanovitch, in condor shape, nailed him on our twenty. Andrevski is the best line werebuck in the Big Ten, and held them for two downs. On the third, Pilsudski got the ball and became a kangaroo. His footwork was beautiful as he dodged a tackle—the guy had a Tarnkappe, but you could see the footprints advance—and passed to Mstislav. The Wyverns swooped low, expecting Mstislav to turn it into a raven for a field goal, but with lightning a-crackle as he fended off their counterspells, he made it into a pig...greased. These were minor transformations, naturally, a quick gesture at an object already sensitized, not the great and terrible Words I was to hear before dawn.

A bit later, unnecessary roughness cost us fifteen yards: Domingo accidentally stepped on a scorecard which had blown to the field and drove his cleats through several of the Wyverns' names. But no real harm was done, and they got the same penalty when Thorsson was carried away by the excitement and tossed a thunderbolt. At the end of the first half, the score was Trismegistus 13, Albertus Magnus 6, and the crowd was nearly ripping up the benches.

I pulled my hat back off my ears, gave the Old Grad a dirty look, and stared into the crystal. Ginny was more of a fan than I; she was jumping and hollering, hardly seeming to notice that Abercrombie had draped an arm around her. Or perhaps she didn't mind...? I took a long, resentful drag at my flask.

The cheering squad paraded out onto the field. Their instruments wove through an elaborate aerial maneuver, drumming and tootling, as they made the traditional march to the Campus Queen. I'm told it's also traditional that she ride forth on a unicorn to meet them, but for some reason that was omitted this year.

The hair rose stiff on my neck and I felt the blind instinctive tug of Skinturning. Just in time I pulled myself back toward human and sat in a cold shudder. The air was suddenly rotten with danger. Couldn't *anyone* else smell it?

I focused my crystal on the cheering squad, looking for the source, only dimly aware of the yell—

> *Aleph, beth, gimel, daleth, he, vau,*
> *Nomine Domini, bow, wow, wow!*
> *Melt 'em in the fire and stick 'em with pins,*
> *Trismegistus always wins...*

MACILWRAITH!

"Hey...what's wrong, mister?" The coed shrank from me, and I realized I was snarling.

"Oh. Nothing...I hope." With an effort I composed my face and kept it human.

The fattish blond kid down among the rooters didn't look harmful, but there was a sense of lightning-shot blackness about his future. I'd dealt with him before, and—

I didn't snitch on him at the time, but it was he who had almost broken up Griswold's chemistry class. Premed freshman, rich boy, not a bad guy at heart but with an unfortunate combination of natural aptitude for the Art and total irresponsibility. Medical students are notorious for merry pranks such as waltzing an animated skeleton through the girls' dorm, and he wanted to start early.

Griswold had been demonstrating the action of a catalyst, and MacIlwraith had muttered a pun-spell to make a cat boil out of the test tube. Only, he slipped quantitatively and got a saber-toothed tiger. Because of the pun, it listed to starboard, but it was still a vicious, panic-raising thing. I ducked into a closet, used my pocket moonflash, and transformed; as a wolf I chased Pussy out the window and up a tree till somebody could call the Exorcism Department.

Having seen MacIlwraith do it, I took him aside an warned him that if he disrupted the class again I'd chew him out in the most literal sense. Fun is fun, but not at the expense of students who really want to learn and a pleasant elderly anachronism who's trying to teach them.

"—TEAM!"

The cheerleader waved his hands and a spurt of many-colored fire jumped out of nothingness. Taller than a man it lifted, a leaping glory of red, blue, yellow, haloed with a wheel of sparks. Slitting my eyes, I could just discern the lizard-like form, white-hot and supple, within the aura.

The coed squealed. "Thrice-blessed Hermes," choked the Old Grad. "What is that? A demon?"

"No, a fire elemental," I muttered. "Salamander. Hell of a dangerous thing to fool around with."

My gaze ran about the field as the burning shape began to do its tricks, bouncing, tumbling, spelling out words in long flame-bands. Yes, they had a fireman close by in full canonicals, making the passes that kept the creature harmless. It ought to be all right...I lit a cigarette, shakily. It is not well to raise Loki's pets, and the stink of menace to come was acrid in my nostrils.

A good show, but—The crystal revealed Abercrombie clapping, but Ginny with a worried frown between the long green eyes. She didn't like it any better than I. Switch the ball back to MacIlwraith, fun-loving MacIlwraith.

I was perhaps the only one in the stadium who saw it. The boy gestured at his baton. It sprouted wings. The fat fireman, swaying back and forth with his gestures, was a natural target for a good healthy goose.

"Yeowp!"

He rocketed heavenward. The salamander wavered. All at once it sprang up, thinning out till it towered over the walls. There was a spinning, dazzling blur, and the thing was gone.

My cigarette burst luridly into flame and I tossed it from me. Hardly thinking, I jettisoned my hipflask. It exploded from a touch of incandescence and the alcohol burned blue. The crowd howled, hurling away their smokes, slapping at pockets where matches had kindled, getting rid of bottles. The Campus Queen shrieked as her thin dress caught fire. She got it off in time to prevent serious injury and went wailing across the field. Under different circumstances, I would have been interested.

The salamander stopped its lunatic shuttling and materialized between goalposts that began to smoke: an intolerable blaze, which scorched the grass and roared. The fireman dashed toward it, shouting the spell of extinguishment. From the salamander's mouth licked a tongue of fire, I heard a distinct Bronx cheer, then it was gone again.

The announcer, who should have been calming the spectators, screeched as it flickered before his booth. That touched off the panic! In one heartbeat, fifty thousand people were clawing and trampling, choking each other in the gates, blind with horror and trying only to fight their way out.

I vaulted across benches and an occasional head, down to the field. There was death on those jammed tiers. "Ginny! Ginny, come here where it's safe!"

She couldn't have heard me above the din, but came of herself, dragging a terrified Abercrombie by one wrist. We faced each other in a ring of ruin. She drew the telescoping wand from her purse.

The Gryphons came boiling out of their locker room. Boiling is the right word: the salamander had materialized down there and playfully wrapped itself around the shower pipes.

Sirens hooted under the moon and police broomsticks shot above us, trying to curb the stampede. The elemental flashed for a moment across one of the besoms. The rider dove it low enough to jump off, and the burning stick crashed on the grass.

"God!" exclaimed Abercrombie. "It's loose!"

"Tell me more," I snorted. "Ginny, you're a witch. Can you do anything about this?"

"I can extinguish the brute if it'll hold still long enough for me to recite the spell," she said. Disordered ruddy hair had tumbled past her pale, high-boned face to the fur-clad shoulders. "That's our one chance—the binding charm is broken, and it knows that!"

I whirled, remembering friend MacIlwraith and collared him. "Were you possessed?" I shouted.

"I didn't do anything—" he gasped. His teeth rattle as I shook him.

"Don't hand me that guff. I saw it!"

He collapsed on the ground. "It was just for fun," he whimpered. "I didn't know—"

Well, I thought grimly, that was doubtless true. It's the trouble with the Art—with any blind powerful force man uses, fire or dynamite or atomic energy or thaumaturgy. Any meathead can learn enough to begin something; these days, they start them in the third grade with spelling bees. But it's not always so easy to halt the something.

Student pranks were a standing problem at Trismegistus, as at all colleges. They were usually harmless enough—sneaking into the dorms with Tarnkappen, or 'chanting female lingerie out through the windows. Sometimes they could be rather amusing, like the time the statue of a revered and dignified former president was animated and went downtown singing bawdy songs. Often they fell quite flat, as when the boys turned Dean Hornsby into stone and it wasn't noticed for three days.

This one had gotten out of hand. The salamander was quite capable of igniting the whole city.

I turned to the fireman, who was jittering about trying to flag down a police broom. In the dim shifty light, none of the riders saw him. "What d'you figure to do?" I asked.

"I gotta report back for duty," he said harshly. "And then we'll need a water elemental, I guess."

"I have experience with the Hydros," offered Ginny. "I'll come along."

"Me too," I said at once.

Abercrombie glowered. "What can *you* do?"

"I'm were," I snapped. "In wolf shape I can't easily be harmed by fire. That might turn out useful."

"All right, Steve!" Ginny smiled at me, the old smile which had so often gone between us. Impulsively, I grabbed her to me and kissed her.

She didn't waste energy on a slap. I collected an uppercut that tumbled me on my tuchus. "Not allowed," she clipped. That double-damned geas! I could see misery caged within her eyes, but her mind was compelled to obey Malzius' rules.

"It's...ah...no place for a woman—a lady as charming as you," murmured Abercrombie. "Let me take you home, my dear."

"I've work to do," she said impatiently. "What the devil is wrong with those cops? We've got to get a lift out of here."

"Then I shall come too," said Abercrombie. "I am not unacquainted with blessings and curses, though—ha!—I fear that ever-filled purses are a trifle beyond my scope. In any event, the Treasury Department frowns on them."

Even in that moment, with riot thundering and hell let loose on earth, I was pleased to note that Ginny paid no attention to his famous wit. She scowled abstractedly and looked around. The Campus Queen was huddled near the benches, wearing somebody's overcoat. Ginny turned and waved her wand. The Campus Queen shucked the coat and ran toward us. Thirty seconds later, three police broomsticks had landed. The fireman commandeered them and we were all whirled over the stadium and into the street.

During that short hop, I saw three houses ablaze. The salamander was getting around!

We gathered at the district police station, a haggard and sooty crew with desperate eyes. The fire and police chiefs were there, and a junior officer going crazy at the switchboard. Ginny, who had picked up her own broom and come via her apartment, arrived with Svartalf on one shoulder and the *Handbook of Alchemy and Metaphysics* under her arm. Abercrombie was browbeating the terrified MacIlwraith till I told him to lay off.

"My duty—" he began. "I'm a proctor, you know."

I suppose it's necessary to have witch-smellers on campus, to make sure the fellows don't 'chant up liquor in the frat houses or smuggle in succubi. And every year somebody tries to get by an exam with a familiar under his coat whispering the answers from a crib-sheet. Nevertheless, I don't like professional nosy parkers.

"You can deal with him later," I said, and gave the boy a push out the door. "The salamander can fight back."

President Malzius huffed into the room. "What is the meaning of this?" he demanded. His pince-nez bobbed above full jowls. "I'll have you know, sir, I was preparing a most important address. The Lions Totem is holding a luncheon tomorrow, and—"

"Might not be any lunch," grunted the cop who had fetched him. "There's a salamander loose around here."

"Sala—No! It's against the rules! It is positively forbidden to—"

The man at the switchboard looked toward us. "It just kindled the Methodist church at 14th and Elm," he said. "And my God, all our equipment is already working—"

"Impossible!" cried Malzius. "A demon can't go near a church."

"How stupid does a man have to be to get your job?" Ginny fairly spat. "This *isn't* a demon. It's an elemental." Her temper was again sheathed in ice, and she continued slowly: "We haven't much hope of using a Hydro to put out the salamander, but we can raise one to help fight the fires. It'll always be three jumps behind, but at least the whole city won't be ruined."

"Unless the salamander gets too strong," cut in Abercrombie. His face was colorless and he spoke through stiff lips. "Then it can evaporate the Hydro."

"Call up two water beings," stammered Malzius "Call up a hundred. I'll waive the requirement of formal application for permission to—"

"There's a limit, sir," Abercrombie told him. "The restraining force required is an exponential function of the total embodied mass. There probably aren't enough adepts in this town to control more than three at a time. If we raised four...we'd flood the city, and the salamander need merely skip elsewhere."

"Alan—" Ginny laid her handbook on the desk and riffled its pages. Abercrombie leaned over her shoulder, remembering to rest one hand carelessly on her hip. I choked back my prize cusswords. "Alan, just for a starter, can you summon one Hydro and put it to work?"

"Of course, gorgeous one," he smiled. "It is a—ha!—elemental problem."

She gave him a worried glance. "They can be as tricky as Fire or Air," she warned. "It's not enough just to know the theory."

"I have some small experience," he preened. "During the war—After this is over, come around to my place for a drink and I'll tell you about it." His lips brushed her cheek.

"Mr. Matuchek!" yelled Malzius. "Will you please stop growing fangs?"

I shook myself and suppressed the rage which had been almost as potent as moonlight.

"Look here," said the police chief. "I gotta know what's going on. You longhairs started this trouble and I don't want you making it worse."

Seeing that Ginny and Pretty Boy were, after all, legitimately busy, I sighed and whistled for a cigarette. "Let me explain," I offered. "I learned a few things about the subject, during the war. An elemental is not the same as a demon. Any kind of demon is a separate being, as individual as you and I. An elemental is part of the basic force involved: in this case, fire, or more accurately energy. It's raised out of the basic energy matrix, given temporary individuality, and restored to the matrix when the adept is through with it."

"Huh?"

"Like a flame. A flame only exists potentially till someone lights a fire, and goes back to potential existence when you put the fire out. And of course, the second fire you light, even on the same log, is not identical with the first, so you can understand why an elemental isn't exactly anxious to be dismissed. If it ever breaks loose, as this one did, it does its damnedest to stay in this world and to increase its power."

"But how come it can burn a church?"

"Because it's soulless, a mere physical force. Any true individual, human or otherwise, is under certain constraints of a...a moral nature. A demon is allergic to holy symbols. A man who does wrong has to live with his conscience in this world and face judgment in the next. But what does a fire care? And that's what the salamander is—a glorified fire. It's bound only by the physical laws of nature and paranature."

"So how do you, uh, put one out?"

"A Hydro of corresponding mass could do it—mutual annihilation. Earth could bury it or Air withdraw from its neighborhood. Trouble is, Fire is the swiftest of them all; it can flick out of an area before any other sort of elemental can injure it. So we're left with the dismissal spell. But that has to be said in the salamander's presence, and it takes about two minutes."

"Yeh...and when it hears you start the words, it'll burn you down or scram. *Very* nice. What're we gonna do?"

"I don't know, chief," I said, "except it's like kissing a sheepdog." I blew hard and immediately smacked my lips. "You got to be quick. Every fire the critter starts feeds it more energy and makes it that much stronger. There's a critical point somewhere at which it becomes too powerful for anything to affect it."

"And what'd happen next?"

"Ragnarok."

I saw Ginny turn from the desk. Abercrombie was chalking a pentagram on the floor while a sputtering Malzius had been deputized to sterilize a pocket knife with a match—blood is a substitute for the usual powders, since it has the same proteins. The girl laid a hand on mine. "Steve, it'll take too long to get hold of all the local adept and organize them," she said. "God knows what the salamander will be doing meanwhile. Are you game to track it down?"

"Sure," I agreed. "It can't hurt—if I'm careful—till it gets big enough to burn up all the world's oxygen. But you're staying here!"

As we went out the door, I gave Abercrombie a smug look. He had nicked his wrist and sprinkled the Signs; now he was well into the invocation. I felt cold dampness swirl through the room.

Outside, the night was still autumnally sharp, the moon high. Roofs were a saw-toothed silhouette against the leaping red glare at a dozen points around us, and sirens howled in the streets. Overhead, across the small indifferent stars, I saw what looked like a whirl of dry leaves, refugees fleeing on their sticks.

Svartalf jumped to the front end of Ginny's Cadillac, and I took the saddle behind. We rode skyward.

Below us, blue fire spat and the station lights went out. Water poured into the street, a solid roar of it with President Malzius bobbing like a cork in the torrent.

"Unholy Sathanas!" I choked. "What's happened now?"

Svartalf ducked the stick low. "That idiot," groaned Ginny. "He let the Hydro slop all over the floor...short circuits..." She made a few rapid passes with her wand. The stream quieted, drew into itself, became a ten-foot-high blob glimmering in the moonlight. Abercrombie scuttled out and started it squelching toward the nearest fire.

I laughed. "Go on up to his place and listen to him tell about his vast experience," I said.

"Don't kick a man when he's down," Ginny snapped. "You've pulled your share of boners, Steve Matuchek."

Svartalf whisked the broom up again and we went low above the chimneypots. *Oof!* I thought. Could she, really be falling for that troll? A regular profile, a smooth tongue, and proximity...I bit back an inward sickness and squinted ahead, trying to find the salamander.

"There!" Ginny yelled it over the whistle of cloven air. Svartalf bottled his tail and hissed.

The University district is shabby-genteel: old pseudo-Gothic caves of wood which have slipped from mansions to rooming houses, fly-specked with minor business establishments. It was burning merrily, a score of angry red stars flickering in the darkness between street lamps. As I watched, one of the stars exploded in a puff of steam—the Hydro must have clapped a sucker onto a fireplug and blanketed the place. I had a brief heretical thought that the salamander was doing a public service by eliminating those architectural teratologies...but lives and property were involved—

Tall and terrible, the elemental wavered beside the house on which it was feeding. It had doubled in size and its core was too bright to look at. Flames whirled about the reptile head.

Svartalf braked and we hovered a few yards off, twenty feet in the air and level with the hungry mouth. Ginny was etched wild against night by that intolerable radiance. She braced herself in the stirrups began the spell, her voice almost lost in the roar as the roof caved in. *"O Indra, Abaddon, Lucifer, Moloch, Hephaestos, Loki..."*

It heard. The seething eyes swung toward us and it leaped.

Svartalf squalled as his whiskers shriveled—perhaps it was only hurt vanity—and put the stick through an Immelmann turn and whipped away. The salamander bawled with the voice of a hundred blazing forests. Suddenly the heat scorching my back was gone, and the thing had materialized in front of us.

"That way!" I hollered, pointing. "In there!"

I covered Ginny's face and buried my own against her back as we went through the plate-glass front of Stub's Beer Garden. The flame-tongue licked after us, recoiled, and the salamander ramped beyond the door.

We tumbled off the broom and looked around. The place was empty, full of a fire-spattered darkness. Everyone had fled. I saw a nearly full glass of beer on the counter and tossed it off.

"You might have offered me a drink," said Ginny. "Alan would have." Before I could recover enough to decide whether she was taunting or testing me, she went on in a rapid whisper: "It isn't trying to escape. It's gained power—confidence—it means to kill us!"

Even then, I wanted to tell her that tousled red hair and a soot-smudge across an aristocratic nose were particularly enchanting. But the occasion didn't seem appropriate. "Can't get in here," I panted. "Can't do much more than ignite the building by thermal radiation, and that'll take a while. We're safe for the moment."

"Why...oh, yes, of course. Stub's is cold-ironed. All these college beer parlors are, I'm told."

"Yeh." I peered out the broken window. The salamander peered back, and spots danced before my eyes. "So the clientele won't go jazzing up the brew above 3.2—Quick, say your spell."

Ginny shook her head. "It'll just flicker away out of earshot. Maybe we can talk to it, find out—"

She trod forth to the window, and the thing crouched in the street, extended its neck and hissed at her. I stood behind my girl, feeling boxed and useless. Svartalf, lapping spilled beer off the counter, looked toward us and sneered.

"Ohé, Child of Light!" she cried.

A ripple went down the salamander's back. Its tail switched restlessly, and a tree across the way kindled. I can't describe the voice that answered...crackling, bellowing, sibilant, it was Fire given a brain and a throat. "Daughter of Eve, what have you to say to the likes of Me?"

"I command you by the Most High, return to your proper bonds and cease from troubling the world."

"Ho—oh, ho, ho, ho!" The thing sat back on its haunches—asphalt bubbled—and shuddered its laughter into the sky. "*You* command me, combustible one?"

"I have at my beck powers so mighty they could wither your little spark into the nothingness whence it came. Cease and obey, lest worse befall you than dismissal."

I think the salamander was, for a moment, honestly, surprised. "Greater than *Me?*" Then it howled so the tavern shook. "You dare say there are mightier forces than Fire? Than Me, who am going to consume the earth?"

"Mightier and more beautiful, O Ashmaker. Think—you cannot even enter this house. Water will extinguish you. Earth will smother you, Air alone can keep you alive. Best you surrender now—"

I remembered the night we had faced an afreet together. Ginny must be pulling the same trick—feeling out the psychology of the thing that raged and flared beyond the door—but what could she hope to gain?

"More beautiful!" The salamander's tail beat furrows in the street. It threw out bursting fireballs and a rain of sparks, red, blue, yellow, a one-being Fourth of July. I thought crazily of a child kicking the floor in a tantrum.

"More beautiful! Stronger! You dare say— Haaaaa—" Teeth of incandescence gleamed in a mouth that was jumping fire. "We shall see how beautiful you are when you lie a choked corpse!" Its head darted to the broken glass front. It could not pass the barrier of cold iron, but it began to suck air, in and out. A furnace wave of heat sent me gasping back.

"My God...it's going to use up all our oxygen.... Stay here!" I sprang for the door. Ginny shrieked, but I scarcely heard her "No!" as I went through.

Moonlight flooded me, cool and tingling between the unrestful guttering fires. I crouched to the hot sidewalk and felt a shudder when my body changed.

Wolf I was, and a wolf which my enemy could not kill...I hoped. My abbreviated tail thrust against the seat of my pants, and I remembered that some injuries are beyond the healing powers of even the were shape.

Pants! Hell and damnation! Have you ever tried being a wolf while wrapped in shirt, trousers, underwear, and topcoat designed for a man?

I went flat on my moist black nose. My suspenders slid down and wrapped themselves about my hind legs. My tie tripped me in front and my coat gleefully wrapped itself around the whole bundle.

Frantic, I snapped at the cloth, rolling over and tearing it with my fangs. The salamander grew aware of me, and its tail slapped contemptuously across my back. For a moment of searing agony, hair and skin went up with the fabric…then I was free and the fluid molecules rebuilt themselves. Hardly realizing what I did, I picked up a shoe which had dropped from my now smaller foot, laid it on the salamander's white-hot toe, and bore down.

It roared and swung about to attack me afresh. Those jaws gaped wide enough to bite me in half. I skittered away. It paused, gauged the distance, flicked into nothingness, and materialized right on top of me.

I *think* I got a tooth-grip in the obvious place to bite a salamander when it is sitting on you, but the pain was too great for me to know. Then it was gone, the street lay bare and quiet between burning houses, and I gasped my way back toward wholeness.

Sanity returned. My shaggy head was in Ginny's lap, and she was stroking it and crying. Feebly, I licked her hand. Strength flowed back. As a man, I'd naturally have stayed where I was, but being a wolf with lupine instincts, I sat up and yipped.

"Steve…Almighty Father, Steve, you saved our lives," whispered Ginny. "Another minute and we'd have been suffocating. My lungs still feel like mummy dust."

Svartalf trotted from the bar, looking as smug as a cat with singed whiskers can. He meowed. Ginny gave a trembling laugh and explained:

"But you owe Svartalf a pint of cream or something. He saved you too. A few more seconds and you'd have been dead—but he showed me how to drive the beast off."

I cocked my ears inquiringly.

"He manned the beer taps," she said. "I filled stein after stein and went out and threw them at the salamander. Not enough to do more than discommode it…but added to the trouble you were making, enough to make it skip."

Horrible waste of beer, I thought. But there was still work to do.

Penalties attach to everything. The trouble with being were is that in the other shape you have, essentially, an animal brain, with only a superficial layer of human personality. Or in plain language, as a wolf I'm a rather stupid man. I was only able to think I'd better reassume human form…and I did.

Ever see a cat grin? "Omigawd!" I groaned, and started to change back.

"Never mind that," said Ginny crisply, peeling off her fur coat. I broke all records donning it. Pretty tight fit around the shoulders, but it went low enough…if I was careful. The night wind nipped my shanks, but my face was of salamander temperature.

"Now where?" I asked quickly. "The damned critter could be anyplace."

"I think it will hang around the campus," she said. "Plenty of grazing, and it's not very smart. Let's get back on our stick,"

She fetched it from the smoldering barroom and we lifted. "All we've done so far," I said, "is lose time."

"No, not entirely. I did get a line on its mind." Ginny turned her head back to face me as we cleared the rooftops. "I wasn't sure into just what form it had been conjured—you can mold the elemental forces into almost anything. But apparently the cheerleader was satisfied to give it a knowledge of English and a rudimentary intelligence. Add to that the volatile nature of Fire, and what have you got? A child."

"Some child," I muttered, hugging her coat to me.

"No, no, Steve, this is important. It has all the child's traits. Improvidence, complete lack of foresight...a wise salamander would lie low, gathering strength slowly, and would never think of burning the entire planet. Because what would it use for oxygen when that was finished? You'll note, too, its fantastic vanity; it went into an insane rage when I said there were powers stronger and more beautiful than it, and the crack about beauty hurt as much as the one about strength. Short span of attention...it could have smothered us easily before attending to as minor a nuisance as you provided. At the same time, within that span of attention, it focuses on one issue only, to the exclusion of everything else." She nodded thoughtfully, and the long blowing hair tickled my face. "I don't know just how, but some way its psychology must provide us with a lever."

My own vanity is not small. "I wasn't such a minor nuisance," I grumbled.

Ginny smiled and reached around to pat my cheek. "All right. Steve, all right. I love you just the same, and now I *know* you'll make a good husband."

That left me in a comfortable glow until I wondered precisely what she was thinking of.

We spotted the salamander below us, igniting a theater, but it flicked away even as I watched, and a mile off it appeared next to the medical research center. Glass brick doesn't burn so well. As we neared, I saw it petulantly kick the wall and vanish again. Ignorant and impulsive...a child...a brat from Hell!

Sweeping over the campus, we saw lights in the Administration Building. "Probably that's HQ for our side, said Ginny. "We'd better report." Svartalf landed us on the Mall in front of the place and strutted ahead toward the stairs.

A squad of cops armed with fire extinguishers guarded the door. "Hey, there!" One of them barred our path. "Where you going?"

"To the meeting," said Ginny, smoothing her tangled hair.

"Yeh?" The policeman's eye fell on me. "Really dressed for it, too, aren't you? Haw, haw, haw!"

I'd had about enough for one night. I wered and peeled off his own trousers. As he lifted his billy, Ginny turned it into a small boa constrictor. I switched back to human; we left the squad to its own problems and went down the hall.

The faculty meeting room was packed. Malzius had summoned all of his professors. As we entered, I heard his orotund tones: "...disgraceful. The authorities won't so much as listen to me. Gentlemen, it is for us to vindicate the honor of Gown against Town." He blinked when Ginny and Svartalf came in, and turned a beautiful Tyrian purple as I followed in the full glory of mink coat and stubbly chin. "*Mister* Matuchek!"

"He's with me," said Ginny curtly. "We were out fighting the salamander while you sat here."

"Possibly something other than brawn, even lupine brawn, is required," smiled Dr. Alan Abercrombie. "I see that Mr. Matuchek lost his pants in a more than vernacular sense."

Like Malzius, he had changed his wet clothes for the inevitable tweeds. Ginny gave him a cold look. "I thought you were directing the Hydro," she said.

"Oh, we got enough adepts together to use three water elementals," he said. "Mechanic's work. I felt my job was here. We can control the fires easily enough—"

"—if the salamander weren't always lighting fresh ones," clipped Ginny. "And each blaze it starts, it gets bigger and stronger, while you sit here looking beautiful."

"Why, thank you, my dear," he laughed.

I jammed my teeth together so they hurt. She had actually smiled back at him.

"Order, order!" boomed President Malzius. "Please be seated, Miss Graylock. Have you anything to contribute to the discussion?"

"Yes. I understand the salamander now." She took a place at the end of the table. That was the last vacant chair, so I hovered miserably in the background wishing her coat had more buttons.

"Understand it sufficiently well to extinguish it?" asked Professor van Linden of Alchemy.

"No. But I know how it thinks—"

"We're more interested in how it operates," said van Linden. "How can we make it hold still for a dismissal?" He cleared his throat. "Obviously, we must first know by what process it shuttles around so fast—"

"Oh, that's simple enough," piped up little Griswold timidly. He was drowned by van Linden's fruity bass:

"—which is, of course, by the well-known affinity of Fire for Quicksilver. Since virtually every home these days has at least one thermometer—"

"With due respect, my good sir," interrupted Vittorio of Astrology, "you are talking utter hogwash. It is simple matter of the conjunction of Mercury and Neptune in Scorpio—"

"You're wrong, sir!" declared van Linden. "Dead wrong! Let me show you the *Ars Thaumaturgica.*" He glared around after his copy, but of course it had been mislaid and he had to use an adaptation of the Dobu yam-calling chant to find it. Meanwhile Vittorio was screaming:

"No, no, no! The conjunction, with Uranus opposing in the ascendant...as I can easily prove—" He went to the blackboard and started to draw a diagram.

"Oh, come now!" snorted Jasper of Metaphysics. "I don't understand how you can both be so wrong. As I showed in the paper I read at the last A.A.A.S. meeting, the intrinsic nature—"

"That was disproved ten years ago!" roared van Linden. "The affinity—"

"Ding an sich—"

"—up Uranus—"

I sidled over and tugged at Griswold's sleeve. He pattered into a corner with me. "Okay, how *does* the bloody thing work?" I asked.

"Oh...merely a question of wave mechanics," he whispered. "According to the Heisenberg Uncertainty Principle, a photon has a finite probability of being at any point of space. The salamander uses a simple diffraction process to change the spatial coordinates of psi squared, in effect going from point to point without crossing the intervening distance, much like an electron making a quantum jump, though of course the analogy is not precise due to the modifying influence of—"

"Never mind," I sighed. "This confab is becoming a riot. Wouldn't we do better to—"

"—stick by the original purpose," agreed Abercrombie, joining us. Ginny followed. Van Linden blacked Vittorio's eye while Jasper threw chalk at both of them. Our little group went over near the door.

"I've already found the answer to our problem," said Abercrombie, "but I'll need help. A transformation spell—turn the salamander into something we can handle more easily."

"That's dangerous," said Ginny. "You'll need a really strong T-spell, and that sort can backfire. Just what happens then is unpredictable."

Abercrombie straightened himself with a look of pained nobility. "For you, my dear, no hazard is too great."

She regarded him with admiration. It does take guts to use the ultimate runes. "Let's go," she said. "I'll help."

Griswold plucked at my arm. "I don't like this, Mr. Matuchek," he confided. "The Art is too unreliable. There ought to be some method grounded in nature and nature's quantitative laws."

"Yeh," I said disconsolately. "But what?" I paddled out after Ginny and Abercrombie, who had their heads together over the handbook. Griswold marched beside me and Svartalf made a gesture with his tail at the Trismegistus faculty. They were too embroiled to notice.

We went out past an enraged but well-cowed squad of cops. The Physical Sciences hall was nearby, and its chemistry division held stuff that would be needed. We entered an echoing gloom.

The freshman lab, a long room full of workbenches; shelves, and silence, was our goal. Griswold switched on the lights and Abercrombie looked around. "But we'll have to bring the salamander here," he said. "We can't do anything except in its actual presence."

"Go ahead and make ready," the girl told him. "I know how to fetch the beast. A minor transformation—" She laid out some test tubes, filled them with various powders, and sketched her symbols on the floor. Those ball-point wands are useful.

"What's the idea?" I asked.

"Oh, get out of the way," she snapped. I told myself she was only striking at her own weariness and despair, but it hurt. "We'll use its vanity, of course. I'll prepare some Roman candles and rockets and stuff—shoot them off, and naturally it'll come to show it can do more spectacular things."

Griswold and I withdrew into a corner. This was big-league play. I was frankly scared, and the little scientist's bony knees were beating a tattoo in march time. Even Ginny—yes, there was sweat beading that smooth forehead. If this didn't work, we here were probably done for: either the salamander or the backlash of the spell could finish us. And we had no way of knowing whether the beast had grown too strong for a transformation.

The witch got her fireworks prepared, and went to an open window and leaned out. Hissing balls of blue and red, streamers of golden sparks, flew skyward and exploded.

Abercrombie had completed his diagrams. He turned to smile at us. "It's all right," he said. "Everything under control. I'm going to turn the salamander's energy into matter. E equals mc squared, you know. Just light me a Bunsen burner, Matuchek, and set a beaker of water over it. Griswold, you turn off these lights and use the Polaroid bulbs. We need polarized radiation."

We obeyed—I hated to see an old and distinguished man acting as lab assistant to this patronizing slick-paper adman's dream. "You *sure* it'll work?" I asked.

"Of course," he smiled. "I've had experience. I was in the Quartermaster Corps during the war, till they tapped me for the propaganda division…broadcasting nightmares, you know."

"Yeh," I said, "but turning dirt into K-rations isn't the same thing as transforming that hell-born monster. You and your experience!"

Suddenly and sickly, remembering how he had bungled with the Hydro, I realized the truth. Abercrombie was confident, unafraid—because he didn't *know* enough!

For a minute I couldn't unfreeze my muscles. Griswold stood fiddling unhappily with some metallic samples. He'd been using them the other day for freshman experiments, trying to teach us the chemical properties—Lord, it seemed a million years ago…

"Ginny!" I stumbled toward her where she stood at the window throwing rainbows into the air. "My God, darling, stop—"

Crack! The salamander was in the room with us.

I lurched back from it, half-blinded. Grown hideously bigger, it filled the other end of the lab, and the bench tops smoked.

"Oh, so!" The voice of Fire blasted our eardrums. Svartalf shot to a shelf top and began upsetting bottles of acid onto the varmint. It didn't notice. "So, small moist pests, you would try to outdo Me!"

Abercrombie and Ginny lifted their wands and shouted the few brief words of transformation.

Crouched back into my corner, peering through a sulfurous reek of fumes, I saw Ginny lurch and then jump for safety. She must have sensed the backlash. There was a shattering explosion and the air was full of flying glass.

My body shielded Griswold, and the spell didn't do more to me than turn me lupine. I saw Ginny nearly on her hands and knees, behind a bench, half-unconscious...but unhurt, unhurt, praise all Powers forever. Svartalf—a Pekingese dog yapped on the shelf. Abercrombie was gone, but a chimpanzee in baggy tweeds scuttered wailing toward the door.

A fire-blast rushed before the ape. He whirled, screamed, and shinnied up a steam pipe. The salamander arched its back and howled with laughter.

"You would use your tricks on Me? Almighty Me, terrible Me, beautiful Me? Ha, they bounce off like water from a hot skillet! And I, I, I am the skillet which is going to fry you!"

Somehow, the low-grade melodrama of its speech was not at all ridiculous. For this was the childish, vainglorious, senselessly consuming thing which was loose on earth to turn our broad fair home into one white blaze among the planets.

Under the polaroids, I switched back to human and stood up behind the bench. Griswold turned on a water faucet and squirted a jet with his finger. The salamander hissed in annoyance—yes, water still hurt, but there wasn't enough liquid here to quench it, you'd need a whole lake by this time...It swung its head, gape-mouthed, aimed at Griswold, and drew a long breath.

All is vanity...

I reeled over to the Bunsen burner that was heating a futile beaker of water. Ginny sat up and looked at me through scorched locks. The room shimmered in heat, my lungs were one great anguish. I didn't have any flash of genius, I acted on raw instinct and tumbled memories.

"Kill us," I croaked. "Kill us if you dare. Our servant is more powerful than you. He'll hound you to the ends of creation."

"Your servant?" Flame wreathed the words.

"Yeh...I mean yes...our servant, that Fire which fears not water!"

The salamander stepped back a pace, snarling. It was not yet so strong that the very name of water didn't make it flinch. "Show Me!" it chattered. "Show Me! I dare you!"

"Our servant...small, but powerful," I rasped. "Brighter and more beautiful than you, and above taking harm from the Wet Elements." I staggered to the jars of metal samples and grabbed a pair of tongs. "Have you the courage to look on him?"

The salamander bristled. "Have I the *courage?* Ask rather, does it dare confront Me?"

I flicked a glance from the corner of my eye. Ginny had risen and was gripping her wand. She scarcely breathed, but her eyes were narrowed.

There was a silence. It hung like a world's weight in that room, smothering what noises remained: the crackle of fire, Abercrombie's simian gibber, Svartalf's indignant yapping. I took a strip of magnesium in the tongs and held it to the burner flame.

It burst into a blue-white actinic radiance from which I turned dazzled eyes. The salamander was not so viciously brilliant. I saw the brute accomplish the feat of simultaneously puffing itself up and shrinking back.

"Behold!" I lifted the burning strip. Behind me, Ginny's rapid mutter came: "*O Indra, Abaddon, Lucifer...*"

The child mind, incapable of considering more than one thing at a time…but for how long a time? I had to hold its full attention for the hundred and twenty seconds required.

"Fire," said the salamander feverishly. "Only another fire, one tiny piece of that Force from which I came."

"Can you do this, buster?"

I plunged the strip into the beaker. Steam puffed from the water, it boiled and bubbled—and the metal went on burning!

"*…abire ex orbis terrestris…*"

"Mg plus H_2O yields MgO plus H_2," whispered Griswold reverently.

"Keek-eek!" said Abercrombie.

"Yip-yip-yip!" said Svartalf.

"It's a trick!" screamed the salamander. "It's impossible! If even I cannot—*No!*"

"Stay where you are!" I barked in my best Army manner. "Do you doubt that my servant can follow you where you may flee?"

"I'll kill that little monster!"

"Go right ahead, chum," I agreed. "Want to fight the duel under the ocean?"

Whistles skirled above our racket. The police had seen through these windows.

"I'll show you, I will!" There was almost a sob. I ducked behind the bench, pulling Griswold with me as a geyser of flame rushed where I had been.

"Nyaah, nyaah, nyaah," I called. "You can't catch me! Scaredy cat!"

Svartalf gave me a hard look.

The floor trembled as the elemental came toward me, not going around the benches but burning its way through them. Heat clawed at my throat. I spun down toward darkness.

And it was gone. Ginny cried her triumphant *"Amen!"* and displaced air cracked like thunder.

I lurched to my feet. Ginny fell into my arms. The police entered the lab and Griswold hollered something about calling the fire department before his whole building whiffed off in smoke. Abercrombie scampered out a window and Svartalf jumped down from the shelf. He forgot that a Pekingese isn't as agile as a cat, and his pop eyes bubbled with righteous wrath.

Outside, the Mall was cool and still. We sat on dewed grass and looked at the moon and thought what a great and simple wonder it is to be alive.

The geas held us apart, but tenderness lay on Ginny's lips. We scarcely noticed when somebody ran past us shouting that the salamander was gone, nor when church bells began pealing the news to all men.

Svartalf finally roused us with his barking. Ginny chuckled. "Poor fellow. I'll change you back as soon as I can, but there's more urgent business now. Come on, Steve."

Griswold, assured that his priceless hall was safe, followed us at a tactful distance. Svartalf merely sat where he was...too shocked to move, I guess, at the idea that there could be more important affairs than turning him back into a cat.

Dr. Malzius met us halfway, under one of the campus elms. Moonlight spattered his face and gleamed on the pince-nez. "My dear Miss Graylock," he began, "is it indeed true that you have overcome that menace to society? Most noteworthy. Accept my congratulations. The glorious annals of this great institution of which I have the honor to be president—"

Ginny faced him, arms akimbo, and nailed him with the chilliest gaze I have ever seen. "The credit belongs to Mr. Matuchek and Dr. Griswold," she said. "I shall so inform the press. Doubtless you'll then see fit to recommend a larger appropriation for Dr. Griswold's outstanding work."

"Oh, now, really," stammered the scientist. "I didn't—"

"Be quiet, you ninnyhammer," hissed Ginny. Aloud: "Only through his courageous and farsighted adherence to the basic teachings of natural law—Well, you can fill in the rest for yourself, Malzius. I don't think you'd be very popular if you went on starving his department."

"Oh...indeed...after all..." The president blew himself up. "I have given careful consideration to the matter. Was going to recommend it at the next meeting of the board, in fact."

"I'll hold you to that," said Ginny. "Now there is this stupid rule against student-faculty relationships. Mr. Matuchek is shortly going to be my husband—"

Whoosh! I tried to regain my breath.

"My dear Miss Graylock," sputtered Malzius, "decorum...propriety...why, he isn't even decent!"

I realized with horror that somehow in all the excitement, I'd lost Ginny's expensive mink coat.

A pair of cops approached, dragging a small hairy form that struggled in their arms. One of them carried the garments the chimp had shed. "Begging your pardon, Miss Graylock." The tone was pure worship. "We found this monkey loose and—"

"Oh, yes." She laughed. "We'll have to restore him. But not right away. Steve needs those pants worse."

I got into them in a hurry. Ginny turned back to smile with angelic sweetness at Malzius.

"Poor Dr. Abercrombie," she sighed. "These things will happen when you deal with paranatural forces. Now I believe, sir, that there is no rule against faculty members conducting research."

"Oh, no," said the president shakily. "Of course not. On the contrary! We expect our people to publish—"

"To be sure. Now I have in mind a most interesting research project involving transformations. I'll admit it's just the least bit dangerous. It could backfire as Dr. Abercrombie's spell did." Ginny leaned on her wand and regarded the turf thoughtfully. "It could even…yes, there's even a small possibility that it could turn you into an ape, dear Dr. Malzius. Or, perhaps, a worm. A long slimy one. But we mustn't let that stand in the way of Science, must we?"

"What? But—"

"Naturally," purred the witch, "if I were allowed to conduct myself as I wish with my fiancé, I shouldn't have time for research."

It took Malzius a bare fifty words to admit surrender. He stumped off in tottery grandeur while the last fire-glow died above the campus roofs.

Ginny gave me a long slow glance. "The rule can't officially be stricken till tomorrow," she murmured. "Think you can cut a few classes then?"

"Keek-eek-eek," said Dr. Alan Abercrombie. Then Svartalf showed up full of resentment and chased him up the tree.

UNTITLED LIMERICK

(Dedicated to Fritz Leiber)

A mathematician named Jones
was fonder of cubes than of cones.
Said he on his rambles:
"When I travels, I gambles.
Gonna roll them Napierian bones!"

Sam Hall

Click. Bzzz. Whrrr.

Citizen Blank Blank, Any town, Somewhere, U.S.A., approaches the hotel desk. "Single with bath."

"Sorry, sir, our fuel ration doesn't permit individual baths. We can draw one for you; that will be twenty-five dollars extra."

"Oh, is that all? Okay."

Citizen Blank takes out his wallet, extracts his card, gives it to the registry machine, an automatic set of gestures. Aluminum jaws close on it, copper teeth feel for the magnetic encodings, electronic tongue tastes the life of Citizen Blank.

Place and date of birth. Parents. Race. Religion. Educational, military, and civilian service records. Marital status. Children. Occupations, from the beginning to the present. Affiliations. Physical measurements, fingerprints, retinals, blood type. Basic psychotype. Loyalty rating. Loyalty index as a function of time to moment of last test given. Click, click. Bzzz.

"Why are you here, sir?"

"Salesman. I expect to be in Cincinnati tomorrow night."

The clerk (32 yrs., married, two children; NB confidential: Jewish. To be kept out of key occupations) punches buttons.

Click, click. The machine returns the card. Citizen Blank puts it back in his wallet.

"Front!"

The bellboy (19 yrs., unmarried; NB confidential: Catholic. To be kept out of key occupations) takes the guest's suitcase. The elevator creaks upstairs. The clerk resumes his reading. The article is entitled "Has Britain Betrayed Us?" Companion articles in the magazine include "New Indoctrination Program for the Armed Forces," "Labor Hunting on Mars," "I Was a Union Man for the Security Police," "More Plans for YOUR Future."

The machine talks to itself. Click, click. A bulb winks at its neighbor as if they shared a private joke. The total signal goes out over the wires.

Accompanied by a thousand others, it shoots down the last cable and into the sorter unit of Central Records. Click, click. Bzzz. Whrrr. Wink and glow. The distorted molecules in a particular spool show the pattern of Citizen Blank, and this is sent back. It enters the comparison unit, to which the incoming signal corresponding to him has also been shunted. The two are perfectly in phase; nothing wrong. Citizen Blank is staying in the town where, last night, he said he would, so he has not had to file a correction.

The new information is added to the record of Citizen Blank. The whole of his life returns to the memory bank. It is wiped from the scanner and comparison units, that these may be free for the next arrival.

The machine has swallowed and digested another day. It is content.

Thornberg entered his office at the usual time. His secretary glanced up to say "Good morning," and looked closer. She had been with him for enough years to read the nuances in his carefully controlled face. "Anything wrong, chief?"

"No." He spoke harshly, which was also peculiar. "No, nothing wrong. I feel a bit under the weather, maybe."

"Oh." The secretary nodded. You learned discretion in the government. "Well, I hope you get better soon."

"Thanks. It's nothing." Thornberg limped over to his desk, sat down, and took out a pack of cigarettes. He held one for a moment in nicotine-yellowed fingers before lighting it, and there was an emptiness in his eyes. Then he puffed ferociously and turned to his mail. As chief technician of Central Records, he received a generous tobacco ration and used it all.

The office was a windowless cubicle, furnished in gaunt orderliness, its only decorations pictures of his son and his late wife. Thornberg seemed too big for the space. He was tall and lean, with thin straight features and neatly brushed graying hair. He wore a plain version of the Security uniform, insignia of Technical Division and major's rank but none of the ribbons to which he was entitled. The priesthood of Matilda the Machine were a pretty informal lot.

He chain-smoked his way through the mail. Most was related to the changeover. "Come on, June," he said. Recording and later transcription sufficed for routine stuff, but best that his secretary take notes as well while he dictated anything unusual. "Let's get this out of the way fast. I've got work to do."

He held a letter before him. "To Senator E. W. Harmison, S.O.B., New Washington. Dear Sir: In re your communication of the 14th inst., requesting my personal opinion of the new ID system, may I say that it is not a technician's business to express opinions. The directive that every citizen shall have a single number for his records—birth certificate, education, rations, taxes, wages, transactions, public service, family, travel, etc.—has obvious long-range advantages, but naturally entails a good deal of work both in reconversion and interim data control. The president having decided that the gain justifies our present difficulties, the duty of citizens is to conform, not complain. Yours, and so forth." He let a cold smile flicker. "There, that'll fix him! I don't know what use Congress is anyway, except to plague honest bureaucrats."

Privately, June decided to modify the letter. Maybe a senator was only a rubber stamp, but you couldn't brush him off that curtly. Part of a secretary's job is to keep the boss out of trouble.

"Okay, let's get to the next," said Thornberg. "To Colonel M. R. Hubert, Director of Liaison Division, Central Records Agency, Security Police, etc. Dear Sir: In re your memorandum of the 14th inst. requiring a definite date for completion of the ID conversion, may I respectfully state that it is impossible for me honestly to set one. You realize we must develop a memory modification unit which will make the changeover in our records without our having to take out and alter each of three hundred million spools. You realize too that we cannot predict the exact time needed to complete such a project. However, research is progressing satisfactorily (refer him to my last report, will you?), and I can confidently say that conversion will be finished and all citizens notified of their numbers within three months at the latest. Respectfully, and so on. Put that in a nice form, June."

She nodded. Thornberg continued through his mail, throwing most into a basket for her to answer alone. When he was done he yawned and lit a fresh cigarette. "Praise Allah that's over. Now I can get down to the lab."

"You have afternoon appointments," she reminded him.

"I'll be back after lunch. See you." He got up and went out of the office.

Down the escalator to a still lower sublevel, walking along a corridor, he returned the salutes of passing subordinates automatically. His expression did not bespeak anything; perhaps the stiff swinging of his arms did.

Jimmy, he thought. *Jimmy, boy.*

At the guard chamber, he presented hand and eye to the scanners. Finger and retinal patterns were his pass. No alarm sounded. The door opened for him and he walked into the temple of Matilda.

She squatted huge, tier upon tier of control panels, meters, indicator lights to the lofty ceiling. The spectacle always suggested to Thornberg an Aztec pyramid, whose gods winked red eyes at the acolytes and suppliants creeping about base and flanks. But they got their sacrifices elsewhere.

For a moment Thornberg stood and watched. He smiled again, a tired smile that creased his face on the left side only. A recollection touched him, booklegged stuff from the forties and fifties of the last century which he had read: French, German, British, Italian. The intellectuals had been fretful about the Americanization of Europe, the crumbling of old culture before the mechanized barbarism of soft drinks, hard sells, enormous chrome-plated automobiles (dollar grins, the Danes had called them), chewing gum, plastics...None of them had protested the simultaneous Europeanization of America: bloated government, unlimited armament, official nosiness, censors, secret police, chauvinism...Well, for a while there had been objectors, but first their own excesses and sillinesses discredited them, then later...

Oh, well.

But Jimmy, lad, where are you now, what are they doing to you?

Thornberg sought a bench where his top engineer, Rodney, was testing a unit. "How're you coming along?" he asked.

"Pretty good, chief." Rodney didn't bother to salute. Thornberg had, in fact, forbidden it in the labs as a waste of time. "A few bugs yet, but we're chasing them out."

The project was, essentially, to develop a gimmick that would change numbers without altering anything else—not too easy a task, since the memory banks depended on individual magnetic domains. "Okay," said Thornberg. "Look, I want to run a few checks myself, out of the main coordinator. The program they've written for Section Thirteen during the conversion doesn't quite satisfy me."

"Want an assistant?"

"No, thanks. I just want not to be bothered."

Thornberg resumed his way across the floor. Hardness resounded dully under his shoes. The main coordinator was in a special armored booth nestled against the great pyramid. He must go through a second scan before the door admitted him. Not many were allowed in here. The complete archives of the nation were too valuable to risk.

Thornberg's loyalty rating was AAB-2—not absolutely perfect, but the best available among men and women of his professional caliber. His last drugged checkup had revealed certain doubts and reservations about government policy, but there was no question of disobedience. *Prima facie,* he was certainly bound to be loyal. He had served with distinction in the war against Brazil, losing a leg in action; his wife had been killed in the abortive Chinese rocket raids ten years ago; his son was a rising young Space Guard officer on Venus. He had read and listened to illegal stuff, blacklisted books, underground and foreign propaganda—but then, every intellectual dabbled with that; it was not a serious offense if your record was otherwise good and if you laughed off what the things said.

He sat for a moment regarding the board inside the booth. Its complexity would have baffled most engineers, but he had been with Matilda so long that he didn't even need the reference tables.

Well...

It took nerve, this. A hypnoquiz was sure to reveal what he was about to do. But such raids were, necessarily, in a random pattern. He wouldn't likely be called up again for years, especially given his rating. By the time he was found out, Jack should have risen far enough in the guard ranks to be safe.

In the privacy of the booth Thornberg permitted himself a harsh grin. "This," he murmured to the machine, "will hurt me worse than it does you."

He began punching buttons.

Here were circuits which could alter the records, take out an entire spool and write whatever was desired in the molecules. Thornberg had done the job a few times for high officials. Now he was doing it for himself.

Jimmy Obrenowicz, son of his second cousin, had been hustled off at night by Security Police on suspicion of treason. The file showed what no private citizen was supposed to know: the prisoner was in Camp Fieldstone. Those who returned from there, not a big percentage, were very quiet, and said absolutely nothing about their experiences. Sometimes they were incapable of speech.

The chief of the Technical Division, Central Records, had damn well better not have a relative in Fieldstone. Thornberg toiled at the screens and buttons for an hour, erasing, changing. The job was tough; he had to go back several generations, altering lines of descent. But when he was through, James Obrenowicz had no kinship whatsoever to the Thornbergs.

And I thought the world of that boy. Well, I'm not doing this for me, Jimmy. It's for Jack. When the cops pull your file, later today no doubt, I can't let them find you're related to Captain Thornberg on Venus and a friend of his father.

He slapped the switch that returned the spool to the memory banks. *With this act do I disown thee.*

After that he sat for a while, relishing the quiet of the booth and the clean impersonality of the instruments. He didn't even want to smoke. Presently, though, he began to think.

So now they were going to give every citizen a number, one number for everything. Already they discussed tattooing it on. Thornberg foresaw popular slang referring to the numbers as "brands" and Security cracking down on those who used the term. Disloyal language.

Well, the underground was dangerous. It was supported by foreign countries who didn't like an American-dominated world—at least, not one dominated by today's kind of America, though once "U.S.A." had meant "hope." The rebels were said to have their own base out in space somewhere and to have honeycombed the country with their agents. That could well be. Their propaganda was subtle: we don't want to overthrow the nation; we simply want to restore the Bill of Rights. It could attract a lot of unstable souls. But Security's spy hunt was bound to drag in any number of citizens who had never meditated treason. Like Jimmy—or had Jimmy been an undergrounder after all? You never knew. Nobody ever told you.

There was a sour taste in Thornberg's mouth. He grimaced. A line of a song came back to him. *"I hate you one and all."* How had it gone? They used to sing it in his college days: Something about a very bitter character who'd committed a murder.

Oh, yes. "Sam Hall." How did it go, now? You needed a gravelly bass to sing it properly.

> *Oh, my name it is Sam Hall, it is Sam Hall.*
> *Yes, my name is Sam Hall, it is Sam Hall.*
> *Oh, my name it is Sam Hall,*
> *And I hate you one and all,*
> *Yes, I hate you one and all, God damn your eyes.*

That was it. And Sam Hall was about to swing for murder. Thornberg remembered now. He felt like Sam Hall himself. He looked at the machine and wondered how many Sam Halls were in it.

Idly, postponing his return to work, he punched for the data-name, Samuel Hall, no further specifications. The machine mumbled. Presently it spewed out a stack of papers, microprinted on the spot from the memory banks. Complete dossier on every Sam Hall, living and dead, from the time the records began to be kept. To hell with it. Thornberg chucked the sheets down the incinerator slot.

"Oh, I killed a man, they say, so they say—"

The impulse was blinding in its savagery. They were dealing with Jimmy at this moment, probably pounding him over the kidneys, and he, Thornberg, sat here waiting for the cops to requisition Jimmy's file, and there was nothing he could do. His hands were empty.

By God, he thought, *I'll give them Sam Hall!*

His fingers began to race; he lost his nausea in the intricate technical problem. Slipping a fake spool into Matilda wasn't easy. You couldn't duplicate numbers, and every citizen had a lot of them. You had to account for each day of his life.

Well, some of that could be simplified The machine had only existed for twenty-five years; before then, records had been kept in a dozen different offices. Let's make Sam Hall a resident of New York, his dossier there lost in the bombing thirty years ago. Such of his papers as were in New Washington had also been lost, in the Chinese attack. That meant he simply reported as much detail as he could remember, which needn't be a lot.

Let's see. "Sam Hall" was an English song, so Sam Hall should be British himself. Came over with his parents, oh, thirty-eight years ago, when he was three, and got naturalized with them; that was before the total ban on immigration. Grew up on New York's Lower East Side, a tough kid, a slum kid. School records lost in the bombing, but he claimed to have gone through the tenth grade. No living relatives. No family. No definite occupation, just a series of unskilled jobs. Loyalty rating BBA-O, which meant that purely routine questions showed him to have no political opinions that mattered.

Too colorless. Give him some violence in his background. Thornberg punched for information on New York police stations and civilian-police officers destroyed in the last raids. He used them as the source of records that Sam Hall had been continually in trouble—drunkenness, disorderly conduct, brawls, a suspicion of holdups and burglary, but not strong enough to warrant calling in Security's hypnotechnicians for quizzing him.

Hmm. Better make him 4-F, no military service. Reason? Well, a slight drug addiction; men weren't so badly needed nowadays that hop heads had to be cured. Neo-coke didn't impair the faculties too much. Indeed, the addict was abnormally fast and strong under the influence, though he suffered a tough reaction afterwards.

Then he would have had to put in an additional term of civilian service. Let's see. He spent his four years as a common laborer on the Colorado Dam project. In such a mess of men, who would remember him? At any rate, it would be hard finding somebody who did.

Now to fill in. Thornberg called on a number of automatic devices to help him. He must account for every day in twenty-five years; but of course the majority would show no change of circumstances. Thornberg punched for cheap hotels, the kind which didn't bother keeping records of their own after the data went to Matilda. Who could remember a shabby individual patron? For Sam Hall's current address he chose the Triton, a glorified flophouse on the East Side not far from the craters. At present his man was unemployed, putatively living off savings, likelier off odd jobs and petty crime. Oh, blast! Income tax returns. Thornberg could be sketchy in creating those, however. The poor weren't expected to be meticulous, nor were they audited annually like the middle class and the rich.

Hmm…physical ID. Make him of average height, stocky, black-haired and black-eyed, a bent nose, a scar on his forehead—tough-looking, though not enough to be unusually memorable. Thornberg entered the precise measurements. Fingerprints and retinals being encoded, they were easy to fake; he wrote a censor into his ongoing program, lest he duplicate somebody else's by chance.

Finally he leaned back and sighed. The record was still shot full of holes, but he could plug those at his leisure. The main job was done—a couple of hours' hard work, utterly pointless, except that he had blown off steam. He felt a lot better.

He glanced at his watch. *Time to get back on the job, son.* For a rebellious moment he wished no one had ever invented clocks. They had made possible the science he loved, but they had then proceeded to mechanize man. Oh, well, too late now. He left the booth. The door closed itself behind him.

About a month later, Sam Hall committed his first murder.

The night before, Thornberg had been at home. His rank entitled him to good housing in spite of his living alone: two rooms and bath on the ninety-eighth floor of a unit in town not far from the camouflaged entrance to Matilda's underground domain. The fact that he was in Security, even if he didn't belong to the man-hunting branch, got him so much deference that he often felt lonely. The superintendent had offered him his daughter once—"Only twenty-three, sir, just released by a gentleman of marshal's rank, and looking for a nice patron, sir." Thornberg had refused, trying not to be prissy about it. *Autres temps, autres moeurs*—but still, she wouldn't have had any choice about getting client status, the first time anyway. And Thornberg's marriage had been a long and happy one.

He had been looking through his bookshelves for something to read. The Literary Bureau was trumpeting Whitman as an early example of Americanism, but though Thornberg had always liked the poet, his hands strayed perversely to a dog-eared volume of Marlowe. Was that escapism? The L.B. was very down on escapism. These were tough times. It wasn't easy to belong to the nation which was enforcing peace on a sullen world. You must be realistic and energetic and, all the rest, no doubt.

The phone buzzed. He clicked on the receiver. Martha Obrenowicz's plain plump face showed in the screen: her gray hair was wild and her voice a harsh croak.

"Uh—hello," he said uneasily. He hadn't called her since the news of her son's arrest. "How are you?"

"Jimmy is dead," she told him.

He stood for a long while. His skull felt hollow.

"I got word today that he died in camp," said Martha. "I thought you'd want to know."

Thornberg shook his head, back and forth, quite slowly. "That isn't news I ever wanted, Martha," he said.

"It isn't *right!*" she shrieked. "Jimmy wasn't a traitor. I knew my son. Who ought to know him better? He had some friends I was kind of doubtful of, but Jimmy, he wouldn't ever—"

Something cold formed in Thornberg's breast. You never knew when calls were being tapped.

"I'm sorry, Martha," he said without tone. "But the police are careful about these things. They wouldn't act till they were sure. Justice is in our traditions."

She regarded him for a long time. Her eyes held a hard glitter. "You too," she said at last.

"Be careful, Martha," he warned her. "I know this is a blow to you, but don't say anything you might regret later. After all, Jimmy may have died accidentally. Those things happen."

"I—forgot," she said jerkily. "You…are in Security…yourself."

"Be calm," he said. "Think of it as a sacrifice for the national interest."

She switched off on him. He knew she wouldn't call him again. And he couldn't safely see her.

"Good-bye, Martha," he said aloud. It was like a stranger speaking.

He turned back to the bookshelf. *Not for me,* he told himself. *For Jack.* He touched the binding of *Leaves of Grass. Oh, Whitman, old rebel,* he thought, a curious dry laughter in him, *are they calling you Whirling Walt now?*

That night he took an extra sleeping pill. His head still felt fuzzy when he reported for work, and after a while he gave up trying to answer the mail and went down to the lab.

While he was engaged with Rodney, and making a poor job of understanding the technical problem under discussion, his eyes strayed to Matilda. Suddenly he realized what he needed for a cathartic. He broke off as soon as possible and went into the coordinator booth.

For a moment he paused at the keyboard. The day-by-day creation of Sam Hall had been an odd experience. He, quiet and introverted, had shaped a rowdy life and painted a rugged personality. Sam Hall was more real to him than many of his associates. *Well, I'm a schizoid type myself. Maybe I should have been a writer.* No, that would have meant too many restrictions, too much fear of offending the censor. He had done exactly as he pleased with Sam Hall.

He drew a breath and punched for unsolved murders of Security officers, New York City area, during the past month. They were surprisingly common. Could dissatisfaction be more general than the government admitted? But when the bulk of a nation harbors thoughts labeled treasonous, does the label still apply?

He found what he wanted. Sergeant Brady had incautiously entered the Crater district after dark on the twenty-seventh on a routine checkup mission; he had worn the black uniform, presumably to give himself the full weight of authority. The next morning he had been found in an alley, his skull shattered.

> *Oh, I killed a man, they say, so they say.*
> *Yes, I killed a man, they say, so they say.*
> *I beat him on the head,*
> *And I left him there for dead,*
> *Yes, I left him there for dead, God damn his eyes.*

Newspapers had no doubt deplored this brutality perpetrated by the treacherous agent of enemy powers. (*"Oh, the parson, he did come, he did come."*) A number of suspects had been rounded up and given a stiff quizzing. (*"And the sheriff, he came too, he came too."*) Nothing was proven as yet, though a Joe Nikolsky (fifth generation American, mechanic, married, four children, underground pamphlets found in his room) had been arrested yesterday on suspicion.

Thornberg sighed. He knew enough of Security methods to be sure they would get somebody for such a killing. They couldn't allow their reputation for infallibility to be smirched by a lack of conclusive evidence. Maybe Nikolsky had done the crime—he couldn't *prove* he had simply been out for a walk that evening—and maybe he hadn't. But, hell's fire, why not give him a break? He had four kids. With such a black mark, their mother would find work only in a recreation house.

Thornberg scratched his head. This had to be done carefully. Let's see. Brady's body would have been cremated by now, but of course there had been a thorough study first. Thornberg withdrew the dead man's file from the machine and microprinted a replica of the evidence—zero. Erasing that, he entered the statement that a blurred thumbprint had been found on the victim's collar and referred to ID labs for reconstruction. In the ID file he inserted the report of such a job, finished only yesterday due to a great press of work. (Plausible. They were busy lately on material sent from Mars, seized in a raid on a rebel meeting place.) The probable pattern of the whorls was—and here he inserted Sam Hall's right thumb.

He returned the spools and leaned back in his chair. It was risky; if anyone thought to query the ID lab, he was in trouble. But that was unlikely. The chances were that New York would accept the findings with a routine acknowledgement which some clerk at the lab would file without studying. The more obvious dangers were not too great either: a busy police force would not stop to ask if any of their fingerprint men had actually developed that smudge; and as for hypnoquizzing showing Nikolsky really was the murderer, well, then the print would be assumed that of a passerby who had found the body and not reported it.

So now Sam Hall had killed a Security officer—grabbed him by the neck and smashed his brainpan with a weighted club. Thornberg felt considerably happier.

New York Security shot a request to Central Records for any new material on the Brady case. An automaton compared the codes and saw that fresh information had been added. The message flashed back, plus the dossier on Sam Hall and two others—for the reconstruction could not be absolutely accurate.

The two were safe, as it turned out. Both had alibis. The squad that stormed into the Triton Hotel and demanded Sam Hall met blank stares. No such person was registered. No one of that description was known there. A thorough quizzing corroborated this. Then Sam Hall had managed to fake an address. He could have done that easily by punching the buttons on the hotel register when nobody was looking. Sam Hall could be anywhere!

Joe Nikolsky, having been hypnoed and found harmless, was released. The fine for possessing subversive literature would put him in debt for the next few years—he had no influential friends to get it suspended—but he'd be all right if he watched his step. Security sent out an alarm for Sam Hall.

Thornberg derived a sardonic amusement from watching the progress of the hunt as it came to Matilda. No man with that ID card had bought tickets on any public transportation. That proved nothing. Of the hundreds who vanished every year, some at least must have been murdered for their cards, and their bodies disposed of. Matilda was set to give the alarm when the ID of a disappeared person showed up somewhere. Thornberg faked a few such reports, just to give the police something to do.

He slept more poorly each night, and his work suffered. Once he met Martha Obrenowicz on the street—passed by hastily without greeting her—and couldn't sleep at all, even after maximum permissible drugging.

The new ID system was completed. Machines sent notices to every citizen, with orders to have their numbers tattooed on the right shoulder blade within six weeks. As each center reported that such-and-such a person had had the job done, Matilda changed the record appropriately. Sam Hall, AX-428-399-075, did not report for his tattoo. Thornberg chuckled at the AX symbol.

Then the telecasts flashed a story that made the nation exclaim. Bandits had held up the First National Bank in Americatown, Idaho (formerly Moscow), collecting a good five million dollars in assorted bills. From their discipline and equipment it was assumed that they were rebel agents, possibly having come in a spaceship from their unknown interplanetary base, and that the raid was intended to help finance their nefarious activities. Security was cooperating with the armed forces to track down the evildoers, and arrests were expected hourly, etc., etc.

Thornberg went to Matilda for a complete account. It had been a bold job. The robbers had apparently worn plastic face masks and light body armor under ordinary clothes. In the scuffle of the getaway one man's mask had slipped aside—only for a moment, but a clerk who saw had, under hypnosis, given a fairly good description. A brown-haired, heavyset fellow, Roman nose, thin lips, toothbrush mustache.

Thornberg hesitated. A joke was a joke; and helping poor Nikolsky was perhaps morally defensible; but aiding and abetting a felony which was in all likelihood an act of treason—

He grinned to himself, with scant humor. It was too much fun playing God. Swiftly he changed the record. The crook had been of medium height, dark, scarfaced, broken-nosed...He sat for a while wondering how sane he was. How sane anybody was.

Security Central requisitioned complete data on the incident and any correlations the logic units could make. The description they got could have fitted many men, but geography left just a single possibility. *Sam Hall.*

The hounds bayed forth. That night Thornberg slept well.

Dear Dad,
Sorry I haven't written before. We've been too busy here. I myself was on patrol duty in the Austin Highlands. The idea was, if we can take advantage of reduced atmospheric pressure at that altitude to construct a military spaceport, a foreign country might sneak in and do the same, probably for the benefit of our domestic insurrectionists. I'm glad to say we found nothing. But it was grim going for us. Frankly, everything here is. Sometimes I wonder if I'll ever see the sun again. And lakes and forests—life; who wrote that line about the green hills of Earth? My mind feels rusty as well. We don't get much to read, and I don't care for the taped shows. Not that I'm complaining, of course. This is a necessary job.

We'd hardly gotten back when we were bundled into bathyplanes and ferried to the lowlands. I'd never been there before—thought Venus was awful, but you have to get down in that red-black ocean of hell-hot air, way down, before you know what "awful" means. Then we transferred straight to mobile sealtanks and went into action. The convicts in the new thorium mine were refusing to work on account of conditions and casualties. We needed guns to bring them to reason. Dad, I hated that. I actually felt sorry for the poor devils, I don't mind admitting it. Rocks and hammers and sluice hoses against machine guns! And conditions are rugged. They DELETED BY CENSOR *someone has to do that job too, and if no one will volunteer, for any kind of pay, they have to assign convicts. It's for the state.*

Otherwise nothing new. Life is pretty monotonous. Don't believe the adventure stories. Adventure is weeks of boredom punctuated by moments of being scared gutless. Sorry to be so brief, but I want to get this on the outbound rocket. Won't be another for a couple of months. Everything well, really. I hope the same for you and live for the day we'll meet again. Thanks a million for the cookies—you know you can't afford to pay the freight, you old spendthrift! Martha baked them, didn't she? I recognized the Obrenowicz touch. Say hello to her and Jim for me. And most of all, my kindest thoughts go to you.

As ever,
Jack

The telecasts carried "Wanted" messages for Sam Hall. No photographs of him were available, but an artist could draw an accurate likeness from Matilda's description, and his truculent face began to adorn public places. Not long thereafter, the Security offices in Denver were wrecked by a grenade tossed from a speeding car that vanished into traffic. A witness said he had glimpsed the thrower, and the fragmentary picture given under hypnosis was not unlike Sam Hall's. Thornberg doctored the record a bit to make it still more similar. The tampering was risky; if Security ever became suspicious, they could easily check back with their witnesses. But the chance was not too big to take, for a scientifically quizzed man told everything germane to the subject which his memory, conscious, subconscious, and cellular, held. There was never any reason to repeat such an interrogation.

Thornberg often tried to analyze his motives. Plainly, he disliked the government. He must have contained that hate all his life, carefully suppressed from awareness, and recently it had been forced into his conscious mind. Not even his subconscious could have formulated it earlier, or he would have been caught by the loyalty probes. The hate derived from a lifetime of doubts (Had there been any real reason to fight Brazil, other than to obtain those bases and mineral concessions? Had the Chinese attack perhaps been provoked—or even faked, for their government denied it?) and the million petty frustrations of the garrison state. Still—the strength of his feelings! The violence!

By creating Sam Hall he had struck back. But that was an ineffectual blow, a timid gesture. Most likely his basic motive was simply to find a halfway safe release. In Sam Hall he lived vicariously the things that the beast within him wanted to do. Several times he had intended to discontinue his sabotage, but it was like a drug: Sam Hall was becoming necessary to his own stability.

The thought was alarming. He ought to see a psychiatrist—but no, the doctor would be bound to report his tale, he would go to camp, and Jack, if not exactly ruined, would be under a cloud for the rest of his life. Thornberg had no desire to go to camp, anyway. His existence had compensations, interesting work, a few good friends, art and music and literature, decent wine, sunsets and mountains, memories. He had started this game on impulse, and now he was simply too late to stop it.

For Sam Hall had been promoted to Public Enemy Number One.

Winter came, and the slopes of the Rockies under which Matilda lay were white beneath a cold greenish sky. Air traffic around the nearby town was lost in that hugeness: brief hurtling meteors against infinity, ground traffic that could not be seen from the Records entrance. Thornberg took the special tubeway to work every morning, but he often walked the ten kilometers back, and his Sundays were usually spent in long hikes over slippery trails. That was a foolish thing to do alone in winter, except that he felt reckless.

He was in his office shortly before Christmas when the intercom said: "Major Sorensen to see you, sir. From Investigation."

Thornberg felt his stomach tie itself into a cold knot. "All right," he answered in a voice whose levelness surprised him. "Cancel any other appointments." Security Investigation took AAA priority.

Sorensen strode in with a clack of bootheels. He was a big blond man, heavy-shouldered, face expressionless, eyes pale and remote as the winter sky. His black uniform fitted him like a skin; against it, the lightning badge of his service glittered frosty. He halted before the desk. Thornberg rose to give him an awkward salute.

"Please sit down, Major Sorensen. What can I do for you?"

"Thanks." The agent's tone crackled. He lowered his bulk into a chair and let his gaze drill Thornberg. "I've come about the Sam Hall case."

"Oh, the rebel?" Thornberg's flesh prickled. He could barely meet those eyes.

"How do you know he's a rebel?" Sorensen demanded. "That's never been stated officially."

"Why—I assumed—bank raid—attacks on personnel in your service—"

Sorensen slightly inclined his cropped head. When he spoke again, he sounded relaxed, almost casual. "Tell me, Major Thornberg, have you followed the Hall developments in detail?"

Thornberg hesitated. He was not supposed to do so unless ordered; he only kept the machine running. He remembered a principle from reading and, yes, furtively cynical conversation. "When suspected of a major sin, admit minor ones frankly. That may satisfy them."

"As a matter of fact, I have," he said. "I know it's against regs, but I was interested and—well, I couldn't see any harm in it. I've not discussed it with anybody, of course."

"No matter." Sorensen waved a muscular hand. "If you hadn't, I'd have ordered you to. I want your opinion on this."

"Why—I'm not a detective—"

"You know more about Records, though, than any other person. I'll be frank with you—under the rose, naturally." Sorensen seemed almost friendly now. *Was it a trick to put his prey off guard?* "You see, there are some puzzling features about this case."

Thornberg kept silent. He wondered if Sorensen could hear the thudding of his heart.

"Sam Hall is a shadow," said the agent. "The most careful checkups eliminate any chance of his being identical with anyone else of that name. In fact we've learned that the name occurs in a violent old drinking song. Is this coincidence, or did the song suggest crime to Sam Hall, or did he by some incredible process get that alias into his record instead of his real name? Whatever the answer there, we know that he's ostensibly without military training, yet he's pulled off some beautiful pieces of precision attack. His IQ is only 110, but he evades our traps. He has no politics, yet he turns on Security without warning. We have not been able to find a single individual who remembers him—not one, and believe me, we have been thorough. Oh, there are a few subconscious memories which might be of him, but probably aren't; and so aggressive a personality should be remembered consciously. No undergrounder or foreign operative we've caught had any knowledge of him, which defies probability. The whole business seems impossible."

Thornberg licked his lips. Sorensen, the hunter of men, must know he was frightened; but would he assume that to be the normal nervousness of a man in the presence of a Security officer?

Sorensen's face broke into a hard smile. "As Sherlock Holmes remarked," he said, "when you have eliminated every other hypothesis, then the one which remains, however improbable, must be right."

Despite himself, Thornberg was jolted. Sorensen hadn't struck him as a reader.

"Well," he asked slowly, "what is your remaining hypothesis?"

His visitor watched him for a long time, it seemed forever, before replying. "The underground is more powerful and widespread than people realize. They've had seventy years to prepare, and many good brains in their ranks. They carry on scientific research of their own. It's top secret, but we know they have perfected a type of weapon we cannot duplicate yet. It seems to be a hand gun throwing bolts of energy—a blaster, you might call it—of immense power. Sooner or later they're going to wage open war against the government.

"Now, could they have done something comparable in psychology? Could they have found a way to erase or cover up memories selectively, even on the cellular level? Could they know how to fool a personality tester, how to disguise the mind itself? If so, we may have any number of Sam Halls in our midst, undetectable until the moment comes for them to strike."

Thornberg felt almost boneless. He couldn't help gasping his relief, and hoped Sorensen would take it for a sign of alarm.

"The possibility is frightening, no?" The blond man laughed metallically. "You can imagine what is being felt in high official circles. We've put all the psychological researchers we could get to work on the problem—bah! Fools! They go by the book; they're afraid to be original even when the state tells them to.

"This may just be a wild fancy, of course. I hope it is. But we have to *know*. That's why I approached you personally, instead of sending the usual requisition. I want you to make a search of the records—everything pertaining to the subject, every man, every discovery, every hypothesis. You have a broad technical background and, from your psychorecord, an unusual amount of creative imagination. I want you to do what you can to correlate your data. Co-opt whoever you need. Submit to my office a report on the possibility—or should I say probability—of this notion; and if you find any likelihood of its being true, sketch out a research program which will enable us to duplicate the results and counteract them."

Thornberg fumbled for words. "I'll try," he said lamely. "I'll do my best."

"Good. It's for the state."

Sorensen had finished his official business, but he didn't go at once. "Rebel propaganda is subtle stuff," he said quietly, after a pause. "It's dangerous because it uses our own slogans, with a twisted meaning. Liberty, equality, justice, peace. Too many people can't appreciate that times have changed and the meanings of words have necessarily changed likewise."

"I suppose not," said Thornberg. He added the lie: "I never thought much about that kind of question."

"You should," said Sorensen. "Study your history. When we lost World War III we had to militarize to win World War IV, and after that mount guard on the whole human race. The people demanded it at the time."

The people, thought Thornberg, *never appreciated freedom till they'd lost it. They were always willing to sell their birthright. Or was it merely that, being untrained in thinking, they couldn't see through demagoguery, couldn't visualize the ultimate consequences of their wishes?* He was vaguely shocked at the thought; wasn't he able to control his mind any longer?

"The rebels," said Sorensen, "claim that conditions have changed, that militarization is no longer necessary—if it ever was—and that America would be safe in a union of free countries. Devilishly clever propaganda, Major Thornberg. Watch out for it."

He got up and took his leave. Thornberg sat for a long time staring at the door. Sorensen's last words had been odd, to say the least. Were they a hint—or a bait?

The next day Matilda received a news item which was carefully edited for the public channels. An insurrectionist force had landed aircraft in the stockade of Camp Forbes, in Utah, gunned down the guards, and taken away the prisoners. The institution's doctor had been spared, and related that the leader of the raid, a stocky man in a mask, had said to him: "Tell your friends I'll call again. My name is Sam Hall."

Space Guard ship blown up on Mesa Verde Field. On a fragment of metal someone has scrawled: "Compliments of Sam Hall!"

Squad of Security Police, raiding a suspected underground hideout in Philadelphia, cut down by tommy-gun fire. Voice from a hidden bullhorn cries: "My name, it is Sam Hall!"

Matthew Williamson, chemist in Seattle, suspected of subversive connections, is gone when the arresting officers break into his home. A note left on his desk says: "Off to visit Sam Hall. Back for liberation. M.W."

Defense plant producing important robomb components near Miami is sabotaged by a planted bomb, after a phone warning gives the workers time to evacuate. The caller, who leaves the visio circuit off, styles himself Sam Hall. Various similar places get similar warnings. These are fakes, but each costs a day's valuable work in the alarm and the search.

Scribbled on walls from New York to San Diego, from Duluth to El Paso: Sam Hall, Sam Hall, Sam Hall.

Obviously, thought Thornberg, the underground had seized on the invisible and invincible man of legend and turned him to their own purposes. Reports of him poured in from all over the country, hundreds every day—Sam Hall seen here, Sam Hall seen there. Ninety-nine percent could be dismissed as hoaxes, hallucinations, mistakes; it was another national craze, fruit of a jittery time, like the sixteenth- and seventeenth-century witch-hunts or the twentieth-century flying saucers. But Security and civilian police had to check on everyone.

Thornberg planted a number of them himself.

Mostly, though, he was busy on his assignment. He could understand what it meant to the government. Life in the garrison state was inevitably founded on fear and mistrust, every man's eye on his neighbor; but at least psychotyping and hypnoquizzing had given a degree of surety. Now, that staff knocked out from under them—

His preliminary studies indicated that an invention such as Sorensen had hypothesized, while not impossible, was too far beyond the scope of contemporary science for the rebels to have perfected. Such research carried on nowadays would, from the standpoint of practicality if not of knowledge, be a waste of time and trained men.

He spent a good many sleepless hours and a month's cigarette ration before he could decide what to do. All right, he'd aided insurrection in a small way, and he shouldn't boggle at the next step. Still—nevertheless—did he want to?

Jack—his son had a career lined out for himself. He loved the big deeps beyond the sky as he would love a woman. If things changed, what then of Jack's career?

Well, what was it now? Stuck on a dreary planet as guardsman and executioner of homesick starvelings poisoned by radioactivity; never even seeing the sun. Come the day, Jack could surely wrangle a berth on a real spacer. They'd need bold men to explore beyond Saturn. Jack was too honest to make a good rebel, but Thornberg felt that after the initial shock he would welcome a new government.

But treason! Oaths!

When in the course of human events...

It was a small thing that decided Thornberg. He passed a shop downtown and noticed a group of the Youth Guard smashing the windows and spattering yellow paint over the goods, O Moses, Jesus, Mendelssohn, Hertz, and Einstein! Once he had chosen his path, a curious serenity possessed him. He stole a vial of prussic acid from a chemist friend and carried it in his pocket; and as for Jack, the boy would have to take his chances too.

The work was demanding and dangerous. He had to alter recorded facts which were available elsewhere, in books and journals and the minds of men. Nothing could be done about basic theory. But quantitative results could be juggled a little to set the overall picture subtly askew. He would co-opt carefully chosen experts, men whose psychotypes indicated they would take the easy course of relying on Matilda instead of checking original sources. And the correlation and integration of innumerable data, the empirical equations and extrapolations thereof, could be tampered with.

He turned his regular job over to Rodney and devoted himself entirely to the new one. He grew thin and testy; when Sorensen called, trying to hurry him, he snapped back: "Do you want speed or quality?" and wasn't too surprised at himself afterward. He got little sleep, but his mind seemed unnaturally clear.

Winter faded into spring while Thornberg and his experts labored and while the nation shook, psychically and physically, under the growing violence of Sam Hall. The report Thornberg submitted in May was so voluminous and detailed that he didn't think the government researchers would bother referring to any other source. Its conclusion: Yes, given a brilliant man applying Belloni matrices to cybernetic formulas and using some unknown kind of colloidal probe, a psychological masking technique was plausible.

The government yanked every man it could find into research. Thornberg knew it was only a matter of time before they realized they had been had. How much time, he couldn't say. But when they were sure…

> *Now up the rope I go, up I go,*
> *Now up the rope I go, up I go.*
> *And the bastards down below,*
> *They say, "Sam, we told you so."*
> *They say, "Sam, we told you so," God damn their eyes.*

REBELS ATTACK
SPACESHIPS LAND UNDER COVER OF RAINSTORM
SEIZE POINTS NEAR N DETROIT
FLAME WEAPONS USED AGAINST ARMY BY REBELS

"The infamous legions of the traitors have taken ground throughout the nation, but already our gallant forces have hurled them back. They have come out in early summer like toadstools, and will wither as fast—WHEEEEEEOOOOOO!" Silence.

"All citizens will keep calm, remain loyal to their country, and stay at their usual tasks, until otherwise ordered. Civilians will report to their local defense officers. Military reservists will report immediately for active duty."

"Hello, Hawaii! Are you there? Come in, Hawaii! Calling Hawaii!"

"CQ, Mars GHQ calling…bzzz, wheeee…seized Syrtis Major Colony and…whoooo…help needed…"

The lunar rocket bases are assaulted and carried. The commander blows them up rather than surrender. A pinpoint flash on the moon's face, a new crater; what will they name it?

"So they've got Seattle, have they? Send a robomb flight. Scrub the place off the map…Citizens? To hell with citizens! This is war!"

"…in New York. Secretly drilled rebels emerged from the notorious Crater district and stormed…"

"…assassins were shot down. The new president has already been sworn in and…"

BRITAIN, CANADA, AUSTRALIA REFUSE
ASSISTANCE TO GOV'T

"…no, sir. The bombs reached Seattle all right. But they were stopped before they hit—some kind of energy gun…"

"COMECO to army commanders in Florida and Georgia: Enemy action has made Florida and the keys temporarily untenable. Your units will withdraw as follows…"

"Today a rebel force engaging a military convoy in Donner Pass was annihilated by a well-placed tactical atomic bomb. Though our own men suffered losses on this account."

"COMWECO to army commanders in California: the mutiny of units stationed around San Francisco poses a grave problem…"

SP RAID REBEL HIDEOUT,
BAG FIVE OFFICERS

"Okay, so the enemy is about to capture Boston. We *can't* issue weapons to the citizens. They might turn them on us!"

SPACE GUARD UNITS EXPECTED FROM VENUS

Jack, Jack, Jack!

It was strange, living in the midst of a war. Thornberg had never thought it would be like this. Drawn faces, furtive looks, chaos in the telecast news and the irregularly arriving papers, blackouts, civil defense drills, shortages, occasional panic when a rebel jet whistled overhead—but nothing else. No gunfire, no bombs, no more than the unreal combats you heard about. The only local casualty list was due to Security; people kept disappearing, and nobody spoke about them.

But then, why should the enemy bother with this unimportant mountain town? The self-styled Libertarian Army was grabbing key points of manufacture, transportation, communication, was engaging in pitched battles, sabotaging buildings and machines, assassinating officials. By its very purpose, it couldn't wage total war, couldn't annihilate the folk it wanted to free—an attitude historically rare among revolutionaries, Thornberg knew. Rumor said the defenders were less finicky.

Most citizens were passive. They always are. Probably no more than one-fourth of the population was ever in earshot of an engagement. City dwellers might see fire in the sky, hear crump and whistle and crash of artillery, scramble aside from soldiers and armored vehicles, cower in shelters when rockets arced overhead; but the action was outside of town. If matters came to street fighting, the rebels never pushed far in. They would either lay siege or they would rely on agents inside the town. Then a citizen might hear the crack of rifles and grenades, rattle of machine guns, sizzle of lasers, and see corpses. But the end was either a return of military government or the rebels marching in and setting up their own provisional councils. (They rarely met cheers and flowers. Nobody knew how the war would end. But they heard words whispered, and usually got good service.) As nearly as possible, the average American continued his average life.

Thornberg stayed on his personal rails. Matilda, the information nexus, was in such demand that users queued for their shared time. If the rebels ever learned where she was—

Or did they know?

He got few opportunities to conduct his private sabotages, but on that account planned each of them extra carefully. The Sam Hall reports were almost standardized in his mind—Sam Hall here, Sam Hall there, pulling off this or that incredible stunt. But what did one superman count for in these gigantic days? He needed something more.

Television and newspapers jubilantly announced that Venus had finally been contacted. Luna and Mars had fallen, but the Guard units on Venus had quickly smashed a few feeble uprisings. Mere survival there demanded quantities of powerful, sophisticated equipment, readily adaptable to military purposes. The troops would be returning at once, fully armed. Given present planetary configurations, the highest boost could not deliver them on Earth for a good six weeks. But then they might prove a decisive reinforcement.

"Looks like you may see your boy soon, chief," Rodney remarked.

"Yes," said Thornberg, "I may."

"Tough fighting." Rodney shook his head. "I'd sure as hell hate to be in it."

If Jack is killed by a rebel gun, when I have aided the rebels' cause...

Sam Hall, reflected Thornberg, had lived a hard life, all violence and enmity and suspicion. Even his wife hadn't trusted him.

> *...And my Nellie dressed in blue,*
> *Says, "Your trifling days are through.*
> *Now I know that you'll be true, God damn your eyes.*

Poor Sam Hall. No wonder he had killed a man.

Suspicion!

Thornberg stood for a moment while a tingle went through him. The police state was founded on suspicion. Nobody could trust anybody else. And with the new fear of psychomasking, and research on that project suspended during the crisis—

Steady, boy, steady. Can't rush into action. Have to plan very carefully.

Thornberg punched for the dossiers of key men in the administration, in the military, in Security. He did this in the presence of two assistants, for he thought that his own frequent sessions alone in the coordination booth were beginning to look funny.

"Top secret," he warned them, pleased with his cool manner. He was becoming a regular Machiavelli, "You'll be skinned alive if you mention it to anyone."

Rodney gave him a shrewd glance. "So they're not even sure of their top men now, are they?" he murmured.

"I've been told to make some checks," snapped Thornberg. "That's all you need to know."

He studied the files for many hours before coming to a decision. Secret observations were, of course, made of everyone from time to time. A cross check with Matilda showed that the cop who filed the last report on Lindahl had been killed the next day in a spontaneous and abortive uprising. The report was innocuous: Lindahl had stayed at home, studying various papers; he had been alone in the house except for a bodyguard in another room who had not seen him. And Lindahl was Undersecretary of Defense.

Thornberg changed the record. A masked man—stocky, black-haired—had come in and talked for three hours with Lindahl. They had spoken low, so that the cop's ears, outside the window, couldn't catch what was said. After the visitor left, Lindahl had retired. The cop went back in great excitement, made out his report, and gave it to the signalman, who had sent it on to Matilda.

Tough on the signalman, thought Thornberg. *They'll want to know why he didn't tell this to his chief in New Washington, if the observer was killed before doing so. He'll deny every such report, and they'll hypnoquiz him—but they don't trust that method anymore!*

His sympathy quickly faded. What counted was having the war over before Jack got home. He refiled the altered spool and did a little backtracking, shifting the last report of Sam Hall from Salt Lake City to Atlanta. More plausible. Then, as opportunity permitted, he worked on real men's records.

He must wait two haggard days before the next order came from Security for a check on Sam Hall. The scanners trod out their intricate measure, transistors awoke, in due course a cog turned. LINDAHL unrolled before the microprinter. Cross references ramified in all directions. Thornberg attached a query to the preliminary report: this looked interesting; did his superiors want more information?

They did!

Next day the telecast announced a shake-up in the Department of Defense. Nobody heard more about Lindahl.

And I, Thornberg reflected, *have grabbed a very large tiger by the tail. Now they'll have to check everybody. How does a solitary man keep ahead of the Security Police?*

Lindahl is a traitor. How did his chief ever let him get such a sensitive position? Secretary Hoheimer was a personal friend of Lindahl, too. Have Records check Hoheimer.

What's this? Hoheimer himself! Five years ago, yes, but even so—the dossier shows he lived in an apartment unit where *Sam Hall* was janitor. Grab Hoheimer! Who'll take his place? General Halliburton? That stupid old bastard? Well, at least his nose is clean. Can't trust those slick characters.

Hoheimer has a brother in Security, general's rank, good detection record. A blind? Who knows? Slap the brother in jail, at least for the duration. Better check his staff...Central Records shows that his chief field agent, Jones, has five days unaccounted for a year ago; he claimed Security secrecy at the time, but a double-cross check shows it wasn't true. Shoot Jones! He has a nephew in the army, a captain. Pull that unit out of the firing line till we can study it man by man! We've had too many mutinies already.

Lindahl was also a close friend of Benson, in charge of the Tennessee Atomic Ordnance Works. Haul Benson in! Check every man connected with him! No trusting those scientists; they're always blabbing secrets.

The first Hoheimer's son is an industrialist, owns a petroleum-synthesis plant in Texas. Nab him! His wife is a sister of Leslie, head of the War Production Coordination Board. Get Leslie too. Sure, he's doing a good job, but he may be sending information to the enemy. Or he may just be waiting for the signal to sabotage the whole works. We can't trust *anybody*, I tell you!

What's this? Records relays an Intelligence report that the mayor of Tampa was in cahoots with the rebels. It's marked "Unreliable, Rumor"—but Tampa did surrender without a fight. The mayor's business partner is Gale, who has a cousin in the army, commanding a robomb base in New Mexico. Check both the Gales, Records…So the cousin was absent four days without filing his whereabouts, was he? Military privilege or not, arrest him and find out where he was!

- Attention, Records, attention, Records, urgent. Brigadier John Harmsworth Gale, etc., etc., refused to divulge information required by Security Officers, claiming to have been at his base all the time. Can this be an error on your part?
- Records to Security Central, ref: etc., etc. No possibility of error exists except in information received.
- To Records, ref: etc., etc. Gale's story corroborated by three of his officers.

Put that whole damned base under arrest! Recheck those reports! Who sent them in, anyway?

- To Records, ref: etc., etc. On attempt to arrest entire personnel, Robomb Base 37-J fired on Security detachment and repulsed it. At last reports Gale was calling for rebel forces fifty miles off to assist him. Details will follow for the files as soon as possible.

So Gale was a traitor. Or was he driven by fear? Have Records find out who filed that information about him in the first place.

We can't trust anybody!

Thornberg was not much surprised when his door was kicked open and the Security squad entered. He had been expecting it for days, maybe weeks. A solitary man can't keep ahead of the game forever. No doubt accumulated inconsistencies had finally drawn suspicion his way; or, ironically, the chains of accusation he forged had by chance led to him; perhaps somebody here, like Rodney, had decided something was amiss and lodged a tip.

Were that last the case, he laid no blame. The tragedy of civil war was that it turned brother against brother. Millions of decent people were with the government because they had pledged themselves to be, or simply because they didn't believe in the alternative. Mostly, Thornberg felt tired.

He looked down the barrel of a revolver and up to the eyes of the blackcoat behind. They were equally empty of feeling. "I assume I'm under arrest?" he said tonelessly.

"On your feet," the leader snapped.

June could not hold back a whimper of pain. The man who held her was twisting her arm behind her back, obviously enjoying himself. "Don't do that," Thornberg said. "She's innocent. Had no idea what I was carrying out."

"On your feet, I told you." The leader thrust his gun closer.

"I suggest you leave me alone, too." Thornberg lifted his right hand, to show a ball he had taken from his desk when the squad arrived. "Do you see this? A thing I made against contingencies. Not a bomb *per se*—but a radio trigger. If my fingers relax, the rubber will expand and close a circuit. I believe such a device is called a dead-man switch."

The squad stiffened. Thornberg heard an oath. "Release the lady," he said.

"You surrender first!" said June's captor. He wrenched. She screamed.

"No," Thornberg said. "June, dear, I'm sorry. But have no fears. You see, I expected this visit, and made my preparations. The radio signaller won't touch off anything as melodramatic as a bomb. No, instead it will close a relay which will activate a certain program in Matilda—the Records computer, you know, the data machine. Every spool will be wiped. The government will have not a record left. Myself, I am prepared to die. But if you men let me complete that circuit, I imagine you'll wish there had been a bomb. Now do let go of the lady."

The blackcoat did, as if she had suddenly turned incandescent. She slumped sobbing to the floor.

"A bluff!" the leader shouted. Sweat made his face shiny.

"Do you wish to call it?" Thornberg made a smile. "By all means."

"You traitor—"

"I prefer 'patriot,' if you please. But be the semantics as they may, you must admit I was effective. The government has been turned end for end and upside down. The army is breaking apart, officers deserting right and left for fear they'll be arrested next, or defecting, or leading mutinies. Security is chasing its own tail around half a continent. Far more administrators are being murdered by their colleagues than the underground could possibly assassinate. The Libertarians take city after city without resistance. My guess is that they will occupy New Washington inside another week."

"Your doing!" Finger quivered on trigger.

"Oh, no. Spare my blushes. But I did make a contribution of some significance, yes. Unless you say Sam Hall did, which is fine by me."

"What...will...you do now?"

"That depends on you, my friend. Whether I am killed or only rendered unconscious, Matilda dies. You could have the technicians check out whether I'm telling the truth, and if I am, you could have them yank that program. However, at the first sign of any such move on your part, I will naturally let the ball go. Look in my mouth." He opened it briefly. "Yes, the conventional glass vial of prussic acid. I apologize for the cliché, but you will understand that I have no wish to share the fate that you people bring on yourselves."

Bafflement wrestled rage in the countenances before Thornberg. They weren't used to thinking, those men.

"Of course," he went on, "you have an alternative. At last reports, a Liberation unit was established less than two hundred kilometers from here. We could call and ask them to send a force, explaining the importance of this place. That would be to your advantage too. There is going to be a day of reckoning with you blackcoats. My influence could help you personally, however little you deserve to get off the hook."

They stared at each other. After a very long while, wherein the only sounds were June's diminishing sobs, unevenly drawn breaths among the police, and Thornberg's pulse rapid in his ears, the leader spat, "No! You lie!" He aimed his gun.

The man behind him drew and shot him in the head.

The result was ugly to see. As soon as he knew he was fully in charge, Thornberg did his best to comfort June.

"As a matter of fact," he told Sorensen, "I *was* bluffing. That was just a ball; the poison alone was real. Not that it made much difference at that stage, except to me."

"We'll need Matilda for a while yet," said Sorensen. "Want to stay on?"

"Sure, provided I can take a vacation when my son comes home."

"That shouldn't be long now. You'll be glad to hear we've finally contacted the Venus units of the Space Guard, on their way back. The commander agreed to stay out of the fighting, on the grounds that his service's obligation is to the legitimate government and we'll need an election to determine what that is. Your boy will be safe."

Thornberg could find no words of response. Instead he remarked with hard-held casualness, "You know, I'm surprised to learn you were an undergrounder."

"We got a few into Security, who wrangled things so they gave each other clearances and loyalty checks." Sorensen grimaced. "That was the only part of it I enjoyed, though, till quite lately."

He leaned back in his chair, which creaked under his weight. In civilian clothes which nothing but an armband made into the uniform of a Libertarian officer, he did seem an altogether different man. Where his bulk had formerly crowded Thornberg's office, today his vitality irradiated it.

"Then Sam Hall came along," he said. "They had their suspicions at first in Security. My bosses were evil but not stupid. Well, I got myself assigned to the job of checking you out. Right away I guessed you harbored disruptive thoughts; so I gave you a clean bill of health. Afterward I cooked up that fantasy of the psychological mask and got several high-ranking men worried. When you followed my lead, I was sure you were on our side. Consequently, though the Libertarian command knew all along where Matilda was, of course they left her alone!"

"You must have joined them in person very recently."

"Yeah, the witch-hunt you started inside of Security was getting too close to me. Well worth a risk, though, to see those cockroaches busily stepping on each other."

Thornberg sat quiet awhile, then leaned over his desk. "I haven't enlisted under your banner yet," he said gravely. "I had to assume the Libertarian words about freedom were not mere rhetoric. But...you mentioned Matilda. You want me to continue in my work here. What are your plans for her?"

Sorensen turned equally serious. "I was waiting for you to ask that, Thorny. Look. Besides needing her to help us find some people we want rather badly, we are responsible for the sheer physical survival of the country. I'd feel easier too if we could take her apart this minute. But—"

"Yes?"

"But we've got to transcribe a lot of information first, strictly practical facts. *Then* we wipe everything else and ceremoniously dynamite this building. You're invited, no, urgently asked to sit on the board that decides the details—in other words, we want you to help work yourself out of a job."

"Thank you," Thornberg whispered.

After a moment, in a sudden tide of happiness, he chuckled. "And that will be the end of Sam Hall," he said. "He'll go to whatever Valhalla there is for the great characters of fiction. I can see him squabbling with Sherlock Holmes and shocking the hell out of King Arthur and striking up a beautiful friendship with Long John Silver. Do you know how the ballad ends?" He sang softly: *"Now up in heaven I dwell, in heaven I dwell..."*

Unfortunately, the conclusion is pretty rugged. Sam Hall never was satisfied.

Robin Hood's Barn

Svoboda was about sixty years old. He did not know his exact age. The Lowlevel seldom counted such things, and his earliest memory was of weeping in an alley while rain fell past an overhead beltway that roared. Afterward his mother died and someone, who claimed to be his father, but probably wasn't, sold him to Inky the thiefmaster.

Sixty was ancient for a man of the masses, whether he slunk cat-fashion through soot and noise and sudden death in a city Lowlevel or—more healthfully if with less freedom—squirmed along a mine shaft or tended engine on a plankton reaper. For an upperlevel Citizen, or a Guardian, sixty was only middle-aged. Svoboda, who had spent half his life in either category, looked as old as Satan but could hope for another two decades.

If you wanted to call it hope, he thought wryly.

His left foot was paining him again. It was a lump within the special shoe. When he was twelve or so, scrambling over a garden wall with a silver chalice contributed by one Engineer Harkavy, an explosive slug from a guard's pistol had smashed all the bones. He got away somehow, but it was a cruel thing to happen to one of the most agile and promising lads in the Brotherhood. Inky reapprenticed him to a fence, which forced him to learn reading and writing and thus started him on a long road up. Twenty-five years afterward, when Svoboda was Commissioner of Astronautics, a medic recommended prosthetizing the broken foot.

"I could make you one that you could hardly tell from the real thing, sir," he offered.

"Undoubtedly," said Svoboda. "I have seen our older Guardians tottering around with prosthetic hearts and prosthetic stomachs and a sort of prosthetic eye. I am sure the onward march of science will soon come to a prosthetic brain, which can hardly be told from the real thing. Some of my colleagues led me to think this has already been achieved." He shrugged skinny shoulders. "No. I'm too busy. Later, perhaps."

The busyness consisted in breaking out of the Astronautical Department, a notorious dead-end street into which nervous superiors had maneuvered him. And having done so, he was at once preoccupied with something else. There had never been time. You had to run pretty fast just to stay where you were.

How many people nowadays had read "Alice"? he wondered.

But the foot often did pain him. He stopped to let the throbbing ease.

"Are you all right, sir?" asked Iyeyasu.

Svoboda looked at the gray-clad giant and smiled. His other six guards were nonentities, the usual efficient impersonal killing machines. Iyeyasu did not pack a gun; he was a karate man, and he could reach into your rib cage and pull your lungs out if you displeased Svoboda.

"I'll do," said the Commissioner of Psychologics. "Don't inquire exactly what I'll do, but there must be something."

Iyeyasu offered an arm and his master leaned on it. The contrast was ridiculous. Svoboda stood barely one hundred fifty centimeters tall, with a hairless dome of skull and a face all dark wrinkles and scimitar nose. His childish frame was gaudy in a cloak like fire, iridescent high-collared tunic, and deep-blue trousers cut in the latest bell-bottomed style. Whereas the Okinawan wore gray, and had a shoulder-length black mane and hands deformed by a lifetime's cracking bricks and punching through boards.

Svoboda fumbled with yellow-stained fingers after a cigarette. He stood on a landing terrace, immensely high up. Below was none of the parkscape which most Commissioners chose for their buildings; Svoboda had put his departmental tower in the same city which spawned him. It stretched under his feet, as far as he could gaze through air-borne filth. But past the floating docks, on the world's very eastern edge, he could see a mercury gleam that was the open Atlantic.

Dusk was creeping over the planet, spires etched themselves black across a surly red sundown. Highlevel walls and streets began to glow. Lowlevel was a darkness beneath, and a muted unending growl of beltways, generators, auto factories, sparks to show a window waking to life or a pedicar headlamp or the flashes of men going in cudgel-armed parties for fear of the Brotherhood.

Svoboda drew smoke through his nostrils. His eyes wandered past the aircar which had borne him here from his oceanic house to the sky. Venus stood forth, white against royal blue. He sighed and gestured at it. "Do you know," he said, "I'm almost glad the colony there has been discontinued. Not because it wasn't paying for itself, but for a better reason."

"What is that, sir?" Iyeyasu sensed that the commissioner wanted to talk. They had been together for many years.

"Now there's one place you can go to get away from humankind."

"Venus air is no good, sir. You can go to the stars and get away, and not wear armor."

"But nine years in deepsleep to the nearest star. A bit extreme for a vacation."

"Yes, sir."

"And then the planets you find are as bad as Venus...or they're like Earth, but not *enough* like Earth, and men break their hearts. Come on, let's go play at being important."

Svoboda leaned back onto his crutch and went quickly over the terrace, through an arched portal and down a long luminous-walled corridor. His guards fanned out, ahead and behind, their eyes never still; Iyeyasu stayed close. Not that Svoboda expected assassins. There was a night shift here, because Psychologics was a major fief within the Federation government, but no one on this floor.

At the hall's end was a teleconference room. Svoboda hobbled to an easy-chair, Iyeyasu helped him into it and set a desk in front of him. Most of the men who looked from the screens had advisors beside them. Svoboda was alone, except for his guards. He had always worked alone.

Premier Selim nodded. Behind his image was a window opening on palm trees. "Ah, there you are, Commissioner," he said. "We were just beginning to wonder."

"I apologize for lateness," said Svoboda. "As you know, I never transact business from my home, so I had to come here for the conference. Well, a caisson under my house sprang a leak, the gyrostabilizers failed, and before I knew what had happened I was reading the time off a seasick octopus. It was ten minutes slow."

Security Chief Chandra blinked, opened a bearded mouth to protest, then nodded. "Ah, you make a joke. I see. Ha." He sat in India at sunrise; but the rulers of Earth were used to irregular hours.

"Let us begin," said Selim. "We will dispense with formalities. However, before we start the business at hand, is there anything else of urgency?"

"Er—" Rathjen, the present Commissioner of Astronautics, spoke timidly. He was the weak son of the late Premier; his father had given him the post and nobody since had cared to take it away. "Er, yes, gentlemen, I should again like to raise the question of repair funds for...I mean to say, we have several perfectly good spaceships which only need a few million in repair funds to, er, reach the stars again. And then all the astronautical academies, really, the quality of new recruits is as low as the quantity. I should think, that is, if we—Mr. Svoboda especially, it seems to be in his department—an intensive propaganda campaign, directed at younger sons of the Guardian families...or Citizens of professional Status...persuading them of the importance, giving the profession the, er, the glamor it once had—"

"Please," interrupted Selim. "Another time."

"I might make a remark, though," said Svoboda.

"What?" Novikov of Mines turned a surprised eye on him. "You are the one who brought this special conference about. Do you want to waste it on irrelevancies?"

"'Nothing is irrelevant,'" murmured Svoboda.

"What?" said Chandra.

"I was only quoting Anker, the philosophical father of Constitutionalism," Svoboda told him. "Some day you might try understanding the things you want to suppress. I have been assured that it works wonders."

Chandra flushed with annoyance. "But I don't want—" he began, and decided otherwise.

Selim looked baffled. Rathjen said plaintively, "You were going to comment on my business, Mr. Svoboda."

"So I was." The small man struck a fresh cigarette and inhaled deeply. His eyes, a startling electric blue in the mummy face, leaped from screen to screen. "Commissioner Novikov could give you a good reason for the decay of astronautics: more people and fewer resources every day. We can no more afford interstellar exploration than we can afford representative government. The vestiges of both are being eliminated as fast as the anguish of yourself, and the Constitutionalists, permits. Which I know is not as fast as some of you gentlemen would like. But by pushing social change too hard, the government provoked the North American Rebellion twenty years ago." He grinned. "Therefore we must take the lesson to heart and not goad the Astronautical Department into revolt. It is easier to operate a few spaceships for a few more generations than to storm barricades of filing cabinets manned by desperate bureaucrats waving the bloody flag in triplicate. But you on your side must not expect us to expand, or even maintain, your fleet."

"Mr. Svoboda!" gasped Rathjen.

Selim cleared his throat. "We all know the Psychologics Commissioner's sense of humor," he said ponderously. "But since he has mentioned the Constitutionalists, I trust he means to proceed to our real business."

The dozen faces turned upon Svoboda and did not let go. He veiled his own stare in smoke and answered, "Very well. I daresay Commissioner-baiting is a cruel sport, and we'd all do better to pick good-looking Citizen girls off the streets for several weeks of Special Instruction." Now Larkin of Pelagiculture was the one who glared. "Perhaps you aren't all familiar with the issue on hand. I've submitted a special report on the Constitutionalists to Premier Selim, Mr. Chandra, and the Commandant of North America. It proved so controversial that the whole Guardian Commission has been asked to debate it."

He nodded at Selim. The Premier's harsh gray face looked a bit startled; it was almost as if Svoboda had given him permission to go ahead. He harrumphed, glanced at the paper on his desk, and said:

"The trouble is, the Constitutionalists are not a political group. If they were, we could round them up tomorrow. They are not even formally organized, and there are all shades of agreement among them. It's a philosophy."

"Bad!" murmured Svoboda. "Philosophies only rationalize emotional attitudes. The very name of this one is a Freudian slip."

"What's that?" asked Novikov.

"You ought to know," said Svoboda sweetly. "You're rather an expert. To continue, though. Officially, the name 'Constitutionalism' only refers to an attitude toward the physical universe, an advocacy of basing thought patterns on the constitution of reality. But I grew up here, where half the population still speaks English. And in English, that word Constitution is loaded! The North American insurrection was brought on when the Federation government persistently and flagrantly violated—not the spirit of their poor old much-amended Constitution; they were always good at that themselves—but the letter of it."

"I know that much," said Chandra. "Don't think I haven't investigated these philosophers, as you call them. I know that many were in the revolt, or had fathers who were. But they aren't dangerous. They may grumble to themselves, but as a class they're not doing so badly. They've no reason to start another futile uprising." He shrugged. "Actually, most of them must be intelligent enough to see that that bill of rights or whatever it was simply doesn't work when there are half a billion people on their continent, eighty per cent illiterate."

"What are they, anyway?" asked Dilolo of Agriculture.

"Mostly North American," said Svoboda. "I mean of the old stock, not the more recent immigrants. But their doctrines are spreading through the educated Citizens all over the world. I imagine if you quizzed, you'd find a fourth of the literate population, rather more than that among scientists and technicians, in substantial agreement with Constitutionalist doctrine. Though, of course, they wouldn't think of themselves under that name, usually."

"In other words," said Chandra, "it's not just another new religion. Not for the yuts. Nor for Guardians, as a rule"—he gave Svoboda a lingering glance—"or top-level Citizens. So I agree it merited investigation. But I found Constitutionalism appealed to the hard-working, prosperous-but-not-rich man: the sober, solid type, who has won a little more status than his father and hopes his son may have just a little more than himself. Such people aren't revolutionaries."

"And yet," said Svoboda, "Constitutionalism is becoming a great deal stronger than you would expect from the small number of formal adherents."

"How?" asked Larkin.

"You leave your engineers' daughters alone, don't you?" said Svoboda.

"What has that...I mean, explain yourself before I lodge a criticism!"

Svoboda grinned. He could break Larkin any time he chose. "The Guardians have the power," he said, "but what's left of Earth's middle class has the influence. There's a distinction. The masses don't try to imitate the Guardians, or really listen to us; the gap is too great. Their natural leaders are the lower-middle-class Citizenry. As for us, we may decree the irrigation of Morocco, and round up a million convicts to dig canals and die; but only if the upper-middle-class specialist has assured us it's feasible. He probably advised it in the first place!

"The trouble with Constitutionalism is, it's all too likely to give this middle class an awareness of their potential power, and thereby start them agitating for a corresponding voice in the government. Which could be more than a little bit lethal to us."

There was a pause. Svoboda finished his cigarette and struck another. He felt the air wheeze in his throat. All the world's biomedics couldn't make up the abuse he visited on lungs and bronchial tubes. *But what else was there to do?* he thought somewhere in a private darkness.

Selim said, "This is not a question of personal menace, gentlemen. But the Psychologies Commissioner has persuaded me that if we care about our children and grandchildren, we must think seriously on this matter."

"You don't mean to arrest all the Constitutionalists?" asked Larkin, alarmed. "But you can't do that! I know how many of my key technical personnel are...I mean, it could be a disaster to every pelagic city on Earth!"

"You see?" smiled Svoboda. He shook his head. "No, no. Besides such practical, immediate difficulties, mass arrests involve a danger of provoking new conspiracies to overthrow the Federation. I'm not that stupid, my friends. I propose to undermine the Constitutionalist movement, not batter at it."

"But see here," objected Chandra, "if it's a simple question of a propaganda campaign, you don't need all of us to—"

"More than propaganda. I want to close the Constitutionalist schools. Never mind the adults; it's the next generation that we're worried about anyway."

"You wouldn't let their brats into *our* schools, would you?" gasped Dilolo.

"I assure you, they don't have vermin," said Svoboda. "Of course, they might be infected with a little originality. But no, I'm not that drastic. However, my idea is radical enough to need full Commission approval. It involves reviving the old concept of free compulsory education."

After the hubbub had faded, which it did because he sat and ignored it, he went on: "Oh, modified, to be sure. I don't plan to rope in the hopeless seventy-five per cent of the population. Let them go their merry way. We can rig admission standards to keep them out, easily enough. What I do want is a decree that all basic education will be financed by the government and must meet official requirements. Which means my requirements. I'll leave the apprentice centers, academies, monasteries, and other useful or harmless institutions alone. But the schools maintained according to Constitutionalist principles will be found to have a deplorably low academic level. I'll fire their teachers and put in some good loyal hacks and some good loyal propaganda."

"There'll be trouble," warned Dilolo.

"Yes. But not too much. Of course the parents will object. But what can they say? Here the state, in a sudden gush of benevolence, is lifting the burden of school costs off their shoulders—never mind where the taxes come from—and making sure that their children will be properly taught and properly adjusted to society. If they want to instill their funny little beliefs in addition, why, they can do it in the evenings and on holidays."

"Ha!" Chandra laughed. "A lot of good that will do."

"Just so," agreed Svoboda. "A philosophy has to be lived; you can't acquire it in an hour a day from a weary father who lectures you while you'd rather be out playing ball. Your non-Constitutionalist classmates are going to ridicule your oddities. And at the same time, the parents will scarcely be able to stir up popular support. This simply isn't the kind of issue which brings on revolutions. We will, almost literally, kill Constitutionalism in its cradle."

"You haven't yet proven that it's worth the trouble of killing," said Novikov.

Larkin put in vindictively: "I know why it is. Because Mr. Svoboda's only son is a Constitutionalist, that's the reason. Because they broke up over the issue ten years ago and haven't spoken since!"

Svoboda's eyes turned quite pale. He held them on Larkin for a very long time. Finally Larkin squirmed, twisted a pencil in his fingers, looked away, looked back, and wiped sweat off his face.

Svoboda continued to stare. It grew very still in the room—in all the rooms.

At the end, Svoboda sighed. "I shall lay the detailed facts and analysis before you, gentlemen," he said. "I shall prove that Constitutionalism has the seeds of social change in it: radical change. Do you want the World Wars back again? Or even a *bourgeoisie* strong enough to try for a voice in government? That sounds less dramatic, but I assure you, the Guardians will be killed just as dead. Now, in order to prove my contention, I shall begin with—"

The address which Theron Wolfe had given turned out to be on the fiftieth floor in a district once proud. Joshua Coffin could remember almost a century back, how the sky town had reared alone among trees and gardens, and only a dun cloud in the east bespoke the city. But now the city had engulfed this tower with mean plastic shells of tenement. In another generation, this would be Lowlevel.

"However," said Wolfe, "I have lived here all my life, and gotten a sentimental attachment to the place."

"I beg your pardon?" Coffin was startled.

"It might be hard for a spaceman to realize." Wolfe smiled. "Or for most better-to-do Citizens, as far as that goes. They are even more nomadic than you, First Officer. Generally you have to be of Guardian family, with an estate, or one of the nameless mass too poor to move anywhere, to strike roots nowadays. But I am a middle-class exception." He stroked his beard and added after a moment, sardonically: "Besides which, it would be hard to find a comparable apartment. You must realize that Earth's population has doubled since you left."

"I know," said Coffin. It emerged harsher than he had intended.

"But come in." Wolfe took his arm and led him off the terrace. They entered a living room archaic with broad windows, solid furniture, paneling which might be actual wood, shelves of books both folio and micro, a few age-cracked oil paintings. The merchant's wife, plain and fiftyish, bowed to her guest and went back to the kitchen. She actually cooked her own food? Coffin was irrationally touched.

"Please sit down." Wolfe waved a hand at a worn, ugly chair—an antique, but highly functional. "Unless of course you prefer the modern fashion of sitting cross-legged on a rug. Even Guardians are beginning to think it's stylish." Horsehair rustled under Coffin's weight. "Smoke?"

"No, thank you." The spaceman realized his tone had been too prim, and tried to rationalize. "It's not a common habit in my profession. Mass-ratio, you know, approximately nine to one for an interstellar journey—" He stopped. "Pardon me. I did not mean to talk shop."

"Oh, but I would much prefer you did. That's why I invited you here, after catching your lecture." Wolfe took a cigarillo from the box. "How about a drink?"

Coffin accepted a small glass of dry sherry. The genuine article, doubtless fabulously expensive. In a way it was a shame to waste it on his unappreciative palate.

He looked at Wolfe. The merchant was big, plump, still hearty in middle age, with a neat gray Vandyke on an unusual broad face. The space between his eyes gave him a curious withdrawn look, as if a part of him always stood aside from the world and watched. He wore a formal robe over dress pajamas, but his feet were bare in slippers. The colors were as sober as the rest of this room.

Wolfe sat down, sipped, rolled smoke around his mouth, and said, "A shame so few people heard your lecture, First Officer. It was most interesting."

"I am not a very good speaker," said Coffin, correctly enough.

"The subject matter, though. To think, a planet of Epsilon Eridani where men can live!"

Coffin felt a thickness of anger. Before he could stop himself, his tongue threw out: "You must be the thousandth person who has said I was at Epsilon Eridani. For your information, Epsilon is a miserable dwarf of no use to any Christian. It is *e* Eridani which the *Ranger* visited. I thought you heard my lecture."

"Slip of my mind. Sorry." Wolfe was more urbane than contrite.

Coffin bowed his head, hot-faced. "No. I beg your pardon, sir. I was heedless and ill-mannered."

"Forget it," said Wolfe. "I believe I understand why you're so tense. How long were you away, now? Eighty-seven years, of which eighty-two, less watches, were spent in deepsleep. It was the climax of your career, an experience such as it is granted few men to have. Then you came back. Your home was gone, your kinfolk scattered, the people and mores changed almost beyond recognition. Worst of all, there's hardly a soul who cares. You offer them a new world, and they yawn at you when they do not jeer."

Coffin sat quiet a while, twirling the sherry glass in his fingers. He was a long man with a jagged Yankee face under hair just starting to be grizzled. He still affected snug-fitting tunic and trousers of black, buttons with an American eagle, everything knife-creased, though even in the space service the uniform was now ludicrously archaic.

"Well," he said at last, struggling for words, "I expected a…a different world… when I came back. Of course. But somehow I did not expect it would be different in this fashion. We, my companions and I, like all interstellar spacemen, we knew we had chosen a special way of life. But it was in the service of man, which is the service of God. We expected to return to the Society, at least, our own spacemen's nation within all nations—do you understand that?" It ripped from him: "But the Society was so *dwindled*!"

Wolfe nodded. "Not many people realize it yet, First Officer," he said, "but space travel is dying."

"Why?" mumbled Coffin. "What have we done, that this is visited upon us?"

"We have eaten up our resources with the same abandon with which we have increased our numbers. Therefore the Four Horsemen have ridden out. Exploration is becoming too costly."

"But…substitutes…new alloys, aluminum…must still be abundant…thermonuclear energy, thermionic conversion, dielectric storage—"

"Oh, yes," said Wolfe. He blew a smoke ring. "But it's not enough. Theoretically, we can supply unlimited amounts of fusion power. But there is so little for that power to work on. Light metal and plastics can only do so much, then you need steel. Machines need oil. Well, lean ores can be processed, organics can be synthesized, and so forth. But all at a steadily rising cost. And what you do produce has to be spread thinner every year: more people. Of course, there's no longer any pretense at equal sharing. If we tried that, we'd all be down on Lowlevel. Instead, the rich get richer and the poor get poorer. The usual historic pattern, Egypt, Babylon, Rome, India, China, now all Earth. So the conscientious Guardian—there are more than you might think—doesn't feel right about spending millions, which could be used to alleviate quite a bit of Citizen misery, on mere discovery. And the non-conscientious Guardian doesn't give a damn."

Coffin was startled. He looked hard at the other.

"I have heard mention of something called, er, Constitutionalism," he said slowly. "Do you subscribe to the doctrine?"

"More or less," admitted Wolfe. "Though that's a rather gaudy name for a very simple thing, an ideal of seeing the world as it actually is and behaving accordingly. Anker never called his system anything in particular. Laird was a rather gaudy man, and—" He paused, smoked with the care of a thrifty person remembering what tobacco cost, and went on: "You're probably as much of a Constitutionalist, First Officer, as the average among us."

"I beg your pardon, no. It seems, from what I've heard, to be a hea...a Gentile belief."

"But it isn't a belief. That's the whole point. We're among the last holdouts against a rising tide of Faith. The masses, and lately even a few upper-levels, turn via mysticism and marijuana toward a more tolerable pseudo-existence. I prefer to inhabit the objective universe."

Coffin grimaced. He had seen abominations. There was a smiling idol where his father's white church had overlooked the sea.

He changed the subject: "But don't the leaders, at least, understand that space travel is the only way to escape the economic trap? If Earth is growing exhausted, we have an entire galaxy of planets."

"That doesn't help Earth much," said Wolfe. "Consider the problem of hauling minerals nine years from the nearest star, with a nine-to-one mass ratio. Or how much bottom do you think it would take to drain off population faster than it could be replaced here at home? No, no, even interplanetary exploitation has about stopped paying for itself. As for colonizing—Rustum is the first planet yet found where men could live without special apparatus."

Coffin said, driven by a reluctant honesty: "As I explained, sir, a good deal of equipment would still be needed. With one or two exceptions, we didn't find any native life forms in five years of study which can be eaten by man. And then of course the gravity is wearing, and only the highlands are really habitable,"

"There you are," said Wolfe.

"But it could be done!" exploded Coffin. "My lectures have outlined the methods. And it would keep the tradition alive—knowing that there was a colony, a place where a man could still find elbow room—and we could keep looking for still better planets."

"We won't," said Wolfe bluntly. "There's another trouble with your emigration idea. The wage slave Citizen—sometimes, on Lowlevel, an actual slave, in spite of fancy doubletalk about contract—he can't afford such an expensive passage. And why should the state pay his fare? It won't lessen the number of mouths at home; it will only make the state that much poorer, in its efforts to fill those mouths. Nor is the Citizen himself interested, as a rule. Do you think an ignorant, superstitious child of crowds and walls and machines can survive, plowing soil on an empty world under an alien sun? Do you think he even wants to try?" He spread his hands. "As for the literate, technically minded class of people, they have it pretty good so far. Why should they uproot?"

"I am becoming aware of all this," nodded Coffin.

Wolfe's wide face tightened into a grin. "Another thing, First Officer. Suppose, somehow, this colony were established. Would you want to go live there yourself?"

"Good heavens, no!" Coffin jerked upright.

"Why not?"

"Because…because I'm a spaceman. And there wouldn't be any spaceships operating out of Rustum for generations. The colonists will, uh, would have too much else to do."

"Exactly. And I am a dealer in fabrics. And my neighbor Israel Stein thinks space travel is a glorious thing, but he teaches music. My friend John O'Malley is a protein chemist, who would certainly be useful as such on a new planet and he goes skindiving and blew several years' savings once on a hunting trip—but his wife has ambitions for their children. And there are others who love their comfort, such as it is; or are afraid; or feel too deeply rooted; or name your own reason. All interested, all sympathetic, but let someone else do it. The people you could get who are ready, willing, and able to go, can't finance the trip. Q. E. D."

"So it seems." Coffin stared into his empty glass.

"But I've seen all this for myself," he said after a while, his words wrenched and slow. "I realize my profession is on the way out. And it's the only profession open to me. More important, to my children, if I ever have any; for of course I would have to marry within the Society, I just can't find a decent home life anywhere else—" He stopped.

"I know," gibed Wolfe, not very sharply. "You beg my pardon. Never mind. Times change, and you are from out of time. I shall not dwell upon the fact that my older daughter is a Guardian's mistress, nor will I raise your hair by remarking that this does not trouble me in the least. Because there are some rather more important changes in recent months, of which I do disapprove with all my soul, and they are the main reason I invited you here tonight."

Coffin looked up. "What?"

Wolfe cocked his head. "I believe dinner is about ready. Come, First Officer." He took his guest's arm again. "Your lectures have been admirably dry and factual, but what I would like from you now is a still more detailed description. Just what Rustum is like, and what equipment would be needed to establish a colony of what minimum size, and the cost…everything. I assume you would rather talk that kind of shop than make polite noises at me. Well, here's your chance!"

Even among his admirers, there were many people who would have been astonished to learn that Torvald Anker was still alive. They knew he was born a century ago, that he had never been rich enough to afford elaborate medical care—for he would give a pauper boy with intelligence the same right to sit at his feet and question him that he refused a wealthy young dullard who offered good fees. So it seemed natural that he would have died.

His writings bore out that impression. The magnum opus, which men were still debating, was now sixty years old. The last book, a small volume of essays, was published twenty years back, and even it had been a gentle anachronism, the style as easy and the thought as careful as if Earth still held a few countries where speech was free. Since then he had lived in a tiny house on the Sognefjord, avoiding the publicity which he had never courted. The district was a fragment of an older world, where a sparse population still lived largely by individual effort, men spoke with deliberateness in a beautiful language and cared that their children be educated. Anker taught elementary school for a few hours a day, received food and housekeeping in return, and divided the rest of his time between a garden and a final book.

On a morning in early summer, when dew still lay on his roses, he entered the cottage. It was centuries old, with a red tile roof above ivied walls. From here a man could look down hundreds of meters, wind, sun, and stone, a patch of wildflowers, a single tree, until he saw cliff and cloud reflected in the fjord. Sometimes a gull sailed just in front of the study window.

Anker sat down at his desk. For a moment he rested, chin in hand. It had been a long climb up from the water's edge, and he had often been forced to stop for breath. His tall thin body had grown so frail he sometimes thought he could feel the sunshine streaming through. But it needed little sleep, and when the light nights came—*the sky was like white roses*, someone had written—he must go down to the fjord.

Well. He sighed, brushed an unruly lock off his forehead, and swiveled the writer into position. The letter from young Hirayama was first on the correspondence pile. It was not very well written, but it had been written, with an immense will to say, and that was what counted. Anker was not opposed to the visiphone *per se*, but quite apart from avoiding interruptions of thought, he had a duty not to own one. The young men must be forced to write if they wanted contact with him, because writing was as essential to the orderly training of the mind as conversation, perhaps more so, and elsewhere it was a vanishing skill.

His fingers tapped the keys.

> *My dear Saburo,*
> *Thank you for your confidence in me. I fear it is misplaced. My reputation, such as it is, has been gained largely by imitating Socrates. The longer I think upon matters, the more I believe that the touchstone is the epistemological question. How do we know what we know, and what is it we know?*

From this query a degree of enlightenment sometimes comes. But I am not at all certain that enlightenment is very similar to wisdom.

However, I shall try to give positive answers to the problems you bring me, keeping always in mind that the only real answers are those a person finds for himself. But remember that these are the opinions of one who has long shut himself away from modern reality. I think it has afforded a gain in perspective, but I look out of an old reality, now becoming quite alien, out of salt water and rowan trees and huge winter nights, on the active human world. Surely you are far more competent to handle its practical details than I.

First, then, I do not recommend that you devote your life to philosophy, or to basic scientific research. "The time is out of joint," and there would be nothing for you but a sterile repetition of what other men have said and done. In this judgment I am guided by no Spenglerian mystique of an aged civilization, but by the very hardheaded observation of Donne that no man is an island. Be you never so gifted, you cannot work alone; the cross-fertilization of equally interested colleagues, the whole atmosphere must be there, or originality becomes impossible. Doubtless the biological potential of a Periclean era or a Renaissance always exists: genetic statistics guarantee that. But social conditions must then determine the extent to which this potential is realized, and even the major forms of expression it takes. I hope I am not being a sour old man in thinking that the present age is as universally barren as the Rome of Commodus. These things happen.

But—second—you ask implicitly if something can be done to change this. In all frankness, I have never believed so. There may be theoretical ways, just as it is theoretically possible to turn winter into summer by hastening the planet along its orbit. But practical limitations intervene; and it is just as well that mortal men with mortal scope do not have the power of destiny.

You seem to think that I was, on the contrary, once active in politics, a founder of the Constitutionalist movement. This is a popular fallacy; I had nothing to do with it, and never even met Laird. (He is rather a mysterious figure anyway, I gather, suddenly appearing without any background—presumably of Lowlevel birth, self-educated—and vanishing as completely after a decade. Murdered, perhaps?) He was an enthusiastic and understanding reader of mine, but made no attempt at personal contact. He said he was only applying my principles to a concrete situation. His phenomenal rise came after the suppression of the North American revolt, when a crushed, despairing socioeconomic-ethnic group turned toward a leader who put their inchoate beliefs into sharp focus and who offered them a practical set of rules to live by. Actually these rules amounted to little more than the traditional virtues of patience, courage, thrift, industry, with an interwoven scientific rationalism, but if it has heartened them in their comeback I am honored that Laird quoted me.

However, I see no long-range hope for them. The tide is ebbing too strongly. And now, I hear, the masters have decided to eliminate Constitutionalism as a danger to the status quo. *It is being very cleverly done, in the guise of free education; but it amounts to absorbing the next generation into the common ruck. Let me be grateful that this poor district does not qualify for a public school.*

If we cannot reform society, then, can we save ourselves? There is a traditional way. As the Old Americans would have put it: Get the hell out! The monastic orders of the post-Roman past, or of feudal China, India, and Japan, did this, in effect; and I note that their latter-day equivalent is becoming more prominent every decade. It has been my own solution too, though I prefer being an anchorite to a cenobite. The advice grieves me, Saburo, but this may be the only answer for you.

There was once another way out, Christian leaving the City of Destruction in the most literal sense. American history is full of examples, Puritan, Quaker, Catholic, Mormon. And today the stars are a new and more splendid America.

But I fear this is not the right century. The pioneering misfits I speak of departed from a vigorous society which took expansion for granted. It is not characteristic of moribund cultures to export their radicals. The radicals themselves have little interest in departure. I would personally love to end my days on this new planet Rustum, deep though my roots are here, but who would come with me?

Therefore, Saburo, we can only endure, until

Anker's hands fell off the keys. The pain through his breast seemed to rip it open.

He stood up, somehow, clawing for air. Or his body did. His mind was suddenly remote, knowing that it had perhaps a minute to look down upon the fjord and out to the sky. And he said to himself, with a strange thankful joy, the promise three thousand years old, Odysseus, death will come to you out of the sea, death in his gentlest guise.

Everybody knew Jan Svoboda was estranged from his father the Commissioner. But no orders for his arrest or even his harassment, had ever come, so presumably the parent retained a certain affection for the child and a reconciliation was possible. This would in fact, if not officially, re-elevate the young Citizen to Guardian status. Therefore it was advisable to stay on the right side of him.

And thus Jan Svoboda could never be sure how much of his rise was due to himself and how much to some would-be sycophant in the Oceanic Minerals office. With few exceptions, he could not even be sure how many of his friends really meant it. Nor did his attempts to find out, or his occasional blunt questions, lead anywhere. Certainly not! He became a bitter man.

His father's educational decree provoked a tirade from him which brought envy to the eyes of his fellow Constitutionalists. They would have liked to make those remarks, but they weren't Commissioner's sons. Their own formal appeals were denied, and they settled down to make the best of a foul situation.

After all, they were a literate, well-to-do, pragmatically oriented class; they could give supplemental instruction at home, or even hire tutors.

The new system was established. A year passed.

On a gusty fall evening, Jan Svoboda set his aircar down at home. Great gray waves marched from the west and roared among the house caissons.

Their spume and spindrift went over the roof. The sky streamed past, low and ragged. Visibility was so narrow that he could see no other houses at all.

Which suited him, he thought. A sea dwelling was expensive, and though well paid, he could only afford this one because a Constitutionalist normally led a quiet life. Even so, he felt the pinch. But where else could a man live these days without a horizon cluttered by oafs?

His car touched wheels to the main deck, the garage door opened for him and closed behind, he got out into an insulated quietness. Faintly came a whisper that was gymbal mountings, gyrostabilizers, air conditioner, power plant; louder were the hoot of wind and the ocean where it brawled. He had a wish to step out and take the cold wet air in his face. Those idiots in the office today, couldn't they *see* that the ion exchange system now in use was inefficient at tropical concentrations, and a little basic research could produce a design which—Svoboda hit the car with a knotted fist. It was no use. There was nothing to fight, you might as well try to catch water in a net.

He sighed and entered the kitchen. He was a medium-sized, rather slender man, dark, with high cheekbones and hooked nose and a deep, premature wrinkle between his eyes.

"Hullo, darling." His wife gave him a kiss, "Ouch," she added. "That was like bussing a brick wall. What happened?"

"The usual," grunted Svoboda. He heard startling silence, "Where're the kids?"

"Jocelyn wanted to stay ashore overnight with a girl friend. I said it was all right."

Svoboda stopped, He stared at her for a long time. Judith took a backward step. "Why, what's the matter?" she asked.

"What's the matter?" His voice rose as he spoke. "Do you realize we broke off yesterday in the middle of the conformal-mapping theorem? She just can't get it through her head. No wonder, with her whole day given to Homemaking or some such ridiculous thing, as if her only choice in life fell between being a rich man's toy and a poor man's slave. And how do you expect she'll ever be able to think without knowing how language functions? Great horny toads! By tomorrow night she'll have forgotten everything I said!"

Svoboda grew aware he was shouting. He stopped, swallowed, and considered the situation objectively. "All right," he said. "I'm sorry. You did not know, I guess."

"Perhaps I did," said Judith slowly.

"What?" Svoboda, who had been leaving the kitchen, spun on his heel.

She braced herself and told him: "There's more to life than just discipline. You can't expect healthy youngsters to go to the mainland four days a week, six hours a day, meeting other children who *live* there, hearing games planned, excursions, parties—after school—and then return here, where there isn't anyone their age, nothing but your lessons and your books."

"We go sailing," he argued, taken aback. "Diving, fishing...visiting, even. The Lochabers have a boy David's age, and the de Smets—"

"Somebody they meet once a month!" interrupted Judith. "Their friends are on the mainland!"

"Fine lot of friends," snapped Svoboda. "Who's Jocelyn staying with?" She hesitated. "Well?"

"She didn't say."

He nodded, stiff in the neck muscles. "I thought so. You see, we're old fogies. We wouldn't approve of a fourteen-year-old girl at a harmless little marijuana party. If that's all they have planned." He shouted again: "Well, this is the last time it happens. Any more such requests are to be turned down flat, and hell take their precious social lives!"

Judith caught a shaky lower lip between her teeth. She looked away from him and said, "It was so different last year."

"Of course it was. We had our own schools then. No need for extra instruction, because the right things were taught during the regular hours. No need to worry about their schoolmates—all our kind, with decent behavior and sensible prestige symbols. But now, what can we do?"

Svoboda passed a hand across his eyes. His head ached. Judith came over and rubbed her cheek across his breast. "Don't take it so hard, sweetheart," she murmured. "Remember what Laird always used to say. 'Co-operate with the inevitable.'"

"You're omitting what he meant by 'co-operation,'" replied Svoboda gloomily. "He meant to use it the way a judo master uses his opponent's attack. We're forgetting his advice, all of us are forgetting, now that he's gone."

She held him close for a wordless minute. The glory came back, he looked beyond the wall and whispered, "You don't know what it was like, coming into the movement as late as you did. I was just a child myself, and my father jeered at him all the time, but I saw the man speak, both video and live, and even then I knew. Not that I really understood. But I knew here was a tall man and a beautiful voice, talking about hope to people whose kin lay dead in bombed-out houses. I think afterward, when I began to study the theory of it, I was trying to get back the feeling I had had then...And my father could do nothing but make fun of it!" He stopped. "I'm sorry, dear. You've heard this from me often enough."

"And Laird is dead," she sighed.

He blurted in reborn anger what he had never told her before: "Murdered. I'm sure of it. Not just some chance Brother, on a dark street...no, I got a word here, a hint there, my father had spoken to Laird privately, Laird had grown too big…I accused him to his face of having had Laird done away with. He grinned and did not deny it. That was when I left him. And now he's trying to murder Laird's work!"

He tore free of her and stormed from the kitchen, through the dining room on his way out. A taste of the gale might cool the boiling in him.

On the living room floor, his son David sat cross-legged, swaying with half shut eyes.

Svoboda stopped. He was not noticed.

"What are you doing?" he said at last.

The nine-year-old face turned up to him, briefly dazed as if wakened from sleep. "Oh…hello, sir."

"I asked what you were doing," rapped Svoboda.

David's lids drooped. Looking from beneath them, he had a curious sly appearance. "Homework," he muttered.

"What kind of homework is that? And since when has that flatheaded wretch of a teacher made any demand on your intellect?"

"We're to practice, sir."

"Quit evading me!" Svoboda planted himself above the boy, fists on hips, and glared down. "Practice what?"

David's expression was half mutinous, but he seemed to decide on co-operation. "El, el, elementary attunement," he said. "Just to get the technique. It takes years to have the actual experience."

"Attunement? Experience?" Svoboda stood back. He had again the sense of trying to net a river. "Explain yourself. Attunement to what?"

David flushed. "The Ineffable All." It was a defiance.

"Now wait," said Svoboda, fighting for calm. "You're in a secular school. By law. You're not being taught a religion, are you?" For a moment, he hoped so. If the government ever started favoring one of the million cults and creeds over another, it would guarantee trouble—which might make a wedge for—

"Oh, no, sir. This is fact. Mr. Tse explained it all."

Svoboda sat down beside his son. "What kind of fact?" he asked. "Scientific?"

"No. No, not exactly. You told me yourself, science don't have all the answers."

"Doesn't," corrected Svoboda mechanically. "Agreed. To maintain that proposition is equivalent to maintaining that the discovery of structured data is the sum total of human experience; which is a self evident absurdity." He felt pleased at the control in his own voice. There was some childish misunderstanding here, which could be cleared up with sensible talk. Looking down on the curly brown head, Svoboda was almost overwhelmed by tenderness. He wanted to rumple the boy's hair and invite him to the sun porch for a game of catch. However—

"In normal usage," he explained, "the word 'fact' is reserved for empirical data and well-confirmed theories. This Ineffable All is an obvious metaphor, and thus has no place in factual discourse. You must mean you're studying some form of aesthetics."

"Oh, no, sir. " David shook his head vigorously. "It's *true.* A higher truth than science."

"But then you are speaking of religion!"

"No, sir. Mr. Tse told us about it, and all the older kids in his school are already in, uh, in some degree of attunement. I mean, by these exercises you not only ap, ap, apprehend the All but become the All, which you aren't every day, I mean—"

Svoboda leaped back to his feet. David stared. The father said in a tone that shook: "What sort of nonsense is this? What do those words All and Attunement mean? What structure has this identification, which is somehow only an identification on alternate Thursdays, got? Go on! You know enough basic semantics to explain it to me clearly. You can at least show me where definitions fail and ostensive experience takes over. Go on, tell me!"

David sprang up, too. His fists were clenched at his sides and tears stood in his eyes. "That don't mean anything!" he yelled. "You don't! Mr. Tse says you don't! He says all this playing with words and d-d-definitions, logic, it's all a lot of hooey! He says it's all down on the material plane, and the real fact is Attunement and I'm only hindering myself by studying logic and, and, and the older kids all laughed at me! I don't want to study your old semantics! I don't want to! I won't!"

Svoboda regarded him for an entire minute. Then he strode back through the kitchen. "I'm going out," he said. "Don't wait for me." The garage door shut behind him. Moments afterward, Judith heard his car take off into the storm.

Theron Wolfe shook his head. *"Tsk-tsk-tsk,"* he scolded. "Temper, temper."

"Don't tell me it's immature to get angry," said Jan Svoboda in a dull voice. "Anker never wrote any such thing. Laird said once it was nonsane not to get angry, in atrocious situations."

"Agreed," said Wolfe. "And no doubt you relieved your glands considerably by flying to the mainland, storming into poor little Tse's one-room apartment, and beating him up before the eyes of his wife and children. I don't see that you accomplished much else, though. Come on, let's get out of here."

They left the jail. A respectful policeman bowed them toward Wolfe's car. "Sorry about the misunderstanding, sir," he said.

"That's all right," said Wolfe. "You had to arrest him, since he wasn't doing his brawling in Lowlevel and you didn't know he was the Psychologics Commissioner's son."

Svoboda lifted a tired lip. "But you did well to call me as he insisted."

"Do you wish to file any charges against the Tse person?" asked the officer. "We'll take care of him, sir."

"No," said Svoboda.

"You might even send him some flowers," suggested Wolfe. "He's only a hack, executing his orders."

"He doesn't have to be a hack," clipped Svoboda, "I'm sick of this whine, 'Don't blame me, blame the System.' There isn't any system: there are men, who act in certain ways."

Wolfe's jovian form preceded him into the car. The merchant took the controls and they murmured up the ramp. Presently they were airborne. It was still night, still windy; the jeweled web of Highlevel illumination stretched thin above the city darkness; low in the east, a hunchbacked moon sent flickers of light off a black, restless Atlantic.

"I had your car picked up and shot a message to Judith," said Wolfe. "How about staying overnight with me and taking a holiday tomorrow?"

"All right." Svoboda slumped.

Wolfe put the autopilot on Cruise, offered a cigar, and struck one for himself. Its red glow as he sucked sketched his features upon shadow, a goateed Buddha with a faint Mephistophelean smile. "Look here," he said, "you were always a hairtrigger type, but basically levelheaded. Otherwise you wouldn't be a Constitutionalist. Let's examine the situation. Why do you care what your children become? I mean, naturally you want them to be happy and so on, but does it have to be your kind of happiness?"

"Let's not get into the hedonistic fallacy," said Svoboda with a weary sort of annoyance. "I want my kids to become the right sort of human adults."

"In other words, not only individuals, but cultures have an instinct to survive," said Wolfe. "Very good. I agree with you. Our particular culture emphasizes the conscious mind, perhaps too much for perfect health but there you are. It's being swallowed up in a new culture which exalts a set of as-yet-undefined subconscious functions. We're like the Jewish Zealots, English Puritans, Russian Old Believers, all trying to restore certain basics they felt had been corrupted. (And actually, like them, creating something altogether new, but let's not dim that fine fresh purposefulness of yours with too much analysis.) Also like them, we're more and more at odds with the surrounding society. At the same time, our beliefs are becoming popular with a certain class of people, all over Earth. This in turn alarms the custodians of things-as-they-are."

"Well?" said Svoboda.

"Well," said Wolfe, "I don't see how conflict is to be avoided, and physical force is still the *ultima ratio*. But I don't advise putting well-meaning little teachers in the hospital."

Svoboda sat up straight. "You don't mean another rebellion?" he exclaimed.

"Not like the last fiasco," said Wolfe. "Let's not end up like the Old Believers. The Puritan Commonwealth is the analogy we desire. It'll take patience...yes, and prudence, my friend. What we must do is organize. Not too formally, but we must be able to act as a group. It won't be hard to achieve that much; you aren't the only man who resents what's being done to his children. Once organized, we can start making our weight felt. Boycotts, for instance; bribes to the right officials; and please don't look shocked when I point out that Lowlevel is full of skilled assassins with very reasonable fees."

"I see." Svoboda was calmer now. "Pressure. Yes. We may be able to get our schools restored, if nothing else."

"Don't forget," said Wolfe, "pressure provokes counterpressure. If we act, the government will react, and then we must react to that. The possible, even probable end result is war."

"What? No!"

"Or a *coup d'état*. Most likely civil war, though. Since a few military and police personnel already subscribe to Constitutionalism, and we can hope to recruit more, we've a chance to win. If we proceed with care. This can't be hurried. But…we might start quietly caching weapons."

Again Svoboda was jarred. He had seen dead men in the streets, when he was a child. Next time there might even be the ultimate violence of the nuclear bomb or the artificial plague. And how much rebuilding would be possible afterward, on this impoverished globe?

"We've got to find another way," he whispered. "We can't let it go that far."

"We may have to," said Wolfe. "We will most certainly have to threaten to. Or else go under." He glanced at the profile beside him. It stood sharp against a few stars, already stiffening with resolution which, nourished, could become fanaticism. Wolfe nearly declared what was really in his mind, but stopped himself.

Commissioner Svoboda looked at the clock. "Get out," he said. "All of you."

The guards obeyed in surprise. Only Iyeyasu remained; that went without saying. For a moment the big office was quiet.

"Your son comes now, yes?" asked the Okinawan.

"In five minutes," said Svoboda. "He'll be prompt, if I know him. To be sure, men change, and we haven't spoken for a good many years."

He felt a nervous tic in the corner of his mouth. It wouldn't stop. The dwarfish man scrambled from his chair and limped across to the full-wall transparency. The towers and ways shimmered below him, heated, but winter lay in pale sky and far-looking frosty sun. A late winter this year. Svoboda wondered if it would ever end.

Not that the season mattered when your life ran out in offices. But he would like to see the cherry orchard crowning this building bloom once more. He had never allowed the roof to be greenhoused. Let's keep a little unscientific nature in the world!

"I wonder if that's why technological civilization is dying," he mused. "It may not be the loss of resources, or the uncontrolled obsession to reproduce, or the decline of literacy, or the rise of mysticism, or any such thing at all. Those may only be effects, and the real cause be a collective unconscious revolt against all this steel and machinery. If we evolved among forests, do we dare cut down every tree on Earth?"

Iyeyasu didn't answer. He was used to his master's moods. He looked at him with compassionate small eyes.

"If this be so," said Svoboda, "then perhaps my maneuverings have served no real purpose. But come, we Practical Men have no time to stop and think."

The sardonicism uplifted him. He went back and sat down behind his desk and waited, a cigarette between his fingers.

The door opened for Jan on the stroke of 0900. Svoboda's first shocked thought was *Bernice*. Oh, God, he had forgotten how the boy had Bernice's eyes, and she fifteen years in the earth. He sat for a moment in an aloneness that stung.

"Well?" said Jan coldly.

Svoboda braced his thin shoulders. "Sit down," he invited.

Jan perched on a chair's edge and stared across the desk. He had grown a lot thinner, his father noticed, and tense, but the youthful awkwardness was gone. An uncompromising harsh face jutted above that plain gray' tunic.

"Smoke?" asked the Commissioner.

"No," said Jan.

"I hope everything is all right at home? Your wife? Your children?" *Most men are privileged to see their own grandchildren. Ah, stop sniveling, you tinpot Machiavelli.*

"We are in physical health," said Jan. His voice was like iron. "You are a busy man, Commissioner. I don't wish to take up your time unduly."

"No, I suppose not. " Svoboda put another cigarette between his lips, remembered he was still holding the first, and ground it out with needless violence. Self-control returned, to parch his tones. "I imagine, when the question of a conference between myself and a representative of your new Constitutionalist Association first arose, it seemed most natural for me to have your president, Mr. Wolfe, come see me. You may wonder why I specified you instead, who are only the engineering delegate on your policy committee."

Jan's mouth tightened. "I hope you did not plan a sentimental appeal."

"Oh, no. The fact is, Wolfe and I have had several discussions." Svoboda chuckled. "Ah-ha. That startled you, eh? Now if I were determined to wreck your organization, I would let you stew over the fact. But the truth is merely that Wolfe talked to me on the 'phone, unofficially, and sounded me out on various points. Of course, that entailed me sounding him out too, but we came to a tacit agreement."

Svoboda leaned on his elbows, puffed smoke, and went on: "It's been several months since your organization was formed. Constitutionalists have been joining it by the thousands, all over the world. What they want from it varies—some, a spokesman for their grievances; some, doubtless, a revolutionary underground; the majority probably have no more than vague unformulated expectations of help. Since you have not yet adopted any clear-cut program, you have disappointed no one. But now your committee must soon come up with a definite plan of action, or see the outfit revert to jelly."

"We will," said Jan. "Since you know so much, I can tell you what our first step will be. We're going to make a formal petition for repeal of your so-called school decree. We're not without influence on several of our fellow Commissioners. If the petition is denied, we will call for stronger measures."

"The economic squeeze." Svoboda's big bald head nodded. "Thereafter strikes, disguised as mass resignation. Boycotts. Civil disobedience, if that fails. And then—Oh, well. It's a classic pattern."

"Classic because it works," said Jan. The blood crept up his dark cheeks, making him heartbreakingly boylike again.

"Sometimes."

"You could save a lot of trouble all around by canceling the decree at once. In that case, we might be willing to compromise on a few points."

"Oh, but I'm not going to," Svoboda folded his hands as if in prayer, rolled his eyes upward, and chanted piously around his cigarette, "The public interest demands the public school."

Jan jumped erect. "You know that's only a hypocritical way of destroying us!" he exclaimed.

"As a matter of fact," said Svoboda, "I plan to have the curriculum modified next fall. The time now devoted to critical analysis of certain classics could better be spent in rote memorization. And then, with hallucinogens becoming so important socially, a practical course in their proper use—"

"You shriveled-up son of a sewer!" screamed Jan. He lunged across the desk.

Iyeyasu was there, without seeming to cross the floor between. The edge of a hand cracked down on Jan's wrist. The other hand, stiff-fingered, poked him in the solar plexus. Jan gasped out his wind and collapsed backward.

"Careful, there," warned Svoboda.

"No harm done, sir," Iyeyasu assured him. He eased Jan into the chair and began kneading his shoulders and the base of his skull. "He gets air back in a minute." With an ill concealed rage: "Is not a way to speak to your father."

"For all I know," said Svoboda "he may have been literally correct."

The glaze left Jan's eyes, but no one talked for a while. Svoboda lit another cigarette and stared into space. He wanted to look at the boy, there might never be another chance, but it would be poor tactics. Jan slumped under Iyeyasu's mountainous form. At last he spoke, sullenly:

"I don't apologize. What else could you expect?"

"Nothing, perhaps." Svoboda made a bridge of his fingers and regarded his son across them. "There will certainly be resistance to such measures. And yet I am only underlining a conflict which would otherwise proceed to the same inevitable end. You did not let me explain why you, rather than Wolfe, are your people's representative today. The fact is that you are young and hot-headed, a much better spokesman for the upcoming Constitutionalist generation than an older, more cautious, less indoctrinated man. The extremists in your party might repudiate any agreement Wolfe made, simply because he is Wolfe, notoriously all things to all men. But if you endorse a plan of action, they will listen."

"What agreement can we make?" he snarled back at him. "Unless you return our children to us—"

"No maudlin figures of speech, please. Let me explain the difficulty. You and the government represent opposing ways of life. They simply cannot be reconciled. Once, perhaps, there was a possibility of co-existence. There may be again in the future, when the issues no longer seem vital. But not now. Just suppose that we did give in, repealed the education decree and reinstated your school system. It would be a victory for you and a defeat for us. You would gain not only your objective, but confidence, support, strength; we would lose correspondingly.

How long before you made your next demand? You have other grudges beside this. Having gotten back your schools, you may next want back the right to criticize political basics. If you gain that, you will want the right to agitate publicly. Having gotten that, you will want representation on the Commission. Then you will want laws against dope. Then—But I need not elaborate—It seems best to settle the issue now, once and for all, before you get too strong. And that's why you won't get as much support from my colleagues as you expect."

Jan bristled. "If you think this is the final word—"

"Oh, no. I have already indicated how you will fight. I'm also well aware of your potential for accumulating weapons, subverting military units, and at last resorting to force. A number of Guardians want to arrest the lot of you right now. But alas, you are too important. Imagine the chaos, if suddenly a fourth of the technical personnel in Minerals or Pelagiculture vanished, without even training their successors! Or if Wolfe was suddenly removed from his devious routes of supply, where would half the mistresses on Highlevel get new gowns to outshine the other half? Then, also, it's notorious that martyrs are a stimulant to any cause. There would be plenty of young men, who had never cared one way or another about your philosophy, suddenly fired by the vision of a thing bigger than themselves—Yes, we might provoke the very war we were setting out to forestall."

Svoboda leaned back. He had the boy on the ropes now, he saw: bewildered eyes, half parted lips, a hand raised as if uncertain whether to defend or appeal or offer thanks.

"There is a possible compromise," he said.

"What?" The question was barely audible, in that big room which faced a winter sky.

"Rustum. E Eridani II."

"The new planet?" Jan's head snapped up. "But—"

"If the most dissatisfied Constitutionalists left voluntarily, after making proper arrangements for replacement personnel and so on, the pressure would be off us. Then, in time, we could back down on the school issue and please your stay-at-home fellows, without actually being defeated on it. Or, even if we didn't, *you* would be quit of us. The successful planting of a colony would be kudos for the Commission, a shot in the arm for space travel, and therefore well worth our support and encouragement. As for the considerable expense involved—you all own valuable property which couldn't be taken with you, so you can sell out and thereby finance the passage and the necessary equipment.

"It's an old pattern in history. Massachusetts, Maryland, Pennsylvania, were all promoted by a government which was hostile to the ideals involved. Why not a repeat performance?"

"But twenty light-years," whispered Jan. "Never to see Earth again."

"You'll have to give up a lot," agreed Svoboda. "But in return, you will escape the risk of destruction by force or absorption by my evil schemes." He shrugged. "Of course, if your nice radiant-heated sea house is more important than your philosophy, by all means stay home."

Jan shook his head, as if it had taken a blow. "I'll have to think about it," he mumbled.

"Consult Wolfe," said Svoboda. "He's already looked into the matter."

"What?" The eyes that were Bernice's grew candid with surprise.

"I told you Wolfe is not a fire-eater," said Svoboda, grinning. "I gather he's discussed the possibility of war, and done some organizing for it, but I suspect he's really been trying for no more than a strong bargaining position—so he can make us send you to Rustum."

This was the right note, he saw. If Wolfe the mentor had really been operating behind the scenes, Jan would have less fear of a bomb in whatever scheme was proposed.

"I'll have to talk to him." The boy stood up. He was suddenly trembling. "To all of them. We'll have to think—Good-by."

He turned and stumbled toward the door.

"Good-by, kid," said Svoboda.

He didn't think Jan heard him. The door closed.

Svoboda sat without moving for a long time. The cigarette between his fingers burned so low that it scorched him. He swore, dropped it in the disposer, and struggled to his feet. The broken foot was hurting him again.

Iyeyasu glided around the desk. Svoboda leaned on the tree trunk arm, shuffling to the clear wall until he could stare out and catch a glitter of open ocean.

"Your son comes back, yes?" asked Iyeyasu finally.

"I doubt it," said Svoboda.

"You wanting them to go to the planet?"

"Yes. And they will. I haven't been working all these years without getting to know my machinery."

The sun out there was pale, but its light hurt Svoboda's eyes, so he had to rub them with a knuckle. He said aloud, in a precise but somehow not steady tone: "Old Inky was an educated man in his way. He used to claim that the only axiom in human geometry is, the straight line is not the shortest distance between two points. In fact, there are no straight lines. I find that's pretty true."

"This was your plan, sir?" Iyeyasu's voice held more sympathy than intellectual interest.

"Uh-huh. Anker's work showed me there was no hope for Earth in the foreseeable future. Maybe something will evolve here a thousand years hence, but that won't help my son much. I wanted to get him out while there was still time. But he couldn't go alone. It would have to be as part of a colony. And the colonists would have to be healthy, independent, able people—nothing else was likely to survive. I was gambling that a habitable planet would be discovered, but I could not gamble that it would be very hospitable...But why should such people leave? On the whole, given half a chance, they would do rather well at home."

"So there had to be an obstacle on Earth which sheer drive and intelligence could not overcome. What sort would that be? Well, it's in the nature of intercultural conflicts to be insoluble. When axioms clash, logic is helpless. So I set up a rival society within the Federation. That wasn't hard. Here in North America, a dying culture had just tried to assert itself by rebellion, and failed; but it wasn't dead yet. It only needed to be given a new spirit and a sense of direction. I had

Anker's philosophy for a background. I had Laird, a marvelous actor with much brains and no conscience. He proved expensive, but faithful, largely because I made it plain what would happen if he wasn't. When his work was finished, I retired him—a new face, a new name, and a lavish pension. He caroused himself to death four years ago. Of course, the possibility that I had had Laird murdered was always left open: the first irritating wound. Among others."

Svoboda remembered a boy who raged from the house and never came back. He sighed. One can't foresee every detail. At least Bernice's grandchildren would grow up as thinking individuals, if Rustum didn't eat them first.

"I think we're over the hump now," he said. "From now on, we can sit back and watch the wagon roll downhill. With stars at the bottom of the hill."

"We go south," suggested Iyeyasu clumsily. "We will get a telescope and you can watch his new sun."

"I imagine I'll be dead before he gets there," said Svoboda. He gnawed his lip a moment, then straightened and hobbled from the window. "Come on. Let's go visit some fellow Commissioner and be nasty to him."

UNTITLED LIMERICK
(Dedicated to Robert A. Heinlein}

Poor Joe-Jim, with one extra head,
could not have a woman in bed.
   "Since I cannot abet you,
   I never will let you,
for I'm no voyeur," each head said.

The Only Game in Town

John Sandoval did not belong to his name. Nor did it seem right that he should stand in slacks and aloha shirt before an apartment window opening on mid-twentieth-century Manhattan. Everard was used to anachronism, but the dark hooked face confronting him always seemed to want war paint, a horse, and a gun sighted on some pale thief.

"Okay," he said. "The Chinese discovered America. Interesting, but why does the fact need my services?"

"I wish to hell I knew," Sandoval answered.

His stocky form turned about on the polar bear rug which Bjarni Herjulfsson had once given to Everard, until he was staring outward. Towers were sharp against a clear sky; the noise of traffic was muted by height. His hands clasped and unclasped behind his back.

"I was ordered to co-opt an Unattached agent, go back with him and take whatever measures seemed indicated," he went on after a while. "I knew you best, so…" His voice trailed off.

"But shouldn't you get an Indian like yourself?" asked Everard. "I'd seem rather out of place in thirteenth-century America."

"So much the better. Make it impressive, mysterious…It won't be too tough a job, really."

"Of course not," said Everard. "Whatever the job actually is."

He took pipe and tobacco pouch from his disreputable smoking jacket and stuffed the bowl in quick, nervous jabs; one of the hardest lessons he had had to learn, when first recruited into the Time Patrol, was that every important task does not require a vast organization. That was the characteristic twentieth-century approach; but earlier cultures, like Athenian Hellas and Kamakura Japan—and later civilizations too, here and there in history—had concentrated on the development of individual excellence. A single graduate of the Patrol Academy (equipped, to be sure, with tools and weapons of the future) could be the equivalent of a brigade.

But it was a matter of necessity as well as aesthetics. There were all too few people to watch over all too many thousands of years.

"I get the impression," said Everard slowly, "that this is not a simple rectification of extratemporal interference."

"Right," said Sandoval in a harsh voice. "When I reported what I'd found, the Yuan milieu office made a thorough investigation. No time travelers are involved. Kublai Khan thought this up entirely by himself. He may have been inspired by Marco Polo's accounts of Venetian and Arab sea voyages, but it was legitimate history, even if Marco's book doesn't mention anything of the sort."

"The Chinese had quite a nautical tradition of their own," said Everard. "Oh, it's all very natural. So how do we come in?"

He got his pipe lit and drew hard on it. Sandoval still hadn't spoken, so he asked, "How did you happen to find this expedition? It wasn't in Navajo country, was it?"

"Hell, I'm not confined to studying my own tribe," Sandoval answered. "Too few Amerinds in the Patrol as is, and it's a nuisance disguising other breeds. I've been working on Athabascan migrations generally." Like Keith Denison, he was an ethnic Specialist, tracing the history of peoples who never wrote their own so that the Patrol could know exactly what the events were that it safeguarded.

"I was working along the eastern slope of the Cascades, near Crater Lake," he went on. "That's Lutuami country, but I had reason to believe an Athabascan tribe I'd lost track of had passed that way. The natives spoke of mysterious strangers coming from the north. I went to have a look, and there the expedition was, Mongols with horses. I checked their back trail and found their camp at the mouth of the Chehalis River, where a few more Mongols were helping the Chinese sailors guard the ships. I hopped back upstairs like a bat out of Los Angeles and reported."

Everard sat down and stared at the other man. "How thorough an investigation did get made at the Chinese end?" he said. "Are you absolutely certain there was no extratemporal interference? It could be one of those unplanned blunders, you know, whose consequences aren't obvious for decades."

"I thought of that too, when I got my assignment," Sandoval nodded. "I even went directly to Yuan milieu HQ in Khan Baligh—Cambaluc, or Peking to you. They told me they'd checked it clear back to Genghis's lifetime, and spatially as far as Indonesia. And it was all perfectly okay, like the Norse and their Vinland. It simply didn't happen to have gotten the same publicity. As far as the Chinese court knew, an expedition had been sent out and had never returned, and Kublai decided it wasn't worthwhile to send another. The record of it lay in the Imperial archives, but was destroyed during the Ming revolt which expelled the Mongols. Historiography forgot the incident."

Still Everard brooded. Normally he liked his work, but there was something abnormal about this occasion.

"Obviously," he said, "the expedition met a disaster. We'd like to know what. But why do you need an Unattached agent to spy on them?"

Sandoval turned from the window. It crossed Everard's mind again, fleetingly, how little the Navajo belonged here. He was born in 1930, had fought in Korea and gone through college on the GI bill before the Patrol contacted him, but somehow he never quite fit the twentieth century.

Well, do any of us? Could any man with real roots stand knowing what will eventually happen to his own people?

"But I'm not supposed to spy!" Sandoval exclaimed. "When I'd reported, my orders came straight back from Danellian headquarters. No explanation, no excuses, the naked command: to arrange that disaster. To revise history myself!"

Anno Domini One Thousand Two Hundred Eighty:

The writ of Kublai Khan ran over degrees of latitude and longitude; he dreamed of world empire, and his court honored any guest who brought fresh knowledge or new philosophy. A young Venetian merchant named Marco Polo had become a particular favorite, but not all peoples desired a Mongol overlord. Revolutionary secret societies germinated throughout those several conquered realms lumped together as Cathay. Japan, with the Hojo family an able power behind the throne, had already repelled one invasion. Nor were the Mongols unified, save in theory. The Russian princes had become tax collectors for the Golden Horde; the Il-Khan Abaka sat in Baghdad.

Elsewhere, a shadowy Abbasid Caliphate had refuge in Cairo; Delhi was under the Slave Dynasty; Nicholas III was Pope; Guelphs and Ghibellines were ripping up Italy; Rudolf of Habsburg was German Emperor, Philip the Bold was King of France, Edward Longshanks ruled England. Contemporaries included Dante Alighieri, Joannes Duns Scotus, Roger Bacon, and Thomas the Rhymer.

And in North America, Manse Everard and John Sandoval reined their horses to stare down a long hill.

"The date I first saw them is last week," said the Navajo. "They've come quite a ways since. At this rate, they'll be in Mexico in a couple of months, even allowing for some rugged country ahead."

"By Mongol standards," Everard told him, "they're proceeding leisurely."

He raised his binoculars. Around him, the land burned green with April. Even the highest and oldest beeches fluttered bright young leaves. Pines roared in the wind, which blew down off the mountains cold and swift and smelling of melted snow, through a sky where birds were homebound in such flocks that they could darken the sun. The peaks of the Cascade range seemed to float in the west, blue-white, distant, and holy. Eastward the foothills tumbled in clumps of forest and meadow to a valley, and so at last, beyond the horizon, to prairies thunderous under buffalo herds.

Everard focused on the expedition. It wound through the open areas, more or less following a small river. Some seventy men rode shaggy, dun-colored, short-legged, longheaded Asian horses. They led pack animals and remounts. He identified a few native guides, as much by their awkward seat in the saddle as by their physiognomy and clothing. But the newcomers held his attention most.

"A lot of pregnant mares toting packs," he remarked, half to himself. "I suppose they took as many horses in the ships as they could, letting them out to exercise and graze wherever they made a stop. Now they're breeding more as they go along. That kind of pony is tough enough to survive such treatment."

"The detachment at the ships is also raising horses," Sandoval informed him. "I saw that much."

"What else do you know about this bunch?"

"No more than I've told you, which is little more than you've now seen. And that record which lay for a while in Kublai's archives. But you recall, it barely notes that four ships under the command of the Noyon Toktai and the scholar Li Tai-Tsung were dispatched to explore the islands beyond Japan."

Everard nodded absently. No sense in sitting here and rehashing what they'd already gone over a hundred times. It was only a way of postponing action.

Sandoval cleared his throat. "I'm still dubious about both of us going down there," he said. "Why don't you stay in reserve, in case they get nasty?"

"Hero complex, huh?" said Everard. "No, we're better off together. I don't expect trouble anyhow. Not yet. Those boys are much too intelligent to antagonize anyone gratuitously. They've stayed on good terms with the Indians, haven't they? And we'll be a far more unknown quantity...I wouldn't mind a drink beforehand, though."

"Yeh. And afterward, too!"

Each dipped in his saddlebag, took out a half-gallon canteen and hoisted it. The Scotch was pungent in Everard's throat, heartening in his veins. He clucked to his horse and both Patrolmen rode down the slope.

A whistling cut the air. They had been seen. He maintained a steady pace toward the lead of the Mongol line. A pair of outriders closed in on either flank, arrows nocked to their short powerful bows, but did not interfere.

I suppose we look harmless, Everard thought. Like Sandoval, he wore twentieth-century outdoor clothes: hunting jacket to break the wind, hat to keep off the rain. His own outfit was a good deal less elegant than the Navajo's Abercrombie & Fitch special. They both bore daggers for show, Mauser machine pistols and thirtieth-century stun-beam projectors for business.

The troop reined in, so disciplined that it was almost like one man halting. Everard scanned them closely as he neared. He had gotten a pretty complete electronic education in an hour or so before departure—language, history, technology, manners, morals—of Mongols and Chinese and even the local Indians. But he had never before seen these people close up.

They weren't spectacular: stocky, bowlegged, with thin beards and flat, broad faces that shone greased in the sunlight. They were all well equipped, wearing boots and trousers, laminated leather cuirasses with lacquer ornamentation, conical steel helmets that might have a spike or plume on top. Their weapons were curved sword, knife, lance, compound bow. One man near the head of the line bore a standard of gold-braided yak tails. They watched the Patrolmen approach, their narrow dark eyes impassive.

The chief was readily identified. He rode in the van, and a tattered silken cloak blew from his shoulders. He was rather larger and even more hard-faced than his average trooper, with a reddish beard and almost Roman nose. The Indian guide beside him gaped and huddled back; but Toktai Noyon held his place, measuring Everard with a steady carnivore look.

"Greeting," he called, when the newcomers were in earshot. "What spirit brings you?" He spoke the Lutuami dialect, which was later to become the Klamath language, with an atrocious accent.

Everard replied in flawless, barking Mongolian: "Greeting to you, Toktai son of Batu. The Tengri willing, we come in peace."

It was an effective touch. Everard glimpsed Mongols reaching for lucky charms or making signs against the evil eye. But the man mounted at Tokai's left was quick to recover a schooled self-possession. "Ah," he said, "so men of the Western lands have also reached this country. We did not know that."

Everard looked at him. He was taller than any Mongol, his skin almost white, his features and hands delicate. Though dressed much like the others, he was unarmed. He seemed older than the Noyon, perhaps fifty. Everard bowed in the saddle and switched to North Chinese: "Honored Li Tai-Tsung, it grieves this insignificant person to contradict your eminence, but we belong to the great realm farther south."

"We have heard rumors," said the scholar. He couldn't quite suppress excitement. "Even this far north, tales have been borne of a rich and splendid country. We are seeking it that we may bring your Khan the greeting of the Kha Khan, Kublai son of Tuli, son of Genghis; the earth lies at his feet."

"We know of the Kha Khan," said Everard, "as we know of the Caliph, the Pope, the Emperor, and all lesser monarchs." He had to pick his way with care, not openly insulting Cathay's ruler but still subtly putting him in his place. "Little is known in return of us, for our master does not seek the outside world, nor encourage it to seek him. Permit me to introduce my unworthy self. I am called Everard and am not, as my appearance would suggest, a Russian or Westerner. I belong to the border guardians."

Let them figure out what that meant.

"You didn't come with much company," snapped Toktai.

"More was not required," said Everard in his smoothest voice.

"And you are far from home," put in Li.

"No farther than you would be, honorable sirs, in the Kirghiz marches."

Toktai clapped a hand to his sword hilt. His eyes were chill and wary. "Come," he said. "Be welcome as ambassadors, then. Let's make camp and hear the word of your king."

The sun, low above the western peaks, turned their snowcaps tarnished silver. Shadows lengthened down in the valley, the forest darkened, but the open meadow seemed to glow all the brighter. The underlying quiet made almost a sounding board for such noises as existed: rapid swirl and cluck of the river, ring of an ax, horses cropping in long grass. Woodsmoke tinged the air.

The Mongols were obviously taken aback at their visitors and this early halt. They kept wooden faces, but their eyes would stray to Everard and Sandoval and they would mutter formulas of their various religions—chiefly pagan, but some Buddhist, Moslem, or Nestorian prayers. It did not impair the efficiency with which they set up camp, posted guard, cared for the animals, prepared to cook supper. But Everard judged they were more quiet than usual. The patterns impressed on his brain by the educator called Mongols talkative and cheerful as a rule.

He sat cross-legged on a tent floor. Sandoval, Toktai, and Li completed the circle. Rugs lay under them, and a brazier kept a pot of tea hot. It was the only tent pitched, probably the only one available, taken along for use on ceremonial occasions like this. Toktai poured *kumiss* with his own hands and offered it to Everard, who slurped as loudly as etiquette demanded and passed it on. He had drunk worse things than fermented mare's milk, but was glad that everyone switched to tea after the ritual.

The Mongol chief spoke. He couldn't keep his tone smooth, as his Chinese amanuensis did. There was an instinctive bristling: what foreigner dares approach the Kha Khan's man, save on his belly? But the words remained courteous: "Now let our guests declare the business of their king. First, would you name him for us?"

"His name may not be spoken," said Everard. "Of his realm you have heard only the palest rumors. You may judge his power, Noyon, by the fact that he needed only us two to come this far, and that we needed only one mount apiece."

Toktai grunted. "Those are handsome animals you ride, though I wonder how well they'd do on the steppes. Did it take you long to get here?"

"No more than a day, Noyon. We have means."

Everard reached in his jacket and brought out a couple of small gift-wrapped parcels. "Our lord bade us present the Cathayan leaders with these tokens of regard."

While the paper was being removed, Sandoval leaned over and hissed in English: "Dig their expressions, Manse. We goofed a bit."

"How?"

"That flashy cellophane and stuff impresses a barbarian like Toktai. But notice Li. His civilization was doing calligraphy when the ancestors of Bonwit Teller were painting themselves blue. His opinion of our taste has just nosedived."

Everard shrugged imperceptibly. "Well, he's right, isn't he?"

Their colloquy had not escaped the others. Toktai gave them a hard stare, but returned to his present, a flashlight, which had to be demonstrated and exclaimed over. He was a little afraid of it at first, even mumbled a charm; then he remembered that a Mongol wasn't allowed to be afraid of anything except thunder, mastered himself, and was soon as delighted as a child. The best bet for a Confucian scholar like Li seemed to be a book, the *Family of Man* collection, whose diversity and alien pictorial technique might impress him. He was effusive in his thanks, but Everard doubted if he was overwhelmed. A Patrolman soon learned that sophistication exists at any level of technology.

Gifts must be made in return: a fine Chinese sword and a bundle of sea otter pelts from the coast. It was quite some time before the conversation could turn back to business. Then Sandoval managed to get the other party's account first.

"Since you know so much," Toktai began, "you must also know that our invasion of Japan failed several years ago."

"The will of heaven was otherwise," said Li, with courtier blandness.

"Horse apples!" growled Toktai. "The stupidity of men was otherwise, you mean. We were too few, too ignorant, and we'd come too far in seas too rough. And what of it? We'll return there one day."

Everard knew rather sadly that they would, and that a storm would destroy the fleet and drown who knows how many young men. But he let Toktai continue:

"The Kha Khan realized we must learn more about the islands. Perhaps we should try to establish a base somewhere north of Hokkaido. Then, too, we have long heard rumors about lands farther west. Fishermen are blown off course now and then, and have glimpses; traders from Siberia speak of a strait and a country beyond. The Kha Khan got four ships with Chinese crews and told me to take a hundred Mongol warriors and see what I could discover."

Everard nodded, unsurprised. The Chinese had been sailing junks for hundreds of years, some holding up to a thousand passengers. True, these craft weren't as seaworthy as they would become in later centuries under Portuguese influence, and their owners had never been much attracted by any ocean, let alone the cold northern waters. But still, there were some Chinese navigators who would have picked up tricks of the trade from stray Koreans and Formosans, if not from their own fathers. They must have a little familiarity with the Kuriles, at least.

"We followed two chains of islands, one after another," said Toktai. "They were bleak enough, but we could stop here and there, let the horses out, and learn something from the natives. Though the Tengri know it's hard to do that last, when you may have to interpret through six languages! We did find out that there are two mainlands, Siberia and another, which come so close together up north that a man might cross in a skin boat, or walk across the ice in winter sometimes. Finally we came to the new mainland. A big country; forests, much game and seals. Too rainy, though. Our ships seemed to want to continue, so we followed the coast, more or less."

Everard visualized a map. If you go first along the Kuriles and then the Aleutians, you are never far from land. Fortunate to avoid the shipwreck which had been a distinct possibility, the shallow-draft junks had been able to find anchorage even at those rocky islands. Also, the current urged them along, and they were very nearly on a great-circle course. Toktai had discovered Alaska before he quite knew what had happened. Since the country grew ever more hospitable as he coasted south, he passed up Puget Sound and proceeded clear to the Chehalis River. Maybe the Indians had warned him the Columbia mouth, farther on, was dangerous—and, more recently, had helped his horsemen cross the great stream on rafts.

"We set up camp when the year was waning," said the Mongol. "The tribes thereabouts are backward, but friendly. They gave us all the food, women, and help we could ask for. In return, our sailors taught them some tricks of fishing and boatbuilding. We wintered there, learned some of the languages, and made trips inland. Everywhere were tales of huge forests and plains where herds of wild cattle blacken the earth. We saw enough to know the stories were true. I've never been in so rich a land." His eyes gleamed tigerishly. "And so few dwellers, who don't even know the use of iron."

"Noyon," murmured Li warningly. He nodded his head very slightly toward the Patrolmen. Toktai clamped his mouth shut.

Li turned to Everard and said, "There were also rumors of a golden realm far to the south. We felt it our duty to investigate this, as well as explore the country in between. We had not looked for the honor of being met by your eminent selves."

"The honor is all ours," Everard purred. Then, putting on his gravest face: "My lord of the Golden Empire, who may not be named, has sent us in a spirit of friendship. It would grieve him to see you meet disaster. We come to warn you."

"What?" Toktai sat up straight. One sinewy hand snatched for the sword which, politely, he wasn't wearing. "What in the hells is this?"

"In the hells indeed, Noyon. Pleasant though this country seems, it lies under a curse. Tell him, my brother."

Sandoval, who had a better speaking voice, took over. His yarn had been concocted with an eye to exploiting that superstition which still lingered in the half-civilized Mongols, without generating too much Chinese skepticism. There were really two great southern kingdoms, he explained. Their own lay far away; its rival was somewhat north and east of it, with a citadel on the plains. Both states possessed immense powers, call them sorcery or subtle engineering as you wished. The northerly empire, Badguys, considered all this territory as its own and would not tolerate a foreign expedition. Its scouts were certain to discover the Mongols before long, and would annihilate them with thunderbolts. The benevolent southern land of Goodguys could offer no protection, could only send emissaries warning the Mongols to turn home again.

"Why have the natives not spoken of these overlords?" asked Li shrewdly.

"Has every little tribesman in the jungles of Burma heard about the Kha Khan?" responded Sandoval.

"I am a stranger and ignorant," said Li. "Forgive me if I do not understand your talk of irresistible weapons."

Which is the politest way I've ever been called a liar, thought Everard. Aloud: "I can offer a small demonstration, if the Noyon has an animal that may be killed."

Toktai considered. His visage might have been scarred stone, but sweat filmed it. He clapped his hands and barked orders to the guard who looked in. Thereafter they made small talk against a silence that thickened.

A warrior appeared after some endless part of an hour. He said that a couple of horsemen had lassoed a deer. Would it serve the Noyon's purpose? It would. Toktai led the way out, shouldering through a thick and buzzing swarm of men. Everard followed, wishing this weren't needful. He slipped the rifle stock onto his Mauser. "Care to do the job?" he asked Sandoval.

"Christ, no."

The deer, a doe, had been forced back to camp. She trembled by the river, the horsehair ropes about her neck. The sun, just touching the western peaks, turned her to bronze. There was a blind sort of gentleness in her look at Everard. He waved back the men around her and took aim. The first slug killed her, but he kept the gun chattering till her carcass was gruesome

When he lowered his weapon, the air felt somehow rigid. He looked across all the thick bandy-legged bodies, the flat, grimly controlled faces; he could smell them with unnatural sharpness, a clean odor of sweat and horses and smoke. He felt himself as nonhuman as they must see him.

"That is the least of the arms used here," he said. "A soul so torn from the body would not find its way home."

He turned on his heel. Sandoval followed him. Their horses had been staked out, the gear piled close by. They saddled, unspeaking, mounted and rode off into the forest.

The fire blazed up in a gust of wind. Sparingly laid by a woodsman, in that moment it barely brought the two out of shadow—a glimpse of brow, nose, and cheekbones, a gleam of eyes. It sank down again to red and blue sputtering above white coals, and darkness took the men.

Everard wasn't sorry. He fumbled his pipe in his hands, bit hard on it and drank smoke, but found little comfort. When he spoke, the vast soughing of trees, high up in the night, almost buried his voice, and he did not regret that either.

Nearby were their sleeping bags, their horses, the scooter—antigravity sled *cum* space-time hopper—which had brought them. Otherwise the land was empty; mile upon mile, human fires like their own were as small and lonely as stars in the universe. Somewhere a wolf howled.

"I suppose," Everard said, "every cop feels like a bastard occasionally. You've just been an observer so far, Jack. Active assignments, such as I get, are often hard to accept."

"Yeh." Sandoval had been even more quiet than his friend. He had scarcely stirred since supper.

"And now this. Whatever you have to do to cancel a temporal interference, you can at least think you're restoring the original line of development." Everard fumed on his pipe. "Don't remind me that 'original' is meaningless in this context. It's a consoling word."

"Uh-huh."

"But when our bosses, our dear Danellian supermen, tell *us* to interfere…We know Toktai's people never came back to Cathay. Why should you or I have to take a hand? If they ran into hostile Indians or something and were wiped out, I wouldn't mind. At least, no more than I mind any similar incident in that god-damned slaughterhouse they call human history."

"We don't have to kill them, you know. Just make them turn back. Your demonstration this afternoon may be enough."

"Yeah. Turn back…and what? Probably perish at sea. They won't have an easy trip home—storm, fog, contrary currents, rocks—in those primitive ships meant mostly for rivers. And we'll have set them on that trip at precisely that time! If we didn't interfere, they'd start home later, the circumstances of the voyage would be different…Why should we take the guilt?"

"They could even make it home," murmured Sandoval.

"What?" Everard started.

"The way Toktai was talking. I'm sure he plans to go back on a horse, not on those ships. As he's guessed, Bering Strait is easy to cross; the Aleuts do it all the time. Manse, I'm afraid it isn't enough simply to spare them."

"But they aren't going to get home! We know that!"

"Suppose they do make it." Sandoval began to talk a bit louder and much faster. The night wind roared around his words. "Let's play with ideas awhile. Suppose Toktai pushes on southeastward. It's hard to see what could stop him. His men can live off the country, even the deserts, far more handily than Coronado or any of those boys. He hasn't terribly far to go before he reaches a high-grade neolithic people, the agricultural Pueblo tribes. That will encourage him all the more. He'll be in Mexico before August. Mexico's just as dazzling now as it was—will be in Cortez's day. And even more tempting: the Aztecs and Toltecs are still settling who's to be master, with any number of other tribes hanging around ready to help a newcomer against both. The Spanish guns made, will make, no real difference, as you'll recall if you've read Diaz. The Mongols are as superior, man for man, as any Spaniard…Not that I imagine Toktai would wade right in. He'd doubtless be very polite, spend the winter, learn everything he could. Next year he'd go back north, proceed home, and report to Kublai that some of the richest, most gold-stuffed territory on earth was wide open for conquest!"

"How about the other Indians?" put in Everard. "I'm vague on them."

"The Mayan New Empire is at its height. A tough nut to crack, but a correspondingly rewarding one. I should think, once the Mongols got established in Mexico, there'd be no stopping them. Peru has an even higher culture at this moment, and much less organization than Pizarro faced; the Quechua-Aymar, the so-called Inca race, are still only one power down there among several.

"And then, the land! Can you visualize what a Mongol tribe would make of the Great Plains?"

"I can't see them emigrating in hordes," said Everard. There was that about Sandoval's voice which made him uneasy and defensive. "Too much Siberia and Alaska in the way."

"Worse obstacles have been overcome. I don't mean they'd pour in all at once. It might take them a few centuries to start mass immigration, as it will take the Europeans. I can imagine a string of clans and tribes being established in the course of some years, all down western North America. Mexico and Yucatan get gobbled up—or, more likely, become khanates. The herding tribes move eastward as their own population grows and as new immigrants arrive. Remember, the Yuan dynasty is due to be overthrown in less than a century. That'll put additional pressure on the Mongols in Asia to go elsewhere. And Chinese will come here too, to farm and to share in the gold."

"I should think, if you don't mind my saying so," Everard broke in softly, "that you of all people wouldn't want to hasten the conquest of America."

"It'd be a different conquest," said Sandoval. "I don't care about the Aztecs; if you study them, you'll agree that Cortez did Mexico a favor. It'd be rough on other, more harmless tribes, too—for a while. And yet, the Mongols aren't such devils. Are they? A Western background prejudices us. We forget how much torture and massacre the Europeans were enjoying at the same time.

"The Mongols are quite a bit like the old Romans, really. Same practice of depopulating areas that resist, but respecting the rights of those who make submission. Same armed protection and competent government. Same unimaginative, uncreative national character; but the same vague awe and envy of true civilization. The *Pax Mongolica*, right now, unites a bigger area, and brings more different peoples into stimulating contact, than that piddling Roman Empire ever imagined.

"As for the Indians—remember, the Mongols are herdsmen. There won't be anything like the unsolvable conflict between hunter and farmer that made the white man destroy the Indian. The Mongol hasn't got race prejudices, either. And after a little fighting, the average Navajo, Cherokee, Seminole, Algonquin, Chippewa, Dakota, will be glad to submit and become allied. Why not? He'll get horses, sheep, cattle, textiles, metallurgy. He'll outnumber the invaders, and be on much more nearly equal terms with them than with white farmers and machine-age industry. And there'll be the Chinese, I repeat, leavening the whole mixture, teaching civilization and sharpening wits…

"Good God, Manse! When Columbus gets here, he'll find his Grand Cham all right! The Sachem Khan of the strongest nation on earth!"

Sandoval stopped. Everard listened to the gallows creak of branches in the wind. He looked into the night for a long while before he said, "It could be. Of course, we'd have to stay in this century till the crucial point was past. Our own world wouldn't exist. Wouldn't ever have existed."

"It wasn't such a hell of a good world anyway," said Sandoval, as if in dream.

"You might think about your…oh…parents. They'd never have been born either."

"They lived in a tumbledown hogan. I saw my father crying once, because he couldn't buy shoes for us in winter. My mother died of TB."

Everard sat unstirring. It was Sandoval who shook himself and jumped to his feet with a rattling kind of laugh. "What have I been mumbling? It was just a yarn, Manse. Let's turn in. Shall I take first watch?"

Everard agreed, but lay long awake.

The scooter had jumped two days futureward and now hovered invisibly far above to the naked eye. Around it, the air was thin and sharply cold. Everard shivered as he adjusted the electronic telescope. Even at full magnification, the caravan was little more than specks toiling across green immensity. But no one else in the Western Hemisphere could have been riding horses.

He twisted in the saddle to face his companion. "So now what?"

Sandoval's broad countenance was unreadable. "Well, if our demonstration didn't work—"

"It sure as hell didn't! I swear they're moving south twice as fast as before. Why?"

"I'd have to know all of them a lot better than I do, as individuals, to give you a real answer, Manse. But essentially it must be that we challenged their courage. A warlike culture, nerve and hardihood its only absolute virtues…what choice have they got but to go on? If they retreated before a mere threat, they'd never be able to live with themselves."

"But Mongols aren't idiots! They didn't conquer everybody in sight by bull strength, but by jolly well understanding military principles better. Toktai should retreat, report to the Emperor what he saw, and organize a bigger expedition."

"The men at the ships can do that," Sandoval reminded. "Now that I think about it, I see how grossly we underestimated Toktai. He must have set a date, presumably next year, for the ships to try and go home if he doesn't return. When he finds something interesting along the way, like us, he can dispatch an Indian with a letter to the base camp."

Everard nodded. It occurred to him that he had been rushed into this job, all the way down the line, with never a pause to plan it as he should have done. Hence this botch. But how much blame must fall on the subconscious reluctance of John Sandoval? After a minute Everard said: "They may even have smelled something fishy about us. The Mongols were always good at psychological warfare."

"Could be. But what's our next move?"

Swoop down from above, fire a few blasts from the forty-first-century energy gun mounted in this timecycle, and that's the end…No, by God, they can send me to the exile planet before I'll do any such thing. There are decent limits.

"We'll rig up a more impressive demonstration," said Everard.

"And if it flops too?"

"Shut up! Give it a chance!"

"I was just wondering." The wind harried under Sandoval's words. "Why not cancel the expedition instead? Go back in time a couple of years and persuade Kublai Khan it isn't worthwhile sending explorers eastward. Then all this would never have happened."

"You know Patrol regs forbid us to make historical changes."

"What do you call this we're doing?"

"Something specifically ordered by supreme HQ. Perhaps to correct some interference elsewhere, elsewhen. How should I know? I'm only a step on the evolutionary ladder. They have abilities a million years hence that I can't even guess at."

"Father knows best," murmured Sandoval.

Everard set his jaw. "The fact remains," he said, "the court of Kublai, the most powerful man on earth, is more important and crucial than anything here in America. No, you rang me in on this miserable job, and now I'll pull rank on you if I must. Our orders are to make these people give up their exploration. What happens afterward is none of our business. So they don't make it home. We won't be the proximate cause, any more than you're a murderer if you invite a man to dinner and he has a fatal accident on the way."

"Stop quacking and let's get to work," rapped Sandoval.

Everard sent the scooter gliding forward. "See that hill?" he pointed after a while. "It's on Toktai's line of march, but I think he'll camp a few miles short of it tonight, down in that little meadow by the stream. The hill will be in his plain view, though. Let's set up shop on it."

"And make fireworks? It'll have to be pretty fancy. Those Cathayans know about gunpowder. They even have military rockets."

"Small ones. I know. But when I assembled my gear for this trip, I packed away some fairly versatile gadgetry, in case my first attempt failed."

The hill bore a sparse crown of pine trees. Everard landed the scooter among them and began to unload boxes from its sizable baggage compartments. Sandoval helped, wordless. The horses, Patrol trained, stepped calmly off the framework stalls which had borne them and started grazing along the slope.

After a while the Indian broke his silence. "This isn't my line of work. What are you rigging?"

Everard patted the small machine he had half assembled. "It's adapted from a weather-control system used in the Cold Centuries era upstairs. A potential distributor. It can make some of the damnedest lightning you ever saw, with thunder to match."

"Mmm...the great Mongol weakness." Suddenly Sandoval grinned. "You win. We might as well relax and enjoy this."

"Fix us a supper, will you, while I put the gimmick together? No fire, naturally. We don't want any mundane smoke...Oh, yes, I also have a mirage projector. If you'll change clothes and put on a hood or something at the appropriate moment, so you can't be recognized, I'll paint a mile-high picture of you, half as ugly as life."

"How about a PA system? Navajo chants can be fairly alarming, if you don't know it's just a *yeibichai* or whatever."

"Coming up!"

The day waned. It grew murky under the pines; the air was chill and pungent. At last Everard devoured a sandwich and watched through his binoculars as the Mongol vanguard checked that campsite he had predicted. Others came riding in with their day's catch of game and went to work cooking. The main body showed up at sundown, posted itself efficiently, and ate. Toktai was indeed pushing hard, using every daylight moment. As darkness closed down, Everard glimpsed outposts mounted and with strung bows. He could not keep up his own spirits, however hard he tried. He was bucking men who had shaken the earth.

Early stars glittered above snow peaks. It was time to begin work.

"Got our horses tethered, Jack? They might panic. I'm fairly sure the Mongol horses will! Okay, here goes." Everard flipped a main switch and squatted by the dimly lit control dials of his apparatus.

First there was the palest blue flicker between earth and sky. Then the lightnings began, tongue after forked tongue leaping, trees smashed at a blow, the mountainsides rocking under their noise. Everard threw out ball lightning, spheres of flame which whirled and curvetted, trailing sparks, shooting across to the camp and exploding above it till the sky seemed white hot.

Deafened and half blinded, he managed to project a sheet of fluorescing ionization. Like northern lights the great banners curled, bloody red and bone white, hissing under the repeated thunder cracks. Sandoval trod forth. He had stripped to his pants, daubed clay on his body in archaic patterns; his face was not veiled after all, but smeared with earth and twisted into something Everard would not have known. The machine scanned him and altered its output. That which stood forth against the aurora was taller than a mountain. It moved in a shuffling dance, from horizon to horizon and back to the sky, and it wailed and barked in a falsetto louder than thunder.

Everard crouched beneath the lurid light, his fingers stiff on the control board. He knew a primitive fear of his own; the dance woke things in him that he had forgotten.

Judas priest! If this doesn't make them quit...

His mind returned to him. He even looked at his watch. Half an hour...give them another fifteen minutes, in which the display tapered off...They'd surely stay in camp till dawn rather than blunder wildly out in the dark; they had that much discipline. So keep everything under wraps for several hours more, then administer the last stroke to their nerves by a single electric bolt smiting a tree right next to them...Everard waved Sandoval back. The Indian sat down, panting harder than his exertions seemed to warrant.

When the noise was gone, Everard said, "Nice show, Jack." His voice sounded tinny and strange in his ears.

"I hadn't done anything like that for years," muttered Sandoval. He struck a match, startling noise in the quietness. The brief flame showed his lips gone thin. Then he shook out the match and only his cigarette end glowed.

"Nobody I knew, on the reservation, took that stuff seriously," he went on after a moment. "A few of the older men wanted us boys to learn it to keep the custom alive, to remind us we were still a people. But mostly our idea was to pick up some change by dancing for tourists."

There was a longer pause. Everard doused the projector completely. In the murk that followed, Sandoval's cigarette waxed and waned, a tiny red Algol.

"Tourists!" he said at last.

After more minutes: "Tonight I was dancing for a purpose. It meant something. I never felt that way before."

Everard was silent.

Until one of the horses, which had plunged at its halter's end during the performance and was still nervous, whinnied.

Everard looked up. Night met his eyes. "Did you hear anything, Jack?"

The flashlight beam speared him.

For an instant he stared blinded at it. Then he sprang erect, cursing and snatching for his stun pistol. A shadow ran from behind one of the trees. It struck him in the ribs. He lurched back. The beam gun flew to his hand. He shot at random.

The flashlight swept about once more. Everard glimpsed Sandoval. The Navajo had not donned his weapons again. Unarmed, he dodged the sweep of a Mongol blade. The swordsman ran after him. Sandoval reverted to Patrol judo. He went to one knee. Clumsy afoot, the Mongol slashed, missed, and ran straight into a shoulder block to the belly. Sandoval rose with the blow. The heel of his hand jolted upward to the Mongol's chin. The helmeted head snapped back. Sandoval chopped a hand at the Adam's apple, yanked the sword from its owner's grasp, turned and parried a cut from behind.

A voice yammered above the Mongol yipping, giving orders. Everard backed away. He had knocked one attacker out with a bolt from his pistol. There were others between him and the scooter. He circled to face them. A lariat curled around his shoulders. It tightened with one expert heave. He went over. Four men piled on him. He saw half a dozen lance butts crack down on Sandoval's head; then there wasn't time for anything but fighting. Twice he got to his feet, but his gun was gone by now, the Mauser plucked from its holster—the little men were pretty good at *yawara*-style combat themselves. They dragged him down and hit him with fists, boots, dagger pommels. He never quite lost consciousness, but he finally stopped caring.

Toktai struck camp before dawn. The first sun saw his troop wind between scattered copses on a broad valley floor. The land was turning flat and arid, the mountains to the right farther away, fewer snow peaks visible and those ghostly in a pale sky.

The hardy small Mongol horses trotted ahead—plop of hoofs, squeak and jingle of harness. Looking back, Everard saw the line as a compact mass; lances rose and fell, pennants and plumes and cloaks fluttered beneath, and under that were the helmets, with a brown slit-eyed face and a grotesquely painted cuirass visible here and there. No one spoke, and he couldn't read any of those expressions.

His brain felt sandy. They had left his hands free, but lashed his ankles to the stirrups, and the cord chafed. They had also stripped him naked—sensible precaution, who knew what instruments might be sewn into his garments?—and the Mongol garb given him in exchange was ludicrously small. The seams had had to be slit before he could even get the tunic on.

The projector and the scooter lay back at the hill. Toktai would not take any risks with those things of power. He had had to roar down several of his own frightened warriors before they would even agree to bring the strange horses, with saddle and bedroll, riderless among the pack

Hoofs thudded rapidly. One of the bowmen flanking Everard grunted and moved his pony a little aside. Li Tai-Tsung rode close.

The Patrolman gave him a dull stare. "Well?" he said.

"I fear your friend will not waken again," answered the Chinese. "I made him a little more comfortable."

But lying strapped on an improvised litter between two ponies, unconscious... Yes, concussion, when they clubbed him last night. A Patrol hospital could put him to rights soon enough. But the nearest Patrol office is in Cambaluc, and I can't see Toktai letting me go back to the scooter and use its radio. John Sandoval is going to die here, six hundred and fifty years before he was born.

Everard looked into cool brown eyes, interested, not unsympathetic, but alien to him. It was no use, he knew; arguments which were logical in his culture were gibberish today; but one had to try. "Can you, at least, not make Toktai understand what ruin he is going to bring on himself, on his whole people, by this?"

Li stroked his fork beard. "It is plain to see, honored sir, your nation has arts unknown to us," he said. "But what of it? The barbarians—" He gave Everard's Mongol guards a quick glance, but evidently they didn't understand the Sung Chinese he used. "—took many kingdoms superior to them in every way but fighting skill. Now already we know that you, ah, amended the truth when you spoke of a hostile empire near these lands. Why should your king try to frighten us away with a falsehood, did he not have reason to fear us?"

Everard spoke with care: "Our glorious emperor dislikes bloodshed. But if you force him to strike you down—"

"Please." Li looked pained. He waved one slender hand, as if brushing off an insect. "Say what you will to Toktai, and I shall not interfere. It would not sadden me to return home; I came only under Imperial orders. But let us two, speaking confidentially, not insult each other's intelligence. Do you not see, eminent lord, that there is no possible harm with which you can threaten these men? Death they despise; even the most lingering torture must kill them in time; even the most disgraceful mutilation can be made as naught by a man willing to bite through his tongue and die. Toktai sees eternal shame if he turns back at this stage of events, and a good chance of eternal glory and uncountable wealth if he continues."

Everard sighed. His own humiliating capture had indeed been the turning point. The Mongols had been very near bolting at the thunder show. Many had groveled and wailed (and from now on would be all the more aggressive, to erase that memory). Toktai charged the source as much in horror as defiance; a few men and horses had been able to come along. Li himself was partly responsible: scholar, skeptic, familiar with sleight-of-hand and pyrotechnic displays, the Chinese had helped hearten Toktai to attack before one of those thunderbolts did strike home.

The truth of the matter is, son, we misjudged these people. We should have taken along a Specialist, who'd have an intuitive feeling for the nuances of this culture. But no, we assumed a brainful of facts would be enough. Now what? A Patrol relief expedition may show up eventually, but Jack will be dead in another day or two... Everard looked at the stony warrior face on his left. *Quite probably I'll be also. They're still on edge. They'd sooner scrag me than not.*

And even if he should (unlikely chance!) survive to be hauled out of this mess by another Patrol band—it would be tough to face his comrades. An Unattached agent, with all the special privileges of his rank, was expected to handle situations without extra help. Without leading valuable men to their deaths.

"So I advise you most sincerely not to attempt any more deceptions."

"What?" Everard turned back to Li.

"You do understand, do you not," said the Chinese, "that our native guides did flee? That you are now taking their place? But we expect to meet other tribes before long, establish communication…"

Everard nodded a throbbing head. The sunlight pierced his eyes. He was not astonished at the ready Mongol progress through scores of separate language areas. If you aren't fussy about grammar, a few hours suffice to pick up the small number of basic words and gestures; thereafter you can take days or weeks actually learning to speak with your hired escort.

"…again obtain guides from stage to stage, as we did before," continued Li. "Any misdirection you may have given will soon be apparent. Toktai will punish it in most uncivilized ways. On the other hand, faithful service will be rewarded. You may hope in time to rise high in the provincial court, after the conquest."

Everard sat unmoving. The casual boast was like an explosion in his mind.

He had been assuming the Patrol would send another force. Obviously something was going to prevent Toktai's return. But was it so obvious? Why had this interference been ordered at all, if there were not—in some paradoxical way his twentieth-century logic couldn't grasp—an uncertainty, a shakiness in the continuum right at this point?

Judas in hell! Perhaps the Mongol expedition was going to succeed! Perhaps all the future of an American Khanate which Sandoval had not quite dared dream of…was the real future.

There are quirks and discontinuities in space-time. The world lines can double back and bite themselves off, so that things and events appear causelessly, meaningless flutters soon lost and forgotten. Such as Manse Everard, marooned in the past with a dead John Sandoval, after coming from a future that never existed as the agent of a Time Patrol that never was.

At sundown their unmerciful pace had brought the expedition into sagebrush and greasewood country. The hills were steep and brown; dust smoked under hoofs; silvery-green bushes grew sparse, sweetening the air when bruised but offering little else.

Everard helped lay Sandoval on the ground. The Navajo's eyes were closed, his face sunken and hot. Sometimes he tossed and muttered a bit. Everard squeezed water from a wetted cloth past the cracked lips, but could do nothing more,

The Mongols established themselves more merrily than of late. They had overcome two great sorcerers and suffered no further attack, and the implications were growing upon them. They went about their chores chattering to each other, and after a frugal meal they broke out the leather bags of *kumiss*.

Everard remained with Sandoval, near the middle of camp. Two guards had been posted on him. They sat with strung bows a few yards away but didn't talk. Now and then one of them would get up to tend the small fire. Presently silence fell on their comrades too. Even this leathery host was tired; men rolled up and went to sleep, the outposts rode their rounds drowsy-eyed, other watch fires burned to embers while stars kindled overhead, a coyote yelped across miles. Everard covered Sandoval against the gathering cold; his own low flames showed rime frost on sage leaves. He huddled into a cloak and wished his captors would at least give him back his pipe.

A footfall crunched dry soil. Everard's guards snatched arrows for their bows. Toktai moved into the light, his head bare above a mantle. The guards bent low and moved back into shadow.

Toktai halted. Everard looked up and then down again. The Noyon stared a while at Sandoval. Finally, almost gently, he said: "I do not think your friend will live to next sunset."

Everard grunted.

"Have you any medicines which might help?" asked Toktai. "There are some queer things in your saddlebags."

"I have a remedy against infection, and another against pain," said Everard mechanically. "But for a cracked skull, he must be taken to skillful physicians."

Toktai sat down and held his hands to the fire. "I'm sorry we have no surgeons along."

"You could let us go," said Everard without hope. "My chariot, back at the last camp, could get him to help in time."

"Now you know I can't do that!" Toktai chuckled. His pity for the dying man flickered out. "After all, Eburar, you started the trouble."

Since it was true, the Patrolman made no retort.

"I don't hold it against you," went on Toktai. "In fact, I'm still anxious to be friends. If I weren't, I'd stop for a few days and wring all you know out of you."

Everard flared up. "You could try!"

"And succeed, I think, with a man who has to carry medicine against pain." Toktai's grin was wolfish. "However, you may be useful as a hostage or something. And I do like your nerve. I'll even tell you an idea I have. I think maybe you don't belong to this rich southland at all. I think you're an adventurer, one of a little band of shamans. You have the southern king in your power, or hope to, and don't want strangers interfering." Toktai spat into the fire. "There are old stories about that sort of thing, and finally a hero overthrew the wizard. Why not me?"

Everard sighed. "You will learn why not, Noyon." He wondered how correct that was.

"Oh, now." Toktai clapped him on the back. "Can't you tell me even a little? There's no blood feud between us. Let's be friends."

Everard jerked a thumb at Sandoval.

"It's a shame, that," said Toktai, "but he would keep on resisting an officer of the Kha Khan. Come, let's have a drink together, Eburar. I'll send a man for a bag."

The Patrolman made a face. "That's no way to pacify me!"

"Oh, your people don't like *kumiss*? I'm afraid it's all we have. We drank up our wine long ago."

"You could let me have my whisky." Everard looked at Sandoval again, and out into night, and felt the cold creep inward. "God, but I could use that!"

"Eh?"

"A drink of our own. We had some in our saddlebags."

"Well…" Toktai hesitated. "Very well. Come along and we'll fetch it."

The guards followed their chief and their prisoner, through the brush and the sleeping warriors, up to a pile of assorted gear also under guard. One of the latter sentries ignited a stick in his fire to give Everard some light. The Patrolman's back muscles tensed—arrows were aimed at him now, drawn to the barb—but he squatted and went through his own stuff, careful not to move fast. When he had both canteens of Scotch, he returned to his own place.

Toktai sat down across the fire. He watched Everard pour a shot into the canteen cap and toss it off. "Smells odd," he said.

"Try." The Patrolman handed over the canteen.

It was an impulse of sheer loneliness. Toktai wasn't such a bad sort. Not on his own terms. And when you sit by your dying partner, you'd bouse with the devil himself, just to keep from thinking. The Mongol sniffed dubiously, looked back at Everard, paused, and then raised the bottle to his lips with a bravura gesture.

"*Whoo-oo-oo!*"

Everard scrambled to catch the flask before too much was spilled. Toktai gasped and spat. One guardsman nocked an arrow, the other sprang to lay a hard hand on Everard's shoulder. A sword gleamed high. "It's not poison!" the Patrolman exclaimed. "It's only too strong for him. See, I'll drink some more myself."

Toktai waved the guards back and glared from watery eyes. "What do you make that of?" he choked. "Dragon's blood?"

"Barley." Everard didn't feel like explaining distillation.

He poured himself another slug. "Go ahead, drink your mare's milk."

Toktai smacked his lips. "It does warm you up, doesn't it? Like pepper." He reached out a grimy hand. "Give me some more."

Everard sat still for a few seconds. "Well?" growled Toktai.

The Patrolman shook his head. "I told you, it's too strong for Mongols."

"What? See here, you whey-faced son of a Turk—"

"On your head be it, then. I warn you fairly, with your men here as witnesses, you will be sick tomorrow."

Toktai guzzled heartily, belched, and passed the canteen back. "Nonsense. I simply wasn't prepared for it, the first time. Drink up!"

Everard took his time. Toktai grew impatient. "Hurry along there. No, give me the other flask."

"Very well. You are the chief. But I beg you, don't try to match me draught for draught. You can't do it."

"What do you mean, I can't do it? Why, I've drunk twenty men senseless in Karakorum. None of your gutless Chinks, either: they were all Mongols." Toktai poured down a couple of ounces more.

Everard sipped with care. But he hardly felt the effect anyway, save as a burning along his gullet. He was too tightly strung. Suddenly he was glimpsing what might be a way out.

"Here, it's a cold night," he said, and offered his canteen to the nearest guardsman. "You lads have one to keep you warm."

Toktai looked up, a trifle muzzily. "Good stuff, this," he objected. "Too good for..." He remembered himself and snapped his words off short. Cruel and absolute the Mongol Empire might be, but officers shared equally with the humblest of their men.

The warrior grabbed the jug, giving his chief a resentful look, and slanted it to his mouth. "Easy, there," said Everard. "It's heady."

"Nothin's heady to me." Toktai poured a further dose into himself. "Sober as a bonze." He wagged his finger. "That's the trouble bein' a Mongol. You're so hardy you can't get drunk."

"Are you bragging or complaining?" said Everard. The first warrior fanned his tongue, resumed a stance of alertness, and passed the bottle to his companion. Toktai hoisted the other canteen again.

"Ahhh!" He stared, owlish. "That was fine. Well, better get to sleep now. Give him back his liquor, men."

Everard's throat tightened. But he managed to leer. "Yes, thanks, I'll want some more," he said. "I'm glad you realize you can't take it."

"Wha' d'you mean?" Toktai glared at him. "No such thing as too much. Not for a Mongol!" He glugged afresh. The first guardsman received the other flask and took a hasty snort before it should be too late.

Everard sucked in a shaken breath. It might work out after all. It might.

Toktai was used to carousing. There was no doubt that he or his men could handle *kumiss*, wine, ale, mead, *kvass*, that thin beer miscalled rice wine—any beverage of this era. They'd know when they'd had enough, say good night, and walk a straight line to their bedrolls. The trouble was, no substance merely fermented can get over about twenty-four proof—the process is stopped by its waste product—and most of what they brewed in the thirteenth century ran well under five percent alcohol, with a high foodstuff content to boot.

Scotch whisky is in quite a different class. If you try to drink that like beer, or even like wine, you are in trouble. Your judgment will be gone before you've noticed its absence, and consciousness follows soon after.

Everard reached for the canteen held by one of the guards. "Give me that!" he said. "You'll drink it all up!"

The warrior grinned and took another long gulp, before passing it on to his fellow. Everard stood up and made an undignified scrabble for it. A guard poked him in the stomach. He went over on his backside. The Mongols bawled laughter, leaning on each other. So good a joke called for another drink.

When Toktai folded, Everard alone noticed. The Noyon slid from a cross-legged to a recumbent position. The fire sputtered up long enough to show a silly smile on his face. Everard squatted wire-tense.

The end of one sentry came a few minutes later. He reeled, went on all fours, and began to jettison his dinner. The other one turned, blinking, fumbling after a sword. "Wha's mattuh?" he groaned. "Wha' yuh done? Poison?"

Everard moved.

He had hopped over the fire and fallen on Toktai before the last guard realized it. The Mongol stumbled forward, crying out. Everard found Toktai's sword. It flashed from the scabbard as he bounded up. The warrior got his own blade aloft. Everard didn't like to kill a nearly helpless man. He stepped close, knocked the other weapon aside, and his fist clopped. The Mongol sank to his knees, retched, and slept.

Everard bounded away. Men stirred in the dark, calling. He heard hoofs drum, one of the mounted sentries racing to investigate. Somebody took a brand from an almost extinct fire and whirled it till it flared. Everard went flat on his belly.

A warrior pelted by, not seeing him in the brush. He glided toward deeper darknesses. A yell behind him, a machine-gun volley of curses, told that someone had found the Noyon.

Everard stood up and began to run.

The horses had been hobbled and turned out under guard as usual. They were a dark mass on the plain, which lay gray-white beneath a sky crowded with sharp stars. Everard saw one of the Mongol watchers gallop to meet him. A voice barked: "What's happening?"

He pitched his answer high. "Attack on camp!" It was only to gain time, lest the horseman recognize him and fire an arrow. He crouched, visible as a hunched and cloaked shape. The Mongol reined in with a spurt of dust. Everard sprang.

He got hold of the pony's bridle before he was recognized. Then the sentry yelled and drew sword. He hewed downward. But Everard was on the left side. The blow from above came awkwardly, easily parried. Everard chopped in return and felt his edge go into meat. The horse reared in alarm. Its rider fell from the saddle. He rolled over and staggered up again, bellowing. Everard already had one foot in a pan-shaped stirrup. The Mongol limped toward him, blood running black in that light from a wounded leg. Everard mounted and laid the flat of his own blade on the horse's crupper.

He got going toward the herd. Another rider pounded to intercept him. Everard ducked. An arrow buzzed where he had been. The stolen pony plunged, fighting its unfamiliar burden. Everard needed a minute to get it under control again. The archer might have taken him then, by coming up and going at it hand to hand. But habit sent the man past at a gallop, shooting. He missed in the dimness. Before he could turn, Everard was out of night view.

The Patrolman uncoiled a lariat at the saddlebow and broke into the skittish herd. He roped the nearest animal, which accepted it with blessed meekness. Leaning over, he slashed the hobbles with his sword and rode off, leading the remount. They came out the other side of the herd and started north.

A stern chase is a long chase, Everard told himself inappropriately. *But they're bound to overhaul me if I don't lose 'em. Let's see, if I remember my geography, the lava beds lie northwest of here.*

He cast a glance behind. No one pursued yet. They'd need a while to organize themselves. However...

Thin lightnings winked from above. The cloven air boomed behind them. He felt a chill, deeper than the night cold. But he eased his pace. There was no more reason for hurry. That must be Manse Everard—

—who had returned to the Patrol vehicle and ridden it south in space and backward in time to this same instant.

That was cutting it fine, he thought. Patrol doctrine frowned on helping oneself thus. Too much danger of a close causal loop, or of tangling past and future.

But in this case, I'll get away with it. No reprimands, even. Because it's to rescue Jack Sandoval, not myself. I've already gotten free. I could shake pursuit in the mountains, which I know and the Mongols don't. The time-hopping is only to save my friend's life.

Besides, (an upsurging bitterness), *what's this whole mission been, except the future doubling back to create its own past? Without us, the Mongols might well have taken over America; and then there'd never have been any us.*

The sky was enormous, crystalline black; you rarely saw that many stars. The Great Bear flashed above hoar earth; hoofbeats rang through silence. Everard had not felt so alone before now.

"And what am I doing back there?" he asked aloud. The answer came to him, and he eased a little, fell into the rhythm of his horses and started eating miles. He wanted to get this over with. But what he must do turned out to be less bad than he had feared.

Toktai and Li Tai-Tsung never came home. But that was not because they perished at sea or in the forests. It was because a sorcerer rode down from heaven and killed all their horses with thunderbolts, and smashed and burned their ships in the river mouth. No Chinese sailor would venture onto those tricky seas in whatever clumsy vessel could be built here; no Mongol would think it possible to go home on foot. Indeed, it probably wasn't. The expedition would stay, marry into the Indians, live out their days. Chinook, Tlingit, Nootka, all the potlatch tribes, with their big seagoing canoes, lodges and copperworking, furs and cloths and haughtiness...well, a Mongol Noyon, even a Confucian scholar might live less happily and usefully than in creating such a life for such a race.

Everard nodded to himself. So much for that. What was harder to take than the thwarting of Toktai's bloodthirsty ambitions was the truth about his own corps, which was his own family and nation and reason for living. The distant supermen turned out to be not quite such idealists after all. They weren't merely safeguarding a perhaps divinely ordained history which led to them. Here and there they, too, meddled, to create their own past...Don't ask if there ever was any "original" scheme of things. Keep your mind shut. Regard the rutted road mankind had to travel, and tell yourself that if it could be better in places, in other places it could be worse.

"It may be a crooked game," said Everard, "but it's the only one in town."

His voice came so loud, in that huge rime-white land, that he didn't speak any more. He clucked at his horse and rode a little faster northward.

UNTITLED SONG
(Melody obvious)

Black bodies give off radiation,
and ought to continuously.
Black bodies give off radiation,
but do it by Planck's theory.

(Chorus)
Bring back, bring back,
oh, bring back that old continuity!
Bring back, bring back,
oh, bring back Clerk Maxwell to me!

Though now we have Schrödinger functions,
dividing up h by 2π,
that damn differential equation
still has no solution for ψ.

(Chorus)

Supernova

For who knows how long, the star had orbited quietly in the wilderness between Betelgeuse and Rigel. It was rather more massive than average—about half again as much as Sol—and shone with corresponding intensity, white-hot, corona and prominences a terrible glory. But there are no few like it. A ship of the first Grand Survey noted its existence. However, the crew were more interested in a neighbor sun which had planets, and could not linger long in that system either. The galaxy is too big; their purpose was to get some hint about this spiral arm which we inhabit. Thus certain spectroscopic omens escaped their notice.

No one returned thither for a pair of centuries. Technic civilization had more than it could handle, let alone comprehend, in the millions of stars closer to home. So the fact remained unsuspected that this one was older than normal for its type in its region, must indeed have wandered in from other parts. Not that it was very ancient, astronomically speaking. But the great childless suns evolve fast and strangely.

By chance, though, a scout from the Polesotechnic League, exploring far in search of new markets, was passing within a light-year when the star exploded.

Say instead—insofar as simultaneity has any meaning across interstellar distances—that the death agony had occurred some months before. Even more fierce, thermonuclear reaction had burned up the last hydrogen at the center. Unbalanced by radiation pressure, the outer layers collapsed beneath their own weight. Forces were released which triggered a wholly different order of atomic fusions. New elements came into being, not only those which may be found in the planets but also the short-lived transuranics; for a while, technetium itself dominated that anarchy. Neutrons and neutrinos flooded forth, carrying with them the last balancing energy. Compression turned into catastrophe. At the brief peak, the supernova was as radiant as its entire galaxy.

So close, the ship's personnel would have died had she not been in hyperdrive. They did not remain there. A dangerous amount of radiation was still touching them between quantum microjumps. And they were not equipped to study the phenomenon. It is rare; this was the first chance in our history to observe a new supernova. Earth was too remote to help. But the scientific colony on Catawrayannis could be reached fairly soon. It could dispatch laboratory craft.

Now to track in detail what was going to happen, considerable resources were demanded. Among these were a place where men could live and instruments be made to order as the need for them arose. Such things could not well be sent from the usual factories. By the time they arrived, the wave front carrying information about rapidly progressing events would have traveled so far that inverse-square enfeeblement would create maddening inaccuracies.

But a little beyond one parsec from the star—an excellent distance for observation over a period of years—was a G-type sun. One of its planets was terrestroid to numerous points of classification, both physically and biochemically. Survey records showed that the most advanced culture on it was at the verge of an industrial-scientific revolution. Ideal!

Except, to be sure, that Survey's information was less than sketchy, and two centuries out of date.

"No."

Master Merchant David Falkayn stepped backward in startlement. The four nearest guards clutched at their pistols. Peripherally and profanely, Falkayn wondered what canon he had violated now.

"Beg, uh, beg pardon?" he said.

Morruchan Long-Ax, the Hand of the Vach Dathyr, leaned forward on his dais. He was big even for a Merseian, which meant that he overtopped Falkayn's rangy height by a good fifteen centimeters. Long, shoulder-flared orange robes and horned miter made his bulk almost overwhelming. Beneath them, he was approximately anthropoid, save for a slanting posture counterbalanced by the tail which, with his booted feet, made a tripod for him to sit on. The skin was green, faintly scaled, totally hairless. A spiky ridge ran from the top of his skull to the end of that tail. Instead of earflaps, he had deep convolutions in his head. But the face was manlike, in a heavy-boned fashion, and the physiology was essentially mammalian.

How familiar the mind was, behind those jet eyes, Falkayn did not know.

The harsh basso said: "You shall not take the rule of this world. If we surrendered the right and freehold they won, the God would cast back the souls of our ancestors to shriek at us."

Falkayn's glance flickered around. He had seldom felt so alone. The audience chamber of Castle Afon stretched high and gaunt, proportioned like nothing men had ever built. Curiously woven tapestries on the stone walls, between windows arched at both top and bottom, and battle banners hung from the rafters, did little to stop echoes. The troopers lining the hall, down to a hearth whose fire could have roasted an elephant, wore armor and helmets with demon masks. The guns which they added to curved swords and barbed pikes did not seem out of place. Rather, what appeared unattainably far was a glimpse of ice-blue sky outside.

The air was chill with winter. Gravity was little higher than Terrestrial, but Falkayn felt it dragging at him.

He straightened. He had his own sidearm, no chemical slug-thrower but an energy weapon. Adzel, abroad in the city, and Chee Lan, aboard the ship, were listening in via the transceiver on his wrist. And the ship had power to level all Ardaig. Morruchan must realize as much.

But he had to be made to cooperate.

Falkayn picked his words with care: "I pray forgiveness, Hand, if perchance in mine ignorance I misuse thy...uh...your tongue. Naught was intended save friendliness. Hither bring I news of peril impending, for the which ye must busk yourselves betimes less ye lose everything ye possess. My folk would fain show your folk what to do. So vast is the striving needed, and so scant the time, that perforce ye must take our counsel. Else can we be of no avail. But never will we act as conquerors. 'Twere not simply an evil deed, but 'twould boot us naught, whose trafficking is with many worlds. Nay, we would be brothers, come to help in a day of sore need."

Morruchan scowled and rubbed his chin. "Say on, then," he replied. "Frankly, I am dubious. You claim...Valenderay is about to become a supernova—"

"Nay, Hand, I declare it hath already done so. The light therefrom will smite this planet in less than three years."

The time unit Falkayn actually used was Merseian, a trifle greater than Earth's. He sweated and swore to himself at the language problem. The Survey xenologists had got a fair grasp of Eriau in the several months they spent here, and Falkayn and his shipmates had acquired it by synapse transform while en route. But now it turned out that, two hundred years back, Eriau had been in a state of linguistic overturn. He wasn't even pronouncing the vowels right.

He tried to update his grammar. "Would ye, uh, I mean if your desire is...if you want confirmation, we can take you or a trusty member of your household so near in our vessel that the starburst is beheld with living eyes."

"No doubt the scientists and poets will duel for a berth on that trip," Morruchan said in a dry voice. "But I believe you already. You yourself, your ship and companions, are proof." His tone sharpened. "At the same time, I am no Believer, imagining you half divine because you come from outside. Your civilization has a technological head start on mine, nothing else. A careful reading of the records from that other brief period when aliens dwelt among us shows they had no reason more noble than professional curiosity. And that was fitful; they left, and none ever returned. Until now.

"So: what do you want from us?"

Falkayn relaxed a bit. Morruchan seemed to be his own kind despite everything, not awestruck, not idealistic, not driven by some incomprehensible non-human motivation, but a shrewd and skeptical politician of a pragmatically oriented culture.

Seems to be, the man cautioned himself. *What do I really know about Merseia?*

Judging by observations made in orbit, radio monitoring, initial radio contact, and the ride here in an electric groundcar, this planet still held a jumble of societies, dominated by the one which surrounded the Wilwidh Ocean. Two centuries ago, local rule had been divided among aristocratic clans. He supposed that a degree of continental unification had since been achieved, for his request for an interview with the highest authority had got him to Ardaig and a confrontation with this individual. But could Morruchan speak for his entire species? Falkayn doubted it.

Nevertheless, you had to start somewhere.

"I shall be honest, Hand," he said. "My crew and I are come as naught but preparers of the way. Can we succeed, we will be rewarded with a share in whatever gain ensueth. For our scientists wish to use Merseia and its moons as bases wherefrom to observe the supernova through the next dozen years. Best for them would be if your folk could provide them with most of their needs, not alone food but such instruments as they tell you how to fashion. For this they will pay fairly; and in addition, ye will acquire knowledge.

"Yet first must we assure that there remaineth a Merseian civilization. To do that, we must wreak huge works. And ye will pay us for our toil and goods supplied to that end. The price will not be usurious, but it will allow us a profit. Out of it, we will buy whatever Merseian wares can be sold at home for further profit." He smiled. "Thus all may win and none need fear. The Polesotechnic League compriseth nor conquerors nor bandits, naught save merchant adventurers who seek to make their"—more or less—"honest living."

"*Hunh!*" Morruchan growled. "Now we bite down to the bone. When you first communicated and spoke about a supernova, my colleagues and I consulted the astronomers. We are not altogether savages here; we have at least gone as far as atomic power and interplanetary travel. Well, our astronomers said that such a star reaches a peak output about fifteen billion times as great as Korych. Is this right?"

"Close enough, Hand, if Korych be your own sun."

"The only nearby one which might burst in this manner is Valenderay. From your description, the brightest in the southern sky, you must be thinking of it, too."

Falkayn nodded, realized he wasn't sure if this gesture meant the same thing on Merseia, remembered it did, and said: "Aye, Hand."

"It sounded terrifying," Morruchan said, "until they pointed out that Valenderay is three and a half light-years distant. And this is a reach so enormous that no mind can swallow it. The radiation, when it gets to us, will equal a mere one-third of what comes daily from Korych. And in some fifty-five days" (Terrestrial) "it will have dwindled to half...and so on, until before long we see little except a bright nebula at night.

"True, we can expect troublesome weather, storms, torrential rains, perhaps some flooding if sufficient of the south polar ice cap melts. But that will pass. In any case, the center of civilization is here, in the northern hemisphere. It is also true that, at peak, there will be a dangerous amount of ultraviolet and X radiation. But Merseia's atmosphere will block it.

"Thus." Morruchan leaned back on his tail and bridged the fingers of his oddly humanlike hands. "The peril you speak of scarcely exists. What do you really want?"

Falkayn's boyhood training, as a nobleman's son on Hermes, rallied within him. He squared his shoulders. He was not unimpressive, a tall, fair-haired young man with blue eyes bright in a lean, high-cheekboned face. "Hand," he said gravely, "I perceive you have not yet had time to consult your folk who are wise in matters—"

And then he broke down. He didn't know the word for "electronic."

Morruchan refrained from taking advantage. Instead, the Merseian became quite helpful. Falkayn's rejoinder was halting, often interrupted while he and the other worked out what a phrase must be. But, in essence and in current language, what he said was:

"The Hand is correct as far as he goes. But consider what will follow. The eruption of a supernova is violent beyond imagining. Nuclear processes are involved, so complex that we ourselves don't yet understand them in detail. That's why we want to study them. But this much we do know, and your physicists will confirm it.

"As nuclei and electrons recombine in that supernal fireball, they generate asymmetrical magnetic pulses. Surely you know what this does when it happens in the detonation of an atomic weapon. Now think of it on a stellar scale. When those forces hit, they will blast straight through Merseia's own magnetic field, down to the very surface. Unshielded electric motors, generators, transmission lines…oh, yes, no doubt you have surge arrestors, but your circuit breakers will be tripped, then intolerable voltages will be induced, and the entire system will be wrecked. Likewise telecommunications lines. And computers. If you use transistors…ah you do…the flipflop between p and n type conduction will wipe every memory bank, stop every operation in its tracks.

"Electrons, riding that magnetic pulse, will not be long in arriving. As they spiral in the planet's field, their synchrotron radiation will completely blanket whatever electronic apparatus you may have salvaged. Protons should be slower, pushed to about half the speed of light. Then come the alpha particles, then the heavier matter: year after year after year of cosmic fallout, most of it radioactive, to a total greater by orders of magnitude than any war could create before civilization was destroyed. Your planetary magnetism is no real shield. The majority of ions are energetic enough to get through. Nor is your atmosphere any good defense. Heavy nuclei, sleeting through it, will produce secondary radiation that does reach the ground.

"I do not say this planet will be wiped clean of life. But I do say that, without ample advance preparation, it will suffer ecological disaster. Your species might or might not survive; but if you do, it will be as a few starveling primitives. The early breakdown of the electric systems on which your civilization is now dependent will have seen to that. Just imagine. Suddenly no more food moves into the cities. The dwellers go forth as a ravening horde. But if most of your farmers are as specialized as I suppose, they won't even be able to support themselves. Once fighting and famine have become general, no more medical service will be possible, and the pestilences will start. It will be like the aftermath of an all-out nuclear strike against a country with no civil defense. I gather you've avoided that on Merseia. But you certainly have theoretical studies of the subject, and—I have seen planets where it did happen.

"Long before the end, your colonies throughout this system will have been destroyed by the destruction of the apparatus that keeps the colonists alive. And for many years, no spaceship will be able to move.

"Unless you accept our help. We know how to generate force screens, small ones for machines, gigantic ones which can give an entire planet some protection. Not enough—but we also know how to insulate against the energies that get through. We know how to build engines and communications lines which are not affected. We know how to sow substances which protect life against hard radiation. We know how to restore mutated genes. In short, we have the knowledge you need for survival.

"The effort will be enormous. Most of it you must carry out yourselves. Our available personnel are too few, our lines of interstellar transportation too long. But we can supply engineers and organizers.

"To be blunt, Hand, you are very lucky that we learned of this in time, barely in time. Don't fear us. We have no ambitions toward Merseia. If nothing else, it lies far beyond our normal sphere of operation, and we have millions of more profitable planets much closer to home. We want to save you, because you are sentient beings. But it'll be expensive, and a lot of the work will have to be done by outfits like mine, which exist to make a profit. So, besides a scientific base, we want a reasonable economic return.

"Eventually, though, we'll depart. What you do then is your own affair. But you'll still have your civilization. You'll also have a great deal of new equipment and new knowledge. I think you're getting a bargain."

Falkayn stopped. For a while, silence dwelt in that long dim hall. He grew aware of odors which had never been on Earth or Hermes.

Morruchan said at last, slowly: "This must be thought on. I shall have to confer with my colleagues, and others. There are so many complications. For example, I see no good reason to do anything for the colony on Ronruad, and many excellent reasons for letting it die."

"What?" Falkayn's teeth clicked together. "Meaneth the Hand the next outward planet? But meseems faring goeth on apace throughout this system."

"Indeed, indeed," Morruchan said impatiently. "We depend on the other planets for a number of raw materials, like fissionables, or complex gases from the outer worlds. Ronruad, though, is of use only to the Gethfennu."

He spoke that word with such distaste that Falkayn postponed asking for a definition. "What recommendations I make in my report will draw heavily upon the Hand's wisdom," the human said.

"Your courtesy is appreciated," Morruchan replied: with how much irony, Falkayn wasn't sure. He was taking the news more coolly than expected. But then, he was of a different race from men, and a soldierly tradition as well. "I hope that, for now, you will honor the Vach Dathyr by guesting us."

"Well—" Falkayn hesitated. He had planned on returning to his ship. But he might do better on the spot. The Survey crew had found Merseian food nourishing to men, in fact tasty. One report had waxed ecstatic about the ale.

"I thank the Hand."

"Good. I suggest you go to the chambers already prepared, to rest and refresh yourself. With your leave, a messenger will come presently to ask what he should bring you from your vessel. Unless you wish to move it here?"

"Uh, best not…policy—" Falkayn didn't care to take chances. The Merseians were not so far behind the League that they couldn't spring a nasty surprise if they wanted to.

Morruchan raised the skin above his brow ridges but made no comment. "You will dine with me and my councillors at sunset," he said. They parted ceremoniously.

A pair of guards conducted Falkayn out, through a series of corridors and up a sweeping staircase whose bannister was carved into the form of a snake. At the end, he was ushered into a suite. The rooms were spacious, their comfort-making gadgetry not greatly below Technic standards. Reptile-skin carpets and animal skulls mounted on the crimson-draped walls were a little disquieting, but what the hell. A balcony gave on a view of the palace gardens, whose austere good taste was reminiscent of Original Japanese, and on the city.

Ardaig was sizable, must hold two or three million souls. This quarter was ancient, with buildings of gray stone fantastically turreted and battlemented. The hills which ringed it were checkered by the estates of the wealthy. Snow lay white and blue-shadowed between. Ramparted with tall modern structures, the bay shone like gunmetal. Cargo ships moved in and out, a delta-wing jet whistled overhead. But he heard little traffic noise; nonessential vehicles were banned in the sacred Old Quarter.

"Wedhi is my name, Protector," said the short Merseian in the black tunic who had been awaiting him. "May he consider me his liege man, to do as he commands."

"My thanks," Falkayn said. "Thou mayest show me how one maketh use of facilities." He couldn't wait to see a bathroom designed for these people. "And then, mayhap, a tankard of beer, a textbook on political geography, and privacy for some hours."

"The Protector has spoken. If he will follow me?"

The two of them entered the adjoining chamber, which was furnished for sleeping. As if by accident, Wedhi's tail brushed the door. It wasn't automatic, merely hinged, and closed under the impact. Wedhi seized Falkayn's hand and pressed something into the palm. Simultaneously, he caught his lips between his teeth. A signal for silence?

With a tingle along his spine, Falkayn nodded and stuffed the bit of paper into a pocket.

When he was alone, he opened the note, hunched over in case of spy eyes. The alphabet hadn't changed.

> *Be wary, star dweller. Morruchan Long-Ax is no friend. If you can arrange for one of your company to come tonight in secret to the house at the corner of Triau Street and Victory Way which is marked by twined fylfots over the door, the truth shall be explained.*

As darkness fell, the moon Neihevin rose full. Luna size and copper color, above eastward hills whose forests glistened with frost. Lythyr was already up, a small pale crescent. Rigel blazed in the heart of that constellation named the Spear Bearer.

Chee Lan turned from the viewscreen with a shiver and an unladylike phrase. "But I am not equipped to do that," said the ship's computer.

"The suggestion was addressed to my gods," Chee answered.

She sat for a while, brooding on her wrongs. Ta-chih-chien-pih—O_2 Eridani A II or Cynthia to humans—felt even more distant than it was, warm ruddy sunlight and rustling leaves around treetop homes lost in time as well as space. Not only the cold outside daunted her. Those Merseians were so bloody *big*!

She herself was no larger than a medium-sized dog, though the bush of her tail added a good deal. Her arms, almost as long as her legs, ended in delicate six-fingered hands. White fur fluffed about her, save where it made a bluish mask across the green eyes and round, blunt-muzzled face. Seeing her for the first time, human females were apt to call her darling.

She bristled. Ears, whiskers, and hair stood erect. What was she—descendant of carnivores who chased their prey in five-meter leaps from branch to branch, xenobiologist by training, trade pioneer by choice, and pistol champion because she liked to shoot guns—what was she doing, feeling so much as respect for a gaggle of slewfooted bald barbarians? Mainly she was irritated. While standing by aboard the ship, she'd hoped to complete her latest piece of sculpture. Instead, she must hustle into that pustulant excuse for weather, and skulk through a stone garbage dump that its perpetrators called a city, and hear some yokel drone on for hours about some squabble between drunken cockroaches which he thought was politics...and pretend to take the whole farce seriously!

A narcotic cigarette soothed her, however ferocious the puffs in which she consumed it. "I guess the matter is important, at that," she murmured. "Fat commissions for me if the project succeeds."

"My programming is to the effect that our primary objective is humanitarian," said the computer. "Though I cannot find that concept in my data storage."

"Never mind, Muddlehead," Chee replied. Her mood had turned benign. "If you want to know, it relates to those constraints you have filed under Law and Ethics. But no concern of ours, this trip. Oh, the bleeding hearts do quack about Rescuing a Promising Civilization, as if the galaxy didn't have too many chaos civilizations already. Well, if they want to foot the bill, it's their taxes. They'll have to work with the League, because the League has most of the ships, which it won't hire out for nothing. And the League has to start with us, because trade pioneers are supposed to be experts in making first contacts and we happened to be the sole such crew in reach. Which is our good luck, I suppose."

She stubbed out her cigarette and busied herself with preparations. There was, for a fact, no alternative. She'd had to admit that, after a three-way radio conversation with her partners. (They didn't worry about eavesdroppers, when not a Merseian knew a word of Anglic.) Falkayn was stuck in what's-his-name's palace. Adzel was loose in the city, but he'd be the last one you'd pick for an undercover mission. Which left Chee Lan.

"Maintain contact with all three of us," she ordered the ship. "Record everything coming in tonight over my two-way. Don't stir without orders—in a galactic language—and don't respond to any native attempts at communication. Tell us at once whatever unusual you observe. If you haven't heard from any of us for twenty-four hours at a stretch, return to Catawrayannis and report."

No answer being indicated, the computer made none.

Chee buckled on a gravity harness, a tool kit, and two guns, a stunner and a blaster. Over them she threw a black mantle, less for warmth than concealment. Dousing the lights, she had the personnel lock open just long enough to let her through, jumped, and took to the air.

It bit her with chill. Flowing past, it felt liquid. An enormous silence dwelt beneath heaven; the hum of her grav was lost. Passing above the troopers who surrounded *Muddlin' Through* with armor and artillery—a sensible precaution from the native standpoint, she had to agree, sensibly labeled an honor guard—she saw the forlorn twinkle of campfires and heard a snatch of hoarse song. Then a hovercraft whirred near, big and black athwart the Milky Way, and she must change course to avoid being seen.

For a while she flew above snowclad wilderness. On an unknown planet, you didn't land downtown if you could help it. Hills and woods gave way at length to a cultivated plain where the lights of villages huddled around tower-jagged castles. Merseia—this continent, at least—appeared to have retained feudalism even as it swung into an industrial age. Or had it?

Perhaps tonight she would find out.

The seacoast hove in view, and Ardaig. That city did not gleam with illumination and brawl with traffic as most Technic communities did. Yellow windows strewed its night, like fireflies trapped in a web of phosphorescent paving. The River Oiss gleamed dull where it poured through town and into the bay, on which there shone a double moonglade. No, triple; Wythna was rising now. A murmur of machines lifted skyward.

Chee dodged another aircraft and streaked down for the darkling Old Quarter. She landed behind a shuttered bazaar and sought the nearest alley. Crouched there, she peered forth. In this section, the streets were decked with a hardy turf which ice had blanketed, and lit by widely spaced lamps. A Merseian went past, riding a horned gwydh. His tail was draped back across the animal's rump; his cloak fluttered behind him to reveal a quilted jacket reinforced with glittering metal disks, and a rifle slanted over his shoulder.

No guardsman, surely; Chee had seen what the military wore, and Falkayn had transmitted pictures of Morruchan's household troops to her via a hand scanner. He had also passed on the information that those latter doubled as police. So why was a civilian going armed? It bespoke a degree of lawlessness that fitted ill with a technological society...unless that society was in more trouble than Morruchan had admitted. Chee made certain her own guns were loose in the holsters.

The *clop-clop* of hooves faded away. Chee stuck her head out of the alley and took bearings from street signs. Instead of words, they used colorful heraldic emblems. But the Survey people had compiled a good map of Ardaig, which Falkayn's gang had memorized. The Old Quarter ought not to have changed much. She loped off, seeking cover whenever she heard a rider or pedestrian approach. There weren't many.

This corner! Squinting through murk, she identified the symbol carved in the lintel of a lean gray house. Quickly, she ran up the stairs and rapped on the door. Her free hand rested on the stunner.

The door creaked open. Light streamed through. A Merseian stood black against it. He carried a pistol himself. His head moved back and forth, peering into the night. "Here I am, thou idiot," Chee muttered.

He looked down. A jerk went through his body. *"Hu-ya!* You are from the star ship?"

"Nay," Chee sneered, "I am come to inspect the plumbing." She darted past him, into a wainscoted corridor. "If thou wouldst preserve this chickling secrecy of thine, might one suggest that thou close yon portal?"

The Merseian did. He stood a moment, regarding her in the glow of an incandescent bulb overhead. "I thought you would be...different."

"They were Terrans who first visited this world, but surely thou didst not think every race in the cosmos is formed to those ridiculous specifications. Now I've scant time to spare for whatever griping ye have here to do, so lead me to thine acher."

The Mersian obeyed. His garments were about like ordinary street clothes, belted tunic and baggy trousers, but a certain precision in their cut—as well as blue-and-gold stripes and the double fylfot embroidered on the sleeves—indicated they were a livery. Or a uniform? Chee felt the second guess confirmed when she noted two others, similarly attired, standing armed in front of a door. They saluted her and let her through.

The room beyond was baronial. Radiant heating had been installed, but a fire also roared on the hearth. Chee paid scant attention to rich draperies and carven pillars. Her gaze went to the two who sat awaiting her.

One was scarfaced, athletic, his tailnip restlessly aflicker. His robe was blue and gold, and he carried a short ceremonial spear. At sight of her, he drew a quick breath. The Cynthian decided she'd better be polite. "I hight Chee Lan, worthies, come from the interstellar expedition in response to your kind invitation."

"Khraich." The aristocrat recovered his poise and touched finger to brow. "Be welcome. I am Dagla, called Quick-to-Anger, the Hand of the Vach Hallen. And my comrade: Olgor hu Freylin, his rank Warmaster in the Republic of Lafdigu, here in Ardaig as agent for his country."

That being was middle-aged, plump, with skin more dark and features more flat than was common around the Wilwidh Ocean. His garb was foreign, too; a sort of toga with metal threads woven into the purple cloth. And he was soft-spoken, imperturbable, quite without the harshness of these lands. He crossed his arm—gesture of greeting?—and said in accented Eriau:

"Great is the honor. Since the last visitors from your high civilization were confined largely to this region, perhaps you have no knowledge of mine. May I therefore say that Lafdigu lies in the southern hemisphere, occupying a goodly part of its continent. In those days we were unindustrialized, but now, one hopes, the situation has altered."

"Nay, Warmaster, be sure our folk heard much about Lafdigu's venerable culture and regretted they had no time to learn therefrom." Chee got more tactful the bigger the lies she told. Inwardly, she groaned: *Oh, no! We haven't troubles enough, there has to be international politicking too!*

A servant appeared with a cut-crystal decanter and goblets. "I trust that your race, like the Terran, can partake of Merseian refreshment?" Dagla said.

"Indeed," Chee replied. "'Tis necessary that they who voyage together use the same stuffs. I thank the Hand."

"But we had not looked for, *hurgh,* a guest your size," Olgor said. "Perhaps a smaller glass? The wine is potent."

"This is excellent." Chee hopped onto a low table, squatted, and raised her goblet two-handed. "Galactic custom is that we drink to the health of friends. To yours, then, worthies." She took a long draught. The fact that alcohol does not affect the Cynthian brain was one she had often found it advantageous to keep silent about.

Dagla tossed off a yet larger amount, took a turn around the room, and growled: "Enough formalities, by your leave, Shipmaster." She discarded her cloak. "Shipmistress?" He gulped. His society had a kitchen-church-and-kids attitude toward females. "We...*kh-h-h*...we've grave matters to discuss."

"The Hand is too abrupt with our noble guest," Olgor chided.

"Nay, time is short," Chee said. "And clearly the business hath great weight, sith ye went to the length of suborning a servant in Morruchan's very stronghold."

Dagla grinned. "I planted Wedhi there eight years ago. He's a good voice-tube."

"No doubt the Hand of the Vach Hallen hath surety of all his own servitors?" Chee purred.

Dagla frowned. Olgor's lips twitched upward.

"Chances must be taken." Dagla made a chopping gesture. "All we know is what was learned from your first radio communications, which said little. Morruchan was quick to isolate you. His hope is plainly to let you hear no more of the truth than he wants. To use you! Here, in this house, we may speak frankly with each other."

As frankly as you two klongs choose, Chee thought. "I listen with care," she said.

Piece by piece, between Dagla and Olgor, the story emerged. It sounded reasonable, as far as it went.

When the Survey team arrived, the Wilwidh culture stood on the brink of a machine age. The scientific method had been invented. There was a heliocentric astronomy, a post-Newtonian pre-Maxwellian physics, a dawning chemistry, a well-developed taxonomy, some speculations about evolution. Steam engines were at work on the first railroads. But political power was fragmented among the Vachs. The scientists, the engineers, the teachers were each under the patronage of one or another Hand.

The visitors from space had too much sense of responsibility to pass on significant practical information. It wouldn't have done a great deal of good anyway. How do you make transistors, for instance, before you can refine ultra-pure semimetals? And why should you want to, when you don't yet have electronics? But the humans had given theoretical and experimental science a boost by what they related—above all, by the simple and tremendous fact of their presence.

And then they left.

A fierce, proud, people had their noses rubbed in their own insignificance. Chee guessed that here lay the root of most of the social upheaval which followed. And belike a more urgent motive than curiosity, or profit, began to drive the scientists: the desire, the need to catch up, to bring Merseia in one leap onto the galactic scene.

The Vachs had shrewdly ridden the wave. Piecemeal they shelved their quarrels, formed a loose confederation, met the new problems well enough that no movement arose to strip them of their privileges. But rivalry persisted, and cross purposes, and often a reactionary spirit, a harking back to olden days when the young were respectful of the God and their elders.

And meanwhile modernization spread across the planet. A country which did not keep pace soon found itself under foreign domination. Lafdigu had succeeded best. Chee got a distinct impression that the Republic was actually a hobnail-booted dictatorship. Its own imperial ambitions clashed with those of the Hands. Nuclear war was averted on the ground, but space battles had erupted from time to time, horribly and inconclusively.

"So here we are," Dagla said. "Largest, most powerful, the Vach Dathyr speak loudest in this realm. But others press upon them, Hallen, Ynvory, Rueth, yes, even landless Urdiolch. You can see what it would mean if any one of them obtained your exclusive services."

Olgor nodded. "Among other things," he said, "Morruchan Long-Ax would like to contrive that my country is ignored. We are in the southern hemisphere. We will get the worst of the supernova blast. If unprotected, we will be removed from his equations."

"In whole truth, Shipmistress," Dagla added, "I don't believe Morruchan wants your help. *Khraich,* yes, a minimum, to forestall utter collapse. But he has long ranted against the modern world and its ways. He'd not be sorry to see industrial civilization reduced so small that full-plumed feudalism returns."

"How shall he prevent us from doing our work?" Chee asked. "Surely he is not fool enough to kill us. Others will follow."

"He'll bet the knucklebones as they fall," Dagla said. "At the very least, he'll try to keep his position—that you work through him and get most of your information from his sources—and use it to increase his power. At the expense of every other party!"

"We could predict it even in Lafdigu, when first we heard of your coming," Olgor said. "The Strategic College dispatched me here to make what alliances I can. Several Hands are not unwilling to see my country continue as a force in the world, as the price for our help in diminishing their closer neighbors."

Chee said slowly: "Meseems ye make no few assumptions about us, on scant knowledge."

"Shipmistress," said Olgor, "civilized Merseia has had two centuries to study each word, each picture, each legend about your people. Some believe you akin to gods—or demons—yes, whole cults have flowered from the expectation of your return, and I do not venture to guess what they will do now that you are come. But there have also been cooler minds; and that first expedition was honest in what it told, was it not?

"Hence: the most reasonable postulate is that none of the starfaring races have mental powers we do not. They simply have longer histories. And as we came to know how many the stars are, we saw how thinly your civilization must be spread among them. You will not expend any enormous effort on us, in terms of your own economy. You cannot. You have too much else to do. Nor have you time to learn everything about Merseia and decide every detail of what you will affect. The supernova will flame in our skies in less than three years. You must cooperate with whatever authorities you find, and take their word for what the crucial things are to save and what others must be abandoned. Is this not truth?"

Chee weighed her answer. "To a certain degree," she said carefully, "ye have right."

"Morruchan knows this," Dagla said. "He'll use the knowledge as best he can." He leaned forward, towering above her. "For our part, we will not tolerate it. Better the world go down in ruin, to be rebuilt by us, than that the Vach Dathyr engulf what our ancestors wrought. No planet-wide effort can succeed without the help of a majority. Unless we get a full voice in what decisions are made, we'll fight."

"Hand, Hand," reproved Olgor.

"Nay, I take not offense," Chee said. "Rather, I give thanks for so plain a warning. Ye will understand, we bear ill will toward none on Merseia, and have no partisanship—" *in your wretched little jockeyings.* "If ye have prepared a document stating your position, gladly will we ponder on the same."

Olgor opened a casket and took out a sheaf of papers bound in something like snakeskin. "This was hastily written," he apologized. "At another date we would like to give you a fuller account."

"'Twill serve for the nonce." Chee wondered if she should stay a while. No doubt she could learn something further. But chaos, how much propaganda she'd have to strain out of what she heard! Also, she'd now been diplomatic as long as anyone could expect. Hadn't she?

They could call the ship directly, she told them. If Morruchan tried to jam the airwaves, she'd jam him, into an unlikely posture. Olgor looked shocked. Dagla objected to communication which could be monitored. Chee sighed. "Well, then, invite us hither for a private talk," she said. "Will Morruchan attack you for that?"

"No...I suppose not...but he'll get some idea of what we know and what we're doing."

"My belief was," said Chee in her smoothest voice, "that the Hand of the Vach Hallen wished naught save an end to these intrigues and selfishnesses, an openness in which Merseians might strive together for the common welfare."

She had never cherished any such silly notion, but Dagla couldn't very well admit that his chief concern was to get his own relatives on top of everybody else. He made wistful noises about a transmitter which could not be detected by Merseian equipment. Surely the galactics had one? They did, but Chee wasn't about to pass on stuff with that kind of potentialities. She expressed regrets—nothing had been brought along—so sorry—good night, Hand, goodnight, Warmaster.

The guard who had let her in escorted her to the front door. She wondered why her hosts didn't. Caution, or just a different set of mores? Well, no matter. Back to the ship. She ran down the frosty street, looking for an alley from which her takeoff wouldn't be noticed. Someone might get trigger happy.

An entrance gaped between two houses. She darted into darkness. A body fell upon her. Other arms clasped tight, pinioning. She yelled. A light gleamed briefly, a sack was thrust over her head, she inhaled a sweet-sick odor and whirled from her senses.

Adzel still wasn't sure what was happening to him, or how it had begun. There he'd been, minding his own business, and suddenly he was the featured speaker at a prayer meeting. If that was what it was.

He cleared his throat. "My friends," he said.

A roar went through the hall. Faces and faces and faces stared at the rostrum which he filled with his four and a half meters of length. A thousand Merseians must be present: clients, commoners, city proletariat, drably clad for the most part. Many were female; the lower classes didn't segregate sexes as rigidly as the upper. Their odors made the air thick and musky. Being in a new part of Ardaig, the hall was built plain. But its proportions, the contrasting hues of paneling, the symbols painted in scarlet across the walls, reminded Adzel he was on a foreign planet.

He took advantage of the interruption to lift the transceiver hung around his neck up to his snout and mutter plaintively, "David, what *shall* I tell them?"

"Be benevolent and noncommittal," Falkayn's voice advised. "I don't think mine host likes this one bit."

The Wodenite glanced over the seething crowd, to the entrance. Three of Morruchan's household guards stood by the door.

He didn't worry about physical attack. Quite apart from having the ship for a backup, he was too formidable himself: a thousand-kilo centauroid, his natural armorplate shining green above and gold below, his spine more impressively ridged than any Merseian's. His ears were not soft cartilage but bony, a similar shelf protected his eyes, his rather crocodilian face opened on an alarming array of fangs. Thus he had been the logical member of the team to wander around the city today, gathering impressions. Morruchan's arguments against this had been politely overruled. "Fear no trouble, Hand," Falkayn said truthfully. "Adzel never seeketh any out. He is a Buddhist, a lover of peace who can well afford tolerance anent the behavior of others."

By the same token, though, he had not been able to refuse the importunities of the crowd which finally cornered him.

"Have you got word from Chee?" he asked.

"Nothing yet," Falkayn said. "Muddlehead's monitoring, of course. I imagine she'll contact us tomorrow. Now don't you interrupt me either. I'm in the middle of an interminable official banquet."

Adzel raised his arms for silence, but here that gesture was an encouragement for more shouts. He changed position, his hooves clattering on the platform, and his tail knocked over a floor candelabrum. "Oh, I'm sorry," he exclaimed. A red-robed Merseian named Gryf, the chief nut of this organization—Star Believers, was that what they called themselves?—picked the thing up and managed to silence the house.

"My friends," Adzel tried again. "Er...my friends. I am, er, deeply appreciative of the honor ye do me in asking for some few words." He tried to remember the political speeches he had heard while a student on Earth. "In the great fraternity of intelligent races throughout the universe, surely Merseia hath a majestic part to fulfill."

"Show us...show us the way!" howled from the floor. "The way, the truth, the long road futureward!"

"Ah...yes. With pleasure." Adzel turned to Gryf. "But perchance first your, er, glorious leader should explain to me the purposes of this...this—" What was the word for "club"? Or did he want "church"?

Mainly he wanted information.

"Why, the noble galactic jests," Gryf said in ecstasy. "You know we are those who have waited, living by the precepts the galactics taught, in loyal expectation of their return which they promised us. We are your chosen instrument for the deliverance of Merseia from its ills. Use us!"

Adzel was a planetologist by profession, but his large bump of curiosity had led him to study in other fields. His mind shuffled through books he had read, societies he had visited...yes, he identified the pattern. These were cultists, who'd attached a quasi-religious significance to what had actually been quite a casual stopover. Oh, the jewel in the lotus! What kind of mess had ensued?

He had to find out.

"That's, ah, very fine," he said. "Very fine indeed. Ah...how many do ye number?"

"More than two million, Protector, in twenty different nations. Some high ones are among us, yes, the Heir of the Vach Isthyr. But most belong to the virtuous poor. Had they all known the Protector was to walk forth this day—Well, they'll come as fast as may be, to hear your bidding."

An influx like that could make the pot boil over, Adzel foresaw. Ardaig had been restless enough as he quested through its streets. And what little had been learned about basic Merseian instincts, by the Survey psychologists, suggested they were a combative species. Mass hysteria could take ugly forms.

"No!" the Wodenite cried. The volume nearly blew Gryf off the podium. Adzel moderated his tone. "Let them stay home. Calm, patience, carrying out one's daily round of duties, those are the galactic virtues."

Try telling that to a merchant adventurer! Adzel checked himself. "I fear we have no miracles to offer."

He was about to say that the word he carried was of blood, sweat, and tears. But no. When you dealt with a people whose reactions you couldn't predict, such news must be released with care. Falkayn's first radio communications had been guarded, on precisely that account.

"This is clear," Gryf said. He was not stupid, or even crazy, except in his beliefs. "We must ourselves release ourselves from our oppressors. Tell us how to begin."

Adzel saw Morruchan's troopers grip their rifles tight. *We're expected to start some kind of social revolution?* he thought wildly. *But we can't! It's not our business. Our business is to save your lives, and for that we must not weaken but strengthen whatever authority can work with us, and any revolution will be slow to mature, a consequence of technology—Dare I tell them this tonight?*

Pedantry might soothe them, if only by boring them to sleep. "Among those sophonts who need a government," Adzel said, "the basic requirement for a government which is to function well is that it be legitimate, and the basic problem of any political innovator is how to continue, or else establish anew, a sound basis for that legitimacy. Thus newcomers like mineself cannot—"

He was interrupted—later he was tempted to say "rescued"—by a noise outside. It grew louder, a harsh chant, the clatter of feet on pavement. Females in the audience wailed. Males snarled and moved toward the door. Gryf sprang from the platform, down to what Adzel identified as a telecom, and activated the scanner. It showed the street, and an armed mob. High over them, against snow-laden roofs and night sky, flapped a yellow banner.

"Demonists!" Gryf groaned. "I was afraid of this."

Adzel joined him. "Who be they?"

"A lunatic sect. They imagine you galactics mean, have meant from the first, to corrupt us to our destruction. I was prepared, though. See." From alleys and doorways moved close-ranked knots of husky males. They carried weapons.

A trooper snapped words into the microphone of a walkie-talkie. Sending for help, no doubt, to quell the oncoming riot. Adzel returned to the rostrum and filled the hall with his pleas that everyone remain inside.

He might have succeeded, by reverberation if not reason. But his own transceiver awoke with Falkayn's voice: "Get here at once! Chee's been nabbed!"

"What? Who did it? Why?" The racket around became of scant importance.

"I don't know. Muddlehead just alerted me. She'd left this place she was at. Muddlehead received a yell, sounds of scuffling, then no more from her. I'm sending him aloft, to try and track her by the carrier wave. He says the source is moving. You move too, back to Afon."

Adzel did. He took part of the wall with him.

Korych rose through winter mists that turned gold as they smoked past city towers and above the river. Kettledrums rolled their ritual from Eidh Hill. Shutters came down off windows and doors, market circles began to fill, noise lifted out of a hundred small workshops. Distantly, but deeper and more portentous, sounded the buzz of traffic and power from the new quarters, hoot of ships on the bay, whine of jets overhead, thunder of rockets as a craft left the spaceport for the moon Seith.

Morruchan Long-Ax switched off the lights in his conference chamber. Dawnglow streamed pale through glass, picking out the haggardness of faces. "I am weary," he said, "and we are on a barren trail."

"Hand," said Falkayn, "it had better not be. Here we stay until we have reached some decision."

Morruchan and Dagla glared. Olgor grew expressionless. They were none of them accustomed to being addressed thus. Falkayn gave them stare for stare, and Adzel lifted his head from where he lay coiled on the floor. The Merseians slumped back onto their tails.

"Your whole world may be at stake, worthies," Falkayn said. "My people will not wish to spend time and treasure, aye, some lives, if they look for such ungrateful treatment."

He picked up the harness and kit which lay on Morruchan's desk and hefted them. Guided by Muddlehead, searchers from this household had found the apparatus in a ditch outside town and brought it here several hours ago. Clearly Chee's kidnappers had suspected a signal was being emitted. The things felt pitifully light in his hand.

"What more can be said?" Olgor argued. "We have each voiced a suspicion that one of the others engineered the deed to gain a lever for himself. Or yet a different Vach, or another nation, may have done it; or the Demonists; or even the Star Believers, for some twisted reason." He turned to Dagla. "Are you certain you have no inkling who that servant of yours may have been working for?"

"I told you before, no," said the Hallen chief. "It's not our way in this country to pry into lives. I know only that Dwyr entered my service a few years ago, and gave satisfaction, and now has also vanished. So I presume he was a spy for someone else, and told his masters of a chance to seize a galactic. A telecom call would be easy to make, and they needed only to cover the few possible routes she could take on leaving me."

"In sum," Morruchan declared, "he acted just like your spy who betrayed my doings to you."

"Enough, worthies," Falkayn sighed. "Too stinking often this night have we tracked the same ground. Perchance investigation will give some clues to this Dwyr, whence he came and so forth. But such taketh time. We must needs look into every possibility at once. Including your very selves. Best ye perform a mutual checking."

"And who shall do the like for you?" Morruchan asked.

"What meaneth the Hand?"

"This might be a trick of your own."

Falkayn clutched his hair. "For what conceivable reason?" He wanted to say more, but relations were strained already.

"How should I know?" Morruchan retorted. "You are unknowns. You *say* you have no imperial designs here, but your agents have met with rivals of mine, with a cult whose main hope is to upset the order of things—and with how many else? The Gethfennu?"

"Would the Hand be so gracious as to explain to me who those are?" said Adzel in an oil-on-the-waves voice.

"We described them already," Dagla answered.

"Then 'twas whilst I was out, Hand, directing our ship in its search and subsequent return to base. Indulge a humble fool's request, I beg you."

The idea of someone equipped like Adzel calling himself a humble fool took the Merseians so much aback that they forgot to stay angry. Falkayn added: "I'd not mind hearing about them again. Never suspected I their existence ere now."

"They are the criminal syndicate, spread across the world and on into space," Morruchan said. "Thieves, assassins, harlots, tricksters, corrupters of all good."

He went on, while Falkayn analyzed his words. No doubt the Gethfennu were a bad influence. But Morruchan was too prejudiced, and had too little historical sense, to see why they flourished. The industrial revolution had shaken foundation stones loose from society. Workers flocking to the cities found themselves cut off from the old feudal restrictions…and securities. Cultural and material impoverishment bred lawlessness. Yet the baronial tradition survived, in a distorted form; gangs were soon gathered into a network which offered members protection and purpose as well as loot.

The underground kingdom of the Gethfennu could not be destroyed by Vachs and nations divided against each other. It fought back too effectively, with money and influence more often than with violence. And, to be sure, it provided some safety valve. A commoner who went to one of its gambling dens or joy houses might get fleeced, but he would not plot insurrection.

So a tacit compromise was reached, the kind that many planets have known, Earth not least among them. Racketeering and vice were held to a tolerable level, confined to certain areas and certain classes, by the gang lords. Murder, robbery, and shakedown did not touch the aristocratic palace or the high financial office. Bribery did, in some countries, and thereby the Gethfennu was strengthened.

Of late, its tentacles had stretched beyond these skies. It bought into established interplanetary enterprises. And then there was Ronruad, the next planet out. Except for scientific research, it had scant intrinsic value, but bases upon it were of so great strategic importance that they had occasioned wars. Hence the last general peace treaty had neutralized it, placed it outside any jurisdiction. Soon afterward the Gethfennu took advantage of this by building a colony there, where anything went. A spaceship line, under the syndicate's open-secret control, offered passenger service. Luridor became the foremost town for respectable Merseians to go in search of unrestrained, if expensive, fun. It also became a hatchery of trouble, and Falkayn could understand why Morruchan didn't want it protected against the supernova.

Neither, he found, did Dagla. Probably few if any Hands did. Olgor was less emphatic, but agreed that, at best, Ronruad should get a very low priority.

"The Gethfennu may, then, have seized Chee Lan for ransom?" Adzel said.

"Perhaps," Dagla said. "Though the ransom may be that you galactics help them. If they've infiltrated Hand Morruchan's service too, they could know what the situation is."

"But," Falkayn objected, "they are scarcely so naive as to think—"

"I shall investigate," Morruchan promised. "I may make direct inquiry. But channels of communication with the Gethfennu masters are devious, therefore slow."

"In any event," Falkayn said bleakly, "Adzel and I do not propose to leave our partner in the grip of criminals—for years, after which they may cut her throat."

"You do not know they have her," Olgor reminded him.

"True. Yet may we prowl somewhat through space, out toward their colony. For little can we do on Merseia, where our knowledge is scant. Here must ye search, worthies, and contrive that all others search with you."

The command seemed to break Morruchan's thin-stretched patience. "Do you imagine we've nothing better to do than hunt for one creature? We, who steer millions?"

Falkayn lost his temper likewise. "If ye wish to keep on doing thus, best ye make the finding of Chee Lan your foremost concern!"

"Gently, gently," Olgor said. "We are so tired that we are turning on allies. And that is not well." He laid a hand on Falkayn's shoulder. "Galactic," he said, "surely you can understand that organizing a system-wide hunt, in a world as diverse as ours, is a greater task than the hunt itself. Why, no few leaders of nations, tribes, clans, factions will not believe the truth if they are told. Proving it to them will require diplomatic skill. Then there are others whose main interest will be to see if they cannot somehow maneuver this affair to give them an advantage over us. And yet others hope you do go away and never return; I do not speak merely of the Demonists."

"If Chee be not returned safely," Falkayn said, "those last may well get their wish."

Olgor smiled. The expression went no deeper than his lips. "Galactic," he murmured, "let us not play word games. Your scientists stand to win knowledge and prestige here, your merchants a profit. They will not allow an unfortunate incident, caused by a few Merseians and affecting only one of their folk…they will not let that come between them and their objectives. Will they?"

Falkayn looked into the ebony eyes. His own were the first to drop. Nausea caught at his gullet. The Warmaster of Lafdigu had identified his bluff and called it.

Oh, no doubt these who confronted him would mount some kind of search. If nothing else, they'd be anxious to learn what outfit had infiltrated agents onto their staffs, and to what extent. No doubt, also, various other Merseians would cooperate. But the investigation would be ill-coordinated and lackadaisical. It would hardly succeed against beings as wily as those who captured Chee Lan.

These three here—nigh the whole of Merseia—just didn't give a damn about her.

She awoke in a cell.

It was less than three meters long, half that in width and height: windowless, doorless, comfortless. A coat of paint did not hide the basic construction, which was of large blocks. Their unresponsiveness to her fist-pounding suggested a high density. Brackets were bolted into the walls, to hold equipment of different sorts in place. Despite non-Technic design, Chee recognized a glow lamp, a thermostated air renewer, a waste unit, an acceleration couch…space gear; by Cosmos!

No sound, no vibration other than the faint whirr of the air unit's fan, reached her. The walls were altogether blank. After a while, they seemed to move closer. She chattered obscenities at them.

But she came near weeping with relief when one block slid aside. A Merseian face looked in. Behind was polished metal. Rumble, clangor, shouted commands resounded through what must be a spaceship's hull, from what must be a spaceport outside.

"Are you well?" asked the Merseian. He looked still tougher than average, but he was trying for courtesy, and he wore a neat tunic with insignia of rank.

Chee debated whether to make a jump, claw his eyes out, and bolt for freedom. No, not a chance. But neither was she going to embrace him. "Quite well, I thank thee," she snarled, "if thou'lt set aside trifles such as that thy heart-rotten varlets have beaten and gassed me, and I am athirst and anhungered. For this outrage, methinks I'll summon my mates to blow thy pesthole of a planet from the universe it defileth."

The Merseian laughed. "You can't be too sick, with that kind of spirit. Here are food and water." He passed her some containers. "We blast off soon for a voyage of a few days. Do you need anything?"

"Where are we bound? Who art thou? What meaneth—"

"*Hurh,* little one, I'm not going to leave this smugglehole open very long, for any spillmouth to notice. Tell me this instant what you want, so I can try to have it sent from the city."

Later Chee swore at herself, more picturesquely than she had ever cursed even Adzel. Had she specified the right things, they might have been a clue for her partners. But she was too foggy in the head, too dazed by events. Automatically, she asked for books and films which might help her understand the Merseian situation better. And a grammar text, she added in haste. She was tired of sounding like a local Shakespeare. The Merseian nodded and pushed the block back in place. She heard a faint click. Doubtless a tongue-and-groove lock, operated by a magnetic key.

The rations were revivifying. Before long, Chee felt in shape to make deductions. She was evidently in a secret compartment, built into the wall of a radiation shelter.

Merseian interplanetary vessels ran on a thermonuclear-powered ion drive. Those which made landings—ferries tending the big ships, or special jobs such as this presumably was—set down in deep silos and departed from them, so that electromagnetic fields could contain the blast and neutralize it before it poisoned the neighborhood. And each craft carried a blockhouse for crew and passengers to huddle in, should they get caught by a solar storm. Altogether, the engineering was superb. Too bad it would go by the board as soon as gravity drive and force screens became available.

A few days, at one Merseian G: hm-m-m, that meant an adjacent planet. Not recalling the present positions, Chee wasn't sure which. A lot of space traffic moved in the Korychan System, as instruments had shown while *Muddlin' Through* approached. From a distance, in magniscreens, she had observed some of the fleet, capacious cargo vessels and sleek naval units.

Her captor returned with the materials she had requested and a warning to strap in for blastoff. He introduced himself genially as Iriad the Wayfarer, in charge of this dispatch boat.

"Who art thou working for?" Chee demanded.

He hesitated, then shrugged. "The Gethfennu." The block glided back to imprison her.

Lift was nothing like the easy upward floating of a galactic ship. Acceleration rammed Chee down into her couch and sat on her chest. Thunder shuddered through the very blockhouse. Eternal minutes passed before the pressure slacked off and the boat fell into steady running.

After that, for a timeless time, Chee had nothing to do but study. The officers brought her rations. They were a mixed lot, from every part of Merseia; some did not speak Eriau, and none had much to say to her. She considered tinkering her life support apparatus into a weapon, but without tools the prospect was hopeless. So for amusement she elaborated the things she would like to do to Iriad, come the day. Her partners would have flinched.

Once her stomach, the only clock she had, told her she was far overdue for a meal. When finally her cell was opened, she leaped forward in a whirlwind of abuse. Iriad stepped back and raised a pistol. Chee stopped and said: "Well, what happened? Hadn't my swill gotten moldy enough?"

Iriad looked shaken. "We were boarded," he said low.

"How's that?" Acceleration had never varied.

"By…your people. They laid alongside, matching our vector as easily as one runner might pace another. I did not know what armament they had, so—He, who came aboard, was a dragon."

Chee beat her fists on the shelter deck. Oh, no, no, no! Adzel had passed within meters of her, and never suspected…the big, ugly, vacuum-skulled bumblemaker!

Iriad straightened. "But Haguan warned me it might happen," he said with a return of self-confidence. "We know somewhat about smuggling. And you are not gods, you galactics."

"Where did they go?"

"Away. To inspect other vessels. Let them."

"Do you seriously hope to keep me hidden for long?"

"Ronruad is full of Haguan's boltholes." Iriad gave her her lunch, collected the empty containers, and departed.

He came back several meals later, to supervise her transferral from the cell to a packing crate. Under guns, Chee obeyed his instructions. She was strapped into padding, alongside an air unit, and left in darkness. There followed hours of maneuver, landing, waiting, being unloaded and trucked to some destination.

Finally the box was opened. Chee emerged slowly. Weight was less than half a standard G, but her muscles were cramped. A pair of workers bore the crate away. Guards stayed behind, with a Merseian who claimed to be a medic. The checkup he gave her was expert and sophisticated enough to bear him out. He said she should rest a while, and they left her alone.

Her suite was interior but luxurious. The food brought her was excellent. She curled in bed and told herself to sleep.

Eventually she was taken down a long, paneled corridor and up a spiral ramp to meet him who had ordered her caught.

He squatted behind a desk of dark, polished wood that looked a hectare in area. Thick white fur carpeted the room and muffled footsteps. Pictures glowed, music sighed, incense sweetened the air. Windows gave a view outside; this part of the warren projected aboveground. Chee saw ruddy sand, strange wild shrubbery, a dust storm walking across a gaunt range of hills and crowned with ice crystals. Korych stood near the horizon, shrunken, but fierce through the tenuous atmosphere. A few stars also shone in that purple sky. Chee recognized Valenderay, and shivered a little. So bright and steady it looked; and yet, at this moment, death was riding from it on the wings of light.

"Greeting, galactic." The Eriau was accented differently from Olgor's. "I am Haguan Eluatz. Your name, I gather, is Chee Lan."

She arched her back, bottled her tail, and spat. But she felt very helpless. The Merseian was huge, with a belly that bulged forward his embroidered robe. He was not of the Wilwidh stock, his skin was shiny black and heavily scaled, his eyes almond-shaped, his nose a scimitar.

One ring-glittering hand made a gesture. Chee's guards slapped tails to ankles and left. The door closed behind them. But a pistol lay on Haguan's desk, next to an intercom.

He smiled. "Be not afraid. No harm is intended you. We regret the indignities you have suffered and will try to make amends. Sheer necessity forced us to act."

"The necessity for suicide?" Chee snorted.

"For survival. Now why don't you make yourself comfortable on yonder couch? We have talk to forge, we two. I can send for whatever refreshment you desire. Some arthberry wine, perhaps?"

Chee shook her head, but did jump onto the seat. "Suppose you explain your abominable behavior," she said.

"Gladly." Haguan shifted the weight on his tail. "You may not know what the Gethfennu is. It came into being after the first galactics had departed. But by now—" He continued for a while. When he spoke of a system-wide syndicate, controlling millions of lives and uncounted wealth, strong enough to build its own city on this planet and clever enough to play its enemies off against each other so that none dared attack that colony: he was scarcely lying. Everything that Chee had seen confirmed it.

"Are we in this town of yours now?" she asked.

"No. Elsewhere on Ronruad. Best I not be specific. I have too much respect for your cleverness."

"And I have none for yours."

"*Khraich?* You must. I think we operated quite smoothly, and on such short notice. Of course, an organization like ours must always be prepared for anything. And we have been on special alert ever since your arrival. What little we have learned—" Haguan's gaze went to the white point of Valenderay and lingered. "That star, it is going to explode. True?"

"Yes. Your civilization will be scrubbed out unless—"

"I know, I know. We have scientists in our pay." Haguan leaned forward. "The assorted governments on Merseia see this as a millennial chance to rid themselves of the troublesome Gethfennu. We need only be denied help in saving our colony, our shipping, our properties on the home planet and elsewhere. Then we are finished. I expect you galactics would agree to this. Since not everything can be shielded in time, why not include us in that which is to be abandoned? You stand for some kind of law and order too, I suppose."

Chee nodded. In their mask of dark fur, her eyes smoldered emerald. Haguan had guessed shrewdly. The League didn't much care who it dealt with, but the solid citizens whose taxes were to finance the majority of the rescue operations did.

"So to win our friendship, you take me by force," she sneered halfheartedly.

"What had we to lose? We might have conferred with you, pleaded our cause, but would that have wrought good for us?"

"Suppose my partners recommend that no help be given your whole coprophagous Merseian race."

"Why, then the collapse comes," Haguan said with chilling calm, "and the Gethfennu has a better chance than most organizations of improving its relative position. But I doubt that any such recommendation will be made, or that your overlords would heed it if it were. So we need a coin to buy technical assistance. You."

Chee's whiskers twitched in a smile of sorts. "I'm scarcely that big a hostage."

"Probably not," Haguan agreed. "But you are a source of information."

The Cynthian's fur stood on end with alarm. "Do you have some skew-brained notion that I can tell you how to do everything for yourself? I'm not even an engineer!"

"Understood. But surely you know your way about in your own civilization. You know what the engineers can and cannot do. More important, you know the planets, the different races and cultures upon them, the mores, the laws, the needs. You can tell us what to expect. You can help us get interstellar ships—hijacking under your advice should succeed, being unlooked for—and show us how to pilot them, and put us in touch with someone who, for pay, will come to our aid."

"If you suppose for a moment that the Polesotechnic League would tolerate—"

Teeth flashed white in Haguan's face. "Perhaps it won't, perhaps it will. With so many stars, the diversity of peoples and interests is surely inconceivable. The Gethfennu is skilled in stirring up competition among others. What information you supply will tell us how, in this particular case. I don't really visualize your League, whatever it is, fighting a war—at a time when every resource must be devoted to saving Merseia—to prevent someone else rescuing us."

He spread his hands. "Or possibly we'll find a different approach," he finished. "It depends on what you tell and suggest."

"How do you know you can trust me?"

Haguan said like iron: "We judge the soil by what crops it bears. If we fail, if we see the Gethfennu doomed, we can still enforce our policy regarding traitors. Would you care to visit my punishment facilities? They are quite extensive. Even though you are of a new species, I think we could keep you alive and aware for many days."

Silence dwelt a while in that room. Korych slipped under the horizon. Instantly the sky was black, strewn with the legions of the stars, beautiful and uncaring.

Haguan switched on a light, to drive away that too enormous vision. "If you save us, however," he said, "you will go free with a very good reward."

"But—" Chee looked sickly into sterile years ahead of her. And the betrayal of friends, and scorn if ever she returned, a lifetime's exile. "You'll keep me till then?"

"Of course."

No success. No ghost of a clue. She was gone into an emptiness less fathomable than the spaces which gaped around their ship.

They had striven, Falkayn and Adzel. They had walked into Luridor itself, the sin-bright city on Ronruad, while the ship hovered overhead and showed with a single, rock-fusing flash of energy guns what power menaced the world. They had ransacked, threatened, bribed, beseeched. Sometimes terror met them, sometimes the inborn arrogance of Merseia's lords. But nowhere and never had anyone so much as hinted he knew who held Chee Lan or where.

Falkayn ran a hand through uncombed yellow locks. His eyes stood bloodshot in a sunken countenance. "I still think we should've taken that casino boss aboard and worked him over."

"No," said Adzel. "Apart from the morality of the matter, I feel sure that everyone who has any information is hidden away. That precaution is elementary. We're not even certain the outlaw regime is responsible."

"Yeh. Could be Morruchan, Dagla, Olgor, or colleagues of theirs acting unbeknownst to them, or any of a hundred other governments, or some gang of fanatics, or—Oh, *Judas*!"

Falkayn looked at the after viewscreen. Ronruad's tawny-red crescent was dwindling swiftly among the constellations, as the ship drove at full acceleration back toward Merseia. It was a dwarf planet, an ocherous pebble that would not make a decent splash if it fell into one of the gas giants. But the least of planets is still a world: mountains, plains, valleys, arroyos, caves, waters, square kilometers by the millions, too vast and varied for any mind to grasp. And Merseia was bigger yet; and there were others, and moons, asteroids, space itself.

Chee's captors need but move her around occasionally, and the odds against a fleetful of League detectives finding her would climb for infinity.

"The Merseians themselves are bound to have some notion where to look, what to do, who to put pressure on," he mumbled for the hundredth time. "We don't know the ins and outs. Nobody from our cultures ever will—five billion years of planetary existence to catch up with! We've got to get the Merseians busy. I mean really busy."

"They have their own work to do," Adzel said.

Falkayn expressed himself at pungent length on the value of their work. "How about those enthusiasts?" he wondered when he had calmed down a trifle. "The outfit you were talking to."

"Yes, the Star Believers should be loyal allies," Adzel said. "But most of them are poor and, ah, unrealistic. I hardly expect them to be of help. Indeed, I fear they will complicate our problem by starting pitched battles with the Demonists."

"You mean the anti-galactics?" Falkayn rubbed his chin. The bristles made a scratchy noise, in the ceaseless gentle thrum that filled the cabin. He inhaled the sour smell of his own weariness. "Maybe they did this."

"I doubt that. They must be investigated, naturally—a major undertaking in itself—but they do not appear sufficiently well organized."

"Damnation, if we don't get her back I'm going to push for letting this whole race stew!"

"You will not succeed. And in any event, it would be unjust to let millions die for the crime of a few."

"The millions jolly well ought to be tracking down the few. It's possible. There have to be some leads somewhere. If every single one is followed—"

The detector panel flickered. Muddlehead announced: "Ship observed. A chemical carrier, I believe, from the outer system. Range—"

"Oh, dry up," Falkayn said, "and blow away."

"I am not equipped to—"

Falkayn stabbed the voice cutoff button.

He sat for a while, then, staring into the stars. His pipe went out unnoticed between his fingers. Adzel sighed and laid his head down on the deck.

"Poor little Chee," Falkayn whispered at last. "She came a long way to die."

"Most likely she lives," Adzel said.

"I hope so. But she used to go flying through trees in an endless forest. Being caged will kill her."

"Or unbalance her mind. She is so easily infuriated. If anger can find no object, it turns to feed on itself."

"Well...you were always squabbling with her."

"It meant nothing. Afterward she would cook me a special dinner. Once I admired a painting of hers, and she thrust it into my hands and said, 'Take the silly thing, then,' like a cub that is too shy to say it loves you."

"Uh-huh."

The cutoff button popped up. "Course adjustment required," Muddlehead stated, "in order to avoid dangerously close passage by ore carrier."

"Well, do it," Falkayn rasped. "Destruction, but they've got a lot of space traffic!"

"Well, we are in the ecliptic plane, and as yet near Ronruad," Adzel said. "The coincidence is not great."

Falkayn clenched his hands. The pipestem snapped. "Suppose we strafe the ground," he said in a cold strange voice. "Not kill anyone. Burn up a few expensive installations, though, and promise more of the same. if they don't get off their duffs and start a real search for her."

"No. We have considerable discretion, but not that much."

"We could argue with the board of inquiry later."

"Such a deed would produce confusion and antagonism, and weaken the basis of the rescue effort. It might actually make rescue impossible. You have observed how basic pride is to the dominant Merseian cultures. An attempt to browbeat them, with no face-saving formula possible, might compel them to refuse galactic assistance. We would be personally, criminally responsible. I cannot permit it, David."

"So we can't do anything, not anything, to—"

Falkayn's words chopped off. He smashed a fist down on the arm of his pilot chair and surged to his feet. Adzel rose also, sinews drawn taut. He knew his partner.

Merseia hung immense, shining with oceans, blazoned with clouds and continents, rimmed with dawn and sunset and the deep sapphire of her sky. Her four small moons made a diadem. Korych flamed in plumage of zodiacal light.

Space cruiser *Yonuar*, United Fleet of the Great Vachs, swung close in polar orbit. Officially she was on patrol to stand by for possible aid to distressed civilian vessels. In fact she was there to keep an eye on the warcraft of Lafdigu, Wolder, the Nersan Alliance—any her masters mistrusted. And, yes, on the newcome galactics, if they returned hither. The God alone knew what they intended. One must tread warily and keep weapons close to hand.

On his command bridge, Captain Tryntaf Fangryf-Tamer gazed into the simulacrum tank and tried to imagine what laired among those myriad suns. He had grown up knowing that others flitted freely between them while his people were bound to this one system, and hating that knowledge. Now they were here once again—why? Too many rumors flew about. But most of them centered on the ominous spark called Valenderay.

Help; collaboration; were the Vach Isthyr to become mere clients of some outworld grotesque?

A signal fluted. The intercom said: "Radar Central to captain. Object detected on an intercept path." The figures which followed were unbelievable. No meteoroid, surely, despite an absence of jet radiation. Therefore, the galactics! His black uniform tunic grew taut around Tryntaf's shoulders as he hunched forward and issued orders. Battle stations: not that he was looking for trouble, but he was prudent. And if trouble came, he'd much like to see how well the alien could withstand laser blasts and nuclear rockets.

She grew in his screens, a stubby truncated raindrop, ridiculously tiny against the sea-beast hulk of *Yonuar*. She matched orbit so fast that Tryntaf heard the air suck in through his lips. Doom and death, why wasn't that hull broken apart and the crew smeared into a red layer? Some kind of counterfield…The vessel hung a few kilometers off and Tryntaf sought to calm himself. They would no doubt call him, and he must remain steady of nerve, cold of brain.

For his sealed orders mentioned that the galactics had left Merseia in anger, because the whole planet would not devote itself to a certain task. The Hands had striven for moderation; of course they would do what they reasonably could to oblige their guests from the stars, but they had other concerns, too. The galactics seemed unable to agree that the business of entire worlds was more important than their private wishes. Of necessity, such an attitude was met with haughtiness, lest the name of the Vachs, of all the nations, be lowered.

Thus, when his outercom screen gave him an image, Tryntaf kept one finger on the combat button. He had some difficulty hiding his revulsion. Those thin features, shock of hair, tailless body, fuzzed brown skin, were like a dirty caricature of Merseiankind. He would rather have spoken to the companion, whom he could see in the background. That creature was honestly weird.

Nonetheless, Tryntaf got through the usual courtesies and asked the galactic's business in a level tone.

Falkayn had pretty well mastered modern language by now. "Captain," he said, "I regret this and apologize, but you'll have to return to base."

Tryntaf's heart slammed. Only his harness prevented him from jerking backward, to drift across the bridge in the dreamlike flight of zero gravity. He swallowed and managed to keep his speech calm. "What is the reason?"

"We have communicated it to different leaders," said Falkayn, "but since they don't accept the idea, I'll also explain to you personally."

"Someone, we don't know who, has kidnapped a crew member of ours. I'm sure that you, Captain, will understand that honor requires we get her back."

"I do," Tryntaf said, "and honor demands that we assist you. But what has this to do with my ship?"

"Let me go on, please. I want to prove that no offense is intended. We have little time to make ready for the coming disaster, and few personnel to employ. The contribution of each is vital. In particular, the specialized knowledge of our vanished teammate cannot be dispensed with. So her return is of the utmost importance to all Merseians."

Tryntaf grunted. He knew the argument was specious, meant to provide nothing but an acceptable way for his people to capitulate to the strangers' will.

"The search for her looks hopeless when she can be moved about in space," Falkayn said. "Accordingly, while she is missing, interplanetary traffic must be halted."

Tryntaf rapped an oath. "Impossible."

"Contrariwise," Falkayn said. "We hope for your cooperation, but if your duty forbids this, we two can enforce the decree."

Tryntaf was astonished to hear himself, through a tide of fury, say just: "I have no such orders."

"That is regrettable," Falkayn said. "I know your superiors will issue them, but that takes time and the emergency will not wait. Be so good as to return to base."

Tryntaf's finger poised over the button. "And if I don't?"

"Captain, we shouldn't risk damage to your fine ship—"

Tryntaf gave the signal.

His gunners had the range. Beams and rockets vomited forth.

Not one missile hit. The enemy flitted aside, letting them pass, as if they were thrown pebbles. A full-power ray struck: but not her hull. Energy sparked and showered blindingly off some invisible barrier.

The little vessel curved about like an aircraft. One beam licked briefly from her snout. Alarms resounded. Damage Control cried, near hysteria, that armorplate had been sliced off as a knife might cut soft wood. No great harm done; but if the shot had been directed at the reaction-mass tanks—

"How very distressing, Captain," Falkayn said. "But accidents will happen when weapons systems are overly automated, don't you agree? For the sake of your crew, for the sake of your country whose ship is your responsibility, I do urge you to reconsider."

"Hold fire," Tryntaf gasped.

"You will return planetside, then?" Falkayn asked.

"I curse you, yes," Tryntaf said with a parched mouth.

"Good. You are a wise male, Captain. I salute you. Ah...you may wish to notify your fellow commanders elsewhere, so they can take steps to assure there will be no further accidents. Meanwhile, though, please commence re-entry."

Jets stabbed into space. *Yonuar*, pride of the Vachs, began her inward spiral.

And aboard *Muddlin' Through*, Falkayn wiped his brow and grinned shakily at Adzel. "For a minute," he said, "I was afraid that moron was going to slug it out."

"We could have disabled his command with no casualties," Adzel said, "and I believe they have lifecraft."

"Yes, but think of the waste; and the grudge." Falkayn shook himself. "Come on, let's get started. We've a lot of others to round up."

"Can we—a lone civilian craft—blockade an entire globe?" Adzel wondered. "I do not recall that it has ever been done."

"No, I don't imagine it has. But that's because the opposition has also had things like grav drive. These Merseian rowboats are something else again. And we need only watch this one planet. Everything funnels through it." Falkayn stuffed tobacco into a pipe. "Uh, Adzel, suppose you compose our broadcast to the public. You're more tactful than I am."

"What shall I say?" the Wodenite asked.

"Oh, the same guff as I just forked out, but dressed up and tied with a pink ribbon."

"Do you really expect this to work, David?"

"I've pretty high hopes. Look, all we'll call for is that Chee be left some safe place and we be notified where. We'll disavow every intention of punishing anybody, and we can make that plausible by pointing out that the galactics have to prove they're as good as their word if their mission is to have any chance of succeeding. If the kidnappers don't oblige—Well, first, they'll have the entire population out on a full-time hunt after them. And second, they themselves will be suffering badly from the blockade meanwhile. Whoever they are. Because you wouldn't have as much interplanetary shipping as you do, if it weren't basic to the economy."

Adzel shifted in unease. "We must not cause anyone to starve."

"We won't. Food isn't sent across space, except gourmet items; too costly. How often do I have to explain to you, old thickhead? What we will cause is that everybody loses money. Megacredits per diem. And Very Important Merseians will be stranded in places like Luridor, and they'll burn up the maser beams ordering their subordinates to remedy that state of affairs. And factories will shut down, spaceports lie idle, investments crumble, political and military balances get upset…You can fill in the details."

Falkayn lit his pipe and puffed a blue cloud. "I don't expect matters will go that far, actually," he went on. "The Merseians are as able as us to foresee the consequences. Not a hypothetical disaster three years hence, but money and power eroding away right now. So they'll put it first on their agenda to find those kidnappers and take out resentment on them. The kidnappers will know this and will also, I trust, be hit in their personal breadbasket. I bet in a few days they'll offer to swap Chee for an amnesty."

"Which I trust we will honor," Adzel said.

"I told you we'll have to. Wish we didn't."

"Please don't be so cynical, David. I hate to see you lose merit."

Falkayn chuckled. "But I make profits. Come on, Muddlehead, get busy and find us another ship."

The teleconference room in Castle Afon could handle a sealed circuit that embraced the world. On this day it did.

Falkayn sat in a chair he had brought, looking across a table scarred by the daggers of ancestral warriors, to the mosaic of screens which filled the opposite wall. A hundred or more Merseian visages lowered back at him. On that scale, they had no individuality. Save one: a black countenance ringed by empty frames. No lord would let his image stand next to that of Haguan Eluatz.

Beside the human, Morruchan, Hand of the Vach Dathyr, rose and said with frigid ceremoniousness: "In the name of the God and the blood, we are met. May we be well met. May wisdom and honor stand shield to shield…" Falkayn listened with half an ear. He was busy rehearsing his speech. At best, he was in for a cobalt bomb's worth of trouble.

No danger, of course. *Muddlin' Through* hung plain in sight above Ardaig. Television carried that picture around Merseia. And it linked him to Adzel and Chee Lan, who waited at the guns. He was protected.

But what he had to say could provoke a wrath so great that his mission was wrecked. He must say it with infinite care, and then he must hope.

"…Obligation to a guest demands we hear him out," Morruchan finished brusquely.

Falkayn stood up. He knew that in those eyes he was a monster, whose motivations were not understandable and who had proven himself dangerous. So he had dressed in his plainest gray zipsuit, and was unarmed, and spoke in soft words.

"Worthies," he said, "forgive me that I do not use your titles, for you are of many ranks and nations. But you are those who decide for your whole race. I hope you will feel free to talk as frankly as I shall. This is a secret and informal conference, intended to explore what is best for Merseia.

"Let me first express my heartfelt gratitude for your selfless and successful labors to get my teammate returned unharmed. And let me also thank you for indulging my wish that the, uh, chieftain Haguan Eluatz participate in this honorable assembly, albeit he has no right under law to do so. The reason shall soon be explained. Let me, finally, once again express my regret at the necessity of stopping your space commerce, for however brief a period, and my thanks for your cooperation in this emergency measure. I hope that you will consider any losses made good, when my people arrive to help you rescue your civilization.

"Now, then, it is time we put away whatever is past and look to the future. Our duty is to organize that great task. And the problem is, how shall it be organized? The galactic technologists do not wish to usurp any Merseian authority. In fact, they could not. They will be too few, too foreign, and too busy. If they are to do their work in the short time available, they must accept the guidance of the powers that be. They must make heavy use of existing facilities. That, of course, must be authorized by those who control the facilities. I need not elaborate. Experienced leaders like yourselves, worthies, can easily grasp what is entailed."

He cleared his throat. "A major question, obviously, is: With whom shall our people work most closely? They have no desire to discriminate. Everyone will be consulted, within the sphere of his time-honored prerogatives. Everyone will be aided, as far as possible. Yet, plain to see, a committee of the whole would be impossibly large and diverse. For setting overall policy, our people require a small, unified Merseian council, whom they can get to know really well and with whom they can develop effective decision-making procedures.

"Furthermore, the resources of this entire system must be used in a coordinated way. For example, Country One cannot be allowed to hoard minerals which Country Two needs. Shipping must be free to go from any point to any other. And all available shipping must be pressed into service. We can furnish radiation screens for your vessels, but we cannot furnish the vessels themselves in the numbers that are needed. Yet at the same time, a certain amount of ordinary activity must continue. People will still have to eat, for instance. So—how do we make a fair allocation of resources and establish a fair system of priorities?

"I think these considerations make it obvious to you, worthies, that an international organization is absolutely essential, one which can *impartially* supply information, advice, and coordination. If it has facilities and workers of its own, so much the better.

"Would that such an organization had legal existence! But it does not, and I doubt there is time to form one. If you will pardon me for saying so, worthies, Merseia is burdened with too many old hatreds and jealousies to join overnight in brotherhood. In fact, the international group must be watched carefully, lest it try to aggrandize itself or diminish others. We galactics can do this with one organization. We cannot with a hundred.

"So." Falkayn longed for his pipe. Sweat prickled his skin. "I have no plenipotentiary writ. My team is merely supposed to make recommendations. But the matter is so urgent that whatever scheme we propose will likely be adopted, for the sake of getting on with the job. And we have found one group which transcends the rest. It pays no attention to barriers between people and people. It is large, powerful, rich, disciplined, efficient. It is not exactly what my civilization would prefer as its chief instrument for the deliverance of Merseia. We would honestly rather it went down the drain, instead of becoming yet more firmly entrenched. But we have a saying that necessity knows no law."

He could feel the tension gather, like a thunderstorm boiling up; he said fast, before the explosion came; "I refer to the Gethfennu."

What followed was indescribable.

But he was, after all, only warning of what his report would be. He could point out that he bore a grudge of his own, and was setting it aside for the common good. He could even, with considerable enjoyment, throw some imaginative remarks about ancestry and habits in the direction of Haguan—who grinned and looked smug. In the end, hours later, the assembly agreed to take the proposal under advisement. Falkayn knew what the upshot would be. Merseia had no choice.

The screens blanked.

Wet, shaking, exhausted, he looked across a stillness into the face of Morruchan Long-Ax. The Hand loomed over him. Fingers twitched longingly near a pistol butt. Morruchan said, biting off each word: "I trust you realize what you are doing. You're not just perpetuating that gang. You're conferring legitimacy on them. They will be able to claim they are now a part of recognized society."

"Won't they, then, have to conform to its laws?" Falkayn's larynx hurt, his voice was husky.

"Not them!" Morruchan stood brooding a moment. "But a reckoning will come. The Vachs will prepare one, if nobody else does. And afterward—Are you going to teach us how to build stargoing ships?"

"Not if I have any say in the matter," Falkayn replied.

"Another score. Not important in the long run. We're bound to learn a great deal else, and on that basis...well, galactic, our grandchildren will see."

"Is ordinary gratitude beneath your dignity?"

"No. There'll be enough soft-souled dreambuilders, also among my race, for an orgy of sentimentalism. But then you'll go home again. I will abide."

Falkayn was too tired to argue. He made his formal farewells and called the ship to come get him.

Later, hurtling through the interstellar night, he listened to Chee's tirade: "...I still have to get back at those greasepaws. They'll be sorry they ever touched me."

"You don't aim to return, do you?" Falkayn asked.

"Pox, no!" she said. "But the engineers on Merseia will need recreation. The Gethfennu will supply some of it, gambling, especially, I imagine. Now if I suggest our lads carry certain miniaturized gadgets which can, for instance, control a wheel—"

Adzel sighed. "In this splendid and terrible cosmos," he said, "why must we living creatures be forever perverse?"

A smile tugged at Falkayn's mouth. "We wouldn't have so much fun otherwise," he said.

Men and not-men were still at work when the supernova wave front reached Merseia.

Suddenly the star filled the southern night, a third as brilliant as Korych, too savage for the naked eye to look at. Blue-white radiance flooded the land, shadows were etched sharp, trees and hills stood as if illuminated by lightning. Wings beat upward from forests, animals cried through the troubled air, drums pulsed and prayers lifted in villages which once had feared the dark for which they now longed. The day that followed was lurid and furious.

Over the months, the star faded, until it became a knifekeen point and scarcely visible when the sun was aloft. But it waxed in beauty, for its radiance excited the gas around it, so that it gleamed amidst a whiteness which deepened at the edge to blue-violet and a nebular lacework which shone with a hundred faerie hues. Thence also, in Merseia's heaven, streamed huge shuddering banners of aurora, whose whisper was heard even on the ground. An odor of storm was blown on every wind.

Then the nuclear rain began. And nothing was funny any longer.

Untitled Song
(Melody obvious)

I wandered today to the hill, Maggie,
although it has been bulldozed low.
The creek's thick with gunk from the mill, Maggie,
the tract houses jammed row on row.
The air is mephitic and gray, Maggie,
the grass dead where concrete has been flung.
Let us sing of the progress they've made, Maggie,
since you and I were young.

Sunjammer

Ol' Jonah was a transporteer, he was, he was.
Ol' Jonah was a transporteer, he was, he was.
  A storm at sea was getting mean,
  So he invented the submarine.
Bravo, bravo, hurrah for the transporteers!

Lazing along a cometary orbit, a million-odd miles from Earth, herdship *Merlin* resembled nothing so much as a small bright spider which had decided to catch an elephant and had spun its web accordingly. The comparison was not too farfetched. Sometimes a crew on the Beltline found they had gotten hold of a very large beast indeed.

Stars crowded the blackness in the control cabin viewports, unwinking wintry points of brilliance; the Milky Way cataracted around the sky, the Andromeda galaxy shimmered mysterious across a million and a half lightyears. The sunward port had automatically closed off, refusing so gross an overload for itself and its men. But Earth was visible in the adjacent frame, a cabochon of clear and lovely blue, with Luna a tarnished pearl beyond.

Sam Storrs, who was on watch, didn't sit daydreaming over the scene as Edward West would probably have done. He admitted there were few better sights in the System, but he'd seen it before and that wasn't his planet yonder. He was a third-generation asterite, a gaunt, crease-cheeked, prematurely balding man who remembered too well the brother he had lost in the Revolution.

Since there was no work for him at the moment, he was trying to read Levinsohn's "Principles of Modern Political Economy." It took concentration, and the whanging of a guitar from the saloon didn't help. He scowled as Andy Golescu's voice continued to butcher the melody.

King Solomon was a transporteer, he was, he was.
King Solomon was a transporteer, he was, he was.
  He shipped his wood on a boat for hire,
  'Cuz a wheel's no good without a Tyre.
Bravo, bravo, hurrah for the transporteers!

"Ye gods," Storrs muttered, "how sophomoric is an adult allowed to get?"

He reached for the intercom switch, with the idea of asking Golescu to stop. But his hand withdrew. Better not. It'd be a long time yet before their orbit brought them back to Pallas and the end of their patrol, even though the run would be finished under power. Crew solidarity was as important to survival as the nuclear generator.

And Andy's O.K., Storrs argued to himself. *He just happens to be from Ceres. What do you expect of anyone growing up in that kind of hedonistic boom town atmosphere? It was different for me, out on the Trojans.* His mouth bent wryly upward. *There puritanism still has survival value.*

No doubt the company psychomeds had known what they were doing when they picked Storrs, West, and Golescu to operate *Merlin*. You needed a balance of personality types...Storrs wondered about asking for a transfer when they returned to base.

Ulysses was a transporteer, he was, he was...

The long-range radio receiver buzzed and flashed a red light. Storrs jerked in his seat. What the hell? That was no distress signal from a sunjammer. A widebeam call on the common band—He sucked in a breath and snapped the Accept switch.

...He stopped at Calypso's isle for beer,
And, didn't proceed for ten more years...

The loud-speaker seethed with cosmic static. A voice cut through. "International Space Control Central calling Beltline Transportation Company maintenance ship number 11, computed to be in Sector Charlie. Come in, number 11...International Space Control—"

"Here we are." Storrs recollected his dignity. No Earthling was going to say that a citizen of the Asteroid Republic didn't know the rituals. "Maintenance ship 11, *Merlin* out of Pallas, Storrs on duty, acknowledging call from International Space Control Central," he intoned. "My precise position and orbit are—" He read the figure off the autonavigator screen.

There was no need for him to adjust the transceiver web outside the hull. Its detector antenna had already fixed the direction of the incoming beam, and now the maser swung itself about to face squarely that way. The ship counter-rotated a trifle. Storrs touched the controls. The generator purred, power ran into the Emetts, the field drive dissipated angular momentum into the general mass-energy background of the universe.

Columbus was a transporteer, he was, he was.
Columbus was a transporteer, he was, he was.
 They put the royal crown in pawn.
 To shut him up and move him on.
Bravo...

Golescu must have noticed the motion all at once, to judge from how his singing cut off. Storrs flipped the intercom open. "Got a call from Earth," he said hurriedly. "I don't know why, but assume condition red."

Feet clattered on the decks. Storrs' skin began to prickle. What the blazes was going on? Earth's SCC knew approximately where *Merlin* was, of course. Every herdship's orbit went on file in every traffic monitoring station throughout the System. If an orbit was changed, that news was also beamcast between the planets. But it was strictly an in-case precaution. The messages which drew a herdship off her path had always been automatic: beeps from a sailship whose interior sensors had registered trouble.

Always—until now?

His signal had leaped forth. Half a dozen seconds later it had reached the relay stations orbiting Earth. The operator stopped chanting, heard Storrs out, and began to talk back.

"International Space Control Central acknowledging reply from maintenance ship 11. Stand by, please. I'm going to switch you over to the main office, groundside."

A low whistle drifted from the intercom. Golescu, posted at the engine, had heard. West came in the door, puffing from the climb up the companionway. He was a large man, his hair grizzled, face and stomach sagging a bit with middle age. But he was still highly able, Storrs admitted, and decent for an Earthman. To be sure, it helped that he was British. The Revolution had been fought mostly against North Americans.

"Must be something big, eh?" West said. "Headquarters and all that." He settled himself in the navigator's chair.

"Hello, *Merlin*," said a new voice on the radio. It was a deep baritone, clipped but heavy with authority. "Evan Bailey speaking, assistant director of ISCC's Bureau of Safety." This time it was West who whistled. A message from so high an official of the World Interplanetary Commission, relayed straight from his personal desk—!

"A serious emergency has come up," Bailey went on. "There's no time to lose. Calculate an interception curve for sailship number 128, that's one-two-eight. Assume that you start acceleration at maximum thrust in, well, fifteen minutes. As soon as possible, anyhow. Is there by any chance another craft like yours reasonably near? We have no record of one ourselves, but there might have been some filing error. And you'll want every piece of help you can get."

"No," Storrs answered. "Nothing. The herdships are few and far between. You're lucky we happen to be this close to you right now."

That was not entirely coincidence. The orbits of the maintenance ships were planned to keep them never too distant from the great vessels of the Beltline. Some of the best mathematicians in the Republic had worked out the formulas for optimization of paths followed by sail and power craft: an intricate, forever changing figure dance across half the Solar System.

Storrs sat up straight. "So what's the trouble?" he finished.

West's fingers had been playing a tattoo on the keys before him. A tape popped out with the information he wanted. "One-two-eight," he murmured. "Yes, here we are. Cargo of...I say, this is an odd one. She's carrying eight hundred metric tons of isonitrate from the Sword's Jovian-orbit plant. Right now she's approaching Earth, only about six thousand miles away, in fact. There were no indications of trouble during her passage."

"Isonitrate what?" Golescu inquired over the intercom.

"An important industrial chemical," West explained. "Alkali complex of 2,4-benzoisopro—"

"Never mind," Golescu said. "I'm sorry I asked. Uh, everything's O.K. with our engines, if the gauges aren't liars."

Bailey had hesitated a while at the other end. Storrs could visualize the man, plump in a lounger behind several acres of mahogany desk, sweating with fear that something might happen to interrupt his placid climb through the bureaucracy. His words, when they came, wavered slightly.

"The sun is going to flare."

"What?" Storrs jumped to his feet. An oath from Golescu bounced through the intercom. West paused at his work, hands frozen on the keys. After a second he grunted, like someone struck a body blow, and went back to setting up the computation of thrust vectors.

"No!" Storrs protested. "Can't be! This is a clear weather season." His eyes went past the stars, sought the one blank port, and clung there.

"My office issues more storm warnings than you perhaps realize," Bailey told him. "The big flare cycles are predictable far in advance these days, but indications that a small, short-lived one is going to occur are often not observable more than forty-eight hours ahead." His tone grew patronizing. "'Clear weather season' means only a period in which there will be no major flares and the probability of minor ones is low. Still finite, however. You asterites don't have to worry about solar radiation out where you are, so perhaps you forget these details. Around Earth, we're highly conscious of them."

You smug planethugger! Storrs hung onto politeness with both hands. "I know the details well enough," he said stiffly. "After all, Mr. Bailey, every man aboard a herdship holds a master's certificate. I was only shocked. It seemed unbelievable that a cargo of isonitrate would be shipped, if there was any measurable chance of a flare while the vessel was inside the orbit of Mars."

The beam went forth. While they waited for reply, West said in a mild voice, "Call it an unmeasurable chance, then, Sam. The chap's right, you know. Solar meteorology is still not a completed science. It's either assume the hazard, knowing you'll lose an occasional ship, or else have no space traffic whatsoever. A coincidence like this one was bound to happen sooner or later."

"But for crying in the beer!" exclaimed Golescu from aft. "Why couldn't it have happened to a cargo of metal?"

"It does, quite often," Storrs reminded him. "Metal isn't hurt by radiation. Remember?" Sarcastically: "I've heard you gripe so often about how dull these cruises are most of the time. Well, here's your chance for some action."

Bailey had hung fire again. A rustle, penetrating the dry star-whisper, suggested he had been searching through a report prepared for him. "The flare is expected in about twelve hours," he said. "Predicted duration is three hours. Estimated peak radiation rate in Earth's vicinity is four thousand roentgens per hour. As you know, that will cause the isonitrate to explode."

Storrs exploded himself. *"Twelve hours!* You must'a known about it at least two days ago! Why didn't you alert us then? It'll take us two of those blithering hours just to make rendezvous!"

"Take it easy there, Sam," West said *sotto voce*. "Some of those high caste officials are even touchier than that isonitrate."

As if in confirmation, Bailey's words turned hard. "Kindly watch your language, captain. The delay is unfortunate, I admit, but no one is to blame. The prediction was issued in the usual way, and records were checked as per regulations. The nearness of 128 was noted. However, it is an unmanned craft. You can't expect an ordinary clerk to know the danger involved in its particular cargo. That was only pointed out when the data reached my office for the routine double check. And then a policy decision had to be reached. We haven't the lugger capacity to unload so much material in time. It would have been simple for us to send a crew out to bleed off the gas and thereby save the sailship from being destroyed. But a staff physicist showed that this was impossible. I was informed of the dilemma the moment I came back from lunch, and immediately ordered that contact be made with the nearest herdship. What more do you want, man?"

Storrs choked. *Though I should have expected this*, he thought in a distant part of himself. *There isn't a government of any importance on Earth these days that isn't based on some version of "social justice." So of course independent thinking, conscientiousness, ordinary competence have gone by the board.*

He unpinched his lips, sat down again, and said, "Well, Mr. Bailey, you might as well order that crew of yours to jettison. We can't do anything more than that ourselves. Or have you some alternative suggestion?"

Waiting out the transmission lag, he heard Golescu say, "Whoof! Looks as if there's going to be more excitement than I bargained for."

West uttered a small chuckle. "Weren't you caroling about the mad, merry life of a transporteer?"

"Shucks, Ed, I was only practicing my act. Those blooming glamour boys from the scoopships and the prospector teams have been latching on to all the girls back home. Something's got to be done for our kind of spaceman."

"That gas must positively not be released so close to Earth." Bailey stated. "It would contaminate the entire inner region, causing damage estimated at ten billion dollars. You may valve it out when you are no less than a hundred thousand miles from Earth sea level and/or basic Lunar surface. That's a direct order, by my authority under this jurisdiction and the Interplanetary Navigation agreement. Are you recording? I repeat—"

"Judas priest!" Golescu yelled. "You expect us to haul away a bomb?"

A humming silence fell over the ship. Storrs became acutely aware of how the stars glistened, the power plant and ventilators murmured, the deck quivered ever so slightly with energies. He felt the roughness of his coverall on his skin, which had become damp and sharp-smelling. He stared at the meters on the pilot panel, and they stared back like troll eyes, and still the silence waxed.

Bailey broke it. "Yes. Unless you have some other plan, we do expect you to remove that stuff to a safe distance. Under terms of your company's franchise for Terrestrial operations, it is your responsibility to dispose of this object in a manner not injurious to the public well-being. What's the problem, anyway? According to your rated thrust, you should be able to get the sailship's cargo section far enough away in four or five hours."

"The hell you say," Storrs barked. "We can't use full power on that big an outside load. Too much inertia. We'd rip our hull open. One third of max'll be risky enough. And we've got to uncouple the sail first, to get proper trim—at least two hours' work." Desperately: "You're giving us no safety margin. You know as well as I do, flare time can't be predicted much closer than an hour. If it happens sooner than you claim, and the radiation sweeps over us before we can disengage and get clear—and *that* takes time—the explosion will destroy us. And you'll still have space contamination. Plus a lot of ship fragments."

"Also people fragments," Golescu chimed in. "We got a legal right to refuse an impossible job, don't we?"

"But not an improbable one," West said. His gaze went to Earth. "I did want to see Blighty again."

"You will," Storrs said. "We're not going to commit suicide for the benefit of a lot of Earthlings."

"Like me, Sam?" West asked softly.

Bailey came back on: "You are not expected to act without due precautions. You can safely tow at the end of a cable several miles long, can't you?"

"Know how much mass that adds?" Storrs snapped. "But never mind. The fact is, our class of ship isn't designed for cable tows. We hook on directly by geegee. A cable 'ud tear us apart, just like hauling under max thrust."

"Wait a bit," West interrupted. He had skippered a European League ship before he reached compulsory retirement age and Beltline made him an offer. Asterite law based retirement on medical data rather than the calendar. "I know what sort of boat can do a cable tow. Not an ordinary tug—I mean the kind that starts a sailship off. It hasn't enough power, considering how fast we'll have to work. But a North American Navy tug of the *Hercules* class would serve. I should think four of them could be hitched on without their drive fields interfering. Or perhaps you can borrow some *Kubilai* types from the Asians. With that many engines at work, we can cover the required distance in ample time. Have 'em there when we arrive, will you? We'll make the attachments and supervise the whole job."

Again the wait was longer than transmission lag would account for. At last Bailey's voice came, so small and shaken that the noise of the universe nearly drowned it. "I...guess you don't know. Both fleets are out near Venus. Joint maneuvers."

After a moment, assuming briskness like a garment: "We'll do what we can. Alert the International Rescue Service. Commandeer whatever else we can find that may be of help. I can't make any promises, with so little time to go through channels. But I'll do whatever is humanly possible."

"Amoebically possible, you mean," Storrs said. He managed to keep it under his breath. Shaking himself, he answered aloud:

"We'll get started now. Have to fold our radio-radar net. Acceleration forces would wreck it otherwise. When we've made rendezvous with 128, we'll call you on the short-range 'caster. Stand by for that. Over."

He didn't wait for a response, but snapped off transmission as if the switch were Evan Bailey's neck.

Once the web had been pulled in by the appropriate machinery and acceleration had commenced, there was little for men to do until the end of the run. But doctrine required that Storrs remain on the bridge during his pilot watch—in which time he was also the captain. He roused from a period of angry lip-gnawing and said, "How about fixing us some chow? God only knows when we'll get our next chance to eat, and he isn't passing the information on."

"Right-o." West heaved his bulk out of the navigator's chair and started aft.

His body dragged at him as he went down the companionway and along the passage to the galley. There was, of course, no sensation of the ten gravities under which *Merlin* hurtled Earthward. The Emetts acted equally on every object inboard, and normally to the internal gyrogravitic field which furnished weight. But sometimes he wished the latter weren't kept at the standard Earth gee. One of the few things he really liked about the asteroids was the sense of buoyancy on a rock where pull generators had not yet been installed. It was almost like being young again.

Oh, stop kidding yourself. Also stop feeling sorry for yourself. He squeezed into the galley and got to work. Herdships always carried a gourmet assortment of food, as one means of keeping up morale on their long lonely cruises. West enjoyed exploring the potentialities, whenever his turn came to cook. And he had the honor of his country to defend as well, against that ancient canard about English cuisine. Even now, he built the sandwiches as elaborately as any Dane. But his mind was elsewhere.

How much risk are we obliged to run?

Under the law, a transporteer crew had the right to refuse a task as being too dangerous. Afterward they would have to face a board of inquiry, and Beltline might well decide to fire them. *(Would I honestly mind that?)* In this particular instance, though, they'd probably be cleared. *Merlin* represented a considerable investment. The company's cost accountants would not be happy if she were lost. In fact, if the isonitrate was simply released into space, a moderately expensive sailship could also be saved.

However, that might well embroil Beltline in legal action, considering how much economic damage Earth would suffer. No one could hold anyone responsible for the sun's picking this day to flare. But a lawyer could argue that Beltline's agents had made no effort to rescue the situation, and therefore a whopping claim should be paid. Earth's SCC might be put under pressure to rescind the

Terrestrial franchise. A protracted court battle, even if won, would doubtless prove more costly than two ships and three men.

West shook his head. *That's another thing I don't like about the Republic. They can brag as much as they want about free enterprise, but it still amounts to the rawest, most cold-blooded kind of capitalism. Maybe the welfare states on Earth have gotten stuffy and over-bureaucratized—nevertheless, we don't let the devil take the hindmost!*

He put the food and a pot of coffee on a tray and went forward. Storrs was busy with a slide rule and some bescribbled sheets of paper. He grabbed a sandwich with an automatic "Thanks," and chewed as he worked on. Rations, to him, were only fuel; West and Golescu never looked forward to his turn in the galley.

"What're you doing?" the Englishman asked.

"Trying to figure if we can't boil off some of the liquid as we tow, so gradually that it won't affect space too much, so fast that we'll shed noticeable mass. But hell and sulfur! I don't have the thrust parameter. Not knowing what sort of tugs we'll have available—How about hitching that Bailey character to the load and cracking a whip over him? A big wire whip hooked up to five hundred volts AC."

West achieved a smile. "What'd he push against?"

"Hm-m·m, yeah, that's right. O.K., we'll get extra reaction by cutting Bailey into small pieces—very, very small pieces—and pitching him aft."

West's look moved out to Earth. The half disk was becoming a crescent as *Merlin* approached the spaceward side, but it was also rapidly growing. He traced bands that were clouds, white in a summer sky, the mirror sheen of ocean and the blurred greenish-brown coast of Europe.

"Don't be too hard on the man, Sam," he said. "When a world gets as crowded as that one there, you have to operate by quite a rigid system. Within the system, I presume he's doing his best."

Storrs spoke an obscenity. "A machine is judged by its output. How's your precious system performing in this mess?"

"Oh, forget the political arguments. There's England."

Storrs' features softened a trifle. "Kind of tough, huh? Passing this close to your wife and not getting a chance to see her."

West thought of the little house in Kent, where the hollyhocks would now be in bloom, so tall that they overshadow the windows. He shrugged. "I knew what I was letting myself in for when I signed up as a transporteer."

Five years on the Beltline. I've waited out not quite three of them so far.

He stared spaceward. Illimitable emptiness gaped at him, from here to the frost-cold stars. Out there plodded the sailships, unmanned, driven by the sun, slowly but cheaply carrying nonperishable cargo from the mineral-rich asteroids and the chemical-rich Jovian atmosphere to an Earth grown gaunt in natural resources, returning with such manufactured goods as the Republic had not yet gotten around to producing for itself. And there, too, flitted the herdships on the interweaving orbits, *Apollonius of Tyana, Simon Magus, Hermes Trismegistus,*

Morgan le Fay, Gandalf, a score of them with radio webs outreaching, listening until an automaton cried for help. It was a chilly concept, somehow. He shivered.

Two more years.

After that, the real retirement, with Mary in flowering Kent. He didn't yet know if his decision had been right. Gardens, green hills, four-hundred-year-old homes, were not anything a man could afford on a space officer's pension. Not with today's land values and taxes. But the pay scale in the asteroids was fantastic, the Republic did not levy on income, and Earth needed outplanet exchange so badly that every Terrestrial government also exempted such earnings from impost. The house would be mortgage free by the time he came back to Mary, and there would be enough in the bank as well for them to do everything they once promised themselves.

On the other hand, they paid for it with five years when they might have been together.

And if he got killed, they never would collect the goods. Mary would have to move in with one of the kids, and—

West picked up the tray. "I'll take Andy his lunch," he said.

Storrs nodded absent-mindedly and returned to his calculations, No doubt they were his form of escape.

Passing through the tiny saloon, West heard the plink of Golescu's guitar. Words bounced after:

> *George Washington was a transporteer, he was, he was.*
> *George Washington was a transporteer, he was, he was.*
> *He paddled across the Delaware*
> *To find the buck he'd shot-put there.*
> *Bravo, bravo, hurrah for the transporteers!*

He entered the workshop just forward of the bulkhead which sealed off the nuclear generator. A man was always supposed to stand by here under acceleration, in case of trouble. But *Merlin* had yet to develop any collywobbles, and Golescu was sitting by. His chair was tilted back against the big lathe, his feet on the rungs and his instrument on his lap. He was a squat, dark young man with squirrel-bright eyes.

"Hi," he said. "Also yum."

West set the tray down and poured two cups of coffee. "By the bye," he said, "I'm not too well up on American folklore, but wasn't it the Potomac that Washington threw the dollar over?"

"Don't ask me. My parents came to Ceres direct from Craiova."

"Wherever that may be…D'you want to go back and visit there some day?"

"Whatever for?" Golescu rose. "Hey, those sandwiches look great."

"Thanks. I'm afraid my heart wasn't in them, though."

Golescu made a face. "Yeah! I should hope not."

"I mean I had the wind up so about this confounded affair—"

"'Wind up?'"

"Forget it. A Briticism." West shook his head. "D'you know, I can't help pitying children who've never felt wind or rain."

"Everything I hear about weather makes it sound more dismal," Golescu said through a mouthful. "Me, I feel sorry for kids that never get to ride a scooter with the whole universe shining around them."

He chewed for a while, then blurted, "Hey, what *is* this problem of ours, Ed? There's no hazard in jettisoning boiloff cargo, not to anybody except the insurance carrier. Is there? It's not like when 43's sail rotation went crazy. I still get nightmares about that one! Why can't we just valve off the isowhatsit, adjust the sail to whatever new track is right, and get back inside *Merlin's* rad screen field long before the sun burps?"

"Space contamination," West said. "Weren't you listening?"

"Yeah, but I didn't get it. Eight hundred long tons of gas aren't going to make any dent in all that hard vacuum."

"The devil they aren't. You'd still need instruments to detect the difference, but—Well, let's figure it out." West extracted paper, pencil, and a slide rule from a workbench drawer. "At a distance of six thousand miles from sea level, Earth has an angular diameter of, um, call it forty-three and a half degrees. Adding in the surrounding volume of space that concerns us, we can say about fifty-seven and a half. If we jettison, nearly all the gas will arrive there; the molecules have an Earthward component of velocity. Between the upper atmosphere limit and, say, a fifteen-hundred mile radius from the surface, the concentration of matter will go about ten molecules per cubic centimeter, if I remember the figure rightly, to... good Lord, I have trouble believing this myself! Over fifteen thousand per cc!"

"And so? That's not going to cause any friction worth mentioning."

"We'd actually do better to let the ship blow up," West mumbled, still bent over his work. "In that case the gas will scatter every which way, and maybe only two per cent or so will come near Earth. That's still intolerable, though."

"Hell, it'll dissipate again."

"Not for months, I'll bet. Remember the trapping effect of a planetary magnetic field. But even a few hours of that kind of contamination means the biggest economic disaster since the Nucleus failed."

"How come?"

"The equipment in orbit, man! There're a couple of hundred assorted devices near Earth these days. Photocells, for instance, directly exposed to space. Monitoring instruments. How d'you think solar meteorologists get their data? One of the primary sources is a set of ultra-clean metal surfaces with characteristic responses to various radiations—automatic spectrometers sending continuous information to the computers Earthside on the relative output of UV, X-rays, the whole band of solar emission. What do you imagine bombardment by so many metallic-complex molecules, and adsorption, are going to do to the work function of these metals? How about the weather satellites, with their electronic insides open to space, shielded against ions but not against vacuum? Or any cybernet constructed along those lines, controlling some such elaborate apparatus as a radio relay or a Mössbauer clock—or even a manned station." West slapped the bulkhead, so hard that it rang. "Bailey said the loss would be ten billion dollars. But I don't believe he was counting in the indirect effects. He probably hasn't the nerve!"

Golescu put down his coffee cup with great care and jammed hands into pockets. A muscle jumped at the corner of his jaw. "I get you," he said.

West discovered that his appetite was gone. *You know,* it occurred to him, *the economic repercussions might even be such that my own government will have to put a surtax on everyone who has any money left, simply to feed the unemployed. Mary could lose that house yet.*

"Remembered an errand," he said thickly. "I'll be back later to fetch this tray." He left fast, stumbling at first.

You don't scramble into a full suit of space armor, no matter what the hurry. You wriggle and grunt your way in. Helping Storrs secure a knee joint, Golescu remarked, "And to think, when I was a kid, I figured it would've been real romantic being one of King Arthur's knights."

"Shut up and keep going," Storrs answered.

Maybe I am, though, in a way, Golescu's mind continued. *Or at least it's a line to feed the ladies. That dragon outside is fixing to spew some mighty hot fire.*

The intercom speaker in the locker room resounded with West's voice from the bridge: *"Merlin* calling International Space Control Central. Come in, Central."

The reply was abrupt. "International Space Control Central acknowledging call from *Merlin*. Stand by for relay from Earthside office."

"So they finally woke Bailey up from his nice nap," Storrs said.

"Nah." Golescu finished assisting and went back to clamping his own boots. "He finally came out of conference. Formulation of policy directive in re Cigars, Standard Officers' Issue of and Correct Angle in Mouth of."

"Relax, you chaps," West said. "You ought to know how hard it is to raise a spaceship of some given type on short notice."

"You mean they don't keep Rescue Service craft in orbit, with full crews?" Golescu asked, astonished.

"Oh, they do that much," Storrs admitted grudgingly. "But—"

"Bailey here," said the speaker. "That you, *Merlin?*"

"No, just us chickens," Golescu muttered.

"West speaking, now in command," said the English man. "We're near rendezvous with 128. I haven't picked up anything else on the radar. You do have tugs here, don't you?"

This close to Earth, there was no time lag that human senses could register. "I'm sorry, no," Bailey said. It was hard to tell whether his tone was curt or merely defensive. "Unfeasible."

"What?" Storrs cried. Golescu watched the sallow face turn quite bloodless. His own heart skipped a beat or two. He got violently busy with his armor. Above the clatter of metal, he heard West:

"But the Rescue Service has tugs."

"I know," Bailey said. "Believe me, Captain West, this decision was not arrived at lightly. The unfortunate fact is, as I told you before, every ship that could tow your load on a cable at a high enough acceleration to give us any chance, is out on maneuvers. You must be aware that a standard rescue tug does not use cables and is not built for them. Just like your own vessel. A cable would add a great deal of dead weight, for no purpose when it is so easy to clamp on directly with a gyrogravitic grapnel. Nor do the tugs have more power than your type. It isn't necessary, in any foreseeable situation. A disabled ship need only be gotten into a stable orbit to wait for a repair crew. This merely happens to be so improbable a situation that it could not be foreseen."

"But three or four to help us—"

"How will you attach more than one hauler by geegee to a load as small in volume as this? If we had a ship available, so big it could take the container aboard, there would be no problem. Its radiation screen would protect the cargo. But we don't. The Navy transports are gone. So is the *Lunar Queen*." Bailey's voice turned cold. "With the asterites taking over so much interplanetary shipping, and with so much Terrestrial bottom destroyed during the war, those are the only such craft left to us."

Silence extended itself. Golescu could imagine West, alone before the pilot board, his sad eyes resting on the stars and unreachable Earth, methodically trying to think his way out of the trap.

"Build a frame around the gasbag, you Oedipal clotbrain!" Storrs snarled.

"Sam, please," West begged. To Bailey: "Forgive us. We are rather overwrought here, you understand. Er…what about it, though? A skeleton of girders around the bag, giving a large effective surface to which several tugs could grapple."

"How long would it take to build?" the man on the ground countered. "You know how ticklish and specialized a job construction in orbit is. The sun would flare hours before any such project could be finished." Something like eagerness came into his speech. "The Rescue Service is prepared to take you aboard one of its own units. You need only detach the sail and other excess mass, hook onto the cargo section, and operate your ship by remote control from ours. Quite safe."

"'Fraid not." West said. "Herdships don't include equipment for unforeseeable cases either. All we could do by remote control is turn the Emetts on and off. Which is insufficient. A ship coupled to an outside mass makes a highly unstable system. We'll need a pilot on deck, to correct every time it starts hunting."

He sighed. "Bring your ship around, though. Only one of us has to be aboard."

Storrs' face had gone from white to red. "Why one of *us?*" he shouted. "It's your problem, Earthling!"

There was a thump that might have been Bailey's fist striking his desk. "Yours, sir, yours," he threw back. "Read the Interplanetary Navigation Treaty, or your own franchise. Beltline sent that cargo here, and until delivery has been made, Beltline is responsible for the consequences. If someone has to risk a ship and, yes, a life, why should it be this Earth you despise so loudly?"

"Gentlemen—" West expostulated.

Bailey's tone smoothed over. "I agree. This is no time for recriminations. Do understand that our decision was a hard one. I sympathize with your feelings. We shall all pray for you. And don't forget, if the, um, the outcome is unfortunate, my own position will be seriously jeopardized."

Storrs swallowed something and clanged his faceplate shut.

"Very well, then," West said tiredly. "We'll proceed as best we can. Dispatch that ship of yours. Maintain contact with us. Let us know if you come up with any better ideas."

"Certainly. Good luck, *Merlin*. Over."

"Over and out, Earth."

Golescu's earplugs registered Storrs' suit radio: "I don't want that one's good wishes."

"Me, I'll take every scrap of luck that's offered me," Golescu said. "I'm not proud." To the intercom: "How long till rendezvous, Ed?"

"About ten minutes," West answered. "Better run off your suit checks fast."

"A checked suit...in space?" Golescu closed his own faceplate.

By the time he and Storrs had verified that everything was in order and had clumped their way to the air lock, deceleration was ended. They stood unspeaking while the chamber exhausted for them. The outer door opened, a cup that brimmed with stars.

Golescu touched the controls of his geegee unit and went forth. Suddenly he was no longer encased in clumsiness; he flitted free as an Earthdweller can only be in dreams. *Merlin* dwindled to a toy torpedo. Blackness surrounded him, lit by twelve thousand visible suns.

He did not look at his own sun. It could have struck him blind before it struck him dead. And Luna was occulted from here. But Earth lay enormous to one side, a dark ball with one dazzling thin edge and a rim of refracted light. There was not much poetry in his makeup, but he found it hard to remove his gaze from the planet.

Storrs' broadcast voice sounded in his receiver. "We're clear, Ed. Stay where you are till we finish."

"Right-o," said West. "Your velocity relative to target is—" He reeled off the figures.

There was scant need. As Golescu swung about, the sailship, which had been at his back, loomed like another Earth.

He had snapped down his glare filter. The stars vanished; he could now have stared Sol in the eye. The disk of the sail reflected with nearly the same brilliance. Protected, he saw it as a great white moon, growing as he sped across the few miles between. The suit radar controlled a series of beeps to inform him of vectors and distance. It made a dry, crickety music for his flight. Not exactly the Ride of the Valkyries, he thought—scarier. He found himself whistling soundlessly, the words running defiant through his head.

Chuck Lindbergh was a transporteer, he was, he was.
Chuck Lindbergh was a transporteer, he was, he was.

> *His lonesome song was in the news:*
> *The Spirit of St. Louis Blues.*
> *Bravo, bravo, hurrah for the transporteers!*

"Hey, Ed," Storrs called. As an afterthought: "You, too, Andy."

"Yes?" West replied.

"I've been considering. The way this job has developed, it's most likely an impossible one."

"We must try."

"Sure, sure, sure. But listen. It won't do us any good to watch telescopically for the commencement of that flare. The highest energy protons don't travel at much under the speed of light. And there's that whopping probable error in the time prediction. One hour in advance, let's cast off, and to hell with those precious satellites."

"Sorry, old chap, no. *Merlin's* going to stay coupled and hauling till the end of the run…or her. I'll pilot. We can dispense with the engine watch. You and Andy wait aboard the rescue ship."

"Stow that," Golescu said. "What kind of guts do you think we have?"

"You're both young men," West said dully.

"And you're a married man. And I got a reputation to keep up."

"Ease off on the heroics, you two," Storrs said. "If it comes to that, maybe we can cut cards. Meanwhile, every mile we can drag that canned stink spaceward will help some, I suppose—so let's get on with it."

The sail now nearly bisected the sky. Four and a half miles across, the foam-filled members that stiffened it marching across the field of view like Brobdingnagian spokes with its slow rotation, that disk massed close to a hundred tons. And yet it was ghostly thin, a micron's breadth of tough aluminized plastic, the spin as necessary as the ribs to keep it from collapsing backward under the torque at its edge.

For while the pressure of sunlight in Earth's neighborhood is only some eighty microdynes per square centimeter, this adds up unbelievably when dimensions stretch out into miles. The sunjammers were slow, their shortest passages measured in months, but that vast steady wind never ended for them; it weakened as they drove starward, but so did solar gravity, and in exact proportion. They cost money to build, out in free space, yet far less than a powered ship; for they required no engines, no crews, simply a metal coating sputtered onto a sheet of carbon compounds, a configuration of sensors and automata, and a means to signal their whereabouts and their occasional needs. Those needs rarely amounted to more than repair of some mechanical malfunction. Otherwise little happened on the long blind voyages. Micrometeorites eroded the sails, which must eventually be replaced; cosmic rays sleeted through the carrier sections, unheeded by unalive cargoes—

Or solar flares blew them to hellangone, Golescu thought.

First time it's ever happened, he reminded himself. *Probably the last time too. Unique event. I'm privileged to be on hand for it. What'm I offered, ladies and gentlemen, for my share of this unique privilege?*

He noticed, with a slight surprise, that he wasn't afraid. Well, nothing very dreadful was going to take place for several hours yet. Except a lot of hard work. Dreadful enough. *I should'a tried for scoopship pilot. Still, you got to make your money somehow, and the pay here is good, to compensate for having nothing to spend it on. A few more cruises, and I'll have me that stake to go prospecting.* Now there's the life!

Passing near the middle of the disk, he noticed the hub in which the sunjammer kept its transmitter and its navigational sensors. Then he had slipped around behind. The monstrous moon turned black for him. He raised his filter and saw it become dim blue with reflected starlight.

Carefully, he moved with Storrs toward the opposite hub. It was linked by a universal joint to a large, dully gleaming cylinder which held the motors. Those drew their power—they didn't need much—from solar batteries in the sunward hub, and used it to control rotation and precession of the sail according to instructions from the pilot computer. For the sunjammer must tack from orbit to orbit, across the ever-radial energy wind. Gravitation helped only on a trip from the outer to the inner System; and even then the reduction vector was a continuously changing thing.

Golescu felt the slight jar as his boots made contact with the precessor hull. They clung, and he rested weightless. The motors beneath had been turned off on radio command from *Merlin*. He stood for a moment letting his eyes complete their adjustment to the wan illumination.

Storrs landed beside him. "Come on," said the impatient voice. "Get the lead out of your rectifier. We'll need every bit of two hours to unhitch the cargo section as is."

"Yes, sure." Golescu began unstrapping the collapsible tool rack from his shoulders. He and his companion were hung about with equipment like a robot family's Christmas tree.

"I haven't worked on one of this type very often," he admitted. "You'd better be straw boss." He grinned. "I'll be the straw."

Storrs made a sour noise.

The gas carriers were a pretty special model at that. Their cargoes must be shaded by the sail, lest temperature go above critical, the liquefied material boil and the containers rupture. The standard form of sunjammer used a curved sail controlled by shroud lines, which pulled rather than pushed the load. Such an arrangement permitted a considerably larger light-catching area and proportionate freight capacity. The drawback was that maintenance crews on a standard vessel had to begin with erecting a shield between them and the reflector...if they didn't want to be fricasseed in their spacesuits.

West called: "Ed speaking. I had to drop behind. The sail was screening me off from you. Everything in order?"

"Just fine," Golescu said. "Apart from having an itch on my back that I can't scratch, and more work ahead of me than I'd dare load on any machine, and a prospect of getting blown to nanosmithereens, and no women in sight, and hell's own need for beer, I can't complain. Or, rather, I can, but it wouldn't do much good."

"Don't you ever stop chattering, Andy?" Storrs grumbled.

"Let him be, Sam," West advised. "We each need some outlet."

"Well…yes. Mine's hating Earth, I suppose. North America, anyway. You Britishers are still human." Storrs carried his tool rack to the farther end of the cylinder and set it in place with what should have been a crash but naturally wasn't. "Those Americans—The muckheads don't even have their regular gas boats out here unloading some of this cargo."

"They can't," West said. "Remember what Bailey told us. They haven't the capacity. Once the container was put in orbit, two or three luggers would have spent a couple of weeks shunting the contents groundside."

"Still," Golescu said, "seems to me that every pound they can save right now would help. Make matters that much less serious if this thing does blow."

"Wouldn't make any significant difference, in the short time available," West said. "And it'd hamper our operations."

"But doesn't the consignee want his stuff? I checked, and this load is worth eight million dollars F.O.B. That works out to quite a bit per pound."

"I just told you, Andy, salvage would interfere with the really important job—keeping those satellites functional!" West's tone became thoughtful. "Y'know, if we do succeed, there ought to be rather a nice bonus for us."

Golescu snorted. "That's about as likely as the Milky Way curdling. Beltline ain't gonna be happy. Sure, they'll have gained good will Earthside. But they'll have lost a sunjammer and a shipment. Somebody'll have to make the loss good. If it's an insurance company as I suppose…well, imagine what the premiums are going to go up to!"

"We might get a pat on the back," Storrs agreed, "and then the Old Man will call us in privately and tell us that the next time we do so poor a job of chestnut pulling, he'll put us on portside duty, latrine detail."

West sounded shocked. "Are you serious?"

"Uh-huh," Golescu said. "Asterites can't afford excuses. If you don't cut the mustard, you're apt to be dead, and so are your mates."

"But I have to cut it for Earth," Storrs said between his teeth.

Golescu's frame was now also in place. He flitted "up" to install a battery of floodlamps, "down" again to plug them in. Light glared, harsh and undiffused, on the spot where the work must be done.

That was the heavy U-joint connecting precessor with cargo section. The latter was also illuminated in part. Hitherto it had appeared only as a circle of blackness. Now, beyond the framework that held it in place, ponderously counter-rotating, the translucent bag glimmered a deep, angry red.

It was not very large to contain so much hell…or so much money, Golescu reflected. Space-cold and liquefied under high pressure, the isonitrate occupied a sphere only some ten yards in diameter. Its substance, even the metal atoms, had been reaped from the atmosphere of Jupiter—a chill great star shining in Gemini, two firefly moons visible beside it, treasure house and grave of more asterites than Golescu cared to think about. They were brave men, too, who manned the orbital station where the Jovian complexes were processed into isonitrate. An accident there would not be quite like a nuclear warhead going off, but the difference was academic.

Yet Earth needed those energy-crammed molecules, as the starting point for a dozen chemical syntheses. And Earth was willing to pay. Demand evoked supply, including a supply of men to keep production and the Beltline moving.

Golescu began to unclip his tools and hang them on the rack where they would be ready to hand. A sense came to him of his own muscles, not merely in arms but in legs and belly and neck, constantly interplaying with centrifugal and Coriolis forces to hold him in balance on this free-falling shell. That led him to notice how the breath went in and out of his nostrils, tasting of recycler chemicals, and how his heart pumped the blood slowly around the intricate circuit of veins and arteries, and how that made an incessant tiny throb in his ears. He was getting hungry again, and had not lied about wanting a beer…ah, cool tickling over his tongue, yes, that was why the asterites must sell to Earth, they hadn't yet succeeded in brewing decent beer themselves…

"Sam," he said, "I've been thinking."

"About time," Storrs grunted.

"No, really. I never wondered about it before. But if this junk is so irritable, how come we can ship it at all? Why doesn't cosmic radiation set it off?"

Storrs sighed. The lamps threw the lean features behind his faceplate into highlights and black gullies. "If you'd spent more time in school learning your science, and less chasing women and beating that guitar—Oh, well." He relented. "I'm no chemist myself, but it's fairly obvious. Isonitrate complex is actually quite reasonably stable. It's plain to see that X-rays and electrons don't bother it. And the probability of a high-energy nucleus breaking up enough molecules to start a chain reaction must be extremely low. Trouble right now is, we're due for one all-time concentration of high-energy nuclei."

"Uh, yes. If we could screen them off—maybe mount a field generator on the frame—"

"Where'd you get hold of one that puts out the right size and shape of field, in the time we've got? I daresay they will be provided in the future. Hindsight versus foresight, as usual. Now hurry it up there."

"Wait a bit," West hailed them. "Just got a signal from the Rescue Service ship. Want me to relay to you?"

"Might as well," Golescu said. "For the laughs."

A new voice, accented English: "'Allo, *Merlin*. International Space Commission Rescue Service cutter *Rajasthan*, commanding officer Villegas speaking. Come in, *Merlin*." Golescu searched for the newcomer, but it must still be only a spark, lost among the stars.

"Acknowledging," said West shortly, and identified himself.

"We 'ave your position and path, *Merlin*. Do you plan to maintain same for t'e present? Yes? T'en we will adopt t'e same orbit, with thirty kilometer lag. Unless we can do something to 'elp."

"Tell him to send over anybody he's got along who has sailship experience," Storrs said. "With an extra man or two, we'll finish sooner."

West passed the idea on. Villegas hemmed for a moment before answering, "I am most sorry, but we 'ave no such persons with us. You should 'ave asked for t'em before."

"We assumed you weren't infinitely dunderheaded," Storrs bit off. "Our mistake."

"Don't blow your gaskets, Sam," Golescu counseled. "Sunjammers are oddball craft. Earth hasn't got any. How could they know?"

"Beltline's got offices and personnel on Earth! Didn't that Bailey snerd even consult them?"

"Maybe no one was on hand except a secretary. This boat wasn't due to make final approach for another two, three weeks. Maybe all our people who could be of any help are out fleshpotting around Earth and not tuning in any newscasts. I hear they've got some mighty fine places there for that sort of thing."

The byplay had not been relayed. Villegas was saying: "No use to send any of my engineers, yes? T'ey 'ave not t'e special skills. By t'e time t'e men you want could arrive, yours will 'ave finished uncoupling and you will be under acceleration, I trust."

"Well, you'll take mine aboard first," West said. "We only need a pilot here for that maneuver."

"I never thought of Ed as the hero type," Golescu remarked. He squatted to fit a wrench around a bolthead. "Shall we oblige him?"

"What a dilemma," Storrs said acridly. "If I do, I'm a coward. If I don't, and we cut cards, I might end up risking my neck for Mother Earth."

"Come off that shtick, Sam. The war's over, or hadn't you heard? Besides, we may reach jettisoning distance before the flare pops. It's just as likely to be later than prediction as earlier. Or...you know, in armor, with a strong metal shield around him, a man might even survive the explosion. There's no air to carry blast. When *Merlin* breaks apart, he could be tossed into space in one piece."

"Sure. Into four thousand roentgens per hour. That means nine minutes for a lethal dose. The other ship isn't going to find him in any nine minutes, chum."

"Hm-m-m...true. Damn! What we need is a pocket size rad screen generator. Or something very thick to hide behind—"

Golescu's words cut off. He stared before him, into the icy light of Jupiter, until its after-image danced through his vision.

All the stars danced.

"What's eating you now?" Storrs growled. "Get to work."

Golescu's yell nearly shattered his own eardrums. Its echoes were still flying around in his helmet when West cried, "What is it? I say, what happened? I'm coming, be there in a few minutes, hang on, boys!"

"No…wait…hold everything," Golescu stammered. "Not so fast. We're O.K. Better than O.K."

Storrs closed gauntlet fingers on the other man's shoulderpieces and shook him. "What's the matter, you clown?"

"Don't you see?" Golescu howled. "We can save the whole shooting match!"

Words flew between sunjammer and herdship. The decision was quickly reached; a spaceman who could not make up his mind from a standing start was unlikely to clutter his profession very long. West called *Rajasthan*. "…Send us every hand you can possibly spare," he concluded. "I'll raise Bailey and have him rush us more crews from your service's fleet in orbit. But they can hardly arrive for a few hours yet, and we've got to make what progress we can meanwhile."

"Um-m-m…*nombre de Dios*…no, captain," Villegas said. "I am sorry, but I 'ave no authority to do t'is."

"Eh? You're in command of your own ship, aren't you?"

"Yes, but my orders were only to—"

West surprised Storrs and Golescu with a choice recital of Anglo-Saxon monosyllables. "Very well, we'll get your orders changed," he said. "Hello, hello, *Merlin* calling International—"

On the sailship, the asterites were hastily clipping tools back onto their armor. They didn't bother with any they didn't expect to need. Those could be collected afterward, if there was an afterward.

"Craziest thing I ever heard of," Storrs panted. "It *ought* to work, but—Why didn't anybody think of it on Earth?"

"Same reason you and Ed didn't, I guess," Golescu said. "It's so crude and obvious, only a low wattage brain like mine 'ud see it. At least see it quick-like. I suppose somebody would've hit on it eventually."

"That would have been too late." Storrs' gaze traveled across the awesome blue plain that wheeled before him, curtaining off half the universe. "May be too late already. Hell's kettles, what a huge job!"

"Don't remind me. I got troubles of my own. Ready? O.K., let's stop rotation."

Storrs opened the shield over the manual controls, made several adjustments, replaced the cover, and used the handle of a small crescent wrench to push a deeply recessed button. At once he leaped back, off the cylinder. Golescu went simultaneously.

They were none too soon. Gears meshed, flywheels began to spin, the motor and cargo sections took up the angular momentum which was being removed from the sail. At the same time, the disk was precessed to face the sun directly.

So great a mass could not be stopped fast. Storrs and Golescu flitted clear, out into the fierce light. Their thermostatic units began to labor, converting heat into electricity and storing it in the suit capacitors. That energy would be needed; the men were going to be at work for quite a spell.

"You know," Storrs said, "you weren't right about saving everything. The sail will be lost."

"So?" Golescu returned. "The kit is what matters. A couple of hundred thousand bucks worth of caboodle is cheap for salvaging the rest."

"If we do."

"Talk about pessimists! Sam, I'm surprised you don't wear a belt and suspenders both…At that, come to think of it, the pieces of sail ought to command fancy prices as souvenirs."

West contacted them: "I'm having a bit of a tussle with Bailey. Let me cut you into the circuit." A pause. "Here they are. You'll have to argue with them as well as me. Equal ranks."

"Ridiculous arrangement," Bailey said.

"Not in the least. Each of us has to be able to do any task that comes along. But let's not waste time. What precisely are your objections to our proposal?"

"Why, the whole concept is fantastic."

"Look," Storrs crackled, "this is our line of work, not yours. We know what's possible and what isn't."

"Eight hours—less than that—to handle sixteen square miles of material?" Bailey protested.

"One micron thick," West pointed out. "A hundred square yards masses only about a pound. It's not like building a frame for tugs to grapple. This job is elementary. Any spacehand with a geegee unit on his suit can do it."

"But—no, you can't."

"Not if you don't send us a swarm of men to help," West admitted. "And soon."

"If you think I'm going to authorize that kind of expense to the taxpayer, think again. I forbid this lunacy. You're hereby ordered to carry on with standard procedures."

An inarticulate sound vibrated in Storrs' throat. Golescu said bad words. West spoke with complete calm:

"You can't forbid it, or issue any order except for us to do our best. Please read the texts you've been citing to me. If Beltline is responsible for this operation, Beltline's agents have to have authority to decide how it shall be carried out. And our decision is to go for broke, as I believe you Americans say. Without your cooperation, we are bound to fail. And what excuse will you offer then? I respectfully suggest, Mr. Bailey, that you get cracking."

Stillness hummed, except for the noise of the crowding, flashing stars. Earth rolled tremendous against an ultimate dark. The sail began to bend at the edges as centrifugal force waned. Had it not faced the sun head on, it could have buckled into a hopeless tangle. As matters stood, when rotation ended it would approximate a section of a sphere.

Bailey's gulp gurgled in earplugs. "You win. I'll get several crews to you within a couple of hours, and meanwhile tell Captain Villegas to put his men under your direction. What equipment will be needed?"

"Torches, mainly," West said. "Quickest way of slicing up that stuff. We have metal rods aboard, so I can construct a frame to hold the whole mess in position myself, rather fast. Your gang will also want—"

Golescu signaled Storrs to switch bands. *"Whew!"* he said. "That was a nasty minute. I didn't think old Ed had it in him."

"Ed's a good fellow," Storrs said. "Uh, we'll still only require one man aboard *Merlin,* but—"

"Hell with that bleat. We're in this together. I'm sticking with him when the time comes."

"Right. Me, too."

It was necessary for the herdship to grapple and apply power, lest spin expose the bag to the radiation storm. Golescu should have been at the pilot board then, but he and Storrs were too exhausted. The work had been brutal. They sat in the saloon with untasted mugs of coffee, staring emptily at the bulkheads, while West rode the controls.

Outside, Lucifer ran free. Coughed from the sun, ions with energies in the millions of electron volts flooded all space. Down on Earth, tourists in the Antarctic lodges crowded into the observation domes to watch the winter sky come alive with vast flapping curtains of aurora. Elsewhere, men who had heard the news huddled near their television screens, waiting for word. Reception was poor. The nuclear generators of ships beyond the atmosphere poured power into screen fields, deflecting that murderous torrent from their hulls. The engineers' eyes never left the gauges.

Merlin throbbed. Now and then, as she moved to keep the load at the end of her grapnel on an even keel, her members groaned with stress. That was the only token granted the men in the saloon. They dared not interrupt the pilot with questions.

"It's got to work," Storrs said stupidly, for the dozenth time. He rubbed his chin. The bristles of beard made an audible scratching.

"Sure it will," Golescu said. "My idea, wasn't it?" The cockiness had left his voice.

"Well," Storrs said, "If it doesn't…if that cargo explodes…we'll never know." He laid his fist on the table and regarded the knobby knuckles. "I'd like to know, though. How I'd laugh at those fat Earthlings."

Golescu reached for his coffee. It had gone cold. "They aren't that bad. And if you've got to be such a hot-bottomed patriot, don't forget that trouble on Earth would affect the Republic. We need them, same as they need us."

"Bull. I can show you economic statistics…Damn and double damn! It isn't right! How many men's lives is it proper to risk, to save ten billion or so lousy dollars?"

"That dinero represents a lot more man-years than we three will rack up, even if I achieve my ambition to become a dirty old man."

"Work years. Not deaths."

"Scared?"

Storrs spat in the ashcatcher. "No. Tired and angry. This means one thing to Ed. Economic breakdown on Earth would hurt him directly. But you and me—"

"You didn't have to be aboard."

"I sure did."

"Oh, fork all those fancy moral issues," Golescu said. "This is what we get paid for."

"Hm-m-m...yeah...Another half hour to go, by the clock, if the prediction is right. I hope Ed can stand the strain."

"He'd better. That's the real chance we take. We knew right along the shield would be more than ample. Well, I saw him swallow a whole medicine chest full of anti-fatigue pills and psychodrugs." Golescu stirred in his seat. "Feel like a game of rummy?"

"No."

The sun's arrows rushed on through vacuum. Where they encountered *Merlin's* screen, they swerved, with a spiteful gout of X-radiation that her internal shielding drank up. Where they struck at the cargo section—

They hit a barrier of plastic and aluminum: the sail, cut into fifteen-yard squares that were layered within a welded framework. The shielding factor came to about fifty grams per square centimeter. Light metals and hydrogen-rich carbon compounds are highly effective stoppers of stripped small atoms like the hydrogen and helium ions which make up nearly the whole of flare emission. For example, 32.7 grams per square centimeter of aluminum will halt protons of two hundred million electron volts. The recoil characteristics are such that secondary radiation is not a serious problem—at least, not to isonitrate, which is only touched off by a nucleus plowing into its giant molecule.

But the whole clumsy ensemble of shield, cargo section, and herdship must be kept facing directly into the blast. And gravitation kept trying to swing it into orbit, which brought gyroscopic forces into play. Control was exercised at the end of a long arm; the mass had considerable turning moment, nor was it perfectly balanced. Compensation could become over-compensation with gruesome ease.

"If we ride this one out," Golescu said, "we really will get that bonus Ed was faunching for."

"Uh-huh." Storrs raised dark-rimmed eyes. "Andy, you're a good oscar and I hope we can ship out together again, but right now I've got some thinking to do. Keep quiet, huh?"

"O.K." Golescu said. "Though thinking's the last thing I want to do."

He prowled aft to have a look at the engine-room meters. Not that he could improve matters much if anything was going awry in his present condition. Why had not one single man, out of the scores who divided the sail, volunteered to ride along and help? Earthlings, of course, had no great cause to love asterites. Golescu caught himself wondering if the Revolution had really been justified—if anything ever was that raised such bitterness between men. *Now stow that! Break out the guitar and—No, it'd bother Ed. Sam too, I guess.*

I should'a taken a sleeping pill…Uh-uh, none o' that either.

His bleared vision focused on the bank of indicators. Everything operating smoothly—good ship—wait a second! The external radiation count—

"Yi-yi-yip!" he screamed. "She's going down! The flare's dying!" And he did a war dance around the workshop and up the length of the corridor beyond.

Slowly, slowly, the storm faded. Until at last West said from the intercom, "It's over with. We're alive, boys."

Storrs began to dance, too.

After a while West reported, "Earth called in. Congratulations and so forth. They'll send a tug at once for this cargo, and hold it in the Moon's shadow while they unload. We're invited groundside for a celebration." Wistfulness tinged his voice. "D'you think the company would mind if we accepted?"

"They better not," Storrs said.

"We need a checkout anyway, after putting the ship to so much stress," Golescu added. "And they'll have to compute a new orbit for the rest of our mission. We're bound to have a few days' layover." Exhaustion dropped from him. "Fleshpots, here I come!"

He snatched up his guitar and bellowed forth:

> *Ol' Einstein was a transporteer, he was, he was*
> *Ol' Einstein was a transporteer, he was, he was.*
> *His racing car used too much gas;*
> *It shrank the time but it raised the mass,*
> *Bravo, bravo, hurrah for the transporteers!*

Now he had a story to embroider for the girls in Pallas town.

ARSENAL PORT

-1-

When the Earth ship came, Gunnar Heim was bargaining with a devil-winged messenger from a nuclear smithy. The Aerie of Trebogir, for which Ro spoke, had weapons to sell; but there were conditions.

Non-human words hissed and whistled into the man's helmet pickup. Gregorios Koumanoudes translated into English. "—missile gets so large an initial velocity by drawing on the ship's own gravitrons for a launch impetus."

Heim wished he could show horse trader reluctance, as by thoughtfully scratching his head. But it would look silly under present circumstances. Damn this need to wear air-suits! Even on the lift platform where he stood, which kept his weight Earth normal, and even with the strength of a two-meter-tall body which he had gotten back into first-class condition on the voyage hither, the mass of equipment he must carry was tiring. Originally he had planned to stay inboard, put a 3V two-way outside *Connie Girl*, and thus meet with the Staurni; but Koumanoudes warned him against it. "They'll respect you more, Captain, for coming out into their own environment," the Greek had said. "Irrational, sure, but they make a big thing of physical toughness. And they'll give a better deal to someone they respect."

So—Heim scowled into harsh blue sunlight. "I see the advantage," he answered. "However, with my own maneuvering handicapped, I'd be a sitting duck."

Koumanoudes put his objection into the language that prevails between Kimreth Heights and the Iron Sea. Ro spread his taloned hands, a startlingly humanlike gesture. "The loss of maneuverability is negligible," he said, "as only a fractional second is needed for launch. Thereafter one immediately has full accelerative power available again. To be sure, the system must be synchronized with the engine complex, but it should not take long to make the necessary modifications on your ship."

Unconsciously, Heim glanced skyward. Somewhere beyond that deep purple vault, those icily blue-tinged clouds, *Fox II* swung in orbit around Staurn; tenders flitted back and forth with cargoes of hell, men and not-men swarmed over the cruiser, working together to fit her for war. There was not much left to do. And every nerve in him throbbed to be away. Each day he spent here, Alerion grew stronger, the cause of men on New Europe more hopeless.

Still, he was going to be dreadfully alone when he got there; one commerce raider, whose letters of marque depended on a legal technicality, bound off to harass an enemy whom most of Earth's politicians would rather placate. He could not hope for others to follow him. Ultimately, the liberation of that colony planet which Alerion had seized must depend on Earth herself setting the regular Navy in motion. And that would not happen soon, if ever.

Fox needed any microscopic advantage he could find for her. Like this missile sling which Ro claimed they could make in the Aerie of Trebogir. It did sound promising…"How long to install?" Heim asked.

Again four claw fingers, set around the entire palm of the hand, gestured. "Some days. One cannot tell exactly without more knowledge than my kinfather's technologists possess about vessels of your particular class. May I suggest that the captain send his honored chief engineer to discuss such matters with our folk?"

"Um-m-m." Heim considered. His gaze went past Ro, to Galveth, who waited impassively for something to be said that might concern the Lodge. But the blast gun remained idly cradled in the observer's arms. If Galveth had any expression, it was of sleepiness, his yellow eyes drooping. A human could never be sure, though, what went on in the narrow Staurni skulls.

It was even hard to tell individuals apart. A common alienness outweighed variable details. Ro and Galveth were each about three meters long; but half that was in the thick, rudder-tipped tail, on whose coil the legless torso sat. The keelbone jutted like a prow. The face was sharp-muzzled, with wolfishly fanged mouth and small round ears. Its mask appearance came less from the dark band across the eyes than from the nostrils being hidden under the chin. A gray growth, neither hair nor feathers but something in between, covered the entire hide. No clothes were worn except two pouched belts crossing from shoulder to waist. All was overshadowed by the immense chiropteran wings, seven meters in span.

When you looked closely, you saw differences, mainly that Galveth had grown lean and frosty-tinged while Ro was still in the fierceness of youth. And Galveth wore the gold-ornamented harness reserved for Lodge members, Ro the red and black geometry of Trebogir's pattern.

Heim turned to Koumanoudes. "What do you think?" he asked.

The stocky man shrugged. "I'm no engineer."

"But damnation, you and Wong have spent a couple of months here. You must have some notion who's honest and competent, who isn't."

"Oh, that. Sure. Trebogir isn't one of the robber barons. He has a good name. You can deal with him."

"Okay." Heim reached a decision. "Tell this messenger, then, that I am interested. I'll call C.E. down from *Fox* as soon as possible—right now he's got to help the contractor from the Hurst of Wenilwain install our fire-control computers —and we'll come to the Aerie and talk further about the proposal."

"You can't be that blunt," Koumanoudes said. "Lodge members are, but they're different. A Nester is worse than an Arab or a Japanese for wanting flowery language." He turned and began to form syllables.

Through the wind that rustled the low red-leaved forest surrounding the spaceport, through the beat of surf a kilometer distant, a sudden whine smote. It grew, became thunderous, the heavy air was split and a shadow fell across concrete field and lava-block buildings. Every head swung up.

A blunt-nosed cylinder was descending. The blue-white radiance was savage off its metal, spots danced before Heim's eyes when he turned them away. But he recognized the make. The heart jumped in his breast. "A spaceship! Human built—What's going on?"

"I…don't…know." Behind the dark faceplate, Koumanoudes' big-nosed countenance harshened. "Nobody said a word. Galveth!" He rattled off a question.

The Lodge agent made a bland reply. "He says he didn't think it mattered," Koumanoudes said.

"Blaze," Heim said in anger, "he knows about the Aleriona crisis! He must have at least some inkling of our trouble with our own government. The Lodge must've stopped that ship for inspection no later than yesterday. Why haven't we been warned?"

"I'm not sure how much the Staurni ever understood," Koumanoudes said. "To them it's ridiculous that we couldn't arm ourselves at home and take off whenever we wanted. Besides, those people can't have any real weapons along, or they wouldn't've been allowed to land."

"They can have small arms," Heim snapped. "We do. Get rid of these bucks as fast as you can, Greg, and come inboard. I've got to alert the boys."

He strode rapidly across the platform to the landing ramp and up to the airlock. There he must fume while pumps replaced the atmosphere of Staurn with something he could breathe, and he himself was decompressed. The baffled rage that he had thought was left behind on Earth came back to possess him. So much could have happened in the couple of weeks that *Fox II* had needed to cross the hundred-odd light-years to this star, or in the three weeks that followed while she was being refitted. If the appeasement party had won out, if his privateering venture had been declared illegal—

Of course, he told himself, over and over, *that's not a Federation Navy ship. She's a small civilian ranger. But then, the Staurni don't let any warcraft but their own near this planet. If she's simply bringing an official order for me to come home… Well, all right, face the question: what then? Do I go on anyway—as a pirate?*

Sickly: *Wouldn't be much use. The hope was to create a situation that Earth could take advantage of. If Earth refuses the chance and disowns us, we can only be troublemakers to Alerion, until at last we're cornered and killed. I'll never see Lisa again.* It was as if once more he could feel a small body pressed against him in farewell. *They'll tell her, the whole rest of her life, her father was a criminal.*

But maybe, maybe even a pirate could accomplish something. There was Drake of the Golden Hind—*He sailed in another day, when men weren't afraid.*

The inner door opened. He moved on into his yacht, that was now an auxiliary for the starship, and opened his helmet.

Endre Vadász had the bridge. Technically he was no more than the steward; the life of a troubadour tramping the starways had not equipped him to be anything else. But in practice he was the captain's right hand, and had been since he came back with his eyewitness account of what really happened on New Europe and thus planted the seed of this expedition. His thin dark face was turned outward, staring through the viewport as the other vessel neared in a gravitron-distorted shimmer of light. When Heim's boots rang on the deck, he didn't look around, but said tonelessly, "I have ordered the crew into battle gear, and brought your own rifle from your cabin."

"Good man." Heim took the weapon in the crook of an arm. There was assurance in that weight and solidity and beautiful deadly shape. It was a .30-caliber Browning cyclic, able to send forty rounds a minute through any atmosphere or none, the pride of his collection. Vadász, also in a collapsed airsuit with faceplate unlocked, had settled for a laser pistol.

"I am not certain," the Hungarian remarked, "what six men can do if they try to storm us. Yonder ship can easily hold five times as many."

"We can stand 'em off till the boys arrive from *Fox*," Heim said, "and they total almost a hundred. Assuming the Lodge doesn't stop the fight."

"Oh, that I doubt," Vadász murmured with a slight smile. "We aren't likely to damage their nice spaceport, and from everything I hear, they have no rules against bloodshed." He pointed to several winged shapes, wheeling black against the clouds over the western end of Orling Island. "They will come enjoy the spectacle."

Heim directed the radioman to get in touch with *Fox*. It would take a while. The beam must go through a ground station and a couple of relay satellites. Wong was in orbit to interpret between human and native workers, while Sparks' command of the language was slight. And the newcomer would be down in another minute.

I'm borrowing trouble, Heim tried to believe. *Yet why would any Terrestrial come here, except in connection with me?*

To trade? Yes, yes, an occasional merchant does call, from Earth or Naqsa or one of the other spacefaring worlds. That's why the weaponmakers of Staurn will accept my Federation credits. But surely not while the Aleriona trouble is so near explosion.

Beside him, Vadász was softly whistling. *The Blue Danube,* now of all times? Well, maybe he wanted to remember, while he still could....

The least quiver ran through ground and hull and Heim's bones as the stranger touched jacks to concrete. Her shadow fell engulfingly over *Connie Girl*. Through the intercom he heard a few oaths from his men, Sparks' mumble at the transmitter, the snore of a nuclear engine on stand-by. A ventilator gusted air across his cheeks, which were sweating.

When Koumanoudes clumped in, Heim spun about with a jerkiness that revealed to him how tense he was. "So?" the captain barked. "Did you get any information?"

The Greek looked relieved. "I think we can freefall, sir. According to Galveth, they want to stay awhile, look around, and ask questions. A xenological expedition, in other words."

"To this planet?" Heim scoffed.

"Well, after all, we are in Hydrus," Vadász pointed out. "The trouble is going on in the Phoenix. Quite some distance from here."

"No further from The Eith than Alpha Eridani," Heim said, "where we had our biggest skirmish with the Aleriona. And that was many years ago. They're prowling through this whole sector. Besides, it takes time to organize an expedition. Why didn't we hear of it on Earth?"

"We were rather occupied," Vadász said dryly. He went to the radiophone. "Shall I try to call them?"

"What?—Oh, yes. Of course." Heim swore at himself for forgetting so simple an act.

The connection was made at once. "MDS *Quest* of the U.S.A.," said a mild young man. "Captain Gutierrez is still busy, sir, but I can switch you to Dr. Bragdon. He's the head of the scientific team."

The release was like a blow. Heim sagged in his suit. "You're only here to make studies, then?"

"Yes, sir, for the University of Hawaii, under contract to the Federation Research Authority. One moment, please."

The screen flickered to a view of a cabin, crowded with references both fullsize and micro. The man in the foreground was also young, husky, with black hair and cragged profile. "Victor Bragdon speaking," he said, and then, his mouth falling open, "Good heavens! Aren't you Gunnar Heim?"

The privateer captain didn't reply. His own astonishment was too much. The woman behind Bragdon leaned over the man's shoulder and met Heim's stare with wide hazel eyes. She was tall; an informal gray zipsuit clung to a figure strong and mature. Her face had strength too, rather than conventional good looks: straight nose, wide mouth, arching bones, framed by curly chestnut hair. But some years back it had troubled his sleep. When he saw the name Jocelyn Lawrie on the letterhead of a flyer from World Militants for Peace, an old hurt had awakened, and he went on still more intensely with his preparations for war.

"Gunnar!" she exclaimed. "Of all people—How's your daughter? I was so horrified when I heard—"

"She's all right now," he said automatically. Surprise faded. Suspicion tightened his muscles. "What are you doing here?" he rapped.

-2-

Afterward he remembered with irony and sadness how careful he had been. Pleading an urgent requirement for his presence on *Fox II,* he raised his yacht within the hour. But Koumanoudes volunteered to stay behind, aboard the *Quest* on a "courtesy call." Heim knew the Greek had done a good job of preliminary arrangement-making on Staurn; how good he would be with his fellow humans was uncertain, but there was scant choice. It had to be him or Wong, the only ones who spoke the local language fluently and hence could use the spaceport's eavesdrop-proof maser line.

His report came after two watches. "They're clean, skipper. I was toured around the whole ship and talked to everybody. There're five in the crew, plus captain, mate, and C.E. They're plain spacehands, who signed on for this cruise the same as they would for any other exploratory trip. You can't fake that. Anybody who's so good an actor works on 3V, not in the black."

"They don't have to act," Heim said. "They only have to wear a poker face."

"But these bucks didn't. They swarmed over me, asking every kind of question about us. On the whole, they thought we had a hell of a fine idea here. A couple of them wished they'd joined us."

"Uh-huh. I'm not surprised. The common man often shows more common sense than the intellectual elite. But wait, now, do you include their officers in this?"

"The engineer, yes. Captain Gutierrez and the first officer…well, they were stiff as meteorite plating. I don't know what they think. Probably they don't like us on principle, figure war should be left to the regular Navy. But I did make an excuse to see the articles of the expedition. It's bona fide, official papers and everything."

"How about the scientific passengers?"

"A mixed bag. I think Bragdon and Mrs. Lawrie must be the only ones who've ever been out of the Solar System. There's another xenologist, a semanticist, a glossanalyst, a biologist, and half a dozen graduate students to help. I gather none have visited Staurn before."

"Odd."

"Charlie Wong and I hadn't either, boss, when you sent us off. They did the same as us, boned up on what information was available and learned the main language with RNA-electro cramming, en route. Anyhow, I can tell you there's nothing to fear from these academic types. I don't think any but Bragdon can handle a gun. They don't much care for us and what we stand for, so relationships were a tad strained even if nothing rude got said. But they're no threat."

"They all feel this way?" Heim asked, with a curious little sinking in his spirit.

"No, funny thing, Bragdon and Mrs. Lawrie were both friendly. He remarked once he disagrees with your ideas but has a lot of respect for your guts. And she said she hopes you can come back soon."

"I can," Heim said softly. "Oh, I can."

An hour later, *Connie* accelerated planetward.

Seated on the bridge, Heim listened to the thrum of the yacht and his own pulse, underlying the flamenco that leaped from Vadász's guitar beside him. For a while neither man spoke, nor did their eyes leave the spectacle in the viewports.

Two and a fifth times the diameter of Earth, nine and a half times the mass, Staurn rolled immense against darkness. The seas shone royal blue, the continents, blurred by snow-colored cloud bands, were ocher and cinnabar. Along the horizon, atmosphere made a violet rim; over the whole, under the irradiation of a hot F_5 sun, ran a fluorescence which near the poles became great banners of aurora, shaken aloft into space. Two moons were visible beyond, glacially luminous, and further yet there glittered strange constellations.

"When I see something like that," Heim murmured at length, half to himself, "I wonder."

Vadász stopped playing and cocked a birdlike glance at him. "What do you wonder?"

"Why the hell we waste time hating and killing, that we might use to—Argh, never mind." Heim got out his pipe. "It only takes one to make a quarrel."

Vadász studied him, "I've come to know you somewhat well, Gunnar," he said. "You are not given to the role of Hamlet. What is the real trouble?"

"Nothing!"

"Ah. Excuse me if I pry, but this whole enterprise depends on you. Is it the lady's unexpected arrival that is so disturbing?"

"A surprise, no more. We used to be friends." Heim became busy loading his pipe. The Magyar's steady look forced him to explain further. "My wife and I had quite a bit to do with the Lawries, years ago. They went off to Ourania in the Epsilon Indi System shortly before Connie died, to establish a machine-tool factory in the colony there. Things can't have worked out too well, because she came back last year, divorced. The conflict with Alerion was already serious, even if they hadn't yet attacked New Europe, and she got active in the peace movement. It had her shuttling around the world, so we only met again a few times, briefly, at large loud parties. I half doubted she'd speak to me now, after what I've done."

"And are pleasantly amazed, eh? She is indeed attractive. You must find her especially so."

"What do you mean?" Heim bridled.

"Oh…" Vadász's grin was disarming. "One does not wish to get too personal. However, Gunnar, busy though you were, I felt you were mistaken not to, um, prepare yourself for a long cruise in strictly male society."

Heim grinned back. "I'd trouble enough concocting stories to explain your absences. How could I tell Lisa her hero was out tomcatting?"

"*Touché!*" Vadász went tomato red and attacked his guitar with great vigor.

But he has a point, maybe, Heim thought. *I could have—well, Connie would've understood. The way she understood about Jocelyn. Lord knows there've been other women since—Maybe I was thinking too hard about Madelon on New Europe. Damned foolishness. Or—I don't know, I'm all confused.*

That was what he remembered, afterward.

—His finger was not quite steady when he pressed the button on her door. She opened it while the chime was still sounding. "Gunnar," she said, and took both his hands. "I'm so glad you could come."

"You were nice, to invite me," he said.

"Nonsense. When two old friends meet again, halfway between home and the Southern Cross, what else do they do but have a private gabfest? Come in, man."

The door closed behind them. He looked around. Her cabin was large and comfortable, and she had made it her own. He recognized some things from her lost San Francisco home—a Matisse and a Hiroshige reproduction, some worn volumes of Catullus, Yeats, Tagore, Pasternak, Mosunic-Lopez, the flute he had once loved to heat her play—and there were a few souvenirs of her years in the Epsilon Indi System, less from Ourania than from stark New Mars. His attention returned to her and stayed. She had on an electric blue dress and a Gean necklace of massive silver. The outfit was at once quiet and stunning. Or was that simply the contents?

Whoa, boy! he checked himself. Aloud: "You haven't changed."

"Liar. But thanks." Her eyes dwelt on him. "You have, anyway. Tired and bitter."

"Why, no, I feel happier now than—" His protest was cut off. She let his hands go and went to a table where bottles and ice stood.

"Let's do something about it," she said. "As I recall, you're a Scotch drinker. And here's some sho-nuff Glenlivet."

"Eh? You always preferred light wine."

"Well, Vic—Dr. Bragdon, you know—he shares your taste, and very kindly gave us this from his locker." She poured. For a moment the clear gurgle was the only sound in the universe.

What the devil right have I to feel jealous? "I'm not sure what, uh, you're doing out here with him."

"Officially I'm secretary to the expedition. I have such skills from my job before I married, and got the rust off them working for the peace movement. Then too, I've had experience on other planets, including planets where you need special equipment to live. I used to go to New Mars quite often, ostensibly with Edgar's mineral prospectors, actually to get away—No matter. That's past. When I heard about this expedition, I applied for a berth and, rather to my surprise, got it. I suppose that was partly because most qualified people were scared to come so near the big bad Aleriona, partly because Vic knew me and felt I could handle it." She handed him a glass and raised her own. "Welcome aboard, Gunnar. Here's to the old days."

They clinked rims, wordless.

"When life was simple and splendid," she added. Tossing off a sip of her Chablis, she toasted again, defiantly. "And here's to the future. We'll make it the same."

"Well, let's hope so." His mouth creased upward. She'd always been overly dramatic, but his own stolidity had found it a trait more endearing than otherwise.

"Sit down." She waved him to her lounger, but he took a chair instead. Jocelyn chuckled and relaxed in the form-fitting seat. "Now," she said, "tell me about yourself."

"Didn't you get a bellyful of me in the news?"

"There sure was plenty." She clicked her tongue. "The entire Solar System in an uproar. Half the people wanted to hang you and H-bomb France for commissioning you. The rest—" Her humor waned. "I hadn't known there was so much popular support for your side of the issue. Your departure crystallized it, somehow."

He gathered his nerve and said, "Frankly, that's what I hoped. One decisive gesture, to cut through that wretched muddle...Okay, you can throw me out."

"No, Gunnar. Never." She leaned over and patted his hand. "I think you're wrong, horribly wrong, but I never doubted you mean well."

"Same for you, of course. Wish I could say likewise for some of your associates. And mine, I must admit. I don't like having the approval of some pretty nasty fanatics."

"Nor I. The Militants—I quit them when they started openly applauding mob violence."

"They tried to blackmail me through my daughter," he said.

"Oh, Gunnar!" Her clasp tightened over his knuckles. "And I never came to see you while she was missing. There was this work for the movement, way off on Venus, and by the time I got back and heard, everything was finished and you were gone. But...are you serious? Did Yore's people really—"

"I fixed that," he said. "'Druther not say any more. We had to keep it out of the news. I'm glad, Joss, you broke with them."

"Not with what they meant in the beginning, though," she said. Tears glimmered suddenly in the long hazel eyes; he wondered on whose account. "Another reason I wanted to get off Earth. Everything was such a ghastly mess, no clear rights or wrongs anyplace you searched." She drew a breath before continuing, with swift earnestness:

"But can't you see what harm the French have done? It looked as if the dispute with Alerion could be settled peacefully. Now the Peacemakers have been tied in a legal knot, and it's all they can do to prevent the extremists from taking over control of Parliament. The Aleriona delegation announced they weren't going to wait any longer. They went home. We'll have to send for them when our deadlock is broken."

"Or come after them, if it breaks *my* way," he said. "What you can't see, you won't see, is that they've no intention of making any real peace. They want Earth out of space altogether."

"Why?" she pleaded. "It doesn't make sense!"

He frowned into his glass. "That's something of a puzzle, I admit. It must make sense in their own terms; but they don't think like us. Look at the record, however, not their soft words but their hard deeds ever since we first encountered them. Including the proof that they deliberately attacked New Europe and are deliberately setting out to exterminate the French colonists there. Your faction denied the evidence, but be honest with yourself, Joss."

"You be honest too, Gunnar—No, look at me. What can a single raider do but make the enmity worse? There aren't going to be any more privateers, you realize. France and her allies have been able to keep Parliament from illegalizing your expedition, so far. But the Admiralty has frozen all transfers of ships, and it'll take more of a legislative upheaval than France can engineer to get that authority out of its hands. You'll die out there, Gunnar, alone, for nothing."

"I'm hoping the Navy will move," he said. "If, as you put it, I make enmity worse—Uh-uh, not a delusion of grandeur. Just a hope. But a man has to do what little he can."

"So does a woman," she sighed.

Abruptly, sweeping to her feet, taking his glass for a refill, smiling with an effort but not as a pretense: "No more argument. Let's be only ourselves this evening. It's been such a long time."

"Sure has. I wanted to see you, I mean really see you, when you came back to Earth, but we were both too busy, I guess. Somehow the chance never seemed to come."

"Too busy, because too stupid," she agreed. "Real friends are so rare at best. And we were that once, weren't we?"

"Rawthuh," he said, as anxious as she to walk what looked like a safe road. "Remember our junket to Europe?"

"How could I forget?" She gave him back his glass and sat down again, but upright this time, so that her knee brushed his. "That funny little old tavern in Amsterdam, where you kept bumping your head every time you stood up, till finally you borrowed a policeman's helmet to wear. And you and Edgar roared out something from the *Edda*, and—But you were both awfully sweet outside Sacre Coeur, when we necked and watched the sun rise over Paris."

"You girls were a lot sweeter, believe me," he said, not quite comfortably. A silence fell. "I'm sorry it didn't last between you and him," he ventured.

"We made a mistake, going outsystem," she admitted. "By the time we realized how much the environment had chewed our nerves, it was too late. He's got himself quite a good wife now."

"Well, that's something."

"What about you, Gunnar? It was so dreadful about poor Connie. But after five years, haven't you—?"

"After five years, nothing," he said flatly. "I don't know why."

She withdrew herself a little and asked with much gentleness, "I dare not flatter myself, but could I be to blame?"

He shook his head. His face burned. "No. That was over with long ago. Let's discuss something else."

"Sure. This is supposed to be a merry reunion. *A nuestra salud.*" The glasses clinked again.

She began to talk of things past, and presently he was chiming in, the trivia that are so large a part of friendship—do you remember, whatever became of, we did, once you said, we thought, do you remember, and then there was, we hoped, I never knew that, do you remember, do you remember?—and the time and the words and the emptied glasses passed, and finally somehow she was playing her flute for him, *Au Clair de la Lune* and *Gaudeamus Igitur*, *September* and *Shenandoah*, Pan-notes bright and cool through the whirl in him, while he had moved to the lounger and lay back watching the light burnish her hair and lose itself in the deep shadows below. But when she began *The Skrydstrup Girl*—

Was it her that I ought to have loved, then,
In a stone age's blossoming spring—

the flute sank to her lap and he saw her eyes shut and her mouth go unfirm.

"No," she said. "I'm sorry. Wasn't thinking. You taught it to me, Gunnar."

He sat straight and laid a clumsily tender hand on her shoulder. "Forget that business," he said. "I should've kept my big mouth shut. But there was no real harm done. It was no more than…than one of those infatuations. Connie didn't hold it against you. She nursed me through the spell okay."

"I wasn't so lucky," she whispered.

Dumfounded, he could only stammer: "Joss, you never let on!"

"I didn't dare. But that was the real reason I talked Edgar into leaving Earth. I hoped—Gunnar, when I came back, why were we both such idiots?"

Then suddenly she laughed, low in her throat, came to him and said, "We're not too late, are we? Even now?"

-3-

Saturn rotated once in about eighteen hours. Seven such days had passed when Uthg-a-K'thaq finished work on the naval computers and rode a tender down to Orling spaceport.

As his huge cetaceal form wallowed into the yacht's chart-room, Endre Vadász, who had been waiting for him, backed up. *Phew!* the minstrel thought. *That swamp stench! If only we had been able to get a human chief engineer, not a creature from Naqsa, beached and desperate for a job…Stop it, you. Humans are prejudiced against Naqsans less because they stink, less because they look like an unseemly cross between a walrus and a nightmare, than because they are tough commercial competitors. If the crew is gradually, grudgingly coming to admit he is decent and capable, I can do no less. How do I look and smell to him?*

"Hallo, C.E.," he greeted. "I hope you are not too tired to depart at once. We have spent too much time here already."

"Quite," replied the rumbling, burbling voice. "I am imwatient as you wy now. Ewerything else can 'roceed without me and, I weliewe, reach com'letion simultaneously with this swecial missile tur-ret. That is, iw the Staurni system is as good as claimed."

"Which is what you are supposed to decide." Vadász nodded. Another irritating thing about Naqsans was their habit of solemnly repeating the obvious. In that respect they were almost as bad as humans. "Well, I've seen to your planetside supplies. Get your personal kit together and meet us at the lift platform outside in half an hour."

"Us-s-s? Who goes to this Nest?"

"You and the skipper, of course, to make decisions, and Gregorios Koumanoudes to interpret. Myself…ah, officially this falls in the steward's department also, since the extra armament will affect stowage. But in practice the steward's department is idle, bored, and in dire need of a jaunt. Then there are two from the *Quest,* Victor Bragdon and Jocelyn Lawrie."

"Why come they with?"

"They're here for xenological research, you know. Accompanying us on a business trip to an important kinfather is a unique opportunity to observe laws and customs in action. So Bragdon offered to lend us one of his flyers, provided he and the woman could ride along. He wanted several of his people, actually, but Nesters limit the number of visitors at one time. Suspicious brutes. In any event, by using the flyer, we save this yacht for shuttle work and so expedite our own project."

"I scent. No, you say 'I see' in English." Uthg-a-K'thaq's tone was indifferent. He turned and slap-slapped on webbed feet toward his cabin.

Vadász looked thoughtfully at his back until he had disappeared. *I wonder how much of our interhuman quarrels and tensions come through to him,* the Hungarian reflected. *Perhaps none. Surely he will think the business between Gunnar and Jocelyn is utter triviation, if he even notices.*

And he may well be right. Thus far, at least, it has only amounted to Gunnar's being often absent from our vessel. Which has done no harm at the present stage of things. The men gossip, but the tone I hear is simple good-natured envy. For myself, I am the last to begrudge a friend what scrap of happiness he can stumble upon. Therefore—why does it make me uneasy, this?

He threw off worry and pushed buttons on the radiophone extension. A middle-aged, scholarly-looking man glared from *Quest's* saloon.

"Good day, Dr. Towne," Vadász said cheerily. "Would you please remind Captain Heim that we're leaving in half an hour?"

"Let him remind himself," the glossanalyst snapped.

"Do you so strongly oppose our little enterprise over here that you will not even give a man an intercom call?" Vadász leered. "Then kindly remind Mme. Lawrie."

Towne reddened and cut the circuit. He must have some very archaic mores indeed. Vadász chuckled and strolled off to complete his own preparations, whistling to himself.

"Malbrouck se va-t-en guerre—"

—And aboard the *Quest,* Heim looked at a bulkhead clock, stretched, and said, "We'd better start."

Jocelyn laid a hand on his roan hair, another beneath his chin, and brought the heavy-boned homely face around until it was close to hers. "Do we have to?" she asked.

The trouble in those eyes hurt him. He tried to laugh. "What, cancel this trip and lose Vic his data? He'd never forgive us."

"He'd be nearly as happy as I. Because it's far more important that...that you come out of this lunacy of yours, Gunnar."

"My dear," he said, "the only thing that's marred an otherwise delightful time has been your trying and trying to wheedle me into giving up the raider project. You can't. In the old Chinese advice, why don't you relax and enjoy it?" He brushed his lips across hers.

She didn't respond, but left the bed and walked across the cabin. "If I were young again," she said bitterly, "I might have succeeded."

"Huh? No, now, look—"

"I am looking." She had stopped before a full-length optex beside her dresser. Slowly, she ran her hands down cheeks and breasts and flanks. "Oh, for forty-three I'm quite well preserved. But the crow's feet are there, and the beginnings of the double chin, and without clothes I sag. You've been—good, kind—the last few days, Gunnar. But I noticed you never committed yourself to anything."

He swung to his own feet, crossed the intervening distance in two strides, and towered over her; then didn't know what to do next. "How could I?" he settled for saying. "I've no idea what may happen on the cruise. No right to make promises or—"

"You could make them conditionally," she told him. The moment's despair had left her, or been buried. Her expression was enigmatic, her tone impersonal. "'If I come home alive,' you might say, 'I'll do such and such, if you're agreeable.'"

He had no words. After some seconds she breathed out and turned from him. Her head drooped. "Well, let's get dressed," she said.

He put on the one-piece garment which doubled as under-padding for an airsuit, his motions automatic, his mind awash. *Okay, what do I want? How much of what I felt (do I still feel it?) was genuine and how much was just a grab at the past when lonesomeness had me off balance?*

I plain don't know.

His bewilderment didn't last long, because he was the least self-analytical of men. He shoved his questions aside for later examination and, with them, most of the associated emotions. Affection for Jocelyn remained in the forefront of his awareness, along with regret that she had been hurt and a puzzled wish to do something about it; but overriding all else was eagerness to be away. He'd cooled his heels long enough on this island. The flight to Trebogir's would be a small unleashing.

"C'mon," he said with reborn merriment. His hand slapped the woman playfully. "Should be quite a trip, you know."

She turned about. Grief dwelt in her eyes and on her lips. "Gunnar—" She must look down at her fingers, tensed against each other. "You really don't think I'm...a fool at best, a traitor at worst...for not wanting a war...do you?"

"*Hvad for pokker!*" he exclaimed, rocked back. "When did I give you that idea?"

She swallowed and found no reply.

He took her by the forearms and shook her gently. "You are a fool if you think I ever thought so," he said. "Joss, I don't want war any more than you. I believe a show of force now—one warning snap of teeth—may head off a fatal showdown later. That's all. Okay, you have a different opinion. I respect it, and I respect you. What've I done to make you suppose anything different? Please tell me."

"Nothing." She straightened. "I'm being silly," she said in a machine voice. "We'd better go."

They went silently downhall. At the locker outside Boathouse Three, Victor Bragdon was donning his airsuit. "Hi, there," he called. "I'd begun to wonder what was keeping you. One of your men delivered your stuff last watch, Gunnar. Good thing, too. You'd never fit into anybody else's outfit."

Heim took the stiff fabric, zipped it shut around himself, and put on gloves and ankle-supporting boots with close attention to the fastenings. If the oxygen inside mingled with the hydrogen outside, he'd be a potential torch. Of course, in a flyer it was only a precaution to wear a full outfit; but he'd seen too often how little of the universe is designed for man to neglect any safety measure. Connecting the helmet to high-pressure air bottles and recycler tank, he hung the rig from his shoulders, but left the valves closed and the faceplate open. Now, the belt of food bars and medicines; canteen; waste unit; not the machine pistol, for you did not come armed into a Nest…He saw that Jocelyn was having some trouble with her gear and went to help.

"It's so heavy," she complained.

"Why, you wore much the same type on New Mars," Heim said.

"Yes, but that was under half an Earth gravity."

"Be glad we aren't under the full Staurnian pull, then," Bragdon said genially. He bent to pick up a carrying case.

"What've you got there?" Heim asked.

"Extra camera equipment. A last-minute thought. Don't get alarmed, though. The field survival kit is aboard and double checked." Bragdon was still grinning as he walked to the entry lock. His aquiline profile was rather carefully turned toward Jocelyn. Heim felt amused.

The boathouse seemed cavernous. The space auxiliary intended to rest here had been replaced by three atmospheric flyers built for work on subjovian planets; and one of them was out on a preliminary mapping flight. The humans wriggled through the lock of another bulky fuselage and strapped in, with Bragdon at the controls. He phonespoke to his dispatcher. The boathouse was evacuated, Staurn's air was valved in, the outer doors were opened. With a whirr of power, the vehicle departed.

It set down again immediately, to let in Vadász, Koumanoudes, and Uthga-K'thaq. The Naqsan looked still more ungainly in his own airsuit than he did nude, but it confined most of his odor. Bragdon made a last check of his instruments and lifted skyward.

"I'm excited as a boy," he said. "This'll be the first real look I've had at the planet."

"Well, you should be able to play tourist," Koumanoudes said. "No bad weather's predicted. 'Course, we wouldn't be aloft anyway in a Staurnian storm. Fee-rocious."

"Indeed? I thought wind velocities were low in a high-density atmosphere."

"Staurn's isn't that dense. About three times Earth pressure at sea level, with gravity accounting for a good deal of it. Also, you've got water vapor, which rises to breed thunderstorms. And so damn much solar energy."

"What?" Jocelyn cast a surprised glance aft, not too near the morning sun. At half again the distance of Sol from Earth, the disc had slightly less angular diameter; and, while it was nearly twice as brilliant, throwing a raw blue-tinged light across the world, its total illumination was likewise a little inferior to home. "No, that can't be. Staurn gets only—what is it?—20 percent more irradiation than Earth."

"You forget how much of that is ultraviolet," Heim reminded her, "with no free oxygen to make an ozone barrier."

"A poor site for a nudist colony," Vadász said. "If the hydrogen, helium, and nitrogen don't choke you, or the methane and ammonia poison you, the UV will crisp you like a steak."

"Brrr. When it's so beautiful, too." Jocelyn pressed her nose against the port by her seat and stared downward.

They were high now, with Orling dropping behind at supersonic speed. The island reared Gibraltar-like from an indigo sea, beaches obsidian black, land turned a thousand subtle shades of red by its forest. There was a final glimpse of a radar, skeletal at the spaceport, then that scar was lost to view and one saw only a great peace brooding under westward cliffs of cumulus. On the edge of vision, kilometers away, a flock of Staurni winged in a V on an unknown errand.

As if to escape some thought, Jocelyn pointed at them and said, "Pardon me if I'm dumb, but how can they fly? I mean, aren't hydrogen-breathers supposed to have less active metabolisms than oxygen-breathers? And is the air pressure enough to support them against nearly twice Terrestrial gravity?"

"They got bird-type bones," Koumanoudes explained.

"As for the energy consideration," Heim added, "it's true hydrogen gives less energy per mole than oxygen, reacting with carbon compounds. But there are an awful lot of hydrogen molecules in a lungful, here. Besides, the enzyme systems are efficient. And—well, look. Staurnian plants photosynthesize water and methane to get free hydrogen and carbohydrates. Animals reverse the process. Only with that flood of ultraviolet on them, the plants build compounds more energy-rich than anything on Earth."

"I see, I suppose." She relapsed into her brown study.

The island fell below the wide horizon. They flew over wine-darkness, streaked with foam, until the mainland hove into sight. There mountains climbed and climbed, red with wilderness at the foot, gray and ruggedly shadowed above, snowpeaked at the top. Sunlight glinted off a distant metallic speck. Heim tuned his and Jocelyn's viewport to full magnification. The speck became a flyer, of gaunt unhuman design, patrolling above a cluster of fused-stone towers that clung to a precipice a kilometer over the surf. "The Perch of Rademir," he said. "Better jog a little farther south, Vic. I'm told he's somewhat peeved at us, and he just might get an impulse to attack."

Bragdon adjusted the autopilot. "Why?"

"He wanted to sell us warheads, when Charlie Wong and I arrived to make arrangements," Koumanoudes said. "But the Roost of Kragan offered us a better price."

Bragdon shook his head. "I really don't understand this culture," he said. "Anarchy and atomic power. They can't go together."

"What?" Vadász tautened in his seat. "There is quite a literature on Staurn," he said very slowly. "Have you not even read it?"

"Oh, sure, sure," Bragdon answered in haste. "But it's a jumble. Nothing scientific. My own field work was mainly on Isis."

"We aren't the best-prepared expedition that ever went out," Jocelyn added. "Quite hurriedly organized, in fact. But with all the trouble in this sector, the Research Authority decided it was urgent to get some solid information on the space-traveling societies hereabouts."

"The Staurni aren't that, exactly," Heim said. "They have the capability, but use it only for planetary defense purposes. They'll trade with visitors, but aren't interested in looking for business themselves."

"They must once—Say." Bragdon turned in his seat to face the others. "We've time to kill. Why don't you give us your version of the situation here? Even when I've read it before, it's helpful to have the material put in different words."

Vadász narrowed his eyes and remained silent. Heim was chiefly conscious of Jocelyn's glove resting on his. He thought that somehow she was pleading with him. To keep away from the thing that divided them? He leaned back, easing the weight of his air equipment onto the rest bracket, and said:

"I'm no expert. But as I understand it, the Staurni are a rare thing, a strictly carnivorous intelligent race. Normally carnivores specialize in fighting ability rather than brains, you know. I once talked with a buck who'd visited here and poked around a little. He said he'd noticed fossil outcrops that suggested this continent was invaded long ago by a bigger, related species. Maybe the ancestral Staurni had to develop intelligence to fight back. I dunno. However it happened, you've got a race with high-powered killer instincts and not gregarious. The basic social unit is, uh, a sort of family. A big family, with a system of companionate marriage so complicated that no human has ever figured it out, plus retainers with their own females and cubs; but still, a patriarchal household dominated by one big, tough male."

The flyer rocked in a gust. Heim peered out. At their present speed, they were already crossing the spine of the mountains. In the west he saw foothills, tumbling off to the red and tawny plain of the Uneasy Lands.

"I shouldn't think that would make for advance beyond savagery," Bragdon remarked.

"They managed it on Staurn, for a while. I don't know how. But then, does anybody know for sure what the evolutionary laws of human civilization are? Maybe being winged, more mobile than us, helped the Staurni. In time they got a planet-wide industrial culture, split into confederations. They invented the scientific method and rode the exponential curve of discovery on up to nuclear engines and gravitronics."

"I think," Uthg-a-K'thaq grunted, "those nations were wuilt on conquest and slawery. Unnatural, and hence unstawle."

Heim gave the tendriled face a surprised glance, shrugged, and went on: "Could be. Now there is one stabilizing factor. A Staurni male is fiercer than a man during his reproductive years, but when he reaches middle age he undergoes a bigger endocrine change than we do. Without getting weak otherwise, he loses both sex drive and belligerence, and prefers to live quietly at home. I suppose under primitive conditions that was a survival mechanism, to give the females and cubs some protection around the nest while the young males were out hunting. In civilization it's been a slightly mellowing influence. The oldsters are respected and listened to, somewhat, because of their experience.

"Nevertheless, the industrial society blew itself apart in a nuclear war. Knowledge wasn't lost, nor even most of the material equipment, but organization was. Everywhere the Staurni reverted to these baronial Nests. Between the productivity of its automated machines and the return of big game to hunt, each such community is damn near independent. Nobody's interested in any more elaborate social structures. Their present life suits them fine."

"What about the Lodge?" Jocelyn asked.

"Oh, yes. There has to be some central group to arbitrate between Nests, defend the planet as a whole, and deal with outworlders. The Lodge grew up as a—I suppose quasi-religious organization, though I don't know a thing about the symbolism. Its leaders are old males. The more active jobs are done by what you might call novices or acolytes, younger sons and such, who sign on for the adventure and the concubines and the prospect of eventually becoming full initiates. It works pretty well."

"It wouldn't with humans," Bragdon said.

"Yeh," Koumanoudes answered, "but these people aren't human."

"That's about everything I know," Heim said. "Nothing you haven't found in books and journals, I'm sure."

He looked outside again. The prairie was sliding swiftly beneath; he could hear the whistle and feel the vibration of their passage. A herd of grazing beasts darkened the land and was gone. Eastward the last mountaintops vanished. No one spoke for a considerable period. Heim was in fact startled to note how much time had gone by while they all sat contemplating the view or their own thoughts, before Bragdon ended the silence.

"One item I have not seen explained," he said. "Apparently each Nest maintains a nuclear arsenal and military production equipment. What *for?*"

"To fight," Koumanoudes said. "They get an argument the Lodge can't settle, like over territory, and hoo! They rip up the landscape. We'll probably see a few craters."

"No. That sort of insanity smashed their civilization."

"The last phase of their civilization, you mean," Heim said. "The present one isn't vulnerable. A Nest is mostly underground, and even the topside buildings are nearly blastproof. Radiation affects a Staurni a lot less than a human, he gets so much of it in the normal course of life; and they have medicines for an overdose here, same as us. And there are no incendiary effects, not in a hydrogen atmosphere. In fact, before atomic energy, the only way to smelt metals was to use a volcanic outlet—which there are plenty of on a big planet with a hot core."

"So they have no restrictions," Jocelyn murmured. "Not even on selling the things offworld, for others to kill with."

"We've been over that ground too mucking often," Koumanoudes growled.

"Free-fall, Greg," Heim warned. The woman's face was so unhappy.

Koumanoudes shifted in his seat, glared out, and grew suddenly rigid.

"Hey!" he barked.

"What's the matter?" Bragdon asked.

"Where do you think you're headed?"

"Why, to the Aerie of Trebogir."

The Greek half rose. His forefinger stabbed at the bow viewports. Above the horizon, ghostly in its detachment, floated a white cone. The plain beneath rolled down toward a thread which wound blinding silver through a valley where cloud shadows ran.

"What the hell!" he exploded. "That's the River Morh. Got to be. Only I know the map. Trebogir doesn't live anywhere in sight of a snowpeak. It must belong to Kimreth upland. We're a good five hundred kilometers north of where we should be!"

Sweat sprang forth on Bragdon's forehead. "I did set a roundabout course, to get a better look at the countryside," he admitted.

"And never told us?" Koumanoudes yanked at his harness. "I should've noticed where the sun is. Get away from that pilot board. I'm taking over."

Heim's eyes swung to Jocelyn. Her fists were clamped together and she breathed in deep uneven gulps.

Bragdon darted his hand into the carrying case by his seat. It lifted, and Heim stared down the barrel of a laser pistol.

"Sit back!" Bragdon ordered. "I'll shoot the first one who unstraps himself."

-4-

When he cycled through the airlock, out of the flyer's interior gee-field, Staurn yanked at Heim so violently that he staggered. He tightened his leg muscles and drew himself erect. However well balanced, the load of gear on him was monstrous.

Jocelyn had gone ahead, to cover the prisoners as they emerged. She looked grotesquely different in her airsuit, and the dark faceplate was a mask over her features. He moved toward her.

"Stop!" In spite of the helmet pickups being adjusted to compensate for changed sound-transmission parameters, her voice was eerily different. He halted under the menace of her gun. It was a .45 automatic, throwing soft-nosed slugs at low velocity to rip open a man's protection.

He drew a long breath, and another. His own air was a calculated percentage composition at three atmospheres, both to balance outside pressure and to furnish extra oxygen for the straining cells. It made his words roar in the helmet: "Joss, what is this farce?"

"You'll never know how sorry I am," she said unevenly. "If you'd listened to me, back on the ship—"

"Your whole idea, then, was to wreck my plan," he flung at her.

"Yes. It had to be done. Can't you see, it had to! There's no chance of negotiating with Alerion when...when you're waging war. Their delegates told Earth so officially, before they left."

"And you believed them? Don't you know any more history than that?"

She didn't seem to hear. Words cataracted from her; through all the distortion, he could read how she appealed to him.

"Peace Control Intelligence guessed you'd come here for your weapons. They couldn't send an armed ship. The Staurni wouldn't have allowed it. In fact, France could block any official action. But unofficially—We threw this expedition together and took off after you. I learned about it because PCI found out I was an, an, an old friend of yours and interrogated me. I asked to come along. I thought, I hoped I could persuade you."

"By any means convenient," he bit off. "There's a name for that."

"I failed," she said desolately. "Vic decided this trip was his chance to act. We don't mean to hurt you. We'll take you back to Earth. Nothing more. You won't even be charged with anything."

"I could charge kidnapping," he said.

"If you want to," she mumbled.

Hopelessness gutted him. "What's the use? You'd get yourself a judge who'd put you on probation."

Vadász appeared, then Koumanoudes, then Uthg-a-K'thaq. The Greek cursed in a steady stream.

Without a captain, without a chief engineer, Fox *will have to go home, beaten before one blow is struck,* Heim thought.

He looked around. They had landed on the west bank of the Morh. It ran wide and luminous through a sandy, boulder-strewn dale walled by low bluffs. The mountains of Kimreth reared opposite the sun, still many kilometers distant, not quite real in the blue-gray haze of intervening air, but a titan's rampart, dominated by the volcanic cone he had seen from afar. Underfoot the ground was covered by that springy mosslike red-yellow growth which was this world's equivalent of grass. Overhead the sky arched plum-dark, clouds scudding on a wind that boomed in his audio receptors. A flock of airborne devilfish shapes drifted into sight and out again.

How far have we come? What's going to happen?

Vadász moved to Heim's side, touched helmets, and muttered, "Quickly, can we rush her? I do not think her aim will be good here."

"Nor can we move fast," Heim said. *Though...would you really shoot me, Joss?*

His heart stuttered and sweat smelt sharp in his nostrils. But before he could nerve himself to try, Bragdon was out, and there was no question whether that laser pistol would be used.

"*G'yaaru!*" Uthg-a-K'thaq shouted. "You hawe lewt the airlock owen!"

"I know," Bragdon said. "And I've set the pilot a certain way. Better lie down." He eased himself to a sitting position.

The flyer whined and leaped forward. The glare off its metal blinded Heim. He saw what seemed a comet arc off the ground, to a hundred meters, loop about, and plunge. Instinct sent him flat on his belly.

Some distance away, the flyer crashed. The explosive mixture of hydrogen and oxygen went off. Blue flame spurted upward. Thunder coughed, again and again, and Heim heard shards scream above him. Then there was only a thick pillar of smoke and dust, while echoes tolled away and were lost in the wind.

He strained back to his feet. His head still rang. The other males did likewise. Jocelyn remained seated.

"Great…jumping…Judas," Koumanoudes gasped. "What have you done?"

"Don't be alarmed," said Bragdon. "We have other transportation coming." He paused. "I may as well explain. The object is to cripple your damned piracy by taking you back to Earth. I had various schemes in mind, but this chance suggested a simple method."

"They engineered this, huh?" Koumanoudes snorted. "Yeh. They've got members in government too."

Heim spoke to Jocelyn. "You never actually quit that gang, did you?"

"Please, please," her whisper drifted down the wind.

"We may as well make ourselves comfortable," Bragdon advised. "This gravity will wear us out if we don't The other vessel probably won't arrive for several hours, since we couldn't make exact timing or location arrangements, nor risk radio." He gestured with his gun. "You sit before I do."

Vadász was so near Heim that the captain alone heard the minstrel's indrawn hiss and noticed how he stiffened. "Heigh-ho, Roger!" he murmured. "Hook the first moon by."

"What's that?" Bragdon challenged, for he saw his prisoners go taut.

"I would not translate in a lady's presence," Vadász snarled.

It thrilled through Heim. *Spaceman's slang.* "*Something's about to happen. Take your chance when you see it.*" The blackness and coldness departed him. His pulse slammed with preparation to fight.

"Are you skizzy, though?" Vadász continued. "We can't stay here."

"What d'you mean?" Bragdon demanded.

"Next to a river like this. Flash floods. We will get tumbled around, our suits torn open, we are dead unless we get on higher ground."

"You lie!"

"No, no. Look at those mountains. Think. A dense atmosphere under strong gravity has a high density gradient, therefore a high temperature gradient. This is autumn. It gets cold enough at night, above snowline, to freeze ammonia. But the stuff liquefies again about noon, and pours down into the riverbeds. The gravity pulls it so fast that it goes fifty kilometers or better before it evaporates. Isn't that true, Gregorios? You were the one who told me."

"Sure," Koumanoudes said. "That's what the name Morh means. Floodwater."

"If this is some trick—" Bragdon began.

It sure as blaze is, Heim's thought leaped. *There's no such phenomenon. But the yarn sounds plausible to a newcomer—I hope—how I hope!*

"I swear I'll shoot on any suspicion," Bragdon said.

Heim started to walk away from him. "Do, if you want," he retorted. "That's an easier way to die than in an ammonia flood. You can't stop me trying to get on top of those bluffs."

His back was tense against the firebeam. But only Jocelyn's cry reached him: "Vic, no, don't! What's the harm?"

"I…guess none, except that it's a difficult climb," Bragdon conceded. "Okay. You people go first. Jocelyn will cover me while I follow. If you feel like running away, once you're over the crest, I don't mind too much. You can't get far before the flyer comes, and we'll catch you then. Or if you find some hiding place, Staurn will kill you for me."

Step by heavy step, Heim wound among the scattered rocks until he reached the nearest bank. It was bare gritty earth, mingled with stones, not high or steep but a daunting obstacle when this weight bore on him. He commenced trudging upward. The slope gave way under his boots, slid past in a hiss and a rattle; he lost his footing and went to hands and knees.

Fumbling erect, he proceeded cautiously. Before long he was half drowned in sweat, his heart raced and the air burned his throat. Through blurred eyes he saw Vadász and Koumanoudes toiling behind. Uthg-a-K'thaq made it with less trouble, down on his stomach, pushing with wide feet and scrabbling with powerful swimmer's arms; but still the Naqsan's breath was noisy across the wind.

Somehow they got to the top. Heim and his engineer gave the others a hand. They crouched on the brink and wheezed.

There was a stone under Heim's glove. His fingers closed. As strength returned, he saw Bragdon halfway up. The Peaceman was taking his time, frequent lengthy rests, during which he stood gun in hand and glared at the privateers. Jocelyn waited below. Now and then sand or pebbles skittered around her, dislodged by Bragdon, but she didn't try to dodge. Her suited form looked black in the lightning-blue sun-dazzle; her pistol reflected it moltenly.

Vadász knelt between Heim and Koumanoudes. He squeezed their hands. No other signal or explanation was needed.

Heim threw his stone. An instant later, their own missiles whizzed from his men. Accelerated at nineteen hundred centimeters per second per second, the rocks flew as if catapulted. He didn't know whose hit Bragdon. He saw the man lurch and fall. Then he and his folk were on their way down again.

Leap—slide—run—skip—keep your feet in the little avalanche you make—charge in your weight like a knight at full gallop!

Jocelyn had not been struck. He saw her stumble back, slow and awkward, and bounded past the collision of Bragdon and Koumanoudes. Dust boiled from his boot-soles. Twice he nearly fell. It could have snapped his neck at the speed he now had. Somehow he recovered balance and raged on ahead.

Down to the valley floor! He must tumble or run, faster than man had ever run before. His body was a machine gone wild, he fought to steer it and slow it but the momentum was overwhelming. Each footfall slammed through muscle and bone to rattle his teeth. The blood brawled in his ears.

Jocelyn had shot once while he plunged. The slug whanged wide. He saw the gun slew around to take closer aim. No chance for fear or hope. He had nothing but velocity. Yet it was too great for common sense to perceive. In her panic and her anguish she hesitated before shooting anew. The time was a fractional second. A man attacking her on Earth would have taken the bullet point blank. Heim crashed by before she could squeeze the trigger. His fist shot out. He did not snatch the gun. His blow tore it from her grasp and spun it meters away.

On flat terrain he braked himself to a normal run, a jog, a halt. He wheeled. Jocelyn had been knocked down by his mere brush against her. She was still struggling to regain her feet. Through his own deep gasps, he heard her weep. He plodded to retrieve the pistol.

When he had it, he looked for the others. Uthg-a-K'thaq slumped on his feet in the rubble under the bluff. Two men stood half crouched nearby. One held the laser. A third sprawled unmoving between them, suit rent and blackened.

Heim steadied one shaking hand with the other and took aim. "Endre!" he called, hoarse and in horror.

"We have him," rang back the voice of the armed man. It sank till the wind nearly overrode it. "But Gregorios is done."

Slowly, Heim dragged his way thither. He could not see through the Greek's sooted faceplate. In a dull fashion he was glad of that. The laser beam had slashed open fabric and body, after which gases mixed and exploded. Blood was streaked round about, garish scarlet.

A gruesome keening lifted from the Naqsan. *"Gwurru shka ektrush,* is this war? We do not thus at home. *Rahata, rahata."*

"Bragdon must have recovered himself and shot as Gregorios jumped him," Vadász said drearily. "The impact jarred his gun loose. I got it and came back here, where they both had rolled. C.E. held him pinned meanwhile."

Heim stared long at the Peaceman. Finally, mechanically, he asked, "Any serious injuries?"

"No," Bragdon replied in the same monotone. "At least, no bones broken. I've a headache." He stumbled off, lowered himself to the ground, and lay there with an arm across his faceplate.

"I thought we could get away with this," Vadász said, eyes fixed on the dead man.

"We did," Heim answered. "Wars have casualties." He clapped the minstrel's shoulder and walked toward Jocelyn. Sweat, runneling down his body, squelched in his boots. He felt a tightness in chest and gullet as if he were about to cry, but he wasn't able.

"You all right, Joss?" he asked.

She backed away. "I won't hurt you," he said.

"But I shot at you!" Her voice was as a frightened child's.

"That's in the game." He laid his arms around her and drew the helmet against his breast. She sobbed for minutes. He waited it out from a vague sense of duty. Not that he hated her; there was a strange ashy vacuum where she had been in him. His emotions were engaged with the man who had died, his thoughts with what must be done.

At last he could leave her, seated and silent. He went on to the wrecked flyer. Fragments and cargo were scattered from hell to breakfast. He found an unharmed entrenching tool and several machetes and carried them back.

"Start digging, Bragdon," he said.

"What?" The man jerked where he lay.

"We're not going to leave Greg Koumanoudes unburied. It'll have to be a shallow grave, but—Get busy. Somebody will spell you when you're tired."

Bragdon rose, centimeter by centimeter. "What have you done?" he cried.

"I didn't kill that man. You did, with your insane attempt to—to what? Do you think you can stand off our flyer?"

"No," Heim said. "I don't plan to be here when it arrives."

"But—but—but—"

"You left your motor running." Heim gave him the tool and continued on to Vadász. Uthg-a-K'thaq bestirred himself and came to help, scooping dirt with his hands.

"Did you think of anything beyond getting control?" Heim asked the Magyar.

"No," said Vadász. "A dim idea of—I knew not what, except that my forefathers never quit without a fight."

"Sit down and let's look at the poopsheets." Every suit had a pocket loaded with charts and other local information. There wasn't much about Staurn. Heim unfolded the map of this region. It fluttered and crackled in the wind. He spread it across his knees. "Greg would have known what these symbols mean. But look—" His finger traced the outlines. "Those mountains are the Kimreth boundary and this is the River Morh; we know that. Now, see, Mount Lochan is marked as the highest in the northern sierra. In fact, no other peak stands that much bigger than its neighbors. So yonder old volcano has to be Lochan. Then we're about *here*."

"Yes." A certain life returned to Vadász's speech. "And here is the Hurst of Wenilwain on Lochan's northern slope. About a hundred airline kilometers hence, would you not say? I doubt we can survive that big a walk. But if we can get moderately near, someone flying on patrol or on a hunt ought to spy us."

"And Wenilwain knows us. Uh-huh." Heim shook his head. "It's a long chance to take, I admit. What are these areas marked between us and him? The Walking Forest; the Slaughter Machines; Thundersmoke."

"Let me try—" Vadász riffled through the pitifully thin handbook. "No entry. But then, this is a stat of a map annotated by Gregorios and Charles, on the basis of what they learned while dealing with the natives. They must have planned to pass the information on when they got home. It's a common practice."

"I know. And Greg's dead. Well, we'll find out."

"What of those?" Vadász pointed at Bragdon painfully digging, Jocelyn huddled by herself.

"They'll have to come along, I'm afraid. For one thing, it'll puzzle and delay their friends, not to find anybody here, and so give us time to find cover. For another thing, we'll need every hand we can get, especially when we hit the foothills."

"Wait!" Vadász slapped the ground. His voice bleakened. "Gunnar, we cannot do it. We have air recyclers, but nothing for water except a day's worth in these canteens. That isn't even allowing for what we will need to reconstitute powdered food. And you know that ten kilometers a day, afoot, will be fantastic progress."

Heim actually noticed himself smiling, lopsidedly. "Haven't you ever met that trick? We won't be far from native water at any time; notice these streams on the map. So we fill our canteens, put the laser pistol at wide beam and low intensity, and boil out the ammonia."

"Spending the capacitor charges," Vadász objected. "That leaves only your slugthrower for defense."

"Shucks, Endre, local tigers are no problem. We're as unsavory to them as they'd be to us. Our biggest enemy is the gravity drag; our second biggest the short food and medicine supply; our third, maybe, bad weather if we hit any."

"M-m-m...as you say. I would still like to know precisely what the Slaughter Machines are. But—yes, of course, we will try." The minstrel got up almost bouncily. "In fact, you have made me feel so much better that I think I can take my turn at digging."

They had not much time to spare, enough barely to scrape a little earth over the fallen man and hear Vadász sing the Paternoster. Then they departed.

-5-

Four Staurnian days? Five? Heim wasn't sure. The nightmare had gone on too long.

At first they made good time. The ground rolled quite gently upward, decked with sparse forest that hid them from aerial searchers without hindering their feet. They were all in trim physical shape. And their survival gear, awkward though it seemed, was a miracle of lightness and compactness.

Yet between it and the gravity, each was carrying a burden equal to more than his own Earth weight. "Good time" meant an average of hardly over one kilometer per hour.

Then the land canted and they were on the slopes of Kimreth's foothills. Worse, their bodies were beginning to show cumulative effects of stress. This was nothing so simple as exhaustion. Without a sealtent, they could never take off their airsuits. The recyclers handled volatile by-products of metabolism; but slowly, slowly, the fractional percent that escaped chemical treatment built up. Stench and itch were endurable, somewhat, for a while. Too much aldehyde, ketone, organic acid, would not be.

And high gravity has a more subtle, more deadly effect than overworking the heart. It throws the delicate body-fluid balance—evolved through a billion years on *one* smaller planet—out of kilter. Plasma seeps through cell walls. Blood pools in the extremities, ankles swell while the brain starves. On Staurn this does not happen fast. But it happens.

Without the drugs in their medikits—gravanol, kinesthan, assorted stimulants and analgesics—the travelers would not have traveled three days. When the drugs gave out (and they were getting low) there would be perhaps one day in which to go on, before a man lay down to die.

Is it worth it? gibbered through the guerning in Heim's skull. *Why didn't we go back home? I can't remember now.* His thought fluttered away again. Every remnant of attention must go to the Sisyphian task of picking up one foot, advancing it, putting it down, picking up the other foot, advancing it…Meanwhile a death-heavy weight dragged at his right side. *Oh, yes, Jocelyn,* he recalled from a remote past. *The rest of us have to take turns helping her along.*

She stumbled. Both of them came near falling. "Gotta rest," her air-warped voice wavered.

"You rested…till ten minutes ago…Come!" He jerked brutally on the improvised harness which joined them.

They reeled on for another five hundred seconds. "Time," Vadász called at the end. They lowered themselves down on their backs and breathed.

Eventually Heim rose to his knees. His vision had cleared and his head throbbed a bit less. He could even know, in a detached way, that the scenery was magnificent.

Eastward the hills up which he was laboring swooped in long curves and dales toward the illimitable hazy plain. The gentled light of an evening sun turned their colors—tawny and orange, with red splashes to mark stands of forest—into a smoldering richness. Not far away a brook twisted bright among boulders, until it foamed over in a series of cataracts whose noise was like bells through the still air. A swarm of insectoidal creatures, emerald bodies and rainbow wings, hovered above the pools it made.

Westward the mountains loomed dark and wild against the sun, which was near their ridge. Yet it tinged Lochan's snowcone, a shape as pure as Fuji's, with unearthly greens and blues under a violet heaven. The crags threw their shadows far down the sides, dusking whatever was ahead on Heim's route. But he saw that, a kilometer hence, a wood grew. His field glasses showed it apparently thick with underbrush. But it was too far to go around—he couldn't see the northern or southern end—while it was probably not very wide.

Vadász had also been looking in that direction. "I think best we call this a day," he said.

"It's early yet," Heim objected.

"But the sun will soon go below that high horizon. And we are exhausted, and tomorrow we shall have to cut our way through yonder stuff. A good rest is a good investment for us, Gunnar."

Hell, we've been sleeping nine hours out of the eighteen! Heim glanced at the others. Their suits had become as familiar to him as the seldom-seen faces. Jocelyn was already unconscious. Uthg-a-K'thaq seemed to flow bonelessly across the place where he lay. Vadász and Bragdon sat tailor style, but their backs were bent. And every nerve in Heim carried waves of weariness.

"All right," he said.

He hadn't much appetite, but forced himself to mix a little powder with water and squeeze the mess through his chowlock. When that was done, he stretched himself as well as his backpack allowed. Some time had passed before he realized that he wasn't sleepy. Exhausted, yes; aching and throbbing; but not sleepy. He didn't know whether to blame overtiredness or the itch in undepilated face and unwashed skin. *Lord, Lord, what I'd give for a bath, clean sheets to lie between, clean air to breathe!* He braked that thought. There was danger enough without adding an extra psychological hazard.

Pushing himself to a seated position, he watched the light die on Mount Lochan. The sky darkened toward night, a few stars trembled, the little crescent of the outer moon stood steely near the zenith.

"You too?"

Heim shifted so he could see through his faceplate who had joined him. Bragdon. Reflexively, his hand dropped to his pistol.

Bragdon laughed without humor. "Relax. You've committed us too thoroughly." After a moment: "Damn you."

"Who made this mess in the first place?" Heim growled.

"You did, back in the Solar System…I've heard that Jews believe death itself to be an act of expiation. Maybe when we die here on Staurn, you'll make some amends for him we had to bury."

"I didn't shoot him," Heim said between his teeth.

"You brought about the situation."

"Dog your hatch before I take a poke at you."

"Oh, I don't hold myself guiltless. I should have managed things better. The whole human race is blood guilty."

"I've heard that notion before, and I don't go along with it. The human race is nothing but a species. Individuals are responsible for what they personally do."

"Like setting out to fight private wars? I tell you, Heim, that man would be alive today if you'd stayed home."

Heim squinted through the murk. He could not see Bragdon's face, nor interpret nuances in the transformed voice. But—"Look here," he said, "I could accuse you of murder in the course of making your own little foreign policy. My expedition is legal. It may even be somewhat more popular than otherwise. I'm sorry about Greg. He was my friend. More, he was under my command. But he knew the risks and accepted them freely. There are worse ways to die than in battle for something that matters. You do protest too much."

Bragdon started backward. "Don't say any more!"

Heim hammered pitilessly: "Why aren't you asleep? Could it be that Greg came back in your dreams? Have you been thinking that your noisy breed may be powered less by love than by hate? Would you like to chop off the finger that pulled the trigger on a man who was trying to do his best for Earth? Can you afford to call anyone a murderer?"

"Go to hell!" Bragdon screamed. "Go to hell! Go to hell!" He crawled off on all fours. Some meters distant, he collapsed and shuddered.

Maybe I was too rough on him, Heim thought. *He's sincere...Fout on that. Sincerity is the most overrated virtue in the catalogue.* He eased himself back to the turf. Presently he slept.

Sunrise woke him, level across the Uneasy Lands and tinging Mount Lochan with fire. He felt more stiff and hollow-headed each dawn, but it helped to move about, fix a cold breakfast and boil a fresh supply of water. Bragdon was totally silent; no one else said many words. But as they started the long slog toward the forest—a whole kilometer uphill—Vadász began to sing.

Trois jeunes tambours, s'en revenaient de guerre.
Trois jeunes tambours, s'en revenaient de guerre.
Et ri, et ran, ra-pa-ta-plan, S'en revenaient de guerre.—

When he had finished, he went on to *Rimini, Marching Through Georgia, The British Grenadiers,* and *From Syrtis to Cydonia.* Heim and Jocelyn panted with him in the choruses, and perhaps Uthg-a-K'thaq, or even Bragdon, got some help too from the tramping rhythms and the brave images of home. They reached the woods sooner, in better shape, than expected.

"Thanks, Endre," Heim said.

"My job, you know," Vadász answered.

Resting before they went among the trees, Heim studied the growth more closely. At a distance, by dawnlight, he had seen that it wound across the hills along a fault line, and was as sharply bordered as if artificial. Since the northwestern edge was well above him on a steep rise, he had also made out a curious, churned sweep of soil on that side, which passed around the slopes beyond his purview. Now he was too near to see anything but the barrier itself.

"Not brushy after all," he observed in surprise. "Only one kind of plant. What do you think?"

"We are none xenowotanists," the engineer grunted.

The trees were about four meters tall; nothing grows high on Staurn. And they were no thicker than a man's arm. But numberless flexible branches grew along the stems, from top to bottom, each in turn split into many shoots. In places the entanglement of limbs was so dense as to be nearly solid. Only the upper twigs bore leaves; but those were matted together into a red roof beneath which the inner forest looked night-black.

"This'll be machete work," Heim said. "We shouldn't have to move a lot slower than usual, though. One man cuts—that doesn't look too hard—while the others rest. I'll begin." He unlimbered his blade.

Whick! Whick! The wood was soft, the branches fell right and left as fast as he could wield his tool. In an hour the males ran through a cycle of turns, Jocelyn being excused, and were far into the forest. *With the sun still only a couple of hours up,* Heim exulted.

"Take over, Gunnar," Vadász rattled. "The sweat is gurgling around my mouth."

Heim rose and advanced along the narrow trail. It was hot and still in here. A thick purple twilight soaked through the leaves, making vision difficult where one stood and impossible a few meters off. Withes rustled against him, springily resisting his passage. He felt a vibration go back through the machete and his wrist, into his body, as he chopped.

Huh! Odd. Like the whole interlocked wilderness shivering.

The trees stirred and soughed. Yet there was no breath of wind.

Jocelyn shrieked.

Heim spun on his heel. A branch was coiling down past her, along her airsuit. Something struck his back. He lifted his machete—tried to—a dozen tendrils clutched him by the arm. He tore free.

An earthquake rumble went through the gloom. Heim lost balance under a thrust. He fell to one knee. Pain shot through the point of impact. The tree before his eyes swayed down. Its many-fingered lower branches touched the soil and burrowed. Leaves drew clear of each other with a crackling like fire. He glimpsed sky, then he was blinded by their descent about his head.

He shouted and slashed. A small space opened around him. The tree was pulling loose its roots. Groaning, shuddering, limbs clawed into the earth, it writhed forward.

The entire forest was on the march. The pace wasn't quick, no faster than a man could walk on Staurn, but it was resistless. Heim scrambled up and was instantly thrown against a tangle of whipping branches. Through airsuit and helmet he felt those buffets. He reeled away. A trunk, hitching itself along, smote him in the stomach. He retched and dropped his machete. Almost at once it began to be covered, as limbs pulled from the ground and descended for the next grab along their way. Heim threw what remained of his strength against them. They resisted with demoniac tenacity. He never knew how he managed to part them long enough to retrieve the blade.

Above the crashing and enormous rustle he heard Jocelyn scream again, not in startlement but in mortal terror. He knelt to get under the leaves and peered wildly about. Through swaying, lurching trunks, snakedancing branches, clawing twigs, murk, and incandescent sunlight spears—he saw her. She had fallen. Two trees had her pinned. They could break bones or rip her suit when they crawled across her body.

His blade flew in his hand. A battlecry burst from his mouth. He beat his way to her like a warrior hewing through enemy lines. The stems had grown rigid, as if they had muscles now tightened. His blows rebounded. A sticky fluid spurted from the wounds he made. "Gunnar, help!" she cried in sightlessness. He cleared brush from her until he could stoop and pull her free.

"You okay?" He must shout to be heard in the racket. She lay against him and sobbed. Another tree bent down upon them. He yanked her to her feet.

"To me!" he bellowed. "Over here!"

Uthg-a-K'thaq wriggled to join him. The Naqsan's great form parted a way for Bragdon. Vadász wove lithely through the chaos.

"Joss in the middle," Heim ordered. "The rest of us, back to back around her. We can't outrun this mess, can't stay here either. We'd exhaust ourselves just keeping our feet. Forward!"

His blade caught a sunbeam and burned in its arc.

The rest was chop, wrestle, duck, and dodge, through the moving horror. Heim's awareness had gone coldly lucid; he watched what happened, saw a pattern, found a technique. But the strength to keep on, directly across that tide, came from a deeper source. It was more than the simple fear of death. Something in him revolted against his bones being tumbled forever among these marching trolls.

Bragdon gave way first. "I can't…lift…this…any more," he groaned, and sank to the earth. Wooden fingers closed about one leg.

Uthg-a-K'thaq released him. "Get in the middle, then," the Naqsan said. "Hel' him, you Lawrie."

Later in eternity, Vadász's machete sank. "I am sorry." The minstrel could barely be heard. "Go on."

"No!" Heim said. "We'll all get out, or none."

"Let me try," Jocelyn said. She gave Vadász into the care of Bragdon, who had recovered a little, and took his knife herself. Her blows were weak, but they found she could use the tool as a crowbar to lever a path for herself.

And…sunlight, open sky, turf under Lochan's holy peak. They went a few meters farther before they toppled.

Heim woke a couple of hours afterward. For a while he blinked at heaven and found curious shapes in the clouds, as if again he were a boy on Gea. When memory came back, he sat upright with a choked oath.

The trees were still moving past. He thought, though, they had slowed down. Northwestward, opposite to their direction, he saw their trail of crumbled earth. The most distant part that he could spy was overlaid with pale yellow, the first new growth.

Uthg-a-K'thaq was the only other one awake. The Naqsan flopped down beside him. "Well, skiwwer, now we know what the Walking Worest is."

"I'd like to know how it works," Heim said.

Rest had temporarily cleared his mind. An answer grew. "I'm only guessing, of course," he said after a minute, "but it could be something like this. The ultraviolet sunlight makes plant chemistry hellish energetic. That particular species there needs something, some mineral maybe. Where faulting exposes a vein of it, a woods appears."

"Not likely mineral," Uthg-a-K'thaq corrected. "You cannot hawe liwe dewendent on sheer geological ac-cident."

"Geology operates faster on a big planet than a terrestrial one, C.E.," Heim argued. "Still, I'll agree it makes poor ecology. Let me think…Okay, let's say you get bacteria laying down organic stuff of a particular kind, wherever conditions are right. Such deposits would be fairly common, exposed fairly often. Those trees could broadcast spores that can lie dormant for centuries, waiting for a chance to sprout. All right, then, they consume the deposit at a tremendous rate. Once mature, such a forest has to keep moving because the soil gets exhausted where it stands. Reproduction is too slow; the trees themselves have to move. Evidently sunlight starts them on their way, because you remember they didn't begin till mid-morning and now in the afternoon they're coming to a halt."

"What hawwens when they hawe eaten out the whole wein?"

"They die. Their remains go back to the soil. Eventually everything gets reprocessed into the material they need, and the spores they've left wake to life." Heim grimaced. "Why am I trying to play scientist? Defense mechanism? I've *got* to believe that thing is natural."

"We came through it aliwe," Uthg-a-K'thaq said calmly. "Is that not suwwicient?"

Heim didn't reply. His gaze drifted west, whither he had yet to go. Did he see a vague plume of mist on the lower steeps of Lochan? It was too distant for him to be sure. But—Thundersmoke? *Whatever that is. No need to worry about it now. First we've got to get past the Slaughter Machines.*

-6-

Two more days—twenty kilometers? They could not have done that much were they not crossing a flat space, a plateau on the lap of Lochan.

It was dreary country, treeless, rock-strewn, sparsely covered with low yellowish scrub. Many streams ran down toward the Morh, their tinkle the only sound except for an endless whittering wind; but the banks held no more life than the dusty stretches beyond. Only the ranges that hemmed in the world on three sides, and the splendid upward leap of the snowcone ahead, redeemed this landscape.

The first evening they camped in sight of a crater. Its vitrified walls gleamed reddish black, like clotted blood, in the last sunlight. Vadász pointed and remarked, "I thought this region is barren because runoff from above leached the soil. Now I find otherwise."

"How so?" Heim asked, incurious in his fatigue.

"Why, yonder is plain to see as bombwork. There must have been an industrial center here once, that was destroyed in the war."

"And you'd let the same happen to Earth!" Bragdon's accusation was the first word he had spoken in more than a day.

Heim sighed. "How often must I explain?" he said, more to Jocelyn than the Peaceman. "Earth has space defenses. She can't be attacked—unless we drift on from crisis to crisis till matters get so bad that both sides have to build fleets big enough to take the losses in breaking through. All I want is to head off that day by settling with Alerion now. Unfortunately, Alerion isn't interested in a reasonable settlement. We've got to prove to them that they haven't any alternative."

"Womwardment does not account wor the inwertility here," said Uthg-a-K'thaq. "The war was three or wour Earth centuries ago. Radioactiwity disawweared long since. Something else has kewt nature 'rom recowering."

"Oh, to hell with it," Jocelyn moaned. "Let me sleep."

Heim lay down too. He thought with a dull unease that they should set a watch—but no, everyone was exhausted…Unconsciousness took him.

The next day they saw two metallic shapes at a distance. There was no question of detouring for a closer look, and in any event they had something else to occupy what small part of their minds could be spared from the ever-more-painful onward march. The end of the plateau was coming into sight. Between the edge and the mountain's next upward slope was an escarpment. Right and left stretched those obsidian cliffs, sheer, polished, not high but unscalable in this gravity without equipment the party didn't have. To go around them—at whatever unseen point they stopped—would take days; and the survival drugs could not last for such a journey.

Only in the center of view was the line broken. A bank of vapor roiled from the foot of the scarp for several kilometers up the mountainside above. Like an immense curtain it hid the terrain; plumes blew off the top, blizzard color against the deep sky, and a roaring grew louder as the walkers neared.

"That has to be Thundersmoke," Vadász said. "But what is it?"

"A region ow—I hawe not the English," Uthg-a-K'thaq answered. *"Tsheyyaka.* The ground weneath is hot, and water woils out."

"Geysers and hot springs." Heim said. He whistled. "But I've never seen or heard of anything their size. They make Yellowstone or Dwarf's Forge look like a teakettle. Can we get through?"

"We must." Uthg-a-K'thaq bent his head so that all three eyes could peer through his faceplate. Evolved for the mists of his own planet, they could see a ways into the infrared. "Yes-s-s. The cliwws are crum'led. Makes an incline, though wery rugged and with water rushing everywhere."

"Still, thank God, a high gravity means a low angle of repose. And once into those meadows beyond, we should have a chance of meeting hunters or patrollers from the Hurst." Heim straightened a little. "We'll pull through."

A while later he saw a third gleam of steel among the bushes. This one was so near the line of march that he altered course to pass by. They didn't know exactly where they could best start into Thundersmoke anyway.

The object grew as he plodded. During rest periods he found he could not keep his gaze off. The shape was no uglier than much else he had seen, but in some indescribable fashion it made his spine crawl. When at last he dragged himself alongside and stopped for a look, he wanted to get away again, fast.

"An ancient machine." Vadász spoke almost too softly to be heard through the grumble and hiss from ahead. "Abandoned when the bomb struck."

Corrosion was slow in this atmosphere. Paint had worn off the iron, which in turn was eroded but still shiny in places. The form was boxlike, some two meters square and five long, slanting on top toward a central turret. The ruins of a solar power accumulator system could be identified, together with a radar sweep and, Heim thought, other detector instruments. Several ports in body and turret were shut, with no obvious means of opening them. He parted the brush around the base and saw that this had been a hovercraft, riding an air cushion and propelled by net backward thrust in any direction.

"A vehicle," he said. "After the war it just sat, I guess. Nobody can have moved back to the Lochan region for a long time. Those other things we glimpsed must be similar."

Jocelyn clutched at his hand. He was reminded of his daughter when she was small and got frightened. "Let's go, Gunnar," she begged. "This is too much like dead bones."

"I wonder," he remarked, carefully matter-of-fact, "why the metal wasn't salvaged. Even with atomic energy, I should think the natives on a fireless planet would value scrap iron."

"Taboo?" Vadász suggested. "These wrecks may well have dreadful associations."

"Maybe. Though my impression is that the Staurni look back on their war with a lot less horror than we remember our Exchange—and Earth got off very lightly." Heim shifted the burden of air system and supply pack on his shoulders. "Okay, we'll push on. The sun's low, and I don't fancy camping among ghosts."

"Can you give us a song, Endre?" Jocelyn asked. "I could use one."

"I shall try." The minstrel's voice was flattened as well as distorted in transmission, but he croaked:

> *While goin' the road to sweet Athy, karroo, karroo!—*

Engaged in helping the woman along, Heim paid no attention to the words at first. Suddenly he realized that Vadász was not singing *When Johnny Comes Marching Home* at all, but the cruel old Irish original.

> *—Where are the legs on which ye run*
> *When first ye went to carry a gun?*
> *Indeed your dancing days are done.*
> *Och, Johnny, I hardly knew ye.*
>
> *With their guns and drums and drums and guns*
> *the enemy nearly slew ye.*
> *Och, Johnny, me dear, ye look so queer,*
> *ohnny, I hardly knew ye!*

Heim glanced at Bragdon. One could almost read the thought in that helmet: How can these devils admit to themselves what war really means? The gloved hands clamped into fists: *I know! I had to bury it*!

> *—Ye haven't an arm and ye haven't a leg,*
> *Ye're an eyeless, noseless, chickenless egg.*
> *Ye'll have to be put in a bowl to beg.*
> *Och, Johnny, I hardly knew ye.*

With their guns and drums and drums and guns—

It was not good to hear in this slain land. But maybe Endre had no choice. Whatever haunted the machine receding too slowly into distance, had touched him likewise.

Everyone was unspokenly glad of the exhaustion which tumbled them into sleep that night. Yet Heim rested ill. Dreams troubled him, and several times he started awake…what noise? A change in the geysers? No, something metallic, a creak, a rattle, a buzz, far off but limping closer; imagination, nothing else. He sank back into the feverish dark.

Dawn was wet with mists blown from Thundersmoke, a bare three or four kilometers away. White vapors coiled along the ground and hazed the countryside so that vision faded shortly into grayness. Overhead the sky was a bowl of amethyst and Lochan's cap too bright to look at. Heim closed his chowlock on a mouthful of concentrate—the rest was a lump in his stomach—and stared blearily around. "Where's Joss?"

"She went yonder," Vadász said. "Um-m…she ought to be back now, eh?"

"I'll go find her." Heim settled the weight on his body and lumbered into the fog.

She hunched not far off. "What's the matter?" he called through the gush and burble of water.

Her form scarcely moved. "I can't," she said thinly.

"What can't you?"

"Go any further. I can't. Pain, every joint, every cell. You go on. Get help. I'll wait."

He crouched, balancing on hands as well as feet. "You've got to march," he said. "We can't leave you alone."

"What can hurt me worse? What does it matter?"

Remorse smote him. He laid an arm across her and said without steadiness, "Joss, I was wrong to make you come. I should have left you behind for your friends—But too late now. I don't ask you to forgive me—"

"No need, Gunnar." She leaned against him.

"—but I do tell you you've got to make the trek. Three or four more days." *Can't be any longer, because that's when we run out of supplies.* "Then you can rest as much as you want."

"Rest forever," she breathed. Moisture ran down her faceplate like tears, but she spoke almost caressingly. "I used to dread dying. Now it's sweet."

Alarm cut through his own weariness. "There's another reason you can't stay here by yourself. You'd let go all holds. This is the wrong time of month for you, huh? Okay." He took the waste unit she had not refolded and slung it on his own back. His gloves groped at her pack.

"Gunnar!" She started. "You can't carry my load too!"

"Not your air rig, worse luck. The rest is only a few kilos." The fresh weight gnawed at him. He climbed to his feet again and reached down for her hands. "C'mon. Allez oop."

The breeze shifted and from the north came the sound of his dreams. Clank, bang, groan, close enough to override the thunders. "What's that?" she shrilled.

"I dunno. Let's not find out." His own heart missed a beat, but he was grimly pleased to see how she scrambled erect and walked.

At camp, Vadász and Uthg-a-K'thaq stared vainly for the source of the new noise. Bragdon was already stumping off, lost in an apathy which must stem from more than tiredness. The others followed him without speculating aloud.

The sun swung higher and began to burn off the fog. Steam still shrouded the natural cut in the cliffs, though the Naqsan said he could make out details of the nearer part. The humans saw scores of boulders, some big as houses, and thousands of lesser rocks that littered the final kilometer before the climb began. Among them washed hot, smoking streams, which turned the ground into mud tinted yellow by sulfur. Where pools had formed the hues were red and green, microscopic organisms perhaps…

The pursuing clatter had strengthened. Vadász tried to sing, but no one listened and he soon quit. They tottered on, breathing hard, pausing less often to rest than had been their wont.

The moment came without announcement. Heim cast a glance behind and stopped dead. *"Fanden i helvede!"* he choked. His companions slewed around to see.

Between the lifting of fog and its own nearness, the thing had become visible a kilometer or so to their rear. It was another machine like the one they had found. But a twisted, weather-eaten detector frame still rose above the turret, and the body moved…slowly, cripplingly, loose parts vibrating aloud, airblower spitting and jerking, the whole frame ashudder, it moved in their wake.

Jocelyn suppressed a cry. Bragdon actually jumped backward a step. Panic edged his tone: "What's that?"

Heim beat down his own quick fear. "An abandoned vehicle," he said. "Some kind of automaton. Not quite worn out. Scarcely any moving parts, you know."

"But it's following us!" Jocelyn quavered.

"Probably set to patrol an area, home on any life it detects, and—" A crazy hope fluttered through Heim's brain, unshared by his guts. "Maybe we're being offered a ride."

"Suq?" asked Uthg-a-K'thaq in astonishment. After a moment, thoughtfully: "Yes-s-s, is wossiwle. Or at least, grant a radio that wunctions, we could call."

"No." Vadász's helmet rolled with headshaking. "I do not trust the looks."

Heim ran a tongue which had gone wooden over his lips. "It's moving quicker than we can, I think," he said. "We'll have to settle with it one way or another." Decision came. "Wait here. I'll go back and see."

Vadász and Jocelyn caught his arms simultaneously. He shook them off. "Damnation, I'm still the captain," he rapped. "Let me be. That's an order."

He started off. The hurt in his muscles dwindled. Instead there came an odd, tingling numbness. His mind felt unnaturally clear, he saw each twig and leaf on the haggard bushes around, felt how his feet struck soil and the impact that traveled through shins to knees, smelled his own foulness, heard the geysers boom at his back. Earth seemed infinitely remote, a memory of another existence or a dream he had once had, unreal; yes, despite its vividness this world was unreal too, as hollow as himself. *I'm afraid,* he thought across an unbridgeable abyss. *That machine frightens me worse than anything ever did before.*

He walked on. There was nothing else to do. The detector lattice swiveled stiffly about, focused invisible unfelt energies on him. The robot changed direction to intercept. Several armor plates clashed loose. Blackness gaped behind them. The whole body was leprous with metal decay.

How long has it wandered this upland? For what?

The turret rotated. A port tried to open, got halfway, and stuck. The machine grated inside. Another port at the front of the body slid back. A muzzle poked forth. The slug-thrower spoke.

Heim saw dirt fly where the bullets hit, a hundred meters short. He whipped about and ran. The thing growled. Swaying on an unstable air cushion, it chased him. The gun raved a minute longer before stopping.

The Slaughter Machines! beat through Heim's skull, in time with his gasps for wind and the jar of footfalls. *Robots to guard whatever there was where that crater is now. Guard it by killing anything that moved. But a missile got through, and the robots alone were left, and hunted and killed till they wore out, and a few are still prowling these barrens, and today one of them has found us.*

He reached the others, stumbled, and rolled, in a heap. For a minute he lay half stunned. Vadász and Uthg-a-K'thaq helped him rise. Jocelyn hung onto his hand and wept "I thought you were dead. I thought you were dead."

"He would be," said Vadász, "but explosives have deteriorated...Watch out!"

Another port had opened, another tube thrust clear. Across the distance, through a red blur in his vision, Heim saw coils, a laser projector, and lasers don't age. He grabbed Jocelyn to pull her behind him. A beam sickled, brighter than the sun. It struck well to the left. Bushes became charcoal and smoke. The beam traced a madman's course, boiled a rivulet, shot skyward, winked out.

"The aiming mechanism," Uthg-a-K'thaq said. For once his own voice was shaken. "Has worn to uselessness."

"Not if the thing gets close," Bragdon whimpered. "Or it can slugger us, or crush us, or—Run!"

The terror had gone from Heim. He felt a cold uplifting: no pleasure of combat, for he knew how thin their chance was, but total aliveness. The matter grew crystalline in his mind, and he said: "Don't. You'll wear yourself out in no time. This is a walking race. If we can get to Thundersmoke, or even to those boulders, ahead of the bullets, we may be able to hide. No, don't shed your packs. We won't be allowed to retrieve them. Walk."

They struck out. "Shall I sing for you?" Vadász asked.

"No need," Heim said.

"I thought not. Good. I do need the breath."

Heim took the rear. The engine coughed and banged behind. Again and again he could not control himself, he must stop and turn about for a look. Always death was closer. Old, old, crumbling, crazed, half blind and half palsied, the thing which had never been alive and would not die shivered along just a little faster than a man could stride on Staurn. The noise from it was an endless metal agony. Once he saw an armor plate drop off, once the air drive went awry and almost toppled the ponderous bulk; but it came on, came on. And the rocks of refuge ahead grew nearer with nightmare slowness.

Jocelyn began to stagger. Heim moved to give her support. As if the change in configuration had tripped some relay in a rotted computer, the slug-thrower spat anew. Several of the bullets buzzed past them.

Bragdon joined Heim on the woman's other side. "Let me help," he panted. She leaned on them both. "We…won't make it," Bragdon said.

"We might," Heim snapped, for he dreaded a return of that negation he had seen in Jocelyn this dawn.

"We could…maybe…if we moved steady. You could. Not me. Not her. Got to rest." Bragdon left the remainder unsaid: *The pursuer needs no rest.*

"Get into that water, among those rocks," Vadász said. "Lie low. Then maybe that *pokolgep* cannot see us."

Heim followed his gesture. Somewhat to the left, a scatter of stones lay in a muddy pool. None were bigger than a man, but—A light artillery shell passed overhead. The cannon crack rang back off the unattainable cliffs. The shell struck, splintered a boulder, but did not explode.

"Let's try," he agreed.

They splashed through muck and crouched bellydown in shallow red water. Heim was careful to hold his automatic free, Vadász his laser. Pistols seemed pathetic against the monster's size and armament; but a man took care of his weapons. Mist blown from Thundersmoke pattered upon them. Heim wiped his faceplate and stared between two rocks.

The machine had halted. It snarled to itself, jerked guns right and left, swept detectors through a hemisphere. "Good Lord," Vadász whispered, "I think indeed it has lost us."

"The water cools oww our in'rared radiation," Uthg-a-K'thaq replied as hushedly. "We are maywe under its radar weams, and maywe the owtical circuits are wad. Or the memory system has gone to wieces."

"If only—No." Heim's pistol sank in his fist.

"What did you think?" Jocelyn asked, frantic.

"How to disable what's left of the detector lattice. Could be done by a laser beam—see that exposed power cable? Only you'd never get close enough before you were spotted and killed."

The short pulse-stopping hope, that the machine might give up and go away, crashed. It started grinding about a spiral, a search curve. Heim plotted that path and muttered: "Should be here inside half an hour. However, first it'll move away. Which gains us some slight meterage. Be ready to start when I give you the word."

"We'll never make it, I tell you," Bragdon protested.

"Not so loud, you crudhead. We don't know that the thing hasn't still got ears."

As if in response, the robot stopped. It rested a moment on the whirr from its air blowers; the lattice horns wove around, tilted, came to a halt...It continued along the spiral.

"You see?" Vadász said with disgust. "Keep trying, Bragdon. You may yet destroy us."

The Peaceman made a strangled noise. "Don't," Jocelyn begged. "Please."

Uthg-a-K'thaq stirred. "A thought," he belched. "I do in truth weliewe we cannot outrun the enemy to shelter. But can Slaughter Machines count?"

Vadász's breath hissed inward. "What's this?"

"We hawe lit-tle to lose," the Naqsan said. "Let us run, excewt for one who waits here and keews the laser. Can he get unnoticed in cutting range ow the wistol—"

"He could be killed too easily," Heim said. But hope shuddered anew in him. *Why not? Better go down fighting, whatever happens. And I might even save her.*

"Okay," he said slowly. "Give me the gun and I'll bushwhack our friend."

"No, skipper," Vadász said. "I am no hero, but—"

"Orders," Heim said.

"Gunnar—" broke from Jocelyn.

Uthg-a-K'thaq plucked the laser out of Vadász's grasp. "No time wor human games," he snorted. "We were not here without him, and he is the least usewul. So." He thrust the weapon at Bragdon. "Or dare you not?"

"Gimme!" Heim snatched for it.

Bragdon drew away. "That thing out there," he said in a remote voice. "What comes of war. Think about that, Heim."

Vadász wallowed through the water and silt, after him. Heim saw the robot stop again to listen. "Get out of here!" Bragdon yelled. "I'll let it see me if you don't!"

The machine plowed through the bushes, over streams and stones, directly toward them.

No chance to argue. Bragdon must go ahead and be a damn fool. Heim got to his feet with a sucking splash. "Follow me—everyone!" Jocelyn slithered from the pool with him. They started off together.

Thundersmoke brawled before them. The engine chugged hoarse behind. A gun chattered. Mist swirled in their view, settled on their faceplates, blinded them. Staurn hauled them downward, laid rocks to trip them, brewed mud to glue their boots. Heim's heart smashed at his ribs as if it were also a cannon. He didn't know how much he leaned on Jocelyn or she on him. There was no awareness of anything but noise, weight, and vast drowning waters.

Vadász shouted.

Heim lurched against a boulder, got his back to it, and lifted his automatic. But the hunter machine was not about to pounce.

Near the thing was, most horribly near. Bragdon's tiny form crept from ambush. Up to that iron body the man went, braced himself on widespread legs, aimed his pistol and fired.

The laser sword hewed. Metal framework glowed white where struck. Trigger held fast, Bragdon probed for the power cable.

Something like a bull's bellow rose out of the robot. It swung clumsily around. Bragdon stood where he was, dwarfed under its bulk, steadily firing. Ports opened in the armor, where they were able. Guns came out. A few still worked. Heim hauled Jocelyn to the ground and laid himself above her. A wild beam hit the boulder where he had made his stand. Rock flowed from the wound.

The guns could not reach as low as Bragdon. The machine clanked forward. Bragdon severed the detector powerline. "Run, Victor!" Vadász howled. "Get out of the way!" Bragdon turned and tripped. He went on his face. The robot passed over him.

And on, firing, firing, a sleet of bullets, shells, energy beams, poison gases, destruction's last orgasm; senseless, witless, futureless, the Slaughter Machine rocked south because it chanced to be headed that way.

Heim rose and hurried toward Bragdon. *Maybe he's all right. An air cushion distributes weight over a large area.* Bragdon did not stir. Heim came near and stopped.

Dimly, through the clamor of geysers and departing engine, he heard Jocelyn call, "I'm coming, Gunnar!"

"No," he cried back. "Don't."

There were sharp blades in the bottom of the iron shell. They must move up and down, clearing the ground by a few centimeters. He did not want her to see what lay before his eyes.

-7-

Drumroll in the earth: vapor puffed from a sulfurous cone. Then the spout came, climbing until a pillar for giants stood white and crowned. Another died; but there were more, everywhere among the tumbled black stones, as far as Heim could see through a whirl of fog. There was no distance. He groped in chaos. Water chuckled around his boots; over and over again he slipped on wetness. The damp was interior too, sweat soddened his skin. Strange, he thought in what detachment he could muster from the weariness with which he trembled, strange that his lungs should be a dry fire. Jocelyn's gasps reached him, where she crawled at his side.

Half his strength was spent to help her along. Otherwise he heard nothing but the titanic forces that churned about them. Uthg-a-K'thaq's broad shape was visible ahead, leading the way. Vadász toiled in the rear. Light waned as the sun sank behind the mountain, to end the day after they piled a cairn over their newest dead.

We've got to keep going, chanted idiotically in Heim. *Got to keep going. Got to keep going.* And underneath: *Why?*

For the sake of the battle he intended to fight? That had become meaningless. The only battle was here, now, against a planet. For Lisa, then? A better cause, that she should not be fatherless. But she could well survive him. Grief dies young in the young. To discharge his own responsibility to those he commanded? Better still; it touched a deep-lying nerve. Yet he was no longer in command, when his engineer saw more clearly and moved more surely than any human could.

Reasons blew away like geyser smoke. Death lured him with promises of sleep.

Animal instinct raised his hackles. He cursed the tempter and went on.

A mudpot bubbled on a level stretch. The farther bank was a precarious hill of boulders. Water rushed among them, struck the mud below and exploded in steam. Uthg-a-K'thaq beckoned the others to wait, flopped down on his belly and hitched himself forward. Mineral crusts were treacherous, and whoever fell into one of those kettles might be cooked alive before the rest heaved him out against gravity.

Jocelyn used the pause to lie flat. Maybe she slept, or fainted; small difference any more. Heim and Vadász remained standing. It would have been too much effort to rise again.

On the edge of visibility, among the clouds around the hilltop, Uthg-a-K'thaq waved. Heim and Vadász wrestled Jocelyn back to her legs. The captain led the way, stooped so he could make out the leader's track through gray soft precipitate powders.

When he came to the rise, hands and feet alike must push him over the high-stacked stones. Often a lesser chunk got loose and bounced hollowly down to the mudpot. Safest would have been to go one at a time, his dimmed consciousness realized now—

"*Gunnar!*"

He scrambled around, and almost went down in the same minor avalanche where Jocelyn rolled.

Somehow he was up, bounding through the hot fog as he had plunged to attack centuries ago. Stones turned under his soles, water spurted where he struck. Nothing existed but his need to stop her before she went into the cauldron below.

Her limbs flailed, her fingers clawed, dislodging more rocks that tumbled across her. He reached bottom. His boots sank in ooze. There was not too much heat on this fringe of the pot. But had there been, he would not have noticed. Those boulders which had spun downward faster than the woman and sunk immediately gave footing. He knelt and braced himself.

The mass poured at him, around him. He laid hold on Jocelyn's air cycler and became a wall.

When the landslip was done, he pulled his smeared self clear and fell beside her. Vadász saw they would go no further than the verge of the mudsink, ended his own haste, and picked a cautious way to join them. Presently Uthg-a-K'thaq arrived too.

Heim roused some minutes later. The first he noticed was the Naqsan's voice, weirdly akin to the voice of the kettle: "Wery much harm wor us. Lac-King him, can we long liwe?"

"Joss," he mumbled, and fought to rise. Vadász helped him. He leaned on the Magyar a while until strength returned.

"*Hála Istennek,*" gusted from the helmet beside his. "You are not hurt?"

"I'm okay," Heim said. His entire being seemed one bruise, and blood welled from abrasions. "Her?"

"Broken leg at the minimum." Vadász's fingers touched the unnatural angle between left hip and thigh of the motionless figure. "I don't know what else. She is unconscious."

"Her suit is intact," Uthg-a-K'thaq said. *First silly remark I've heard from him,* trickled through Heim. *If the fabric had torn, we wouldn't worry about bones.*

He shoved Vadász aside and bent over her. When the faceplate had been wiped clean, he could make out her features in the dimming light. Eyes were closed, lips half-parted, skin colorless and sweat-beaded. He was dismayed at how sunken her cheeks were. Laying an audio pickup against her speaker, he was barely able to detect breath, rapid and shallow.

He poised on his knees. To stave off the future, he asked, "Did anyone see what happened?"

"A stone moved when she put her weight on," Vadász said. "She started to roll and half the hillside went with her. Some recent quake must have unstabilized it. I will never know how you got down here so fast, not falling."

"Who cares?" Heim gritted. "She's in shock. I don't know if that's due to nothing more than the leg fracture, she being so weakened to begin with. Could be worse injuries, like spinal. We don't dare move her."

"What then can we do?" the engineer asked.

Heim realized that command had passed back to him. "You two go on," he said. "I'll stay with her."

"No!" Vadász exclaimed involuntarily.

Uthg-a-K'thaq spoke in some remnant of his pedantic way. "You can giwe her no aid, woth sealed in airsuits. We others may well need an ex-tra wair ow hands. A diwwicult wassage is wewore us,"

"As battered as I am, I'd hinder you more than help," Heim said. "Besides, she can't be left alone. Suppose there's another rockslip, or this mudpot boils higher?"

"Cawtain, she is done already. Unconscious, she cannot take her grawanol. Without that, in shock, heart wailure comes quickly. Kindest to owen her helmet now."

Rage and loss flew out of Heim: "Be quiet, you coldblooded bastard! You goaded Bragdon to die, on purpose. One's enough!"

"Gwurru," the Naqsan sobbed, and retreated from him.

The venom dissipated, leaving emptiness. "I'm sorry, C.E.," Heim said dully. "Can't expect you to think like a Terrestrial. You mean well. I suppose men's instincts are less practical than yours." Laughter shook chains in his throat. "Speaking about practicality, though, you've got something like an hour of light. Don't waste it. March."

Vadász considered him long before asking, "If she dies, what will you do?"

"Bury her and wait. I can stretch out the water in these canteens if I sit quiet, but you'll need the laser for your own drink."

"And you will then have nothing to, to fall back on. No, this is foolishness."

"I'll keep the automatic, if that makes you happier. Now get going. I'll hoist a beer with you yet."

Vadász surrendered. "If not on ship," he said, "then in Valhalla. Farewell."

Their hands clasped, pair by pair. Minstrel and engineer began to climb. A geyser spat not far off, steam blew down the wind, the two shapes were lost to sight

Heim settled himself.

A chance for sleep, he thought. But that desire was gone. He checked Jocelyn's breathing—no change—and stretched out beside her, glove upon her glove.

Resting thus, he grew clearer-headed. With neither excitement nor despair he weighed the likelihood of survival. It wasn't great. Zero for Joss, of course, barring miracles. For the other three, about fifty-fifty. The walkers should emerge from Thundersmoke tomorrow evening, more or less. Then they had perhaps two days (allowing those tough bodies one day without chemical crutches) in which to cross the high meadows toward Wenilwain's castle. It was still distant, but the folk of the Hurst ranged widely. Doubtless they even crossed above Slaughter Land now and then, on their way to the plains and the sea. *(Hm, yes, that's why they leave the robots alone. A free defense. Carnivore souls for sure.)* Given a break, the travelers might have been spied days ago.

Well, the break was not given. So Joss must die in this wet hell, under a sun whose light would not reach Earth for a century: Earth of the greenwoods where she had walked, the halls where she danced, the garden where she played her flute for him until he frightened her with babbled impossibilities. As that sun smoldered to extinction behind the fogs, Gunnar Heim pondered the riddle of his guilt toward her.

He had forced her here. But he did so because if she stayed behind she would betray his hopes for his planet. *(Are you certain of that, buck? In fact, are you certain your way is the right one?)* The choice would never have arisen except for the plot she had joined in. Yet that was evoked by his own earlier conspirings.

He gave up. There was no answer, and he was not one to agonize in unclarity. This much he knew: if the time aboard the *Quest* had not matched those dreams he buried long ago for Connie's sake, it had still been more dear than he deserved, and when Joss died a light would forever go out in him.

Blup-blup, said the mudpot beneath. A hot spring seethed louder. A geyser roared in thickening dusk, echoes resounded from unseen walls and water rilled among the shadow shapes of boulders. Heavy as his own flesh pressed against unyielding painful jumble, night flowed across the world.

Gloom lightened when the nearer moon rose, close to full, a shield bigger than Luna seen from Earth, iron bright and mottled with a strange heraldry. Heim dozed a while, woke, and saw it well above him. A thin glow surrounded the disc, diffusion in the upper mists. But most of the sky was open and he could make out stars. The lower fog rolled ashen through Thundersmoke gulch.

His drowsy eyes tried to identify individual suns. Could that bright one near Lochan's ghostlike peak be Achernar? If so, curious to look from here upon his emblem of victory. *I wonder if Cynbe could be watching it too. Wherever he is.*

Better check on Joss. He commenced pulling his stiffened frame off the rocks.

What's that?

WHAT'S THAT?

The sight was a lightning bolt. For a second he could not believe. A long V trailed across the moon—

Staurni, in flight home to the Hurst!

Heim soared erect. "Hey! Hallo-o-o! You up there, come down, help, help, help!"

The bawling filled his helmet, shivered his eardrums, tore his larynx; and was lost within meters of noise-troubled air. He flapped his arms, knew starkly that the blurring vapors made him invisible from so high above, saw the winged ones pass the disc and vanish into darkness. A beast yell broke from him, he cursed every god in the cosmos, drew his automatic and fired again and again at heaven.

That little bark was also nothing. And not even a glint from the muzzle. Heim lifted the useless thing, that could only kill Joss, to hurl it into the mud.

His hand sank. The metal moonlight seemed to pierce his skull, he was instantly cold, utterly aware, tracing the road he must follow as if on a battle map.

No time to lose. Those wings beat fast. He squatted, unbuckled his air system, hauled its packboard around in front of him. The valve on the hose into his suit closed readily, but the coupling beyond resisted. And he had no pliers. He threw all his bear strength into his hands. The screw threads turned. The apparatus came free.

Now he was alone with whatever air his suit contained; the recycler depended on pressure from the reserve bottles. He cracked their valves. Terrestrial atmosphere, compressed more than Staurn's own, streamed forth.

The reaction must be kindled, and he had no laser. Heedless of ricochet or shrapnel, he laid the automatic's mouth, against the cock and pulled the trigger. The bang and the belling came together. Alloy shattered, the bullet screamed free, the air tanks became a lamp.

Its flame was wan blue under the moon. Heim held the packboard steady with one hand and fanned with the other. "Please," he called, "please, look this way, she'll die if yon don't." A far-off part of him observed that he wept.

The fire flickered out. He bent near the pressure gauge, trying to read it in the unpitying moonlight. Zero. Finished.

No, wait, that was zero net. There were still three atmospheres absolute. And hydrogen diffused inward faster than oxygen did outward. Explosive mixture? He scrambled to put the bottles behind a large rock. Leaning across, he shot straight into them and threw himself down.

Flame blossomed anew, one fury and the crash toning away, whine of flying fragments, a grating among lesser stones as they sought new rest, nothingness. Heim got carefully up.

An infinite calm descended upon him. He had done what he could. Now it was only to wait, and live or die as the chance befell. He returned to Jocelyn, listened to her breath, and lay down beside her.

I ought to be in suspense, he thought vaguely. *I'm not. Could my air be poisoned already?—No, I should last an hour or so if I don't move. I'm just...fulfilled, somehow.* His eyes went to the moon, his thoughts to Connie. He had no belief in survival after death, but it was as if she had drawn close to him.

"Hi, there," he whispered.

And—"Hai-i-i-i!" winded down the reaches of heaven, the air sang, and bat wings eclipsed the moon. Weapons flashed clear, the flock whirled around in their search for an enemy, fangs glittered, and devil shapes came to earth.

Only they didn't act like devils, once they saw. A warrior bayed into the midget transceiver he carried. A vehicle from the Hurst descended within minutes. Her mother could not have raised Jocelyn more tenderly onto a stretcher and into the machine. Wolf-gray Wenilwain himself connected an oxygen bottle to Heim's suit. The flyer lifted and lanced eastward for Orling.

"But...listen...*jangir ketleth*—" Heim desisted. His few pidgin phrases couldn't explain about Endre and C.E. No matter, really. He'd soon be at the yacht; Wong could interpret via radio; the last survivors would be found no later than sunrise. Heim fell asleep smiling.

-8-

Her cabin was quiet. Someone had hung a new picture on the bulkhead where she could see it: a beach, probably on Tahiti. Waves came over a sapphire ocean to foam against white sands; in the foreground, palm trees nodded at Earth's mild winds.

She laid down her book as the tall man entered. Color mounted in her face. "Gunnar," she said very low. "You shouldn't be up."

"Our medic wants me on my back till we leave," he said, "but the hell with him. At least, I had to come see you before you go. How're you feeling?"

"All right. Still weak, of course, but Dr. Silva says I'm making a good recovery."

"I know. I asked him. Enzyme therapy is a wonder, eh?" Heim searched for a phrase. Nothing sufficed. "I'm glad."

"Sit down, you idiot!"

He pulled the lounger close to her bed and lowered himself. Even in a flyer, the trip had left him lightheaded. Several days yet must pass before his vigor was restored. The gun at his hip caught on the adjuster console. He pulled it free with a muttered oath.

Amusement touched her lips. "You needn't have brought that. Nobody's going to kidnap you."

"Well, hopefully not. Call it insurance."

Her smile faded. "Are you that angry?"

"No. Two good men died, the rest of us went through a nasty time. I'm sorry it happened, but you can't take an episode in a war to heart."

Her look reminded him of a trapped small animal. "You could press charges of murder."

"Good Lord!" he exclaimed. "What kind of swine do you take me for? We went out together on a field trip. Our engine failed, we made a crash landing where one man was killed, and hiked after help. If your people will stick by that story, mine will."

A thin hand stole toward him. He took it and did not let go. Her hazel eyes caught him in turn. Silence grew.

When he could hold out no more, and still lacked meaningful words, he said, "You're hauling mass at dawn, right?"

"Yes. The scientists—those who thought this was a genuine trip—they want to stay. But Captain Gutierrez overruled them. We've lost our purpose." Quickly: "How long will you remain?"

"About another Earth week, till the new missile units are fitted. To be sure, we'll lose time getting out of the planetary system. The Lodge has to escort us, and won't let us arm our warheads till we're beyond defensive limits. But still, I figure we'll be on the move inside of ten days."

Again muteness, while they looked at each other, and away, and back. "What do you plan on doing at home?" he tried.

"Wait for you," she said. "Pray for you."

"But—no, look, your, uh, your political work—"

"That's no longer relevant. I haven't changed my mind—or have I? It's hard to tell." Her free hand rubbed her forehead confusedly. The motion stirred her hair, awakening light in the chestnut tresses. "I don't think I was wrong in principle," she said after a bit. "Maybe I was in practice. But it doesn't matter any more. You see, you've changed the universe. Earth is committed."

"Nonsense!" His face smoldered. "One ship?"

"With you her captain, Gunnar."

"Thanks, but...but you flatter me and—Wait, Joss, you do have a job. Sentiment at home might swing too far in the other direction. The last thing any sane person wants is a jehad. You keep telling 'em the enemy is not too evil to live.

Remind 'em there'll be peace negotiations eventually, and the more reasonable we are then, the more likely the peace is to last. Okay?"

He saw that she braced herself. "You're right, and I'll do my poor best," she said. "But talking politics is only an evasion."

"What do you mean?" he stalled.

Her mouth quirked afresh. "Why, Gunnar, I do believe you're scared."

"No, no, nothing of the sort. You need rest. I'd better go."

"Sit," she commanded. Her fingers closed about his palm. The touch was light, but it would have been easier to break free of a ship grapple.

Red and white chased each other across her countenance. "I have to explain," she said with, astounding steadiness. "About what happened earlier."

His skin prickled.

"Yes, I hoped to persuade you not to fight," she said. "But I learned more was involved. Infinitely more."

"Uh, uh—the past, sure—"

"When you come back," she asked, "what are *you* going to do?"

"Live quietly."

"Ha! I'd like to make book on that. For a while, though, you will be home on Earth." Her tone dropped. "Oh, God, you must." She raised her head. "I'll be there too."

He must summon so much will to speak that none was left for holding his eyes off the deck. "Joss," he said, word by word, "you remember too many things. So do I. There was that chance once, which we did better to pass up. Now we met again, both free, both lonesome, and I admit I also thought the chance might have come again. Only it hadn't. Time switched the dice on us."

"No, that isn't true. Sure, at first I believed otherwise. Our casual meetings after I returned from Ourania, and the political barrier between us—damn all politics! I thought you were simply attractive, and half that must be because of a friendship we'd never revive. I dreamed a little on the way here, but they seemed like just ordinary woman-type daydreams. How could you hurt me?" She paused. "It turned out you could."

"I'm trying not to," he said desperately. "You're too good for soothing with lies."

She let his hand go. Her own fell open upon the blanket. "So you don't care."

"I do, I do. But can't you see, I didn't break with Connie the way you did with Edgar. When she, well, helped me about you, we pulled still closer together. Then she died. It cut me off at the roots. I guess without thinking about it I've looked ever since for a root that strong. I'm a coward, afraid to settle for anything less, because afterward someone else might happen by who—It wouldn't be fair to you."

She rallied. "You've outgrown believing in permanent infatuation, haven't you? We understand what really matters between two people. If you're trying to warn me you might be restless—I wouldn't be jealous at your wandering a little. As long as you always came back."

"I don't want to wander. Physically isn't important. I wouldn't want to mentally. That one time was bad enough. And when I heard about New Europe, I remembered a girl there. I was young and stupid, skittish about being tied down, which is especially bad for a Navy man. So I left when my leave was up without committing myself. Next time I arrived, she'd moved; I dithered whether to track her down, finally didn't, and soon after got posted too far away to visit that planet. Now—"

"I see. You want to make sure about her."

"I have to."

"But that was twenty years or more ago, wasn't it?"

He nodded. "I've got to find out what happened to her, see her safe if she's still alive. Beyond that, yes, I'm doubtless being foolish."

She smiled then. "Go ahead. I'm not too worried."

He rose. "I must leave now. Neither of us is in any shape for emotional scenes."

"Yes. I'll wait, darling."

"Better not. Not seriously, anyhow. Hell alone knows what'll happen to me. I might not return at all."

"Gunnar!" she cried, as if he had struck her. "Never say that!"

He jollied her as best he could, and kissed her farewell, and departed. While his pilot flitted him the short way back to the yacht, he looked out. A flock of Staurni hunters was taking off. Sunlight flared across their weapons. The turmoil in him changed toward eagerness—to be away, to sail his ship again—as he watched those dragon shapes mount into the sky.

UNTITLED LIMERICK

There was a young man of Calais
who considered himself a gourmet,
eating crocodile roast
and flies' eggs upon toast.
His sex life was more recherché.

Hiding Place

Captain Bahadur Torrance received the news as befitted a Lodgemaster in the Federated Brotherhood of Spacemen. He heard it out, interrupting only with a few knowledgeable questions. At the end, he said calmly, "Well done, Freeman Yamamura. Please keep this to yourself till further notice. I'll think about what's to be done. Carry on." But when the engineer officer had left the cabin—the news had not been the sort you tell on the intercom—he poured himself a triple whisky, sat down, and stared emptily at the viewscreen.

He had traveled far, seen much, and been well rewarded. However, promotion being swift in his difficult line of work, he was still too young not to feel cold at hearing his death sentence.

The screen showed such a multitude of stars, hard and winter-brilliant, that only an astronaut could recognize individuals. Torrance sought past the Milky Way until he identified Polaris. Then Valhalla would lie so-and-so-many degrees away, in that direction. Not that he could see a type-G sun at this distance, without optical instruments more powerful than any aboard the *Hebe G.B.* But he found a certain comfort in knowing his eyes were sighted toward the nearest League base (houses, ships, humans, nestled in a green valley on Freya) in this almost-uncharted section of our galactic arm. Especially when he didn't expect to land there, ever again.

The ship hummed around him, pulsing in and out of four-space with a quasi-speed that left light far behind and yet was still too slow to save him.

Well...it became the captain to think first of the others. Torrance sighed and stood up. He spent a moment checking his appearance; morale was important, never more so than now. Rather than the usual gray coverall of shipboard, he preferred full uniform: blue tunic, white cape and culottes, gold braid. As a citizen of Ramanujan planet, he kept a turban on his dark aquiline head, pinned with the Ship-and-Sunburst of the Polesotechnic League.

He went down a passageway to the owner's suite. The steward was just leaving, a tray in his hand. Torrance signaled the door to remain open, clicked his heels and bowed. "I pray pardon for the interruption, sir," he said. "May I speak privately with you? Urgent!"

Nicholas van Rijn hoisted the two-liter tankard which had been brought him. His several chins quivered under the stiff goatee; the noise of his gulping filled the room, from the desk littered with papers to the Huy Brasealian jewel-tapestry hung on the opposite bulkhead. Something by Mozart lilted out of a taper. Blond, big-eyed, and thoroughly three-dimensional, Jeri Kofoed curled on a couch, within easy reach of him where he sprawled in his lounger. Torrance, who was married but had been away from home for some time, forced his gaze back to the merchant.

"Ahhh!" Van Rijn banged the empty mug down on a table and wiped foam from his mustaches. "Pox and pestilence, but the first beer of the day is good! Something with it is so quite cool and—um—by damn, what word do I want?" He thumped his sloping forehead with one hairy fist. "I get more absent in the mind every week. Ah, Torrance, when you are too a poor old lonely fat man with all powers failing him, you will look back and remember me and wish you was more good to me. But then is too late." He sighed like a minor tornado and scratched the pelt on his chest. In the near tropic temperature at which he insisted on maintaining his quarters, he need wrap only a sarong about his huge body. "Well, what begobbled stupiding is it I must be dragged from my all-too-much work to fix up for you, ha?"

His tone was genial. He had, in fact, been in a good mood ever since they escaped the Adderkops. (Who wouldn't be? For a mere space yacht, even an armed one with ultrapowered engines, to get away from three cruisers was more than an accomplishment; it was nearly a miracle. Van Rijn still kept four grateful candles burning before his Martian sandroot statuette of St. Dismas.) True, he sometimes threw crockery at the steward when a drink arrived later than he wished, and he fired everybody aboard ship at least once a day. But that was normal.

Jeri Kofoed arched her brows. "Your first beer, Nicky?" she murmured. "Now really! Two hours ago—"

"*Ja*, but that was before midnight time. If not Greenwich midnight, then surely on some planet somewhere, *nie*? So is a new day." Van Rijn took his churchwarden off the table and began stuffing it. "Well, sit down, Captain Torrance, make yourself to be comfortable and lend me your lighter. You look like a dynamited custard, boy. All you youngsters got no stamina. When I was a working spaceman, by Judas, we made solve our own problems. These days, death and damnation, you come ask me how to wipe your noses! Nobody has any guts but me." He slapped his barrel belly. "So what is be-jingle-bang gone wrong now?"

Torrance wet his lips. "I'd rather speak to you alone, sir."

He saw the color leave Jeri's face. She was no coward. Frontier planets, even the pleasant ones like Freya, didn't breed that sort. She had come along on what she knew would be a hazardous trip because a chance like this—to get an in with the merchant prince of the Solar Spice & Liquors Company, which was one of the major forces within the whole Polesotechnic League—was too good for an opportunistic girl to refuse. She had kept her nerve during the fight and the subsequent escape, though death came very close. But they were still far from her planet, among unknown stars, with the enemy hunting them.

"So go in the bedroom," van Rijn ordered her.

"Please," she whispered. "I'd be happier hearing the truth."

The small black eyes, set close to van Rijn's hook nose flared. "Foulness and fulminate!" he bellowed. "What is this poppies with cocking? When I say frog, by billy damn, you jump!"

She sprang to her feet, mutinous. Without rising, he slapped her on the appropriate spot. It sounded like a pistol going off. She gasped, choked back an indignant screech, and stamped into the inner suite. Van Rijn rang for the steward.

"More beer this calls for," he said to Torrance. "Well, don't stand there making bug's eyes! I got no time for fumblydiddles, even if you overpaid loafers do. I got to make revises of all price schedules on pepper and nutmeg for Freya before we get there. Satan and stenches! At least ten percent more that idiot of a factor could charge them, and not reduce volume of sales. I swear it! All good saints, hear me and help a poor old man saddled with oatmeal-brained squatpots for workers!"

Torrance curbed his temper with an effort. "Very well, sir. I just had a report from Yamamura. You know we took a near miss during the fight, which hulled us at the engine room. The converter didn't seem damaged, but after patching the hole, the gang's been checking to make sure. And it turns out that about half the circuitry for the infrashield generator was fused. We can't replace more than a fraction of it. If we continue to run at full quasispeed, we'll burn out the whole converter in another fifty hours."

"Ah, s-s-so." Van Rijn grew serious. The snap of the lighter, as he touched it to his pipe, came startlingly loud. "No chance of stopping altogether to make fixings? Once out of hyperdrive, we would be much too small a thing for the bestinkered Adderkops to find. Hey?"

"No, sir. I said we haven't enough replacement parts. This is a yacht, not a warship."

"Hokay, we must continue in hyperdrive. How slow must we go, to make sure we come within calling distance of Freya before our engine burns out?"

"One-tenth of top speed. It'd take us six months."

"No, my captain friend, not that long. We never reach Valhalla star at all. The Adderkops find us first."

"I suppose so. We haven't got six months' stores aboard anyway." Torrance stared at the deck. "What occurs to me is, well, we could reach one of the nearby stars. There barely might be a planet with an industrial civilization, whose people could eventually be taught to make the circuits we need. A habitable planet, at least—maybe…"

"Nie!" Van Rijn shook his head till the greasy black ringlets swirled about his shoulders. "All us men and one woman, for life on some garbagey rock where they have not even wine grapes? I'll take an Adderkop shell and go out like a gentleman, by damn!" The steward appeared. "Where you been snoozing? Beer, with God's curses on you! I need to make thinks! How you expect I can think with a mouth like a desert in midsummer?"

Torrance chose his words carefully. Van Rijn would have to be reminded that the captain, in space, was the final boss. And yet the old devil must not be antagonized, for he had a record of squirming between the horns of dilemmas. "I'm open to suggestions, sir, but I can't take the responsibility of courting enemy attack."

Van Rijn rose and lumbered about the cabin, fuming obscenities and volcanic blue clouds. As he passed the shelf where St. Dismas stood, he pinched the candles out in a marked manner. That seemed to trigger something in him. He turned about and said, "Ha! Industrial civilizations, *ja*, maybe. Not only the pest-begotten Adderkops ply this region of space. Gives some chance perhaps we can come in detection range of an un-beat-up ship, *nie*? You go get Yamamura to jack up our detector sensitivities till we can feel a gnat twiddle its wings back in my Djakarta office on Earth, so lazy the cleaners are. Then we go off this direct course and run a standard naval search pattern at reduced speed."

"And if we find a ship? Could belong to the enemy you know."

"That chance we take."

"In all events, sir, we'll lose time. The pursuit will gain on us while we follow a search-helix. Especially if we spend days persuading some nonhuman crew who've never heard of the human race that we have to be taken to Valhalla immediately if not sooner."

"We burn that bridge when we come to it. You have might be a more hopeful scheme?"

"Well…" Torrance pondered awhile, blackly.

The steward came in with a fresh tankard. Van Rijn snatched it.

"I think you're right, sir," said Torrance. "I'll go and—"

"Virginal!" bellowed van Rijn.

Torrance jumped. "What?"

"Virginal! That's the word I was looking for. The first beer of the day, you idiot!"

The cabin door chimed. Torrance groaned. He'd been hoping for some sleep, at least, after more hours on deck than he cared to number. But when the ship prowled through darkness, seeking another ship which might or might not be out there, and the hunters drew closer…"Come in."

Jeri Kofoed entered. Torrance gaped, sprang to his feet, and bowed. "Freelady! What—what—what a surprise! Is there anything I can do?"

"Please." She laid a hand on his. Her gown was of shimmerite and shameless in cut, because van Rijn hadn't provided any different sort, but the look she gave Torrance had nothing to do with that. "I had to come, Lodgemaster. If you've any pity at all, you'll listen to me."

He waved her to a chair, offered cigarettes and struck one for himself. The smoke, drawn deep into his lungs, calmed him a little. He sat down on the opposite side of the table. "If I can be of help to you, Freelady Kofoed, you know I'm happy to oblige. Uh…Freeman van Rijn…"

"He's asleep. Not that he has any claims on me. I haven't signed a contract or any such thing." Her irritation gave way to a wry smile. "Oh, admitted, we're all his inferiors, in fact as well as in status. I'm not contravening his wishes, not really. It's just that he won't answer my questions, and if I don't find out what's going on I'll have to start screaming."

Torrance weighed a number of factors. A private explanation, in more detail than the crew had required, might indeed be best for her. "As you wish, Freelady," he said, and related what had happened to the converter. "We can't fix it ourselves," he concluded. "If we continued traveling at high quasi-speed, we'd burn it out before we arrived; and then, without power, we'd soon die. If we proceed slowly enough to preserve it, we'd need half a year to reach Valhalla, which is more time than we have supplies for. Though the Adderkops would doubtless track us down within a week or two."

She shivered. "Why? I don't understand." She stared at her glowing cigarette end for a moment, until a degree of composure returned, and with it a touch of humor. "I may pass for a fast, sophisticated girl on Freya, Captain. But you know even better than I, Freya is a jerkwater planet on the very fringe of human civilization. We've hardly any spatial traffic, except the League merchant ships, and they never stay long in port. I really know nothing about military or political technology. No one told me this was anything more important than a scouting mission, because I never thought to inquire. Why should the Adderkops be so anxious to catch us?"

Torrance considered the total picture before framing a reply. As a spaceman of the League, he must make an effort before he could appreciate how little the enemy actually meant to colonists who seldom left their home world. The name "Adderkop" was Freyan, a term of scorn for outlaws who'd been booted off the planet a century ago. Since then, however, the Freyans had had no direct contact with them. Somewhere in the unexplored deeps beyond Valhalla, the fugitives had settled on some unknown planet. Over the generations, their numbers grew, and the numbers of their warships. But Freya was still too strong for them to raid, and had no extraplanetary enterprises of her own to be harried. Why should Freya care?

Torrance decided to explain systematically, even if he must repeat the obvious. "Well," he said, "the Adderkops aren't stupid. They keep somewhat in touch with events, and know the Polesotechnic League wants to expand its operations into this region. They don't like that. It'd mean the end of their attacks on planets which can't fight back, their squeezing of tribute and their overpriced trade. Not that the League is composed of saints; we don't tolerate that sort of thing, but merely because freebooting cuts into the profits of our member companies. So the Adderkops undertook not to fight a full-dress war against us, but to harass our outposts till we gave it up as a bad job. They have the advantage of knowing their own sector of space, which we hardly do at all. And we were, indeed, at the point of writing this whole region off and trying someplace else. Freeman van Rijn wanted to make one last attempt. The opposition to this was so great that he had to come here and lead the expedition himself.

"I suppose you know what he did: used an unholy skill at bribery and bluff, at extracting what little information the prisoners we'd taken possessed, at fitting odd facts together. He got a clue to a hitherto untried segment. We flitted there, picked up a neutrino trail, and followed it to a human-colonized planet. As you know, it's almost certainly their own home world.

"If we bring back that information, there'll be no more trouble with the Adderkops. Not after the League sends in a few Star-class battleships and threatens to bombard their planet. They realize as much. We were spotted; several warcraft jumped us; we were lucky to get away. Their ships are obsolete, and so far we've shown them a clean pair of heels. But I hardly think they've quit hunting for us. They'll send their entire fleet cruising in search. Hyperdrive vibrations transmit instantaneously, and can be detected out to about one light-year distance. So if any Adderkop observes our 'wake' and homes in on it—with us crippled—that's the end."

She drew hard on her cigarette, but remained otherwise calm. "What are your plans?"

"A countermove. Instead, of trying to make Freya—uh—I mean, we're proceeding in a search-helix at medium speed, straining our own detectors. If we discover another ship, we'll use the last gasp of our engines to close in. If it's an Adderkop vessel, well, perhaps we can seize it or something; we do have a couple of light guns in our turrets. It may be a nonhuman craft, though. Our intelligence reports, interrogation of prisoners, evaluation of explorers' observations, *et cetera*, indicate that three or four different species in this region possess the hyperdrive. The Adderkops themselves aren't certain about all of them. Space is so damned huge."

"If it does turn out to be nonhuman?"

"Then we'll do what seems indicated."

"I see." Her bright head nodded. She sat for a while, unspeaking, before she dazzled him with a smile. "Thanks, Captain. You don't know how much you've helped me."

Torrance suppressed a foolish grin. "A pleasure, Freelady."

"I'm coming to Earth with you. Did you know that? Freeman van Rijn has promised me a very good job."

He always does, thought Torrance.

Jeri leaned closer. "I hope we'll have a chance on the Earthward trip to get better acquainted, Captain. Or even right now."

The alarm bell chose that moment to ring.

The *Hebe G.B.* was a yacht, not a buccaneer frigate. When Nicholas van Rijn was aboard, though, the distinction sometimes got a little blurred. Thus she had more legs than most ships, detectors of uncommon sensitivity, and a crew experienced in the tactics of overhauling.

She was able to get a bearing on the hyperemission of the other craft long before her own vibrations were observed. Pacing the unseen one, she established the set course it was following, then poured on all available juice to intercept. If the stranger had maintained quasi-velocity, there would have been contact in three or four hours. Instead, its wake indicated a sheering off, an attempt to flee. The *Hebe G.B.* changed course too and continued gaining on her slower quarry.

"They're afraid of us," decided Torrance. "And they're not running back toward the Adderkop sun. Which two facts indicate they're not Adderkops themselves, but do have reason to be scared of strangers." He nodded, rather grimly, for during the preliminary investigations he had inspected a few backward planets which the bandit nation had visited.

Seeing that the pursuer kept shortening her distance, the pursued turned off their hyperdrive. Reverting to intrinsic sublight velocity, converter throttled down to minimal output, their ship became an infinitesimal speck in an effectively infinite space. The maneuver often works; after casting about futilely for a while, the enemy gives up and goes home. The *Hebe G.B.*, though, was prepared. The known superlight vector, together with the instant of cutoff, gave her computers a rough idea of where the prey was. She continued to that volume of space and then hopped about in a well-designed search pattern, reverting to normal state at intervals to sample the neutrino haze which any nuclear engine emits. Those nuclear engines known as stars provided most; but by statistical analysis, the computers presently isolated one feeble nearby source. The yacht went thither...and wan against the glittering sky, the other ship appeared in her screens.

It was several times her size, a cylinder with bluntly rounded nose and massive drive cones, numerous housings for auxiliary boats, a single gun turret. The principles of physics dictate that the general conformation of all ships intended for a given purpose shall be roughly the same. But any spaceman could see that this one had never been built by members of Technic civilization.

Fire blazed. Even with the automatic stopping-down of his viewscreen, Torrance was momentarily blinded. Instruments told him that the stranger had fired a fusion shell which his own robogunners had intercepted with a missile. The attack had been miserably slow and feeble. This was not a warcraft in any sense; it was no more a match for the *Hebe G.B.* than the yacht was for one of the Adderkops chasing her.

"Hokay, now we got that foolishness out of the way and we can talk business," said van Rijn. "Get them on the telecom and develop a common language. Fast! Then explain we mean no harm but want just a lift to Valhalla." He hesitated before adding, with a distinct wince, "We can pay well."

"Might prove difficult, sir," said Torrance. "Our ship is identifiably human-built, but chances are that the only humans they've ever met are Adderkops."

"Well, so if it makes needful, we can board them and force them to transport us, *nie*? Hurry up, for Satan's sake! If we wait too long here, like bebobbled snoozers, we'll get caught."

Torrance was about to point out they were safe enough. The Adderkops were far behind the swifter Terrestrial ship. They could have no idea that her hyperdrive was now cut off; when they began to suspect it, they could have no measurable probability of finding her. Then he remembered that the case was not so simple. If the parleying with these strangers took unduly long—more than a week, at best—Adderkop squadrons would have penetrated this general region and gone beyond. They would probably remain on picket for months, which the humans could not do for lack of food. When a hyperdrive did start up, they'd detect it and run down this awkward merchantman with ease. The only hope was to hitch a ride to Valhalla soon, using the head start already gained to offset the disadvantage of reduced speed.

"We're trying all bands, sir," he said. "No response so far." He frowned worriedly. "I don't understand. They must know we've got them cold, and they must have picked up our calls and realize we want to talk. Why don't they respond? Wouldn't cost them anything."

"Maybe they abandoned ship," suggested the communications officer. "They might have hyperdriven lifeboats."

"No." Torrance shook his head. "We'd have spotted that...Keep trying, Freeman Betancourt. If we haven't gotten an answer in an hour, we'll lay alongside and board."

The receiver screens remained blank. But at the end of the grace period, when Torrance was issuing space armor, Yamamura reported something new. Neutrino output had increased from a source near the stem of the alien. Some process involving moderate amounts of energy was being carried out.

Torrance clamped down his helmet. "We'll have a look at that."

He posted a skeleton crew—van Rijn himself, loudly protesting, took over the bridge—and led his boarding party to the main air lock. Smooth as a gliding shark (the old swine was a blue-ribbon spaceman after all, the captain realized in some astonishment), the *Hebe G.B.* clamped on a tractor beam and hauled herself toward the bigger vessel.

It disappeared. Recoil sent the yacht staggering.

"Beelzebub and botulism!" snarled van Rijn. "He went back into hyper, ha? We see about that!" The ulcerated converter shrieked as he called upon it, but the engines were given power. On a lung and a half, the Terrestrial ship again overtook the foreigner. Van Rijn phased in so casually that Torrance almost forgot this was a job considered difficult by master pilots. He evaded a frantic pressor beam and tied his yacht to the larger hull with unshearable bands of force. He cut off his hyperdrive again, for the converter couldn't take much more. Being within the force-field of the alien, the *Hebe G.B.* was carried along, though the "drag" of extra mass reduced quasi-speed considerably. If he had hoped the grappled vessel would quit and revert to normal state, he was disappointed. The linked hulls continued plunging faster than light toward an unnamed constellation.

Torrance bit back an oath, summoned his men, and went outside.

He had never forced entry on a hostile craft before, but assumed it wasn't much different from burning his way into a derelict. Having chosen his spot, he set up a balloon tent to conserve air; no use killing the alien crew. The torches of his men spewed flame; blue actinic sparks fountained backward and danced through zero gravity. Meanwhile the rest of the squad stood by with blasters and grenades.

Beyond, the curves of the two hulls dropped off to infinity. Without compensating electronic viewscreens, the sky was weirdly distorted by aberration and Doppler effect, as if the men were already dead and beating through the other existence toward Judgment. Torrance held his mind firmly to practical worries. Once onboard, the nonhumans made prisoner, how was he to communicate? Especially if he first had to gun down several of them...

The outer shell was peeled back. He studied the inner structure of the plate with fascination. He'd never seen anything like it before. Surely this race had developed space travel quite independently of mankind. Though their engineering must obey the same natural laws, it was radically different in detail. What was that tough but corky substance lining the inner shell? And was the circuitry embedded in it, for he didn't see any elsewhere?

The last defense gave way. Torrance swallowed hard and shot a flashbeam into the interior. Darkness and vacuum met him. When he entered the hull, he floated, weightless; artificial gravity had been turned off. The crew was hiding someplace and...

And...

Torrance returned to the yacht in an hour. When he came on the bridge, he found van Rijn seated by Jeri. The girl started to speak, took a closer look at the captain's face, and clamped her teeth together.

"Well?" snapped the merchant peevishly.

Torrance cleared his throat. His voice sounded unfamiliar and faraway to him. "I think you'd better come have a look, sir."

"You found the crew wherever the sputtering hell they holed up? What are they like? What kind of ship is this we've gotten us, ha?"

Torrance chose to answer the last question first. "It seems to be an interstellar animal collector's transport vessel. The main hold is full of cages—environmentally controlled compartments, I should say—with the damnedest assortment of creatures I've ever seen outside Luna City Zoo."

"So what the pox is that to me? Where is the collector himself, and his fig-plucking friends?"

"Well sir." Torrance gulped. "We're pretty sure by now they're hiding from us. Among the other animals."

A tube was run between the yacht's main lock and the entry cut into the other ship. Through this, air was pumped and electric lines were strung, to illuminate the prize. By some fancy juggling with the gravitic generator of the *Hebe G.B.*, Yamamura supplied about one-fourth Earth-weight to the foreigner, though he couldn't get the direction uniform and its decks felt canted in wildly varying degrees.

Even under such conditions, van Rijn walked ponderously. He stood with a salami in one hand and a raw onion in the other, glaring around the captured bridge. It could only be that, though it was in the bows rather than the waist. The viewscreens were still in operation, smaller than human eyes found comfortable, but revealing the same pattern of stars, surely by the same kind of optical compensators. A control console made a semicircle at the forward bulkhead too big for a solitary human to operate. Yet presumably the designer had only had one pilot in mind, for a single seat had been placed in the middle of the arc.

Had been. A short metal post rose from the deck. Similar structures stood at other points, and boltholes showed where chairs were once fastened to them. But the seats had been removed.

"Pilot sat there at the center, I'd guess, when they weren't simply running on automatic," Torrance hazarded. "Navigator and communications officer… here and here? I'm not sure. Anyhow, they probably didn't use a copilot, but that chair bollard at the aft end of the room suggests that an extra officer sat in reserve, ready to take over."

Van Rijn munched his onion and tugged his goatee. "Pestish big, this panel," he said. "Must be a race of bloody-be-damned octopussies, ha? Look how complicated."

He waved the salami around the half circle. The console, which seemed to be of some fluorocarbon polymer, held very few switches or buttons, but scores of flat luminous plates, each about twenty centimeters square. Some of them were depressed. Evidently these were the controls. Cautious experiment had shown that a stiff push was needed to budge them. The experiment had ended then and there, for the ship's cargo lock had opened and a good deal of air was lost before Torrance slapped the plate he had been testing hard enough to make the hull reseal itself. One should not tinker with the atomic-powered unknown, most especially not in galactic space.

"They must be strong like horses, to steer by this system without getting exhausted," went on van Rijn. "The size of everything tells likewise, *nie*?"

"Well, not exactly, sir," said Torrance. "The viewscreens seem made for dwarfs. The meters even more so." He pointed to a bank of instruments, no larger than buttons, on each of which a single number glowed. (Or letter, or ideogram, or what? They looked vaguely Old Chinese.) Occasionally a symbol changed value. "A human couldn't use these long without severe eyestrain. Of course, having eyes better adapted to close work than ours doesn't prove they are not giants. Certainly that switch couldn't be reached from here without long arms, and it seems meant for big hands." By standing on tiptoe: he touched it himself, an outsize double-pole affair set overhead, Just above the pilot's hypothetical seat.

The switch fell open.

A roar came from aft. Torrance lurched backward under a sudden force. He caught at a shelf on the after bulkhead to steady himself. Its thin metal buckled as he clutched. "Devilfish and dunderheads!" cried van Rijn. Bracing his columnar legs, he reached up and shoved the switch back into position. The noise ended. Normality returned. Torrance hastened to the bridge doorway, a tall arch, and shouted down the corridor beyond: "It's okay! Don't worry! We've got it under control!"

"What the blue blinking blazes happened?" demanded van Rijn, in somewhat more high-powered words.

Torrance mastered a slight case of the shakes. "Emergency switch, I'd say." His tone wavered. "Turns on the gravitic field full speed ahead, not wasting any force on acceleration compensators. Of course, we being in hyperdrive, it wasn't very effective. Only gave us a—uh—less than one-G push, intrinsic. In normal state we'd have accelerated several Gs, at least. It's for quick getaways and…and…"

"And you, with brains like fermented gravy and bananas for fingers, went ahead and yanked it open!"

Torrance felt himself redden. "How was I to know, sir? I must've applied less than half a kilo force. Emergency switches aren't hair-triggered, after all. Considering how much it takes to move one of those control plates who'd have thought the switch would respond to so little?"

Van Rijn took a closer look. "I see now there is a hook to secure it by," he said. "Must be they use that when the ship's on a high-gravity planet." He peered down a hole near the center of the panel, about one centimeter in diameter and fifteen deep. At the bottom a small key projected. "This must be another special control, ha? Safer than that switch. You would need thin-nosed pliers to make a turning of it." He scratched his pomaded curls. "But then, why is not the pliers hanging handy? I don't see even a hook or bracket or drawer for them."

"I don't care," said Torrance. "When the whole interior's been stripped—There's nothing but a slagheap in the engine room, I tell you—fused metal, carbonized plastic…bedding, furniture, anything they thought might give us a clue to their identity, all melted down in a jury-rigged cauldron. They used their own converter to supply heat. That was the cause of the neutrino flux Yamamura observed. They must have worked like demons."

"But they did not destroy all needful tools and machines, surely? Simpler then they should blow, up their whole ship, and us with it. I was sweating like a hog, me, for fear they would do that. Not so good a way for a poor sinful old man to end his days, blown into radioactive stinks three hundred light-years from the vineyards of Earth."

"N-n-no. As far as we can tell from a cursory examination, they didn't sabotage anything absolutely vital. We can't be sure, of course. Yamamura's gang would need weeks just to get a general idea of how this ship is put together, let alone the practical details of operating it. But I agree, the crew isn't bent on suicide. They've got us more neatly trapped than they know, even. Bound helplessly through space—toward their home star, maybe. In any event, almost at right angles to the course we want."

Torrance led the way out. "Suppose we go have a more thorough look at the zoo, sir," he went on. "Yamamura talked about setting up some equipment…to help us tell the crew from the animals!"

The main hold comprised almost half the volume of the great ship. A corridor below, a catwalk above, ran through a double row of two-decker cubicles. These numbered ninety-six, and were identical. Each was about five meters on a side, with adjustable fluorescent plates in the ceiling and a springy, presumably inert, plastic on the floor. Shelves and parallel bars ran along the side walls, for the benefit of creatures that liked jumping or climbing. The rear wall was connected to well-shielded machines; Yamamura didn't dare tamper with these, but said they obviously regulated atmosphere, temperature, gravity, sanitation, and other environmental factors within each "cage." The front wall, facing on corridor and catwalk, was transparent. It held a stout air lock, almost as high as the cubicle itself, motorized but controlled by simple wheels inside and out. Only a few compartments were empty.

The humans had not strung fluoros in this hold, for it wasn't necessary. Torrance and Van Rijn walked through shadows, among monsters; the simulated light of a dozen different suns streamed around them: red, orange, yellow, greenish, and harsh electric blue.

A thing like a giant shark, save that tendrils fluttered about its head, swam in a water-filled cubicle among fronded seaweeds. Next to it was a cageful of tiny flying reptiles, their scales aglitter in prismatic hues, weaving and dodging through the air. On the opposite side, four mammals crouched among yellow mists—beautiful creatures the size of a bear, vividly tiger-striped, walking mostly on all fours but occasionally standing up; then you noticed the retractable claws between stubby fingers, and the carnivore jaws on the massive heads. Farther on, the humans passed half a dozen sleek red beasts like six-legged otters, frolicking in a tank of water provided for them. The environmental machines must have decided this was their feeding time, for a hopper spewed chunks of proteinaceous material into a trough and the animals lolloped over to rip it with their fangs.

"Automatic feeding," Torrance observed. "I think probably the food is synthesized on the spot, according to the specifications of each individual species as determined by biochemical methods. For the crew, also. At least, we haven't found anything like a galley."

Van Rijn shuddered. "Nothing but synthetics? Not even a little glass Genever before dinner?" He brightened. "Ha, maybe here we find a good new market. And until they learn the situation, we can charge them triple prices."

"First," clipped Torrance, "we've got to find them."

Yamamura stood near the middle of the hold, focusing a set of instruments on a certain cage. Jeri stood by, handing him what he asked for, plugging and unplugging at a small powerpack. Van Rijn hove into view. "What goes on, anyhows?" he asked.

The chief engineer turned a patient brown face to him "I've got the rest of the crew examining the shop in detail, sir," he said. "I'll join them as soon as I've gotten Freelady Kofoed trained at this particular job. She can handle the routine of it while the rest of us use our special skills to…" His words trailed off. He grinned ruefully. "To poke and prod gizmos we can't possibly understand in less than a month of work, with our limited research tools."

"A month we have not got," said van Rijn. "You are here checking conditions inside each individual cage?"

"Yes, sir. They're metered, of course, but we can't read the meters, so we have to do the job ourselves. I've haywired this stuff together, to give an approximate value of gravity, atmospheric pressure and composition, temperature, illumination spectrum, and so forth. It's slow work, mostly because of all the arithmetic needed to turn the dial readings into such data. Luckily, we don't have to test every cubicle, or even most of them."

"No," said van Rijn. "Even to a union organizer, obvious this ship was never made by fishes or birds. In fact, some kind of hands is always necessary."

"Or tentacles." Yamamura nodded at the compartment before him. The light within was dim red. Several black creatures could be seen walking restlessly about. They had stumpy-legged quadrupedal bodies, from which torsos rose, centaur fashion, toward heads armored in some bony material. Below the faceless heads were six thick, ropy arms, set in triplets. Two of these ended in three boneless but probably strong fingers.

"I suspect these are our coy friends," said Yamamura. "If so, we'll have a deuce of a time. They breathe hydrogen under high pressure and triple gravity, at a temperature of seventy below."

"Are they the only ones who like that kind of weather?" asked Torrance.

Yamamura gave him a sharp look. "I see what you're getting at, Skipper. No, they aren't. In the course of putting this apparatus together and testing it, I've already found three other cubicles where conditions are similar. And in those, the animals are obviously just animals, snakes and so on, which couldn't possibly have built this ship."

"But then these octopus-horses can't be the crew, can they?" asked Jeri timidly. "I mean, if the crew were collecting animals from other planets, they wouldn't take home animals along, would they?"

"They might," said van Rijn. "We have a cat and a couple parrots aboard the *Hebe G.B.*, *nie*? Or, there are many planets with very similar conditions of the hydrogen sort, just like Earth and Freya are much-alike oxygen planets. So that proves nothings." He turned toward Yamamura, rather like a rotating globe himself. "But see here, even if the crew did pump out the air before we boarded, why not check their reserve tanks? If we find air stored away just like these diddlers here are breathing…"

"I thought of that," said Yamamura. "In fact, it was almost the first thing I told the men to look for. They've located nothing. I don't think they'll have any success, either. Because what they did find was an adjustable catalytic manifold. At least, it looks as if it should be, though we'd need days to find out for certain. Anyhow, my guess is that it renews exhausted air and acts as a chemosynthesizer to replace losses from a charge of simple inorganic compounds. The crew probably bled the ship's atmosphere into space before we boarded. When we go away, if we do, they'll open the door of their particular cage a crack, so its air can trickle out. The environmental adjuster will automatically force the chemosynthesizer to replace this. Eventually the ship'll be full of enough of their kind of gas for them to venture forth and adjust things more precisely." He shrugged. "That's assuming they even need to. Perhaps Earth-type conditions suit them perfectly well."

"Uh, yes," said Torrance. "Suppose we look around some more, and line up the possibly intelligent species."

Van Rijn trundled along with him. "What sort intelligence they got, these bespattered aliens?" he grumbled. "Why try this stupid masquerade in the first places?"

"It's not too stupid to have worked so far," said Torrance dryly. "We're being carried along on a ship we don't know how to stop. They must hope we'll either give up and depart, or else that we'll remain baffled until the ship enters their home region. At which time, quite probably a naval vessel—or whatever they've got—will detect us, close in, and board us to check up on what's happened."

He paused before a compartment. "I wonder…"

The quadruped within was the size of an elephant, though with a more slender build, indicating a lower gravity than Earth's. Its skin was green and faintly scaled, a ruff of hair along the back. The eyes with which it looked out were alert and enigmatic. It had an elephantlike trunk, terminating in a ring of pseudodactyls which must be as strong and sensitive as human fingers.

"How much could a one-armed race accomplish?" mused Torrance. "About as much as we, I imagine, if not quite as easily. And sheer strength would compensate. That trunk could bend an iron bar."

Van Rijn grunted and went past a cubicle of feathered ungulates. He stopped before the next. "Now here are some beasts might do," he said. "We had one like them on Earth once. What they called it? Quintilla? No, gorilla. Or chimpanzee, better, of gorilla size."

Torrance felt his heart thud. Two adjoining sections each held four animals of a kind which looked extremely hopeful. They were bipedal, short-legged and long-armed. Standing two meters tall, with a three-meter arm span, one of them could certainly operate that control console alone. The wrists, thick as a man's thighs, ended in proportionate hands, four-digited including a true thumb. The three-toed feet were specialized for walking, like man's feet. Their bodies were covered with brown fleece. Their heads were comparatively small, rising almost to a point, with massive snouts and beady eyes under cavernous brow ridges. As they wandered aimlessly about, Torrance saw that they were divided among males and females. On the sides of each neck he noticed two lumens closed by sphincters. The light upon them was the familiar yellowish white of a Sol-type star.

He forced himself to say, "I'm not sure. Those huge jaws must demand corresponding maxillary muscles, attaching to a ridge on top of the skull. Which'd restrict the cranial capacity."

"Suppose they got brains in their bellies," said van Rijn.

"Well some people do," murmured Torrance. As the merchant choked, he added in haste, "No, actually, sir, that's hardly believable. Neural paths would get too long and so forth. Every animal I know of, if it has a central nervous system at all, keeps the brain close to the principal sense organs, which are usually located in the head. To be sure, a relatively small brain, within limits, doesn't mean these creatures are not intelligent. Their neurons might well be more efficient than ours."

"Humph and hassenpfeffer!" said van Rijn. "Might, might, might!" As they continued among strange shapes; "We can't go too much by atmosphere or light, either. If hiding, the crew could vary conditions quite a bit from their norm without hurting themselves. Gravity, too, by twenty or thirty percent."

"I hope they breathe oxygen, though—hoy!" Torrance stopped. After a moment, he realized what was so eerie about the several forms under the orange glow. They were chitinous-armored, not much bigger than a squarish military helmet and about the same shape. Four stumpy legs projected from beneath to carry them awkwardly about on taloned feet, also a pair of short tentacles ending in a bush of cilia. There was nothing special about them, as extraterrestrial animals go, except the two eyes which gazed from beneath each helmet: as large and somehow human as—well—the eyes of an octopus.

"Turtles," snorted van Rijn. "Armadillos at most."

"There can't be any harm in letting Jer—Freelady Kofoed check their environment too," said Torrance.

"It can waste time."

"I wonder what they eat. I don't see any mouths."

"Those tentacles look like capillary suckers. I bet they are parasites, or overgrown leeches, or something else like one of my competitors. Come along."

"What do we do after we've established which species could possibly be the crew?" said Torrance. "Try to communicate with each in turn?"

"Not much use, that. They hide because they don't want to communicate. Unless we can prove to them we are not Adderkops…but hard to see how."

"Wait! Why'd they conceal themselves at all, if they've had contact with the Adderkops? It wouldn't work."

"I think I tell you that, by damn," said van Rijn. "To give them a name, let us call this unknown race the Eksers. So. The Eksers been traveling space for some time, but space is so big they never bumped into humans. Then the Adderkop nation arises, in this sector where humans never was before. The Eksers hear about this awful new species which has gotten into space also. They land on primitive planets where Adderkops have made raids, talk to natives, maybe plant automatic cameras where they think raids will soon come, maybe spy on Adderkop camps from afar or capture a lone Adderkop ship. So they know what humans look like, but not much else. They do not want humans to know about them, so they shun contact; they are not looking for trouble. Not before they are well prepared to fight a war, at least. Hell's sputtering griddles! Torrance, we have got to establish our bona fides with this crew, so they take us to Freya and afterward go tell their leaders all humans are not so bad as the slime-begotten Adderkops. Otherwise, maybe we wake up one day with some planets attacked by Eksers, and before the fighting ends, we have spent billions of credits." He shook his fists in the air and bellowed like a wounded bull. "It is our duty to prevent this!"

"Our first duty is to get home alive, I'd say," Torrance answered curtly. "I have a wife and kids."

"Then stop throwing sheepish eyes at Jeri Kofoed. I saw her first."

The search turned up one more possibility. Four organisms the length of a man and the build of thick-legged caterpillars dwelt under greenish light. Their bodies were dark blue, spotted with silver. A torso akin to that of the tentacled centauroids, but stockier, carried two true arms. The hands lacked thumbs, but six fingers arranged around a three-quarter circle could accomplish much the same things. Not that adequate hands prove effective intelligence; on Earth, not only simians but a number of reptiles and amphibia boast as much, even if a man has the best, and man's apish ancestors were as well equipped in this respect as we are today. However, the round flat-faced heads of these beings, the large bright eyes beneath feathery antennae of obscure function, the small jaws and delicate lips, all looked promising.

Promising of what? thought Torrance.

Three Earth-days later, he hurried down a central corridor toward the Ekser engine room.

The passage was a great hemicylinder lined with the same rubbery gray plastic as the cages, making footfalls silent and spoken words weirdly unresonant. But a deeper vibration went through it, the almost subliminal drone of the hyperengine, driving the ship into darkness toward an unknown star, and announcing their presence to any hunter straying within a light-year of them. The fluoros strung by the humans were far apart, so that one passed through bands of humming shadow. Doorless rooms opened off the hallway. Some were still full of supplies, and however peculiar the shape of tools and containers might be, however unguessable their purpose, this was a reassurance that one still lived, was not yet a ghost aboard the Flying Dutchman. Other cabins, however had been inhabited. And their bareness made Torrance's skin crawl.

Nowhere did a personal trace remain. Books, both codex and micro, survived, but in the finely printed symbology of a foreign planet. Empty places on the shelves suggested that all illustrated volumes had been sacrificed. Certainly he could see where pictures stuck on the walls had been ripped down. In the big private cabins in the still larger one which might have been a saloon as well as in the engine room and workshop and bridge, only the bollards to which furniture had been bolted were left. Long low niches and small cubbyholes were built into the cabin bulkheads, but when bedding had been thrown into a white-hot cauldron, how could a man guess which were the bunks...if either kind were? Clothing, ornaments, cooking and eating utensils, everything was destroyed. One room must have been a lavatory, but the facilities had been ripped out. Another might have been used for scientific studies, presumably of captured animals, but was so gutted that no human was certain.

By God, you've got to admire them, Torrance thought. Captured by beings whom they had every reason to think of as conscienceless monsters, the aliens had not taken the easy way out, the atomic explosion that would annihilate both crews. They might have, except for the chance of this being a zoo ship. But given a hope of survival, they snatched it, with an imaginative daring few humans could have matched. Now they sat in plain view, waiting for the monsters to depart—without wrecking their ship in mere spitefulness—or for a naval vessel of their own to rescue them. They had no means of knowing their captors were not Adderkops, or that this sector would soon be filled with Adderkop squadrons; the bandits rarely ventured even this close to Valhalla. Within the limits of available information, the aliens were acting with complete logic. But the nerve it took!

I wish we could identify them and make friends, thought Torrance. *The Eksers would be damned good friends for Earth to have. Or Ramanujan, or Freya, or the entire Polesotechnic League.* With a lopsided grin: *I'll bet they'd be nowhere near as easy to swindle as Old Nick thinks. They might well swindle him. That I'd love to see!*

My reason is more personal, though, he thought with a return of bleakness. *If we don't clear up this misunderstanding soon, neither they nor we will be around. I mean soon. If we have another three or four days of grace, we're lucky.*

The passage opened on a well, with ramps curving down either side to a pair of automatic doors. One door led to the engine room, Torrance knew. Behind it, a nuclear converter powered the ship's electrical system, gravitic cones, and hyperdrive; the principles on which this was done were familiar to him, but the actual machines were engines cased in metal and in foreign symbols. He took the other door, which opened on a workshop. A good deal of the equipment here was identifiable however distorted to his eyes: lathe, drill press, oscilloscope, crystal tester. Much else was mystery. Yamamura sat at an improvised workbench, fitting together a piece of electronic apparatus. Several other devices, haywired on breadboards, stood close by. His face was shockingly haggard, and his hands trembled. He'd been laboring this whole time, stimpills holding him awake.

As Torrance approached, the engineer was talking with Betancourt, the communications man. The entire crew of the *Hebe G.B.* were under Yamamura's direction, in a frantic attempt to outflank the Eksers by learning on their own how to operate this ship.

"I've identified the basic electrical arrangement, sir." Betancourt was saying. "They don't tap the converter directly like us; evidently they haven't developed our stepdown methods. Instead, they use a heat exchanger to run an extremely large generator—yeah, the same thing you guessed was an armature-type dynamo—and draw AC for the ship off that. Where DC is needed, the AC passes through a set of rectifier plates which, by looking at 'em, I'm sure must be copper oxide. They're bare, behind a safety screen, though so much current goes through that they're too hot to look at close up. It all seems kind of primitive to me."

"Or else merely different," sighed Yamamura. "We use a light-element fusion converter, one of whose advantages is that it can develop electric current directly. They may have perfected a power plant which utilizes moderately heavy elements with small positive packing fractions. I remember that was tried on Earth a long while ago, and given up as impractical. But maybe the Eksers are better engineers than us. Such a system would have the advantage of needing less refinement of fuel—which'd be a real advantage to a ship knocking about among unexplored planets. Maybe enough to justify that clumsy heat exchanger and rectifier system. We simply don't know."

He stared head-shakingly at the wires he was soldering. "We don't know a damn thing," he said. Seeing Torrance: "Well, carry on, Freeman Betancourt. And remember, *festina lente*."

"For fear of wrecking the ship?" asked the captain.

Yamamura nodded. "The Eksers would've known a small craft like ours couldn't generate a big enough hyperforce field to tug their own ship home," he replied. "So they'll have made sure no prize crew could make off with it. Some of the stuff may be booby-trapped to wreck itself if it isn't handled just right; and how'd we ever make repairs? Hence we're proceeding with the utmost caution. So cautiously that we haven't a prayer of figuring out the controls before the Adderkops find us."

"It keeps the crew busy, though."

"Which is useful. Uh-huh. Well, sir, I've about got my basic apparatus set up. Everything seems to test okay. Now, let me know which animal you want to investigate first." As Torrance hesitated, the engineer explained: "I have to adapt the equipment for the creature in question, you see. Especially if it's a hydrogen breather."

Torrance shook his head. "Oxygen. In fact, they live under conditions so much like ours that we can walk right into their cages. The gorilloids. That's what Jeri and I have named them. Those woolly, two-meter-tall bipeds with the ape faces."

Yamamura made an ape face of his own. "Brutes that powerful? Have they shown any sign of intelligence?"

"No. But then, would you expect the Eksers to? Jeri Kofoed and I have been parading in front of the cages of the possible species, making signs, drawing pictures, everything we could think of, trying to get the message across that we are not Adderkops and the genuine article is chasing us. No luck, of course. All the animals did give us an interested regard, though except the gorilloids...which may or may not prove anything."

"What animals, now? I've been so blinking busy—"

"Well, we call 'em the tiger apes, the tentacle centaurs, the elephantoid, the helmet beasts, and the caterpiggles. That's stretching things, I know; the tiger apes and the helmet beasts are highly improbable, to say the least, and the elephantoid isn't much more convincing. The gorilloids have the right size and the most effective-looking hands, and they're oxygen breathers, as I said, so we may well take them first. Next in order of likelihood, I'd guess, are the caterpiggles and the tentacle centaurs. But the caterpiggles, though oxygen breathers, are from a high-gravity planet; their air pressure would give us narcosis in no time. The tentacle centaurs breathe hydrogen. In either case, we'd have to work in space armor."

"The gorilloids will be quite bad enough, thank you kindly."

Torrance looked at the workbench. "What exactly do you plan to do?" he asked. "I've been too busy with my own end of this affair to learn any details of yours."

"I've adapted some things from the medical kit," said Yamamura. "A sort of ophthalmoscope, for example, because the ship's instruments use color codes and finely printed symbols, so that the Eksers are bound to have eyes at least as good as ours. Then this here's a nervous-impulse tracer. It detects synaptic flows and casts a three-dimensional image into yonder crystal box, shows us the whole nervous system functioning as a set of luminous traces. By correlating this with gross anatomy, we can roughly identify the sympathetic and parasympathetic systems—or their equivalents—I hope. And the brain. And, what's really to the point, the degrees of brain activity more or less independent of the other nerve paths. That is, whether the animal is thinking."

He shrugged. "It tests out fine on me. Whether it'll work on a nonhuman, especially in a different sort of atmosphere, I do not know. I'm sure it'll develop bugs."

"'We can but try,'" quoted Torrance wearily.

"I suppose Old Nick is sitting and thinking," said Yamamura in an edged voice. "I haven't seen him for quite some time."

"He's not been helping Jeri and me either," said Torrance. "Told us our attempt to communicate was futile until we could prove to the Eksers that we know who they are. And even after that, he said, the only communication at first will be by gestures made with a pistol."

"He's probably right."

"He's not right! Logically, perhaps, but not psychologically. Or morally. He sits in his suite with a case of brandy and a box of cigars. The cook, who could be down here helping you, is kept aboard the yacht to fix him his damned gourmet meals. You'd think he didn't care if we're blown out of the sky!"

He remembered his oath of fealty, his official position, and so on and so on. They felt nonsensical, here on the edge of extinction. But habit was strong. He swallowed and said harshly, "Sorry. Please ignore what I said. When you're ready, Freeman Yamamura, we'll test the gorilloids."

Six men and Jeri stood by in the passage with drawn blasters. Torrance hoped fervently they wouldn't have to shoot. He hoped even more that if they did have to, he'd still be alive.

He gestured to the four crewmen at his back. "Okay, boys." He wet his lips. His heart thuttered. Being a captain and a Lodgemaster was very fine until moments like this came, when you must make a return for your special privileges.

He spun the outside control wheel. The airlock motor hummed and opened the doors. He stepped through, into a cage of gorilloids.

Pressure differentials weren't enough to worry about, but after all this time at one-fourth G, to enter a field only ten percent less than Earth's was like a blow. He lurched, almost fell, gasped in an air warm and thick and full of unnamed stenches. Sagging back against the wall, he stared across the floor at the four bipeds. Their brown fleecy bodies loomed unfairly tall, up and up to the coarse faces. Eyes overshadowed by brows glared at him. He clapped a hand on his stun pistol. He didn't want to shoot it, either. No telling what supersonics might do to a nonhuman nervous system; and if these were in truth the crewfolk, the worst thing he could do was inflict serious injury on one of them. But he wasn't used to being small and frail. The knurled handgrip was a comfort.

A male growled deep in his chest, and advanced a step. His pointed head thrust forward, the sphincters in his neck opened and shut like sucking mouths; his jaws gaped to show the white teeth.

Torrance backed toward a corner. "I'll try to attract that one in the lead away from the others," he called softly. "Then get him."

"Aye." A spacehand, a stocky slant-eyed nomad from Altai, uncoiled a lariat. Behind him, the other three spread a net woven for this purpose.

The gorilloid paused. A female hooted. The male seemed to draw resolution from her. He waved the others back with a strangely humanlike gesture and stalked toward Torrance.

The captain drew his stunner, pointed it shakily, resheathed it, and held out both hands. "Friends," he croaked.

His hope that the masquerade might be dropped became suddenly ridiculous. He sprang back toward the air lock. The gorilloid snarled and snatched at him. Torrance wasn't fast enough. The hand ripped his shirt open and left a bloody trail on his breast. He went to hands and knees, stabbed with pain. The Altaian's lasso whirled and snaked forth. Caught around the ankles, the gorilloid crashed. His weight shook the cubicle.

"Get him! Watch out for his arms! Here—"

Torrance staggered back to his feet. Beyond the melee, where four men strove to wind a roaring, struggling monster in a net, he saw the remaining three creatures. They were crowded into the opposite corner, howling in basso. The compartment was like the inside of a drum.

"Get him out," choked Torrance. "Before the others charge."

He aimed his stunner again. If intelligent, they'd know this was a weapon. They might attack anyway...Deftly, the man from Altai roped an arm, snubbed his lariat around the gargantuan torso, and made it fast by a slip knot. The net came into position. Helpless in cords of wire-strong fiber, the gorilloid was dragged to the entrance. Another male advanced, step by jerky step. Torrance stood his ground. The animal ululation and human shouting surfed about him, within him. His wound throbbed. He saw with unnatural clarity the muzzle full of teeth that could snap his head off, the little dull eyes turned red with fury, the hands so much like his own but black-skinned, four-fingered, and enormous...

"All clear, Skipper!"

The gorilloid lunged. Torrance scrambled through the air-lock chamber. The giant followed. Torrance braced himself in the corridor and aimed his stun pistol. The gorilloid halted, shivered, looked around in something resembling bewilderment, and retreated. Torrance closed the airlock.

Then he sat down and trembled.

Jeri bent over him. "Are you okay?" she breathed. "Oh! You've been hurt!"

"Nothing much," he mumbled. "Gimme a cigarette."

She took one from her belt pouch and said with a crispness he admired, "I suppose it is just a bruise and a deep scratch. But we'd better check it anyway and sterilize. Might be infected."

He nodded but remained where he was until he had finished the cigarette. Farther down the corridor Yamamura's men got their captive secured to a steel framework. Unharmed but helpless, the brute yelped and tried to bite as the engineer approached with his equipment. Returning him to the cubicle afterward was likely to be almost as tough as getting him out.

Torrance rose. Through the transparent wall, he saw a female gorilloid viciously pulling something to shreds, and realized he had lost his turban when he was knocked over. He sighed. "Nothing much we can do till Yamamura gives us a verdict," he said. "Come on, let's go rest awhile."

"Sick bay first," said Jeri firmly. She took his arm. They went to the entry hole, through the tube, and into the steady half-weight of the *Hebe G.B.* which van Rijn preferred. Little was said while Jeri got Torrance's shirt off, swabbed the wound with universal disinfectant, which stung like hell, and bandaged it. Afterward he suggested a drink.

They entered the saloon. To their surprise, and to Torrance's displeasure, van Rijn was there. He sat at the inlaid mahogany table, dressed in snuff-stained lace and his usual sarong, a bottle in his right and a Trichinopoly cigar in his left. A litter of papers lay before him.

"Ah, so," he said, glancing up. "What gives?"

"They're testing a gorilloid now." Torrance flung himself into a chair. Since the steward had been drafted for the capture party, Jeri went after drinks. Her voice floated back, defiant:

"Captain Torrance was almost killed in the process. Couldn't you at least come watch, Nick?"

"What use I should watch, like some tourist with haddock eyes?" scoffed the merchant. "I make no skeletons about it, I am too old and fat to help chase large economy-size apes. Nor am I so technical I can twiddle knobs for Yamamura." He took a puff of his cigar and added complacently, "Besides, that is not my job. I am no kind of specialist, I have no fine university degrees, I learned in the school of hard knockers. But what I learned is how to make them do things for me, and then how to make something profitable from their doings."

Torrance breathed out, long and slow. With the tension eased, he was beginning to feel immensely tired. "What're you checking over?" he asked.

"Reports of engineer studies on the Ekser ship," said van Rijn. "I told everybody should take full notes on what they observed. Somewhere in those notes is maybe a clue we can use. If the gorilloids are not the Eksers, I mean. The gorilloids are possible, and I see no way to eliminate them except by Yamamura's checkers."

Torrance rubbed his eyes. "They're not entirely plausible," he said. "Most of the stuff we've found seems meant for big hands. But some of the tools, especially, are so small that—oh, well, I suppose a nonhuman might be as puzzled by an assortment of our own tools. Does it really make sense that the same race would use sledge hammers and etching needles?"

Jeri came back with two stiff Scotch-and-sodas. His gaze followed her. In a tight blouse and half knee-length skirt, she was worth following. She sat down next to him rather than van Rijn, whose jet eyes narrowed.

However, the older man spoke mildly. "I would like if you should list for me, here and now, the other possibilities, with your reasons for thinking of them. I have seen them too, natural, but my own ideas are not all clear yet and maybe something that occurs to you would joggle my head."

Torrance nodded. One might as well talk shop, even though he'd been over this ground a dozen times before with Jen and Yamamura.

"Well," he said, "the tentacle centaurs appear very likely. You know the ones I mean. They live under red light and about half again Earth's gravity. A dim sun and a low temperature must make it possible for their planet to retain hydrogen, because that's what they breathe, hydrogen and argon. You know how they look: bodies sort of like rhinoceri, torsos with bone-plated heads and fingered tentacles. Like the gorilloids, they're big enough to pilot this ship easily.

"All the rest are oxygen breathers. The ones we call caterpiggles—the long, many-legged, blue-and-silver ones, with the peculiar hands and the particularly intelligent-looking faces—they're from an oddball world. It must be big. They're under three Gs in their cage, which can't be a red herring for this length of time. Body fluid adjustment would go out of kilter, if they're used to much lower weight. Nevertheless, their planet has oxygen and nitrogen rather than hydrogen, under a dozen Earth-atmospheres' pressure. The temperature is rather high, fifty degrees. I imagine their world, though of nearly Jovian mass, is so close to its sun that the hydrogen was boiled off, leaving a clear field for evolution similar to Earth's.

"The elephantoid comes from a planet with only about half our gravity. He's the single big fellow with a trunk ending in fingers. He gets by in air too thin for us, which indicates the gravity in his cubicle isn't faked either."

Torrance took a long drink. "The others live under pretty terrestroid conditions," he resumed. "For that reason, I wish they were more probable. But actually, except for the gorilloids, they seem like long shots. The helmet beasts—"

"What's that?" asked van Rijn.

"Oh, you remember," said Jeri. "Those eight or nine things like humpbacked turtles, not much bigger than your head. They crawl around on clawed feet, waving little tentacles that end in filaments. They blot up food through those, soupy stuff the machines dump into their trough. They haven't anything like effective hands—the tentacles could only do a few very simple things—but we gave them some time because they do seem to have better developed eyes than parasites usually do."

"Parasites don't evolve intelligence," said van Rijn. "They got better ways to make a living, by damn. Better make sure the helmet beasts really are parasites—in their home environments—and got no hands tucked under those shells, before you quite write them off. Who else you got?"

"The tiger apes," said Torrance. "Those striped carnivores built something like bears. They spend most of their time on all fours, but they do stand and walk on their hind legs sometimes, and they do have hands. Clumsy, thumbless ones, with retractable claws, but on all their limbs. Are four hands without thumbs as good as two with? I don't know. I'm too tired to think."

"And that's the lot, ha?" Van Rijn tilted the bottle to his lips. After a prolonged gurgling he set it down, belched, and blew smoke through his majestic nose. "Who's to try next, if the gorilloids flunk?"

"It better be the caterpiggles, in spite of the air pressure," said Jeri. "Then... oh...the tentacle centaurs, I suppose. Then maybe the—"

"Horse maneuvers!" Van Rijn's fist struck the table. The bottle and glasses jumped. "How long it takes to catch and check each specimen? Hours, *nie*? And in between times, takes many more hours to adjust the apparatus and chase out the hiccups it develops under a new set of conditions. Also, Yamamura will collapse if he can't sleep soon, and who else we got can do this? All the whiles, the forstunken Adderkops get closer. We have not got time for that method! If the gorilloids don't pan out, then only logic will help us. We must deduce from the facts we have who the Eksers are."

"Go ahead." Torrance drained his glass. "I'm going to take a nap."

Van Rijn purpled. "That's right!" he huffed. "Be like everybody elses. Loaf and play, dance and sing, enjoy yourselfs the liver-long day. Because you always got poor old Nicholas van Rijn there, to heap the work and worry on his back. Oh, dear St. Dismas, why can't you at least make some *one* other person in this whole universe do something useful?"

Torrance was awakened by Yamamura. The gorilloids were not the Eksers. They were color blind and incapable of focusing on the ship's instruments; their brains were small, with nearly the whole mass devoted to purely animal functions. He estimated their intelligence as equal to a dog's.

The captain stood on the bridge of the yacht, because it was a familiar place, and tried to accustom himself to being doomed.

Space had never seemed so beautiful as now. He was not well acquainted with the local constellations, but his trained gaze identified Perseus, Auriga, Taurus, not much distorted since they lay in the direction of Earth (and of Ramanujan, where gilt towers rose out of mists to catch the first sunlight, blinding against blue Mount Gandhi). A few individuals could also be picked out: ruby Betelgeuse, amber Spica, the pilot stars by which he had steered through his whole working life. Otherwise the sky was aswarm with small frosty fires, across blackness unclouded and endless. The Milky Way girdled it with cool silver, a nebula glowed faint and green, another galaxy spiraled on the mysterious edge of visibility. He thought less about the planets he had trod, even his own, than about this faring between them which was soon to terminate. For end it would, in a burst of violence too swift to be felt. Better go out thus cleanly when the Adderkops came, than into their dungeons.

He stubbed out his cigarette. Returning, his hand caressed the dear shapes of controls. He knew each switch and knob as well as he knew his own fingers. This ship was his—in a way, himself. Not like that other, whose senseless control board needed a giant and a dwarf, whose emergency switch fell under a mere slap if it wasn't hooked in place, whose—

A light footfall brought him twisting around. Irrationally, so strained was he, his heart flew up within him. When he saw it was Jeri, he eased his muscles, but the pulse continued quick in his blood.

She advanced slowly. The overhead light gleamed on her yellow hair and in the blue of her eyes. But she avoided his glance, and her mouth was not quite steady.

"What brings you here?" he asked. His tone fell even more soft than he had intended.

"Oh...the same as you." She stared out the viewscreen. During the time since they captured the alien ship, or it captured them, a red star off the port bow had visibly grown. Now it burned baleful as they passed, a light-year distant. She grimaced and turned her back to it. "Yamamura is readjusting the test apparatus," she said thinly. "No one else knows enough about it to help him, but he has the shakes so bad from exhaustion he can scarcely do the job himself. Old Nick just sits in his suite, smoking and drinking. He's gone through that bottle already, and started another. I couldn't breathe in there any longer; it was too smoky. And he won't say a word. Except to himself, in Malay or something. I couldn't stand it."

"We may as well wait," said Torrance. "We've done everything we can, till time to check a caterpiggle. We'll have to do that spacesuited, in their own cage, and hope they don't attack us."

She slumped. "Why bother?" she said. "I know the situation as well as you. Even if the caterpiggles are the Eksers, under those conditions we'll need a couple of days to prove it. I doubt if we have that much time left. If we start toward Valhalla two days from now, I'll bet we're detected and run down before we get there. Certainly, if the caterpiggles are only animals too, we'll never get time to test a third species. Why bother?"

"We've nothing else to do," said Torrance.

"Yes, we do. Not this ugly, futile squirming about, like cornered rats. Why can't we accept that we're going to die, and use the time to...to be human again?"

Startled, he looked back from the sky to her. "What do you mean?"

Her lashes fluttered downward. "I suppose that would depend on what we each prefer. Maybe you'll want to, well, get your thoughts in order or something."

"How about you?" he asked through his heartbeat.

"I'm not a thinker." She smiled forlornly. "I'm afraid I'm just a shallow sort of person. I'd like to enjoy life while I have it." She half turned from him. "But I can't find anyone I'd like to enjoy it with."

He, or his hands, grabbed her bare shoulders and spun her around to face him. She felt silken under his palms. "Are you sure you can't?" he said roughly. She closed her eyes and stood with face tilted upward, lips half parted. He kissed her. After a second she responded.

After a minute, Nicholas van Rijn appeared in the doorway.

He stood an instant, pipe in hand, gun belted to his waist, before he flung the churchwarden shattering to the deck. "So!" he bellowed.

"Oh!" wailed Jeri.

She disengaged herself. A tide of rage mounted in Torrance. He knotted his fists and started toward van Rijn.

"So!" repeated the merchant. The bulkheads seemed to quiver with his voice. "By louse-bitten damn, this is a fine thing for me to come on. Satan's tail in a mousetrap! I sit hour by hour sweating my brain to the bone for the sake of your worthless life, and all whiles you, you illegitimate spawn of a snake with dandruff and a cheese mite, here you are making up to my own secretary hired with my own hard-earned money! Gargoyles and *Götterdämmerung*! Down on your knees and beg my pardon, or I mash you up and sell you for dogfood!"

Torrance stopped, a few centimeters from van Rijn. He was slightly taller than the merchant, if less bulky, and at least thirty years younger. "Get out," he said in a strangled voice.

Van Rijn turned puce and gobbled at him.

"Get out," repeated Torrance. "I'm still the captain of this ship. I'll do what I damned well please, without interference from any loud-mouthed parasite. Get off the bridge, or I'll toss you out on your fat bottom!"

The color faded in van Rijn's cheeks. He stood motionless for whole seconds. "Well, by damn," he whispered at last. "By damn and death, cubical. He has got the nerve to talk back."

His left fist came about in a roundhouse swing. Torrance blocked it, though the force nearly threw him off his feet. His own left smacked the merchant's stomach, sank a short way into fat, encountered the muscles, and rebounded bruised. Then van Rijn's right fist clopped. The cosmos exploded around Torrance. He flew up in the air, went over backward, and lay where he fell.

When awareness returned, van Rijn was cradling his head and offering brandy which a tearful Jeri had fetched. "Here, boy. Go slow there. A little nip of this, ha? That goes good. There, now, you only lost one tooth and we get that fixed at Freya. You can even put it on expense account. There, that makes you feel more happy, *nie*? Now, girl, Jarry, Jelly, whatever your name is, give me that stimpill. Down the hatchworks, boy. And then, upsy-rosy, onto your feet. You should not miss the fun."

One-handed, van Rijn heaved Torrance erect. The captain leaned awhile on the merchant, until the stimpill removed aches and dizziness. Then, huskily through swollen lips, he asked, "What's going on? What d'you mean?"

"Why, I know who the Eksers are. I came to get you, and we fetch them from their cage." Van Rijn nudged Torrance with a great splay thumb and whispered almost as softly as a hurricane, "Don't tell anyone or I have too many fights, but I like a brass-bound nerve like you got. When we get home, I think you transfer off this yacht to command of a trading squadron. How you like that, ha? But come, we still got a damn plenty of work to do."

Torrance followed him in a daze through the small ship and the tube, into the alien ship, down a corridor and a ramp to the zoological hold. Van Rijn gestured at the spacemen posted on guard lest the Eksers make a sally. They drew their guns and joined him, their weary slouch jerking to alertness when he stopped before an air lock.

"Those?" sputtered Torrance. "But—I thought—"

"You thought what they hoped you would think," said van Rijn grandly. "The scheme was good. Might have worked, not counting the Adderkops, except that Nicholas van Rijn was here. Now, then. We go in and carry them all out, making a good show of our weapons. I hope we need not get too tough with them. I expect not, when we explain by drawings how we understand their secret. Then they should take us to Valhalla, as we can show by those pretty astronautical diagrams Captain Torrance has already prepared. They will cooperate under threats, as prisoners, at first. But on the voyage, we can use the standard means to establish alimentary communications…no, terror and taxes, I mean rudimentary…anyhows, we get the idea across that all humans are not Adderkops and we want to be friends and sell them things. Hokay? We go!"

He marched through the airlock, scooped up a helmet beast, and bore it kicking out of its cage.

Torrance didn't have time for anything en route except his work. First the entry hole in the prize must be sealed, while supplies and equipment were carried over from the *Hebe G.B.* Then the yacht must be cast loose under her own hyperdrive; in the few hours before her converter quite burned out, she might draw an Adderkop in chase. Then the journey commenced, and though the Eksers laid a course as directed, they must be constantly watched lest they try some suicidal stunt. Every spare moment must be devoted to the urgent business of achieving a simple common language with them. Torrance must also supervise his crew, calm their fears, and maintain a detector-watch for enemy vessels. If any had been detected, the humans would have gone off hyperdrive and hoped they could lie low. None were, but the strain was considerable.

Occasionally he slept.

Thus he got no chance to talk to van Rijn at length. He assumed the merchant had had a lucky hunch, and let it go at that.

Until Valhalla was a tiny yellow disc, outshining every other star; a League patrol ship closed on them; and, explanation being made, it gave them escort as they moved at sublight speed toward Freya.

The patrol captain intimated he'd like to come aboard. Torrance stalled him. "When we're in orbit, Freeman Agilik, I'll be delighted. But right now, things are pretty disorganized. You can understand that, I'm sure."

He switched off the alien telecom he had now learned to operate. "I'd better go below and clean up," he said. "Haven't had a bath since we abandoned the yacht. Carry on, Freeman Lafarge." He hesitated. "And—uh—Freeman Jukh-Barklakh."

Jukh grunted something. The gorilloid was too busy to talk, squatting where a pilot seat should have been, his big hands slapping control plates as he edged the ship into a hyperbolic path. Barklakh, the helmet beast on his shoulders, who had no vocal cords of his own, waved a tentacle before he dipped it into the protective shaft to turn a delicate adjustment key. The other tentacle remained buried on its side of the gorilloid's massive neck, drawing nourishment from the bloodstream, receiving sensory impulses, and emitting the motor-nerve commands of a skilled space pilot.

At first the arrangement had looked vampirish to Torrance. But though the ancestors of the helmet beasts might once have been parasites on the ancestors of the gorilloids, they were no longer. They were symbionts. They supplied the effective eyes and intellect, while the big animals supplied strength and hands. Neither species was good for much by itself; in combination, they were something rather special. Once he got used to the idea, Torrance found the sight of a helmet beast using its claws to climb up a gorilloid no more unpleasant than a man in a historical stereopic mounting a horse. And once the helmet beasts were used to the idea that these humans were not enemies, they showed a positive affection for them.

Doubtless they're thinking what lovely new specimens we can sell them for their zoo, reflected Torrance. He slapped Barklakh on the shell, patted Jukh's fur, and left the bridge.

A sponge bath of sorts and fresh garments took the edge off his weariness. He thought he'd better warn van Rijn, and knocked at the cabin which the merchant had curtained off as his own.

"Come in," boomed the bass voice. Torrance entered a cubicle blue with smoke. Van Rijn sat on an empty brandy case, one hand holding a cigar, the other holding Jeri, who was snuggled on his lap.

"Well, sit down, sit down," he roared cordially. "You find a bottle somewhere under those dirty clothes in the corner."

"I stopped by to tell you, sir, we'll have to receive the captain of our escort when we're in orbit around Freya, which'll be soon. Professional courtesy, you know. He's naturally anxious to meet the Eks—uh—the TogruKon-Tanakh."

"Hokay, pipe him aboard, lad." Van Rijn scowled. "Only make him bring his own bottle, and not take too long. I want to land, me; I'm sick of space. I think I'll run barefoot over the soft cool acres and acres of Freya, by damn!"

"Maybe you'd like to change clothes?" hinted Torrance.

"Ooh!" squeaked Jeri, and ran off to the cabin she sometimes occupied. Van Rijn leaned back against the wall, hitched up his sarong and crossed his shaggy legs as he said: "If that captain comes to meet the Eksers, let him meet the Eksers. I stay comfortable like I am. And I will not entertain him with how I figured out who they were. That I keep exclusive, for sale to what news syndicate bids highest. Understand?"

His eyes grew unsettlingly sharp. Torrance gulped. "Yes, sir."

"Good. Now do sit down, boy. Help me put my story in order. I have not your fine education, I was a poor lonely hard-working old man from I was twelve, so I would need some help making my words as elegant as my logic."

"Logic?" echoed Torrance, puzzled. He tilted the flask, chiefly because the tobacco haze in here made his eyes smart. "I thought you guessed—"

"What? You know me so little as that? No, no, by damn. Nicholas van Rijn never guesses. I *knew*." He reached for the bottle, took a hefty swig, and added magnanimously, "That is, after Yamamura found the gorilloids alone could not be the peoples we wanted. Then I sat down and uncluttered my brains and thought it over.

"See, it was simple eliminations. The elephantoid was out right away. Only one of him. Maybe, in emergency, one could pilot this ship through space—but not land it, and pick up wild animals, and care for them, and all else. Also, if somethings go wrong, he is helpless."

Torrance nodded. "I did consider it from the spaceman's angle," he said. "I was inclined to rule out the elephantoid on that ground. But I admit I didn't see the animal-collecting aspect made it altogether impossible that this could be a one-being expedition."

"He was pretty too big anyhow," said van Rijn. "As for the tiger apes, like you, I never took them serious. Maybe their ancestors was smaller and more biped, but this species is reverting to quadruped again. Animals do not specialize in being everything. Not brains and size and carnivore teeth and cat claws, all to once.

"The caterpiggles looked hokay till I remembered that time you accidental turned on the bestonkered emergency acceleration switch. Unless hooked in place, what such a switch would not be except in special cases, it fell rather easy. So easy that its own weight would make it drop open under three Earth gravities. Or at least there would always be serious danger of this. Also, that shelf you bumped into—they wouldn't build shelves so light on high-gravity planets."

He puffed his cigar back to furnace heat. "Well, might be the tentacle centaurs," he continued. "Which was bad for us, because hydrogen and oxygen explode. I checked hard through the reports on the ship, hoping I could find something that would eliminate them. And by damn, I did. For this I will give St. Dismas an altar cloth, not too expensive. You see, the Eksers is kind enough to use copper oxide rectifiers, exposed to the air. Copper oxide and hydrogen, at a not very high temperature such as would soon develop from strong electricking, they make water and pure copper. Poof, no more rectifier. Therefore ergo, this shop was not designed for hydrogen breathers." He grinned. "You has had so much high scientific education you forgot your freshlyman chemistry."

Torrance snapped his fingers and swore at himself. "By eliminating, we had the helmet beasts," said van Rijn. "Only they could not possible be the builders. True, they could handle certain tools and controls, like that buried key, but never all of it. And they are too slow and small. How could they ever stayed alive long enough to invent spaceships? Also, animals that little don't get room for real brains. And neither armored animals nor parasites ever get much. Nor do they get good eyes. And yet the helmet beasts seemed to have very good eyes, as near as we could tell. They looked like human eyes, anyhows.

"I remembered there was both big and little cubbyholes in these cabins. Maybe bunks for two kinds of sleeper? And I thought, is the human brain a turtle just because it is armored in bone? A parasite just because it lives off blood from other places? Well, maybe some people I could name but won't, like Juan Harleman of the Venusian Tea & Coffee Growers, Inc., has parasite turtles for brains. But not me. So there I was. Q.," said van Rijn smugly, "E.D."

Hoarse from talking, he picked up the bottle. Torrance sat a few minutes more, but as the other seemed disinclined to conversation, he got up to go.

Jeri met him in the doorway. In a slit and topless blue gown which fitted like a coat of lacquer, she was a fourth-order stunblast. Torrance stopped in his tracks. Her gaze slid slowly across him, as if reluctant to depart.

"Mutant sea-otter coats," murmured van Rijn dreamily. "Martian firegems. An apartment in the Stellar Towers."

She scampered to him and ran her fingers through his hair. "Are you comfortable, Nicky, darling?" she purred. "Can't I do something for you?"

Van Rijn winked at Torrance. "Your technique, that time on the bridge—I watched and it was lousy," he said to the captain. "Also, you are not old and fat and lonesome; you have a happy family for yourself."

"Uh—yes," said Torrance. "I do." He let the curtain drop and returned to the bridge.

A Tragedy of Errors

-1-

Once in ancient days, the then-King of England told Sir Christopher Wren, whose name is yet remembered, that the new Cathedral of St. Paul which he had designed was "awful, pompous and artificial." Kings have seldom been noted for perspicacity.

Later ages wove a myth about Roan Tom. He became their archetype of those star rovers who fared forth while the Long Night prevailed. As such, he was made to fit the preconceptions and prejudices of whoever happened to mention him. To many scholars, he was a monster, a murderer and thief, bandit and vandal, skulking like some carrion animal through the ruins of the Terran Empire. Others called him a hero, a gallant and romantic leader of fresh young peoples destined to sweep out of time the remnants of a failed civilization and build something better.

He would have been equally surprised, and amused, by either legend.

"Look," one can imagine his ghost drawling, "we had to eat. For which purpose, it's sort o' helpful to keep your throat uncut, no? That was a spiny-tail period. Society'd fallen. And havin' so far to fall, it hit bottom almighty hard. The ee-conomic basis for things like buildin' spaceships wasn't there any more. That meant little trade between planets. Which meant trouble on most of 'em. You let such go on for a century or two, snowballin', and what've you got? A kettle o' short-lived dwarf nations, that's what—one-planet, one-continent, one-island nations; all of 'em one-lung for sure—where they haven't collapsed even further. No more information-collatin' services, so nobody can keep track o' what's happenin' amongst those millions o' suns. What few spaceships are left in workin' order are naturally the most valuable objects in sight. So they naturally get acquired by the toughest men around, who, bein' what they are, are apt to use the ships for conquerin' or plunderin'…and complicate matters still worse.

"Well," and he pauses to stuff a pipe with Earth-grown tobacco, which is available in his particular Valhalla, "like everybody else, I just made the best o' things as I found 'em. Fought? Sure. Grew up fightin'. I was born on a spaceship. My dad was from Lochlann, but outlawed after a family feud went sour. He hadn't much choice but to turn pirate. One day I was in a landin' party which got bushwhacked. Next I heard, I'd been sold into slavery. Had to take it from there. Got some lucky breaks after a while and worked 'em hard. Didn't do too badly, by and large.

"Mind you, though, I never belonged to one o' those freaky cultures that'd taken to glorifyin' combat for its own sake. In fact, once I'd gotten some power on Kraken, I was a lot more int'rested in startin' trade again than in anything else. But neither did I mind the idea o' fightin', if we stood to gain by it, nor o' collectin' any loose piece o' property that wasn't too well defended. Also, willy-nilly, we were bound to get into brawls with other factions. Usually those happened a long ways from home. I saw to that. Better there than where I lived, no?

"We didn't always win, either. Sometimes we took a clobberin'. Like finally, what I'd reckon as about the worst time, I found myself skyhootin' away from Sassania, in a damaged ship, alone except for a couple o' wives. I shook pursuit in the Nebula. But when we came out on the other side, we were in a part o' space that wasn't known to us. Old Imperial territory still, o' course, but that could mean anything. And we needed repairs. Once my ship'd been self-fixin', as well as self-crewin', self-pilotin', self-navigatin', aye-ya, even self-aware. But that computer was long gone, together with a lot of other gear. We had to find us a place with a smidgin of industrial capacity, or we were done for."

The image in the viewscreens flickered so badly that Tom donned armor and went out for a direct look at the system he had entered.

He liked being free in space anyway. He had more esthetic sense than he publicly admitted. The men of Kraken were quick to praise the beauty of a weapon or a woman, but would have considered it strange to spill time admiring a view rather than examining the scene for pitfalls and possibilities. In the hush and dreamlike liberty of weightlessness, Tom found an inner peace; and from this he turned outward, becoming one with the grandeur around him.

After he had flitted a kilometer from it, *Firedrake's* lean hull did not cut off much vista. But reflections, where energy beams had scored through black camouflage coating to the steel beneath, hurt his eye...He looked away from ship and sun alike. It was a bright sun, intrinsic luminosity of two Sols, though the color was ruddy, like a gold and copper alloy. At a distance of one and a half astronomical units, it showed a disc thirty-four minutes wide; and no magnification, only a darkened faceplate, was necessary to see the flares that jetted from it. Corona and zodiacal light made a bronze cloud. That was not a typical main sequence star, Tom thought, though nothing in his background had equipped him to identify what the strangeness consisted of.

Elsewhere glittered the remoter stars, multitudinous and many-colored in their high night. Tom's gaze circled among them. Yes, yonder was Capella. Old Earth lay on the far side, a couple of hundred light-years from here. But he wanted home, to Kraken: much less of a trip, ten parsecs or so. He could have picked out its sun with the naked eye, as a minor member of that jewel-swarm, had the Nebula not stood between. The thundercloud mass reared gloomy and awesome athwart a quarter of heaven. And it might as well be a solid wall, if his vessel didn't get fixed.

That brought Tom's attention back to the planet he was orbiting. It seemed enormous at this close remove, a thick crescent growing as the ship swung dayward, as if it were toppling upon him. The tints were green, blue, brown, but with an underlying red in the land areas that wasn't entirely due to the sunlight color. Clouds banded the brightness of many seas; there was no true ocean. The southern polar cap was extensive. Yet it couldn't be very deep, because its northern counterpart had almost disappeared with summer, albeit the axial tilt was a mere ten degrees. Atmosphere rimmed the horizon with purple. A tiny disc was heaving into sight, the further of the two small moons.

Impressive, yes. Habitable, probably according to the spectroscope, certainly according to the radio emissions on which he had homed. (They'd broken off several light-years away, but by then no doubt remained that this system was their origin, and this was the only possible world within the system.) Nonetheless—puzzling. In a way, daunting.

The planet was actually a midget. Its equatorial diameter was 6810 kilometers, its mass 0.15 Terra. Nothing that size ought to have air and water enough for men.

But there were men there. Or had been. Feeble and distorted though the broadcasts became, away off in space, Tom had caught Anglic words spoken with human mouths.

He shrugged. One way to find out. Activating his impellers, he flitted back. His boots struck hull and clung. He free-walked to the forward manlock and so inboard.

The interior gee-field was operational. Weight thrust his armor down onto his neck and shoulders. Yasmin heard him clatter and came to help him unsuit. He waved her back. "Don't you see the frost on me? I been in planet shadow. Your finger'd stick to the metal, kid." Not wearing radio earplugs, she didn't hear him, but she got the idea and stood aside. Gauntleted, he stripped down to coverall and mukluks and lockered the space equipment. At the same time, he admired her.

She was slight and dark, but prettier than he had realized at first. That was an effect of personality, reasserting itself after what happened in Anushirvan. The city had been not only the most beautiful and civilized, but the gayest on all Sassania; and her father was Nadjaf Kuli, the deputy governor. Now he was dead and his palace sacked, and she had fled for her life with one of her Shah's defeated barbarian allies. Yet she was getting back the ability to laugh. Good stock, Tom thought; she'd bear him good sons.

"Did you see trace of humans?" she asked. He had believed her Anglic bore a charming accent—it was not native to her—until he discovered that she had been taught the classical language. Her gazelle eyes flickered from the telescope he carried in one fist on to his battered and weatherbeaten face.

"Trace, yes," he answered bluntly. "Stumps of a few towns. They'd been hit with nukes."

"Oh-h-h..."

"Ease off, youngster." He rumpled the flowing hair. "I couldn't make out much, with nothin' better'n these lenses. We'd already agreed the planet was likely raided, what time the broadcasts quit. Don't mean they haven't rebuilt a fair amount. I'd guess they have. The level o', shall I say in two words, radio activity—" Tom paused. "You were supposed to smile at that," he said in a wounded tone.

"Well, may I smile at the second joke, instead?" she retorted impishly. They both chuckled. Her back grew straighter, in the drab one-piece garment that was all he had been able to give her, and somehow the strength of the curving nose dominated the tenderness of her mouth. "Please go on, my lord."

"Uh, you shouldn't call me that. They're free women on Kraken."

"So we were on Sassania. In fact, plural marriage—"

"I know, I know. Let's get on with business." Tom started down the corridor. Yasmin accompanied him, less gracefully than she had moved at home. The field was set for Kraken weight, which was 1.25 standard. But she'd develop the muscles for it before long.

-2-

He had gone through a wedding ceremony with her, once they were in space, at Dagny's insistence. "Who else will the poor child have for a protector but you, the rest of her life? Surely you won't turn her loose on any random planet. At the same time, she *is* aristocratic born. It'd humiliate her to become a plain concubine."

"M-m-m...but the heirship problem—"

"I like her myself, what little I've seen of her; and the Kuli barons always had an honorable name. I don't think she'll raise boys who'll try to steal house rule from my sons."

As usual, Dagny was no doubt right.

Anxious to swap findings with her, Tom hurried. The passage reached empty and echoing; air from the ventilators blew loud and chilled him; the stylized murals of gods and sea beasts had changed from bold to pathetic—now that only three people crewed this ship. But they were lucky to be alive—would not have been so, save for the primitive loyalty of his personal guardsmen, who died in their tracks while he ran through the burning city in search of Dagny—when the Pretender's nonhuman mercenaries broke down the last defenses. He found his chief wife standing by the ship with a Mark IV thunderbolter, awaiting his return. She would not have left without him. Yasmin huddled at her feet. They managed to loose a few missiles as they lifted. But otherwise there was nothing to do but hope to fight another day. The damage that *Firedrake* sustained in running the enemy space fleet had made escape touch and go. The resulting absence of exterior force-fields and much interior homeostasis made the damage worse as they traveled. Either they found the wherewithal for repair here, or they stayed here.

Tom said to Yasmin while he strode: "We couldn't've picked up their radio so far out's we did, less'n they'd had quite a lot, both talk and radar. That means they had a pretty broad industrial base. You don't destroy that by scrubbin' cities. Too many crossroads machine shops and so forth; too much skill spread through the population. I'd be surprised if this planet's not on the way back up."

"But why haven't they rebuilt any cities?"

"Maybe they haven't gotten that far yet. Been less'n ten years, you know. Or, 'course, they might've got knocked clear down to savagery. I've seen places where it happened. We'll find out."

Walking beside the girl, Roan Tom did not look especially note-worthy, certainly not like the rover and trader chieftain whose name was already in the ballads of a dozen planets. He was of medium height, though so broad in shoulders and chest as to look stocky. From his father, he had the long head, wide face, high cheekbones, snub nose and beardlessness of the Lochlanna. But his mother, a freedwoman said to be of Hermetian stock, had given him dark-red hair, which was now thinning, and star-blue eyes. Only the right of those remained; a patch covered where the left had been. (Some day, somewhere, he'd find someone with the knowledge and facilities to grow him a new one!) He walked with the rolling gait of a Krakener, whose planet is mostly ocean, and bore the intertwining tattoos of his adopted people on most of his hide. A blaster and knife hung at his waist.

Dagny was in the detector shack. Viewscreens might be malfunctioning, along with a lot else, but such instruments as the radionic, spectroscopic, magnetic and sonic were not integrated with ship circuitry. They had kept their accuracy, and she was expert—not educated, but rule of-thumb expert—in their use.

"Well, there," she said, looking around the console at which she sat. "What'd you see?"

Tom repeated in more detail what he had told Yasmin. Since Dagny spoke no Pelevah and only a little pidgin Anglic, while Yasmin had no Eylan, these two of his wives communicated with difficulty. Maybe that was why they got along so well. "And how 'bout you?" he finished.

"I caught a flash of radiocast. Seemed like two stations communicating from either end of a continental-size area."

"Still, somebody is able to chat a bit," Tom said. "Hopeful." He lounged against the doorframe. "Anyone spot us, d' you think?"

Dagny grinned. "What do *you* think?"

His lips responded. A positive answer would have had them in action at once, he to the bridge, she to the main fire control turret. They couldn't be sure they had not been noticed—by optical system, quickly brushing radar or maser, gadget responsive to the neutrino emission of their proton converter, several other possible ways—but it was unlikely.

"Any further indications?" Tom asked. "Atomic powerplants?"

"I don't know."

"How come?"

"I don't know what the readings mean that I get, particle flux, magnetic variations and the rest. This is such a confoundedly queer sun and planet. I've never seen anything like them. Have you?"

"No."

They regarded each other for a moment that grew very quiet. Dagny, Od's daughter in the House of Brenning, was a big woman, a few years his senior. Her shoulder-length yellow mane was fading a bit, and her hazel eyes were burdened with those contact lenses that were the best help anyone on Kraken knew how to give. But her frame was still strong and erect, her hands still clever and murderously quick. It had been natural for an impoverished noble family to make alliance with an energetic young immigrant who had a goodly following and a spaceship. But in time, voyages together, childbirths and child-rearings, the marriage of convenience had become one of affection.

"Well...s'pose we better go on down," Tom said. "Sooner we get patched, sooner we can start back. And we'd better not be gone from home too long."

Dagny nodded. Yasmin saw the grimness that touched them and said, "What is wrong, my...my husband?"

Tom hadn't the heart to explain how turbulent matters were on Kraken also. She'd learn that soon enough, if they lived. He said merely, "There's some kind o' civilization goin' yet around here. But it may exist only as traces o' veneer. The signs are hard to figure. This is a rogue planet, you see."

"Rogue?" Yasmin was bemused. "But that is a loose planet—sunless—isn't it?"

"You mean a bandit planet. A rogue's one that don't fit in with its usual type, got a skewball orbit or composition or whatever. Like this'n."

"Oh. Yes, I know."

"What?" He caught her shoulder, not noticing how she winced at so hard a grip. "You've heard o' this system before?"

"No...please...no, my people never came to this side of the Nebula either, with what few ships we had. But I studied some astrophysics and planetography at Anushirvan University."

"Huh?" He let her go and gaped. "Science? Real, Imperial-era science, not engineerin' tricks?" She nodded breathlessly. "But I thought—you said you'd studied classics."

"Is not scientific knowledge one of the classic arts? We had a very complete collection of tapes in the Royal Library." Forlornness came upon her. "Gone, now, into smoke."

"Never mind. Can you explain how come this globe is as it is?"

"Well, I...well, no. I don't believe I could. I would need more information. Mass, and chemical data, and—And even then, I would probably not be able. I am not one of the ancient experts."

"Hardly anybody is," Tom sighed. "All right. Let's get us a snack, and then to our stations for planetfall."

A Tragedy of Errors

-3-

Descent was tricky. Sensor-computer-autopilot linkups could no longer be trusted. Tom had to bring *Firedrake* in on manual controls. His few instruments were of limited use, when he couldn't get precise data by which to recalibrate them for local conditions. With no viewscreens working properly, he had no magnification, infrared and ultraviolet presentations, any of the conventional aids. He depended on an emergency periscope, on Dagny's radar readings called via intercom and on the trained reflexes of a lifetime.

Yasmin sat beside him. There was nothing she could do elsewhere, and he wanted to be able to assist her in her inexperience if they must bail out. The spacesuit and gravity impellers surrounded her with an awkward bulk that made the visage in the helmet look like a child's. Neither one of them had closed a faceplate. Her voice came small through the gathering throb of power: "Is it so difficult to land? I mean, I used to watch ships do it, and even if we are partly crippled—we could travel between the stars. What can an aircar do that we can't?"

"Hyperdrive's not the same thing as kinetic velocity, and most particular not the same as aerodynamic speed," Tom grunted. "To start with, I know the theory o' sublight physics."

"You do?" She was frankly astounded.

"Enough of it, anyhow. I can read and write, too." His hands played over the board. Vibration grew in the deck, the bulkheads, his bones. A thin shrilling was heard, the first cloven atmosphere. "A spaceship's a sort o' big and clumsy object, once out o' her native habitat," he said absently. "Got quite a moment of inertia, f'r instance. Means a sudden, hard wind can turn her top over tip and she don't right easy. When you got a lot o' sensitive machinery to do the work, that's no problem. But we don't." He buried his face in the periscope hood. Cloudiness swirled beneath. "Also," he said, "we got no screens and nobody at the guns. So we'd better be choosy about where we sit down. And...we don't have any way to scan an area in detail. Now do be quiet and let me steer."

Already in the upper air, he encountered severe turbulence. That was unexpected, on a planet which received less than 0.9 Terran...insolation, with a lower proportion of UV to boot. It wasn't that the atmosphere was peculiar. The spectroscope readout had said the mixture was ordinary oxy-nitro-CO_2, on the thin and dry side—sea-level pressure around 600 mm.—but quite breathable. Nor was the phenomenon due to excessive rotation; the period was twenty-five and a half hours. Of course, the inner moon, while small, was close in and must have considerable tidal effect—*Hoy!*

The outercom buzzed. Someone was calling. "Take that, Yasmin," Tom snapped. The ship wallowed. He felt it even through the cushioning internal gee-field, and the attitude meters were wavering crazily. Wind screamed louder. The clouds roiled near, coppery-headed blue-shadowed billows on the starboard horizon, deep purple below him. He had hoped that night and overcast would veil his arrival, but evidently a radar had fingered him. Or—"The knob marked A, you idiot! Turn it widdershins. I can't let go now!"

Yasmin caught her lower lip between her teeth and obeyed. The screen flickered to life. "Up the volume," Tom commanded. "Maybe Dagny can't watch, but she'd better hear. You on, Dagny?"

"Aye." Her tone was crisp from the intercom speaker. "I doubt if I'll understand many words, though. Hadn't you better start aloft and I leave the radar and take over fire control?"

"No, stand where you are. See what you can detect. We're not after a tussle, are we?" Tom glanced at the screen for the instant he dared. It was sidewise to him, putting him outside the pickup arc, but he could get a profile of the three-dimensional image.

The man who gazed out was so young that his beard was brownish fuzz. Braids hung from beneath a goggled fiber crash helmet. But his features were hard; his background appeared to be an aircraft cockpit; and his green tunic had the look of a uniform.

"Who are you?" he challenged. Seeing himself confronted by a girl, he let his jaw drop. "Who *are* you?"

"Might ask the same o' you," Tom answered for her. "We're from offplanet."

"Why did you not declare yourselves?" The Anglic was thickly accented but comprehensible, roughened with tension.

"We didn't know anybody was near. I reckon you had to try several bands before hittin' the one we were tuned to. Isn't a standard signal frequency any more." Tom spoke with careful casualness, while the ship bucked and groaned around him and lightning zigzagged in the clouds he approached. "Don't worry about us. We mean no harm."

"You trespass in the sky of Karol Weyer."

"Son, we never heard o' him. We don't even know what you call this planet."

The pilot gulped. "N-Nike," he said automatically. "The planet Nike. Karol Weyer is our Engineer, here in Hanno. Who are you?"

Dagny's voice said, in Eylan, "I've spotted him on the scope, Tom. Coming in fast at eleven o'clock low."

"Let me see your face," the pilot demanded harshly. "Hide not by this woman."

"Can't stop to be polite," Tom said. "S'pose you let us land, and we'll talk to your Engineer. Or shall we take our business elsewhere?"

Yasmin's gauntlet closed convulsively on Tom's sleeve. "The look on him grows terrible," she whispered.

"Gods damn," Tom said, "we're friends!"

"What?" the pilot shouted.

"Friends, I tell you! We need help. Maybe you—"

"The screen went blank," Yasmin cried.

Tom risked yawing *Firedrake* till he could see in the direction Dagny had bespoken. The craft was in view. It was a one- or two-man job, a delta wing whose contrail betrayed the energy source as chemical rather than atomic or electric. However, instruments reported it as applying that power to a gravity drive. At this distance he couldn't make out if the boat had guns, but hardly doubted that. For a moment it glinted silvery against the darkling clouds, banked and vanished.

"Prob'ly hollerin' for orders," Tom said. "And maybe reinforcements. Chil'ren, I think we'd better hustle back spaceward and try our luck in some place more sociable than Hanno."

"Is there any?" Dagny wondered.

"Remains to be seen. Let's hope it's not our remains that'll be seen." Tom concentrated on the controls. Lame and weakened, the ship could not simply reverse. She had too much downward momentum and was too deep in Nike's gravity well. He must shift vectors slowly and nurse her up again.

After minutes, Dagny called through the racket and shudderings: "Several of them—at least five—climbing faster than us, from all sides."

"I was afraid o' that," Tom said. "Yasmin, see if you can eavesdrop on the chit-chat between 'em."

"Should we not stay tuned for their call?" the Sassanian asked timidly.

"I doubt they aim to call. If ever anybody acted so scared and angry as to be past reason—No, hold 'er."

The screen had suddenly reawakened. This time the man who stared forth was middle-aged, leonine, bearded to the waist. His coat was trimmed with fur and, beneath the storm in his voice, pride rang. "I am the Engineer," he said. "You will land and be slaves."

"Huh?" Tom said. "Look, we was goin' away—"

"You declared yourselves friends!"

"Yes. We'd like to do business with you. But—"

"Land at once. Slave yourselves to me. Or my craft open fire. They have tommics."

"Nukes, you mean?" Tom growled. Yasmin stifled a shriek. Karol Weyer observed and looked grimly pleased. Tom cursed without words.

The Nikean shook his head. Tom got a glimpse of that, and wasn't sure whether the gesture meant yes, no, or maybe in this land. But the answer was plain: "Weapons that unleash the might which lurks in matter."

And our force-screen generator is on sick leave, Tom thought. *He may be lyin'. But I doubt it, because they do still use gravs here. We can't outrun a rocket, let alone an energy beam. Nor could Dagny, by herself, shoot down the lot in time to forestall 'em.*

"You win," he said. "Here we come."

"Leave your transceiver on," Weyer instructed. "When you are below the clouds, the fish will tell you where to go."

"Fish?" Tom choked. But the screen had emptied, save for the crackling and formlessnesses of static.

"D-d-dialect?" Yasmin suggested.

"Uh, yeh. Must mean somethin' like squadron leader. Good girl!" Tom spared her a grin. The tears were starting forth.

"Slaves?" she wailed. "Oh, no, no."

"'Course not, if I can help it," he said, *sotto voce* lest the hostiles be listening. "Rather die."

He did not speak exact truth. Having been a slave once, he didn't prefer death—assuming his owner was not unreasonable, and that some hope existed of getting his freedom back. But becoming property was apt to be worse for a woman than a man: much worse, when she was a daughter of Sassania's barons or Kraken's sea kings. As their husband, he was honor bound to save them if he could.

"We'll make a break," he said. "Lot o' wild country underneath. One reason I picked this area. But first we have to get down."

"What's gone by me?" Dagny called.

Tom explained in Eylan while he fought the ship. "But that doesn't make sense!" she said "When they know nothing about us—"

"Well, they took a bad clobberin', ten years back. Can't expect 'em to act terribly sensible about strangers. And s'posin' this is a misunderstandin'…we have to stay alive while we straighten it out. Stand by for a rough jaunt."

-4-

The aircraft snarled into sight, but warily, keeping their distance in swoops and circles that drew fantastic trails of exhaust. For a moment Tom wondered if that didn't prove the locals were familiar with space-war techniques. Those buzzeroos seemed careful to stay beyond reach of a tractor or pressor beam that could have seized them…But no. They were exposed to his guns and missiles, which had far greater range, and didn't know that these were unmanned.

Nevertheless, they were at least shrewd on this planet. From what Tom had let slip, and the battered condition of the vessel, Weyer had clearly guessed that the newcomers were weak. They could doubtless wipe out one or two aircraft before being hit, but could they handle half a dozen? That Weyer had taken the risk and scrambled this much of what must be a very small air fleet suggested implacable enmity. (Why? He couldn't be so stupid as to assume that everyone from off-planet was a foe. Could he?) What was worse, his assessment of the military situation was quite correct. In her present state, *Firedrake* could not take on so many opponents and survive.

She entered the clouds.

For a while Tom was blind. Thunder and darkness encompassed him. Metal toned. The instrument dials glowed like goblin eyes. Their needles spun; the ship lurched; Tom stabbed and pulled and twisted controls, sweat drenched his coverall and reeked in his nostrils.

Then he was through, into windy but uncluttered air. Fifteen kilometers beneath him lay that part of the north temperate zone he had so unfortunately chosen. The view was of a valley, cut into a checkerboard pattern that suggested large agricultural estates. A river wound through, shining silver in what first dawn-light reddened the eastern horizon. A few villages clustered along it, and traffic moved, barge trains and waterships. A swampy delta spread at the eastern end of a great bay.

That bay was as yet in the hour before sunrise, but glimmered with reflections. It had a narrow mouth, opening on a sea to the west. Lights twinkled on either side of the gate, and clustered quite thickly on the southern bayshore. Tom's glance went to the north. There he saw little trace of habitation. Instead, hills humped steeply toward a mountain which smoked. Forests covered them, but radar showed how rugged they were.

The outercom flashed with the image of the pilot who had first hailed him. Now that conditions were easier, Tom could have swiveled it around himself to let the scanner cover his own features. Yasmin could have done so for him at any time. But he refrained. Anonymity wasn't an ace in the hole—at most, a deuce or a trey—but he needed every card he had.

"You will bear east-northeast," the "fish" instructed. "About a hundred kilos upriver lies a cave. Descend there."

"Kilos?" Tom stalled. He had no intention of leaving the refuges below him for the open flatlands.

"Distances. Thousand-meters."

"But a cave? I mean, look, I want to be a good fellow and so forth, but how'm I goin' to spot a cave from the air?"

"Spot?" It was the Nikean's turn to be puzzled. However, he was no fool. "Oh, so, you mean espy. A cave is a stronghouse. You will know it by turrets, projectors, setdown fields."

"Your Engineer's castle?"

"Think you we're so whetless we'd let you near the Great Cave? You might have a tommic boom aboard. No. Karol Weyer dwells by the bay gate. You go to the stronghouse guarding the Nereid River valley. Now change course, I said, or we fire."

Tom had used the talk-time to shed a good bit of altitude. "We can't," he said. "Not that fast. Have to get low first, before we dare shift."

"You go no lower, friend! Those are our folk down there."

"Be reasonable," Tom said. "A spaceship's worth your havin', I'm sure, even a damaged one like ours. Why blang us for somethin' we can't help?"

"Um-m-m...hold where you are."

"I can't. This is not like an aircraft. I've got to either rise or sink. Ask your bosses."

The pilot's face disappeared.

"But—" Yasmin began.

"Shhh!" Tom winked his good eye at her.

He was gambling that they hadn't had spacecraft on Nike for a long time. Otherwise they wouldn't have taken such a licking a decade ago; and they'd have sent a ship after him, rather than those few miserable, probably handmade gravplanes. So if they didn't have anyone around who was qualified in the practical problems of handling that kind of vessel—

Not but what *Firedrake* wasn't giving him practical problems of his own. Wind boomed and shoved.

The pilot returned. "Go lower if you must," he said. "But follow my word, go above the northshore hills."

"Surely." *Right what I was hopin' for!* Tom switched to Eylan. "Dagny, get to the forward manlock."

"What do you say?" rapped the pilot.

"I'm issuin' orders to my crew," Tom said. "They don't speak Anglic."

"No! You'll not triple-talk me!"

Tom let out a sigh that was a production. "Unless they know what to do, we'll crash. Do you want live slaves and a whole spaceship, or no? Make up your mind, son."

"Um-m...well. At first ill-doing, we shoot."

Tom ignored him. "Listen, Dagny. You're not needed here any more. I can land on my altimeter and stuff. But I've got to set us down easy, and not get us hit by some overheated gunner. They must have what we need to make our repairs, but not to build a whole new ship, even s'posin' we knew how. So we can't risk defendin' ourselves, leastwise till we get away from the ship."

"She will be theirs," Dagny said, troubled. "And we will be hunted. Shouldn't we surrender peacefully and bargain with them?"

"What bargainin' power has a slave got? Whereas free, if nothin' else, I get we're the only two on Nike that can run a spacecraft. Besides, we don't know what these fellows are like. They could be mighty cruel. No, you go stand by that manlock along with Yasmin. The minute we touch dirt, you two get out—fast and far."

"But Tom, you'll be on the bridge. What about you?"

"Somebody's got to make that landin'. I dunno how they'll react. But you girls won't have much time to escape yourselves. I'll come after you. If I haven't joined you soon, figure I won't, and do whatever comes natural. And look after Yasmin, huh?"

Silence dwelt for a moment amidst every inanimate noise. Until: "I understand. Tom, if we don't see each other again, it was good with you." Dagny uttered a shaken laugh. "Tell her to kiss you for both of us."

"Aye-ya." He couldn't, of course, with that suspicious countenance glowering out of the screen. But in what little Pelevan he had, he gave Yasmin her orders. She didn't protest, too stunned by events to grasp the implications.

Down and down. The tilted wilderness swooped at him.

"The steerin's quit on me!" Tom yelled in Anglic. "Yasmin, go fantangle the dreelsprail! Hurry!" She flung off her safety webbing and left the bridge, as fast as possible in her clumsy armor. "I've got to make an emergency landin'," Tom said to the Nikean officer.

Probably that caused them to hold their fire as he had hoped. He didn't know, nor wonder. He was too busy. The sonoprobe said firm solid below. The altimeter said a hundred meters, fifty, twenty-five, ten—Leaves surged around. Boughs and boles splintered. The further trees closed in like a cage. Impact shook, drummed, went to silence. Tom cut the engines and gee-field. Native gravity, one-half standard, hit him with giddiness. He unharnessed himself. The deck was canted. He slipped, skidded, got up and pounded down the companionway.

-5-

The manlock valves opened at Dagny's control while *Firedrake* was still moving. The drop in air pressure hurt her eardrums. She glimpsed foliage against a sky red with dawn, gray with scattering stormclouds. The earthquake landing cast her to hands and knees. She rose, leaning against a bulkhead. Yasmin stumbled into sight. The faceplate stood open before the terrified young visage. "Chaos! Dog that thing!" Dagny cried. "We'll be at top speed." She was not understood. She grabbed the girl and snapped the plate shut herself. "You…know…fly?" she asked in her fragment of Anglic.

"Yes. I think so." Yasmin wet her lips. Her radio voice was unsteady in the other's earplugs. "I mean…Lord Tom explained how."

"No practice, though?" Dagny muttered in Eylan. "You're about to get some." In Anglic: "Follow I."

She leaned out of the lock. High overhead she descried the gleam of a wheeling delta wing. The forest roared with wind. A little clearing surrounded the ship where trees had been flattened. Beyond the shadowy tangle of their trunks and limbs, their neighbors made a wall of night.

"Go!" Dagny touched her impeller stud and launched herself. She soared up. Flight was tricky in these gusts. Curving about, she saw Yasmin's suit helplessly cartwheel. She returned, caught the Sassanian girl, laid one arm around her waist and used the other to operate her drive units for her in the style of an instructor. They moved off, slowly and awkwardly.

A scream split the air. Dagny glanced as far behind as she could. Two of the aircraft were stooping…One took a hoverstance above *Firedrake,* the other came after her and Yasmin. She saw the muzzle of an energy gun and slammed the two impeller sets into full forward speed. Alone, she might have dived under the trees. But Yasmin hadn't the skill, and two couldn't slip through those dense branches side by side. Tom had told her to look after Yasmin, and Dagny was his sworn woman.

She tried to summon before her the children they had had together, tall sons and daughters, the baby grandchildren, and Skerrygarth, their home that was the dowry she had brought him, towers steadfast above a surf that played white among the reefs—

Explosion smashed at her. Had she been looking directly aft, she would have been dazzled into momentary blindness. As it was, the spots before her eyes and the tolling in her ears lasted for minutes. A wave of heat pushed through her armor.

She yelled, clung somehow to Yasmin, and kept the two of them going. Fury spoke again and again. It dwindled with distance as they fled.

Finally it was gone. By that time the women had covered some twenty kilometers, more or less eastward. The sea-level horizon of Nike was only about six kilometers off; and this was not flat country. They were well into morning light and far beyond view of the spaceship. Dagny thought she could yet identify an aircraft or two, but maybe those sparks were something else.

Beneath her continued hills and ravines, thickly wooded, and rushing streams. The volcano bulked in the north; smoke plumed from a frost-rimmed crater. Southward the land rolled down to the quicksilver sheet of the bay. Its shore was marshy—an effect of the very considerable tides that the nearer moon raised—but a village of neat wooden houses stood there on piles. Sailboats that doubtless belonged to fishermen were putting out. They must exist in such numbers because of a power shortage rather than extreme backwardness; for Dagny saw a good-sized motorship as well, crossing the bay from the gate to the lower, more populous south side. Its hull was of planks and its wake suggested the engine was minimal. At the same time, its lines and the nearly smokeless stack indicated competent design.

Here the wind had gentled, and the clouds were dissipating fast. (Odd to have such small cells of weather, she thought in a detached logical part of herself. Another indication of an atmosphere disturbed by violent solar conditions?) They shone ruddy-tinted in a deep purple vault of sky. The sun stood bright orange above mists that lay on the Nereid River delta.

"Down we go, lass," Dagny said, "before we're noticed."

"What happened? Lord Tom, where is he?"

The sob scratched at Dagny's nerves. She snapped, biting back tears: "Use your brain, you little beast, if it's anything except blubber! He went first to the main fire-control turret. When he saw us attacked, he cut loose with the ship's weapons. I don't see how he could have gotten all those bastards, though. If they didn't missile him, they've anyhow bottled him up. On *our* account!"

She realized she'd spoken entirely in Eylan. Suppressing a growl, she took over the controls of both suits. With no need for haste, she could ease them past the branches that tried to catch them, down to the forest floor.

"Now," she said in Anglic. "Out." Yasmin gaped. Dagny set the example by starting to remove her own armor.

"Wh-why?"

"Find us. In...in...in-stru-ments. Smell metal, no? Could be. Not take chance. We got—got to—" Dagny's vocabulary failed her. She had wanted to explain that if they stayed with the suits, they ran the risk of detection from afar. And even if the Nikeans didn't have that much technology left, whatever speed and protection the equipment lent wasn't worth its conspicuousness.

She was almost grateful for every difficulty. It kept her mind—somewhat—off the overwhelming fact that Tom, her Roan Tom, was gone.

Or maybe not. Just maybe, not. He might be a prisoner, and she might in time contrive to bargain for his release. No, she would not remember what she had seen done to prisoners, here and there in her wanderings, by vengeful captors!

Were that the case, though...Her hand went first to the blaster at one coveralled hip, next to the broad-bladed knife; and there it lingered. If she devoted the rest of her days to the project, and if the gods were kind, she might eventually get his murderers into her clutch.

Yasmin shed the last armor. She hugged herself and shivered in a chill breeze. "But we haven't any radios except in our helmets," she said. "How can he contact us?"

Dagny framed a reply: "If he'd been able to follow us, he'd already be here, or at least have called. I left my squealer circuit on, for him to track us by. That was safe; its frequency varies continuously, according to synchronized governors in both our suits. But he hasn't arrived, and we daren't stay near this much metal and resonant electronic stuff." Somehow, by words and gestures, she conveyed the gist. Meanwhile she filled their pockets with rations and medications, arranged the weapons beneath their garments, checked footgear. Last she hid the armor under leaf mould and canebrake, and took precise note of landmarks.

Yasmin's head drooped until the snarled dark locks covered her face. "I am so tired," she whispered.

Think I'm not? My lips are numb with it. "Go!" Dagny snapped.

She had to show the city-bred girl how to conceal their trail through the woods.

After a couple of hours, unhounded, the air warming and brightening around them, both felt a little better. It was up-and-down walking, but without much underbrush to combat, for the ground was densely carpeted with a soft mossy growth. Here and there stood clumps of fronded gymnosperm plants. This native vegetation was presumably chlorophyll-bearing, though its greenness was pale and had a curious bluish overcast. Otherwise the country had been taken over by the more efficient, highly developed species that man commonly brought with him. Oaks cast sun-speckled shadows; birches danced and glistened; primroses bloomed in meadows, where grass had overwhelmed a pseudo-moss that apparently had a competitive advantage only in shade. A sweet summery smell was about, and Yasmin spoke of her homeland. Even Dagny, bred in salt winds and unrestful watery leagues, felt a stirring of ancient instinct.

She was used to denser atmosphere. Sounds—sough in leaves, whistle of birds, rilling of brooks they crossed, thud of her own feet—came as if muffled to her ears; and on a steep upgrade, her heart was apt to flutter. But oxygen shortage was more or less compensated for by a marvelous, almost floating low-gravity lightness.

A good many animals were to be seen. Again, terrestroid forms had crowded out most of the primitive native species. With a whole ecology open to them, they were now in the process of explosive evolution. A few big insect-like flyers, an occasional awkward amphibian, gave glimpses of the original biosphere. But thrushes, bulbuls, long-winged hawks rode the wind. Closer down swarmed butterflies and bees. A wild boar, tusked and rangy, caused Dagny to draw her blaster; but he went by, having perhaps learned to fear man. Splendid was the more distant sight of mustangs, carabao, an entire herd of antlered six-legged tanithars.

A measure of peace came upon Dagny, until at last she could say, "All right, we stop, eat, rest."

They sat under a broad-spreading hilltop cedar that hid them from above while openness, halfway down the heights to the forest, afforded ample ground vision. They had made for the bay and were thus at a lower altitude. The waters sheened to south, ridges and mountains stood sharply outlined to north. In this clear air, the blueness of their distance was too slight to hide the basic ocherous tint of rocks and soil.

Dagny broke out a packet of dehydrate. She hesitated for a moment before adding water to the tray from a canteen she had filled en route. Yasmin, slumped exhausted against the tree trunk, asked, "What is the matter?" And, her eyes and mind wandering a little, she tried to smile. "See, yonder, apples. They are green but they can be dessert."

"No," Dagny said.

"What? Why not?"

"Heavy metal." Dagny scowled. How to explain? "Young planet. Dense. Lots heavy metals. Not good."

"Young? But—"

"Look around you," Dagny wanted to say. "That sun, putting out radiation like an early Type F—in amount—but the color and spectral distribution are late G or early K. I've never seen anything like it. The way it flares, I don't believe it's quite stabilized at its proper position on the main sequence yet. Because of anomalous chemical composition, I suppose. You get that with very young suns, my dear. They've condensed out of an interstellar medium made rich in metals by the thermonuclear furnaces of earlier star generations. Or so I've been told.

"I know for fact that planets with super-abundant heavy elements can be lethal to men. So much…oh, arsenic, selenium, radioactives. Slow poison in some areas, fast and horrible death in others. This water, that fruit, may have stuff to kill us."

But she lacked words or inclination. She said, "Iron. Makes red in rocks. No? Lots iron. Could be lots bad metal. Young planet. Lots air, no?"

She had, in truth, never heard of a dwarf world like this, getting such an amount of sunlight, that had hung onto a proper atmosphere. Evidently, she thought, there had not been time for the gas to leak into space. The primitive life forms were another proof of a low age.

Beyond this, she didn't reason. She did not have the knowledge on which to base logic, nor did she have the scientific way of thinking. What little cosmology and cosmogony she had learned, for instance, was in the form of vague, probably distorted tradition—latter-day myth. And she was intelligent enough to recognize this.

Once, she imagined, any Imperial space officer had been educated in the details of astrophysics and planetology. And he would have seen, or read about, a far greater variety of suns than today's petty travels encompassed. So he would have known immediately what sort of system this was; or, if not, he would have known how to find out.

But that was centuries ago. The information might not actually be lost. It might even be moldering in the damp, uncatalogued library of her own Skerrygarth. Surely parts of it were taught in the universities of more civilized planets, though as a set of theoretical ideas, to be learned by rote without any need for genuine comprehension.

Practical spacefarers, like her and Tom, didn't learn it. They didn't get the chance. A rudiment of knowledge was handed down to them, largely by word of mouth, the minimum they needed for survival.

And speaking of survival—

She reached her decision. "Eat," she said. "Drink." She took the first sample. The water had a woodsy taste, nothing unfamiliar.

After all, humans did flourish here. Perhaps they were adapted to metal-rich soil. But the adaptation could scarcely be enormous. Had that been the case, terrestroid species would not be so abundant and dominant, after a mere thousand years or whatever on this planet.

Thus Nike was biochemically safe—at least, in this general region—at least, for a reasonable time. Perhaps, if outworlders stayed as long as one or two decades, they might suffer from cumulative poisoning. But she needn't worry that far ahead, when a hunt was on immediately and when Tom—

Grimly, she fueled her body. Afterward she stood watch while Yasmin caught a nap. What she thought about was her own affair.

When the Sassanian awoke, they held a lengthy conference. The order Dagny had to issue was not complicated:

"We're in enemy territory. But I don't believe it covers the whole planet, or even the whole area between this sea and the next one east. 'The Engineer of Hanno' is a typical feudal title. I've not heard before that 'engineer' changed meaning to the equivalent of 'duke' or 'king,' but it's easy to see how that could've happened, and I've met odder cases of wordshift. Well, our darling Engineer made it plain he regarded us as either the worst menace or the juiciest prey that'd come by in years. Maybe both. So he'd naturally call his full air power, or most of it, against us. Which amounted to half a dozen little craft, with gravmotors so weak they need wings! And look at those sailboats, and the absence of real cities, and the fact there's scarcely any radio in use...yes, they've fallen far on Nike. I'm sure that raid from space was only the latest blow. They must have a small half-educated class left, and some technicians of a sort; but the bulk of the people must've been poor and ignorant for many generations.

"And divided. I swear they must be divided. I've seen so many societies like this, I can practically identify them by smell. A crazy-quilt pattern of feudalisms and sovereignties, any higher authority a ghost. If as rich a planet as this one potentially is were united, it'd have made a far greater recovery by now, after the space attack, than it has done. Or it would have beaten the raiders off at least.

"So, if we have enemies here in Hanno, we probably have automatic friends somewhere else. And not dreadfully far away. At any rate, we're not likely to be pursued beyond the nearest border, nor extradited back here. In fact, the Engineer's rivals are apt to be quite alarmed when they learn he's clapped hands on a real space warship. They're apt to join forces to get it away from him. Which'll make you and me, my dear, much-sought-after advisors. We may or may not be able to get Tom back unhurt. I vow the gods a hundred Blue Giant seabeasts if we do! But we'll be free, even powerful.

"Or so I hope. We've nothing to go on but hope. And courage and wits and endurance. Have you those, Yasmin? Your life was too easy until now. But he asked me to care for you.

"You'll have to help. Our first and foremost job is to get out of Hanno. And I don't speak their damned language for diddly squat. You'll talk for both of us. Can you? We'll plan a story. Then, if and when you see there must be a false note in it, you'll have to cover—at once—with no ideas from me. Can you do that, Yasmin? You must!"

—But conference was perforce by single words, signs, sketches in the red dirt. It went slowly. And it was repeated, over and over, in every possible way, to make certain they understood each other.

In the end, however, Yasmin nodded. "Yes," she said, "I will try, as God gives me strength…and as you do." The voice was almost inaudible, and the eyes she turned on the bigger, older woman were dark with awe.

-6-

In midafternoon they reached a farm. Its irregular fields were enclosed by forest, through which a cart track ran to join a dirt road that, in turn, twisted over several kilometers until it entered the fisher village.

Dagny spent minutes peering from a thicket. Beside her, Yasmin tried to guess what evaluations the Krakener was making. *I should begin to learn these ways of staying alive,* the Sassanian thought. *More is involved than my own welfare. I don't want to remain a burden on my companions, an actual danger to them.*

And to think, not one year ago I took for granted the star rovers were ignorant, dirty, cruel, quarrelsome barbarians!

Yasmin had been taught about philosophic objectivity, but she was too young to practice it consistently. Her universe having been wrecked, herself cast adrift, she naturally seized upon the first thing that felt like a solid rock and began to make it her emotional foundation. And that thing happened to be Roan Tom and Dagny, Od's daughter.

Not that she had intellectual illusions. She knew very well that the Krakeners had come to help the Shah of Sassania because the Pretender was allied with enemies of theirs. And she knew that, if successful, they would exact good pay. She had heard her father grumble about it.

Nevertheless, the facts were: First, compatriots of hers, supposedly civilized, supposedly above the greed and short-sightedness that elsewhere had destroyed civilization...had proven themselves every bit as animalistic. Second, the starrover garrison in Anushirvan turned out to be jolly, well-scrubbed, fairly well-behaved. Indeed, they were rather glamorous to a girl who had never been past her planet's moon. Third, they had stood by their oaths, died in their ships and at their guns, for her alien people. Fourth, two of them had saved her life, and offered her the best and most honorable way they could think of to last out her days. Fifth (or foremost?), Tom was now her husband.

She was not exactly infatuated with him. A middle-aged, battle-beaten, one-eyed buccaneer had never entered her adolescent dreams. But he was kind in his fashion, and a skillful lover, and...and perhaps she did care for him in a way beyond friendship...if he was alive—oh, let him be alive!

In any event, here was Dagny. *She* certainly felt grief like a sword in her. But she hid it, planned, guided, guarded. She had stood in the light of a hundred different suns, had warred, wandered, been wife and mother and living sidearm. She knew everything worth knowing (what did ancient texts count for?) except one language. And she was so brave that she trusted her life to what ability an awkward weakling of a refugee might possess.

Please don't let me fail her.

Thus Yasmin looked forth too and tried to make inferences from what she saw.

The house and outbuildings were frame, not large, well-built but well-weathered. Therefore they must have stood here for a good length of time. Therefore Imperial construction methods—alloy, prestressed concrete, synthetics, energy webs—had long been out of general use in these parts, probably everywhere on Nike. That primitiveness was emphasized by the agromech system. A couple of horses drew a hay-cutter. It also was wooden; even the revolving blades were simply edged with metal. From its creaking and bouncing, the machine had neither wheel bearings nor springs. A man drove it. Two half-grown boys, belike his sons, walked after. They used wooden-tined rakes to order the windrows. The people, like the animals, were of long slim deep-chested build, brown-haired and fair-complexioned. Their garments were coarsely woven smock and trousers.

No weapons showed, which suggested that the bay region was free of bandits and vendettas. Nevertheless Dagny did not approach. Instead, she led a cautious way back into the woods and thence toward the house, so that the buildings screened off view of the hayfield.

The Krakener woman scowled. "Why?" she muttered.

"Why what...my lady?"

"Why make—" Dagny's hands imitated whirling blades. "Here. Planet... canted?...little. No cold?"

"Oh. Do you mean, why do they bother making hay? Well, there must be times when their livestock can't pasture."

Dagny understood. Her nod was brusque. "Why that?"

"Um-m-m...oh, dear, let me think. Lord Tom explained to me what he—what you two had learned about this planet. Yes. Not much axial tilt. I suppose not an unusually eccentric orbit. So the seasons oughtn't to be very marked. And we are in a rather low latitude anyway, on a seacoast at that. It should never get too cold for grass. Too dry? No, this *is* midsummer time. And, well, they'd hardly export hay to other areas, would they?"

Dagny shrugged.

It is such a strange world, Yasmin thought. *All wrong. Too dense. That is, if it had a great many heavy metals, humans would never have settled here permanently. So what makes it dense should be a core of iron, nickel and things, squeezed into compact quantum states. The kind that terrestroid planets normally have. Yes, and the formation of a true core causes tectonic processes, vulcanism, the outgassing of a primitive atmosphere and water. Later we get chemical evolution, life, photosynthesis, free oxygen—*

But Nike is too small for that! It's Mars type. We have a Mars type planet in our own system—oh, lost and loved star that shines upon Sassania—*and it's got a bare wisp of unbreathable air. Professor Nasruddin explained to us. If a world is small, it has weak gravity. So the differential migration of elements down toward the center, that builds a distinct core, is too slow. So few gas molecules get unlocked from mineral combination by heat...Nike isn't possible!*

(How suddenly, shockingly, real came back to her the lecture hall, and the droning voice, young heads bent above notebooks, sunlight that streamed in through arched windows, and the buzz of bees, odor of roses, a glimpse of students strolling across a greensward that stretched between beautiful buildings.)

Dagny's fingers clamped about Yasmin's arm. "Heed! Fool!"

Yasmin started from her reverie. They were almost at the house. "Heavens! I'm sorry."

"Talk well." Dagny's voice was bleak with doubt of her.

Yasmin swallowed and stepped forth into the yard. She felt dizzy. The knocking of her heart came remote as death. Penned cows, pigs, fowl were like things in a dream. There was something infinitely horrible about the windmill that groaned behind the barn.

Neither shot nor shout met her. The door opened a crack, and the woman who peered out did so fearfully.

Why, she's nervous of us!

Relief passed through Yasmin in a wave of darkness. But an odd, alert calm followed. She perceived with utter clarity. Her thoughts went in three or four directions at once, all coherent. One chain directed her to smile, extend unclenched hands, and say: "Greeting to you, good lady." Another observed that the boards of the house were not nailed but pegged together. A third paid special heed to the windmill. It too was almost entirely of wood, with fabric sails. She saw that it pumped water into an elevated cistern, whence wooden pipes ran to the house and a couple of sheds. Attachments outside one of the latter indicated that there the water, when turned on, drove various machines, like the stone quern she could see.

No atomic or electric energy, then. Nor even solar or combustion power. And yet the knowledge of these things existed: if not complete, then sufficient to make aircraft possible, radio, occasional motorships, doubtless some groundcars. Why was it no longer applied by the common people? The appearance of this farm and of the fisher village as seen from a distance suggested moderate prosperity. The Engineer's rule could not be unduly harsh.

Well, the answer must be, Nike's economy had collapsed so far that hardly anyone could afford real power equipment.

But why not? Sunlight, wood, probably coal and petroleum were abundant. A simple generator, some batteries…Such things took metal. A broken-down society might not have the resources to extract much…Nonsense! Elements like iron, copper, lead, and uranium were surely simple to obtain, even after a thousand years of industrialization. Hadn't Dagny, who knew, said this was a young planet? Weren't young planets metal-rich?

Meanwhile the woman mumbled, "Day. You're from outcountry?"

"Yes," Yasmin said. No use trying to conceal that. Quite apart from accent and garments (the Hannoan woman wore a broad-sleeved embroidered blouse and a skirt halfway to her ankles), they were not of the local racial type. But it was presumably not uniform over the whole planet. One could play on a peasantry's likely ignorance of anything beyond its own neighborhood.

"I am from Kraken," Yasmin said. "My friend is from Sassania." If no one on those comparatively cosmopolitan planets had heard of Nike, vice versa was certain. "We were flying on a mission when our aircraft crashed in the hills."

"That…was the flare…noises…this early-day?" the woman asked. Yasmin confirmed it. The woman drew breath and made a shaky sign in the air. "High 'Uns I thank! We feared, we, 'twas *them* come back."

It was obvious who "they" were, and therefore impossible to inquire about them. A little hysterical with relief, the wife flung wide her door. "Enter you! Enter you! I call the men."

"No need, we thank you," Yasmin said quickly. The fewer who saw them and got a chance later to wonder and talk about them, the better. "Nor time. We must hurry. Do you know of our countries?"

"Well, er, far off." The woman was embarrassed. Yasmin noted that the room behind her was neat, had a look of primitive wellbeing—but how primitive! Two younger children stared half frightened from an inner doorway. "Yes, far, and I, poor farmwife, well, hasn't so much as been to the Silva border—"

"That's the next country?" Yasmin pounced.

"Why…next cavedom, yes, 'tother side of the High Sawtooths east'ard…Well, we're both under the Emp'ror, but they do say as the Prester of Silva's not happy with our good Engineer…You! A-travel like men!"

"They have different customs in our part of the world," Yasmin said. "More like the Empire. Not your Empire. The real one, the Terran Empire, when women could do whatever a man might." That was a safe claim. Throughout its remnants, no one questioned anything wonderful asserted about the lost Imperium—except, perhaps, a few unpleasant scholars, who asked why it had fallen if it had been so great. "Yes, we're from far parts. My friend speaks little Anglic. They don't, in her country." That was why Dagny, clever Dagny, had said they should switch national origins. Krakener place names sounded more Anglic than Sassanian ones did, and Yasmin needed a ready-made supply.

"We have to get on with our mission as fast as possible," she said. "But we know nothing about these lands."

"Storm blow you off track?" the woman queried. As she relaxed, she became more intelligent. "Bad storm-time coming, we think. Lots rain already. Hope the hay's not ruined before it dries."

"Yes, that's what happened." *Thank you, madam, for inventing my explanation.* Yasmin could not resist probing, further the riddle of Nike. "Do you really expect many storms?"

-7-

One child hustled after his father while they went in and took leather-covered chairs. The woman made a large to-do about coffee and cakes. Her name was Elanor, she said, and her husband was Petar Landa, a freeholder. One must not think them backwoods people. They were just a few hours from the town of Sea Gate, which lay nigh the Great Cave itself and was visited by ships from this entire coast. Yes, the Landa family went there often; they hadn't missed a Founders' Festival in ten years, except for the year after the friends came, when there had been none—

"You only needed a year to recover from something like that?" Yasmin exclaimed.

Dagny showed alarm, laying a hand on the Sassanian's and squeezing hard. Elanor Landa was surprised. "Well, Sea Gate wasn't hit. Not that important. Nearest place was...I forgot, all the old big cities went, they say, bombed after being looted, but seems me I heard Terrania was nearest to Hanno. Far off, though, and no man I know was ever there, because 'twas under the Mayor of Bollen and he wasn't any camarado to us western cavedoms, they say—"

Yasmin saw her mistake. Unthinkingly, she had taken "year" to mean a standard, Terran year. It came the more natural to her because Sassania's wasn't very different. *Well,* thought the clarified brain within her, *we came here to get information that might help us escape. And surely, if we're to pretend to be Nikeans, we must know how the planet revolves.*

"I've forgotten," she said. "Exactly when was the attack?"

Elanor was not startled. Such imprecision was common in a largely illiterate people. Indeed, it was somewhat astonishing that she should say, "A little over five years back. Five and a quarter, abs'lut, come Petar's father's birthday;

I remember, for we planned a feast, and then we heard the news. We had radio news then. Everyone was so scared. Later I saw one black ship roar over us, and waited for my death, but it just went on."

"I think we must use a different calendar from you in Kraken," Yasmin said. "And—being wealthier, you understand—not that Hanno *isn't*—but we did suffer worse. We lost records and—Well, let's see if Kraken and Sassania were attacked on the same day you heard about it. That was…let me think…dear me, how, how many days in a year?"

"What? Why, why, five hundred and ninety-one."

Yasmin allayed Elanor's surprise by laughing: "Of course. I was simply trying to recollect if an intercalary date came during the period since."

"A what?"

"You know. The year isn't an exact number of days long. So they have to put in an extra day or month or something, every once in a while." That was a reasonable bet.

It paid off, too. Elanor spoke of an extra day every eleventh Nikean year. Yasmin related how in Kraken they added a month—"What do you call the moons hereabouts?…I mean by a month, the time it takes for them both to get back to the same place in the sky…We add an extra one every twentieth year." Her arithmetic was undoubtedly wrong, but who was going to check? The important point was that Nike circled its sun in 591 days of 25.5 hours each, as near as made no difference.

And hadn't much in the way of seasons, but did suffer from irregular, scarcely predictable episodes when the sun grew noticeably hotter or cooler.

And was poor in heavy metals. Given all the prior evidence, what Yasmin wormed from the chattersome Elanor was conclusive. Quite likely iron oxides accounted for the basic color. But they were too diffuse to be workable. Metals had never been mined on this globe; they were obtained electrochemically from the sea and from clays. (Aluminum, beryllium, magnesium and the like; possibly a bit of heavy elements too, but only a bit. For the most part, iron, copper, silver, uranium, *etc.,* had been imported from outsystem, in exchange for old-fashioned Terrestrial agroproducts that must have commanded good prices on less favored worlds. This would explain why, to the very present, Nike had such a pastoral character.)

The Empire fell. The starships came less and less often. Demoralization ruined the colonies in their turn; planets broke up politically; in the aftermath, most industry was destroyed, and the social resources were no longer there to build it afresh. Today, on Nike, heavy metals were gotten entirely through reclaiming scrap. Consequently they were too expensive for anything but military and the most vital civilian uses. Even the lighter elements came dear; some extractor plants remained, but not enough.

Elanor did not relate this directly. But she didn't need to. Trying to impress her distinguished guests, she made a parade of setting an aluminum coffeepot on the ceramic stove and mentioning the cost. (A foreigner could plausibly ask what that amounted to in real wages. It was considerable.) And, yes, Petar's grandmother had had a lot of ironware in her kitchen. When he inherited, Petar was offered enormous sums for his share. But he had it made into cutting-edge implements. He cared less about money than about good tools, Petar did. Also for his wife. See, ladies, see right here, I use a real steel knife.

"Gold," Dagny said, low and harsh in Yasmin's ear. "Animals, buy, ride."

The younger girl jerked to alertness. Tired, half lulled by Elanor's millwheel voice, she had drifted off into contemplation. Dagny said this was a young world. Nevertheless it was metal-poor. The paradox had an answer. This system could have formed in the galactic halo, where stars were few and the interstellar dust and gas were thin, little enriched. Yes, that must be the case. It had drifted into this spiral arm...But wouldn't it, then, have an abnormal proper motion? Tom hadn't mentioned observing any such thing. Nor had he said there was anything peculiar about Nike's own orbit. Yet he had remarked on less striking facts...

"Tell! Buy!"

Yasmin nodded frantically. "I understand. I understand." They carried a number of Sassanian gold coins. In an age when interstellar currency and credit had vanished, the metal had resumed its ancient economic function. The value varied from place to place, but was never low, and should be fabulous on Nike.

"Good lady," Yasmin said; "we are grateful for your kindness. But we have imposed too much. We should not take any of your men away from the hayfields when storms may be coming. If you will spare us two horses, we can make our own way to Vala and thence, of course, to your Engineer."

Like fun we will! We'll turn east. Maybe we'll ride horseback, maybe we'll take passage on a river boat—whatever looks safest—but we're bound for his enemy, the Prester of Silva!

"We'll pay for them," Yasmin said. "Our overlords provided us well with money. See." She extended a coin. "Will this buy two horses and their gear?"

Elanor gasped. She made a sign again, sat down and fanned herself. Her youngest child sensed his mother's agitation and whimpered.

"Is that gold?" she breathed. "Wait. Till Petar comes. He comes soon. We ask him."

That was logical. But suppose the man got suspicious.

Yasmin glanced back at Dagny. The Krakener made an imperceptible gesture. Beneath their coveralls were holstered energy weapons.

No! We can't slaughter a whole, helpless family!
I hope we won't need to.
I won't! Not for anything!

-8-

Tom reached the fire-control turret as two aircraft peeled off their squadron and dove.

The skyview was full of departing stormclouds, tinged bloody with dawn. Against them, his space-armored women looked tiny. Not so their hunters. Those devilfish shapes swelled at an appalling speed. Tom threw himself into a manual-operation seat and punched for Number Two blastcannon. A cross-hair screen lit for him with what that elevated weapon "saw." He twisted verniers. The auxiliary motors whirred. The vision spun giddily. There…the couple was separating…one to keep guard on him, its mate in a swoop after Dagny and Yasmin. Tom got the latter centered and pressed the discharge button.

The screen stepped down the searing brightness of the energy bolt. Through the open manlock crashed the thunderclap that followed. The Hannoan craft exploded into red-hot shards that rained down upon the trees.

"Gotcha!" Tom exulted. He fired two or three more times, raking toward the other boat where it hung on its negafield some fifty meters aloft. His hope was to scare it off and bluff its mates into holding their bombs—or whatever they had to drop on him. He didn't want to kill again. The first shot had looked necessary if the girls were to live. But why add to the grudge against him?

Not that he expected to last another five minutes.

"No! Wait!" Tom swiveled around to another set of controls. Why hadn't he thought of this at once?

The nearby pilot had needed a couple of seconds to recover from the shock of what happened to his companion. Now he was bound hastily back upward. He was too late. Tom focused a tractor beam on him. Its generator hummed with power. Ozone stung the nostrils; rewiring job needed, a distant aspect of Tom took note. Most of him was being a fisherman. He'd gotten his prey, and on a heavy line—the force locked onto the airboat was meant to grab kilotons moving at cosmic velocities—but his catch was a man-eater. And he wanted to land it just so.

The vessel battled futilely to escape. Tom pushed it down near *Firedrake's* hull, into the jumble of broken trees and canebrake that his own landing had made. Their branches probably damaged wings and fuselage, but their leaves, closing in above, hid any details of what was going on from the pilots overhead. Having jammed his capture against a fence of logs and brush, he held it there with a beam sufficiently narrow that the cockpit canopy wouldn't be pulled shut. Quickly, with a second tractor-pressor projection, he rearranged the tangle in the clearing, shifting trunks, snapping limbs and tossing them about, until he had a fairly good view through a narrow slot that wouldn't benefit observers in heaven. He trusted they were too poorly instrumented—or too agitated, or both—to see how useful the arrangement was for him, and would take the brief stirring they noticed as a natural result of a crash, heaped wood collapsing into a new configuration.

Thereafter he left the turret and made his way to the forward manlock. It was rather high off the ground; the access ladder had automatically extruded, plunging down into the foliage that fluttered shadowy around the base of the hull. Tom placed himself in the chamber, invisible from the sky, hardly noticeable from beneath, and studied his fish more closely.

Fish: yes, indeed. In two senses.

The pilot was that youthful squadron leader with whom he had spoken before. Tom tuned his helmet radio in on the frantic talk that went between the downed man, his companions and Karol Weyer in Sea Gate. He gathered they had no prehensile force-beams on Nike, and only vaguely inferred the existence of such things from their experience with "friends."

Friends? The raiders from space? Tom scowled.

But he couldn't stop to think beyond this moment. His notion had been to take a man and an aircraft—the latter probably the more highly valued—as hostages. They'd not nuke him now. But as for what followed, he must play his cards as he drew them. At worst, he'd gotten the girls free. Perhaps he could strike some kind of bargain, though it was hard to tell why any Nikean should feel bound to keep a promise made to an outworlder. At best…

Hoy!

The canopy slid back. Tom got a look at the plane's interior. There was room for two in the cockpit, if one scrooched, and aft of the seat was a rack of—something or other, he couldn't see what, but it didn't seem welded in place. His pulses leaped.

The pilot emerged, in a dive, flattening himself at once behind a fallen tree. Weyer had said, after several fruitless attempts to get a reply from Tom: "You in the ship! You killed one of ours. Another, and your whole ship goes. Do you seize me?" (That must mean "understand.") Next, to the flyboy: "Fish Aran, use own discretion."

So the young man, deciding he couldn't sit where he was forever, was trying to reach the woods. That took nerve. Tom laid his telescope to his good eye—his faceplate was open—and searched out details. Fiber helmet, as already noted; green tunic with cloth insignia, no metal; green trousers tucked into leather boots; a sidearm, but no indication of a portable communicator or, for that matter, a watch. Tom made sure his transmitter was off, trod a little further out in the lock chamber, and bawled from lungs that had often shouted against a gale at sea:

"Halt where you are! Or I'll chop the legs from under you!"

The pilot had been about to scuttle from his place. He froze. Slowly, he raised his gaze. Tom's armored shape was apparent to him, standing in the open lock, but not discernible by his mates. Likewise the blaster Tom aimed. The pilot's hand hovered at the butt of his own weapon.

"Slack off, son," the captain advised. "You wouldn't come near me with that pipgun—I said 'pip,' not even 'pop'—before I sizzled you. And I don't want to. C'mon and let's talk. That's right; on your feet; stroll over here and use this nice ladder."

The pilot obeyed, though his scramble across the log jam was hardly a stroll. As he started up, Tom said: "They'll see in a minute what you're doin', I s'pose, when you come above the foliage…Belay, there, *I* can see you quite well already…I want you to draw your gun, as if you'd decided to come aboard and reconnoiter 'stead o' headin' for the nearest beer hall. Better not try shootin' at me, though. My friends'd cut you down."

The Hannoan paused a moment, rigid with outrage, before he yielded. His face, approaching, showed pale and wet in the first light. He swung himself into the lock chamber. For an instant, he and Tom stood with guns almost in each other's bellies. The spaceman's gauntleted left hand struck like a viper, edge on, and the Nikean weapon clattered to the deck.

"You—you broke my wrist!" The pilot lurched back, clutching his arm and wheezing.

"I think not. I gauge these things pretty good, if I do say so myself. And I do. March on ahead o' me, please." Tom conducted his prisoner into the passageway, gathering the fallen pistol en route. It was a slugthrower, ingeniously constructed with a minimum of steel. Tom found the magazine release and pressed it one-handed. The clip held ten high-caliber bullets. But what the hoo-hah! The cartridge cases were wood, the slugs appeared to be some heavy ceramic, with a mere skirt of soft metal for the rifling in the barrel to get a grip on!

"No wonder you came along meek-like," Tom said. "You never could've dented me."

The prisoner looked behind him. Footfalls echoed emptily around his words. "I think you are alone," he said.

"Aye-ya. I told you my chums *could* whiff you…if they were present. In here." Tom indicated the fire control turret. "Sit yourself. Now, I'm goin' 'tother side o' this room and shuck my armor, which is too hot and heavy for informal wear. Don't get ideas about plungin' across the deck at me. I can snatch my blaster and take aim quicker'n that."

The young man crouched in a chair and shuddered. His eyes moved like a trapped animal's, around and around the crowding machines. "'What do you mean to do?" he rattled. "You can't get free. You're alone. Soon the Engineer's soldiers come, with 'tillery, and ring you."

"I know. We should be gone by then, however. Look here, uh, what's your name?"

An aristocrat's pride firmed the voice. "Yanos Aran, third son of Rober Aran, who's chief computerman to Engineer Weyer's self. I am a fish in the air force of Hanno—and you are a dirty friend!"

"Maybe so. Maybe not." Tom stripped fast, letting the pieces lie where they fell. He hated to abandon his suit, but it was too bulky and perhaps too detectable for his latest scheme.

"Why not? Didn't you business Evin Sato?"

"You mean that plane I gunned?"

"Yes. Evin Sato was my camarado."

"Well, I'm sorry about that, but wasn't he fixin' to shoot two o' my people? We came down frien—intendin' no harm, and you set on us like hungry eels. I don't want to hurt you, Yanos, lad. In fact; I hope betwixt us we can maybe settle this whole affair. But—" Tom's features assumed their grimmest look, which had terrified stronger men than Aran—"you try any fumblydiddles and you'll find out things about friendship that your mother never told you."

The boy seemed to crumple. "I…yes, I slave me, to you," he whispered.

He wouldn't stay crumpled long, Tom knew. He must be the scion of a typical knightly class. Let him recover from the dismay of the past half hour, the unbalancing effect of being surrounded by unknown powers, and he'd prove a dangerous pet. It was necessary to use him while he remained useable.

Wherefore Tom, having peeled down to coveralls, gave him his orders in a few words. A slight demurral fetched a brutal cuff to the cheek. "And if I shoot you with this blaster, short range, low intensity," Tom added, "you won't have a neat hole drilled through your heart. You'll be cooked alive, medium rare, so you'll be some days about dyin'. Seize me?"

He didn't know if he'd really carry out his threat, come worse to worst. Probably not.

Having switched off the tractor beam, he brought Aran far down into the ship, to an emergency lock near the base. It was well hidden by leaves. The vague dawnlight aided concealment. They crept forth, and thence to the captured aircraft.

It had taken a beating, Tom saw. The wingtips were crumpled, the fuselage punctured. (The covering was mostly some fluoro-synthetic. What a metal shortage they must have here!) But it ought to fly anyhow, after a fashion. Given a gravity drive, however weak, airfoils were mainly for auxiliary lift and control.

"In we go," Tom said. He squeezed his bulky form behind Aran's seat so that it concealed him. The blaster remained in his fist, ready to fire through the back.

But there was no trouble. Aran followed instructions. He called his squadron: "—Yes, you're right, I did 'cide I'd try looking at the ship. And no one! None aboard. 'Least, none I saw. Maybe robos fought us, or maybe the rest of the crew got away on foot, not seen. I found a switch, looked like a main powerline breaker, and opened it. Maybe now I can rise."

And he started the engine. The airboat climbed, wobbling on its damaged surfaces. A cheer sounded from the receiver. Tom wished he could see the face in the screen, but he dared not risk being scanned himself.

"You land, if Engineer Weyer approves," Aran directed. "Go aboard. Be careful. Me, best I take my craft back to base immediately."

Tom had figured that would be a natural move for a pilot on Nike, even a squadron leader. A plane was obviously precious. It couldn't get to the repair shop too fast.

He must now hope that Aran's expression and tone didn't give him away. The "fish" was no actor. But everyone was strung wire-taut. Nobody noticed how much more perturbed this fellow was. After a few further words had passed, Aran signed off and started west.

"Keep low," Tom said. "Like you can't get much altitude. Soon's you're out o' their sight here, swing north. Find us a good secret place to land. I think we got a bucketful to say to each other, no?"

One craft was bound eagerly down. The rest stayed at hover. They'd soon learn that the spaceship was, indeed, deserted. Hence they wouldn't suspect what had happened to Aran until he failed to report. However, that wasn't a long time. He, Roan Tom, had better get into a bolthole quick!

-9-

The volcano's northern side was altogether wild. On the lower flanks, erosion had created a rich lava soil and vegetation was dense. For some reason it was principally native Nikean, dominated by primitive but tree-sized "ferns." An antigrav flyer could push its way under their soft branches and come to rest beneath the overhang of a cliff, camouflaged against aerial search.

Tom climbed out of the cockpit and stretched to uncramp himself. The *abris* was rough stone at his back, the forest brooded shadowy before him. Flecks of copper sunlight on bluish-green fronds and the integuments of bumbling giant pseudo-insects made the scene look as if cast in metal. But water rilled nearby, and the smells of damp growth were organic enough.

"C'mon, son. Relax with me," Tom invited. "I won't eat you. 'Specially not if you've packed along a few sandwiches."

"Food? No." Yanos Aran spoke as stiffly as he moved.

"Well, then we'll have to make do with what iron rations I got in my pockets." Tom sighed. He flopped down on a chair-sized boulder, took out pipe and tobacco pouch, and consoled himself with smoke.

He needed consolation. He was a fugitive on an unknown planet. His ship had been taken. His wives were out of touch; an attempt to raise Dagny on the plane's transmitter, using the Krakener military band, had brought silence. She must already have discarded her telltale space armor.

"And all 'count of a stupid lingo mistake!" he groaned.

Aran sat down on another rock and regarded him with eyes in which alertness was replacing fear. "You say you are not truly our friend?"

"Not in your sense. Look, where I come from, the Anglic word 'friend' means…well, a fellow you like, and who likes you. When I told your Engineer. we were friends, I wanted him to understand we didn't aim at any harm, in fact we could do good business with him."

"Business!" Aran exploded.

"Whoops-la. Sorry. Said the wrong thing again, didn't I?"

"I think," Aran replied slowly, "what you have in mind is what we would call 'change.' You wanted to 'change goods and services with our people. And to you, a 'friend' is what we call a 'camarado.'"

"Reckon so. What're your definitions?"

"A friend is a space raider, such as did business with our planet some five years agone. They destroyed the last great cities we had left from the Terran Empire days, and none knows how many million Nikeans they killed."

"Ah, now we're gettin' somewhere. Let's straighten out for me what did happen."

Aran's hostility had not departed, but it had diminished. He was intelligent and willing to cooperate within the limits of loyalty to his own folk. Information rushed out of him.

Nike did not appear to be unique, except in its planetology. Tom asked about that. Aran was surprised. Was his world so unusual *per se*?

He knew only vague traditions and a few fragmentary written accounts of other planetary systems. Nike was discovered and colonized five hundred-odd years ago—about a thousand standard years. It was always a backwater. Fundamentally agricultural because of its shortage of heavy metals, it had no dense population, no major libraries or schools. Thus, when the Empire fell apart, knowledge vanished more quickly and thoroughly here than most places. Nikean society disintegrated; what had been an Imperial sub-province became hundreds of evanescent kingdoms, fiefs and tribes.

The people were on their way back, Aran added defiantly. Order and a measure of prosperity had been restored in the advanced countries. As yet, they paid mere lip service to an "Emperor," but the concept of global government did now exist. Technology was improving. Ancient apparatus was being repaired and put back into service, or being reproduced on the basis of what diagrams and manuals could be found. Schemes had been broached for making interplanetary ships. Some dreamers had hoped that in time the Nikeans might end their centuries-long isolation themselves, by re-inventing the lost theory and practice of hyperdrive.

For that, of course, as for much else, the tinkering of technicians was insufficient. Basic scientific research must be done. But this also was slowly being started. Had not Aran remarked that his father was head computerman in the Engineer's court? He used a highly sophisticated machine which had survived to the present day and which two generations of modern workers had finally learned how to operate.

Its work at present was mainly in astronomy. While some elementary nuc-leonics had been preserved through the dark ages—being essential to the maintenance of what few atomic power plants remained—practically all information about the stars had vanished. Today's astronomers had learned that their sun (as distinguished from their planet) was not typical of its neighborhood. It was unpredictably variable, and not even its ground state could be fitted onto the main sequence diagram. No one had yet developed a satisfactory theory as to what made this sun abnormal, but the consensus was that it must be quite a young star.

One geologist had proposed checking this idea by establishing the age of the planet. Radioactive minerals should provide a clock. The attempt had failed, partly because of the near-nonexistence of isotopes with suitable half-lives and partly, Tom suspected, because of lousy laboratory technique. But passing references in old books did seem to confirm the idea held by latter-day theorists, that stars and planets condensed out of interstellar gas and dust. If so, Nike's sun could be very new, as cosmic time went, and not yet fully stabilized.

"Aye, I'd guess that myself," Tom nodded.

"Good! Important to be sure. You seize, can we make a mathematical model of our sun, then we can predict its variations. Right? And we will never predict our weather until then. Unforeseen storms are our greatest natural woe. Hanno's self, a southerly land, can get killing frosts any season."

"Well, don't take my authority, son. I'm no scientist. The Imperialists must've known for sure what kind o' star they had here. And a scholar of astronomy, from a planet where they still keep universities and such, should could tell you. But not me." Tom struck new fire to his pipe. "Uh, we'd better stay with less fun topics. Like those 'friends.'"

Aran's enthusiasm gave way to starkness. He could relate little. The raiders had not come in any large fleet, a dozen ships at most. But there was no effective opposition to them. They smashed defenses from space, landed, plundered, raped, tortured, burned, during a nightmare of weeks. After sacking a major city, they missiled it. They were human, their language another dialect of Anglic. Whether in sarcasm or hypocrisy or because of linguistic change, they described themselves to the Nikeans as "your friends, come to do business with you." Since "friend" and "business" had long dropped out of the local speech, Tom saw the origin of their present meaning here.

"Do you know who they might have been?" Aran asked. His tone was thick with unshed tears.

"No. Not sure. Space's full o' their kind." Tom refrained from adding that he too wasn't above a bit of piracy on occasion. After all, he observed certain humane rules with respect to those whom he relieved of their portable goods. The really bestial types made his flesh crawl, and he'd exterminated several gangs of them with pleasure.

"Will they return, think you?"

"Well…prob'ly not. I'd reckon they destroyed your big population centers to make sure no one else'd be tempted to come here and start a base that might be used against 'em. They bein' too few to conquer a whole world, you see. 'Course, I wouldn't go startin' major industries and such again without husky space defenses."

"No chance. We hide instead," Aran said bitterly. "Most leaders dare allow naught that might draw other friends. Radio a bare minimum; no rebuilding of cities; yes, we crawl back to our dark age and cower."

"I take it you don't pers'nally agree with that policy."

Aran shrugged. "What matter my thoughts? I am but a third son. The chiefs of the planet have 'cided. They fought a war or two, forcing the rest to go with them in this. I myself bombed soldiers of Silva, when its Prester was made to stop building a big atomic power plant. Our neighbor cavedom! And we had to fight them, not the friends!"

Tom wasn't shocked. He'd seen human politics get more hashed than that. What pricked his ears up was the information that, right across the border, lived a baron who couldn't feel overly kindly toward Engineer Weyer.

"You can seize, now, why we feared you," Aran said.

"Aye-ya. A sad misunderstandin'. If you hadn't been so bloody impulsive, though—if you'd been willin' to talk—we'd've quick seen what the lingo problem was."

"No! You were the ones who refused talk. When the Engineer called on you to be slaves—"

"What the muck did he expect us to do after that?" Tom rumbled. "Wear his chains?"

"Chains? Why...wait—oh-oh!"

"Oh-oh, for sure," Tom said. "Another little shift o' meanin', huh? All right, what does 'slave' signify to you?"

It turned out that, on Nike, to be "enslaved" was nothing more than to be taken into custody: perhaps as a prisoner, perhaps merely for interrogation or protection. In Hanno, as in every advanced Nikean realm, slavery in Tom's sense of the word had been abolished a lifetime ago.

The two men stared at each other. "Events got away from both sides," Tom said. "After what'd happened when last spacemen came, you were too spooked to give us a chance. You reckoned you had to get us under guard right away. And we reacted to that. We've seen a lot o' cruelty and treachery. We couldn't trust ourselves to complete strangers, 'specially when they acted hostile. So...neither side gave the other time to think out the busi—the matter o' word shift. If there'd been a few minutes' pause in the action, I think I, at least, would've guessed the truth. I've seen lots o' similar cases. But I never had any such pause, till now."

He grinned and extended a broad hard hand. "All's well that ends well, I'm told," he said. "Let's be camarados."

Aran ignored the gesture. The face he turned to the outworlder was only physically youthful. "We cannot," he said. "You wrecked a plane and stole another. Worse, you killed a man of ours."

"But—well, self-defense!"

"I might pardon you," Aran said. "I do not think the Engineer would or could. It is more than the damage you worked. More than the anger of the powerful Sato family, who like it not if a son of theirs dies unavenged because of a comic mix in s'mantics. It is the policy that he, Weyer's self, strove to bring."

"You mean...nothin' good can come from outer space...wall Nike off...treat anyone that comes as hostile...right?" Tom rubbed his chin arid scowled sullenly.

Weyer was probably not too dogmatic, nor too tightly bound by the isolationist treaty, to change his mind in time. But Tom had scant time to spare. Every hour that passed, he and his womenfolk risked getting shot down by some hysteric. Also, a bunch of untrained Nikeans, pawing over his spaceship, could damage her beyond the capacity of this planet's industry to repair.

Also, he was needed back on Kraken *soon*, or his power there would crumble. And that would be a mortally dangerous situation for his other wives, children, grandchildren, old and good comrades...

In short, there was scant value in coming to terms with Weyer eventually. He needed to reach agreement fast. And, after what had happened this day, he didn't see how he could.

Well, the first thing he must do was reunite his party. Together, they might accomplish something. If nothing else, they could seek refuge in the adjacent country, Silva. Though that was doubtless no very secure place for them, particularly if Weyer threatened another war.

"You should slave yourself," Aran urged. "Afterward you can talk."

"As a prisoner—a slave—I'd have precious little bargainin' leverage," Tom said. "Considerin' what that last batch o' spacers did, I can well imagine we bein' tortured till I cough up for free everything I've got to tell. S'posin' Weyer himself didn't want to treat me so inhospitable, he could break down anyhow under pressure from his court or his fellow bosses."

"It may be," Aran conceded, reluctantly, but too idealistic at his age to violate the code of his class and lie.

"Whereas if I can stay loose, I can try a little pressure o' my own. I can maybe find somethin' to offer that's worth makin' a deal with me. That'd even appease the Sato clan, hm?" Tom fumed on his pipe. "I've got to contact my women. Right away. Can't risk their fallin' into Weyer's hands. If they do, he's got me! Know any way to raise a couple o' girls who don't have a radio and 're doin' their level best to disappear?"

-10-

Sunset rays turned the hilltops fiery. Further down, the land was already blue with a dusk through which river, bay, and distant sea glimmered argent. Cloud banks towered in the east, blood-colored, dwarfing the Sawtooth Mountains that marked Hanno's frontier.

At the lowest altitude where this was visible—the highest to which a damaged, overloaded flyer could limp—the air was savagely cold. It wasn't too thin for breathing; the atmospheric density gradient is less for small than for large planets. But it swept through the cracked canopy to sear Tom's nostrils and numb his fingers on the board. Above the drone of the combustion powerplant, he heard Yanos Aran's teeth clatter. Stuffed behind the pilot chair, the boy might have tried to mug his captor. But he wasn't dressed for this temperature and was chilled half insensible. Tom's clothes were somewhat warmer. Besides, he felt he could take on any two Nikeans hand-to-hand.

The controls of the plane were simple to a man who'd used as wide a variety of machines as he. Trickiness came from the broken and twisted airfoil surfaces. And, of course, he must keep a watch for Weyer's boys. He didn't think they'd be aloft, nor that they could scramble and get here in the few minutes he needed. But you never knew. If one did show up, maybe Tom could pot him with a lucky blast from the guns.

He swung through another carousel curve. That should be that. Now to skate away. He throttled the engine back. The negafield dropped correspondingly, and he went into a glide. But he was no longer emitting enough exhaust for a visible trail.

The tracks he had left were scribbled over half the sky. The sun painted them gold-orange against that deepening purple.

Abruptly, turbulence across the buckled delta wing gained mastery. The glide became a tailspin. Aran yelled.

"Hang on," Tom said. "I can ride 'er."

Crazily whirling, the dark land rushed at him. He stopped Aran's attempt to grab the stick with a karate chop and concentrated on his altimeter. At the last possible moment, allowing for the fact that he must coddle this wreck lest he tear her apart altogether, he pulled out of his tumble. A prop, jet or rocket would never have made it, but you could do special things with gravs if you had the knack in your fingers. Or whatever part of the anatomy it was.

Finally the plane whispered a few meters above the bay. Its riding lights were doused, and the air here was too warm for engine vapor to condense. Tom believed his passage had a fair chance of going unnoticed.

Hills shouldered black around the water. Here and there among them twinkled house lamps. One cluster bespoke a village on the shore. Tom's convoluted contrail was breaking up, but slowly. It glowed huge and mysterious, doubtless frightening peasants and worrying the military.

Aran stared at it likewise, as panic and misery left him. "I thought you wrote a message to your camarados," he said. "That's no writing."

"Couldn't use your alphabet, son, seein' I had to give 'em directions to a place with a local name. Could I, now? Even Kraken's letters look too much like yours. But those're Momotaroan phonograms. Dagny can read 'em. I hope none o' Weyer's folk'll even guess it is a note. Maybe they'll think I went out o' control tryin' to escape and, after staggerin' around a while, crashed…Now, which way is this rendezvous?"

"Rendez—oh. The togethering I advised. Follow the north shore eastward a few more kilos. At the end of a headland stands Orgino's Cave."

"You absolutely sure nobody'll be there?"

"As sure as may be; and you have me for hostage. Orgino was a war chief of three hundred years agone. They said he was so wicked he must be in pact with the Wanderer, and to this day the commons think he walks the ruins of his cave. But it's a landmark. Let your camarados ask shrewdly, and they can find how to get there with none suspecting that for their wish."

The plane sneaked onward. Twilight was short in this thin air. Stars twinkled splendidly forth, around the coalsack of the Nebula. The outer moon rose, gradually from the eastern cloudbanks, almost full but its disk tiny and corroded-bronze dark. An auroral glow flickered. This far south? Well, Nike had a fairly strong magnetic field—which, with the mean density, showed that it possessed the ferrous core it wasn't supposed to—but not so much that charged solar particles couldn't strike along its sharp curvature clear to the equator.

If they were highly energetic particles, anyhow. And they must be. Tom had identified enormous spots as well as flares on that ruddy sun disk. Which oughtn't to be there! Not even when output was rising. A young star, its outer layers cool and reddish because they were still contracting, shouldn't have such intensity. Should it?

Regardless, Nike's sun did.

Well, Tom didn't pretend to know every kind of star. His travels had really not been so extensive, covering a single corner of the old Imperium, which itself had been insignificant compared to the whole. And his attention had naturally always been focused on more or less Sol-type stars. He didn't know what a very young or very old, very large or very small sun was like in detail.

Most certainly he didn't know what the effects of abnormal chemical composition might be. And the distribution of elements in this system was unlike that of any other Tom had ever heard about. Conditions on Nike bore out what spectroanalysis had indicated in space: impoverishment with respect to heavy elements. Since it had formed recently, the sun and its planets must therefore have wandered here from some different region. Its velocity didn't suggest that. However, Tom hadn't determined the galactic orbit with any precision. Besides, it might have been radically changed by a close encounter with another orb. Improbable as the deuce, yes, but then the whole crazy situation was very weird.

The headland loomed before him, and battlements against the Milky Way. Tom made a vertical landing in a courtyard. "All right." His voice sounded jarringly loud. "Now we got nothin' much to do but wait."

"What if they come not?" Aran asked.

"I'll give 'em a day or two," Tom said. "After that, we'll see." He didn't care to dwell on the possibility. His unsentimental soul was rather astonished to discover how big a part of it Dagny had become. And Yasmin was a good kid. He wished her well.

He left the crumbling flagstones for a walk around the walls. Pseudo-moss grew damp and slippery on the parapet. Once mail-clad spearmen had tramped their rounds here, and the same starlight sheened on their helmets as tonight, or as in the still more ancient, vanished glory of the Empire, or the League before it, or—And what of the nights yet to come? Tom shied from the thought and loaded his pipe.

Several hours later, the nearer moon rose from the hidden sea; its apparent path was retrograde and slow. Although at half phase, with an angular diameter of a full degree it bridged the bay with mercury.

Rising at the half—local midnight, more or less—would the girls never show? He ought to get some sleep. His eyelids were sandy. Aran had long since gone to rest in the tumbledown keep. He must be secured, of course, before Tom dozed off...*No. I couldn't manage a snooze even if I tried. Where are you, Dagny?*

The cold wind lulled, the cold waves lapped, a winged creature fluttered and whistled. Tom sat down where a portcullis had been and stared into the woods beyond.

There came a noise. And another. Branches rustled. Hoofbeats clopped. Tom drew his blaster and slid into the shadow of a tower. Two riders on horseback emerged from the trees. For a moment they were unrecognizable, unreal. Then the moon's light struck Dagny's tawny mane. Tom shouted.

Dagny snatched her own gun forth. But when she saw who lumbered toward her, it fell into the rime-frosted grass.

-11-

Afterward, in what had been a feasting hall, with a flashlight from the aircraft to pick faces out of night, they conferred. "No, we had no trouble," Dagny said. "The farmer sold us those animals without any fuss."

"If you gave him a thirty-gram gold piece, on this planet, I reckon so," Tom said. "You could prob'ly've gotten his house thrown into the deal. He's bound to gossip about you, though."

"That can't be helped," Dagny said. "Our idea was to keep traveling east and hide in the woods when anyone happened by. But we'd no strong hope, especially with that wide cultivated valley to get across. Tom, dear, when I saw your sky writing, it was the second best moment of my life."

"What was the first?"

"You were involved there too," she said. "Rather often, in fact."

Yasmin stirred. She sat huddled on the floor, chilled, exhausted, wretched, though nonetheless drawing Aran's appreciative gaze. "Why do you grin at each other?" she wailed. "We're hunted!"

"Tell me more," Tom said.

"What can we *do*?"

"You can shut up, for the gods' sake, and keep out o' my way!" he snapped impatiently. She shrank from him and knuckled her eyes.

"Be gentle," Dagny said. "She's only a child."

"She'll be a dead child if we don't get out o' here," Tom retorted. "We got time before dawn to slip across the Silvan border in yon airboat. After that, we'll have to play 'er as she lies. But I been pumpin' my—shall I say, my friend, about politics and geography and such. I think with luck we got a chance o' stayin' free."

"What chance of getting our ship back, and repaired?" Dagny asked.

"Well, that don't look so good, but maybe somethin'll come down the slot for us. Meanwhile, let's move."

They went back to the courtyard. The inner moon was so bright that no supplement was needed for the job on hand. This was to unload the extra fuel tanks, which were racked aft of the cockpit. The plane would lose cruising range, would indeed be unable to go past the eastern slope of the Sawtooths. But it would gain room for two passengers.

"You stay behind, natural," Tom told Aran. "You been a nice lad, and here's where I prove I never aimed at any hurt for you. Have a horse on me, get a boat from the village to Weyer's place, tell him what happened—and to tell him we want to be his camarados and 'change with him."

"I can say it." Aran shifted awkwardly from foot to foot. "I think no large use comes from my word."

"The prejudice against spacemen—"

"And the damage you worked. How shall you repay that? Since 'tis been 'cited there's no good in spacefaring, I expect your ship'll be stripped for its metal."

"Try, though," Tom urged.

"Should you leave now?" Aran wondered. "Weather looks twisty."

"Aye, we'd better. But thanks for frettin' 'bout it."

A storm, Tom thought, was the least of his problems. True, conditions did look fanged about the mountains. But he could sit down and wait them out, once over the border, which ought to remain in the bare fringes of the tempest. Who ever heard of weather moving very far west, on the western seacoast of a planet with rotation like this? What was urgent was to get beyond Weyer's pursuit.

Yasmin and Dagny fitted themselves into the rear fuselage as best they could, which wasn't very. Tom took the pilot's seat again. He waved good-by to Yanos Aran and gunned the engine. Overburdened as well as battered, the plane lifted sluggishly and made no particular speed. But it flew, and could be out of Hanna before dawn. That sufficed.

Joy at reunion, vigilance against possible enemies, concentration on the difficult task of operating his cranky vessel, drove weariness out of him. He paid scant attention to the beauties of the landscape sliding below, though they were considerable—mist-magical delta, broad sweep of valley, river's sinuous glow, all white under the moons. He must be one with the wind that blew across this sleeping land.

And blew.

Harder.

The plane bucked. The noise around it shrilled more and more clamorous. Though the cloud wall above the mountains must be a hundred kilometers distant, it was suddenly boiling zenith-ward with unbelievable speed.

It rolled over the peaks and hid them. Its murk swallowed the outer moon and reached tendrils forth for the inner one. Lightning blazed in its caverns. Then the first raindrops were hurled against the plane. Hail followed, and the snarl of a hurricane.

East wind! Couldn't be! Tom had no further chance to think. He was too busy staying alive.

As if across parsecs, he heard Yasmin's scream, Dagny's profane orders that she curb herself. Rain and hail made the cockpit a drum, himself a cockroach trapped between the skins. The wind was the tuba of marching legions. Sheathing ripped loose from wings and tail. Now and then he could see through the night, when lightning burned. The thunder was like bombs, one after the next, a line of them seeking him out. What followed was doomsday blackness.

His instrument panel went dark. His altitude control stick waggled loose in his hand. The airflaps must be gone, the vessel whirled leaf-fashion on the wind. Tom groped until his fingers closed on the grav-drive knobs. By modulating fields and thrust beams, he could keep a measure of command. Just a measure; the powerplant had everything it could do to lift this weight, without guiding it. But let him get sucked down to earth, that was the end!

He must land somehow, and survive the probably hard impact. How?

The river flashed lurid beneath him, He tried to follow its course. Something real, in this raving night—There was no more inner moon, there were no more stars.

The plane groaned, staggered, and tilted on its side. The starboard wing was torn off. Had the port one gone too, Tom might have operated the fuselage as a kind of gravity sled. But against forces as unbalanced as now fought him, he couldn't last more than a few seconds. Minutes, if he was lucky.

Must be black above the river-mouths, thought the tiny part of him that stood aside and watched the struggle of the rest. *Got to set down easy-like. And find some kind o' shelter. Yasmin wouldn't last out this night in the open.*

Harshly: *Will she last anyway? Is she anything but a dangerous drag on us? I can't abandon her, I swore her an oath, but I almost wish—*

The sky exploded anew with lightnings and showed him a wide vista of channels among forested, swampy islands. Trees tossed and roared in the wind, but the streams were too narrow for great waves to build up and—Hoy!

Suddenly, disastrously smitten, a barge train headed from Sea Gate to the upriver towns had broken apart. In the single blazing moment of vision that he had, Tom saw the tug itself reel toward safety on the northern side of the main channel. Its tow was scattered, some members sinking, some flung aground, and one—yes, driven into a tributary creek, woods and waterplants closing behind it, screening it—

Tom made his decision.

He hoped for nothing more than a bellyflop in the drink, a scramble to escape from the plane and a swim to the barge. But lightning flamed again and again, enormous sheets of it that turned every raindrop and hailstone into brass. And once he was down near the surface of that natural canal, a wall of trees on either side, he got some relief. He was actually able to land on deck.

The barge had ended on a sandbar and lay solid and stable. Tom led his women from the plane. He and Dagny found some rope and lashed their remnant of a vehicle into place. The cargo appeared to be casks of petroleum. A hatch led below, to a cabin where a watchman might rest. Tom's flashlight picked out bunk, chair, a stump of candle.

"We're playin' a good hand," he said.

"For how long?" Dagny mumbled.

"Till the weather slacks off." Tom shrugged. "What comes after that, I'm too tired to care. I don't s'pose…gods, yes!" he whooped. "Here, on the shelf! A bottle—lemme sniff—aye-ya, booze! Got to be booze!" And he danced upon the deckboards till he cracked his pate on the low overhead.

Yasmin regarded him with a dull kind of wonder. "What are you so happy about?" she asked in Anglic. When he had explained, she slumped. "You can laugh…at that…tonight? Lord Tom, I did not know how alien you are to me."

Through hours the storm continued.

They sat crowded together, the three of them, in the uneasy candlelight, which threw huge misshapen shadows across the roughness of bulkheads. Rather, Dagny sat on the chair, Tom on the foot of the bunk, while Yasmin lay. The wind-noise was muffled down here, but the slap of water on hull came loud. From time to time, thunder cannonaded, or the barge rocked and grated on the sandbar.

A Tragedy of Errors

Wet, dirty, haggard, the party looked at each other. "We should try to sleep," Dagny said.

"Not while I got this bottle," Tom said. "You do what you like. Me, though, I think we'd better guzzle while we can. Prob'ly won't be long, you see."

"Probably not," Dagny agreed, and took another pull herself.

"What will we do?" Yasmin whispered.

Tom suppressed exasperation—she had done a good job in Petar Landa's house, if nowhere else—and said, "Come mornin', we head into the swamps. I s'pose Weyer'll send his merry men lookin' for us, and whoever owns this hulk'll search after it, so we can't claim squatter's rights. Maybe we can live off the country, though, and eventually, one way or another, reach the border."

"Would it not be sanest…They do seem to be decent folk…should we not surrender to them and hope for mercy?"

"Go ahead, if you want," Tom said. "You may or may not get the mercy. But you'll for sure have no freedom. I'll stay my own man."

Yasmin tried to meet his hard gaze, and failed. "What has happened to us?" she pleaded.

He suspected that she meant, "What has become of the affection between you and me?" No doubt he should comfort her. But he didn't have the strength left to play father image. Trying to distract her a little, he said, with calculated misunderstanding of her question:

"Why, we hit a storm that blew us the exact wrong way. It wasn't s'posed to. But this's such a funny planet. I reckon, given a violent kind o' sun, you can get weather that whoops out o' the east, straight seaward. And, o' course, winds can move almighty fast when the air's thin. Maybe young Aran was tryin' to warn me. He spoke o' twisty weather. Maybe he meant exactly this, and I got fooled once more by his Nikean lingo. Or maybe he just meant what I believed he did, unreliable weather. He told me himself, their meteorology isn't worth sour owl spit, 'count o' they can't predict the solar output. Young star, you know. Have a drink."

Yasmin shook her head. But abruptly she sat straight. "Have you something to write with?"

"Huh?" Tom gaped at her.

"I have an idea. It is worthless," she said humbly, "but since I cannot sleep, and do not wish to annoy my lord, I would like to pass the time."

"Oh. Sure." Tom found a pad and penstyl in a breast pocket of his coverall and gave them to her. She crossed her legs and began writing numbers in a neat, foreign-looking script.

"What's going on?" Dagny said in Eylan.

Tom explained. The older woman frowned. "I don't like this, dear," she said. "Yasmin's been breaking down, closer and closer to hysteria, ever since we left those peasants. She's not prepared for a guerrilla existence. She's used up her last resources."

"You reckon she's quantum-jumpin' already?"

"I don't know. But I do think we should force her to take a drink, to put her to sleep."

"Hm." Tom glanced at the dark head, bent over some arithmetical calculations. "Could be. But no. Let her do what she chooses. She hasn't bubbled her lips yet, has she? And—we are the free people."

He went on with Dagny in a rather hopeless discussion of possibilities open to them. Once they were interrupted, when Yasmin asked if he had a trigonometric slide rule. No, he didn't. "I suppose I can approximate the function with a series," she said, and returned to her labors.

Has she really gone gollywobble? Tom wondered. *Or is she just soothin' herself with a hobby?*

Half an hour later, Yasmin spoke again. "I have the solution."

"To what?" Tom asked, a little muzzily after numerous gulps from the bottle. They distilled potent stuff in Hanno. "Our problem?"

"Oh, no, my lord. I couldn't—I mean, I am nobody. But I did study science, you remember, and…and I assumed that if you and Lady Dagny said this was a young system, you must be right, you have traveled so widely. But it isn't."

"No? What're you aimed at?"

"It doesn't matter, really. I'm being an awful picky little nuisance. But this *can't* be a young system. It has to be old."

Tom put the bottle down with a thud that overrode the storm-yammer outside. Dagny opened her mouth to ask what was happening. He shushed her. Out of the shadows across his scarred face, the single eye blazed blue. "Go on," he said, most quietly.

Yasmin faltered. She hadn't expected any such reaction. But, encouraged by him, she said with a waxing confidence:

"From the known average distance of the sun, and the length of the planet's year, anyone can calculate the sun's mass. It turns out to be almost precisely one Sol. That is, it has the mass of a G_2 star. But it has twice the luminosity, and more than half again the radius, and the reddish color of a late G or early K type. You thought those paradoxes were due to a strange composition. I don't really see how that could be. I mean, any star is something like 98 per cent hydrogen and helium. Variations in other elements can affect its development some, but surely not this much. Well, we know from Nikean biology that this system must be at least a few billion years old. So the star's instability cannot be due to extreme youth. Any solar mass must settle down on the main sequence far quicker than that. Otherwise we would have many, many more variables in the universe than we do.

"And besides, we can explain all the paradoxes so simply if we assume this system is old. Incredibly old, maybe almost as old as the galaxy itself."

"Belay!" Tom exclaimed, though not loudly. "How could this planet have this much atmosphere after so long a time? Or any? Don't sunlight kick gases into space? And Nike hasn't got the gravity to nail molecules down for good. Half a standard gee; and the potential is even poorer, the field strength droppin' off as fast as it does."

"But my lord," Yasmin said, "an atmosphere comes from within a planet. At least, it does for the smaller planets, that can't keep their original hydrogen like the Jupiter types. On the smaller worlds, gas gets forced out of mineral compounds. Vulcanism and tectonism provide the heat for that, as well as radioactivity. But the major planetological forces originate in the core. And a core originates because the heavier elements, like iron, tend to migrate toward the center. We know Nike has some endowment of those. Perhaps more, even, than the average planet of its age.

"Earth-sized planets have strong gravity. The migration is quick. The core forms in their youth. But Mars-sized worlds...the process has to be slow, don't you think? So much iron combines first in surface rocks that they are red. Nike shows traces of this still today. The midget planets can't outgas more than a wisp until their old age, when a core finally has taken shape."

Tom shook his head in a stunned fashion. "I didn't know. I took for granted—I mean, well, every Mars-type globe I ever saw or heard of had very little air—I reckoned they'd lost most o' their gas long ago."

"There are no extremely ancient systems in the range that your travels have covered," Yasmin deduced. "Perhaps not in the whole Imperial territory. They aren't common in the spiral arms of the galaxy, after all. So people never had much occasion to think about what they must be like."

"Uh, what you been sayin', this theory...you learned it in school?"

"No. I didn't major in astronomy, just took some required basic courses. It simply appeared to me that some such idea is the only way to explain this system we're in." Yasmin spread her hands. "Maybe the professors at my university haven't heard of the idea either. The truth must have been known in Imperial times, but it could have been lost since, not having immediate practical value." Her smile was sad. "Who cares about pure science any more? What can you buy with it?

"Even the original colonists on Nike—Well, to them the fact must have been interesting, but not terribly important. They knew the planet was so old that it had lately gained an atmosphere and oxygen-liberating life. So old that its sun is on the verge of becoming a red giant. Already the hydrogen is exhausted at the core, the nuclear reactions are moving outward in a shell, the photosphere is expanding and cooling while the total energy output rises. But the sun won't be so huge that Nike is scorched for—oh, several million years. I suppose the colonists appreciated the irony here. But on the human time-scale, what difference did it make? No wonder their descendants have forgotten and think, like you, this has to be a young system."

Tom caught her hands between his own. "And...that's the reason...the real reason the sun's so rambunctious?" he asked hoarsely.

"Why, yes. Red giants are usually variable. This star is in a transition stage, I guess, and hasn't 'found' its period yet." Yasmin's smile turned warm. "If I have taken your mind off your troubles, I am glad. But why do you care about the aspect of this planet ten megayears from now? I think best I do try to sleep, that I may help you a little tomorrow."

Tom gulped. "Kid," he said, "you don't know your own strength."

"What's she been talking about?" Dagny demanded.

Tom told her. They spent the rest of that night laying plans.

-12-

Now and then a mid-morning sunbeam struck coppery, through the fog. But otherwise a wet, dripping, smoking mystery enclosed the barge. Despite its chill, Tom was glad. He didn't care to be interrupted by a strafing attack.

To be sure, the air force might triangulate on the radio emission of his ruined plane and drop a bomb. However—

He sat in the cockpit, looked squarely into the screen, and said, "This is a parley. Agreed?"

"For the moment." Karol Weyer gave him a smoldering return stare. "I talked with Fish Aran."

"And he made it clear to you, didn't he, about the lingo scramble? How often your Anglic and mine use the same word different? Well, let's not keep on with the farce. If anybody thinks 'tother's said somethin' bad, let's call a halt and thresh out what was intended. Aye?"

Weyer tugged his beard. His countenance lost none of its sternness. "You have yet to prove your good faith," he said. "After what harm you worked—"

"I'm ready to make that up to you. To your whole planet."

Weyer cocked a brow and waited.

"S'pose you give us what we need to fix our ship," Tom said. "Some of it might be kind of expensive—copper and silver and such, and handicrafted because you haven't got the dies and jigs—but we can make some gold payment. Then let us go. I, or a trusty captain o' mine, will be back in a few months…uh, a few thirty-day periods."

"With a host of friends to do business?"

"No. With camarados to 'change. Nike lived on trade under the Terran Empire. It can once more."

"How do I know you speak truth?"

"Well, you'll have to take somethin' on my word. But listen. Kind of a bad storm last night, no? Did a lot o' damage, I'll bet. How much less would've been done if you'd been able to predict it? I can make that possible." Tom paused before adding cynically, "You can share the information with all Nike, or keep it your national secret. Could be useful, if you feel like maybe the planet should have a really strong Emperor, name of Weyer for instance."

The Engineer leaned forward till his image seemed about to jump from the screen. "How is this?"

Tom related what Yasmin had told him. "No wonder your solar meteorologists never get anywhere," he finished. "They're usin' exactly the wrong mathematical model."

Weyer's eyes dwelt long upon Tom. "Are you giving this information away in hopes of my good will?" he said.

"No. As a free sample, to shake you loose from your notion that every chap who drops in from space is necessarily a hound o' hell. And likewise this. Camarado Weyer, your astronomers'll tell you my wife's idea makes sense. They'll be right glad to hear they've got an old star. But they'll need many years to work out the details by themselves. You know enough science to realize that, I'm sure. Now I can put you in touch with people that *already* know the details—that can come here, study the situation for a few weeks, and predict your weather like dice odds.

"That's my hole card. And you can only benefit by helpin' us leave. Don't think you can catch us and beat what we know out of us. First, we haven't got the information. Second, we'll die before we become slaves, in any meanin' o' the word. If it don't look like we can get killed fightin' the men you send to catch us, why, we'll turn our weapons on ourselves. Then all you've got is a spaceship that to you is nothin' but scrap metal."

Weyer drew a sharp breath. But he remained cautious. "This may be," he said. "Nonetheless, if I let you go, why should you bring learned people back to me?"

"Because it'll pay. I'm a trader and a warlord. The richer my markets, the stronger my allies, the better off I am." Tom punched a forefinger at the screen. "Get rid o' that conditioned reflex o' yours and think a bit instead. You haven't got much left that's worth anybody's lootin'. Why should I bother returnin' for that purpose? But your potential, that's somethin' else entirely. Given as simple a thing as reliable weather forecasts—you'll save, in a generation, more wealth than the 'friends' ever destroyed. And this's only one for instance o' what the outside universe can do for you. Man, you can't afford not to trust me!"

They argued, back and forth, for a long time. Weyer was intrigued but wary. Granted, Yasmin's revelation did provide evidence that Tom's folk were not utter savages like the last visitors from space. But the evidence wasn't conclusive. And even if it was, what guarantee existed that the strangers would bring the promised experts?

The wrangle ended as well as Tom had hoped, in an uneasy compromise. He and his wives would be brought to Sea Gate. They'd keep their sidearms. Though guarded, they were to be treated more or less as guests. Discussions would continue. If Weyer judged, upon better acquaintance, that they were indeed trustworthy, he would arrange for the Ship's repair and release.

"But don't be long about makin' up your mind," Tom warned, "or it won't do us a lot o' good to come home."

"Perhaps," Weyer said, "you can depart early if you leave a hostage."

"You'll be all right?" Tom asked for the hundredth time.

"Indeed, my lord," Yasmin said. She was more cheerful than he, bidding him good-by in the Engineer's castle. "I'm used to their ways by now, comfortable in this environment—honestly! And you know how much in demand an outworlder is."

"That could get dull. I won't be back too bloody soon, remember. What'll you do for fun?"

"Oh," she said demurely, "I plan to make arrangements with quite a number of men."

"Stop teasin' me." He hugged her close. "I'm goin' to miss you."

And so Roan Tom and Dagny, Od's daughter left Nike.

He fretted somewhat about Yasmin, while *Firedrake* made the long flight back to Kraken, and while he mended his fences there, and while he voyaged back with his scholars and merchants. Had she really been joking, at the very last? She'd for sure gotten almighty friendly with Yanos Aran, and quite a few other young bucks. Tom was not obsessively jealous, but he could not afford to become a laughing stock.

He needn't have worried. When he made his triumphant landing at Sea Gate, he found that Yasmin had been charming, plausible, devious and, in short, had convinced several feudal lords of Nike that it was to their advantage that the rightful Shah be restored to the throne of Sassania. They commanded enough men to do the job. If the Krakeners could furnish weapons, training, and transporation—

Half delighted, half stunned, Tom said, "So this time we had a lingo scramble without somethin' horrible happenin'? I don't believe it!"

"Happy endings do occur," she murmured, and came to him. "As now."

And everyone was satisfied except, maybe, some few who went to lay a wreath upon a certain grave.

In the case of the King and Sir Christopher, however, a compliment was intended. A later era would have used the words "awe-inspiring, stately and ingeniously conceived."

"What'll You Give?"

K–B2.
      Q–K7. "Check," said Roy Pearson.
      Captain Elias ben Judah did not swear, because it was against his principles. But his comment was violent enough. "Second blinking check in a row," he added, moving the black king to refuge at Kt3.

"*And* the third," said his operations manager with a parched chuckle. The white queen jumped in his artificial hand to Q8.

"Do you mean that?" asked ben Judah, astonished. He was a medium-sized man, fifty Earth-years old, his hair gray, his eyes brown and gentle in a face that sagged a little with weariness. The blue uniform of the Jupiter Company sat neatly on him; insignia of rank and service, ribbons of past achievement, glowed beneath the fluorescent overhead of his cabin. It was more homelike than most, that cabin. Besides the usual pictures of wife and children, he had a shelf of books, not microspools but old-style volumes, for the pleasure of binding and typography. In a corner stood a little workbench where he had half completed a clipper ship model. Above was a flower box bright with poppies and violets.

Pearson's ruined features twisted into a grimace. "I do," he snapped. "Want to resign?" He was small and hunched, five years younger than the captain, but looked ten years older—not entirely because a goodly fraction of him was prosthetic.

"Certainly not." R X Q.

"I expected that, you know," said Pearson. His bishop scuttled across the board and captured the black queen. "Check…and mate."

Ben Judah studied the board for a moment before he sighed. "Right. Good game."

"You could have had me a while back," Pearson said, "when—"

"Never mind." Ben Judah got up and moved across the deck, heavily under the ship's internal gyrogravitic field, to his dresser. He began to load an old pipe. "I'm afraid I can't concentrate on chess. I keep thinking about the pilots."

Pearson observed him narrowly. "Don't," he said.

"I must. I'm the captain."

"Not in their case. I am."

"*Nu?*" Ben Judah swung about, indignant. This was his first Jupiter-diving cruise, and he admitted there was much he didn't yet know. But—

"You are the captain of the mother ship," Pearson said. "However, we're in orbit now. Only the scoopships are under weigh. And I direct their operations. Under the laws of the Republic, they're my responsibility. You'll find working for the Jupiter Company is a lot different from an inner-plant merchant run."

Ben Judah relaxed. "You needn't tell me," he said with a rather wan laugh. "Everything in the Belt is different. I don't envy you, trying to keep those wildcats of yours under control." He sobered. "But what disturbs me—now that I'm here with the actuality, not a textbook abstraction; now that I *feel* what is involved—what makes me wonder if I should have come at all, is the business of sending men out time after time, ordering them to possible death, while we sit safely here."

"They aren't ordered," Pearson reminded him. "Any pilot may refuse any flit. Of course, if he does it repeatedly, he'll be fired. We can't afford to ship deadheads."

"I know, I know. And yet, well, you asterites are obsessed with economics." The captain lifted a hand to forestall the manager's retort. "I am quite aware of how closely you must figure costs. But there's a...a callousness in your attitude. You often seem to think a machine is worth more than a human life."

"It is, if several other human lives depend on it." Pearson gave him a quizzical look. Himself an introvert, he had not yet gotten to know the new skipper very well. "Why did you come to the Belt, anyhow?"

Ben Judah shrugged. "I was approaching compulsory retirement age. Earth's too crowded for my liking. Besides, spacing is my trade, the thing I want most to do. JupeCo offered me good pay for as long as I'm able to stay in harness. Also a downright luxurious homeship for my family. I've no personal complaints. But sometimes I can't help wondering, meaning no offense, if I want my children to grow up as asterites."

He flipped a switch on his viewscreen. The panel darkened into a simulacrum of the outside, uncountably many frost-cold stars, the curdled ice of the galaxy, and Jupiter. The planet hung monstrous in its nearness, amber with multitudinous colored bands, blotted by storms that could have gulped all Earth, the Red Spot a glowing ember. One moon was coming into sight around that terrible horizon. Its face was tinted saffron by reflection.

"Live men, diving into yonder kettle of hell," ben Judah said low. The susurrus of the ventilators made an undercurrent to his words, as if the ship tried to tell him something. "And it isn't necessary. You could automate the operation."

"Doubling the capital investment in every scoopship," Pearson said. "Also increasing the rate of loss by an estimated twenty-five per cent. Too many unforeseeable things can go wrong down there. An autopilot can only act within the limits of its programming. A man can do more. Sometimes, when he runs into trouble, he can bring his ship back."

"Sometimes." Ben Judah's hands returned blindly to his pipe. He finished stuffing it, touched an igniter to the tobacco, and blew nervous puffs.

"We get more applications than we can find qualified men to accept," Pearson said. "Pay, prestige. And most of the boys actually enjoy the work."

"Maybe that's why I'm scared," ben Judah said. A corner of his mind observed that his English, hitherto Oxford with an Israeli accent, was slipping into the Belt dialect. The citizens of the young Asteroid Republic had every national origin, but North Americans predominated and put their stamp on language and folkways. "When my sons are grown, they might put in for those berths...and get them."

Master Pilot Thomas Hashimoto eased his craft away from the mother ship with a deftness born less of experience in this job than of several years of Earthside test piloting. His motions at the control board were nearly unconscious. Most of his attention was on the view before him.

His heart knocked. *I'm not afraid,* he assured himself. *I can't be. At least I'd better not be. This isn't any more dangerous than what I did back home.*

The thing is, though, I was doing those things there.

"Clear track," said the dispatcher's radio voice. Static buzzed around the words. No tricks of modulation could entirely screen out the interference of Jovian electrical storms. "Good gathering, Tom."

"Thanks," said Hashimoto, mechanical response to a ritual farewell. "Roger and out." His eyes focused on instrument needles, his fingers jumped over switches. The computer clicked and muttered. Otherwise the cockpit was silent, making the beat of blood loud in his ears. He grew conscious of the spacesuit enclosing him, a thick rubbery grip. Its helmet was left off, like its gloves, until such time as an emergency arose. So his nostrils drank smells of machine oil and that ozone tinge which recycled air always has in close quarters. For the minute or two that he traveled in free fall he felt weightlessness; scoopships didn't waste mass on internal field generators. But there was no dreamlike ease to the sensation, such as he had known in other days. The seat harness held him too tightly.

The computer gave him his vectors and he applied power. The nuclear reactor aft was noiseless, but the Emetts of the gyrogravitic generators whirred loudly enough to be heard through the radiation bulkhead which sealed off the engine compartment. Field drive clutched at that fabric of relationships which men call space. Acceleration shoved Hashimoto back into his seat. *Mary Girl* leaped Jupiterward.

He had a while, then, to sit and think. This interval of approach under autopilot was the worst time. Later the battle with the atmosphere would occupy all of him, and still later there would be the camaraderie of shipboard. But now he could only watch Jupiter grow until it filled the sky. Until it became the sky.

The trouble is, he realized, *I'm so near the end of my hitch. I didn't count the days and the separate missions at first, when I began this job. But now that there's only a few more months to go—*

Three years!

He hadn't needed to stay in the Belt that long, as far as his wife was concerned. She wanted desperately to have children, yes, and her frail body would miscarry again and again unless she spent each pregnancy under next-to-zero weight, and obstetrical facilities for that kind of condition existed nowhere but in the Asteroid Republic. (No country on Earth would spend money to establish a gee-gee-equipped maternity hospital, or an orbital one; anything that increased population, however minutely, was too unpopular these days.) Hashimoto had been more than glad to land a contract with JupeCo that enabled them to move out here. But two healthy children were plenty. Now they wanted to return home.

However, JupeCo insisted on a minimum of three years' service, and the bonus he would lose by quitting before the term was over amounted to half his total pay. He couldn't afford it. No contract that harsh would have been allowable in North America. But once they concluded their war of independence, the asterites had gone their own way.

It was not Hashimoto's. He remembered too well how sunset touched the mists in San Francisco Bay and made it a bowl of gold, how gardens lay vivid and trees stood rustling about his house in the Marin County hills, how men moved and spoke and exchanged friendship according to rules worn gentle with long usage. The asterites were as raw and stark as their own flying mountains.

He did not fear Jupiter because it could kill him. Any untried spaceflitter might do that at home. But it would be horrible to die without having slept once more in the house that had been his grandfather's, and having walked Earth's living soil and felt Earth's wind on his face.

Or without seeing his and Mary's children grow into the heritage that was theirs.

Throttle down, Hashimoto told his mind. *You've got work to do.*

The scoopship thrummed around him. Through the low, thick inertrans canopy he looked forward along the flaring nose. By twisting his neck he could have looked aft to the tapered stern. The metal shimmered blue in the light that poured from Jupiter. He could not see that open mouth which was the bow, gaping upon emptiness, but he could well visualize it. He had watched the service crew often enough, to make sure that their periodic inspections of every accessible part were thorough. *Mary Girl* was getting along in years, as divers went—which wasn't very far. (She had been *Star Pup* when passed on to him, but every pilot had the right to name his own craft.) Hashimoto didn't trust his life to someone else's estimate of her soundness. Most of his fellows did; but then, most scoopship pilots played a hell-for-leather role that he secretly considered rather childish.

They were good Joes, though, he thought. He must admit he would miss that gang. Often on Earth he would remember escapades and shared laughter.

And by the Lord Harry, it was something to steal from Jupiter himself and come back to brag about it!

The ship drove onward.

Eventually the planet filled his entire vision. But then it was no more a planet, hanging in heaven; it had become the world. It was not ahead but below. Cloudfields stretched limitless underneath him, layered, seething, golden-hued but streaked with the reds and browns, greens and blues of free radicals. To port he saw a continent-sized blot of darkness that was a storm, and shifted course.

Deceleration tugged angrily at him, and the planet's own pull, nearly three times Earth's. His muscles fought back. The first thin keening of cloven air penetrated to him. The ship quivered.

He switched off the autopilot and plunged downward on manual. The noise grew until it was thunder, booming and banging, rattling his teeth in the jaws and his brain in the skull. Winds did not buffet this craft traveling at many supersonic speeds, but gigantic air pockets did, back and forth, up and down, till metal groaned. Darkness overwhelmed him as he passed through a cloud bank. He emerged below it, looked up and saw the masses towering kilometer upon kilometer overhead, mountainous, lightning leaping across blue-black cavern mouths and down the faces of roiling slaty cliffs, against a distant sky that was hell-red. Briefly an ammonia storm pelted him, the hull drummed with the blows of gigantic poisonous hailstones. Then he was past, still screaming downward.

Presently he was too deep for sunlight to touch his eyes. He flew through a darkness that howled. He ceased to be Tom Hashimoto, husband, father, North American citizen, registered Conservative, tennis player, beer drinker, cigarette smoker, detective-story fan, any human identity. He and the ship were one, robbing a world that hit back.

The instruments, lanterns in utter murk, told him he was at sufficient depth. He leveled off and snapped the intake gate switch. The atmosphere ceased to whistle through the open tube of the hull—for now the tube was closed at the rear. A shock of impact strained him against his harness. The ship bucked and snarled. He reduced the drive to let the atmosphere brake him.

That air was mostly hydrogen and helium, but rich in methane, ammonia, carbon dioxide, water vapor; less full of ethylene, benzene, formaldehyde, and a dozen other organics, but nonetheless offering them in abundance. This far down, none of them were frozen out. The greenhouse effect operated. Jupiter's surface was warm enough to have oceans like Earth's. No man had seen them. The weight of atmosphere would have crumpled any hull like tinfoil. Even at this altitude, *Mary Girl* sped through an air pressure several times that of sea-level Earth.

Rammed into her open bow by sheer speed, the gases poured through a narrower throat. The wind of their passage operated an ionizer and a magnetic separator. Most of the hydrogen and helium were channeled off into a release duct and thrown away aft. Some of the other gases were too, of, course, but there was more where they came from. An enriched mixture flowed—hurtled—through rugged check valves into the after tanks.

The process did not take long. This was actually not the time of maximum hazard—though ships had been known to break up when the stress proved too much for some flaw in their metal. The dive downward from orbit had killed most men, and the climb back was not always completed. Gales, lightning, hailstorms, supersonics, chemical corrosives, and less well understood traps could be sprung. If the pilot was simply knocked unconscious, or lost control for a couple of minutes, Jupiter ate him.

A needle crossed the Full mark. The intake gate opened again and the tank valves shut. Hashimoto swung the ship's nose toward the hidden sky and poured power into the field drive.

He was once more out in sunlight, a storm-yellow dusk that showed him nothing but a cloud wrack tattered by wind, when his engine began to fail.

Master Pilot Charles de Gaulle d'Andilly approached the mother ship with a song. What a dive that last one had been! He was still ashiver from it, tumbling end over end in a doomsday blackness until he found an updraft that he rode toward safety. Within the spacesuit, his Long John sopped sweat. He wanted a drink in the worst way. There were only two kinds of occasion when every cell of a man's body was absolutely alive, and Jupiter expeditions didn't take women along.

He'd compensate himself for that when he got back to Ceres. Few girls could resist a scoopman's uniform and reputation. Especially when Charles de Gaulle d'Andilly wore them.

> ...*Dans le jardin d' mon père*
> *Les lilas sont fleuris.*
> *Tous les oiseaux du monde*
> *Y viennent fair' leur nid.*
> *Aupres de ma blonde*
> *Qu'il fait bon, fait bon, fait bon...*

The radio receiver buzzed. He flipped the switch. "*Vesta Castle* calling ship detected at—" The dispatcher's voice gave co-ordinates which indicated him. "Come in, please."

"*Mignonne* responding to *Vesta Castle*," said d'Andilly. "Everything O.K."

"Hi, Chuck. How was the trip?"

"Rough. Later I shall elaborate my experiences for you at some length. But being me, I had no unconquerable problems. So give me a guide beam to discharge, please."

"Roger." Cartesian axes flickered to life within the globe of a signal 'scope. D'Andilly aligned the dot that represented his own craft and rode on in. Approach must be under his personal control, with Jupiter's radio interference potentially so great. Nevertheless, he needed to devote little of his mind to it. After a dive, the matching of vectors in space was nothing but relaxation.

> *Aupres de ma blonde*
> *Qu'il fait bon dormir!*

His thoughts drifted back to that certain blonde who was responsible for his having left the United European Space Corps a few years ago. He didn't blame her. He should have known better than to play games with the daughter of his commanding officer. But she was so very tempting. He might try to find her again, when at last he must retire; Jupiter-diving was not for men past thirty-five or so. No, she was doubtless married by now. Well, there would be many others. And it would be good to stroll along the Seine, nurse an aperitif in a cafe on the Champs-Elysées, dine on civilized food before proceeding to the opera. He had no intention of staying in the Belt forever. With his accumulated pay he could buy into a good small business on Earth and live like a gentleman.

Not that he regretted his time out here. It had been glorious fun, mostly.

The *Vesta Castle* grew before his eyes, a great metal egg with softly glowing ports, the smooth curve broken by turrets, air locks, and boat blisters. Her orbit had carried her near the Jovian terminator line, so that the shrunken sun glared hard by the vast hazy crescent of the planet, but there was still ample light. Shadows lay sharp across the hull. Large though it was, it was dwarfed by the balloon harnessed to the stern. And the latter would double its present radius before it was considered full.

D'Andilly edged close to the gas bag. He could see stars through it. The plastifilm had to be thin, to save mass. He didn't worry about ripping it in case of collision. That elastomer was quite incredibly tough, could even bounce back small meteorites. But one could all too easily start the whole awkward ship-and-balloon system twisting around three simultaneous axes, and have the devil's own job getting rid of that angular momentum.

On such a whisper of drive that he felt no weight worth mentioning, he matched velocities. A radar at the balloon's main valve locked onto him. He followed the beam to within meters of target. A hose snaked out from *Mignonne's* stern, its nozzle driven by a miniature geegee and homing on the valve. They coupled. Between them, the pilots of the two ships killed what slight rotation was induced.

Pumps throbbed, forcing the scoopship's cargo of Jovian gas into the balloon. The sphere did not expand much; a single load was a small fraction of its total capacity. D'Andilly continued working to balance forces and hold the entire system steady in orbit.

At the end, he directed the hose to uncouple and retract. Then he slipped smoothly toward his assigned blister on the mother ship. This far spaceward there was seldom need to operate hydromagnetic screens against solar particle radiation, so approach and contact were simple. While he got out of his harness and suit, the final adjustments of angular momentum were made. The balloon waited quietly for the next arrival.

Who would not be d'Andilly. He had twenty hours off till he dove again.

Whistling, he climbed through joined air locks into the *Vesta Castle*. Two maintenance men waited in the companionway to clean his gear. Afterward the ship would be inspected. That was no concern of d'Andilly's. He gave the tech monkeys a greeting less condescending than compassionate—imagine so dreary a job!—and sauntered to pilot's country: a short, stocky man, brown hair carefully waved and mustache carefully trimmed, blue eyes snapping in a hook-nosed square face.

Ulrich von Raaben, tall, blond, and angular, was emerging from the showers as d'Andilly entered. "Whoof!" he exclaimed. "You smell like an uncleaned brewer's vat." He saw the condition of the undersuit that the Frenchman began to strip off, and paused. "Bad down there?"

"I hit an unobserved storm," d'Andilly said, as casually as he could manage.

Von Raaben stiffened. "We shall have a word with the weather staff about that."

"Oh, I will report the matter, of course. But they cannot be blamed. It must have risen from the depths faster than normal. Our meteorologists can only observe so far down."

"A cyclonic disturbance does not rise for no reason. Surrounding conditions ought to give a clue, at least to the probability of such a thing happening. If they tell us a given region looks calm, and it proves not to be, by heaven they will have some explanations to make!"

D'Andilly cocked his head at the other. "You are too Prussian to believe. Where were you born…Milwaukee?" Von Raaben reddened. D'Andilly slapped his back and laughed. "No matter, *mon vieux*. For a filthy Boche you are quite a good fellow."

He ducked under the shower and wallowed in an extravagance of hot water. That was one of numerous special privileges enjoyed by the scoopship pilots. Others included private cabins, an exclusive recreation room, seats at the officers' mess with wine if desired, high pay, and a dashing uniform that one was free to modify according to taste. In exchange they made a certain number of dives per Earth-year, into Jupiter.

One must be young and heedless to strike such a bargain. Sensible men, even among the asterites, preferred a better chance of reaching old age. No wonder that scoopship pilots off duty tended to act like ill-disciplined sophomores. *Including me, no doubt.*

There are exceptions, to be sure. Like poor Tom Hashimoto. I should take him out with me when we reach Ceres and show him the proper way to valve off accumulated pressure. But no, he is much too married.

In his own quarters d'Andilly put on lounging pajamas. From there he proceeded to the rec room. He found von Raaben, battered and eagle-decorated military cap shoved back on his head, playing rummy with Bill Wisner. The latter, who affected loud clothes and foul stogies, was one of the few native-born asterites aboard. Immigration was still ahead of birth in expanding the population of the Republic.

"Hi," Wisner said. "I hear you hit some weather."

"Yes. I'd best report it before someone else dives into that region." D'Andilly observed the glasses on the table and headed for the liquor cabinet himself. "Are we the only ones here?"

"The only divers, yes," von Raaben said in his meticulous way. "None others are due for several hours, I believe." The scoopships operated on a staggered but loose schedule, and no one liked to discharge by starlight alone.

Those who had completed a flit would assume parking orbits and rendezvous when the *Vesta Castle* was back in the sunshine.

"Well, the more for us, then." D'Andilly poured a stiff drink, tossed it off, and sipped appreciatively at a second. "Ah! Praise be that the cognac is holding out. When we are reduced to asterite booze, then it is time to head for Ceres, and never mind whether the balloon is full or not."

"Oh, Comet Blood isn't that bad," said Wisner defensively,

"It is for any man whose palate was not burned out by it in infancy. Your synthetic liquor is one excellent reason I shall not remain in the Belt after they shelve me as a diver."

"You ought to, though, Chuck," Wisner said with characteristic patriotism. "The life's rough and risky, sure. But with any luck at all, you stand to make a fortune. And no bureaucrat's going to tax most of it away and tell you how you can spend the rest, either."

"True. I admire the pioneer spirit, in an abstract fashion. But do you see, I am not interested enough, myself, in wealth or fame or power. There are so many other things to do."

"If one lives that long. Well—" von Raaben raised his own glass. *"Prosit."*

"May we love all the women we please," Wisner toasted, "and please all the women we love."

D'Andilly was about to propose something equally traditional when the emergency summons cut loose.

The wardroom was also used for briefings and conferences. Captain ben Judah stood looking down the green length of the table. Roy Pearson sat on his right, the chief engineer on his left, other officers not on watch beyond them. But the three scoopship pilots, clustered at the foot, were those whose eyes he must meet.

He felt sick. The words dragged from his throat:

"Gentlemen, we have received a call. Hashimoto is down."

There could be no adding to the silence that followed. But Wisner lost color and von Raaben slowly took off his cap.

"Not exactly down, yet," ben Judah went on. "His engine quit on him. But not too suddenly. When it first began misbehaving, he got as high as he could and threw himself into orbit. That's how we were able to receive his 'cast. He was above the sources of atmospheric interference, though it was still bad enough."

D'Andilly half rose. *"Pardieu!* Why do we sit here? I can go fetch him myself."

"If he were in clear space, yes," ben Judah said. "But he didn't get that far. There's still a trace of gas where he is. Frictional resistance—He's spiraling inward."

"How fast?" von Raaben barked.

"That can only be estimated. We know his approximate altitude, from the orbital velocity as given by Doppler shift of his signal. That is thirty-one-point-five kilometers per second, in the same sense as our own path. On the basis of the average density-altitude relationship in the Jovian atmosphere, the weathermen figure he should…should start burning in five or six hours."

"No chance that Stuart or Dykstra or any of the others can give a hand?" asked Wisner.

"We've tried to raise them," said ben Judah. "No luck, as expected." Only a tight beam could drive a recognizable message from the *Vesta Castle* to a scoopship deep in the radio chaos of Jupiter's air. And the exact position of such a ship was never known—constantly and unpredictably changing, anyway. A broadcast could be received by a man in clear space, over considerable distances. But the parking orbits of those who had taken on full loads and were waiting to rendezvous on dayside were eccentric ellipses, crossing the mother ship's circle at the space-time point of the meeting. Now Jupiter lay between, a wall to block off any cry. Unless some man still in its neighborhood should find some reason to call, and come around the edge of the radio shadow for that purpose, there was no measurable probability of getting in touch.

"We could accelerate toward dayside ourselves, couldn't we, till we can get a 'cast through?" asked the engineer.

"Don't be ridiculous," Pearson snorted. "We could, sure. But they'd all be far out, farther out than we are now. It would only waste time."

"So the problem's ours," Wisner said. "Well, I don't see why you're looking so down in the nose about it. What the hell, even at one gee a scoopship gets from here to the atmospheric fringes inside of two hours. Let's see…if you got his call a few minutes ago, he must still be on our side of Jupe, and his period just about three hours. You don't gain much by flitting a high-acceleration curve over such a short distance, seeing that you also have to brake, but you do gain a little. Yes, I think I can meet him in something like two hours. Three at the most, to allow for matching speeds and so forth…Sure, we can do it. Assume I start out half an hour from this moment at five gees, and have a curve computed for me. It'll take me that long to get ready. Got to dope up with stim and gravanol—"

"No, I shall go," said d'Andilly, and, *"Nein, ich,"* von Raaben. They began to rise.

"Sit down!" rapped Pearson.

Men's gazes focused on him, the ship's officers' with incomprehension, the pilots' with flaring resentment. The manager clamped his lips together for a space before he asked, "Precisely what do you propose to do?"

"Equalize velocities, couple air locks, and take him aboard," said d'Andilly. *"Voilà!"*

"Easy in space," Pearson said. "But do you realize that he's in atmosphere?"

"Very thin atmosphere thus far," the engineer said. "Nearly a vacuum."

"He'll be down where it's thicker by the time another ship can arrive," Pearson said.

"If he has five hours to go before he hits such a density that metal volatilizes," d'Andilly said, "it will not be too thick three hours from now for a scoopship hull to stand orbital speeds."

"No. You can't do it, I tell you,"

D'Andilly reddened. "Well, perhaps not. But we must try, or stop claiming to be men."

"Very dramatic," Pearson scoffed. "Too bad the laws of physics don't sympathize."

"What do you mean?"

"Look, I admit the air friction is slight where he is now. If only we could contact one of the men now diving, rescue would not be hard. But by the time you can reach him, he'll be down to a level where it's considerably worse. Oh, the air will still be tenuous, upper stratosphere density or less. Aerodynamic forces will tend to keep the hull aloft, preventing an extremely quick plunge to destruction.

"But...at thirty-odd KPS, that thin air is equivalent to an Earthside wind of more than hurricane force. It doesn't much resist the smooth, streamlined shape of a hull with an open gate; they're designed that way. But how does your screw engine open an air lock against such pressure? How can a tube be extended and secured? You'd accomplish nothing except to generate so much turbulence that your own craft would spin out of control."

D'Andilly sank back in his chair.

"Grapple onto his hull, then, and bring home ship and everything," von Raaben said.

"You can't do that either, for the same reason. The grapnel field doesn't seize hold till it's within a centimeter or so of metal. Otherwise the thing would be unmanageable in space. In such a wind, you'd never be able to swing it into contact."

"Are you certain of that?" Wisner asked.

"Certain enough," Pearson said.

"That means you aren't one hundred per cent sure. Who could be, with so many unknowns in the equation? O.K., we'll see. Personally, I think that we three between us might well be able to slap a claw or two on him."

"No. You'll only get tossed against each other in the attempt. I don't consider suicide heroic."

"You just can't understand, can you?" Wisner said in a soft voice. "Tom Hashimoto is one of ours."

"He isn't, really. He's not planning to renew his contract."

"So what? I've drunk his beer too often. His wife's a hell of a sweet girl. You think I can go back to Ceres and tell her we didn't even try to rescue her husband?"

"If it will make you feel better," Pearson said coldly, "I'll turn that into an order. You stay put."

"*Tu chameau pouilleux,*" d'Andilly whispered. He climbed erect, with a loud suggestion for the manager's private recreation. "Let us get started, friends."

"Sit down!" Pearson shouted. A vein pulsed in his temple, above the plastic that replaced his right cheek. "Or do you want to face charges of mutiny?"

"Monsieur le capitaine." D'Andilly turned to ben Judah. "I appeal to you."

"I…no, I am not a diver," the Israeli croaked. Sweat glittered on his forehead. "I can't go against a man who knows the subject better than I do."

D'Andilly spat on the deck. "He's no diver himself."

Von Raaben tugged at his companion's sleeve. "Sit, Charles. Contain yourself. This does nothing." By main strength he dragged d'Andilly back into his chair, then looked squarely at Pearson and said:

"Perhaps you do not know what morale means. I have heard a story about the British in one of their wars with my ancestors. Their army was beaten on the Continent and had to evacuate or be captured. The men were taken onto ships off Dunkirk. Afterward the naval commander whose warships had given what help they could was reproached for taking so great a risk. If we had brought up our own battleships and heavy artillery to the narrows, or if a storm had arisen, he would have lost his entire fleet. Let me tell you what he replied. 'We could build another fleet in four or five years. But it would have taken us three hundred years to build another tradition.'"

Pearson's eyes dropped. He stared for a space at his artificial hand, inert on the table. Finally he said, "But I do know. I was a space pilot once myself. Not scoopships, no, but prospecting, which is pretty dangerous, too, in a rock cluster. Some good friends of mine died in the same collision that shelved me. I managed to get into an intact compartment, alone. But I'd soon have died too, if the survivors hadn't risked their necks to search the debris for casualties.

"But…that was sound doctrine. The ship was a total loss. Nothing more was being hazarded except men, who'd die in any event if they couldn't pool their efforts to jury-rig sufficient shelter until help came. This case is different. You have to multiply values to be gained or lost by the probability of success or failure. Exposing three ships and three men to a very high chance of destruction, for the sake of one ship and one man whom there's only the smallest likelihood of saving…no, that's much too bad economics."

"Economics?" d'Andilly exploded.

"That's what I said," Pearson answered. Steel underlay his tone. "The dollar cost of building and outfitting a ship, of training and equipping a man. It's the only basis we've got.

"Wisner, you're an asterite born, and von Raaben has been one for a number of years. But I guess I'll have to spell the facts out for you, Pilot d'Andilly. You're kept like a fighting cock, because that's the only way to attract men to your job. So you aren't aware, I suppose, how thin a margin we asterites live on. Can you imagine what it means to carve a living from airless rocks? Sure, they're rich in metal; atomic power is cheap and solar power is free; but what is there otherwise? Why raid Jupiter at such enormous effort, if we didn't have to have those gases to form the basis of chemical synthesis, of our whole chemical industry, which equals our survival?

"O.K. It's barely possible that three ships working together could grapple onto Hashimoto's and haul him into clear space. I don't believe they could, but I'll grant a slight possibility. So if you did pull off that stunt, every boy on every asteroid would cheer himself hoarse for you, and every girl would fall into your arms, and every *man* would curse you for a pack of dangerous idiots. Because any operation which consistently gambled at those odds would soon go broke—and we've got to have the operation or the whole Republic dies.

"Now do you understand?"

D'Andilly's look traveled wildly from one pilot to the other. Von Raaben's face had congealed, Wisner's fingers twisted together like snakes. But each of them nodded.

After a time when no one spoke, Pearson turned his head toward ben Judah. The captain stood unmoving, backed against the bulkhead. "Are we still in contact with Hashimoto?" the manager asked.

"I believe so," ben Judah said dully.

"Then I suggest you return to the radio room and offer him what consolation you can. If he has a co-religionist aboard—" Pearson had raised his prosthetic hand a little. He let it fall. The clatter was so loud that he jerked in his seat.

"I wonder what happened to conk out Tom's engine?" Wisner muttered.

"We'll never know," the chief engineer said. "That compartment's sealed off behind a rad shield, remember. It's only cracked for direct inspection at refueling time, every five years or so—Why am I telling you what everybody knows?"

"I'll have nightmares thinking it might happen any time, to me or…or anyone."

"Me, I shall have nightmares about Tom," d'Andilly said. "Whirling so utterly helpless, yes, the helplessness is the real horror."

"He did not stop to think we could not get him out of orbit," von Raaben said, "or he might not have bothered."

"Well, we could, if he'd gotten into clear space," Wisner said. "Or, of course, if Jupe's mass didn't produce that kind of orbital speed." His chuckle was without humor. "But then, if Jupe were a minor planet, it wouldn't have an atmosphere worth exploiting, and this would never have happened in the first place."

"If we could slow him somehow," von Raaben floundered. "By aerodynamic braking? No, he has no control surfaces, and with his engine dead—"

D'Andilly sprang to his feet. His chair fell over backwards. *"Mon Dieu!"* he shouted.

"Huh? What?" Startlement ran around the table. "Control surfaces!" d'Andilly chattered. He waved his arms and forgot to put his torrent of words in English.

"Climb down from the mast, you nut," Wisner exclaimed. "Do you have an idea?"

"Oui…yes, yes…the balloon, *n'est-ce pas?* Dump the gas out, make a drogue. Ha, quick, draw some plans, *Monsieur l'ingènieur,* time is a-wasteful!"

"You're crazy!" Pearson snapped. He, too, leaped up.

"No, wait," ben Judah said. Hope kindled in his face.

"I do know something about this. The first experimental spacecraft were retrieved in some such way. It might work. And it doesn't look too risky to the men."

"You'd abort this whole cruise," Pearson said. "Not to mention the whopping cost of the balloon. Even getting Hashimoto's vessel back, we'd stick the Company for a terrific net loss."

"Economics can only go so far," ben Judah said.

"But don't you see?" Pearson's voice turned pleading. "It's not that I'm inhumane. Dollars and cents are nothing but shorthand for resources and human effort. And the Republic has only so much of either to go around. To us, an unprofitable operation is a socially evil one. We've got to operate under economic doctrine!"

"Not every time." Ben Judah's eyes were no longer mild. "If these pilots are willing to go, they shall."

Pearson bit his lip. "All right," he said. "Somebody has to take the blame of all the emotional morons. It may as well be me. I haven't any family to ostracize. So I directly forbid any attempt."

"As captain, I overrule you."

"You can't. This isn't in your province."

"Isn't it?" Ben Judah murmured. His officers, who had crowded close, moved nearer Pearson. The second mate laid a hand on the manager's thin shoulder. "You heard the captain," he said.

Pearson shook himself loose, stumbled back to his chair and buried his face in his hands.

Presently the gang went aft to begin work. Pearson raised his head. The cabin had grown very still again. Only ben Judah remained, puffing his pipe at the opposite side of the table.

"I'm sorry, Roy," the skipper said.

"I'm sorrier," Pearson told him. "When we reach Ceres, I'm going to prefer charges of incompetence against you."

"Really?"

"Yes. I don't want to. How I don't want to! But we can't keep sentimentalists on the payroll, and we need an object lesson. It's my duty to get you fired." Pearson rubbed his live hand over his plastic jaw. His voice was empty. "What have I got to live for, except my duty?"

The atmosphere of a high-gravity planet has a correspondingly high-density gradient. Streaking downward, the scoopships hit perceptibly thick air—still thin even by Martian standards, but thick enough to matter at this speed—almost before the pilots realized they were about to do so. Then it was all their drug-stimulated bodies could do to maintain formation.

There ought to be an art to this, d'Andilly thought amid thunder. Given time, an art could be developed, a whole profession of...droguedragging? His teeth gleamed behind his faceplate, a taut and short-lived grin. God grant this was the last as well as the first occasion the thing was tried!

Mignonne reared like a whipped horse. The cable had pulled on her. D'Andilly applied sidewise field thrust. Give that line some slack or it'll yank the guts out of her! But not too much slack, or you'll lose control of the whole crazy package.

Then you and your comrade may tumble into Jupiter, ready wrapped in a plastic shroud. Death as a shooting star sounds romantic, but any man of sense prefers to die in bed, at the end of a long and misspent life.

"Whoa, there!" Wisner's voice came to d'Andilly's earphones, barely audible over the interference, the wind, and the cry of tormented metal. "You're pulling on me now."

The Frenchman cast a glance outside. They were still so high that heaven was clear. Stars glittered inhumanly serene and a moon rode in an ice-crystal halo, turning the cloud layers far below into snow mountains. That Jovian horizon stretched further than a man could see; it did not lose itself in curvature but in mists and blacknesses. He saw his companion ships above him, *Sky Thief* to starboard and *Seeadler* to port—himself at the lowest point of an equilateral triangle—as shimmering curves where the light struck them, occulting shadows elsewhere.

The cables trailing aft of the three vessels were harder to see. They'd been smeared with luminous paint; but in this howling, shuddering chaos, one's head slapped back and forth in the helmet—Yes, there. Wisner's line was too taut, von Raaben's too slack. More by feel than brain, d'Andilly decided how he should adjust his own place in the formation.

Mignonne groaned and lurched when he touched the controls. Her Emetts whined, nearly as loudly as the air she split at orbital speed, feeding energy into the drive field. Any change of course under these conditions was like slugging through a brick wall. Sweat stung the pilot's eyes, half blinding him. His tongue was a block of wood and his nose full of his own stink. Vibration quivered his bones. Wind shrieked and hooted. Now and again there came a great flat smack of noise.

But...so! He'd completed the shift. The dive proceeded more smoothly.

The balloon snakedanced at the end of the cables. Deflated, slashed open, rolled in a sausage shape and stuffed into a long metal tube, the thing had not been hard to manage in space. But now when they slanted through atmosphere—d'Andilly hoped the plastic wouldn't he damaged. But no, that stuff was intended for spatial conditions. The engineers had needed a laser torch to cut it.

"Tom," he said into his radio, for the dozenth time. "Tom, are you there? Do you read us?"

We should *be headed to intercept him, according to the last fix the mother ship relayed us. But anything can have happened.* "Tom! Rescue party from *Vesta Castle* calling *Mary Girl*. Come in!"

"He may have passed out," said von Raaben's tiny drowned voice in the earphones. "He may be dead."

"We'll never find him without some kind of signal to home on," Wisner predicted, through teeth clenched against shock waves. "Too big a search field, not enough light to see by."

Everything would have been easier on dayside and at a greater altitude, d'Andilly thought. His mind was buffeted into stupidity, able only to repeat the obvious, over and over. Where the air was thinner than here, less unpredictable variation of windage and density, adequate light, Tom would have been more readily seen as well as rescued. But preparing the drogue had been a maddeningly slow task, when one must stop and plan out every step. The rescuers had arrived very late. Perhaps too late. *Mary Girl* might already have taken the final plunge.

If she wasn't found within the next few minutes, the attempt must be abandoned. They were too near the burnup point. The instrument panel showed outside temperature rapidly rising. Soon the intake scoops would be redly glowing dragon mouths. And soon after that—

"*Hei! Dort!*" von Raaben bellowed. "Eleven o'clock low, see him? There, I say!"

"Jumping Judas, yes," Wisner exclaimed. "I was wrong. We really and truly located him with our own bare eyeballs." Crispness entered his tone. "O.K., Chuck, you still want to be squadron leader?"

"*Mais oui.* Who is better qualified?" D'Andilly had now spotted the distant shape himself. With a pilot's sense of dynamic relationships he gauged how to intercept, and issue his instructions. He knew that he was in fact not superior to his associates. But a single command was essential to co-ordinated effort.

And they would have to do one all-time job of co-ordination!

The three ships slewed about, fighting for every degree of rotation, and dove on *Mary Girl.* Relative velocities were not great, and they established position quickly. There they flew not far ahead of the wreck, which they surrounded by the tow lines. For a moment, then, a kind of stability prevailed.

"Tom, can you hear me? Come in, Tom," Wisner called.

"Stow the conversation," d'Andilly said. "Are you ready? Let's brake a little… back, back, easy does it…not so fast, Krauthead…raise a bit, Bill…ah, we're snagging him."

About halfway between ships and balloon, the three cables were linked by three connecting strands, which in turn supported a flexible metal net. *Mary Girl* was just behind that net. Inchmeal, struggling with a turbulence that threatened to tangle their lines and dash them together, the rescuers allowed the net to move more slowly than the wreck. The scoop nose entered; the mesh snugged close around; the fish was caught.

"Everything seems O.K., true?" d'Andilly said. "*Bien,* let her go."

The hastily adapted hose mechanisms in *Mignonne, Sky Thief,* and *Seeadler* cast loose. The tow lines whipped backward. A radio instruction went to a small package in the balloon's container. It detonated. The metal peeled away. As the furious thrust of air entered its folds, the parachute opened.

D'Andilly brought his staggering ship under control, glanced back, and forgot all else in his awe. High over the stormclouds that looked like white mountains, a transparent hemisphere with a ghostly moon-shimmer across its surface began to bloom. Ever wider it swelled, until d'Andilly thought surely the fabric must rip across and release the shooting star.

But the fabric held. Expanding that elastomer took a great deal of energy, which *Mary Girl* supplied from her velocity. She started to fall more steeply, but at a fast-diminishing rate. Decelerating under power to keep pace, d'Andilly found himself under almost three gravities, besides Jupiter's own pull. Well, that shouldn't be too hard on Tom's body for the short time it must continue.

His live body, one hopes. "Tom, are you there? Do you read us?"

The four ships fled on eastward. They crossed the sunrise line and saw long light, the color of roses, across endless vapor fields. The dwarfed sun climbed higher for them. They descended toward the clouds, until they saw lightning lick its chops.

But by that time nearly their whole speed had been lost. The wreck was parachuting quite gently. It was downright anticlimactic when they closed in on *Mary Girl* and grappled fast. A second radio command ignited thermite cartridges on the cables and burned them loose from the net.

Engines strained skyward. Looking aft, d'Andilly saw the parachute seized by a wind and sent fluttering in the direction of a thunderhead a thousand kilometers tall. *Jupiter wants revenge,* he thought weirdly. *Well, to hell with him. We'll be back.*

After a while, stars crowded a clear darkness. A great silence opened up. The planet seemed no more than some painted backdrop. D'Andilly shook himself gingerly, as if afraid that the bruised flesh would drop off. But no permanent harm seemed done. "Let's go into orbit," he said. His voice sounded odd to him, heard through ears that still tolled. "I want to board and see how Tom is."

He dreaded what he might find.

"Shucks," said Wisner, with a shaken catch of laughter, "I can tell you that. I can see into his cockpit from here. He's waving and shaking hands with himself like a lunatic. Nothing wrong with him."

Joy jumped in d'Andilly.

"It must just be that his radio went out," von Raaben said. "With a dead engine he was depending on the emergency accumulators for everything, and I think they must be drained. Come on, let us take a sight and lay a course and get back as fast as possible. I want some beer."

"Beer you shall have," d'Andilly warbled, "all the beer you wish, you foam-at-the-mouth Boche, beer in Jupiter-sized steins until it cataracts from your ears. Provided, of course, that I get as much cognac."

He adjusted thrust vectors according to navigational directions. The three ships and their load moved toward rendezvous. D'Andilly could almost taste the liquor now. He filled his cockpit with hoarsened song.

..."*Que donn'rez vous, ța belle,*
Pour le voir revenir?"
Auprès de ma blonde
Qu'il fait bon, fait bon, fait bon,
Auprès de ma blonde
Qu'il fait bon dormir!

The *Vesta Castle* throbbed with energy, accelerating homeward.

Captain ben Judah wreathed his head in smoke and squinted at a tiny spar. With much care he brought it to the clipper foremast and held it in place a moment until the glue began to set. His inner eye visualized this W*itch of the Waves as* a real thing, soon to be commissioned, to raise her cloud of sails and ride the wind across the world. Gulls wheeled above, no whiter than the wake she cut through infinitely blue water...He sighed. One might as well face facts. Romance had long died out of the universe.

There was diffident knock. He laid down his tweezers and said, "Come in."

Roy Pearson shuffled through. Ben Judah was shocked at the man's drawn appearance. "Hello, there! What the blazes have you had afoot?" he asked, as heartily as he was able. "Taking your meals in your cabin like that, the past half dozen watches. If I hadn't been so busy getting us under weigh, I'd have come to see what ailed you."

"Oh, save it." Pearson lowered himself to the edge of the bunk and stared between his knees at the deck. His voice was hardly audible. "You know why I kept out of sight."

"Come, now. Nobody's angry at you for giving advice that turned out to be mistaken. You should know your pilots better than that. They might crow a little, as they well deserve to, but nobody that extroverted can nurse a grudge. Even Tom Hashimoto remarked at mess, when he'd heard the story, that in your place he'd have done exactly as you did."

"It isn't that." The voice grew louder, saw-edged. "It's you. I thought I could be smug about filing my complaint. But it's no use, I can't be." Pearson achieved an upward glance. "But I'm still going to do so," he said. "I've got to. If we don't stand by doctrine, how many other young men will die, or be crippled?"

"Well, for everything's sake!" Ben Judah broke into laughter. "Is that what was eating you? Roy, Roy, we need you for comic relief. Haven't you heard the C.E.'s report on the salvaged vessel?"

"N-no. What—" Pearson tried to rise, but his legs wouldn't obey.

"He made a cursory inspection, and found immediately what had caused the trouble. In the engine, of course. Sulfuric acid fumes had corroded the cross-linkages between reactor and geegee generator."

"Where in confusion did it come from?"

"That's clear, too. There have been similar incidents in the past, Mac tells me, involving other kinds of machinery. You see, steel is usually pickled in sulfuric acid, and some of the acid seeps in, gets right in between the crystals. Then, in a sealed environment like that engine compartment, and under the encouragement of nuclear radiation and stray field-drive impulses...the acid leaks out again. Very, very slowly, but it does. Precautions had been taken against that type of thing, but evidently they weren't thorough enough. You recall M*ary Girl is* one of the oldest scoopships in service. She'd had a long time for the effects to accumulate."

"But this means—" Pearson's brain began to click in accustomed patterns. "Yes, it shouldn't be hard to deal with. Install pH meters, or something of the sort, to give warning."

"I thought of that, too," ben Judah said. "Hindsight is always so much sharper than foresight, isn't it? O.K. Suppose I had not countermanded your orders and we had not gotten that ship back. How many more would have been lost before the cause was found?"

Pearson stared at him. "That's right."

"Therefore my decision resulted in a net profit for the Company, or at least in avoiding a serious net loss. So your duty is to give me the highest commendation and nominate me for a raise in pay."

Pearson sprang clumsily to his feet and extended a hand that quivered. Tears touched his eyelids. "You can bet I'll do that, Eli!"

"Now, now," rumbled ben Judah, embarrassed. "No need to make a fuss. Relax. Have a drink."

Before long, Pearson had recovered enough self-possession to suggest a game of chess.

UNTITLED LIMERICK

(Dedicated to Isaac Asimov)

On Lagash, after Stars come in view,
the rebuilders by daylight are few.
Staying cultured is hard
when all cities are charred
and paternities dubious, too.

A Sun Invisible

The invaders had deployed their fleet in standard patrol orbits. Otherwise they did nothing to camouflage themselves. It bespoke a confidence that chilled David Falkayn.

As his speedster neared Vanessa, he picked up ship after ship on his instruments. One passed so close that his viewscreens needed little magnification to show details. She was a giant, of Nova class, with only subtle outward indications that the hands which built her were not human. Her guns thrust across blackness and crowding constellations; sunlight blazed off her flanks; she was beautiful, arrogant, and terrifying.

Falkayn told himself he was not duly terrified. Himself wondered how big a liar he was.

His receiver buzzed, a call on the universal band. He flipped to Accept. The dial on the Doppler compensator indicated that the battleship was rapidly matching vectors with him. The image which looked out of the screen was—no, scarcely that of a Vanessan, but a member of the same species. It gabbled.

"Sorry, no spikka da—" Falkayn braked. Conquerors were apt to be touchy, and yonder chap sat aboard a vessel which could eat a continent with nuclear weapons and use his boat afterward for a toothpick. "I regret my ignorance of your various languages."

The Kraok honked. Evidently he, she, or yx did not know Anglic. Well, the interspeech of the Polesotechnic League... *"Loquerisne Latine?"*

The being reached for a vocalizer. Without such help, humans and Kraoka garbled each other's sounds rather badly. Adjusting it, the officer asked, *"Sprechen Sie Deutsch?"*

"Huh?" Falkayn's jaw hit his Adam's apple.

"Ich haben die Deutsche Sprache ein wenig gelehrt," said the Kraok with more pride than grammar, *"bein der grosse Kapitän."*

Falkayn gripped tight to his pilot seat, and his sanity, and gaped.

Aside from being hostile, the creature was not an unpleasing sight. About two meters tall, the body resembled that of a slim tyrannosaur, if one can imagine tyrannosaurs with brown fur. From the back sprang a great, ribbed dorsal fin, partly folded but still shimmering iridescent. The arms were quite anthropoid, except for four-fingered hands where each digit had an extra joint. The head was round, with tufted ears, blunt muzzle, eyes smaller than a man's.

Clothing amounted to a brassard of authority, a pouchbelt, and a sidearm. Falkayn, therefore, could search his memory and discover which of the three Kraokan sexes the officer belonged to: the so-called transmitter, which was fertilized by the male and in turn impregnated the female. *I should've guessed.* he thought, *even if the library on Ganstang's didn't have much information on them. The males are short and meek, and raise the young. The females are the most creative and make most of the decisions. The transmitters are the most belligerent.*

And right now are tracking me with guns. He felt altogether isolated. The throb and murmur of the boat, the odors of recycled air and his own sweat, his weight under the interior G-field, were like an eggshell of life-sensation around him. Outside lay starkness. The power of the League was distant by multiple parsecs. and these strangers had declared themselves its enemies.

"*Antworten Sie   ,*" demanded the Kraok.

Falkayn groped with half-forgotten bits of Yiddish that he had sometimes heard from old Martin Schuster, his master during his apprenticeship. "*Ikh... veyss...nit keyn...Deitch,*" he said, as slowly and clearly as possible. "Get me... *ah mentsch*...uh, *zeit azay git.*" The other sat motionless. "Damn it, you've got humans with you," Falkayn said. "I know the name of one. Utah Horn. Understand? Utah Horn."

The Kraok switched him over to another, who squatted against a background of electronic apparatus. Unhuman tones whistled from an intercom. The new one turned to Falkayn.

"I know some Latin," yx said. In spite of a vocalizer, the accent was thick enough to spread on pumpernickel. "You identify."

Falkayn wet his lips. "I am the Polesotechnic League's factor on Garstang's," he said. "A messenger capsule brought me word about your, uh, advent. It said I had permission to come here."

"So." More whistles. "Indeed. One boat, unarmed, we allow to make landing at Elan-Trrl. You make trouble, we kill."

"Of course I won't," Falkayn promised. *Unless I get a chance.* "I will proceed directly. Do you want my route plan?"

Yx did. The boat's pilot computer sent numbers to the battleship's. The track was approved. Maser beams flashed through space, alerting other vessels to keep an eye on the speedster. "You go," said the Kraok.

"But this Utah Horn—"

"Commander Horn see you when want to. Go." The screen blanked and Falkayn went. The acceleration strained his internal field compensators.

He gusted air from his lungs and stared outward. Hitherto, as he sped toward Thurman's Star, the view had been dominated by Beta Centauri, unwinking, almost intolerably brilliant across two-score lightyears. But now the sun of Vanessa showed a visible disk. It wasn't that kind of type B supergiant but nevertheless impressive, a white F_7, seething with prominences, shimmering with corona. If his shield screens should fail, its radiation would strike through the hull and destroy him.

Well, he gulped, *I wanted to be a dashing adventurer. So here I am, and mostly I want to dash.*

He stretched, opposed muscles to each other, worked out some of his tension. Then he felt hungry, and went aft to build a sandwich; and when he had eaten and lit his pipe, a certain ebullience returned. For he was a bare twenty years old.

When he got his journeyman's papers, he was one of the youngest humans ever to do so. In large part, that was thanks to his role in the trouble on Ivanhoe. To set a similar record for a Master Merchant's certificate, he needed another exploit or two. Beljagor's message had made him whoop for glee.

Now it turned out that he was up against something more formidable than he had imagined. But he remained a scion of a baronial house in the Grand Duchy of Hermes. Mustn't let the side down, eh, what?

At a minimum, if he did nothing but convey word to Sector HQ about what had happened, that would bring him to the notice of the higher-ups. Maybe old Nick van Rijn himself would hear about this David Falkayn, who was so obviously being wasted in that dismal little outpost on Garstang's.

He practiced a reckless grin. It looked better than last year. While his face remained incurably snubnosed, it had lost the chubbiness that used to distress him. And he was large and blond and rangy, he told himself, and had excellent taste in clothes and wine. Also women, he added, becoming more smug by the minute. If only he weren't the sole human on his assigned planet—Well, perhaps this mysterious Horn person had brought along some spare females…

Vanessa grew in the vision ports, a reddish globe mottled with green and blue, sparked with reflections off the small seas. Falkayn wondered what the inhabitants called it. Being colonists themselves, whose civilization had not fallen apart during the long hiatus in Kraokan space travel as had happened on other settlements, they doubtless had a single language. Why hadn't Thurman done the usual thing in such cases, and put the native name of his discovery into the catalogues?

Quite probably because men couldn't wrap their larynxes around it. Or maybe he just felt like dubbing the planet "Vanessa." Judas, what a radium-plated opportunity an explorer had! What girl could possibly resist an offer to name a whole world for her?

Another warship in sentry orbit became discernible. Falkayn stopped daydreaming.

In the lost great days of their expansion, the Kraoka had never founded a city. The concept of so small a unit having an identity of its own—and composed of still lesser individual sub-units, each with *its* separateness—was too alien to them. However, they did give names to the interconnected warrens they built at various sites. Falkayn's Bible—"Terrestrial Pilot's Guide to the Beta Centauri Region"—informed him that Elan-Trrl, in any of several possible spellings, could be found in the middle northern latitudes and was marked by a League radio beacon.

So crowded a microreel could say little about the planet. The only important hazards mentioned were ozone and ultraviolet. He got into a hooded coverall and donned a filter mask with goggles. The tiny spaceport swooped up at him. He landed and debarked.

For a moment he stood orienting himself, getting accustomed to strangeness. The sky overhead was cloudless, very pale blue, the sun too dazzling for him to look near. Colors seemed washed out in that cruel illumination. Beyond the port, hills rolled down to a lake from which irrigation canals seamed a landscape densely cultivated in bluish-green shrubs. Gnarled, feathery-leaved trees grew along the canal banks and high-prowed motorboats glided on the water. The agricultural machines in the fields, and the occasional gravity craft that flitted overhead, must have been imported by League traders. On the horizon there bulked a dry brown mountain range.

Falkayn felt heavy, under the pull of one-point-two G's. A wind boomed around him, casting billows of heat. But in this parched air he wasn't grossly uncomfortable.

On the other side of the port, Elan-Trrl lifted bulbous towers. Their gray stone was blurred in outline, from millennia of weathering. He didn't see much traffic; mainly underground, he believed. His eyes went gratefully to the homelike steel-and-vitryl facades of the League compound at the edge of the spacefield. They wavered in the heat shimmers.

Two vessels rested near his. One was a stubby Holbert, evidently Beljagor's; the second, lean and armed, modeled after a Terrestrial chaser, must belong to the invaders. Several Kraoka stood guard in her shade. They must have been told to expect Falkayn, for they made no move toward him. Nor did they speak. As he walked to the compound, he felt their eyes bore at his back. His boots made a loud, lonely noise beneath the wind.

The door of the factor's quarters opened for him. The air in the lobby was no less hot and sere than outside, the light scarcely less harsh. But naturally the League would put someone from an F-type star here. Falkayn began to think more kindly about cool green Garstang's. And why hadn't this Beljagor unko come out to meet him?

An intercom said, "Down the hall to your right," in Latin and a gravelly bass.

Falkayn proceeded to the main office. Beljagor sat behind his desk, puffing a cigar. Above him hung the emblem of the Polesotechnic League, an early Caravel spaceship on a sunburst and the motto *All The Traffic Will Bear.* Computers, vocascribes, and other equipment were familiar, too. The boss was not. Falkayn had never met anyone from Jaleel before.

"So there you are," Beljagor said. "Took you long enough."

Falkayn stopped and looked at him. The factor was somewhat anthropoid. That is, his stocky form sported two legs, two arms, one head, and no tail. But he was little over a meter tall; his feet each had three thick toes, his hands three mutually opposed fingers; the kilt which was his solitary garment revealed gray scales and yellow abdomen. His nose could best be likened to a tapir's snout, his ears to a sort of bat wings. A bunch of carroty cilia sprouted from the top of his pate, a pair of fleshy chemosensor tendrils from above his eyes. Those eyes were as small as a Kraok's; animals which see a ways into the ultraviolet, and don't use the red end of man's spectrum, have no need for large orbs.

As if for comparison, a Vanessan squatted on yxs—no, her, this time—tail before the desk. Beljagor gestured with his cigar. "This here is Quillipup, my chief liaison officer. And you are…what is your silly name, now?"

"David Falkayn!" The newcomer could do nothing but snap a bit, when he was a mere journeyman face to face with a Master.

"Well, sit. Have a beer? You Earthtypes dehydrate easy."

Falkayn decided Beljagor wasn't such a bad fellow after all. "Thank you, sir." He folded his lean frame into a lounger.

The Jaleelan ordered through his intercom. "Have any trouble on your way?" he asked.

"No."

"I didn't expect you would. You're not worth bothering with. Also, Horn wanted you to come, and he seems to rank high in their fleet." Beljagor shrugged: "Can't say I wanted you myself. An unlicked cub! If there'd been an experienced man anywhere nearby, we might have got something done."

Falkayn swallowed another chunk of pride. "Regrets, sir. But when the League has only been operating hereabouts for a few decades—I'm not sure what you have in mind. Your message just said the Thurmanian System had been invaded by a force of Kraoka who're ordering the League out of the whole Beta Centauri region."

"Well, somebody has to go warn HQ," Beljagor grunted, "and I won't myself. That is, I figure to stay here and stall, maybe even argue them into changing their minds. Your own post won't miss *you.*" He fumed in silence for a while. "First, though, before you leave, I want you to try and make a few elementary observations. That's why I sent to Garstang's for help, instead of Roxlatl. Snarfen is probably ten times as able as you—he being a Master—but you are a human and there are humans in high positions among the Antoranites. Like Utah Horn, who said he'd want to interview you, after I mentioned your origin. So maybe you can get a line on what's going on. Takes one member of your ridiculous race to understand another, I always say."

Falkayn stuck grimly to the point. "The Antoranites…sir?"

"The invaders call their base Antoran. They won't describe it beyond the name."

Falkayn glanced at Quillipup. "Don't you have some idea where they come from?" he asked.

"No," said the Kraok into her vocalizer. "It can be no world that the Race was known to have settled. But records are incomplete."

"I don't understand how—"

"I shall explain. Ages before your species or Master Beljagor's were aught but savages, our great ancestors on Kraokanan—"

"Yes, I know about them."

"Don't interrupt your superiors, cub," Beljagor growled. "Besides, I'm not sure you do know the history. And won't hurt you to hear it again, whether or not you've waded through a book or two." His nose twitched in disdain. "You're with Solar Spice & Liquors, right? They don't deal here. Nothing for them. As far as interstellar trade goes, Vanessa doesn't produce anything but drugs and fluorescents that aren't useful to your type of life. Me, I'm not only here as agent for General Motors of Jaleel, I often represent other companies from similar planets. So I have to know the situation inside out. Go on, Quillipup."

"Now you are interrupting," sulked the Vanessan.

"When I speak, it is not an interruption, it's an enlightenment. Go on, I said. But make it short. None of your singing chronicles, you hear?"

"The majesty of the Race cannot well be conveyed without the Triumph Ballads."

"Stuff the majesty of the Race! Carry on."

"Oh, well, he probably could not appreciate the splendor anyway."

Falkayn gritted his teeth. Where the hell was that promised beer?

"Thousand upon thousands of years ago, then," Quillipup quietly began, "the Race mastered space flight and set forth to colonize among the stars. Long and mighty was that striving, and the tales of the hero-crews echo down the ages. As for example, Ungn—"

"Vector back," ordered Beljagor, for Quillipup seemed about to burst into song.

Falkayn wondered if her bragging was due to an inferiority complex. The fact of the matter was that the Kraoka never had learned how to build a hyperdrive engine. Everything must be done at sublight speeds: decades or centuries, from star to star. And then only the bright F-types, which are comparatively rare, were reasonable goals. Smaller suns, like Sol, were too cool and dim, too poor in the ultraviolet radiation on which a high-energy biochemistry depended. Bigger ones like Beta Centauri—indeed, any above F_5 in the main sequence—lacked planets. The Kraoka were lucky to have found fourteen new systems they could use.

"Try to imagine the ancestral achievement," Quillipup urged. "Not merely did they cross the unthinkable interstellar abysses, they often transformed the atmosphere and ecology of entire worlds, to make them habitable. Never another species has gained the skill in that art which they possessed."

Well, naturally not, Falkayn thought. Modern spacefarers had no reason to be planetary engineers. If they didn't like a globe, they flitted off to look for another. Sublight travelers could not be so choosy.

He must admit that the Kraokan past had a certain grandeur. Men would hardly have mounted so vast a project for so long; they had more individual but less racial pride.

"When the Dark Ages descended," Quillipup said, "we remembered. Whatever else slipped from our grasp, we were yet able to look into the night sky and know what stars shone upon our kindred."

According to what Falkayn had read, the collapse had been gradual but inevitable. The sphere of operations simply became too big for expeditions so slow; it grew too costly, in time and labor and resources, to attain the next white sun. Thus exploration ended.

And likewise did trade between the colonies. It couldn't be made to pay. The Polesotechnic League exists merely because—given hyperdrive and gravity control

—interstellar freight costs less for numberless planetary products than manufacture at home would cost. Though the ancient Kraoka had lacked a profit motive, they were not exempt from the laws of economics.

So they built no more star ships. In time, most of the colonies even quit interplanetary travel. Several fell into chaos and ultimate barbarism. Vanessa was luckier: civilization persisted, ossified and changeless but on a fairly high technological level, for some three hundred centuries. Then Thurman came. And now the Kraoka again had news from their lost brothers, and dreamed of reunifying the Race.

Which required money. A spaceship is not exactly cheap, and the League is no charitable organization. Let the Vanessans accumulate sufficient credit, and shipyards elsewhere in the galaxy would be glad to take their orders. But not before.

Falkayn grew aware that Quillipup was droning on about more immediately significant business.

"…Neither chronicle nor tradition identifies a world that might be Antoran. Phonetic analysis of clandestinely recorded speech, and certain details of custom that have been observed, suggest that the planet was settled from Dzua. But Dzua was one of the first worlds on which civilization disintegrated, and no record remains of enterprises which might once have begun there. Antoran must, accordingly, be a fifteenth colony, forgotten at home and never mentioned to the rest of us."

"Are you sure?" Falkayn ventured. "I mean, could one of the known Kraokan planets not—"

"Certainly not," Beljagor said. "I've been on all of them and I know their capabilities. A fleet like this one—and I was taken into space, shown how big a fleet it is and what it can do—can't be built without more industry than anybody could hide."

"The invaders…what have they said?"

"Not a clue-giving word, I told you. They don't belong to your blabbermouth species. Kraoka have too much tribal-identity instinct to break security."

"They must at least have explained their reasons."

"Oh, that. Yes. They're hell-bent to reestablish the old society, as an empire this time. And they want the League out of the entire region because they say we're a bunch of dominators, exploiters, corrupters of the pure tradition, and I don't know what stinking else."

Falkayn stole a look at Quillipup. He couldn't read expressions on her face, but the dorsal fin—a body-cooling surface—was erecting itself and the tail switched. Vanessa had offered no resistance to the takeover. Quite probably Quillipup would not be a bit sorry if her present employers got booted out.

The human said carefully, "Well, sir, in a way they're justified, aren't they? This is their home, not ours. We've done nothing for the Kraoka that we didn't make a fat profit on. And if they want to deal with us, they have to change a high, ancient culture—"

"Your idealism pierces me to the core; I won't say in what parts of my anatomy," Beljagor sneered. "What matters is that the League stands to lose a mega whopping amount of money. All our facilities in the region are to be confiscated, you hear? So they'll get our trade with the cooler stars, too. And I don't think they'll stop there, either. Those humans who're with them, what do *they* want?"

"Well…yes," Falkayn conceded. There was no denying that his own species was among the most predatory in the universe. "Your message mentioned somebody called Utah Horn. That does sound pretty, uh, Wild West and bandit-like."

"I'll notify him you're here," Beljagor said. "He wants to talk with a League official of his own race. Well, he'll have to settle for you. I wish I could hope you'll manage to worm something out of him."

A servor floated in with bottles, "Here's the beer," Beljagor announced. The machine opened two, Quillipup curtly declining a third. Her sinews were taut and her tail lashed the clawed feet.

"Ad fortunam tuam." Beljagor said with no great sincerity, and tossed off half a liter.

Falkayn opened his mask at the mouth and did the same. Then he spouted the liquid back, choked, coughed, and fought not to vomit.

"Huh?" Beljagor stared. "What in the nine pustulant hells—? Oh. I see. I forgot your breed can't stand Jaleelan proteins." He slapped his thigh with a pistol noise. "Haw, haw, haw!"

Humans being as ubiquitous as they are, nearly every League outpost on a nonterrestroid planet includes a suite conditioned and stocked for such visitors. Falkayn had been afraid that those Antoranite officers who were of his lineage would have taken the quarters over, leaving him to twiddle his thumbs in the cramped speedster. But they preferred their spaceships, he learned. Perhaps they were wary of booby traps. He was free to twiddle his thumbs in a series of rooms.

His phone chimed as Vanessa's nineteen-hour day was drawing to a close. A man in a form-fitting green uniform looked out of the screen. His features were hard, moustached, and so deeply tanned that at first Falkayn took him for an African. "You are the one from the other Polesotechnic station?" he asked. He spoke coldly, with a guttural accent.

"Yes. David Falkayn. And you're Commander Horn?"

"No. Captain Blanck, in charge of Security. Since Commander Horn is to have a conference with you, I am making safe arrangements."

"I'm not quite sure what we are to confer about."

Blanck cracked a smile. It seemed to hurt his face. "Nothing very definite, Freeman Falkayn. We wish certain messages conveyed by you to the League. Otherwise, shall we say that it is mutually advantageous to get some personal impressions of each other, uncomplicated by inherent differences between species. Antoran will fight if need be, but would rather not. Commander Horn wishes to persuade you that we are no monsters, nor engaged in an unreasonable cause. It is hoped that you in turn can convince your superiors."

"Um-m-m…O.K. Where and when?"

"I think best in your billet. We assume you are not so stupid as to attempt any breach of truce."

"With a war fleet sitting right over my head? Don't worry!" Falkayn considered. "How about dinner here? I've checked the supplies, and they're better than anything a spaceship is likely to have."

Blanck agreed, set the time for an hour hence, and switched off. Falkayn got the kitchen servors busy. The fact that he was to dine with an enemy did not mean he couldn't dine well. Of course, a space cowboy like Utah Horn wouldn't know caviar from buckshot; but Falkayn was prepared to savor for two.

While he dressed, in a formal gold outfit, he lined up his thoughts. There didn't seem to be many humans with the invaders, but they all seemed to be key personnel. No doubt they were the ones who had originally shown the Antoranites how to build warcraft, and were the experienced strategists and tacticians of the whole shebang. Horn was willing to come here because a fellow human taken aboard a ship might observe too much, critical little details which would have escaped Beljagor. But Falkayn could try to pump him...

A tender landed from the orbiting flotilla. Dusk had fallen, and Falkayn could barely see that a single human walked toward his lodgings, accompanied by four Kraokan guards. Those took stations at the entrance.

A minute passed while his guest waited in the air lock for ozone to be converted; then Falkayn activated the inner door. The Antoranite had just hung up a filter mask. Falkayn lurched.

"What?" he yelled.

She couldn't be many years older than himself. The uniform was snug around a figure which would have stunned him even if he had not been celibate for months. Blueblack hair fell softly to her shoulders past enormous hazel eyes, tip-tilted nose, the most delightful mouth he had ever—

She turned Blanck's accent to music. "Freeman Falkayn? I am Commander Horn."

"*Utah* Horn?"

"Yes, that is correct, Jutta Horn of Neuheim. You are surprised?"

Falkayn nodded in a blackjacked fashion.

"You see, Neuheim's population being small, any who happen to have some ability must help. Besides, my father was the man who discovered the lost planet and began this whole crusade. The Kraoka, with their feeling for ancestry, revere me on that account; and moreover, they are used to thinking of females as leaders. So I am doubly useful; any orders transmitted by me are sure to be obeyed to the letter. You must have met women spacers before now."

"Uh, it's only that, uh—" *I get it. When he dictated his letter to me, Beljagor was using a 'scribe adjusted for Anglic spelling. Quite understandable, when so few people speak German any more. He did use the masculine pronoun for her. But either he didn't happen to meet her personally, or he's too contemptuous of humans to bother noticing their sex.*

The loss is entirely his.

Falkayn collected himself, smiled his largest smile and bowed his most sweeping bow. "I wish I could be so pleasantly surprised every time," he purred. "Welcome, Commander. Do sit down. What would you like to drink?"

She looked doubtful. "I am not sure if I ought."

"Come, come. A dinner without an aperitif is like a…ahem…a day without sunshine."

"*Ach,* I am not familiar with these things."

"High time you became so, then." Falkayn told the nearest servor to bring old-fashioneds. He preferred a martini himself, by several lightyears, but if her palate was uneducated she'd drink more of something sweet.

She settled primly on a chair. He saw that her wrist communicator was energized, doubtless transmitting to the guards outside. If they heard anything suspicious, they would break in. Still, they wouldn't catch the nuances of what Falkayn was feverishly planning.

He sat down, too. She refused a cigarette. "You must not have had a chance to be corrupted by civilization," he laughed.

"No," she agreed, deadpan. "I was born and raised on Neuheim. My sole visits beyond the system, until now, were to unexplored stars in the course of training cruises."

"What is this Neuheim?"

"Our planet. A part of the Antoranite System."

"Eh? You mean Antoran is a star?"

Jutta Horn bit her lip. "I did not know you had the opposite impression."

In spite of her nearness, or maybe because of being stimulated thereby, Falkayn's mind leaped. "Ah-ha!" he grinned. "This tells me something. We took for granted that the Antoranites were from a single planet and their human allies simply adventurers. Earthmen don't call themselves Solarians. But Earthmen and Martians do collectively. Ergo, there's more than one inhabited planet going around Antoran. Your Neuheim; and how many Kraokan worlds?"

"No matter," she clipped.

He waved his hand. "I'm sorry if I've disturbed you. Here are our cocktails. Let's drink to a better understanding between us."

She sipped, hesitantly at first, then with frank enjoyment. "You are more friendly than I had expected," she said.

"How could I be otherwise toward you, my lady?" She blushed and fluttered her lashes, yet obviously she was not playing coquette. He eased off; never embarrass your target. "We're discussing our differences like two civilized people, trying to reach a compromise. Aren't we?"

"What authority have you to sign treaties?" She might never have been in civilization, but she had been taught how it worked.

"None," Falkayn said. "As the man on the spot, though, I can make recommendations that will have considerable weight."

"You look so young to be so important," she murmured.

"Oh, well," said Falkayn modestly, "I've knocked around a bit, you know. Had the chance to do this and that. Let's talk about you."

She took his pronoun for plural and started off on what must be a prepared lecture.

Antoran did indeed have planets which the Kraoka of Dzua had once colonized. Though the settlers perforce gave up star travel, they had maintained interplanetary commerce down the millennia, keeping more technology than Vanessa did.

Forty-odd years ago, Robert Horn of Nova Germania was being chased by a League cruiser. He laid a course to throw the pursuer off his trail—the old stardodge maneuver—and thus passed so near Antoran that he detected radio emissions. Later he slipped back to investigate, and discovered the planets.

"Yes, he was an outlaw," his daughter said defiantly. "He was a leader in the Landholders' Revolt…so good, so effective, that afterwards they dared not give him amnesty."

Falkayn had heard vaguely about the matter. Something to do with a conspiracy among Nova Germania's first families, descendants of the original pioneers, to get back the power that a new constitution had taken away from them. And, yes, the League was involved; the republican government offered better trading concessions than the Landholders had granted in their day. No wonder this girl was doing the League all the dirt she could.

He smiled and refilled her glass. "I can sympathize," he said. "Being from Hermes, you see. Aristocracy's far and away my favorite system."

Her eyes widened. "You are *adel*…nobly born?"

"Younger son," Falkayn said, modest again. He did not add that he'd been shipped to Earth for his education because he kept kicking over the traces which an aristocrat was expected to carry. "Do go on. You fascinate me."

"The Antoranite System includes one planet which the Kraoka had modified for habitability, but which was too far out, too cold and dark, to be really worth their while. For humans it is better. That is my world, Neuheim."

Hm-m-m, Falkayn thought. This implied at least one planet farther inward which did provide a good Kraokan environment. Very possibly more than one; a war fleet as big as Beljagor claimed he had seen can't be built in a hurry without a lot of population and resources. But this in turn implied a large sun with a wide biothermal zone. Which didn't make sense! Every F-type star in this region had been visited by League surveyors; likewise the G-types; and there definitely was no such system as—

"My father returned in secret to Nova Germania." Jutta Horn said. "He got recruits there and elsewhere. The whole world of Neuheim was given them in exchange for help."

I feel pretty sure they planted the idea of conquest in the first place, Falkayn reflected. *Yeh, I can guess how Kraoka might fall for the foe concept of a reunited Vaterland. And given enough anti-League propaganda, they might well come to believe that the only way to get unification is to expel us first.*

"So Germanian engineers showed the Antoranites how to make hyperdrive ships," he said, "and Germanian officers trained the crews; and Germanian secret agents kept track of events outsystem—my, you've been busy."

She nodded. Two drinks blurred her tone a little. "That is true. Everything comes second to the crusade. Afterward we can relax. How I look forward!"

"Why not start right away?" Falkayn asked. "Why fight the League? We've no objection to the Kraoka building a star marine at their own expense, nor to any social arrangements you've made on Neuheim."

"After the way the League meddled in the past?" she challenged.

"Yes, granted, we do, now and then, when our interests are threatened. But still, Jutta"—there, he'd established a first-name relationship—"the Polesotechnic League is not a state, not even a government. It's nothing but a mutual-benefit association of interstellar merchants, who're probably more wolfish toward each other than toward anybody outside."

"Power is the one basis of negotiation," she said, turning Clausewitzian, "When we and our allies have secured this region, then perhaps we will allow you to operate here again…under our rules. Otherwise you could too easily impose your will on us, if we did not desire the same things as you."

"The League isn't going to take this lying down," he warned.

"I think the League had better do so," she retorted. "We are here, in the region, with interior lines of communication. We can strike from space, anywhere. A League warfleet must come across many parsecs. It will find its bases demolished. And it will not know where our home planets are!"

Falkayn backed off in haste. He didn't want her in that mood. "You certainly have a tremendous advantage," he said. "The League can muster forces greater by orders of magnitude—surely you realize that—but the League may well decide that the cost of defeating you would be greater than any possible gain in doing so."

"Thus my father calculated before he died. Merchants, who lust for nothing but money, can be cowed. *Adelsvolk* are different. They live for an ideal, not for economics."

I wish you'd had a chance to stick that pretty nose out of your smug, ingrown little kingdom and see what working aristocrats are like, Falkayn thought. Aloud: "Well, now, Jutta, I can't quite agree. Remember, I'm both a merchant and a nobleman's son. The psychologies aren't so unlike. A peer has to be a politician, with everything that that entails, or he's no good. And a merchant has to be an idealist."

"What?" She blinked in startlement. "How?"

"Why, you don't think we work for money alone, do you? If that were the object, we'd stay safe and snug at home. No, it's adventure, new horizons, life's conquest of inanimate nature—the universe itself, the grandest enemy of all."

She frowned, but she was softened. "I do not understand, quite."

"Suppose I give you a few examples—"

Dinner was served in the roof turret, which had a view like being outdoors. By night Vanessa took on beauty. Both moons were aloft, small and swift, turning the land to a fantasy of dim silver and moving shadows. The lake gleamed, the native towers looked like giant blossoms. Overhead the sky was splendid with stars, Beta Centauri the king jewel, its blue radiance matching the moons.

And glowpanels caressed Jutta's sun-browned cheeks with their own light; and Beethoven's Seventh lilted softly from a speaker; and bubbles danced in the champagne glasses. Dinner had made its stately progression from hors d'oeuvres and consommé through fish, roast, and salad, to petits fours and now cheeses. Falkayn had kept the magnum flask busy. Not that either party was drunk—Jutta, alas, had so far kept her wits patriotically about her—but they both felt more than cheerful.

"Tell me other things," she urged. "You have had such a wonderful existence, David. Like the hero of an ancient saga—but this is now, which makes it twice as good."

"Let me think," he said, giving her a refill. "Maybe the time I cracked up on a rogue planet?"

"A what?"

"Free planet, sunless. More of them floating around in space than there are stars. The smaller the body, you see, the likelier it was to form when the galaxy coalesced. Normally you find them in groups...to be honest, you don't normally find them, because space is big and they are little and dark. But by sheer chance, on the way from Tau Ceti to 70 Ophiuchi, I—"

The adventure had, in fact, happened to somebody else. So had most of the stories Falkayn had been relating. But he saw no reason to spoil a good yarn with pedantry.

Besides, she continued to sip, in an absentminded and unsuspecting way, while he talked.

"...And finally I replenished my air by boiling and processing frozen gases. And was I glad to leave!"

"I should think so." She shivered. "Space is bleak, Lovely, but bleak. I like planets better." She gazed outward. "The night here is different from home. I don't know which I like best, Neuheim or Vanessa. After dark, I mean," she added. "None of the Kraokan worlds are pleasant by day."

"None whatsoever? You must have seen quite a variety, with three of them for neighbors."

"Five," she corrected. Her hand went to her mouth. "*Lieber Gott!* I didn't mean to tell."

He chuckled, though inwardly he thrummed with a new excitement. Judas! Five planets—six, counting Neuheim—in the thermal zone where water was liquid...around one star! "It doesn't make any practical difference," he said, "when you've evidently found some way to make your whole system invisible. I'd like to know more about you, that's all, and I can't unless you tell me something about your home." He reached across the table and patted her hand. "That's what gave you your dreams, your hopes—your charm, if I may say so. Neuheim must be a paradise."

"No, it is a hard world for humans," she answered earnestly. "In my own lifetime, we have had to move entire villages toward the poles as the planet swung closer to the sun. Even the Kraoka have their troubles for similar reasons." She pulled free of his touch. "But I am talking of what I shouldn't."

"Very well, let's keep to harmless things," he said. "You mentioned that the nights were different at home. In what way?"

"Oh...different constellations, of course. Not greatly, but enough to notice. And then, because of the auroras, we never see the stars so clearly as here, from any location. I *must* not say more. You are far too observing, Davy. Tell me, instead, about your Hermes." She smiled irresistibly. "I would like to know where your own dreams come from."

Nothing loath, Falkayn spoke of mountains, virgin wilderness, plains darkened by horned herds, surfbathing at Thunderstrands—

"What does that mean, Davy?"

"Why, bathing in the surf. You know, the waves caused by tidal action." He decided to disarm her suspicions with a joke. "Now, my poor innocent, you've given yourself away again, You imply Neuheim doesn't have tides."

"No harm in that," she said. "True, we have not any moon. The oceans are like huge, still lakes."

"Doesn't the sun—" He checked himself.

"Not so far away as it is, a tiny point of fire, I can't get used to the disk here." Abruptly Jutta set down her glass. "Listen," she said, "you are either very young and sweet or you are clever as Satan."

"Why not both?"

"I cannot take the chance." She rose. "Best I leave now. I made a mistake to come."

"What?" He scrambled to his own feet. "But the evening's hardly begun. I thought we'd go back to the living room and relax with some more music." The *Liebestod,* for instance.

"No." Distress and determination chased each other across her face. "I enjoy myself too much. I forget to guard my tongue. Take to the League this word from us. Before they can marshal against us, we will have the Kraokan stars, and more. But if the League will be reasonable, *jo,* perhaps we can discuss trade treaties." Her eyes dropped. She flushed. "I would like if you could return."

Politics! Falkayn groaned. He got nowhere trying to change her mind, and must finally see her to the door. There he kissed her hand...and before he could build on that beginning, she had whispered good night and was outside.

He poured himself a stiff whiskey, lit his pipe, and flung himself into a lounger. None were an adequate substitute.

Rats! he brooded. *Giant mutant rats! She'll have me hustled off the planet right away, tomorrow dawn, before I can use any information I might have gathered.*

Well, at least there'll be girls at Sector HQ. And maybe, eventually, I'll find myself back here.

As a journeyman assistant; and Jutta will be at the social apex of an interstellar empire. She wouldn't snub me on that account, but what chance would we ever have to get together?

He puffed hard and scowled at a repro of a Hokusai portrait, an old man, which hung opposite him. The old man smiled back till Falkayn wanted to punch him in the nose.

The long-range significance of the Neuheimer scheme was far nastier than several gigacredits' loss to the merchant princes, Falkayn saw. Suppose it did succeed. Suppose the mighty Polesotechnic League was defied and defeated, and the Kraokan Empire was established. Well, the Kraoka by themselves might or might not be content to stop at that point and settle down to peaceful relationships with everybody else. In any event, they were no direct threat to the human race; they didn't want the same kind of real estate.

But the Neuheimer' humans—Already they spoke of themselves as crusaders. Consider the past history of Homo self-styled sapiens and imagine what so spectacular a success would do to a bunch of ideologically motivated militarists! Oh, the process would be slow; they'd have to increase their numbers, and enlarge their industrial base, and get control of every man-useful planet in this neighborhood. But eventually, for power, and glory, and upset of the hated merchants, and advancement of a Way of Life—war.

The time to squelch them was now. A good healthy licking would discredit the Landholders; peace, mercantilism, and cooperation with others—or, at least, simple cutthroat economic competition would become fashionable on Neuheim; and, incidentally, a journeyman who played a significant part in that outcome could expect early certification as a Master Merchant.

Whereas a mere bearer of bad tidings—

"All right," Falkayn muttered. "Step One in the squelching process: Find their planetary system!"

They couldn't hope to keep its location secret forever. Just long enough to secure a grip on this region; and given the destructive power of a space fleet, that needn't be very long. While it remained hidden, though, the source of their strength was quite efficiently protected. Hence their entire effort could go into purely offensive operations, which gave them a military capability far out of proportion to their actual force.

Nonetheless, if the League should decide to fight, the League would win. No question about that. In the course of the war, the secret was bound to be discovered, one way or another. And then—nuclear bombardment from space—*No!*

The Landholders were gambling that the League, rather than start an expensive battle for a prize that would certainly be ruined in the course of the fighting, would vote to cut its losses and come to terms. Antoran being hidden, the bet looked fairly good. But no matter how favorable the odds, only fanatics played with entire living worlds for stakes. Poor Jutta! What foul company she was mixed up in. How he'd like to introduce her to some decent people.

O.K., then, where was that star?

Some place not far off. Jutta had betrayed nothing by admitting that the constellations at home were almost like the constellations here. The ancient Kraoka could not have traveled any enormous ways, as interstellar distances go. Also, the home base must be in this territory so that its fleet could exploit the advantage of interior communications.

And Antoran must be large and bright, no later in the main sequence than, say, G0. Yet…every possible sun was already eliminated by information the League had long possessed.

Unless—wait a minute—could it be hidden by a thick nebulosity?

No. There'd still be radio indications. And Jutta had spoken of seeing stars from her home.

Aurora. Hm-m-m. She'd mentioned the necessity for certain villagers to migrate toward the poles, as her planet got too near its primary. Which meant their original settlements were a good bit farther toward the equator. Even so, auroras had been conspicuous: everywhere you went, she'd said. This, again, suggested a highly energetic sun.

Funny, about the eccentric orbit. More than one planet in the system, too, with the same problem. Unheard of. You'd almost think that—

Falkayn sat bolt upright. His pipe dropped from his jaws to his lap. "Holy… hyper…Judas," he gasped.

Thereafter he thought most furiously. He did not come back to himself until the coals from his pipe set fire to his trousers.

The door to Beljagor's place, offices-cum-residence, barely had time to get out of Falkayn's way. But as he entered the lobby, he skidded to a stop. In a small room opening on this, two Kraoka were talking. One was armed and brassarded, an invader. The other was Quillipup. They froze.

"Greetings," said the liaison agent after a pause. "What brings you here?"

"I want to see your boss," Falkayn answered.

"I believe he is asleep," Quillipup said.

"Too bad." Falkayn started down the hall.

"Stop!" Quillipup bounded after him. "I told you he is asleep."

"And I told you it's a pity he has to be wakened," Falkayn rapped.

Quillipup regarded him. Her dorsal fin rose. The Antoranite glided close behind, hand not far from blaster.

"What have you to say which is so urgent?" Quillipup asked slowly.

Falkayn gave her eyeball for eyeball and responded, "What's so urgent for you, that it can't wait till Beljagor has risen?"

Silence, under the icy white light. Falkayn grew aware of blood pounding in his ears. His skin prickled. That energy gun looked too businesslike for his taste.

But Quillipup turned on her heel, without a word, and led her companion back to the office. Falkayn let out a hardheld breath and continued on his way.

He hadn't been told where in the building the factor lived, but the layout of places like this was pretty standardized. The suite door was locked. He buzzed. Nothing happened. He buzzed again.

The scanner must have a screen in the bedroom, because the voice from the annunciator rasped, "You! Do you suppose I'd get up for a pestilential human?"

"Yes," Falkayn said. "Urgent."

"Urgent that you jump off the nearest cliff, right. And a bad night to you." The speaker clicked off.

That adjective "urgent" was being overworked, Falkayn decided. He leaned on the buzzer.

"Stop your infernal racket!" howled Beljagor.

"Sure, when you let me in," Falkayn said.

Click.

Falkayn whistled "The Blue Danube" to pass the time while he leaned on the buzzer.

The door flew open. Beljagor bounced forth. Falkayn was interested to note that the Jaleelan slept in pajamas, bright purple ones. "You insolent whelp!" the factor bawled. "Get out of here!"

"Yes, sir," Falkayn said. "You come, too."

"What?"

"I have to show you something in my spaceboat."

Beljagor's eyes turned red. His tendrils stood erect. He drank air until his small round form seemed ready to explode.

"Please, sir," Falkayn begged. "You've got to. It's terribly important."

Beljagor cursed and swung a fist.

Falkayn sidestepped the blow, picked up the Master Merchant by collar and trousers, and bore him kicking and yelling down the hall. "I told you you had to come," the journeyman said patiently.

The two Kraoka in the lobby had left, and those on sentry-go at the warship made no move to interfere. Maybe, behind furry poker faces, they enjoyed the sight. Falkayn had left the gangway ramp extruded from his speedster but had put a recognition lock on the entrance. It opened for him. He carried Beljagor inside, set him down, and waited for the storm to break.

The Jaleelan spoke no word, only looked at him. His snout quivered a little.

"O.K.," Falkayn sighed. "You don't accept my apologies. You'll have my certificate revoked. You'll strangle me with my own guts. Anything else?"

"I suppose you have an explanation," Beljagor said like fingernails going quite slowly over a blackboard.

"Yes, sir. The business won't wait. And I didn't dare speak any place but here. Your Quillipup is acting far too friendly with the self-appointed liberators. Be no trick for her to bug your quarters."

What ozone had come in with them—less than by day—must have been processed into oxygen by now. Falkayn slipped off his filter mask. Beljagor mumbled something about Earth-type atmosphere, otherwise, the factor had cooled off astonishingly fast. "Talk, cub," he ordered.

"You see," Falkayn said, "I know where Antoran is."

"Heh?" Beljagor jumped several centimeters in the pilot chair he occupied.

"They'd never let me go if they found out I know," Falkayn continued. He leaned back against a bulkhead. His gaze drifted beyond the viewports. Both moons had set, and Beta Centauri ruled heaven. "As is, you'll have to come, too."

"What? Impossible! If you think I'll abandon the property of General Motors to a gang of pirates—"

"They'll doubtless send you packing before long in any event," Falkayn said. "Admit that. You just hate to surrender. But we've got to take the bull by the tail and look the situation squarely in the face."

"What do you mean, you know where Antoran is?" Beljagor spluttered. "Did you swallow something the Horn creature told you for a joke?"

"No, sir, she didn't intend to give me any information. Only, well, she was raised in an isolated, dedicated, Spartan society. She wasn't equipped to handle me." Falkayn grinned. "Figuratively, I mean, not literally. Her fellows didn't allow for the effects of alcohol and smooth talk. Not used to such things themselves, I imagine. Could be they also counted on my being so overbowled by her looks that I'd merely gawk and listen to her. They seem to be a very romantic bunch. Dangerous as hell, but romantic."

"Well? Well? What did Horn say?"

"Little items. They gave the show away, though. Like, Antoran isn't a planet but a star. And just one star hereabouts can possibly fit the data." Falkayn let Beljagor rumble for a moment before he pointed skyward and said, "Beta Centauri."

The factor did explode. He hopped around the cabin, flapping his arms and raving. Falkayn filed the choicer epithets in his memory for later use.

At last Beljagor was sufficiently calm to stand in one spot, raise a finger, and say, "You unutterable imbecile, for your information, Beta is a type B blue giant. People knew, before space flight began, giant suns don't have planets. Angular momentum per unit mass proved as much. After the hyperdrive came along, direct expeditions to any number of them clinched the matter. Even supposing, somehow, one did acquire satellites, those satellites never would get habitable. Giant stars burn hydrogen so fast their existence is measured in millions of years. Millions, you hear, not billions. Beta Centauri can hardly be ten million years old. More than half its stable lifetime is past. It'll go supernova and become a white dwarf. Life'd have no chance to evolve before the planets were destroyed. Not that there are any, I repeat. The reason for only the smaller suns having planets is understood. A big protostar, condensing from the interstellar medium. develops too intense a gravitational field for the secondary condensation process to take place outside it.

"I thought even humans learned so much elementary astrophysics in the first grade of school. I was wrong. Now you know."

His voice rose to a scream. *"And for this you got me out of bed!"*

Falkayn moved to block the cabin exit. "But I do know," he said. "Everybody does. The Antoranites have based their whole strategy on our preconception. They figure by the time we discover Beta Centauri is a freak case, they'll control the whole region."

Beljagor hurled himself back into the pilot chair, folded his arms, and grated, "Well, get the farce over with, since you must."

"Here are the facts," Falkayn said. He ticked them off. "One, the Antoranite System was colonized by Kraoka, who couldn't and didn't settle on planets with suns as cool as Sol. Two, Antoran has six planets in the liquid-water zone. No matter how you arrange their orbits, that zone has to be mighty broad—which indicates a correspondingly luminous star. Three, the outermost of those six planets is too cold and weakly irradiated for Kraokan comfort. but suits humans fairly well. Yet it has brilliant auroras even in the temperate zones. For that, you need a sun which shoots out some terrifically energetic particles: again, a giant.

"Four, this human planet, Neuheim, is far out. The proof lies in three separate facts. (a) From Neuheim, the sun doesn't have a naked-eye disk. (b) There are no solar tides worth mentioning. (c) The year is long. I figure something like two Earth centuries. I know the year is long, because Jutta let slip that her people had to shift some towns poleward a while back. Orbital eccentricity was making the lower latitudes too hot, maybe also too much UV was penetrating the ozone layer in those parts and making poisonous concentrations of ozone at the surface, like here. Nevertheless, the original human settlement was forty years ago. In other words, Neuheim's radius vector changes at so leisurely a rate that it was worth settling down in areas which the colonists knew would have to be abandoned later. I suppose they wanted to exploit local minerals.

"O.K. In spite of its enormous distance from the primary, Neuheim *is* habitable, if you don't mind getting a deep suntan. What kind of star can buck the inverse-square law on so grand a scale? What but a blue giant! And Beta Centauri is the only blue giant close by."

He stopped, hoarse and in need of beer. Beljagor sat like a graven image, assuming that anybody would want to grave such an image, while the minutes stretched. A space boat whined overhead, an enemy craft on an unknown errand.

Finally, tonelessly, Beljagor asked, "How could there be planets?"

"I've worked that out," Falkayn replied. "A freak, as I remarked before, perhaps the only case in the universe, but still possible. The star captured a mess of rogue planets."

"Nonsense. Single bodies can't make captures." But Beljagor didn't yell his objection.

"Granted. Here's what must have happened. Beta was condensing, with a massive nucleus already but maybe half its mass still spread over God knows how. many astronomical units, as a nebular cloud. A cluster of rogue planets passed through. Beta's gravity field swung them around. But because of friction with the nebula, they didn't recede into space again. Energy loss, you see, converting hyperbolic orbits into elliptical ones. Could be that there was also a secondary center of stellar condensation, which later spiraled into the main mass. Two bodies can certainly make captures. But I think friction alone would serve.

"The elliptical orbits were almighty eccentric, of course. Friction smoothed them out some. But Jutta admitted that to this day the planets have paths eccentric enough to cause weather trouble. Which is not the normal case either, you recall. Makes another clue for us."

"Hm-m-m." Beljagor tugged his nose and pondered.

"The planets would've exuded gases and water vapor in the early stages of their existence, through vulcanism, like any other substellar globes," Falkayn plowed on. "The stuff froze in space. But Beta unfroze it.

"I don't know how the Kraoka of Dzua learned what the situation was. Maybe they simply didn't know that blue giants don't have planets. Or maybe they sent a telemetric probe for astrophysical research, and it informed them. Anyhow, they discovered Beta had five potentially good worlds plus one that was marginal for them. So they colonized. Sure, the planets were sterile, with poisonous atmospheres. But the ancient Kraoka were whizzes at environmental engineering. You can sketch for yourself what they did: seeded the air with photosynthetic forms of life to consume the primeval organic matter and form the basis of an ecology, *et cetera*. Under those conditions, microbes would multiply exponentially, and it'd take no more than a few centuries for a world to become habitable."

Falkayn shrugged. "Beta will blow up and destroy their work in five or ten million years," he finished. "But that's ample time for anyone, hey?"

"Yes," Beljagor said low.

He raised his head, looked directly at the man, and said, "If this be true, we've got to tell the League. A war fleet that went straight to Beta should catch the enemy by complete surprise. Once the home planets were hostage to us, obviously there'd be no fighting."

"Uh-huh." Falkayn suppressed a yawn. Weariness was beginning to overtake him.

"But this is only a hypothesis," Beljagor said. "Your evidence is all hearsay. Horn could've been putting you on. The League can't base a whole operation on an idea which may turn out wrong. That'd be ruinous. We need positive proof."

"Right," Falkayn nodded. "So we'll both go, in our separate boats. You can easily make some excuse for having changed your mind about staying here. They won't suspect a thing if you throw a temper tantrum and storm off into space."

Beljagor grew rigid. "What are you saying? I'm the most patient, considerate entity in this cosmos."

"Huh?"

"When I think of what I have to put up with, impertinence like yours, stupidity, greed, thievishness, lack of appreciation—" Beljagor's tone mounted to a dull roar. Falkayn smothered a second yawn.

"Well, no matter now," said the factor as a coda. "I'll think of something. What do you propose after we take off?"

"We'll start ostensibly for HQ," Falkayn said. "Once we're out of detector range, we'll head toward Beta. We'll stop at a safe distance. You wait. I'll run in close to the star and make observations. Then I'll come back to you and we really will skite for home and mother."

"Why the separate excursion?"

"I might get caught. In that case—if I haven't rejoined you by the agreed time—you can tell the League what we do know and suggest they investigate Beta themselves."

"Hm-m-m. Ha. Correct. But why do you volunteer for the dangerous part? I doubt that you're competent."

"Sir," Falkayn said tiredly, "I may be young, but I can handle instruments. This speedster is built for humans—you couldn't operate her efficiently—and she's better adapted to a quick job of spying than your craft. So I'm elected. Besides," he added, "if I get clobbered, I'm a mere journeyman, a human at that. You're a Master Merchant from Jaleel."

His sarcasm went to waste. Beljagor sprang erect with tears starting from his porcine eyes. "Right!" he cried, choked by emotion. "How noble of you to admit it!" He wrung Falkayn's hand. "Please don't think badly of me. I may be loud now and then—I may talk rough when my patience wears thin—but believe me, I've got no prejudice against your race. Humans have fine qualities. Why, some of my best friends are human!"

Danger began about one lightyear from goal: the distance within which the instantaneous space-time pulses emitted by a vessel in hyperdrive are detectable. Beljagor's boat lay outside that radius, her own detectors wide open. Not that there was any measurable chance of a speck like her being found by accident. Falkayn would have trouble enough making rendezvous, knowing her location. But, if Beljagor observed the "wake" of another ship, he would be careful not to start his own secondary engines until the stranger was safely remote again.

Falkayn had no like choice. At full quasi-speed, he drove straight for Beta Centauri.

The sun grew and grew before him. Under magnification, he could see the disk, seething with nuclear storms, raging with billion-kilometer prominences, hell-blue and terrible. Eleven times the mass of Sol; fourteen hundred times the luminosity; across a full hundred and ninety light-years, one of the brightest stars in Earth's sky. He tried to whistle a tune, but the sound was too small and scared.

Inward. Inward. Now he could start the cameras. Photographing the viewscreens, which compensated for aberration and Doppler effect, they pictured a stable background of constellations. Planets, though, registered as meteorite streaks—yes, here! Falkayn changed course and repeated his observations. Before long he had the triangulation data to feed his computer.

He'd only spotted a few of the captured worlds, not all of them possible habitations. What he had was sufficient, however, especially when one turned out to be approximately thirty-seven astronomical units from the sun, the right distance and the right diameter for Neuheim. And, uh-huh, his detectors showed hypervibrations crisscrossing local space, comings and goings among the stars.

One indication was too near for his liking, and getting nearer. A patrol craft must have sniffed his trail and be on her way to investigate. Well, she'd have to be fiendishly fast to catch this little beauty of his!

She was.

As he fled spaceward, Falkayn watched the intensity readings creep higher. He scowled, puffed his pipe, and figured. He could rendezvous with Beljagor before he was overhauled, but then the Antoranite would be within a light-year of them, and get a fix on both.

Well, they could separate...

A second needle flickered on the detector panel. Falkayn said bad words. Another ship was closing in. Extrapolating directions and rates of amplitude increase, he found that Number Two couldn't run him down—but could snag Beljagor's ambling Holbert.

So. The thing to do was switch off the secondaries and lie doggo, hidden by the sheer vastness of space... Uh-uh. If those fellows knew their business, they'd identify the point where he stopped—at this range—within several million kilometers. They'd also go sublight, and home on the neutrino emission of his power plant. Or simply finger him with a radar sweep.

"Brother," Falkayn told himself, "you've had it, with pineapples."

He looked into the glory which was space, sun after sun until suns grew so thick that they melted into the great argent flood of the Milky Way. He remembered how light is trapped in the leaves of a wind-tossed tree; and how good the beer had tasted in a funny little Swiss tavern; and how often he had laughed among friends; and he sensed an utter lack of ambition to be a hero.

Don't irritate them. Surrender. Otherwise they'll phase in to your hyperjump frequency and put a warhead between your ears.

Beljagor could still report to the League, after the enemy had returned home. Of course, then he'd have no confirmation of Beta Centauri's nature. Falkayn's not showing up was inadequate proof, when he could have come to grief in any number of ways. So the League must send spies of its own, who would also be detected. Using ultrafast ships, they'd get away, but the enemy would be alerted and would mount strong guard on his home country. If war then came, it would be more savage than one dared think about, whole planets might be incinerated, Jutta be blown to incandescent gas, Falkayn himself... Judas!

Why wasn't there faster-than-light radio, so he could beam a message to the factor before he must stop? Damn the laws of physics!

The boat hummed and quivered with driving energies. Falkayn was maddeningly aware of thirst, an itch between his shoulderblades, a need for a haircut. This was no time to be human. *Think, blast you.*

He couldn't. He prowled the cabin, smoked his tongue leathery, forced down a plateful of rations, and came back to gloom at the detectors. Until finally he said, "To hell with this," killed his last bottle of booze and went to sleep.

He awoke some hours later, and there was his solution. For a while he lay staring at the overhead, awed by his genius. But according to computation, he'd soon reach Beljagor. Which meant he was in detection range right now, and the Jaleelan was certainly cursing a Beta-colored streak as he watched his own instruments. He'd not be asleep under these circumstances—not him.

"No time like the present," Falkayn said, thus proving his originality had limits. He sprang from his bunk and started scribbling notes.

"O.K., chum." He settled into the pilot chair.

Switch off the secondaries and go sublight. One minute later, switch them back on. Thirty seconds later, off again. One minute later, on again.

Polesotechnic pulse code. The needles of whichever detectors were tuned on him must be jumping back and forth, dash-dot-dash-dash-dot. HYPOTHESIS CONFIRMED. F. Repeat the cycle, to be sure Beljagor noticed. And again. Let him wonder if the F was anything but an initial. He'd get the rest of the idea, which was all that mattered. God willing, the Antoranites would not; this particular code was kept secret.

The engines began objecting to abuse. Falkayn whiffed scorched insulation and heard an ominous whine in the power hum. He switched vectors, taking off at a sharp angle to his former path, and drove steadily.

Arithmetic showed that when Enemy Number One pulled alongside him, they'd be well over a light-year from Beljagor. So would Enemy Number Two, who was obligingly coming about also. Falkayn left the board on automatic, showered, dressed in his fanciest clothes, and fixed a leisurely breakfast.

Next he destroyed his photographs, registry, route papers, and certain parts of his log, and did an artistic job of forging substitutes. League vessels are equipped for a variety of emergencies.

The Antoranite hove close, a Comet class with wicked-looking guns. Her probe light flashed the command to halt. Falkayn obeyed. The other went sublight likewise, matched kinetic velocities, and lay at a cautious distance. The radio buzzed. Falkayn accepted.

A long-jawed human officer type with a chestful of ribbons glared from the screen. "Hello," Falkayn said. "Do you speak Anglic or Latin?"

"*Ja,*" said the man. He picked the former. "Yourself identify."

"PL speedster *Greased Lightning* out of Tricorn for Hopewell, journeyman, Sebastian Tombs aboard solo. And who might you be?"

"Neuheim warship *Graf Helmuth Karl Bernhard von Moltke,* Landholder Otto von Lichtenberg commanding, *Oberleutnant* Walter Schmitt speaking."

"Neuheim? Where the devil is Neuheim? Never heard of it."

"Vot iss your purpose? Vy haff you tried to escape?"

"My purpose," Falkayn said, "is a trip from my post on Tricorn to ask for some emergency supplies from the Polesotechnic station on Hopewell. We had a flood and it rather messed us up. As for why I ran from you, when strangers start chasing a fellow, what do you expect him to do?"

"You assumed ve vas unfriendly," Schmitt said, more in anger than in sorrow. "Maybe you iss unfriendly to us, ha?"

"No, ha. If you consult your navigation tables, you'll find Beta Centauri is almost directly between Tricorn and Hopewell. And I was bound for Hopewell, instead of some closer post, because Hopewell is the nearest planet where I can be sure of getting the stuff we need. Zipping past Beta, I noticed a roughness in the engines." It was there yet, thanks to his using them for a radio. "To check the vector control, I changed course a few times, as you probably noticed. Then all at once, *whoosh,* here I detected a ship headed for me where no ship ought to be. Perhaps you were a harmless scientific expedition, anxious for a gabfest. But I wasn't about to chance it. Pirates do exist, you know. I skedaddled. My engines began spontaneously popping in and out of secondary. I got the Lauritzens fixed and tried a change of course, hoping you'd understand I didn't want company and leave me alone. No luck. So here we are."

Falkayn donned an indignant look and pounded the pilot board. "Seems like you're the one who has explaining to do," he barked. "What is this Neuheim comedy? Why are warships hanging around a blue giant? What's the idea, taking off after a harmless passerby? The Polesotechnic League is going to hear about this!"

"Perhaps," said Schmitt. "Shtand by to be boarded."

"Damnation, you certainly have no right—"

"Ve haff several nuclear cannon zeroed on you. Giffs t'at a right?"

"It does," Falkayn sighed.

He cooperated in linking air locks by a gangtube. Schmitt entered with a squad, who pointed their rifles at him, and demanded to see his papers.

Presently: "Fery vell, Herr Tombs. Might be you are honest. I do not know. Ve haff our orders. It vill be necessary to intern you on Neuheim."

"What?" Falkayn bellowed. He held his breath till he turned scarlet and his eyes popped. "Do you realize who I am? I'm a certified member of the Polesotechnic League!"

"Too bad for you," Schmitt said. "Come along." He grabbed Falkayn's wrist.

Falkayn yanked it back, drew himself straight, and blessed his father for teaching him the proper mannerisms. "Sir," he said, and liquid helium dripped from every word, "if I am to be a prisoner, I protest the illegality but I must yield. Nevertheless, there is such a thing as the laws of war. Furthermore, I am heir apparent to the Barony of Dragonshaw, United Kingdom of New Asia and Radagach. You will treat me with the respect according to my station!"

Schmitt paled. He clicked his heels, bowed, and followed with a salute. *"Jawohl, mein Herr,"* he gasped. "I beg for your most gracious pardon. If you had seen fit to tell me more earlier—Landholder von Lichtenberg vill be reqvesting t'e honor uff your pressence at tea."

Schloss Graustein was not the worst place in the cosmos to be a prisoner. Though gaunt and drafty on its high ridge, it was surrounded by forests where the hunting was excellent. The food was heavy but edible, and the local beer superb. Landholder Graustein did his best to make the distinguished, if compulsory, guest feel at home. During long conversations and occasional guided tours of the planet, Falkayn spotted interesting commercial opportunities, once the region had been pacified.

Unless—He didn't want to contemplate the alternative. And after some weeks, time began to hang as leaden as the *knackwurst*.

Thus Falkayn was quite happy when a servant knocked at the door of his suite and announced a visitor. But then she stepped through. He had never thought she would be an unwelcome sight.

"Jutta," he whispered.

She closed the door behind her. Dark wood and granite panels framed her where she stood vivid under the fluorolight. She was in mufti, and if he had thought her beautiful when uniformed, he must now multiply by an astronomical factor.

"So it is indeed you," she said.

"P-p-please sit down," he managed.

She remained standing. Her features were stony, her voice flat. "Those idiots took for granted you were what you claimed, a merchant who simply chanced to pass by and saw too much. They never interrogated you in depth, never notified the fleet command. I only heard of you yesterday, in conversation with Landholder von Lichtenberg, after I came home on leave. The description—" Words trailed off.

Falkayn rallied his courage. "A stratagem of war, my dear," he said gently.

"What have you done?"

He told his pulse to decelerate, took out his pipe, and made a production of loading and kindling it. "You can squirt me full of babble juice, so I might as well Tell All," he smiled. "I guessed the truth and went for a look to make certain."

"That funny little being who left about the same time as you did…he knew?"

Falkayn nodded. "He's reported to HQ long ago. If the League is half as realistic as I think, a battle fleet you can't hope to resist is on its way right now."

She clenched one hand over another. Tears stood in her eyes. "What follows?"

"They should head straight here. I expect them any day. You've nothing in the Beta System except a few patrollers; the rest of your navy is spread over a dozen stars. Right? The League doesn't want to bombard planets, but in the case—" She uttered anguish. He went quickly to her, took both those hands, and said, "No, no. *Realpolitik,* remember? The object of war is not to destroy the enemy but to impose your will on him. Why should we kill people that we might sell things to? We'll simply take the Beta System prisoner, and then bargain about its release.

"I don't make policy, but I can predict what'll happen. The League will demand you disband your armed forces, down to a normal defense level. And, naturally, we'll want to keep our trade concessions. But that's all. Now that some Kraoka have starships, they can go ahead and unify, as long as they do it peacefully. We'd hoped to sell them a cargo and passenger fleet, at a huge markup, but that hope isn't worth fighting for—you do have bargaining power yourselves, in your own capabilities for making trouble, you know. Neuheim can keep any social order it wants. Why not? If you try to maintain this wretched autarchy, you'll be depriving yourselves of so much that inside of ten years your people will throw out the Landholders and yell for us."

He chucked her under the chin. "I understand," he said. "It's tough when a dream dies. But why should you, your whole life, carry your father's grudges?"

She surrendered to tears. He consoled her, and a private hope began to grow in him.

Not that he was in the market for a wife. Judas! At his age? However—

Afterward they found themselves on the balcony. Night had fallen, the auroral night where vast banners shook red and green across the sky, dimming the stars, and the mountain swooped down to a forest which breathed strange sweet odors back upward. Wine glasses were in their hands, and she stood close to him.

"You can report who I am," he said, "and cause me to have an unpleasant time, maybe even be shot." Pale in the shuddering light, her face lost its look of happiness and he heard the breath suck between her teeth. "Your duty, according to the articles of war," he continued. "And it won't make one bit of difference, it'll be too late—except that the League protects its own and will take a stiff price for me."

"What choice have I?" she pleaded.

He flashed a well-rehearsed grin. "Why, to keep your lovely mouth shut, tell everybody you were mistaken and Sebastian Tombs has nothing to do with that Falkayn character. When peace comes—well, you're quite influential on this planet. You could do a lot to help your people adjust."

"And become merchants?" she said, in a dying flare of scorn.

"I remarked once," he said, "that we aren't really so ignoble. We're after a profit, yes. But even a knight must eat, and *our* bread doesn't come from slaves or serfs or anyone who had to be killed. Look beyond those lights. They're fine, sure, but how about the stars on the other side?"

She caught his arm. He murmured, as best he could in Latin, "*Thy merchants chase the morning down the sea...*" and when she turned questioning to him he added, low in the dusk,

> *Their topmasts gilt by sunset, though their sails be whipped to rags,*
> *Who raced the wind around the world go reeling home again,*
> *With ivory, apes, and peacocks loaded, memories and brags,*
> *To sell for this high profit: knowing fully they are Men!*

"Oh-h-h," he heard.

And to think he'd resented his schoolmasters, when he was a kid on Hermes, making him read Flecker and Sanders in the original.

"I will not tell anyone," she said. And: "May I stay here for a while?"

Falkayn was downright regretful a week later, when the League fleet arrived to rescue him.

Mustn't Touch

There got to be too much knowledge; and more kept pouring in. The fusion of disciplines helped for a while. But soon a biophysicist, say, found his head so full of quantum mechanics and advanced stochastics that he couldn't follow the newest revisions of unified field theory, though he knew in a vague way that eventually some aspects were bound to impinge on his own work. Cybernetic information retrieval made anything quickly available to him—but how could he know just what to look up? The development of creatively synthesizing robot brains—a poor term, but "computer" is even less accurate—was helpful; nevertheless, their own capacity, while large, was finite, and in any case a man had to decide what assignment to give them. He couldn't always be sure, or even guess what general type of problem he ought to foresee.

The story goes that in the very earliest days of astronautics, an engineer in a manned-capsule project asked the physiologist on the team how much dissolved material it was necessary to remove from urine in order to reclaim potable water. "All of it," the physiologist replied, "if you want to stay friends with your astronaut." Raise that communication barrier by several orders of magnitude, and you will appreciate the dilemma that evolved.

Until one day—

Luna had fallen behind. The forward viewscreens held only blackness and stars. *Job* moved through space like a whale through the sea, as quietly and smoothly. There was no sound in Emil Eide's cabin other than the hum of a ventilator, the occasional clicking of a switch or relay. Acceleration pressed him into his seat, so gently that he felt buoyant, almost young again.

But his eyes were tired. He racked away the copy of *Scientific American* he had been studying. It was dated several years ago, he had read the lead article before, had simply wanted to refresh his memory. Not that it could tell him much. The magazine had tried valiantly to give a responsible account of the theory behind faster-than-light drive, but you had to be a matrix physicist really to understand.

He rubbed his eyes and rested them with a long look at infinity. So many were the ice-sharp points of light out there that the constellations were drowned. Not to him, of course, with the experience of his youth to guide him. Even after three decades Earthside, he could pick out Orion and the Hounds, the Wain and the Dragon. But it came back to him, suddenly and startlingly, that each of those stars was a sun.

When the ships began to fare yonder, soon now—A couple of lines ran through his head.

> *Bliss was it in that dawn to be alive,*
> *But to be young was very heaven!*

Well, he thought, he had had his own dawn. Noontime, anyhow, while the last bodies in the Solar System that could possibly be colonized were being made ready. His work hadn't been entirely in the lab, either, on the biotechnic problems. Shorthanded as the crews were, he'd often been out with a bullmole; and the preliminary surveys had involved some rough expeditions. There was a sense of fellowship at the end of such a day, the like of which could no longer be found on poor crowded Earth.

To strike out afoot beneath a new sun, clean air and a living landscape—*Ah, stop sniveling, you old idiot. You can always listen to the stories the young men bring back. Besides, you've been handed a share in the enterprise, right here and now.*

He felt an obscure guilt about that. Dow's unexpected death was the reason why Oslo University's professor of bionics had been co-opted into Project Cosmos. Experts in that particular field were so rare, and there was so much eagerness to go ahead with the work, that Eide's briefings were short and he had boarded *Job* with less information than he really ought to have had. *Well, Dow, you were a good man, God rest you—*

He got out his pipe and stuffed it with fingers that were still scarred and big-knuckled. *"Job,"* he said aloud.

"Yes?" said the ship.

"Are you too busy to talk?"

"No." The voice from the cabin speaker had inflections, but no real tone like a man's. There was a faint brazen ring to it. "This is an entirely routine interception curve."

"When will we get there?"

"We will have matched velocities and made contact in another eighteen minutes. Loading the probe aboard should take less than ten minutes. But as for the various tests to be made, at present there is insufficient data for prediction."

The flatness irritated Eide. "Damnation, aren't you excited at all?" he grumbled. "I could wonder if transistors and mesoducers and the rest of robot circuitry ever feel any emotion—No, don't comment." His annoyance faded out. "I'm well aware that an emotion is the perception of a drive in action, and you have drives. Just not my kind. What I really wonder is how it feels to be you."

"There is an extensive literature on robopsychology," *Job* said.

"I know. I've read some. All behavioristic. No use to me."

"Technically your statement is incorrect."

"Never mind technicalities. Behaviorism is what it amounts to. Pure description, from the outside only. We can't get inside our own creations." Eide noticed that his pipe was yet unlit, and flicked a torchie to its bowl. "Ah, well," he said, "I daresay you feel the same way about me, if you ever bother to wonder. And is that intrinsically any different from the way my children and I felt about each other, when they were growing up? There was always a strangeness between us, no matter how much we wanted to bridge it."

Job did not answer. Eide sighed. He'd been attempting to make amends for his outburst. When he remembered, he tried harder than the average person to treat robots courteously. After all, they were rational, conscious beings. However often he was told that they didn't mind their situation, that it was perfectly satisfactory to them in so far as "satisfactory," or any human-emotional word, meant anything in that connection—he could not quite get rid of an uneasy feeling that he was a slavemaster. But his attitude never seemed to affect their responses to him, one way or another.

"Well," he said inanely, "I think I'll go forward." He rose, a short, thick, gnarly man, face gnomish under a ruff of gray hair, clothes a trifle rumpled and shabby. *Job* opened the cabin door for him and he moved along the corridor with the dreamlike ease of low-weight.

Bill Villiers and Dave Urban, the Australians, were seated with spaceman's bombillas of tea in the main observation verandah. Besides Eide, they were the only men aboard. And none were really needed. The laboratory ship could do everything—recover the probe, transcribe data from the instruments, observe and dissect and analyze the living specimens, draw conclusions, prepare a formal report— with electronic speed. But it wasn't psychologically possible for the people at Cosmos' Lunar base to send no representatives. Their presence was justified on the grounds that something unforeseen might arise and men would be needed to make quick executive decisions. Eide suspected that was mere rationalization.

Nonetheless he was glad, with a deep quiet happiness, to be here.

"Hullo, cobber," said Villiers. "Come to watch the show at last?" He was an assistant director of the engineering section, a long lean man given to loud shirts and baggy trousers. "You do take your work seriously." He told the servitor to bring another bombilla.

"Doesn't everyone?" Eide replied, finding a seat for himself. "I know there has been much public complaint at the slowness of progress, but I think Canberra appointed a crew of beavers. Colbert's equations were published only ten years ago, Otway made the first experimental demonstrations three years later, and in a bare five years of work on Luna, you have produced FTL probes. Whoof!"

Villiers chuckled. "Actually," he said, "Otway could have made his breakthrough far sooner, if he'd known about Huang's theory of the relationship of hyperons and gravity currents. But the connection between that and Colbert's equations wasn't obvious enough."

Eide laughed back. "How familiar that sounds! I wasted sixteen months once, working on the genetic code, finding out what I was after in the hardest possible way. And all the time my results were implicit in the Wavicle Theorem—as several biophysicists pointed out with glee as soon as I had published."

"Genetic code?" Urban, medium-sized and blond, looked surprised. He was a biologist himself, though his competence was elsewhere than the submolar level on which Eide worked. "But that was cracked more than a century ago."

"This was a question about its nature," the Norwegian said. "Almost a philosophical question, though the answer is empirically verifiable. You see, it's been known for a long time that the code is the same for every form of life. So either it's not subject to mutation—which doesn't make sense—or there are certain constraints on how an amino acid can pair with a codon on an RNA molecule. But in the latter case, what are the constraints? Well, that's equivalent to asking how the code-reading mechanism works, not just in a chemical sense but as a function of natural law."

Urban shook his head and clicked his tongue: "Fascinating. I never knew before, and I thought I kept up with the field rather well. Just goes to show you, eh?" He paused. "Er...wait a bit. D'you mean that life everywhere in the universe has to use the same code?"

"N-no. We aren't sure about that. I suspect not, but we don't know what the permissible variations are. That's one of the things I hope your starships will come back and tell us."

"Yeih," Villiers drawled. "Which is why the scientists have been on the Authority's back, wanting the project hurried beyond all reason. Impatient to know. There was quite a tussle last year, when we were readying the first instrumented probes. One faction wanted them sent immediately to the nearer stars. We resisted, though. Haste makes waste. We're still a long ways from itemizing every property of warped space."

"Besides," Urban added, "unmanned probes can furnish just enough information to tantalize the hell out of us. We'll send them in advance of the first manned expeditions, naturally—but the men are what we're really counting on."

"And who are counting on you," Eide said quietly.

Villiers blinked. "What? Oh, you mean colonization."

"Well, yes, in part." Eide's mind went back to Earth: too many people, no more wilderness, no escape from your fellow man, individuality strangling in an unavoidable web of law and regulation. Crowding wouldn't increase forever, probably. Put rats in a cage and let them reproduce for a while. Though you feed them well, the overpopulation soon makes them so neurotic that their breeding rate nosedives. He didn't like to think of his grandchildren growing up misanthropic agoraphobes.

As an alternative, you could put the brakes on in time, reduce the numbers of mankind step by step to a reasonable level, finally stabilize birth and death...what a fine, manicured, smug, ingrown future that was!

He struck the bulkhead with a balled fist. Urban started at the thud. "This project will succeed," Eide said, "because it's got to."

"I say, you really do itch for adventure, don't you?" Villiers remarked. "Myself, I'm content to stay in the lab."

"I'm too old to go," Eide shrugged. "But my youngest son, he's the sort that really ought to have shipped out with Leif Erikson. And he's not unique."

"I know," Urban said. "Canberra is counting heavily on us. Not that interstellar emigration can reduce population pressure much at home; but social pressure, restlessness and discontent, that's something else again. Especially when we start feeling the impact of new knowledge about the universe. Bound to have strong effects on society, both direct and indirect."

Eide reached for his bombilla, which the servitor had been patiently holding out to him. He forgot it when Villiers yelled: "Look! There she is!"

The shape grew rapidly in the viewscreen, sharp across the Milky Way. Sunlight dazzled off its slender flank. There went a primitive tingle along Eide's nerves. That object had carried the first living creatures ever to go faster than light, from this orbit to Neptune's and back, in less than one minute.

The seat took a firm grip on him and *Job* shifted acceleration. The probe need not have waited this hour for rendezvous to be made. Its point of return was closely predictable. But the laboratory ship stood a ways off as a routine precaution. Warped space was an eerily new thing to deal with. There were even some cranks who preached that changing the constants of physics was a direct defiance of God. Well, they had said much the same about every fundamental advance; and people did in fact get hurt, by fire and domestic animals and steam engines and fusing atoms. Few physicists completely understood the Colbert-Otway Effect. There was too much else they had to understand.

The probe slipped out of sight as *Job* lay alongside. Acceleration ended. Villiers popped an anti-nausea pill into his mouth, but free fall didn't seem to bother Urban and Eide enjoyed it. The view flickered briefly: induced currents when the radiation screens of the two craft interacted. It steadied again. A quivering sounded through the hull, a series of clanks and a long rumble. Then silence drew a curtain between men and ship.

"Probe taken aboard," *Job* said at length. "If there are no contrary orders, I shall proceed at one-tenth gravity toward Luna. Weight will be useful in carrying out analyses, and that acceleration should allow ample time for the most important preliminary ones."

"Right-o," Villiers said.

The engine purred. Eide's body sank back into the seat cushions. He felt himself released, and bounced up. "Let's go!"

"Where?" Villiers asked.

"Doctrine is that no human shall approach the probe until I have verified that it is safe to do so," *Job* reminded them.

Urban grimaced. "Yes, yes, yes," he muttered. "But you needn't be so coldblooded about it. You tin brains give me the willies sometimes."

"Oh, do relax," Villiers said. "Why should he be emotionally concerned? This isn't his daydream."

Eide felt embarrassed. *Job* was listening. It occurred to him that Ultra Model Electroencephalon Mark IV, serial number such-and-such, was all too well nicknamed.

Villiers took a thoughtful drag at his bombilla. "Y'know," he went on, obviously trying to calm down the biologists—he was sure that the engineering aspect was O.K.—"we've talked for a long time now about making contact with alien races. But I wonder if we'll ever find any as alien as this one we've built ourselves."

"That's beside the point," Eide said. His own purpose was to change the subject. "What we'll gain from extraterrestrial civilizations, besides knowledge, is culture. New insights, new arts, new philosophies, new ways of living. We're getting stagnant now. I say nothing against the Australian Authority—war had to be eliminated somehow—but it isn't enough. Not if we wish to keep mental as well as physical frontiers."

Urban gnawed a knuckle, but managed to say, "True. Another reason, by the way, Eide, why we haven't sent probes to the stars yet. It'd delay development of a manned FTL ship. To understand what those races are about, what their cultures mean, we've got to have people actually living there, getting to know the intimate details, learning to think in extrahuman ways. Otherwise we'll just be collecting a slew of inferior travelogues."

"There's that," Villiers said. "Also, even in purely physical science, the fact is that instruments can only experience what they're designed to experience. You need a conscious being on hand, a being with imagination, who can see something totally unexpected and come back to describe—" Abruptly his own calm broke across. He set his bombilla down on the table so hard that it rattled. "What are we bandying cliches for?" he growled. "Hurry up, will you?"

"I have begun chemical tests," *Job* said. "But you must allow me some time yet to make certain that the environment is safe for you."

"*Hvad?*" Eide exclaimed. Fingers closed around his heart.

"The bacterial and protozoan cultures are dead. The higher plants and metazoans are dying."

The operations hold was vast and dim, but so crowded with instruments that men must walk carefully. Eide passed by a thing of tendrils and tubes which under *Job's* direction was placing a slide in an electron microscope. Just beyond, a centrifuge whirred, and colors crawled up a chromatograph. The fluorescent illumination felt cold on his skin.

The probe lay long and shining in its rack. One side was open and the biological specimens, such as had not been removed so far, were exposed to view. Urban had snatched a sample of algae, turned to brown scum in the past couple of hours, and put it under a microscope of his own. Eide brushed aside a pumpkin leaf—green and unwithered, but the needle on an attached biometer stood at zero—to look at a cageful of rats. Most lay unmoving. A couple of them still panted feebly. Even as Eide watched, one crawled to a water dispenser and drank again. Its belly was bloated. After a moment it gasped, shivered, and fell quiet.

A machine arm reached over Eide's shoulder, opened the cage, and hooked the body out. Wheels trundled. Turning, the bionicist saw the small furry shape popped into a revival chamber. A heart-lung device began to chug. His gaze went back to the other corpses. "You poor dumb devils," he murmured.

Villiers came to stand beside him. The engineer's face was locked into grimness. "I just checked the instrument records for myself," he said. "There is no difference from the probes we sent before. No difference whatsoever."

"Radiation?" Eide groped.

"No. That would have registered. Anything physical known to man would have."

"I thought...perhaps...when you go blasting through the hydrogen in space, faster than light—"

"Those atoms don't penetrate the drive field. The warp is equivalent to too great a potential barrier. You do get aerodynamic effects, which you have to allow for in plotting an orbit. But nothing from the outside universe can directly affect what happens inside the hull." Villiers jammed hands in pockets. "I also made a quick check of the power and pilot systems. As far as I went, it only confirmed *Job's* word that they functioned normally the whole time."

Urban joined them. "I can't find any structural alteration in the cells," he said. His voice fell flatly amidst the hummings and buzzings. "Oh, certain gross pathologies, but no clue to what produced them, nothing like the changes in structure that a virus makes, say. Well, *Job* will have to investigate the submolar details. He's doing that now...The beast is doing *everything*."

"That's what he is for," Eide said.

"But...our own helplessness!"

"We're no use here," Villiers said. "Let's go back."

"And keep on talking in circles?" Urban groaned.

"Not necessarily," Eide answered. "We should start getting some data to work with pretty soon." His feet dragged over the deck.

Job's voice pursued him: "Revival procedures have failed."

"What about the specimens in cold sleep?" Urban demanded.

"What's this?" Eide asked.

"Didn't you know?" Urban said. "We wanted to test that, too. Knocked 'em down close to absolute zero, at the usual speed with the usual drugs. The idea was that spaceship crews should have the equipment available in case of medical emergencies. Maybe cold sleep has inhibited whatever chemical change went on here."

"Come on," Villiers said. "Let's get cracking."

They went topside at a funeral pace and settled back into the verandah seats. Space blazed at them. The pockmarks on Luna were becoming visible.

"Well." Villiers lit a cigarette and drew a ragged puff into his lungs. "What about some tea?"

Eide looked straight at Sirius. *We're coming just the same*, he told it. He shook his shoulders and willed determination into himself.

"This seems to be in your line," Urban said to him tonelessly. "No apparent changes in cell structure. So what happened at a more basic level?"

Eide frowned, gathering his wits. "You must help me there," he said. "I have tried to understand how the spacewarper works, but I couldn't get much through this thick old noggin. What part of its operation might have biological effects?"

"Who knows?" Villiers said. "Theoretically, though, there shouldn't be any important ones."

"What about the minor ones? They may not be so little after all."

"Well, of course the alteration of natural constants is bound to have some influence on the chemistry and physics of an organism."

"Tell me very simply, please; how that works. I think I know, but I need to be sure."

"Tell you without math? Can't." Villiers recollected himself. "Sorry. You must have a fair background in math, for your own work." He reached for a notepad in his shirt pocket. "Uh, the equations—"

"No, no. I've seen them. What I mean is something like this. In modern physics, the laws of nature can be expressed as functions of space-time geometry. For instance, the frequency of emitted light, or of atomic vibration, is affected by the gravitational field, which in turn depends on—or is—the local warping of space. Likewise, the exact form of a particle's psi function, its probability-wave, is conditioned by geometry, by just what curve is locally a geodesic. Now the Colbert-Otway Effect involves the creation of some very peculiar warps indeed. Within the drive field of one of your interstellar probes, light has a different velocity and the mass-energy relationship takes on a new form. Thus speed is no longer limited by the velocity of light in 'flat' space. Am I correct?"

"You're not too far off," Villiers nodded.

"O.K., then, why does this not change the other constants of nature so much that nothing will work?"

"Because there are compensating effects. If one parameter, like dielectric constant, increases, a related one tends to decrease. And the warp is a good bit weaker inside the drive field than at the edge. Oh, we've had our problems. A NiCad battery rated at 1.35 volts delivers 1.42 while the probe is traveling. Photo film sensitivity drops from ASA 1200 to 970. That sort of thing. We had to design a tandem autocontrol, one set of computers to operate under normal drive, another under FTL. But each can feed its data directly into the other, so this still amounts to having only one system, using its 'right' or 'left' half as the need arises. It works fine, now."

"Ah," Eide pounced. "But biological systems are much more complicated—chemically, at least—than anything robotic."

As if on cue, *Job* said: "Analysis shows certain trace compounds in the cells studied. They are proteins, but do not appear to be identical with any described in my memory banks. It will take considerable time to establish their molecular structure. Do you wish me to defer that and proceed at once with the examination of the cold sleep specimens?"

"Yes, yes," Urban almost shouted.

"Wait," Eide said. Excitement fluttered in him. "How much of those proteins is there, quantitatively?"

"Micro quantities," *Job* answered. "I do not know how they were synthesized, but they do not appear sufficient to cause mortality, even if they are poisonous."

"Haven't you found anything else?"

"Further data on observed pathologies. You saw how thirsty the rats were, and how this led to edema. I am tracing out the chemistry of that metabolic imbalance. There appears to be some enzymatic abnormality involved. A full description will be prepared in due course." After a moment: "Despite every effort at treatment, the last metazoan has just died."

"Wasn't there any way to save them?" Villiers asked. His words came harsh and uneven.

Urban spoke an obscenity. "No," he said. "This ship has every kind of apparatus. The Prime Minister couldn't have gotten better care than those wretched animals."

Eide gloomed at the deck. "Let us get back to, um, the background," he said. "Could it simply be that no organism can survive the changes in physical constants under FTL? If, for instance, the rate at which neurones fire, or the oxygen tension, or any such thing, is altered too much—the organism dies."

"But the change isn't that great," Urban replied. "We made plenty of preliminary experiments, believe me. To take your own example, we reduced neural rates and oxygen tension, with drugs, away below what FTL would do; not to speak of pH, osmotic pressure, everything we could think of. No harm. Oh, on a prolonged trip there'd have to be certain precautions. Special diets and so forth. But no trip would be too long. In warped space, transit time between stars is only a few hours. The crew's health should be less affected than it was by weightlessness in the early days."

"And yet," Villiers breathed, "everything on the probe was effectively killed, within sixty seconds."

Eide lifted his eyes to the viewscreen once more. Earth gleamed at one edge. The sun was just rising over Europe.

"Wait a minute!" he said. "Clearly, under the conditions of FTL, some fundamental biological mechanism is deranged. The question is what, and what can we do about it? Now look, suppose some important molecules break up, or simply flip over into a different isomer—"

Urban shook his head violently. "No. We thought of that long ago, and checked it out. Impossible. The changes in relative energy potentials and so forth aren't enough to break any chemical bond that matters. Certainly not enough to alter atomic nuclei. My team even looked into the possibility of ordinarily random hookups acquiring a directedness, so that lethal compounds could be formed. It turned out to be a statistical absurdity." He raised his voice. "What's new, *Job*?"

"Configurational analysis has now been performed on several individual chromosomes," the ship reported. "None have been altered. Nor have ribosomes or any other fundamental structure."

"Hurry up in that cold sleep chamber!" Urban barked.

Villiers laid a warning hand over his.

Eide pulled at the mouthpiece of his bombilla. The tea was strong and scalding. It seemed to glow in his stomach. *This is a bad setback*, he told himself. *But man won't admit he has ever met an unsolvable problem. He can't.*

Yet the silence grew so dense that *Job's* eventual words came as if from a brass angel:

"I have resuscitated assorted specimens. They were alive at the time."

Villiers and Urban looked at each other. A flame went between their eyes. Eide grabbed the arms of his seat. The image of his youngest son flashed across the stars. *So you must go then sleeping, Olav. But go you shall.*

"The bacteria and protozoa died almost immediately," said the cool voice. "The higher plants and metazoans are still alive, but cells are beginning to exhibit the same pathologies as in the previous cases, progressing at a rate which indicates that these organisms will not survive under normal conditions longer than the others. Evidently cold sleep did not prevent the phenomenon but merely postponed its commencement."

Eide sprang to his feet. He began to pace, around and around the narrow circle of the verandah, not in a low-weight glide but with a stamp that shivered the deck.

"*Job*, what's doing it?" Villiers pleaded. "You were built to figure such things out. What's doing it?"

There was no prompt response. "Are you listening?" Villiers said with a rush of anger.

"Yes," the ship acknowledged. A man would have said, "Of course."

"Well, you're supposed to have creativity. Find us an explanation before I tear you apart!"

"I must gather all possible data before attempting to frame a hypothesis," *Job* said.

"But those new proteins—they had to come from somewhere," Villiers choked. "Isn't that a clue? What makes them?"

Eide stopped in his tracks.

He stood there, unmoving, for so long that the others got alarmed and scrambled erect. "Are you all right?" Urban said. "D'you want to lie down a while?"

Eide didn't answer. Urban came over and shook his arm.

Slowly, Eide turned to face them both. His features had changed from gnome to troll.

"I...believe...I...see." The words creaked out of him.

"What? What?"

"I think I have your explanation." Eide stumbled to his chair, sat down and buried his face in his hands.

"You mean—" Villiers began.

"*Hold mund!*" Eide yelled.

They lowered themselves, cautiously, back into their own seats, and watched him tremble.

When at length he looked up again, his eyes seemed blind. "The genetic code," he said, machine fashion.

"Eh?" Urban said. "You mean there's a mutation in the DNA? I just told you that can't be."

"No. In its function."

Eide reached for his pipe with unsteady hands, took out his tobacco pouch and began to fill the bowl. All the while he was staring past them, out at the stars.

"Consider," he said, in the same dead voice. "The DNA molecule of the chromosome has four bases, adenine, guanine, cytosine, and thymine. They make up a four-letter alphabet, whose different combinations each specify an amino acid. The code is transcribed onto a molecule of 'messenger' RNA and carried to the site of protein synthesis, each kind of amino acid being delivered by a particular form of 'transfer' RNA. There, then, proteins are synthesized: enzymes, which go on to control the entire chemistry of the organism. It is usually described as an information transfer mechanism."

Villiers and Urban exchanged a glance. *Has the old man gone dotty? We learned this in the second form.*

Eide ignored them, plowed on, talking to the sky: "But there are certain constraints on the code. You can write the same message in Latin or Greek or runic characters; or you can go over to Chinese and use an altogether different system which cannot ever carry quite the same messages. That's arbitrary. But the genetic code is not. Everywhere, in every life form we know, the same codon, the same sequence of bases, means the same amino acid. Why should this be? It isn't needed by information theory.

"I found out some time ago that it is required by the laws of nature. Given protoplasmic life, at least, no other system will work."

He fell still again. A relay clicked, a ventilator mumbled, the barren moon swelled in the viewscreen.

"Wait!" Urban half rose. He had gone quite pale. "You mean…the FTL field changes the laws of nature?"

"Yes. You told me it does." Eide began to wake up a little. He fumbled in a pocket for his torchie, and was awkward about getting his pipe lit. When at length he had the fire going, he smoked very hard, trying to warm the bowl. It would comfort his cold hands.

"With changed natural constants," he said, "with different laws of chemical interaction, the DNA code has to be different. It's affected far more than energy considerations alone would suggest. New enzymes are produced, to catalyze new reactions that the body isn't meant for; syntheses that it desperately needs don't take place. A unicellular organism dies almost at once. A multicellular one, having some reserves, can live for a while. Not long."

"But cold sleep should prevent that!" Urban protested wildly.

"No," Eide replied. Full consciousness was returning to him, with a sense of ultimate weariness. "You are still thinking just about the chemistry. But don't you see, the chemical changes, the strange compounds *Job* found, they are an epiphenomenon. What was really changed is the whole meaning of the genetic code. Imagine. A set of amino acids is about to be assembled. The FTL field comes on.

Now that set no longer *can* be made; but a different one, useless or poisonous, can be. Even under cold sleep, even at absolute zero, there is intramolecular activity, which sets the stage for the same thing to happen as soon as chemistry starts up again. The time in warped space required for this to be lethal turns out to be less than sixty seconds. Probably much less. You can't disrupt a process meant to be continuous, and then expect it to go ahead in the usual way as if nothing had happened."

He drew a deep breath, let it out slowly, and faced them head on. "No matter what you do," he said, "men will never ride one of your starships."

The stillness waxed until Eide's pipe began to burble. He blew into the mouthpiece, hoping to stop the cricket noise. His body felt heavy, as if already he had returned to Earth.

"That—" Villiers wet his lips. "I say, that's rather jumping to conclusions, isn't it?"

Job's voice said from the verandah speaker: "The hypothesis fits all my data thus far, and does not contradict any now being gathered. I assign it a high probability of being correct."

"But...never to go out there—" Urban whispered.

Villiers knotted his fists. "We can send mobile robots, at least," he said. "The tandem brain system. That would work."

"It would," said *Job* with a sound of triumph.

Elementary Mistake

Hello, Bellegarde! Hello, Earth. Hello, Universe. And to hell with you. Lind speaking. Squeaking. Reeking. Billy Lind. No, 's not dignified enough. Kin'ly call me th' late William J. Lind, sometime of West Newton, Chassamusetts, U.S.A., World Federation, planet Earth, star Sol, Milky Way galaxy...Does every schoolboy write that kin'a 'dress on his books? Not that I'm a schoolboy now. Wish I was...were?...yes, subjunctive, were. *Ay*-llow me t' in'erduce m'self. William J. Lind, officer and putative gentleman of the Space Service, Pioneer Division, electronician aboard *Widsith*, seated at our primary transmitter on the planet they named, in the best romantic tradition, Guinevere—you should hear what we call it—with a lot of big ugly mountains staring over my shoulder and making rude remarks.

Nope, wrong verb form again. I was sitting here. A thing we might's well call a bird was flopping above the mast, in a purplish sky. It had long sweptback wings, sort o' like our aircraft, and they glinted reddish green. Sun did that, big orange disk, and it tinted the clouds gold, and the snows on the peaks around this here now valley where we're parked. (See, if I watch my tongue, I can still pronounce words good, but believe me, 's not easy to watch your own tongue without a mirror.) The shadows were bluish red, too. But the smoke from yonder volcano, black, black...Where was I? Oh, yes. The proper grammar. Past tense. You won't hear me for nigh on five years. By then I'll be, all ten of us'll be one with the beers of yesteryear.

So fly up, little maser beam. Compute, little computer. Keep me locked onto that relay satellite. It'll buck my words on to Bellegarde. Won't it? Sure it will. It passed on the information that got us into this mess in the first place, didn't it? Mean to say, look here, you smug idiots on Bellegarde, on Durindal, on Frodo, on every planet the human race has reached so far—whoa, there, Lind. Save words. The satellite'll be under the horizon pretty soon. Minimize redundancy. Neologize. So: look here, you smidiots, I'm gonna 'splain'a you jus' wha' y' done t' us. An' you'll hafta sit'n listen. How y' gonna discipline me, then? Ha?

I...Shall...Speak...Carefully.

Widsith. Spaceship. Null-null drive. Affect everything simultaneous. Push you up fast, just under speed of light, no acceleration pressure to worry about, good old-time dilation makes a five light-year hop go by in a couple of months.

And meanwhile that lovely, lovely pay accumulating back at home. Good, no? No. Remember the power consumption. Think, just compute out, how many megawatts per ton you need. Stray radiation means heavy shielding, too, in a power factor of the power. And then, coasting across space? Uh-uh! Space is just full of hydrogen. One atom per cubic centimeter. At a speed of c, figure out the resistance. Figure out, also, what power you have to spend to keep those atoms at arm's length. A long, hairy, tattooed arm. Else the radiation from them will fry your aspidistra. Ergo, you need lots of ergs to go. All engine, no comfort. Most certainly no extra isotopes for fueling a return trip, nor any gear for making 'em at the other end. Not when you're carrying a mattercaster.

Nice mattercaster. Good, friendly, obliging mattercaster. Set one up. Tune it. Step through the gate. Step out the other end, whatever other end has a receiver you're tuned for, Bellegarde, Earth, Hell. No transition time. Not whatsoever. One hyperphase step across the galaxy. The universe is ours. 'Course, you do have to erect your gadget first. No transmitter, no reception, right? And the gadget does have to have a strong gravitational field to work. Got to be on a planet.

So. From an advance base, as it might be Bellegarde, you send your roboprobes to the next likely-looking stars. They find the least horrible planet in the system. Take orbit. Maser back data. Mass, magnetic field, temperature, spectra, everything except what we really needed to know. Load up *Widsith*. Minimum 'caster. Minimum everything. All we have to do is get there; land; make a foundation and frame out of local materials; assemble our unit; walk back to Bellegarde and report. Then the parts for a big, industrial-type caster can get sent through— direct from Earth, if you want. So can men. So can any equipment they need, including women. No sweat. 'Nother planet conquered. Hurray.

Hurray for us, 'spesh'lly. 'Stronomers on Bellegarde analyzed this here now sun we're under, they did. Variant composition. Cosmic abundances just a statistical concept. Actual composition can vary like crazy. Look at the R Peculiar stars, f'r example. Or look at this one. High concentration Group Eight metals, platinum, palladium. Catalysts. (A catalyst is the gait of a drunken feline.) Looks like plenty silver, too.

Like mother, like daughter. Planets oughta be loaded with these here now metals. Send roboprobe. Yep, planets, all right, all right. One of 'em even habitable. Earth size, Earth temperature, water oceans, oxynitro air, life, no sign of natives but reflection spectra show protein-based life. Given a li'l chemical apparatus, we could eat it. Not a full diet, but a dietary supplement, anyhow. Good. Ideal. Send *Widsith* off. Captain Ahmad Akbik, mattercaster engineer Miguel Ocampo, electronician William J. Lind...

Has my recital insulted you enough? Hope so. You killed me, you know. I am, I was sitting here in a valley grown over with spongy brownish-green plants. There're trees, of a sort, growing up the mountainsides. Above timberline, the rocks have funny colors, mostly bluish; they're not like any rocks I ever saw before. On the volcano cone, below the snowcap, I do rec'nize black lava and yellow sulfur. The air stinks. It's cool and damp and smells like old cigar butts. Or something. I'm breathing the air. And I'm drunk. Nearest liquor five light-years away, and I'm drunk. Funny? Merciful? Well, I can tell you what kind of gesture the hand of Providence is making at me. In fact, I will tell you—

No, here comes somebody, airsuited to the ears. He looks mad. Guess they heard me, over yonder in the ship. We got a hookup. I was out here to test the air. Chemical and biological tests said O.K., said the stink's just from the plants and harmless, but you never know. We gotta just breathe the air or we're done for. You see—Hell, with it. We're done for. How do you do, Captain Ahmad Akbik, sir? Shall we dance?

Until the holds were unloaded, the bunkroom was the sole place aboard where all ten men could be simultaneously, and then only if they planned each move in advance. Sleeping, of course, was done in relays. They crowded knee to knee on the four bunks, hunched beneath the low overhead, and stared into each other's face.

The captain would have liked to offer a prayer, when God seemed to be their last remaining friend, but Mecca was probably in a ridiculous direction. "How are you now, Fulgosi?" he asked.

"Quite well," the mineralogist said. "No after-effects. To be sure, I didn't become intoxicated like Lind—"

"Hey!" The electronician blushed.

"Don't be so sensitive about that," said the biochemist, Riese. "Not your fault. You merely showed a certain reaction, idiosyncratic but not unheard-of, to anesthesia."

"Anesthesia?" Lind frowned.

"Sure, what else?" Fulgosi said. "When I tried breathing that stuff, I got too drowsy and thick-headed to think. Would've passed out before long if you hadn't brought me back inside the ship. So what's the cause, Riese?"

"I don't know," said the biochemist slowly.

"What?" Akbik exclaimed. "But you must! You've run a complete atmospheric analysis, haven't you?" In the week since *Widsith* landed, each man had had so much preliminary work to do in his particular specialty that this was their first real chance to compare notes.

"Yes, sir. I found nothing significant that the roboprobe hadn't already reported. The air has a rather high proportion of noble gases, but otherwise it's quite Earthlike."

Lind gagged. "Earthlike, you call those stenches?"

"Yes, what about them?" Ocampo asked. "By-products of a different biochemistry from ours. Couldn't something, in trace amounts, have an anesthetic effect on the human nervous system?"

"I don't know," Riese admitted. "For heaven's sake, my brain doesn't have infinite storage capacity. And the reference works we could take with us, even in microspool form, are so limited. Surgical anesthesia has been entirely electronic for the past two centuries or more. Who could have foreseen any need for information about the chemical kind?"

"Could some kind of germ be responsible?" Akbik wondered.

"No, sir, that's one possibility I swear we can rule out. No native life form can eat us for much the same reason that we can't eat it. The selenium and fluorine concentrations in the body of this planet are so high that they have become integral to the metabolism of everything."

"How can you sit here," the cyberneticist Pereira objected, "having barely seen a little of one valley, and talk about the entire planet?"

Riese shrugged. "If my computer doesn't lie," he said, "it's traced out the fundamental cellular energy cycle. And that will not vary. Not unless the well-founded idea is totally wrong, that all life on a given world derives from the materials available there in the beginning. Our kind of organism uses—oh, hydrogen bonding, and phosphorus in ATP. Life here uses fluorine and selenium in its equivalents. I don't need a large sample to prove that. So—every Guineverean plant or animal is violently poisonous to us because of those elements. But by the same token, the phosphorus and iron in our bodies makes us just as poisonous to them."

"And this cuts our time even shorter," the geologist Deschamps said unnecessarily.

"I wonder how you'd taste, sautéed in lubricant," Lind murmured.

"Stop that!" Akbik said.

"Why, is man forbidden food?"

"Not explicitly," grinned the chemosynthesist Nussbaum. "However, since man does not divide the hoof or chew the cud—"

"You're hopeless," Akbik said.

"I'm afraid that's correct," Lind said. Observing that the captain was in no mood to continue playing straight man, he hastily grew serious. "Sir, do we have to breathe that stink anyway? I mean, we can keep on wearing airsuits outdoors, and recharge their bottles from the ship's oxy renewal plant."

"Unless we have to dismantle her," Akbik said.

They stared at each other, ten men alone in unknownness. The silence and the metal shell around them seemed to press inward.

Widsith was a shining tower, tall in the valley. Lind looked up her hull, and up, and up, and reflected what a fraud the damned object was. Enormous fuel tanks: empty. Engines, therefore, useless, aside from the auxiliary generator. Holds: big, yes, but barely able to contain the equipment necessary to establish a minimal space gate. As a result: living quarters, life support systems, rations, personal gear, cut to the bone.

And now, it turned out, Guinevere wasn't going to furnish any supplements. No food, no air—"

"And the ship's not any cornucopia, either," Lind said.

"Beg pardon?" Tao-Chi Huang, the chief mechanic, glanced from the robotractor he was assembling.

"Oh. I was thinking out loud," Lind said. "The hull's nothing but light metals, aluminum, magnesium, beryllium alloys. And those we can get right out of this planet. What we've got to have, that the planet doesn't seem to have, is iron."

"What for? Structural members?"

"Well, that was the original idea. Maybe we can use something else there. But we cannot replace iron—quite a bit of very pure iron—in things like the transformers and magnetic cores of the mattercaster circuits. Not without redesigning the entire system, which would take a special R&D team several years. We are not an R&D team, and we do not have several years."

"I know Gilruth hasn't found any native iron yet," Tao-Chi said. "But there must be some in the planet!"

"So we assumed, before we arrived here. And, actually, I imagine there is some. Down in the core, if nowhere else. Bloated lot of good that does us. What we need is a workable deposit not too far underground. And we haven't the time or the resources to scour an entire world searching for ore."

"Hm-m-m." Tao-Chi started to rub his chin thoughtfully, but his faceplate got in the way. "Maybe our trouble is due to a lack of ferric-reducing bacteria."

"Maybe. Though wouldn't you still get oxide in the soil? I think likelier the iron shortage is just another aspect of the weird element-abundance situation here." Lind shrugged in his airsuit. "If we don't find any, damn soon, we'll have to cannibalize for it—like maybe your construction equipment."

"That will be needed up to the last minute," Tao-Chi protested, "and in any event, it's mostly light alloys, too. Besides, if you did take what steel parts there are, I doubt if you could purify the iron out of modern aligned-crystal materials with anything less than a gaseous diffusion plant."

"Which is too much for us to build. Well, so we'll have to steal from the ship. Take out its transformers and such. We can do that, of course. *But,* the ship is an integrated system. If we remove a vital unit from, say, the engine, then the oxy renewal plant will also stop working."

"I know. So Joe Riese had jolly well better find a way to make the local air breathable. Right?"

"Right. He's working on it. Me, I got business in the shack."

Burdened and uncomfortable in survival gear, Lind's slender form walked on down the valley. Passing the maser mast where he had disgraced himself, he winced. Damn Guinevere! Damn the astronomers, and their bland assumption that every kind of atom would be available here even if the percentages varied. Damn his own foolishness in signing on for the expedition. At best, he'd come back to a list of female vidiphone numbers five years obsolete. At worst...what good was money to a skeleton? Even if the skeleton's owner had died drunk.

A stream burbled along the path. It supplied water and waste removal to the gate construction site, and thus had lost its pristine freshness. Serve it right, Lind, thought viciously. He proceeded to a wide plot which had been cleared of topsoil and was now being leveled. Dust smoked in the orange sunlight, up from a bulldozer which snorted back and forth. That was an automaton, as was nearly every machine. Under no circumstances could ten men's muscles do the brute labor of establishing a base on an uncharted planet. Nor could ten men's brains do the innumerable necessary analyses of data and material samples. Humans were here to look at the instruments, program the robots, read the computer printouts, make the decisions, and perform the finer tasks of installation and adjustment as the mattercaster assembly grew.

Nice theory. Trouble was, Guinevere didn't provide the stuff needed to make the theory work.

Lind entered a prefab which squatted ugly at the field's edge. Sunlight through begrimed windows glittered red-gold off a clutter of apparatus. Ocampo and Fulgosi were turning away from a bulk that Lind identified as a furnace with attached spectroscope, pyrometer, and assorted things to which he could not put a name. Technology, he thought, had made technologists too blooming specialized.

"No." Fulgosi's helmet speaker needed some adjustment, Lind heard. What the mineralogist must have intended as a sigh emerged as a whistle. "This sample has essentially the same composition as the last. Nothing is different except the hydration and a few impurities."

"But we must have calcium minerals!" Ocampo exclaimed.

"Take that up with a higher authority. All I can tell you is that none of the neighborhood rocks are limestone or gypsum or anything reasonable like that. They're universally based on strontium. It must be vastly more common here."

"Well, can't strontium substitute for calcium? In human bones, I've heard—"

"Yes, there is chemical similarity. But not that close. Strontium carbonate won't burn to the oxide at any temperature we can get with available equipment. And even if it did, the oxide won't set to mortar. Nor, for that matter, will strontium sulfate make plaster of paris." Fulgosi regarded the construction chief for a moment. "Must we actually have a massive concrete foundation for the 'caster?"

"Hell, yes!" Ocampo said. "The thing won't work unless it's properly anchored to the planet. Reaction forces would tear it apart otherwise. Without a strong, weatherproof setting—Ah, Lind. What brings you here?"

"I was after the latest analysis, myself," the electronician said.

Sweat glistened behind Fulgosi's faceplate. "I'll sure be glad when we do get our materials together, if we ever do," he said. "Right now, Gilruth, Riese, and I are the only ones working, and we're working our tails off. The rest of you sit and feel sorry for yourselves...No, my friend, we haven't turned up any bismuth for you."

"But I have been working," Lind answered. "With references and my slipstick and—How about antimony? Found some antimony?"

"Why, uh, yes. Quite a bit of stibnite. What do you want it for?"

"*Whew!* I'm glad to hear that. You see, the tuning circuit calls for a large piece of bismuth, as being diamagnetic. But antimony is almost as good in that respect, and I've calculated we can substitute it." Lind turned to Ocampo. "While I was at it, I checked some other possibilities. You need zinc for galvanizing, and we haven't found any decent deposits, right? Well, cadmium will do the same job. You put it on by a different process, but it works fine."

Fulgosi snatched a piece of paper off the bench. "Here," he said with sudden excitement. "A list. What we've found in extractable form and quantity so far. Plenty of cadmium."

"Plenty of gold, silver, platinum, manganese," Ocampo said. His bitterness had not left him. "So we can make busbars of silver instead of copper—but we'd counted on that anyway. So manganese is a good structural metal—but in a moist oxygen atmosphere, it'll crumble to oxide almost as fast as we can cast our members. Where's the iron coming from for the foundation and framework? Not the ship. Barely enough iron in her for your circuits, Lind. Show me how to make concrete without calcium, and several tons of ribs and girders without iron, and a few such items, and I'll kiss you."

"Ugh," said Lind. He studied the engineer's miserable countenance. "You've let this get to you," he said. "Your brain's tramping in circles. Me, I dunno, maybe that anesthesia jag I went on cleared my head somehow. But seems obvious to me, we'll do best to find substitutes for the stuff we can't get."

"I think that's obvious even to a dolt like me," Ocampo snorted. "Name a few."

"I did. Antimony and cadmium. And then—Hm-m-m." Lind went to the window and stared out. The volcano lifted sheer before him. They'd landed here because they couldn't prospect an entire world and a plutonic region was likeliest to have a wide assortment of easily refinable minerals. Which this area did, to be sure; only they were the wrong minerals. Lind's forefinger doodled on a dusty pane. "Why steel?" he murmured. "I mean, for the framework supporting the 'caster on its foundation. You only want mechanical strength there. Why not stone?"

"No boulders are big enough, around here anyway, and we can't assemble small ones into a frame because we can't make mortar."

"But that lava up yonder. We should be able to cast it and machine it to shape. Don't you think so?"

"Well, I'll be—" Ocampo stood silent a while. Fulgosi gulped. Hope had come like a blow.

"Y-yes," Ocampo said at length, quite softly. "For beams, as you say, and bedplates, and so forth. But not for the foundation. We're not set up to cast that big a piece of material with a high melting point; and, as I told you, without mortar—"

"So what else might serve?" Lind swung back. Inside his suit, he quivered. "Let's use our imaginations. Let's ask Gilruth what he's noticed on his exploring trips."

A teakettle whine cut through the sky. "Speaking about devils," Fulgosi said. The expedition's single aircraft, a hover job with considerable range and carrying capacity, bounced to a halt on the field. The three men hurried from the shack.

Gilruth was climbing out. "What'd you find?" Ocampo shouted.

"Brought home some assorted rocks for testing," the pilot said, working hard at imperturbability. "Doubt if they'll be any use, though. What spot checks I carried out, neutron activation and so forth, showed the same bloody distribution of elements upriver as here. No iron, no calcium, no copper, no nothing."

"Never mind, never mind." Lind seized his arm and dragged him away. "We want something different from you."

Gilruth looked alarmed. "Have you left your helmet off again?"

Ocampo explained. Gilruth had landed on the volcano some days ago, near the peak. Well, did the lava beds look mineable? And what else might he have noticed, paying no special heed at the time because what he saw hadn't been what he hoped to see? The conference lasted an hour, and all four returned to the spaceship still chattering into each other's mouth.

They cycled through the personnel lock, racked their suits, and encountered emptiness. Everyone must be outside, performing the jobs that had to be done before actual construction could start. No—a noise below decks—Ocampo's party squeezed down the companionway.

Now that most of the machinery had been unloaded, the holds were echoing caverns. Riese had taken one of them over for a workshop. He stood at a bench, a laser torch glaring in his hand, making a boxlike assembly.

"Hey, Joe!" Lind cried. "Listen! Good news."

"I'm glad somebody has some," the biochemist grumbled. He switched off his torch, wiped his face, and sat down on the bench. It sagged under his weight, being little more than some cobbled-together alumalloy sheeting which wasn't needed elsewhere at the moment. He swore and stood again. "What's happened?"

"We've hit on the answer to our problem," Lind said. "For the native materials we need but don't find, we use ersatz."

"You've taken this long to realize that?"

"Oh, yes, the principle is obvious," Ocampo said, "but we didn't fully accept it until today. We kept hoping we'd be able to proceed according to the book. This afternoon, though, we took a hard look at the possibilities of using what we've actually got on Guinevere. And they seem very hopeful."

"Fine." Riese stared at the apparatus he was making and clicked his tongue. "Maybe I'd better turn this project over to one of you geniuses."

"What's the matter?" The question jerked from Gilruth. "Not working properly?"

"Not yet, anyhow. The basic idea is simple enough. Assuming that one or more of the trace gases, the bio-compounds, in the atmosphere are responsible for anesthetizing us: how do we get them out? They're organic. So, in theory, we blow air through an electric arc energetic enough to break them down into CO_2, and such-like, and bubble the resulting gas through water. What comes out the other end should be good, pure air."

"It had better be," Gilruth said. "Once we've removed the iron from the ship's electrical system...well, I somehow can't visualize us, drunk, or dopey or unconscious, completing that matter gate. Can you?"

"No." Riese scowled. "My problem is this: Apparently, whatever compounds affect us need only be present in micro quantities. Probably they act by inhibiting certain enzymes. Therefore, my purifier has to work perfectly. So it has to be continuously monitored by spectrographic and chromatographic instruments.

Now designing such circuits is not easy." He looked at Lind. "I think, if you can be spared, you'd better devote full time to helping me."

"I guess I'd better," Lind said in a small voice.

The others had too much to do to worry about whether they would have air fit to breathe toward the end of their tasks. That "too much" included, especially, worrying about every other problem. For their food supply, however rationed, was little more than sufficient to carry them through a set of standardized procedures evolved on familiar kinds of planet. Now they must invent a whole new set of ways to install a mattercaster. And a starving man can continue to work for a while, after a fashion, but he can't continue to produce bright ideas, or tinker with the thing he has built until it does what it is supposed to do.

Thus time was precious and the labor schedule brutal.

They did talk a little. Tamping an explosive charge into a lava bed, Fulgosi growled, "Nussbaum's sure got a soft touch."

"What's he doing?" Deschamps leaned wearily on his pick.

"Making glass epoxy out of silicates and organics. Solder substitute."

"Well, we've got to have that, too, and if Nussbaum's the only one of us who can cook up a batch—One man can't carry all human knowledge in his head."

"Not even in his own specialty," Fulgosi sighed. "I suspect that's Joe Riese's problem. If he had the right reference works, he could probably find out in ten minutes what's wrong with the atmosphere and what to do about it. But no one thought to supply him with the one obscure bit of information he needs." He straightened and looked around. Rockfields tilted dark, up beyond snows and glaciers to where the mountain lifted a skyward smoke plume. "O.K., let's get back to the aircraft. When this charge blows, it could touch off an avalanche."

Down in the valley, after nightfall, Gilruth shepherded a truckload of logs to the construction site. A stone-crushing mill thudded, a wood-pulping machine yelled, a chemical vat seethed—improvised, most of it, one way or another. Beyond the lamp posts ringing the field could be seen the stars, cold and strangely constellated and terribly remote.

"How much more timber will you need?" he asked Ocampo. "Robot help or no, lumberjacking is hardly a sinecure."

"Piloting is?" the engineer replied. "I think two more loads should end this job. We had to run quite a series of tests, but we seem to have found the right mixture now."

"Some concrete, eh? Vegetable fiber and asbestos-like rock, bound together with molten sulfur and poured to make your foundation!"

"Well, it serves. In fact, it should be just as good as the ordinary cement-based kind."

"What about reinforcing rods and conductive tie beams?"

"Haven't you heard? No, I guess you've been in the outback too much. Alagau."

"Alagau to you, too. Or was that a death rattle?"

Ocampo laughed a little. Some distance away, an arc furnace was uncovered, and the light glared off his faceplate. "Aluminum-silver-gold alloy," he explained. "Nussbaum suggested it, and it seems to be hard and tough enough for our purposes, in spite of having a mauve color. Al, Ag, Au, see?"

After a moment, he added, "In fact, by now we have an astonishing collection of assorted ersatzes. Beryllium, titanium, lithium, magnesium, thorium, they're more versatile than you'd think, in their different alloys. Then there are organics, plastics, tars—"

Gilruth slumped wearily in the cab and stared at the fire-trickle where molten metal ran into casting forms. "Won't do us a lot of good if we can't get pure air," he said. "How're Riese and Lind coming on that?"

"All right, I guess."

"I was thinking. Suppose they fail. What then? Couldn't we get oxygen by roasting ores?"

"Um-m-m...possibly. That'd be such a huge job, though. Only imagine what equipment we'd have to build, to operate on the scale necessary. We could easily starve to death before we finished. No, I think our friends have plain got to succeed."

And a few mornings later, in *Widsith's* hold, Riese and Lind beamed at each other. On the bench before them stood a cylinder, fantastically piped and wired. A fan whined at the open end. Inside, arcs sizzled and water gurgled. At the farther end, attached instruments certified that clean atmosphere, free of any organic taint except a normal amount of carbon dioxide, was being compressed into a bottle.

"The damned thing is finally in shape," Lind breathed.

"I was beginning to think it never would be," Riese said.

"Maybe now you understand why engineers draw high pay." Lind yawned and stretched. "Me for some sleep, before Akbik puts me in one of the labor gangs!"

"Uh—" Riese hesitated. "A final test."

"What?"

The biochemist took the bottle off the hose and attached it to the shoulder pack of an airsuit. "Take a few lungfuls," he said. "Just to make sure."

"But...I mean...oh, all right." Lind grumbled his way into the suit, sealed the helmet, and cracked the valve on the bottle.

"Well?" asked Riese anxiously.

"Seems O.K. The stink is certainly gone." Lind inhaled again, and again. "Yep, jus' fine." A wide and foolish grin spread over his features. "Won'erful. Great. What a team we are, you know 'at? C'mon, le's dance."

He walked out, alone, into darkness. Under a dim red moon, the valley dews, the stream, and the far snowpeaks glimmered. Somewhere an animal hooted. His footfalls made a hollow thudding.

He felt cold and tired. But sleep escaped him. Everyone else was sacked out, exhausted. Lind envied them. For the moment, they were free of the knowledge that their labor had been for naught and that Guinevere would never let them go.

They'd driven themselves as no one would dare drive a mule. (Of course, no one would care overly much if a mule didn't come home.) Now time was hideously short. There simply weren't enough man-days left to build the oxygen-producing furnace which Gilruth had proposed. The food was practically gone. You could live a while, empty-bellied; but some of that while must go to completing and adjusting the space gate whose framework bulked yonder in the shadows of the field. Already Lind's stomach complained of underemployment.

Earth-prime ribs, baked potatoes smothered in sour cream and chives, apple pie a la mode…No, damn it, before he thought about such things he must think how to return to them.

Basic problem: Find a way to get the anesthetic factor out of Guinevere's atmosphere. The way must needs be simple, the apparatus easy to build and operate. Thereafter everything else would be simple—shutting down the ship's oxy renewer, dismantling the electrical system, installing the needed iron parts in the mattercaster circuits, adding the parts hauled from Bellegarde, tuning and activating the gate and making one stride across the light-years to home.

Well, then, Billy Lind, *solve* the basic problem. It must have a perfectly easy solution. Given it as a question on an exam, not so long ago in college, you'd likely have seen the answer inside of five minutes.

But the situation was different here. Here, everybody had worked too hard. Their brains were numb. He and Riese were the only men who'd been spared much physical labor—because their comrades trusted them to provide the air—and now their failure seemed to have stunned Riese into apathy.

Therefore, Billy Lind, the responsibility is yours. Certainly you're tired. Certainly you're also in a state of mild shock. But you're not too stupefied to think. Are you?

So. What are the facts? It had been obvious that organic compounds were acting as snooze gases. What else could? And yet…Guineverean air processed until sensitive instruments swore it was pure, kept right on kicking the human mind out of orbit. Therefore the taken-for-granted fact had not been a fact after all. So what other possible fact(or) was there?

Lind couldn't imagine. The noble gases? But they were inert! You could breathe oxyhelium without noticing any difference except that your voice sounded squeaky. Oh, yes, you could force one or two other members of that family to take on fluorine atoms or whatever, but they did it grudgingly, under very special laboratory conditions. How could—Lind cursed in the dark. Unfair to demand that he think. He was too tired, too hungry, even in his airsuit too cold.

Cold!

Hello, Earth. Hello, everybody. Whoops!

William J. Lind again. Call me Billy. Call me anything. Bee-cause by th' time you receive me on Bellegarde, I'll've been five years home an' inna diff'rent job an' you can't fire me 'cause I'll long've been in some other line uh work an' so to Guinevere wi' you.

Or else I'll be rich. Might be. Gotta lotta (hey, that rhymes!) gotta lotta new techniques here. Sure to be other planets like this'n. Hey? Hey-hey. Maybe we can patent 'em. At leas' we can write a book. Bes' seller. "I Was Pumpin' On Guinevere." How's 'at sound? Thought so.

I was, y' know. Distillin', anyway. An' then pumpin' the oxy an' the nitro into bottles. My idea. Very simple. You jus' liquefy your air. We'd enough stuff lyin' 'roun' to make an air liquefaction unit. Then we did fractional distillation. Which, muh frien's an' fellow citizens o' the gr-r-reat World Federation, is not distillin' fractions. What an image, though. Li'l numerators an' denominators boilin' off. But all we did was liquid air. I mean to say, now hear this, all we did was *distill* liquid air. After we'd made it inna firs' place. See? No sweat. Mos' abs'lutely no sweat, at minus 107 point one degrees Celsius.

Tha's the boilin' point o' xenon. Guilty party. We foun' out by tryin' different fractions on ourselves. Yep, xenon. Fine anesthetic. Oh, you knew that already, didja? But you gotta big fat shelf uh references handy. So why didn' you tell us? Huh? Answer me that.

Guess we should'a thought o' it before. But so much else to do. An' whole situation complicated. So natur'lly we 'spected anesthesia problem 'ud be complicated, too. Wasted lotta time, we did, lookin' for complicated answer 'fore we hit on simple one. I did. Me. William J. Lind. I'm simple-minded. Ta-ra-la-la-i-tu! I gloat! Hear me!

All set now. Ever' thing ready.

Tomorrow we start the transmitter an' walk through to Bellegarde. Liquor on Bellegarde. Big celebration. But me, I get drunk on xenon, so why not start now? Whoops! How many moons this planet got, anyway?

Jus' one question, you fat smug people. (Dunno whether to call you smats or fugs.) One li'l bitty question. This here now funny elemental composition. Damn near killed us. Jus' a very slight shift in relative abundances, and k-k-kr-r-r! So I ask you. Think about this. Think good 'n hard, because nex' time aroun', you're not gonna have William J. Lind on deck. Nope, you're not. I'll be on Earth, livin' the life o' Riley, an' I don' 'magine Riley'll ever come home. Cause he's one o' these here now onward-the-march-o'-mankind characters. He'll be pioneerin' the stars. I won't.

So, O.K., my question: What you gonna do when you hit the *nex'* crazy kind o' world?

Peek! I See You

The father of Sean F. X. Lindquist was an amiable, easygoing Boston Swede. His mother was, as might be guessed, an O'Kelly with a will of her own. Their genes combined to produce a son who was good-natured, a bit raffish, intelligent, disinclined to toil—but, on occasion, stubborn as Lucifer. And thereby hangs a tale.

Being expelled from college, for reasons having less to do with his grades than the president's daughter, he was drafted. Presently he was shipped to Asia. Though the general truce there had now lasted for several years, it was chronically unstable and everyone concerned maintained large forces close to hand. In due course, however, and with a certain feeling of mutual relief, the Army gave Lindquist his honorable discharge. He was enchanted with Bangkok, where he had been spending his leaves, and pulled wires to be demobbed in that city.

The enchantment wore off—she married someone else—and he made a leisurely way home around the world. Whenever his funds ran out, he did odd jobs. Some were very odd indeed. He was twenty-six before he reached the States again, and long out of touch. So he might have caught up on newspapers and technical journals; but he went instead to Las Vegas and updated himself in other fields. A true cliché calls luck a lady, apt to smile most upon men who do not pursue her. Lindquist departed with several thousand dollars in his pocket.

At this time the southwestern tourist boom was entering the steep part of its exponential curve. Lindquist remembered boyhood camping trips in the area. It occurred to him that he could make a pleasant living, and have his winters free, by starting an airferry service. The Four Corners country is famous for the grandeur and solitude of its uplands. But the time, effort, and expense of packing into those roadless mountains discouraged most potential visitors. Now if they and their gear could be flown in, and out again at an agreed-on time—if the pilot was available by radio in the meanwhile, to handle emergencies like lost can openers...

He took lessons and got his license. Then he bought himself a used VTOL aircraft and went to scout the territory.

Thus it was that he saw the spaceship.

He was droning leisurely along at about twelve thousand feet. The peaks were not extremely far below him. Their landscape was awesome: vast, steep, ragged, a ruddiness slashed by mineral ochers and blues, a starkness little relieved by scattered mesquite, greasewood, and sagebrush. Here and there, a streamlet turned the bottom of a canyon green. But mostly this was desert land, people-empty land, hawk, buzzard, jackrabbit, and coyote land. The sun was westering in a deep, almost purple sky. Updrafts boomed briefly and trickily, shaking the plane in its course.

Lindquist's lean, sandy-haired, shabby-clad form sat relaxed. He puffed a corncob pipe and hummed a bawdy song. But alertness was in him. Before he tried carrying passengers, he must get familiar with this kind of flying. And he needed a place to roost for the night, preferably containing water and firewood. His eyes roved.

The vision slanted down before him. It moved at incredible speed, banked at impossible angles. Yet its passage was so silent that his own motor, his very pulse hammered at him. The shape, as nearly as he could tell, was roughly like a disk thickened in the middle. But the lambent, shifting colors that played across it, enveloped it in aurora, made such things hard to gauge.

It swung around, slid near, and his magnetic compass went crazy. For a moment he stared at what seemed to be a row of ports, glowing as if furnaces burned behind them. Far in the back of his mind, a reckoner clicked: *Diameter something like a hundred feet.* Otherwise he felt sandbagged.

The thing spun off. He grew aware that the pipe had dropped from his jaws. No matter. His hands were a-dance across the radar controls. He locked on. Reflection. Yes! His compass steadied again. The vision dwindled...a mile away, two miles, three, shrinking to a rainbow dot, like the diffraction dots you see when you look sunward through your lashes...vanishing to nothing against mountain flanks and canyon shadows.

But it was real. Not just his rocking mind said so. His instruments did.

Other memories from boyhood and youth boiled up. "Judas priest," he whispered. "That's a sho-nuff flying saucer."

He opened the throttle. His plane leaped forward. roaring and shivering with power. He hadn't a chance of overhauling in a flat-out chase. But the thing did seem to be on a long downward track. Could he but stay within range, would it but land—

"Well, what then, bimbo?" he challenged himself.

He didn't know. But he relived vividly the arguments that had once fascinated him. The radicals had insisted that flying saucers were ships from outer space, operated by benevolent though green little men. The conservatives denied that anyone had ever seen anything. In this hour he, S. F. X. Lindquist, had been handed a chance to investigate personally. He had nothing to lose, and perhaps—if he could solve the mystery—a great deal to gain. Like fame and money.

Though no intellectual, he followed the news around him. Had he not spent the past several years in out-of-the-way places, he would have known that pursuit was a waste of time, that the riddle had, in fact, already been answered. But no one had mentioned this to him. Quite simply and naïvely, he lined out after the vision.

In the different cultures of the galaxy, Dorek's Law is known by many different names. Some call it Shepalour's Rule, some the Basic Law of Thermodynamics, some the Principle of Most Effort, and so on for millions of languages. But the formulation is invariant, because we all inhabit the same universe.

"Everything that can go wrong, will."

On their present voyage, the partners in the hypership had seen it in full glorious operation. There is no need to detail their woes with rickety hull, asthmatic engines, and senile computer. Nor need one describe what cargoes they carried, with what infinite trouble, from planet to planet. A tramp has to take anything she can get, and this is apt to be stuff too weird for the sleek cargo liners.

But they did think their fortunes had turned when they reached Zandar. A message from the brokers lay waiting for them. After discharging their load of sandorads—and, hopefully, getting most of the mercaptan odor out of the vessel—they were to pick up some machine tools for New Ystanikkinikkitantuvo. Plain machine tools, harmless crafted metal! Of course, the destination was far out on the Rim. So much the better, though. It would be a peaceful haul, with lovely pay accumulating; and then, having been gone as long as they'd signed for, they would head home, loaded or not; and the fleshpots of the Core had better be filled in advance for them.

But a summons came from the port coordinator.

Pazilliwheep Finnison went along to the office. The coordinator was not of any species he recognized, possessing three eyes and a good many tentacles. They studied each other for a few seconds.

The spacefarer was from Ensikt. He was a diopt himself, though the eyes were quite large and dark, contrasting with blue stripes upon glabrous orange skin. (The air being thicker, wetter, and hotter than he was used to, he went nude except for a musette bag.) His body was slender, centauroid, with a gracefully waving tail. He breathed through rows of gill-like organs on either side of his long neck, which alternated with aural tympani. Albeit he thus had no nose, he did sport a muscular trunk above his mouth. It split into two arms that ended in boneless four-fingered hands. This was entirely practical on Ensikt, where gravity is comparatively weak and animals comparatively small. Pazilliwheep stood three feet high at the rump.

"Ah...Navigator Pilot Finnison. H/S *Grumdel Castle*...yes, yes. Welcome," said the coordinator in Interlingo-5 with a flatulent accent. He punched a button on his data screen and regarded what appeared. "Yes. Correct what I was informed. You are clearing for...yes, that part of the Rim...with a stopover at... what is the name of the planet?"

Pazilliwheep automatically jerked his tail, then said in haste: "My gesture indicated indifference."

"Were you afraid it might be objectionable in my culture? No, we have no tails. Now about this…yes…confounded planet. Never heard of it till the other day. Catalogued as—But what's the name?"

"Tierra, Earth, Mir, Jorden, die Erde, *et cetera, et cetera.*" Pazilliwheep's vocal apparatus formed the sounds rather well, except for a lack of nasal quality. "Hundreds of autocthonous words. Most of them translate as 'Dirt.'"

"So. Yes. I see." The coordinator had kept one eye on the unrolling data. "Primitive world. What do you call it?"

"Restocking Station 143."

The coordinator waved a tentacle in the air. "I indicate assent and understanding. Well, Navigator Pilot, this is quite fortunate. Yes, fortunate. You came at, shall we say, the strategic moment. You are, therefore, able to be of material assistance to the Galactic Federation. Intergovernmental Department of Planetary Development, Bureau of Supervisions, to be exact."

Oh, oh! thought Pazilliwheep, and braced himself for bad news. But it was worse than he feared:

"Yes, you can, and, therefore, you…are herewith instructed to…furnish transportation and every necessary assistance…to the sector inspector."

"No!" Pazilliwheep cried, His four hooves clattered on the floor when he sprang backward. "Not the sector inspector!"

"Yes. The sector inspector. New one, you know. Anxious to make a good showing in…this latest assignment. Came here to check local records. Found no official investigation of that particular planet had been made for a long time. Yes, much overdue. Entire intelligent species being neglected. Perhaps, even, slyly exploited by the less scrupulous. Eh?"

"Exploited, my lowest left operculum!" Pazilliwheep protested. "What the entropy would there *be* to exploit? Besides, their principal culture belongs to the Federation. If they have any complaints, they can go through regular channels, can't they? And say, why doesn't the inspector go in his own ship?"

Remorselessly, the coordinator answered: "Economy drive at GHQ. Inspectors for outlying regions do not, shall we say, rate their own vessels any longer. They use available transportation. Yes. I know, they're always behind-hand anyway. Too many planets. And a sector like this—not even important enough for records on it to clutter central data banks on any Core world—do you see?"

"But…listen, the *Grumdel's* an old wreck. We've got the stingiest owners in the galaxy. My engineer's trying to repair a fusion tube right now. The interior maintenance units keep breaking down, too. Our top hyperspeed is a hypercrawl. Anything would be better!"

"No doubt. No doubt. But nothing else available. Not soon. Every other vessel due here within the next several weeks is a liner or else on time charter. Or, of course, not crewed by oxygen breathers. You may be old, Navigator Pilot Finnison; you may be rusty; you may be underpowered, vermin-infested, and all but certifiably unspaceworthy: but you are the best I can do for the sector inspector. And, yes, my own career—promotion off this dreary mudball—his reports to

GHQ—you understand. Yes. You are hereby commandeered." And the coordinator handed over the official orders with a flourish.

Thus Hypership *Grumdel Castle* departed Zandar with a third being aboard.

The inspector was a good fellow at heart: young, inclined to take himself and his work overly seriously, but well intentioned. He apologized for the trouble he was causing, and reminded his hosts that their owners would be compensated according to law. His hosts showed no great enthusiasm at this. He explained that a major reason for his having picked their ship was that she was already scheduled to lay over on 143— "And might I inquire, out of a wish to become more intimately acquainted with my companions as well as for the technical information itself, not to mention simple curiosity, what activities you have planned on this planet?"

He used Interlingo-12 rather than any language of his own world, Ittatik. Unfortunately, Pazilliwheep did not speak Interlingo-12. Engineer Supercargo Urgo the Red did, more or less, and translated into his version of Interlingo-7:

"He says what're we gonna do there?"

"Well, no reason not to tell him the truth," Pazilliwheep replied. "Unless you've got some other little racket you haven't told me about."

"When we touch maybe once in three years? Don't make me laugh. It hurts."

In point of fact, Pazilliwheep had a racket of his own. It was a mild one, and might even be legal, for all he knew. He swapped small quantities of ondon oil, which had turned out to have powerful aphrodisiac effects on the natives of 143, for kitchenware. The latter was unusual and artistic enough to command good prices on several more advanced worlds. This was one reason he did his restocking on 143 whenever possible.

"Let's answer his question by reciting common, elementary knowledge," he suggested to Urgo. "Might put him to sleep, at least."

"Is any knowledge common?" wondered the engineer supercargo. "Like, it's a big galaxy. *I* never heard o' whatzisname's muckin' civilization till now. And still he says it fills a whole muckin' star cluster! Maybe he don't know how we operate in this spiral arm."

"Oh, I suppose the basic procedures are similar everywhere. If nothing else, in the course of ten thousand years or however long it's been around, wouldn't the Federation have had some leveling influence on the member species?" Pazilliwheep tail-shrugged. "We haven't anything better to do. Suppose you translate as I talk." He filled his lungs and began:

"It's a long way between stars in this thin outer part of the galaxy. And it's even longer between up-to-date systems that are normal ports of call. So ships are apt to need fresh supplies en route. Maybe the deuterium runs low, or the protein, or—lots of things. Or else, because no ship has perfect biochemical balance, it's necessary to stop on a homelike world and flush out accumulated by-products with fresh air. Planets suitable for the various types of space-going life forms are listed in the 'Pilot's Data Bank and Ephemerides' for each region."

"He says we gotta tank up," Urgo told the inspector.

Klak't'klak of Ittatik nodded, signifying assent in the same way as most 143an cultures. The head he used for this purpose also resembled the 143an, and those of both his shipmates, in that it had two eyes and a mouth. However, mouth and nostrils were set in a beak that brought the narrow skull to a point. A fleshy aileron grew from the top, counterpart to the rudderlike fluke at the end of a thin tail. The body in between had, like Pazilliwheep's, evolved from a hexapod. But on Ittatik the rear limbs had become legs terminating in claws to grasp branches; the middle limbs had become skinny arms with six-digited hands; the forelimbs were now leathery wings. A keelbone jutted from the deep-chested torso. When he stood erect, Klak't'klak's nude gray-skinned frame was of slightly less stature than Pazilliwheep's; but his wingspan was easily twelve feet. Nonetheless, he could not fly here. The ship's G-field was set lower than his home gravity, but the air was so much thinner that he couldn't stay healthy without artificial help. This took the form of a pomander which he kept lifting to his face. The oxygen-generating biochemicals within smelled like rich swamp ooze.

"The requirement is understood," he said, "and obviously biological maintenance problems alone suffice to compel your descent into the planetary atmosphere. The point, however, which it was desired to make, is that a primary reason for the selection of this vessel as my transport was that you were, indeed, planning to restock on the world in question. Furthermore, your cargo is not perishable nor urgently required by the consignee. Thus the sum total of inconvenience and delay is minimized. Admittedly, I may be the cause of your remaining for more than the few 37.538-hour periods you presumably reckoned with. But if all appears to be in order, if there is no clear need at this point in time for further investigation of the possibility that ameliorative action may be required somewhere upon the globe, then we should be able to proceed within two or three months. I will not insist upon being returned to Zandar, but will rather continue with you to the Rim, where I shall debark in order to instigate a study of conditions prevailing upon that frontier."

"Oh," said Urgo. To Pazilliwheep: "He says we'll be stuck there for at least two or three months."

"Oh!" said the navigator pilot, rather more pungently. "Will you ask his unblessed bureaucratship why the inferno he wants to excrete away so loving much time on one unseemly little ball of fertilizer?" Likewise rather more pungently.

"No fair," grumbled Urgo. "I can't talk to him like that."

Klak't'klak explained. He wasn't really much interested in 143. His primary mission was to make sure that things were going well on the civilized planets of the Rim, and recommend remedies to the Federation authorities for whatever he found amiss. Still, 143 was overdue for inspection—seeing that it housed one nation that belonged to the great confraternity.

Such membership confers certain privileges. They are not many, because a galactic-scale league is necessarily a loose one, little more than a set of agencies serving the common interests of wildly diverse cultures. But a member is entitled to some things: for example, technical assistance if it wishes to modernize in any way.

"No," said Pazilliwheep, "our friends on 143 aren't what you would call the go-getter type. They're content to sell us their services, use of landing space, a few kinds of goods. Mainly they take biologicals in exchange—you know, longevity pills and, uh, other medicines. Ask them yourself if you doubt my word."

"I do not, of course," Klak't'klak answered through Urgo. "But I gather the planet holds numerous cultures. Perhaps they are being treated unfairly. Might they not, for example, be worthy of Federation membership too?"

"Chaos, no!" Pazilliwheep paused. "Well, I suppose they're no worse than some I could name. But no better, either. We do make spot checks, we traders, in the hope of finding new potential markets. But the majority of 143ans haven't shown any improvement in the better than two centuries that the blob's been visited. They've got a drab, fragmented, quarrelsome, early-mechanical kind of civilization. Last time I was there, we noticed traces of manned landings on the single moon. That indicates the stage they're at. If they learned the Federation exists—"

"They would have to be admitted to membership if they asked."

"Exactly! And can you imagine the results? Those dismal characters would yell for so much technical assistance that their whole planet would be one gigantic college for the next fifty years. Sector taxes would go up ten percent, I'll bet, to finance it. We'd have to stop using our base, probably, because of their confounded nationalistic regulations about passports and I don't know what other nonsense. And there isn't as handy a planet for us within a hundred light-years." Pazilliwheep gestured violently. "And all this sacrifice on our part for what? To add one more lousy space-traveling species—competing right in our trade lanes to the Rim!"

"You are satisfied with the status quo, then?"

"Right. The 143ans who do know about us and do have membership are friendly, dignified, unaggressive, mind-their-own-business people who'll work for us when we need help at an honest wage for honest labor, and who produce salable handicrafts. Do you wonder that we hide our existence from everyone else?"

"No. Frankly, I cannot help suspecting you underpay your native help; that is what 'honest wage for honest labor' usually means. But I am more concerned with ascertaining whether the planet has other civilizations that would, on balance, prove an asset to the Federation. Rather than read the sporadic reports of untrained and biased observers, I want to investigate and decide for myself."

Even through Urgo's translation, Pazilliwheep noted how Klak't'klak had dropped his elegant periods for shorter sentences in a sharper tone. The navigator pilot sighed and resigned his soul. All right, he'd be hung up for a while on 143, chauffeuring the sector inspector around, assisting with instruments, catching natives for interviews. (This was done in such wise that, after they were released, no one believed their story. Experience had shown that the best ploy on 143 was the Benign Observers of Elder Race.) He and Urgo would be at once busy and bored.

Yet…eventually they'd start drawing overtime pay. And the mission on 143 wouldn't likely be prolonged. If nothing else, *Grumdel Castle* was uncomfortable. Her cramped cabins, vibrating decks, rusty metal, chipped plastic, wheezy ventilators, and uninspired galley saw to that. In addition, she carried so few books and tapes suitable for Klak't'klak that he would have them memorized in weeks. Pazilliwheep and Urgo always laid in recreational materials before a voyage. But what use to an Ittatikan were Ensiktan murder mysteries and Bontuan pornography?

And so *Grumdel Castle* creaked and groaned the long dark way to the Solar System. She took up orbit around the third planet while Pazilliwheep checked for indications of excessive radioactivity, smog, and other hazards of an early-mechanical culture. Meanwhile Urgo the Red went outside to install camouflage tubes on the hull.

His shipmates saw his fur as bright blue; but then, they didn't use a visual spectrum identical with the Bontuan. The engineer supercargo was a tailless biped, eight feet tall and broad to match. His head was round, short-muzzled, big-eyed, fuzzy, and rather endearing. His hands were five-fingered, his feet four-toed. In spite of his hirsute skin, he affected white coveralls, sandals, and an ornate belt.

He clumped in again and shed his spacesuit. "Guess they'll hang together a while," he reported, "but if the owners don't spring for a new set when we get home, I'm gonna look for another berth. How's the planet doin'?"

"About as before. I note more air traffic each time, though, damn it." Pazilliwheep said. "Also, today, what appears to be a manned orbital satellite. We'll have to wait here till the stupid thing's on the opposite side of the globe."

Klak't'klak inquired why they lingered. Urgo explained. *Grumdel Castle* used a camouflage standard on worlds of this atmospheric type, where it was desired to fly unbeknownst. The natives could not detect an operating hyperdrive; if they had that capability, they'd soon be making their own starships! And antiradiation screens served to control air molecules as well as atomic particles, making even the fastest travel soundless. But you were still stuck with the fact that your ship was a solid, visible, radar-reflecting object.

So you wrapped her in the gaudiest ionized gas-discharge effect you could generate. You added powerful magnetic and electrostatic fields, and varied them randomly. You sailed in, alerting every eye and every instrument for a hundred miles around—

Just like a natural traveling plasmoid.

But since those erratic masses of molecules and electrons occur in atmosphere, and the ship was in space, she must first sneak down.

Presently she did. Near her destination, she spied a native aircraft. At Klak't'klak's request, she veered close so he could get a good look. Then she headed off for the home of that 143an people who, during the past two hundred years, had been members in good standing of the Galactic Federation.

On the assumption that the flying saucer would continue in a straight line, Sean Lindquist zigzagged along the same general path. After half an hour he was rewarded. He crossed above an immense red ridge. Its farther slope tumbled into a canyon whose bottom was the most vivid green he'd spied in a long while. Squarish adobe buildings were stacked against one rock wall, overlooking a stream lined with trees. But what made his pulses jump afresh was the object that lay before the houses. The dazzling, confusing play of colors was gone; the shape had definite outlines and a dark gray hue; but it was surely the thing that had buzzed him. And by all the saints and any heathen gods who cared to join in—it *was* a vessel!

He tilted his airplane's wings, crammed on power, and whipped back the way he had come. A thermal nearly tossed him from control. But he must get out of sight before he was observed and—

And what? Some kind of ray gun shot him down? He ran his tongue across lips gone sandpapery. The ship had to be from outer space: real outer space, the unimaginable abysses that held the stars. He'd followed the progress of flybys and landings within the Solar System. Hence he knew that, while the saucerians might be little and emerald-colored, they were not from any neighborhood planet. He also knew enough aerodynamics to be sure no terrestrial organization was experimenting with stuff that advanced. Even if he had been ignorant of the engineering requirements, he was learned in the ways of public relations offices…"Stop maundering, will you?" he croaked.

What to do?

He kept the plane wobbling back and forth on the far side of the mountain while, feverishly, he studied his charts and tried to discover where he was. Uh, yes…"Wuwucimti," plus the symbol for Population 0-1000…evidently a pueblo, and lonely as hell, to judge from the fact that nothing led away from it except a dim mule trail…Numbly, like parts of a machine rather than a body, his fingers activated the radio. If he could raise, oh, Gallup or Durango or wherever…make his location known, so it wouldn't do the aliens any good to destroy him…A distant seething filled his earphones. Whether atmospherics or They were responsible, he couldn't get through.

He got his pipe off the floor, reloaded and relit it, and fumed himself into a measure of calm. A long gulp from a bottle that lived in his sleeping bag was equally helpful. *Consider, Lindquist.* he thought. *You've stumbled on a secret to shake the world. But this is hardly our first visit from yonder. Leaving aside the mistakes, the hoaxes, and the claims of the nut cults, there always was a certain amount of saucer observation that couldn't be explained away. At least, it was easier to believe in spaceships than in some of those concatenations of coincidences that the orthodox scientists postulated! And now you've got proof that the ship hypothesis is right. Only, who's going to take your unsupported word? Supposing you could go fetch witnesses, the thing's bound to be gone when you return. You'd get classed with Adamski and his breed.*

For which same reason, you'll keep your mouth shut.

Hey! he reflected with rising eagerness. *How many people have actually met saucerians, and been disbelieved afterward? And, on that account, how many more have met them and—not wanting to be laughed at—simply kept mum?*

After all…what little consistent evidence there is—indicates the saucerians aren't evil. They're shy, or snobbish, or something, but I can't remember anyone ever claiming that they do any deliberate harm. So maybe, this time, I can—

Allowing himself no second thoughts, Lindquist brought the plane about. He roared back over the mountain, chose his position, tilted wings, and commenced vertical descent.

Updrafts were tricky; and this was a somewhat battered, cranky craft he had. For a while he was too occupied with controls, instruments, hiss and shudder around him, to heed much else. He did see how the saucer squatted imperturbable in the bright late sunlight. Tawny mudbrick walls, red canyon sides, deep blue sky, green meadows and cornfields, green cottonwoods and willows along the quicksilver stream, dusty sage and juniper farther back—and in the middle, a spaceship from the stars!

His landing gear touched. He cut the power. Silence hit him like a thunderclap. He unharnessed, opened the door, and sprang shakily forth. The air was thin, dry, pungent with resinous odors. Except for a breeze, tinkle of water, bleating from a pasture shared by sheep and goats, the silence continued.

It was not broken by the approaching locals. They were ordinary Pueblo types, a few hundred medium-sized dark-complexioned folk of every apparent age. Men and women both wore their hair in braids. Clothing varied, from more or less traditional breechclouts, gowns, and blankets, to levi's and sports shirts. Lindquist's sharpened perceptions noted that the people were better clad, seemed more healthy and prosperous, than the average southwest Indian. And they were strangely uncordial. Not that they threatened him. But they drew up in a kind of phalanx, and stared, and said never a word. Even the littlest children sucked their thumbs in a marked manner.

Lindquist gulped. "Uh…hello," he said. His voice sounded very small to him. "I'm afraid I, uh, don't speak your language." They might know Spanish. *"Buenos dias, mis amigos."* Trouble was, that damn near exhausted his Spanish.

A grizzled, weather-beaten man called softly, "Sikyabotoma." Lindquist said, "I beg your pardon?" but decided it was the name of a young man who stepped to the elder. They put heads together and conferred in mutters.

Lindquist gulped again, nodded, pasted on a smile, and started toward the flying saucer. At once he grew so conscious of it—so astonished, for instance, at the pitted, corroded metal of what had once been a smooth unitized shape—that the Indians faded from his mind. Colliding with them was a shock. Several had moved to intercept him.

They were embarrassed. The pueblo dwellers are among the politest beings on Earth. They smiled, in a forced way, bobbed their heads and waved their hands. They pushed gently on Lindquist's arms, as if to urge him toward their houses.

Anger flared. "No, thanks!" he snapped, and planted his heels.

The young man rescued the situation. He was among those who wore modern clothes, including the gaudiest sombrero Lindquist had ever met. He sauntered forth, tapped the newcomer on the back, and said, "Excuse me, buddy. That's not the way."

"What?" Lindquist whirled to confront him.

"Welcome to Wuwucimti Pueblo," the Indian said. "I'm Sikyabotoma. But in the Army I used the name Joe Andrews. Picked that because it's handy being near the head of the alphabet. So if you want, call me Joe. Come on inside and have a drink."

"I...I thought...you—"

"You needn't be surprised. Sure, the Hopi don't approve of liquor as a rule. But they need somebody like me, who's equipped to handle white men. Like, I interpret when we take the mules to town and stock up on things. And I did do a military hitch. So I've gotten a few outside habits. It's good bourbon."

"But...I mean—" Lindquist twisted his neck to goggle at what lay now behind his back. "I never imagined—"

"Yes, it is unusual," Sikyabotoma agreed cordially. He linked arms with Lindquist, who must needs come along as he ambled in the direction of the village. "We're the most isolated pueblo in the country. Not awful old. A bunch of Shoshonean-speaking Hopi moved here to get away from the Spaniards after the revolt of 1680 was put down. So we have a tradition of minding our own affairs, and we discourage visitors. Nothing rude, you understand. We just don't do anything interesting when the anthropologists come. And we got rid of the missionaries by telling the last padre who showed that we'd already been converted to hard-shell Baptists."

The other Indians trailed after at some distance. They kept their silence. "Please don't think we're hostile," Sikyabotoma urged. "We're only satisfied. We combine the old and the new as suits us best; and we do quite well for ourselves, on the whole; and everybody among us knows it. Regular contact with the outside world would upset our applecart. So we act pretty unanimously to defend our privacy. Unanimity comes natural in the Hopi culture anyhow. If you're in trouble, we'll help you, Mr., uh..."

"Lindquist," said Lindquist feebly.

"We'll do what we can for you. But if you dropped in out of curiosity, well, I hate to sound inhospitable, but the fact is you'd find Wuwucimti a mighty dull place. Lively young fellow like you, huh? I'd suggest you proceed right away. And, uh, I'd take it as a favor if you don't mention this stop you made. We're not after tourist business and that's that. You savvy?"

"Dull?" Lindquist tore loose. He spun, flung out both arms toward the great spaceship, and shouted, "You call that dull?" so echoes rang.

"Well, not to me, of course," Sikyabotoma said. "I get my kicks. And the average pueblo dweller is staid by nature."

"Flying saucers and...and..."

Sikyabotoma regarded Lindquist narrowly. "Do you feel O.K.?" he asked.

"Sure, I feel O.K.! What about that flying saucer over there?"

Sikyabotoma squinted. "What flying saucer?"

"What do you mean? I...I...I chased it...to here...and there it sits!"

"Awa-Tsireh," called Sikyabotoma, "do you see a flying saucer?"

A middle-aged Indian looked solemnly back and shook his head. "No," he grunted. "No see fly sawsuh."

"I'll ask the others in Hopi if you want," Sikyabotoma offered. "But you know, Mr. Lindquist, when people aren't used to this thin air and sun glare, they can mistake mirage effects for some of the damndest things. I'd be careful about that if I were you. Flitting around in an airplane, a guy has to be mighty sure what's real and what's an optical illusion. Doesn't he?"

Lindquist stared for an entire minute into the broad bland face. The others moved closer, and had also begun to smile and murmur soothing words. Briefly, in his tottering mind, he wondered if he was not indeed the crazy one.

No! He sprang back and launched himself. His legs flew. Dust spurted, the footfalls slammed through his shins, and he made an end run around the tribe. Meanwhile he bawled:

"Do radars have illusions? Do compasses? By heaven...let me...at my instruments...and I'll show you!"

He reached the ship. Its curve swelled immense above him, casting a knife-edge shadow. He snatched a rock and pounded the metal. It boomed. A lizard ran away. The sandstone crumbled under repeated impacts. "Is that optical?" he screamed.

The Hopi had been running toward him. But once more they halted at a distance. Sikyabotoma came nearer. The young Indian stopped, regarded Lindquist, and sighed.

"O.K.," he said. "I didn't really expect it'd work. Have your way, Charlie."

He semaphored with his arms.

Lindquist stepped back from the ship, panting, sweating, trembling. The canyon brooded in a quiet immense and eternal; only the wind had voice. Then came a rusty creak.

Someone had been watching from inside, through some kind of television. And in some fashion, a part of the hull detached itself on three sides and unrolled, to make a gangway to the ground. Three creatures came forth. Lindquist saw them and strangled on an oath that was half a prayer.

Sikyabotoma took a philosophical attitude. "You ought to see what membership in the Galactic Federation has done to our kachina dolls," he remarked. "The real ones, that we don't show the anthropologists."

"This is most annoying," Klak't'klak said. He flapped his wings. They made a parchment rustle where he squatted in the sunshine, under the spaceship, confronting the bug-eyed 143an.

"Sure is," Urgo the Red agreed. "We gotta get rid of this bum. And then we gotta stay away from here for several days—prob'ly go into orbit—in case he does somehow talk somebody into comin' back with him. Right when I was hopin' to get that Number Three regulator tuned!"

"I was thinking more personally," the inspector admitted. "I am not prepared to conduct interviews. That is, my translating computer has not yet assimilated the records of this planet's dominant languages which the autochthons brought me from their…ah…what did they call it?…their *kiva*. And I hate working through interpreters."

"So don't."

"No, as long as we have captured this being, I feel my duty is to examine him for whatever information he can give. And, too, I should endeavor to allay his fears. To this poor unsophisticated semi-savage, we must resemble veritable demons. Consider how he staggered to his aircraft for that bottle of tranquilizing medication he now clutches so tightly."

Urgo waved a massive blue hand. Pazilliwheep trotted over, using his nose-tendrils in turn to summon one of the Indians. "I don't speak this barbarian's jabber," the navigator pilot explained, "but Sikyabotoma does." Urgo passed on the datum.

The galactics, including the Pueblo man, formed a semicircle confronting Lindquist. The rest of the village watched aloofly. Klak't'klak lifted one gaunt arm. "Greeting to you, O native." he said in Interlingo-12. "Rest assured that you are in the grasping organs of civilized and benevolent entities who intend you no harm; who may, indeed, prove to be the promoters of a benign revolution upon your planet. Whether this eventuality materializes or not is dependent upon my official judgment as to whether a general announcement of the existence of a galaxy-wide Federation of technologically and sociologically advanced races will serve the larger good, including your own good. Hence the outcome is to a small extent dependent upon what you yourself, individually, today, choose to give me in the way of information. May I therefore initially request—request, mind you; we shall not compel you—and advise that you relate to me in circumstantial detail what I wish to be apprised of, beginning with the events which led to your untoward arrival."

"He wants to know how the bum got here," Urgo said in Interlingo-7.

"The honorable envoy of the Federation's guiding council asks what gods led hither the stranger's path," Pazilliwheep said in Hopi.

"The pterodactyl character is a kind of inspector," Sikyabotoma said in English. "He won't hurt you, but he would like to know a few things, like how come you stopped by."

Lindquist took another pull on his bottle. "I…I saw the flying saucer…and followed it," he whispered.

"Yeah, sure. Look, pal, I don't believe you can tell him a thing that I can't. But let's go through with the game and make him happy, O.K.? The other two are plain merchant sailors. Old buddies of mine; I even made a voyage with 'em once, to help establish an outplanet market for our local handicrafts. But Beak-and-Wings, he's come to find out whether the galactics ought to let the rest of Earth know about them; whether they should invite every country to join their Federation. In other words, he's one of those do-gooder types."

"You…don't think…we should join?" Lindquist got forth.

"Frankly, no." Sikyabotoma shrugged. "Not that this pueblo is selfish, or holds a deep grudge against the white man, or anything. However, you can't expect we'll fall over ourselves to do the white man a favor, can you? Especially when that'd end our own comfortable monopoly on trade and services with the galaxy. We're not ostentatious about it, and, of course, we're pretty small potatoes in the Federation…but you'd be surprised at some of the stuff we keep in our adobes."

Lindquist braced himself. "*I* look at the matter differently," he said. "Can I trust you to give him my side of the story?"

"Sure. I may be prejudiced, but I'm honest. Besides, he figures to study the whole planet. Don't loft your hopes, though. One dollar gets you ten that he turns thumbs down."

"How can he?" Lindquist cried.

Sikyabotoma looked closer. "I'll be damned, you're right. He has thumbs on both sides of his palms…Oh. You mean how can he refuse the U.S.A., and the U.S.S.R., and France, and Britain, and China, and—Well, it's easy. They haven't anything unique to offer. Not in a galaxy loaded with civilizations. All that Wuwucimti has, really, is a convenient location, and people who don't swarm over every ship that lands, stealing things and asking stupid questions. You start letting in the riffraff, and first you've got to disestablish institutions like war, and then you've got to give them technical assistance, and then—Anyhow, it's a mess. That's why secrecy is preserved, you know. If you guys ever found out the truth, collectively, you'd have to be invited to join. Otherwise, the do-gooders say, your precious little egos would be so bruised that what culture you have would fall to pieces." The Hopi checked himself. "Sorry. I didn't mean to sound smug. Or malicious. It's just the way the ball bounces."

"How about my ego?" Lindquist demanded, close to tears.

Sikyabotoma patted his shoulder. "Nothing personal, Charlie," he said. "Individual humans who got interviewed in the past don't seem to've suffered harm. Look at it this way: you won't be any worse off than you were. Huh?"

"I'll tell the world!" Lindquist said furiously. "I'll call in the F.B.I., the news reporters, the—"

"For both our sakes," the Indian answered, "I wish you wouldn't. You'd only make a fool of yourself. At most, you'd bring in somebody else, and the village 'ud have to go through the same old cover up as before. You wouldn't do that to us, would you, now? A nice guy like you?"

"No, I'll keep watch—" Lindquist snapped his mouth shut.

"Till another ship arrives, eh?" Sikyabotoma chuckled. "You'd wait a mighty long time, podner."

"Not many come?"

"Well, it varies. With thousands of shipping outfits plying these lanes, we can expect several craft per year to stop by, though we never know in advance. However, what we do know is if anybody's within twenty-thirty miles. A little gadget that detects thoughts. So you can't monitor us unbeknownst. We can warn off ships: they do radio us from orbit before landing. Chances are they'd come down anyway, but maintain camouflage. All you'd observe, or photograph, would be a colored blur like ordinary ball lightning. If worst comes to worst, a bunch of us can deal with a spy. Nothing violent, understand. We'll kind of escort him away, no more. If we have to break his camera, we'll pay him full value. You see, we're Federation members, so we live by Federation rules."

The inspector spoke words which went along the chain of interpreters. Sikyabotoma nodded and sat down on his haunches. "You might as well relax," he said. "Over here, in the shade. You're about to be interviewed."

Time passed. Shadows lengthened. The Pueblo women cooked dinner. They brought some to Lindquist. It was Hopi food, based on cornmeal tortillas, but the filling was like nothing on Earth. Quite literally so. Sikyabotoma explained that a lot of interstellar trade was in spices.

When the sun went below the mountains, stars leaped arrogantly forth. Coyotes yipped across a gigantic silence. Lindquist stared heavenward, shivering in the cold.

Sikyabotoma rose, yawning. "That's that," he said. "They'll fly you out now, to make sure you don't hang around. Any special place you'd like to go?"

"Colorado Springs?" Lindquist faltered.

"I wouldn't. NORAD headquarters, remember. If they spot your plane on their radars without any flight plan filed, they might get a little unpleasant."

"That's my problem." Lindquist could scarcely keep his tone level. He had not dared hope his precarious plan would work to this extent.

"O.K., so 'tis. Hm-m-m, I think I'll ride along. You might enjoy being shown around a genuine hypership. Something to tell your grandchildren, if you don't mind 'em thinking you're an awful liar."

The three aliens embarked. Lindquist and Sikyabotoma followed, after the village elders had bidden the former goodby with every ritual courtesy. A larger opening gaped elsewhere in the hull; the aircraft rose on some silent, invisible beam of force; it was stowed aboard. The great ship closed herself. Soundlessly, but swathed again in rainbow haze, she lifted and swung north.

Inside, she was less impressive. In fact, she was grimy, battered, noisy, and ill-smelling. Sikyabotoma shrugged when Lindquist dared remark on it. "So what do you expect in an old tramp with cheapskate owners? Red plush toilet seats? C'mon, we better stash you in your plane. Be over Pike's Peak soon."

When Lindquist was harnessed, the Hopi stuck a hand through the open cabin door of the aircraft. His brown face was bent in a wry smile. "Shake," he offered. "I hope there aren't any hard feelings. You're a right guy. I could damn near wish Birdbrain does certify this whole planet for membership. But I know he won't. So long, Charlie, and good luck to you."

He closed the door. For a minute Lindquist sat alone, in the thrumming, coldly lit cavern of the hold. The hull opened. Stars glittered in the aperture, brilliant against crystalline black. Air puffed outward, popping his eardrums, and cold flowed inward. He started his engine. But it was the impalpable force beam that carried him forth and released him.

Town lights glittered far beneath. The spaceship hovered close, like a swirling, shifting, many-hued light-fog. She departed, gathering speed until no human-built rocket could have paced her. Night swallowed the vision.

Lindquist shuddered. His radio earphones squawked with challenge. An interceptor jet winged toward him. "Sure," he said. "I'll come down. Any place you want." Excitement torrented through him. "And then…take me to your leader!"

In the morning they turned him over to Lieutenant Harold Quimby. Maybe that press officer could get rid of him.

Sunlight slanted through a window, beyond which stretched the neat buildings and walked the neat personnel of a United States Air Force base. Light glowed on immaculate office furniture, on Quimby's polished insignia and practiced toothpaste smile. Lindquist grew doubly aware of how unshaven, sweaty, and haggard he was. His eyes burned; the lids felt like sandpaper.

"Cigarette?" Quimby invited. "Coffee?"

"No," Lindquist grated. "Some common sense. That's all I ask. The common sense and common decency of listening to me."

"Why, surely our people—"

"Yeah, they grilled me. For most of the night. Oh, polite enough. But they kept after me and after me."

"Well, you must realize, Mr. Lindquist, when you suddenly appear over a sensitive area like this, you must expect that men charged with the national defense will ask for details."

"Damn it, I *gave* them details! Every last stinking detail I could dredge up. Look, the fact that I did appear, without your fool radars registering me till I was there…doesn't that mean anything?"

"It means that the plasmoid blanketed your approach. Not unknown. An unusually fine plasmoid, wasn't it?" Quimby leaned forward with a sympathetic air. "I can easily understand why you would follow such a beautiful and fascinating object. And, ah, how the interplay of colors…hypnotic, even epileptogenic effects…mistaking a vivid dream for reality—No, wait!" He lifted his hand. "The Air Force is not calling you a lunatic, Mr. Lindquist. What happened to you could happen to anyone. I talked with Major Williams of our psychiatric division before my appointment with you today. He assured me that illusion and confusion are the normal result of lengthy exposure to certain optical phenomena. We lodged you overnight precisely so that our intelligence officers could make a few phone calls, checking on your background and recent activities. I assure you, Mr. Lindquist, we are careful here. We have established that you are sane and well-intentioned. We appreciate the patriotism that led you to seek us out, even in your, ah, slightly delirious condition. You are free to go home, Mr. Lindquist, with the warmest thanks of the United States Air Force." Quimby paused for breath.

"But you saw the spaceship yourselves!" Lindquist groaned. "You radared the thing. You recorded electric and magnetic effects. Your technical man admitted as much to me. How can you call it an illusion?"

"We don't, sir, we don't," Quimby beamed. "It was absolutely real. The Air Force is not dogmatic; also the Air Force has been interested in this subject for many years. When the first so-called 'flying saucer' reports were made in the 1940s, the Air Force mounted its own official investigation. Here"—he handed Lindquist a glossy-paper pamphlet off a stack on his desk—"a brief summary of Project Blue Book. Certain people remained unsatisfied. They charged—quite wrongly, I assure you—distortion and suppression of evidence. Accordingly, to clear its good name, in the late 1960s the Air Force commissioned a new investigation by independent scientific organizations and reputable unaffiliated individuals. An unclassified project, mind you." He gave Lindquist another pamphlet. "Here is a history of that effort. It was crowned by success. Here is a summary of the technical findings. Here is a somewhat more popular account, and here is a reprint of what proved to be the key physical data, and here is a—"

Lindquist slumped. "I know," he said. "They told me last night what they believe. Ball lightning."

"Well, no, not exactly that," Quimby said. "The subject is pretty complicated. Yes, sir, pretty complicated, if I do say so myself. Flying saucer reports had many different sources. Early during the furore, it was shown that most were caused by sightings of weather balloons, or mirages, or reflections, or Venus, or any of several other things. There did remain a certain small percentage which could not be accounted for in that way. But then it was shown—about 1965 or '70, as I recall—that nature can generate plasmoids in the atmosphere. You know, traveling masses of ionized gas, held together for a few hours by a kind of self-generated magnetic bottle. Ball lightning is one kind of plasmoid. There are others. Including the kind that shines, produces erratic magnetic and electric fields, reflects radar, shuttles about at incredible speed but with never a sound, and is roughly disk-shaped. In short, the classical flying saucer apparition. This was *proven,* Mr. Lindquist. It was observed, analyzed, and reproduced in the laboratory. By now, any good electrophysicist who wanted to take the trouble could fake his own flying saucer. Here, take this account by the Nobel Prize winner Dr.—"

"Never mind," Lindquist mumbled. "I don't doubt there are natural neon signs zipping around. So the saucerians don't need anything for camouflage except a false one."

"Well, Mr. Lindquist," Quimby replied, the least bit severely, "don't you believe it's high time you looked at the matter like the reasonable man you are? You had a, ah, an involuntary psychedelic experience. You would not have had it if you had known the truth. Then you would have realized there was no point in chasing that plasmoid. Nobody does any more, you know. Because of your, ah, long foreign residence, you weren't kept up to date. But the truth is that the flying-saucer hysteria vanished years ago. Once the clear light of science was thrown on this murky subject, the American people realized that everything had been due to an easily explainable natural phenomenon. They turned their attention to better topics. You won't find anyone any longer who claims that flying saucers are, ah, spaceships crewed by little green men."

"Would you believe a surly blue giant?"

"No, Mr. Lindquist, I would not. Nor, ah, pterodactyls and centaurs with arms on their noses. Least of all that a bunch of poverty-stricken, mostly illiterate Pueblo Indians are—Well, you have a very imaginative subconscious mind, sir, but I'm afraid no one cares to listen. So you had better settle for reality."

Lindquist raised eyes in which hope still struggled with exhaustion. "No one?" he asked. "Absolutely no one in the world?"

"Oh, I suppose a few cranks are left, like in California," Quimby laughed. "People to whom the outer-space-visitors idea became a sort of religion that they still can't bear to give up." His tone sharpened. "It would not be advisable to prey on their gullibility. Not that you would, Mr. Lindquist. But some confidence man who, ah, tried to squeeze a dollar from those poor deluded souls…yes, I think the authorities might deal rather harshly with him."

Lindquist rose. "I know when I'm licked," he said bitterly. "I won't take any more of your time."

"Well. thank you, that's appreciated." Quimby stood, too—with almost indecent haste. "We are rather busy at the moment, preparing press kits about General Robinson's promotion to four-star rank."

Lindquist ignored the proffered hand and shambled toward the door. "Too busy to bring Earth into the Galactic Federation!" he spat.

"That's not the job of the Air Force," Quimby reminded him. "Foreign relations belong to the State Department."

The bar which Lindquist found was noisy with college students. He didn't mind that. For the most part he sat hunched over his beer. When his awareness did, occasionally, return from interstellar immensities—to order more beer—he got a little encouragement from the sight of coeds passing by. A universe which had produced girls couldn't be all bad.

Contrariwise, it must be a hell of a good universe. Rich, wonderful, various, exciting, mind-expanding, soul-uplifting: if only you could get out into it.

"Rats!" Lindquist muttered around his pipestem. "Got to be *some* way to make a buck with what I know."

He wasn't entirely cynical. *The galactics were*, he thought. They denied to the human race every marvel, opportunity, insight, help, comfort that a millennia-old science must have to give. Not that they were monsters. With—how many suns in the galaxy? A hundred billion? They rated intelligent species at a dime a dozen, and probably this was inevitable. Indeed, it was astonishing how altruistic they were. They could have conquered Earth in an afternoon. But instead, they slunk about in disguise for fear of what the knowledge of their presence might do to men…if, following the revelation, they did not promptly act to lift man to their own level.

Sure, you can't blame them. Why should they solve our problems for us? Especially when it'd be a lot of trouble and expense to them. What did we ever do for the galactics?

Lindquist fumed smoke into the racketing, beer-laden air. *That's not the point,* he thought grimly. *The point as far as I'm concerned is that I and my* whole ever-lovin' species will keep on being poor, ignorant, war-plagued, tyrannized, restricted, short-lived, and I don't know what else—unless the Federation can be forced to take us in.

Which it can be, if we the people of the United States learn for sure that the Federation exists.

How? The galactics, including those Injuns, understand how to keep us blindfolded. They didn't even bother to silence me. Who'd listen?

Maybe, momentarily, the chance had existed. In 1950, or whenever the flying saucer craze started, human civilization had advanced to the point where it could imagine extraterrestrial visitors; and it had not yet gotten the idea of plasmoids, or rather, it was denying that any such thing could be. So the standard spaceship disguise had been ineffective for a decade or two. Unfortunately, though, no one had happened to catch a sitting spaceship during those years. At least, not enough people had happened to do so, and their unsupported word was insufficient. Now research had established that flying saucers could be plasmoids. Therefore, humankind concluded, they were plasmoids. As the galactics had foreseen.

Today no one would believe the crazy truth. Except maybe some pathetic remnants of the discredited saucer cults. They might. But what could they do, except invite the narrator into their mutual admiration society?

What...could...they...do?

Sean Lindquist leaped to his feet. His table went over, scattering beer and broken glass. His pipe fell to the floor. "Eureka!" he bellowed.

The bartender approached. "You had enough, buster," he said ominously. "Start taking off your clothes and I call a cop."

The Reverend Jaxton Muir, pastor of the First United Church of the Cosmic Brotherhood, was a surprise. Though Lindquist had done considerable research beforehand, he had expected someone more, well, far out. Reverend Muir was soft-spoken, self-contained, and conventionally dressed—for Los Angeles, at least. He lived with his wife in an apartment near the shop that earned him his daily bread. The place could have belonged to any middle-class, middle-aged couple. Only the books were unusual. They formed probably as complete a library of sauceriana as existed anywhere on Earth.

"Please sit down, Mr. Lindquist," he invited. "Would you care for some coffee? Smoke if you wish. It's bad for the health, but until the Elder Brethren see fit to raise us to the next rung of evolution's ladder, we can't much help our frailties. Pardon me. I didn't intend to preach at you. You came to tell me something, not *vice versa*."

Lindquist wondered what his best gambit was. From what he could learn of the C. B. Church, its few score active members, and its influence on several hundred saucerists of other kinds, he didn't believe that he could be entirely truthful. Muir's credo held that the extraterrestrials were the benevolent, well-nigh omnipotent agents of a civilization which was the chosen instrument of God. That wouldn't fit so well with a rusty old tramp ship, pinchpenny owners, and so forth. Would it?

"I've had an Experience," he said.

"Really?" Muir's tone did not alter. "Do you know, I never have been vouchsafed one. Few who were are left alive: and the last confirmed report of a talk with Them was fifteen years ago." His gaze was quite steady. Traffic noises came through the window to underscore his voice with muted thunder. "Hoaxes are not unheard of."

Lindquist achieved a smile. "You're skeptical, Reverend?"

"Well, let us say I'm open-minded. I've often stated, in sermons and articles, that I think the Elders have abandoned us for a while because we grew too skeptical. They will come back when faith has come back. But—forgive me—there have been deliberate frauds, and there have been far more honest mistakes. For your sake as well as ours, we must sift your story carefully—whatever you tell."

"You're very tactful, sir." Lindquist's lanky frame relaxed in the armchair. As he felt his way into the situation, he gained confidence. "And I might as well confess at the outset, I want money. Furthermore, I haven't a scrap of physical evidence. Only the recent sighting over Colorado Springs, which thousands of people saw." He drew a breath. "However, if I can get financing, your auditors will keep track of every nickel. What we need is to build and transport a certain device which the Elders have described to me. For this, we'll have to buy materials and hire expensive technicians. We'll have to do a little R&D, perhaps, because the Elders didn't give me any blueprint, only a general verbal account. We'll have to do this on the QT until we're ready to roll, or you can imagine what a field day the news media will have."

Muir opened his mouth. Lindquist hurried on:

"In earnest of my sincerity, as well as to help, I can mortgage what little I own and toss several thousand dollars into the kitty. If you can double that, I believe we'll have the necessary. I checked on your people before I phoned you. They're not rich by a long shot. But between your congregation and, uh, its sympathizers—if you launch an appeal yourself—a few dollars contributed per person—the thing can be swung financially without hurting any individual except me if it fails."

He paused. "I do not guarantee success," he finished.

Muir sat quiet for a long time. His eyes never left his visitor. Finally he whispered, "You're not a con artist. You may be a crank, but you're honest. Go on, in God's name."

Lindquist saw tears. However noble his purpose, he felt a touch guilty as he gave his doctored account. The benevolent Elders had returned. They found Earth in dire straits. Disaster was imminent. Yet they could not destroy the human spirit by acting as dictators. They could only work through such persons as had faith in them.

Nor could they linger here. Other planets also needed their attention. But if enough humans had faith—if the veritable mustard seed existed upon Earth—then they could manifest themselves at last, and lead mankind to salvation. To this end, let the faithful build a communication device such as they demonstrated and explained to Sean F. X. Lindquist. In time, they would receive its message and they would come.

Did no such call reach them, they would sadly know that man was beyond redemption.

Passing through the ship's observation verandah—an elegant phrase for a crummy little cabin outfitted with an exterior visiscreen and a few seats adjustable to most species—Urgo the Red saw Klak't'klak. The sector inspector stood hunched before the view that slid beneath. The scene was of high desert, raw mineral hues under a blazing sun. His winged shape was etched in black by contrast. And yet he looked so frail, bowed, utterly tired and discouraged, that Urgo's equivalent of a heart went out to him. The engineer supercargo had grumbled at length during the past tedious weeks. Nevertheless, against his will, he had come to like the official passenger. It hurt him, now. to see the little Ittatikan stand thus alone. He went and joined him.

"You're really quittin', huh?" he asked inanely.

Klak't'klak uttered a mournful whistle. "Yes. Not that the natives have no potential. They seem about average, insofar as any such concept is meaningful. But I could not justify a recommendation that missions be sent to elevate them."

"Troublemakers. Yeh, I could'a told you that right off," Urgo rumbled.

"No. Not really." Klak't'klak spread his wings and folded them again. "They would not be a detriment to the Federation. But neither would they be an outstanding asset, as far as I can judge on the basis of my examinations. They would, in short, be…merely one more member species. Therefore, as long as they remain in happy ignorance of us, I cannot honestly say that the Federation taxpayer should be burdened with the cost of incorporating them. Let them invent the hyperdrive for themselves, in a thousand or two years."

Urgo belched, which out of him corresponded to a sigh of relief. "That's the spirit, Inspector! I knew you'd decide right. But how come are you lookin' so down in the chops you haven't got?"

"I don't rightly know," Klak't'klak said. "Depression, I suppose. So much time, effort, expense, inconveniencing you and Navigator Pilot Finnison—you've been extraordinarily kind, you two, and I won't forget it when I write my official report—but for nothing."

Urgo spread his mighty arms. "Ah, don't worry. The job was a drag, sure, but it's over with now. We'll stop off at the pueblo to snatch a rest and some trade goods. Then go to the Rim!"

At that moment, the buzzer sounded. Pazilliwheep's voice followed. *"Attenta!"* He had amused himself by acquiring a few 143an phrases as *Grumdel Castle* prowled around the globe. *"Pericolo!* All hands to stations!"

"What the blazes?" Urgo was already loping for the engine room. Klak't'klak flapped and hopped toward his quarters, where he would at least be out of the way. You don't argue when someone calls emergency on a hypership. The deck gonged to the engineer supercargo's footfalls. "What's'a matter?" he roared.

"I don't know," Pazilliwheep said tautly over the intercom. "Electromagnetic field...variable...registered a few seconds ago. Might be a natural plasmoid, but we'd better have a look."

Urgo felt relieved. The news could have been something nasty, like the bottom dropping out of this hull. "Where are we, anyhow?" he asked.

"About fifty miles west of Wuwucimti. Which is to say, the emanations could be from a galactic ship in distress—a little ways beyond mind-detector range from the pueblo." Pazilliwheep swung his craft through a ninety-degree turn. The acceleration compensators were so badly out of phase that Urgo slipped on the deck and hit his nose.

Nevertheless, the engineer supercargo confined his remarks to a muttered *"S nagabagabartbats!"* That was cruel country below, especially for beings who had not evolved on this planet. A vessel grounded helpless in those arid mountains and canyons might soon be crewless. And that—aside from every moral consideration—invited the disaster of discovery by non-Hopi autochthons. It was well that *Grumdel Castle* had happened by in time.

Once in the engine room, Urgo activated his own visiscreen. He saw a wild landscape, heat shimmers and dust devils...and, yes, a saucer shape on a small mesa. Its outlines were blurred by a weak camouflage field, and neither he nor Pazilliwheep could identify the make of ship. But with millions of different makes—

"Why aren't they transmitting?" Pazilliwheep wondered.

"Transmitter busted, I guess," Urgo said. "They could'a lain here for, cometfire, days or weeks, you know. Aimin' to land at Wuwucimti but not makin' it. Expectin' somebody else'd come by eventually, and keepin' their field goin' so's they'd be detectable at a distance."

"But not daring to strike out on foot for the pueblo," Pazilliwheep added.

"Right you are. Let's get down."

Grumdel Castle descended to the mesa and cut her own camouflage and her engines. The galactics emerged into brilliant, silent, sagebrush-pungent air. Hulking Urgo, graceful Pazilliwheep, broadwinged Klak't'klak moved across the sand toward the beached hypership.

Only, now that they were close, it looked less and less like a hypership. It looked more like—

"Surprise, surprise!" caroled a native voice. Sean F. X. Lindquist's lean form sprang from the false hull. He ran to meet them, arms spread in welcome, face wide open in a silly grin. "Am I glad to see you! Two weeks waiting! And you turn out to be the very same guys who—Come on and have a cold beer!"

Klak't'klak had brought his translator machine, which was keyed to several Federation as well as 143an languages. But it was his pomander behind which he retreated. His eyes rolled. He gasped. Urgo bawled, "Oh, no!" and Pazilliwheep looked ill.

Other humans emerged. So did a television camera on a dolly. "We alerted the news services," Lindquist said happily. "Of course they thought this was a lunatic-fringe project, but they did agree to stand by, in case we came up with anything good for laughs. Smile, you're on candid camera! Now we better break the news gently to my assistants, that you aren't quite the godlike beings most of them think you are." He stopped, blushed through his stubble, and beckoned to a companion. "Pardon me. I was so excited I forgot. Here's Professor Rostovtsev from Colorado U. He speaks Hopi."

Klak't'klak had already adjusted his machine to English. He turned it off for a minute, while he expressed himself in his own tongue. Then he closed the circuit again.

"Never mind," he said resignedly. "Welcome to the Galactic Federation."

Untitled Limerick

The jury was out all the day.
Next lunchtime, the foreman did say:
"Bring us five ham-on-ryes,
four chicken pot pies,
two pastramis, and one bale of hay."

Eve Times Four

Arsang talked on. And on. And on.

"It is indeed a pity," he said, "though, of course, long ago foreseeable, through the diversity of protein structures and the consequent development of mutually poisonous biochemistries—not to mention the basic variations in stellar and planetary types—it is, I say, regrettable that the percentage of worlds suitable for any given species is so small. And then, to be sure, this is reduced still further by those planets which already have auto-chthonous, intelligent species. These would hardly welcome alien colonists."

Teresina Fabricant gazed in despair out of that viewport which formed one whole wall of the lounge. Space glittered with suns and suns; but she stood in an almost visible fog of shrill platitudes, and there was no escape. How had she ever been trapped into this? By being kind to Arsang, she decided, by not cutting him off the first time his fingers closed about her arm and his voice began to pipe. But how could she have known? This was her first deep-space voyage. More experienced passengers, aware that every ship has its bore, recognized the dread tokens at once and gave Arsang a wide orbit.

"So the colonies planted by any given race, such as your own, are scattered thinly through that small portion of the galaxy we know," he continued, as importantly as he had earlier informed her that she was, of course, a graduate student of mathematics, bound for a year of study on a newly autonomous human-settled planet as part of an exchange program. "The distance between Earth and Xenophon, 154 light-years approximately, is not an unusual hop for a liner such as this. But the round-trip cruise on which most of our fellow passengers are embarked must necessarily zigzag so much between the systems it visits, that side trips to the less important places lying more or less along our route become impractical. One would not add an extra week of travel time merely to spend a single day looking at the Great Mud Mountain of New Ganymede, the double planet Holmes-Watson, the satellite system of Kepler, or the craters on Jotunheim, even though these are all terrestroid worlds with human colonies and do not lie very far off our path. You see, they are such new colonies: one tiny settlement on each, with little entertainment to offer, and otherwise a nearly unexplored wilderness. Having seen the one spectacular sight, what would our tourists do with their evening? Whereas Xenophon, where you get off, or my own Tau Ceti Two, Numa, which the ship will reach on the homeward arc of its circuit and where, of course, I disembark to report to my colleagues in the diplomatic service of His Awe-Inspiring Refulgence Pipp XI, Supreme Overlord of the United States of Korlaband—"

The high-pitched lecture began to take on a chanting quality. Bemused, half asleep, Teresina had a dreamlike feeling that she stood in the anteroom of eternity and heard a cantor or priest hold some unending ceremony...

She grew conscious that another human had entered the lounge. For a moment her heart fluttered in the hope of deliverance. Even if it was John Jacob Newhouse—fighting off his attentions was better than being talked at by Arsang XXXIII, Lord High Gongbeater to the Prideful Court of His Awe-Inspiring Refulgence Pipp XI—anything was better. She was suffering a fate worse than death and hadn't even been offered an apartment, jewels, money.

The third mate checked his stride an instant. He was a good-looking young man, with dark wavy hair and regular features. His uniform, blue tunic, white pants, peaked cap, didn't hurt those looks a bit. Of all this he was thoroughly cognizant. A moment his eyes lingered on her, frankly admiring.

Teresina was of the tall and willowy persuasion, with long blonde hair and large blue eyes, snub nose and slightly parted lips. Her black kirtle and white mantle had childlike connotations on Earth, protective coloration for a shy girl who didn't know quite what to do when a man spoke to her in any language but mathematics. The trouble was, as Newhouse had quickly observed, such an outfit looked remarkably sexy on a space liner.

But then Arsang had cornered her, and Arsang could out-chaperone any Spanish duenna. Not that the Tau Cetian was unprepossessing. He had a certain elfin quality, big dome of a head and small torso poised on four spidery legs, two slender arms waving in time with his fronded ears, hairless pale-gold skin, the face quasi-human but with great green eyes, the clothing a filmy shimmer of veils. His size, below one meter, added to the charm. However, he talked.

"Ah, Miss Fabricant." Newhouse swept a bow in her direction. "I hope you're enjoying yourself?"

Teresina gritted her teeth. "Yes, thank you!" she said.

Newhouse raised one brow, threw her an outrageous wink, and continued on his way. Teresina stared after him with smoldering eyes. Really, he was inexcusable! Not that she was cold or...or anything...of course she wanted to get married some day, and so on (here she blushed, and even diverted her attention back to Arsang for a moment)...but that scene on the promenade deck, near the start of the voyage, well, after all, a man might wait a little while after being introduced before mauling a girl around.

With a certain malicious pleasure, Teresina saw Hedwig Trumbull rise hastily from her cocktail, to seize the mate's arm. Undoubtedly: "Oh dear Mr. Newhouse—or *may* I call you Jack?—" But the officer seemed to claim urgent business; at any rate, Hedwig Trumbull returned to her table and he went out the other side of the lounge.

"I think," said Teresina, grasping at straws, "I want a before-dinner drink myself."

"By all means," said Arsang. Her faint hopes evaporated as he walked alongside her, still discoursing. Now it was about his special diplomatic mission to the Earth government, undertaken to draw up the protocol of a treaty regulating the quiggsharfen trade. She thought wildly of telling him to go away, he bored her, he reached such heights of dreariness that it was like entering a different continuum...But no. She wasn't capable of it. She would always remember, afterward, that she had hurt a lonely little being for the sake of a few days' pleasure.

She sat down and stared at the pneumoserv. It stated back at her. She remembered vaguely that a martini was gin and, what was it, oh, yes, vermouth, and wondered what proportions. At last she dialed for half and half.

Fortunately, the alarm went off at that exact moment.

Even Arsang stopped talking when the bell-tone racketed between the walls. As it died away, some woman at another table screamed and huddled close to her escort.

A magnified voice boomed out: "Attention, all passengers, attention, all passengers. This is First Mate Lefkowitz on the bridge, addressing all passengers. The captain will speak to you in a moment. Please remain calm," etc., etc. There was a sound of clicking relays. The amplifiers carried a whisper, "Wake up, sir, for God's sake," and an "uh, oh, oof, huh?" in reply, before hurriedly switching back to more alarm bells.

"What is this outrage?" shrilled Arsang.

"I believe—" Teresina wet her lips. Her pulse seemed very noisy, all at once. "I think it's the signal to go to the lifeboats."

"Yes, lifeboats, yes, that's it, lifeboats," roared a sleep-fogged voice from the loudspeaker. "Lifeboats. You all remember your lifeboat drill, uh...ahhh-*hoo*! This is Captain Ironsmiter speaking, ladies and gentlebeings. No need to get alarmed. That is, well, naturally you have been alarmed, by the alarm bells, I mean. That's what they're for, isn't it? But what I want to say, that is to say, don't be afraid. Have faith. Nothing to be afraid of. Some or other little trouble, the automatic alarms went off. We haven't located the trouble yet, but we will. Meanwhile, have faith. Uh, did I tell you this is Captain Ironsmiter speaking? To the passengers, that is, such as hear me, and I do hope that each and every one of you can hear me. All crewmen will report to, what, oh, yes, emergency stations. This is just an automatic alarm. Maybe the converter's developed a slight flutter, maybe the radiation screen has weakened, temporarily, that is, but anyhow, just go to your lifeboat stations; the ones to which you have each and everyone been assigned to, and as soon as we've found the trouble and fixed it—that is, to say, it's only a precaution, and—" The captain was cut out of the circuit in favor of more alarm bells.

"I'm in Fourteen," said Teresina. She leaped to her feet. "I'll be seeing you, Mr. Arsang."

"Oh I'll come along with you," grumbled the Tau Cetian.

"What?" wailed Teresina. "But you aren't...it isn't...I remember the drill distinctly, and your station isn't—"

"I know, I know, I know," snapped Arsang. "But how should I know which one it is? Do they expect me, hereditary Lord High Gongbeater to the Prideful Court of H.A.R. Pipp XI and special diplomatic representative from the United States of Korlaband, to attend some wretched little lifeboat drill? Come along, now, come along." He took her arm and hustled her forward with a strength remarkable in the native of a rather low-gravity planet. "Incompetence!" he shrilled. "Utter unpardonable incompetence! I shall criticize the company in the strongest terms. See if I don't!"

The passageways were a millstream of babbling tourists and valiantly struggling stewards, through which an occasional spaceman battled toward his post of duty. Swirled around a corner, Teresina saw Fred of the Gombar Road and remembered that he was in her section. "Can you give me some help?" she cried. "I can't make any headway in this mess."

"Why, indeed, Miss Fabricant, I shall be honored," said the mild basso, a meter above her. One huge arm bent downward in an inviting crook. Teresina sprang up and settled herself. Fred's shaggy, blue, rhinoceros-like body plowed onward, his centauroid torso breasting a virtual bow wave of humans. Arsang followed close behind, sputtering.

Teresina leaned toward one fan-shaped ear and said above the hubbub: "Do you think this is anything serious, Mr. Fred?"

"I trust not," replied the other. "Dear me, I do trust not. I was so looking forward to visiting Xenophon and seeing a virile pioneer culture at first hand." His small trunk waggled as he lowered his head to get its purple comb under a light fixture. The beady eyes glittered with anxiety. "I must confess to severe disappointment during my stay on Earth. There was no poetic inspiration for me. None whatsoever. Oh don't think I blame your species, please, Miss Fabricant. Everyone was most kind and hospitable. But you see, I had come as an enthusiastic student of Baudelaire. I felt I must live where he lived, just as he lived, fully to understand him. But nobody on Earth seemed interested nowadays in decadence." His meter-wide shoulders gave an earthquake shrug. "And it is not practical to be decadent all by oneself."

Teresina wondered if she had traded the frying pan for the heating coils.

Then they were at the lifeboat, through its airlock and into the seating section. The miniature spaceship would normally have carried ten humans, but since Fred was assigned to it there were only four Terrestrials present. Teresina strapped herself into a chair next to a stewardess, one Marie Quesnay. She was probably the most sensible person aboard. Besides, though it was a nasty trick, Teresina managed thus to slough Arsang off on Fred.

"What do you think the trouble is?" she asked, half fearfully.

Marie spread her hands. She was small, brown-haired, vivacious, the blue kirtle and red tights of her uniform pleasingly stretched by a more than adequate figure. "Oh, la, Ma'm'selle, it is not to say. As the captain announced, some little trouble. These alarms are not uncommon. One is always so vairry careful in space. An hour here we sit, maybe two hours, then it is all over with and they let us go again. And tomorrow all passengers get free champagne with dinner, to make the apology."

"Oh." Teresina relaxed. She achieved a timid greeting across the aisle to the other two humans, Kamala Chatterji and Hedwig Trumbull. The latter was emitting steam-whistle noises of indignation. Kamala answered with soothing admonitions to seek peace of personality.

Teresina remembered that the Indian girl was bound for Xenophon at her own expense (which she could well afford) as an Inner Reformist missionary. She was quite beautiful, in a dark dignified way; her pink sari enhanced a slim form. In fact, Hedwig Trumbull was the only female in this boat who was not better-looking than average. Teresina recalled that Hedwig had traded assignments with a stunning redhead…probably in hopes of a chance at the handsome crewman who was—

Footsteps clacked in the airlock. Third Mate Newhouse strolled in, balanced on his heels, and grinned around an impudently cocked cigarette. "All comfy?" he said.

"Where's our pilot?" demanded the Trumbull.

Newhouse grimaced faintly in her direction and turned eyes on her more decorative seatmate. "A slight reshuffling," he said. "I had reason to think the trouble would require some electronics work, so I ordered Mr. Manfred to stand by in the shop. He's the electronician's mate, you know. And then, naturally, I had to take his place in your boat."

Hedwig simpered. "A fair exchange, I'm sure." She was on the dumpy and dish-faced side, fashionably gowned, hair dyed green according to the very latest mode. She was also a spinster verging on desperation. Teresina realized that her own sufferings before Arsang were perhaps matched by those of one or two eligible bachelors on the cruise.

"Oh this is simply thrilling!" warbled Hedwig.

"Peace is all," said Kamala. "One begins on the mundane level with relaxation techniques."

"—the current status of the quiggsharfen trade is, of course, determined by the following factors," said Arsang,

"Fortunately," said Fred, "I discovered a new Terrestrial poet, the singer of largeness, of democracy, of, in short, non-decadence. I refer to Mr. Walt Whitman.

Marie cocked a suspicious eye at Newhouse. "And what reasons had you, M'sieur, for this action?" she inquired.

"I'm the officer here, Miss Quesnay," huffed Newhouse. Quickly, bowing: "Though I have never before had so charming a crew member under me. His glance lit on Arsang. "Hey, there! What are you doing—"

Teresina closed her eyes and tried to pass the time by mentally integrating $e^x \log^n X \, dx$.

Something buzzed. Newhouse spun on his heel. "God have mercy!" he cried, and vanished forward. The door to the pilot turret slammed behind him.

Seconds later a giant's fist slammed Teresina against her seat. She heard screams, but they seemed infinitely far away. The universe bellowed and pinwheeled around her.

Steadiness came again. Pseudogravity made a floor. Newhouse reached out in a blind automatic fashion and opened the pilot door. Beyond his seated form, Teresina saw an insane whirling in the viewscreens. It steadied as the circuits compensated for spin, aberration, and Doppler effect. She looked into naked space. The immense form of the spaceliner bulked momentarily against the stars. It vanished before she had drawn another breath.

Newhouse came back from his inspection. The passengers stared at him out of a thickened silence.

He held up a small haywired object. Teresina recognized, relays, resistances, and a time switch. "This is it," he said grimly.

"This is what? Do be more explicit," said Arsang, spoiling the whole effect.

"Now, now," soothed Fred, "let Third Mate Newhouse explain in his own words. I, though fetterless, large and various as the people itself, great sprawling clam'rous unsanitary body of Democracy, will hark to the singing mechanic, blithe and strong."

"Quiet!" roared Newhouse. More softly: "If you please. This is a serious matter. We are in danger of our lives."

"Ohh!" wailed Hedwig. She leaped from her chair and flung herself at Newhouse. He was caught off balance. They went down together in a heap. "Save me!" she yammered.

Kamala tugged vainly at her gown, saying, "Peace of soul, peace is all." Fred tried to help, but couldn't push past the crowding humans in the aisle.

It was Marie Quesnay who muttered something like *"Nom d'une vieille vachel!"* and applied a few brisk swats with the hand to the indicated part of Hedwig. While the various untanglements, tears, recriminations, and soothings went on, Teresina crouched back in her own seat.

Great Gauss, she thought in horror, what am I trapped into?

Arsang tugged her sleeve. "I see you have the good sense to remain clear of that disgraceful melee," he said, "Congratulations. You are almost Numan. Numa is, of course, the name of my planet, Tau Ceti Two, in the principal language of my country, the United States of Korlaband. I do not say your mind is quite on a level with, say, that of a baron or a knight, or even a peasant (I use crude English equivalents) of the U.S.K., but you would not make a bad barbarian of the Ortip Highlands. You progress, Miss Fabricant, you show distinct progress."

He was cut short by Newhouse, who bellowed down all others, smoothed his own hair and dignity, and said in a quick harsh voice:

"I found this gimmick hooked into the control circuit of the release mechanism. Obviously there's been sabotage. Doubtless the ship's alarms were tampered with also, to get us aboard this boat at the time it was scheduled to be thrown free. The communication circuit to the ship has been left open. This means our departure didn't register. They don't know we are missing. Since I'm not normally on duty at this time, they probably won't notice we're gone for hours."

"I should think," said Kamala Chatterji with a calm approaching boredom, "that we could follow the ship."

"Oh, we can try," said Newhouse gloomily. "But the top secondary speed of this boat is about 500 lights. The ship is going nearly 2000: we don't share that any longer, now when we're out of its drive field. Furthermore, we've no measurable chance of pursuing it in its own precise track. Imagine us deviating by, oh, ten degrees, which is conservative. Imagine them turning around when they miss us, but having no idea of the time at which we left. At speeds like that, can you visualize the volume of space they'd have to search? It's hopeless."

Hedwig Trumbull huffed. "I must say, if this is someone's idea of a joke, it is very childish," she exclaimed. "I am sure this is all the company's fault, for not giving psychiatric tests before selling tickets. Now we shall have to limp off to some miserable colonial world, and wait weeks until—"

Newhouse set his face into still bleaker, though handsome, lines. "I'm afraid it is sabotage," he said. "For purposes of murder."

"Oh, no," whispered Teresina. "That's impossible. No one would—"

"Every spacecraft is supposed to carry a pilot's manual with navigation tables," said Newhouse. "Ours is missing."

"What?" yelped Fred. It is something to hear a yelp in basso profundo, but no one appreciated the experience very much.

Newhouse waved a hand at the turret viewport, visible through the open door. "Look at all those stars," he said. "This boat carries supplies for about six months, in which time it could go a distance of some 250 light-years. Do you know how many stars lie in that small radius? I estimate it at ten million. No one can remember the coordinates of so many—or even of the rather small percentage which has thus far been visited let alone explored or colonized. I can identify a few super-brilliant giants, such as Rigel, but they're much too far for us to reach. Out in a little-known, thinly settled wilderness like this, you're completely dependent on your navigator's bible. And ours is missing!"

For a while, even Arsang was silent.

"We could look—" offered Teresina at last.

"From star to star? That's precisely what we must do," said Newhouse. "But don't get your hopes up. We'll try G-type suns within a reasonable range, but the probability of our hitting one with a settled planet is so small we might as well forget it."

"A planet which is habitable, though, M'sieur?" asked Marie. "I would be satisfy with that, perhaps, me."

Newhouse shrugged. "If you know any prayers, I advise you to say them."

There were plenty of stars near the middle of the main sequence. There generally are. Newhouse used the pilot instruments, including a spectroscope and a luminosity meter, for a while. Then he swung the boat around and kicked it into full secondary drive.

"I picked a sun largely at random," he said. "All I had to go by was that it should be roughly Sol-type and not too far away. You see, only humans have been pioneering this region, and they'd pick such stars. If we don't find them but do find a comfortable planet, our nonhuman friends here will like it too, though the sunlight may have a peculiar color to them. I can't say just how long it'll take us to get there. The shape of a line-of-sight approach curve depends on such things as the star's intrinsic velocity, which I can't determine accurately. But it shouldn't be more than about ten Earthdays. Meanwhile, we may as well relax and let the autopilot do the work."

"*Could* it be one of the colonized stars?" asked Kamala.

"Of course not!" shrilled Arsang. "Who ever heard of colonizing a star? The imprecision of you lesser races! Might it have a colonized planet, Newhouse?"

"I told you, who knows?" shrugged the officer. "The chances are immensely against it, though. They're not quite so much against a habitable world: one which may even have been visited once, be on record in the Survey files. But if it has aborigines—or simply if no one has gotten around to starting a settlement there—it might not be visited again for a century." He smiled. "It's a bit crowded in the turret, but if you want to join me there, one by one, I can point out our destination. Er...all but you, Mr. Fred, I'm afraid."

"What does it matter?" said the large being in a cheerful tone. "I, Fred, transcend pettiness, I, standing and yodeling on the island Mannahatta (it's really a spaceboat, but that's not very euphonious) I see the brawling westward swarm, I, myself, me, Fred."

Marie accepted the invitation. The door closed behind her and Newhouse. There was a scuffling sound, a slap, and Marie stamped out saying things which made Teresina glad her own French was so limited. Newhouse rubbed his cheek, grinned brashly, and said: "Next."

The grin faded as Hedwig Trumbull pushed her way down the aisle. He carefully left the door open this time. She closed it. There was a sound of more scuffling and Newhouse emerged, looking hunted.

Arsang rapped for order with a three-fingered fist. "Silence!" he squealed. "Quiet! Listen! Attend! Conference!" When he had them looking at him, he swiveled large green eyes from one to another and said angrily: "We have not yet determined who is responsible for this outrage. At a time when the Lord High Gongbeater to the Prideful Court of His Awe-Inspiring Refulgence has been shanghaied, yes, I shall use strong language, kidnapped, I say, with murderous intent, from a mission of vital importance, I could well say of galactic implications, namely the regulation of the quiggsharfen trade, at such a time it is no time to waste time staring at insignificant stars!"

"I don't recall that you were even supposed to be on this boat," clipped Newhouse.

"That has nothing to do with it!" yelled Arsang, turning saffron.

Teresina overcame shyness enough to say, "Yes, it does seem strange. Someone must have wanted to get rid of one of us. I mean, isn't that probable? Maybe?"

Newhouse bowed. "It's impossible that anyone could have wanted to be rid of you, Miss Fabricant," he purred.

"Now wait," said Kamala Chatterji. Her voice and the dark aristocratic face seemed unusually down-to-earth. (No, not that, thought Teresina; no such luck.) "The point is well taken. It is hard to see why anyone would do such a thing, except to eliminate a person expected to be on this lifeboat. From civilization, at least, if not the present plane of existence. That leaves out Mr. Arsang and Mr. Newhouse as intended victims; they only came aboard at the last minute."

"Me?" Marie Quesnay shrugged. "No one would get so angry with one little spaceship stewardess, *n'est-ce-pas*? Or if so—ah, I do remember one Raoul in Marseilles, that was the episode of excitement!—he would surely not elect this coldblooded means." She nodded at Teresina. "Are you not in a like situation, Ma'm'selle Fabricant?"

Teresina nodded back, ruefully. "Even more so." She wondered with a certain wistfulness how girls got involved in the episodes of excitement. She had been snowbound with a boy in a ski cabin once, when they were about fifteen, but he had been so terrified of her they scarcely exchanged a word. Then there was her present dilemma, but to date it had only involved sitting in a cushioned recoil chair.

"And Ma'm'selle Trumbull," continued Marie.

"Well," simpered Hedwig, "I won't say there haven't been men who might—"

"But not with all this sabotage and danger to innocent people. It would be so much simpler to stuff you out an airlock," said Marie rather yearningly.

All eyes moved to Fred, who blushed and murmured, "Oh, now!"

"I don't believe I remember your name," said Hedwig.

"Fred."

"What?"

"Fred. A perfectly good name in the language of my nation. Why shouldn't it be?" His annoyance moderated, Fred continued: "I am a citizen of the Gombar Road. My world we call Kefflach. It is the second planet of the star Groombridge 1830."

"And were you on some important mission?" asked Newhouse.

"I certainly was!" Fred erected his comb and switched his tufted tail. "I was studying Terrestrial poetry."

"Oh."

"You don't understand. At our last national election, the Poetic Party won a clear victory. The Prosaicists retained hardly a dozen saddles in the Assembly."

"Even so—" Newhouse looked back to Kamala with rather more pleasure. "That seems to leave you, Miss Chatterji."

The Indian girl frowned, thoughtful rather than disturbed. "I cannot make logic out of that proposition," she said.

"Speaking of propositions—" Newhouse shut his mouth hastily.

"My family in Calcutta has money," went on Kamala, "but what is the use of kidnapping me with no prospect of returning me? I am engaged in missionary work for the Inner Reformist movement, but that is not likely to arouse fanatical opposition, since one of our major tenets is that all creeds are equally acceptable."

"But there must be some reason—" began Marie.

"Indeed," said Kamala, ignoring her, "creed is irrelevant, except in the universals common to all, such as charity and peace of self. We do, to be sure, rely on the much misunderstood concept of Nirvana, but in somewhat the same sense as Zen Buddhism, in fact still more so, and hence our ideal of oneness with reality is by no means incompatible with, say, Judaeo-Christo-Moslem eschatology, Hindu poly-pantheism, Confucian—"

"I see," interrupted Newhouse.

"—ethics, and so on. You certainly do not see, and since there are, as you say, days to wait before we approach our destination, you all have an unparalleled opportunity to attain a degree of enlightenment. Now to begin with first principles, consider—"

The star had changed from a point of light to a blaze when Newhouse switched over to sublight primary drive. He locked himself in the pilot's turret and forbade interruptions, though it would take some hours to close in on the possibly Terrestroid planet his instruments had registered.

Teresina leaned back wearily and stared at a blank wall. It had been a bad ten days. In retrospect it hazed into a nightmare of monotony and petty bickering. Were it not for Marie, who organized enough activities to keep thought at bay, God knew what would have happened. Now, though, nothing remained but a waiting and the hope that someone's overloaded nerves wouldn't snap.

Such as my own, thought Teresina.

Tension led to silence, and silence was a blessing she had never fully appreciated before. Not even Arsang was as bad as that eternal female clack-clack-clack. Fred's bass and Newhouse's baritone had been such a relief she could have wept to listen. It was wonderful, she reflected that men had deep voices. Otherwise the human race would long ago have died out...She choked off that train of thought in a hurry, jumped back to her Wisconsin girlhood (no, that wouldn't do either, it brought tears too close to the surface), her college and the intoxication of really learning, the times they sat up all night drinking beer and settling the problems of the universe, the unbelievable day when notification came, she could go to Xenophon University for a year, teach, study, see a new planet and get paid for doing so—

And now what? Teresina plugged astrographical statistics into the laws of probability. The usual cheerless answer came out. The star ahead definitely had planets. There was a reasonably good chance that one would lie in a more or less Terrestroid radiation zone. (But a few degrees of average temperature either way could make for frightful danger and discomfort.) The chance was not bad that it would be of roughly Earth's mass. (However, the long-range effects of a gravity or air pressure different by more than, say, 25 percent from that for which man was evolved, were not pleasant to contemplate.) There was a fair probability of protoplasmic, photosynthesizing life, leading to an oxynitrogen atmosphere. Granted such a biochemistry, there was a smaller likelihood that it would be close enough to her own so that she could walk around freely and eat most of the native species.

The trouble was, mathematical law is so inconsiderate as to decree that such probabilities must be multiplied together to get a net result. That still left quite a few planets hospitable to man, even in this one arm of the galaxy. But the individual chance of stumbling on one was somewhere below a single percent.

Wherefore the lifeboat would doubtless make a hasty survey and then start out again for another star; and after that another, and then another; and finally the supplies would all be eaten, though the searchers would have gone crazy long before then—

I will not think this way. Teresina thrust out a small firm chin and began a resolute mental integration of log log arc tan (x^3-k) dx.

Marie, beside her smiled wryly and made a thumbs-up sign. "*Bon,*" she murmured.

And the hours passed. Teresina had almost dozed off when Newhouse's voice came from the intercom to jar her conscious: "We're very close to the planet— No, stay where you are. I can't be bothered now, it's dangerous. I'm making a tight approach curve, taking readings as I go. Don't get your hopes up too much, but it's definitely Earthlike. Mass, surface gravity, gross atmospheric composition; mean overall temperature a little higher, but the subarctic regions should be ideal for—"

"I want to see!" Hedwig leaped to her feet.

"No, I said!" cried Newhouse. "There's something wrong, a flutter in the meter readings. I didn't want to scare you by admitting it, but there is. I haven't the engineering skill to—I'm going to land. It's either that or risk hanging in orbit with a burned-out primary."

"Is it civilized?" whistled Arsang. "I do not mean, is it civilized to hang in orbit, for certainly that is not the case. Nor do I ask if the place itself is civilized, since I know that the United States of Korlaband has no extraplanetary colonies. But do you see any trace of intelligent life?"

"No interstellar colonists," said Newhouse. "The neutrino detector would register their atomic energy plant if that were the case. I haven't seen anything in the viewscreens either—no trace of native culture—Our path will carry us clear around the globe and I'll keep watching. But I'm afraid the chances are against any highly developed autochthons."

"Just to set down, though," whispered Teresina. "To get outdoors!"

"And we will still have the boat," Marie reminded eagerly. "If we can establish a base here, we can make expeditions to other stars hoping in time to find—"

"If the boat hangs together!" Newhouse's voice harshened. "I don't want to frighten you, but the deeper we get into this gravity field, the more the meters are fluttering. Perhaps our saboteur was more thorough than I realized."

"Ohhh!" shrieked Hedwig.

"Do be quiet," said Kamala. "How can our pilot have the requisite inner peace to land successfully under such a handicap, if you fail to show confidence in him?"

"Oh, I'm confident enough in him, dearie," blubbered Hedwig. "It's the machinery that I don't trust."

Kamala frowned. "It is true," she admitted, "that a means of giving inward serenity to a machine has not yet been discovered."

Presently a thin keening sounded through the walls. It became a roar, and Teresina felt waves of frictional heat. Pseudograv could not smooth out all the jerking and buffeting which rocked the boat. "I know it's a lousy landing!" Newhouse called once, raggedly. "But the primary drive is going to pieces! I haven't any more control over the phasing!"

And then at last there was an impact which smacked teeth together, a blunt roar, a scorched smell, and silence.

A wide green valley, where flowers nodded in grass and trees murmured under a gentle wing, swept past a river to forested hills. The sun was a wheel of gold, low in a sky blue and dizzyingly tall, white clouds scudded, birds were a brightness that swooped and darted overhead. Distantly could be seen a herd of animals slender and burning red, with proud horns.

Teresina sighed. "It could almost be Wisconsin."

"Long ago, however," added Fred. "Back when the great pullulating, or perhaps ululating, tide of America which I, Fred of Groombridge 1830 II, sing, had not yet swept west, O pioneers!"

"I know it's wrong of me," said Teresina. "I should be frightened or miserable or something, if only on Mother's and Dad's account." She shook her yellow tresses loose to the wind. "But I'm happy!" After a moment she decided: "I suppose it's due to the exercise and fresh air."

They topped a long ridge and saw the spaceboat flash metallic below them. John Jacob Newhouse came hurrying uphill as the girl and the Kefflachian strode downward. His hair was rumpled and his shirt stained with grease. "What kept you?" he puffed. "I was about to organize a search party. I thought you two were only going to look around a little."

"We did," said Teresina, "and it's unbelievably beautiful. Fertile, too. If they're only edible, we'll have more nuts and berries and wild grains and game than—"

"They are. I've had the analyzers from our survival kit working hard," said Newhouse. "Naturally, we'll want to test an individual specimen of everything before eating it; and doubtless we'll need a larger variety of foods here than we would on Earth, to get all the vitamins and so on. But it's already obvious that this is our kind of biochemistry."

Fred rolled small devout eyes downward. The gods of the Gombar Road are chthonic. "A miracle," he said.

Newhouse caught Teresina's hand. "But you were gone so long!" he protested.

"Oh?" the girl felt confused. "I didn't have a watch...No, it can't be. The sun has hardly moved."

"2° 36′ 14″," said Fred.

Newhouse started. "What? Can you gauge it that close?"

"Why, of course," said the Groombridgean, astonished. "Can't everybody?"

"You've been away more than four hours," said Newhouse, turning back to the girl.

"Good Euler! I must have—" Teresina realized Newhouse was still holding her hands. She jerked them back. Angrily: "I don't see what difference it makes to you!"

"Ah, much, my dear." The man smiled and fell into step with her. "We must all stick close together now. Very close."

"I'm sure Fred could have handled anything dangerous."

"Quite likely." Newhouse ran an approving eye along the gigantic centauroid form. "We're going to be glad that Mr. Fred is with us. We'll need his strength."

"What do you—Wait!" Teresina stopped dead. The blood seemed to drain from her. "Do you mean the boat—"

"Beyond repair," sighed Newhouse. "The central polyphasic of the primary drive has been so mangled we were lucky to get down before it blew out altogether. We've no facilities for making a replacement, even if any of us knew how."

"But—I mean—the secondary—"

"It's all right. That does us no good now, though. You must know we can't try quantum-jumping a mass as great as a spaceboat, or a man, faster than light, when we're this deep, in a gravitational field. Not unless we want to commit suicide. And without a primary, we can't get off the ground and into space." Newhouse paused a moment, then added: "The radio is sabotaged too."

"But—why—"

"The saboteur, of course. Whoever wanted to get rid of one of us. Wrecking the radio was an added precaution. If we landed safely on a planet where we could live...as we've done, in defiance of probability...we might sometime have a faint hope that a search party would come past. The chances are all against that, you realize. No one will know which way we headed; there are so many stars; our *prima facie* chance of survival was so small that they won't spend much time looking. But if we had a radio, we could keep it tuned, and if ever we picked up a signal, we could answer. Now even that tiny possibility has been eliminated. Suppose a rescue vessel should chance on this planet, what is the likelihood of its detecting a flyspeck like our camp by visual means?"

Teresina closed her eyes. When she opened them again, the landscape was blurred for a while.

Fred, who seemed more phlegmatic than most humans, except where poetry was concerned, rumbled calmly: "Is there any trace of native civilization, Mr. Newhouse?"

"I saw nothing in the viewscreens that looked like a road or a city or even like cultivated fields," replied the officer. "If anything exists, it must be on a low paleolithic level, no use to us. We're on our own."

"What conditions can we expect?"

"Favorable. I took care to land in an area whose climate would be good for our type of life. It's near the vernal equinox, so we have summer ahead of us. But as the axial tilt is only some 10°, even the winter will be mild, little more than a rainy season. As you've seen, this world rotates very slowly, the period is more than three Terrestrial weeks. But the nights won't be terribly dark, even if there isn't a moon. This is a rather thickly starred region of space, a loose cluster. Also, we're in a high latitude, the planet has a strong magnetic field in spite of the rotation, and it's closer to its sun than Earth—so we can expect some brilliant auroral displays the year 'round. In short, we'll be able to see what we're about after sunset. And as I said, we'll have no trouble about food. We'll practice agriculture, but won't have to work unduly hard at it."

"Have we tools?"

"Yes, a good assortment, including some guns. Terrestrial seeds, too, in biostatic containers. Regulation survival equipment. Though as far as I know, this is the first time any tourists have ever had need of it."

They were close to the boat now. Newhouse waved at the others. Marie, fed up with the petulant incompetence of Hedwig and Arsang, had taken a hatchet and chopped some firewood herself; Kamala had a small blaze going, and the smell from a kettle suspended above was savory. Teresina realized with a jolt how hungry she was.

"We can bunk in the craft as long as need be," said Newhouse, "but of course we'd like more space and comfort. Tomorrow—I mean later today, local time!—suppose we set up the crane and the power saw. We can erect a very comfortable log cabin, with a private room for everybody, in a week or so. Next sunrise we can begin some basic farming. Why, in a few months we'll all be living like kings!"

"What kind of kings?" asked Fred suspiciously. "I know some tribes on Kefflach who sacrifice the king every harvest season."

"Oh," said Newhouse, "it was only a figure—"

"Not to mention those which have been infected with republicanism and are starting revolutions against their monarchies."

"—a figure of speech—"

"And then there is the King of the Venruth Way. He's always in debt. He can't walk two steps without some moneylender seizing him by the tail and demanding repayment."

"Forget it!"

"And poor old King Horrok of the Jungar Trail. He's expected to lead his warriors in battle, and he's such a coward, and the expensive psychiatrist he imported from Earth got so interested in the symbolism of a nomadic civilization that—"

"Never mind! Never mind!"

"Is it any wonder that I sing the spaciousness of Democracy, I, Fred, contained in all and all-containing, warm and unwashed as the veritable mob?"

Suddenly Teresina giggled.

Life looked more hopeful after a sleep period. The sun remained at late afternoon, the same low winds blew the same woolly clouds, but grief, anger, and hysterics were over with. It was almost a calm group which met outside the boat when breakfast was done.

Newhouse mounted the second rung of the access ladder and looked down on the others, who sat or stood in tree-shaded grass. He made a dashing figure, his hair rumpled by the breeze, shirt open, pants skin-tight above gleaming boots. Teresina suspected he had put in half an hour or better achieving the effect. At least, that was the only way she could account for the riding boots on a planet without horses.

"Ladies and gentlebeings," said Newhouse in his most vibrant voice. "You know now that we're probably here for the rest of our lives. You know how lucky we've been in finding such a Garden of Eden as this. It's up to us to deserve that luck, to be worthy of the human race."

"And the Numan race," piped Arsang.

"Of course," said Newhouse, annoyed. "I wasn't forgetting the Kefflachian race either. But, well, anyhow, to continue. We can make what we will of this planet. Right now we're a community with no definite authority, no clear-cut legal rights, no…uh…anything. We have work to do. It won't be backbreaking: We have basic power tools, and the boat's converter will supply all the energy we can ever use. But it will be work. A challenge!" he cried, trumpetlike.

"You needn't shout," said Kamala. "We are not deaf." Newhouse looked disconcerted, smoothed it over, and resumed swiftly: "We have to agree, maybe not on anything as elaborate as a constitution, but on a few rules. The way we start will determine the tradition, the whole structure, of our society in the future. Our descendants can bless us or curse us—"

"Une pause!" Marie leaped to her feet. "What is that it is that which you say? Whose descendants?"

Newhouse folded his arms, leaned back against the ladder, and smiled. "Ours. Yours and the other ladies'. And mine."

"Ohhh!" quavered Hedwig pinkly.

Teresina jumped up also. "Now wait a minute, Newhouse!" she yelled, and stopped, appalled at her own boldness.

"You know the law," said the officer.

"What law?" asked Kamala through an otherwise stunned silence.

"Number 298376, Statutes of the United Commonwealths," said Newhouse.

The girl shook her dark head. "I never heard of it, and my father has held a seat in Parliament since—"

"Popularly known as the Reproductive Act."

"No, I can't say—"

Teresina exchanged glances with Marie. The stewardess shrugged and made a face. Who could keep track of all the laws there were?

"I imagine it isn't too familiar to civilians at that," said Newhouse. "Spacemen are of course very much aware of it, though even in their case the issue seldom arises. But, briefly, the law requires that Terrestrial citizens cast away on any planet where reproduction is at all practical must reproduce, and in such a way as to assure the greatest distribution of all available sound heredity."

Teresina shrank back against the comforting bulk of Fred. Newhouse swept a grin across her.

"But this is outrageous!" screamed Hedwig Trumbull. "Indecent!"

"Conditions in space don't always permit the same behavior as at home," said Newhouse blandly. "The law has several purposes. First, since any band of castaways is sure to be small, inbreeding has to be avoided as much as possible, lest the descendants start degenerating in a century or two. There has to be as much genetic variety made available as circumstances allow: interbreeding in all individual combinations. Second, by enforcing reproduction, the law makes use even of disasters like this one to spread civilization throughout the galaxy. By the time our world is discovered, for instance, there may be quite a flourishing colony. Third, it's for your own protection. Do you want to be the last survivor, growing old with no one to take care of you?"

"But—prior marriages—" objected Kamala.

"They're automatically annulled," said Newhouse, "though all children born to the castaways are automatically legitimate."

"Somehow," complained Arsang, "the logic of this escapes me."

"Anyway, none of us are married." Newhouse leered. "Yet."

"I will not do it!" exploded Marie. "You—*jeune bouc!*" When he didn't seem impressed, she translated: "Young goat."

The officer said sternly: "There's a severe penalty for noncompliance, Miss Quesnay."

"But I thought no one was going to rescue us," said Teresina.

"If we are rescued, the penalties will apply. Besides…well, let's face it, I am the only man for God knows how many parsecs." Newhouse buffed his nails on his shirt, regarded them critically, and smiled again.

"It's outrageous!" Hedwig waddled toward him, shaking her fists. It's indecent, I say, immoral, improper! When do you start?"

Newhouse's composure cracked a little. "Oh," he said. Hedwig fluffed her green hair, revealing gray roots. "I want it known that I am complying only under protest" she said. "Furthermore, if we should be rescued, you must make an honest woman of—"

"Well," said Newhouse, jumping down from the ladder and backing away, "let's not be hasty. I, er, didn't want to embarrass any of you ladies. I know you'll, uh, need time to get used to this. To the idea. I'll t-t-talk to you separately… later…"

"Don't think I am afraid," said Hedwig. "I am prepared to do my duty to civilization, however distasteful."

"Fred," gabbled Newhouse, "we'd better start unloading those power tools. Right away."

Since there was nothing obviously dangerous in the neighborhood, Teresina was handed a light rifle just in case and a basket for specimens of potential edibles, to be brought back and analyzed. She was out for some hours, more grateful to be alone than she dared admit.

Returning through the sun-spattered shade of a little wood, bird song overhead and soft leaf mold underfoot, she felt tired enough to put down alertness. She had plenty of samples, no reason to keep an eye out for more. But that, she soon discovered, was a mistake: she began thinking about her own situation.

It looked bleaker by the minute. You could make this damned planet as idyllic as you liked, but it was still a jail. She had thought herself asocial, not really unfriendly but fonder than average of curling up with a book in the evening. She had imagined her own interests were centered on analysis situs and the theory of equations. Only now did she realize how much she had been a part of human society—how much everyone is—from teatime chitchat to nightlong argument, from stranger in the street to lifetime friend—and the whole structure of society, not so much its buildings and machines as its books, paintings, concerts…Great Lagrange! She thought of herself as a mathematician, but without a reference library and at least one monthly journal she wasn't…She shivered in the knowledge.

Camping and hiking and so on, she thought with a swing back from terror to resentment, were fun as a hobby. As a career, they had no appeal.

A rustling ahead made her snatch for the rifle. "Hey, what have I done?" grinned Newhouse, emerging from a screen of brush.

Teresina slung the weapon back over her shoulder. "What are you doing?" she blurted. Her heart didn't stop jumping.

"Is that a shift of emphasis?" He fell into step beside her. "Why, we called it a day, or work period, or whatever the term is under these crazy conditions, back at camp. So I thought I'd stroll out and see if I could meet you."

Teresina's face burned. "It's a big area. The chances were against finding me."

"I'm a great one for lopping the odds," chuckled Newhouse. He tapped a small instrument hung at his belt. "You're carrying an energy compass, which picks up the weak steady emission from the boat's converter. I simply tuned this one to yours. Ahem! Speaking of pickups—"

"Why—What…"

"Why? You yourself are the answer to that." Newhouse slipped an arm about her waist.

Teresina jerked free. "Stop that!"

He laughed aloud, not in the least abashed. "All right, I won't be the big bad wolf. Not yet. Though if I chose to be, there wouldn't be much you could do about it, would there?"

"What do you mean?"

"Well, as I've remarked before, I'm the only human male around. And you are not a girl who'd defy the law."

"Oh." Teresina looked away. "The law."

Newhouse moved up behind her. "Don't be bitter. Am I so horrible?"

Teresina struggled to speak. She still faced away from him when she got out: "No."

"Ah," said Newhouse and laid his hands on her waist.

Teresina continued, word by dogged word: "It isn't personal. Not much. It's the general idea of it all."

"Now, wait," purred Newhouse, nuzzling her hair. "Don't fool yourself. I know the female of our species fairly well if I do say so, and I could tell right away you aren't cold. Reserved, a bluestocking type, sure, but underneath everything, very much a woman."

Teresina stared down rustling leafy arches. "I always expected to get married," she said. She could only think how hard it was to talk so freely about herself to a near stranger. The subject matter seemed almost irrelevant by contrast. "Yes, of course. But I meant married."

"If it's that you're worried about, I've explained the law—"

"Yes, and of all the stupid, vicious laws there ever were…I'm not interested in what some damned Act of Parliament says. I was talking about marriage. A relationship between me and one man, for all our lives; something that was ours alone. I don't mean I'd be possessive. I hope not. But, well, I suppose I am a monogamist."

"However, since things have worked out otherwise—" Newhouse snuggled her close against him. "What was it George Bernard Shaw wrote, centuries ago?" he said complacently. "A woman would rather have part of a superior man than all of an inferior one."

"*What?*"

"Being the only man, I think I can safely call myself superior. Believe me, lass, I'd far rather have been abandoned alone with you. But even as it is, we could get quite abandoned, the two of us—"

Teresina realized, like a fist in her stomach, how she was being held. She tried to jerk free. Newhouse laughed again and held her tightly. She couldn't break away. He swung her around to face him and lowered his lips toward hers.

She smacked his nose with her forehead.

He let go and staggered back, gasping. She unlimbered her rifle. "I don't want to shoot you," she choked. "Please don't make me." Hastily: "I mean, please don't force me to shoot!"

Newhouse dabbed at his nose. "Put that thing away," he groaned. "You want to commit murder?"

Her pulse hammered, but she felt an upsurge of strength and self-command, i.e., adrenalin. "And what you were about to commit?" she snapped.

"My lawful duty," said Newhouse with as great an air of virtue as possible when one has a nosebleed.

"To hell with that bleat," said Teresina, surprising herself. "To hell with that law, also. Do you think I'm so afraid of lonesomeness, now or in my old age, that I'll sign up in your harem? Give me one good reason why I should help perpetuate *your* chromosomes!"

"The survival of this community," said Newhouse primly.

Teresina remembered a coarse Anglo-Saxon monosyllable she had encountered a few times on Earth. Experimentally, she pronounced it. Newhouse looked so delightfully shocked that she said it again. "Whatever bunch of old women in trousers wrote that law," she added, "they must be pretty abject not to have thought that survival isn't worth just any price whatsoever. Enough is enough, for Gauss' sake. Now, git!"

She jerked the rifle. Newhouse stumbled from her. He paused at the edge of a thicket. "What are you going to do?" he asked weakly.

"I'll come back to camp," said Teresina, "after I've cooled off. We needn't say any more about this episode."

Newhouse stood thinking for a moment. "I apologize," he said. "I didn't understand you as well as I thought."

"I suggest you be a little less confident you understand the others."

"But there is still the law. And our group is basically law-abiding. If nothing else, they won't risk the penalties of compounding a felony, if we should be rescued; and that's what they'd be guilty of, if they allowed you to be this obstinate."

Teresina flung back so fast that only later did she have time to admire her own intelligence: "We can argue about that later. The law says this group has to reproduce. All right. It says nothing about the order in which we do so. In fact, it wouldn't be sensible to have all the women pregnant simultaneously. Very well, Mr. Newhouse, you can start elsewhere. When the first infant is well on its way the issue will arise for the rest of us."

He gaped. "Elsewhere?"

"I suggest Hedwig Trumbull," sneered Teresina. "She seemed quite prepared to give her all for the colony."

Recognizing a perfect exit line, she turned her back on his appalled stare and marched off.

The slow sunset came during the next work period. For hours the sky burned red and hot gold. But while Teresina had always regretted the swift fading of such beauty on Earth, she found it rather monotonous when it lasted half her waking time. Blue twilight, the earliest stars blinking to life, was downright welcome.

The party sat outside, under floodlamps rigged near the site of their planned house, and talked. Mostly it was reminiscence, Earth, friends, and do you think we'll ever see home again, until Hedwig began to snivel. Then Marie called rather sharply for a discussion of practical problems. Labor around the boat could continue through the long night, but it was best to suspend hunting and gathering operations. However, it would also be well to venture a way into the forest, get some idea what to expect there after dark. Fred and Newhouse could...no, Newhouse must not be risked...Fred agreed amiably to do some exploring alone. He had little to fear. Teresina offered to accompany him. Newhouse vetoed it: she must not hazard her own germ plasm unnecessarily. Teresina bridled, spoke of her rights as an individual, and was dismayed when the others sided with Newhouse. Only Arsang voted for her, and that chiefly in a spiteful mood. He had been told off to gather berries earlier that session, and did not think it accorded with the dignity of a Lord High Gongbeater.

Presently they all went to bed. Automatic alarms had been set up; there was no need to stand watches. Teresina noted maliciously that Newhouse was still retiring alone to his bunk in the boat. Hedwig made an insinuating remark, but he brushed very quickly past her and the door to the pilot turret was heard to slam shut. Arsang and Hedwig entered the passenger section, the rest preferred to stretch sleeping bags out in the mild night. All but Fred, of course: nothing could be done but hang blankets over him.

Teresina couldn't fall asleep. After an hour or two of twisting in the sack, she got up, donned sandals and cloak, and wandered toward camp limits.

It was now approaching true night. The sky was purple-black overhead. Stars crowded it in great blazing strings and clusters; this was indeed a fairly dense region of space. White auroral shimmers leaped noiselessly between the foreign constellations. Even without a moon, she could see how dew glittered in the grass, how the river flashed some kilometers off and the remote hills shouldered upward. She could hear more noises than in the daytime, rustlings, patterings, whistlings, croakings, warblings, nocturnal life up and about its business. She thought vaguely that the daylight and starlight species must be more sharply divided here, more specialized, than on Earth…Strange that a planet otherwise so homelike should have so lazy a rotation. True, its sun was closer, tidal drag would operate. But that could not even affect the spin as much as Luna had slowed Earth: especially since this world was hardly older than her own and probably younger. Sol is fairly well along in years for its type. The planet appeared to have no satellite, certainly none big enough to create significant drag. The normal distribution of angular momentum would presumably guarantee any moonless planet, not too close to its primary, a rotation period of no more than, say, a hundred hours. So what had slowed this globe down?…But its long luminous night was beautiful.

A closer sound brought Teresina whirling about. For a moment, in the vague tricky light, she stared terrified at a pair of tall black trolls. Then they resolved themselves into Marie Quesnay and Kamala Chatterji, also cloaked.

"Hello," said Teresina, a little shakenly. The big darkness made all voices seem a whisper. "So you can't sleep either?"

"Why, are you suffering from insomnia, my dear?" asked Kamala. "I only came out to admire the view. While total inner peace is not easily attained, I can show you a simple relaxation technique which—"

"It is not to make the matter," interrupted Marie. "I too was tossing wakeful, and when I noticed you leave, Kamala, I got up and joined you. Then we saw Teresina."

"But if you will only," said the Indian girl, "begin by drawing a deep breath—"

"I do not—"

"—eleven times repeated, standing on your toes; then sit down, put your head between your thighs, cross your ankles—"

"I do not want to sleep!" exclaimed Marie. "It is that I have the thinking to do."

"Well, then I should not disturb you," said Kamala. "Goodnight."

"No, stay here. And you, Teresina. It is the thinking we must all do, and we may as well talk it over now, *hein*?"

The cool breeze caressed Teresina's face and sizzled. She said lamely: "You mean…the problem of—"

"Of that *cochon* Newhouse, yes." Marie bit off her words. "He has made the pass at you too, no?"

"No. I mean yes. But I had a gun along and—"

"And I know a few judo arts," said Maria. "In my work, that is always needful. Did he get you alone, Kamala?"

"Yes," answered the Indian girl serenely. "I discoursed to him on the Three Principles. I was starting to develop the Five Basic Philosophies from them when he said we had better get back to camp."

Marie giggled. "That is the easy way out, that!"

"I told him," said Teresina, glad the darkness hid her embarrassment, "that he could, er, well, start with someone who was willing."

"And I the same," nodded Marie. "I think we both suggested the same person, no? Since his interest in her is shall we say, not great, he is so far doing nothing." She shrugged. But that will not last long, *mes amies*. He is a healthy young man, healthier than average in some respects. If nothing else, he will follow our proposal. And then a few months hence, he will have—a'em!—clear title to one of us."

"Just let him dare!" flared Teresina.

Kamala said gently: "He will have the extraterrestrials on his side. They will certainly desire a large community here, especially as a provision for their own old age. And there is the question of law, and even of duty."

"Duty! Law!" Teresina looked out to the river. Finally she spoke, hard-voiced:

"Has it occurred to you just how bad and stupid that law is? Go down the line, tick off the points one by one. First, it's a gross infringement of civil liberties. People have the constitutional right to decide what they'll make of their own lives. An enforced marriage isn't legally a marriage at all. Second, this kind of situation is so wildly improbable that there's no reason for a law regulating it. How sloppy are space crews supposed to be, anyhow? There's almost no excuse for getting marooned. Even explorers, Survey ships, don't head into the wild black yonder. They identify in advance the stars they're going to visit, using astronomical telescopes. If they aren't back within a reasonable time, a rescue expedition will know where to search!"

"True," said Marie. "Though I am surprised that you, a civilian, know so much about Survey procedure."

"I don't, really," confessed Teresina. "I only reasoned it out, on the assumption that space explorers aren't idiots."

"Well," said Kamala, "this is indeed an unnecessary law, as you point out. But that sort of thing is not unknown. There are many regulations providing for the weirdest contingencies. For example, in one of the American states, I have heard, it is illegal to take a bath by the side of the highway on Sunday mornings. So a law regulating castaways is not out of the pattern, even if I have never heard of a situation like ours arising before."

"All right," said Teresina. "Conceded. Fermat knows what will happen when an M.P. gets the bit between his teeth. But let's take this law at face value. It's supposed to guarantee that castaways of mixed sexes will reproduce, if at all possible. Really—" she felt herself blush again, but plowed stubbornly on—"do you think that has to be *required*?"

"The law is also supposed to prevent degeneration by enforcing the greatest outbreeding. Well, after all! I mean, if a band of people are so stupid they can't think of that for themselves, it doesn't matter if they degenerate or not, does it? They don't need to get all promiscuous in the first generation to take care of the genetic drift. All they have to do is regulate who their children and grandchildren marry, make marriage contracts between families. And that's been common practice throughout human history. Our modern custom of leaving it entirely up to the individual is the statistical abnormality."

"Hm, yes," said Marie. "I can also see that if there were several couples shipwrecked together, and they were supposed to change partners all the time, *oui*, the emotional tensions that could make would be more dangerous than any genetic problems!"

"And then, that—" Teresina tried her Anglo-Saxon word again. It seemed to fit, so she let it stand and continued: "—about spreading civilization. Really! If a planet has no natives, it can wait till it's discovered in the usual way. If it does have natives, can you imagine how much trouble a band of aliens like us, calmly filling their land with our own offspring, would make? The explorers who finally did arrive would probably find a full-fledged war waiting for them. In fact, what the law ought to do is forbid reproduction, till the castaways are sure there aren't any aborigines!"

She fell silent. The wind murmured and the forest talked in the night.

Kamala said at last, "You are right, dear, it is a most ridiculous piece of legislation, and if I ever get home I shall certainly have my father introduce a bill to repeal it. But meanwhile—"

"Meanwhile," said Marie as Kamala's voice trailed off, "we have the situation as it is. Forget about the law. We have one man, four women, and no chance of rescue. I am afraid we shall have to agree with what he wants." Wryly: "As you say, the law it is not necessary at all."

"We don't have to!" cried Teresina.

Marie shrugged again. "I do not like M'sieur Newhouse very much. I will not fall into his arms at once. But sooner or later, eh, *bien*, I am a healthy animal myself. And so are you two."

"I am not!" Teresina stamped her foot.

Kamala laughed. Teresina said awkwardly, "Well, I mean, I have some self-discipline."

"We all do, now," said Marie. "A year from now? Two years? Five? I have perhaps seen a little more of the life than you, *chérie*. If nothing else, you will not deny yourself children. And it is true, the community will need those children fifty years from now. You must not be selfish."

"You can delay the inevitable for some months," said Kamala. "During that time I shall instruct you in Inner Reform. These things will seem much less important then."

"Don't you care?" choked Teresina.

Kamala hesitated. "There is a young man, in Calcutta...I was going to come back to him in a year, and—No!" With more violence than her principles allowed: "Forget it! It is past!"

"Cayley and Sylvester!" snarled Teresina. "If you had any will power whatsoever, you'd help me seize the boat! We could keep looking for a human settlement. Better die trying than give up to this, this cotton-candy planet!"

"You forget," said Marie, "the primary drive, she is sabotaged."

"Couldn't we fix it?"

"Not according to what Newhouse says. I have no knowledge of these matters, me. I could fly the boat in atmosphere, but I would not trust myself in space with it."

"What Newhouse says!" rasped Teresina. "How far would you trust that—that—"

"Unintegrated personality," suggested Kamala.

"Cad!" said Teresina.

"Same thing, really," said Kamala.

"We may as well trust in him," said Marie. "He has such luck as never a man in all history. I would rather have a lucky man than a clever one."

"Luck—" Teresina stood as if smitten. Understanding was a thunderbolt.

"All the improbabilities do seem to have operated in his favor," agreed Kamala. "It implies that under his superficially superficial personality there lies some deep unconscious harmony with the All. Yes...yes, perhaps I have been unjust to him. I must get to know him better—"

Teresina grabbed Marie's hands. "Did you say you could fly the boat?" she yelled.

"Yes. A little," said the stewardess. "But what do you—you cannot—"

"The hell I can't!" Teresina whirled and started running downhill. "Come on!"

"*Qu'est-ce que c'est que ça?*" gasped Marie. She stood an instant, then followed. "Kamala, help, she is gone *dérangée!*"

Fred roused at the noise and lumbered to meet the girls. "What has happened?" he boomed. "Is anything wrong little ones?"

"Fred—Fred—" Teresina collapsed shaking against his enormous chest. "Y-y-you don't want to, to, to stay here do you?"

"No. Naturally not. Granted, it is a peaceful scene, but I anticipate an increasing loneliness for my own species. Somehow this planet seems to be lacking in the large, varied, raucous, perspiring qualities of En Masse."

"Well, then, come on!" shrieked Teresina.

Kamala reached her and tugged her arm. "Peace," she urged. "Do be calm, darling. Now just take a long breath."

Marie seized her other arm. "Do you wish a sedative?" she asked.

"I have been studying the recreational microfiles in the boat," Fred rumbled on, "and have decided to take a course of music by Delius and poetry by James Whitcomb Riley."

Steps clanged in the airlock. Newhouse appeared, a pistol in his hand, Hedwig and Arsang behind him. "What is it?" called the man.

"I fear poor Teresina has lost the self-control" said Marie.

"What?" Newhouse hurried down the ladder. After a moment, Hedwig followed. Arsang slithered along, gave the tableau a disdainful look, and began explaining to Hedwig how much better things were regulated at the Prideful Court of H.A.R. Pipp XI.

Newhouse pushed close. "What happened?" he said.

"She began to shout and run," answered Kamala. "The child is overwrought. Let me talk to her alone for a while and—"

"It isn't so!" wailed Teresina. The world trembled in her sight; the noise of her heart filled it with roaring. "The boat! You lied to us! The boat isn't damaged at all!"

"What?" Newhouse's mouth fell open.

"Listen," babbled Teresina, "listen to me for just one minute!"

Newhouse hefted his pistol. "I think she is hysterical," he said. In the wan light, his face was drawn taut. "I'll take her off myself for a chat. I know how to handle these cases."

"No, it is me who have the training," said Marie.

"I'm the captain here!" snapped Newhouse.

Teresina looked at the gun in his fist. It was pointed squarely at her midriff. "Calm down, sweetheart," Newhouse went on. "Be quiet. Relax."

"What is this about the boat?" asked Fred.

"Nothing," said Newhouse. "Nothing at all. Right?" He and his gun looked hard at Teresina.

She never knew where the nerve came from. She kicked upward. Her foot struck his hand. The pistol went soaring off in an arc. Newhouse cursed and ran after it.

Teresina scrambled for the boat. "Come on!" she screamed.

Newhouse was on his hands and knees, casting about in the long, shadowed grass. Marie threw him a single look and scampered up the ladder. "Fred!" shouted Teresina. The Kefflachian snatched up Kamala and made it into the airlock in one jump.

Teresina was still below. She saw Newhouse straighten, the pistol agleam in his grasp. She had no idea whether he would actually use it or not, but her inwards grew cold and lumpy. Then Fred reached down a monster-long arm and hauled her up. The outer airlock valve clashed shut behind her.

She lay a moment gasping before she could say to Marie. "All right...go on to the turret...raise ship."

The stewardess looked at the closed valve, as if to watch the scene beyond. "But Hedwig and Arsang," she said. "Alone with him—"

"He won't dare harm them now. If he ever really intended to." Teresina sat up, shivering, hugging her knees. "They have all the supplies and tools and things. It won't hurt them to wait a while."

Unexpectedly, Kamala grinned. "I cannot think of any three persons I would rather see stranded together," she said.

Sir John Baskerville, legal officer (as well as chief chemist, assistant medico, and Masonic lodgemaster) of Irene, only town on the planet Holmes, stared in astonishment at the beautiful blonde girl on the other side of his desk.

"But this is fantastic!" he exclaimed. "How did you ever deduce it was a hoax?"

"Oh, everything," said Teresina Fabricant. "I mean the whole sabotage business did seem so unlikely. No one could think of a good reason for it. And so clumsy, too! Why not just put a bomb in the boat and make sure of us? And then the chances were so grossly against our finding a planet as good as this."

"Thank you," bowed Sir John. "Frankly, we on Holmes agree, though our neighbors and friendly rivals on Watson—But continue."

"Newhouse, being the third officer, could have arranged lifeboat assignments any way he wanted, within limits," said Teresina. "The original party in Fourteen was four young ladies, all unattached, and, well, at least he thought they were attractive. And then Fred, whose strength would be useful and who wouldn't be a rival. Of course, Newhouse's plans were somewhat thrown akilter. First Miss Trumbull traded places with a very cute redhead he had lined up for our boat. Then Arsang forced himself aboard. But that wasn't too serious. He went ahead. It would have been easy for him to put a timer in the ship's alarm circuit, one that would sound the bells when he wanted. He could also have cut off our boat's communication circuit to the ship. He didn't even have to put another timer in our release mechanism—just a thing he could claim was such a device. Naturally, he had to get rid of the navigation manual. Otherwise there wouldn't have been any excuse not to go to a colony. He must have memorized the coordinates of this star and the orbital elements of this planet beforehand. All he had to do then was disable the radio and neutrino detector, land in the opposite hemisphere from your settlement, and pretend we were on an undiscovered world."

"Did you know where you were, before coming around to this side and seeing Watson in the sky?" asked Sir John.

Teresina nodded bashfully. "I felt pretty sure of it. Once I suspected it was all a trick, I remembered having heard of a double planet in this neighborhood. And a companion of roughly equal mass is about all which could slow the rotation of a reasonably young world this much. I mean, the companions would always face each other. That accounted for the long day and night, and confirmed my suspicions.

"Well, it followed from all this that the boat hadn't really been sabotaged. And I couldn't believe Newhouse had any intention of playing Robinson Crusoe forever. In a year or two or three, when he got bored, he'd pretend to have fixed the primary drive after all. Then he could discover with great astonishment that there had been a colony here all the time, that we never knew about."

"Or he might have taken you all off 'looking' for a colonial planet and 'happened' to find another," nodded Sir John. "Jotunheim isn't far away. Or he might simply have flown off, leaving all of you in the wilderness. A proper villain, Miss! We shall certainly see that he is punished, when we find him. Though I'm afraid, this planet is so big and our police force so small, it may take weeks to identify your camp."

"No matter." Teresina smiled. "He can stay right where he is. I hope he enjoys every minute of it."

"He, ah, would have, if you hadn't been so quick on the uptake," said Sir John.

Teresina blushed. "Yes. I mean, that was his whole intention. To live like a sultan, as long as he wished. And all quite legally, too."

"Why, what do you mean?"

Teresina blushed still more furiously. "You know. That silly rule that castaways must, well, have children,"

"Good heavens!" barked Sir John. "What are you talking about? I'm quite familiar with the statutes relating to space exploration, young lady, and I assure you there is not and never has been any such law!"

Hunter's Moon

We do not perceive reality, we conceive it. To suppose otherwise is to invite catastrophic surprises. The tragic nature of history stems in large from this endlessly recurrent mistake.
—Oskar Haeml, *Betrachtungen über die menschliche Verlegenheit*

Both suns were now down. The western mountains had become a wave of blackness, unstirring, as though the cold of Beyond had touched and frozen it even as it crested, a first sea barrier on the flightway to the Promise; but heaven stood purple above, bearing the earliest stars and two small moons, ocher edged with silvery crescents, like the Promise itself. Eastward, the sky remained blue. There, just over the ocean, Ruii was almost fully lighted, Its bands turned luminous across Its crimson glow. Beneath the glade that It cast, the waters shivered, wind made visible.

A'i'ach felt the wind too, cool and murmurous. Each finest hair on his body responded. He needed but little thrust to hold his course, enough effort to give him a sense of his own strength and of being at one, in travel and destination, with his Swarm. Their globes surrounded him, palely iridescent, well-nigh hiding from him the ground over which they passed; he was among the highest up. Their lifescents overwhelmed all else which the air bore, sweet, heady, and they were singing together, hundreds of voices in chorus; so that their spirits might mingle and become Spirit, a foretaste of what awaited them in the far west. Tonight, when P'a crossed the face of Ruii, there would return the Shining Time. Already they rejoiced in the raptures ahead.

A'i'ach alone did not sing, nor did he lose more than a part of himself in dreams of feast and love. He was too aware of what he carried. The thing that the human had fastened to him weighed very little, but what it was putting into his soul was heavy and harsh. The whole Swarm knew about the dangers of attack, of course, and many clutched weapons—stones to drop or sharp-pointed branches shed by ü trees—in the tendrils that streamed under their globes. A'i'ach had a steel knife, his price for letting the human burden him. Yet it was not in the nature of the People to dread what might sink down upon them out of the future. A'i'ach was strangely changed by that which went on inside him.

The knowledge had come, he knew not how, slowly enough that he was not astonished by it. Instead, a grimness had meanwhile congealed. Somewhere in those hills and forests, a Beast ran that bore the same thing he did, that was also in ghostly Swarmtouch with a human. He could not guess what this might portend, save trouble of some kind for the People. He might well be unwise to ask. Therefore he had come to a resolve he realized was alien to his race: he would end the menace.

Since his eyes were set low on his body, he could not see the object secured on top, nor the radiance beaming upward from it. His companions could, though, and he had gotten a demonstration before he agreed to carry it. The beam was faint, faint, visible only at night and then only against a dark background. He would look for a shimmer among shadows on the land. Sooner or later, he would come upon it. The chance was not bad now at this, the Shining Time, when the Beasts would seek to kill People they knew would be gathered in vast numbers to revel.

A'i'ach had wanted the knife as a curiosity of possible usefulness. He meant to keep it in the boughs of a tree; when the mood struck him, he would experiment with it. A Person did once in a while employ a chance-found object, such as a sharp pebble, for some fleeting purpose, such as scooping open a crestflower pod to release its delicious seedlets upon the air. Perhaps with a knife he could shape wood into tools and have a stock of them always ready.

Given his new insight, A'i'ach saw what the blade was truly for. He could smite from above till a Beast was dead—no, the *Beast.*

A'i'ach was hunting.

Several hours before sundown, Hugh Brocket and his wife, Jannika Rezek, had been preparing for their night's work when Chrisoula Gryparis arrived, much overdue. A storm had first grounded aircraft at Enrique and then, perversely moving west, forced her into a long detour on her way to Hansonia. She didn't even see the Ring Ocean until she had traversed a good thousand kilometers of mainland, whereafter she must bend southward an equal distance to reach the big island.

"How lonely Port Kato looks from the air," she remarked. Though accented, her English—the agreed-upon common language at this particular station—was fluent: one reason she had come here to investigate the possibility of taking a post.

"Because it is," Jannika answered in her different accent. "A dozen scientists, twice as many juniors, and a few support personnel. That makes you extra welcome."

"What, do you feel isolated?" Chrisoula wondered. "You can call to anywhere on Nearside that there is a holocom, can you not?"

"Yeah, or flit to a town on business or vacation or whatever," Hugh said. "But no matter how stereo an image is and sounds, it's only an image. You can't go out with it for a drink after your conference is finished, can you? As for an actual visit, well, you're soon back here among the same old faces. Outposts get pretty ingrown socially. You'll find out, if you sign on." In haste: "Not that I'm trying to discourage you. Jan's right, we'd be more than happy to have somebody fresh join us."

His own accent was due to history. English was his mother tongue, but he was third-generation Medean, which meant that his grandparents had left North America so long ago that speech back there had changed like everything else. To be sure, Chrisoula wasn't exactly up-to-date, when a laser beam took almost fifty years to go from Sol to Colchis and the ship in which she had fared, unconscious and unaging, was considerably slower than that…

"Yes, from Earth," Jannika's voice glowed.

Chrisoula winced. "It was not happy on Earth when I left. Maybe things got better afterward. Please, I will talk about that later, but now I would like to look forward."

Hugh patted her shoulder. She was fairly pretty, he thought: not in a class with Jan, which few women were, but still, he'd enjoy it if acquaintance developed bedward. Variety is the spice of life.

"You really have had bad luck today, haven't you?" he murmured. "Getting delayed till Roberto—uh, Dr. Venosta went out in the field—and Dr. Feng back to the Center with a batch of samples—" He referred to the chief biologist and the chief chemist. Chrisoula's training was in biochemistry; it was hoped that she, lately off the latest of the rare starcraft, would contribute significantly to an understanding of life on Medea.

She smiled. "Well, then I will know others first, starting with you two nice people."

Jannika shook her head. "I am sorry," she said. "We are busy ourselves, soon to leave, and may not return until sunrise."

"That is—how long? About thirty-six hours? Yes. Is that not long to be away in…what do you say?…this weird an environment?"

Hugh laughed. "It's the business of a xenologist, which we both are," he said. "Uh, I think I, at least, can spare a little time to show you around and introduce you and make you feel sort of at home." Arriving as she did at a point in the cycle of watches when most folk were still asleep, Chrisoula had been conducted to his and Jannika's quarters. They were early up, to make ready for their expedition.

Jannika gave him a hard glance. She saw a big man who reckoned his age at forty-one Terrestrial years: burly, a trifle awkward in his movements, beginning to show a slight paunch; craggy-featured, sandy-haired, blue-eyed, close-cropped, clean-shaven, but sloppily clad in tunic, trousers, and boots, the style of the miners among whom he had grown up. "*I* have not time," she stated.

Hugh made an expansive gesture. "Sure, you just continue, dear." He took Chrisoula under the elbow. "Come on, let's wander."

Bewildered, she accompanied him out of the cluttered hut. In the compound, she halted and stared about her as if this were her first sight of Medea.

Port Kato was indeed tiny. Not to disturb regional ecology with things like ultraviolet lamps above croplands and effluents off them, it drew its necessities from older and larger settlements on the Nearside mainland. Moreover, while close to the eastern edge of Hansonia, it stood a few kilometers inland, on high ground, as a precaution against Ring Ocean tides which could get monstrous.

Thus nature walled and roofed and weighed on the huddle of structures, wherever she looked—

—or listened, smelled, touched, tasted, moved. In slightly lesser gravity than Earth's, she had a bound to her step. The extra oxygen seemed to lend energy likewise, though her mucous membranes had not yet quite stopped smarting. Despite a tropical location, the air was balmy and not overly humid, for the island lay close enough to Farside to be cooled. It was full of pungencies, only a few of which she could remotely liken to anything familiar, such as musk or iodine. Foreign too were sounds—rustlings, trills, croakings, mumbles—which the dense atmosphere made loud in her ears.

The station itself had an outlandish aspect. Buildings were made of local materials to local design; even a radiant energy converter resembled nothing at home. Multiple shadows carried peculiar tints; in fact, every color was changed in this ruddy light. The trees that reared above the roof were of odd shapes, their foliage in hues of orange, yellow, and brown. Small things flitted among them or scuttled along their branches. Occasional glittery drifts in the breeze did not appear to be dust.

The sky was deep-toned. A few clouds were washed with faint pink and gold. The double sun Colchis—Castor C was suddenly too dry a name—was declining westward both members so dim that she could safely gaze at them for a short while, Phrixus at close to its maximum angular separation from Helle.

Opposite them, Argo dominated heaven, as always on the inward-facing hemisphere of Medea. Here the primary planet hung low; treetops hid part of the great flattened disc. Daylight paled the redness of its heat, which would be lurid after dark. Nonetheless it was a colossus, as broad to the eye as fifteen or sixteen Lunas above Earth. The subtly chromatic bands and spots upon its face, everchanging, were clouds more huge than continents and hurricane vortices that could have swallowed whole this moon upon which she stood.

Chrisoula shivered. "It...strikes me," she whispered, "more than anywhere around Enrique or—or approaching from space...I have come elsewhere in the universe."

Hugh laid an arm around her waist. Not being a glib man otherwise, he merely said, "Well this *is* different. That's why Port Kato exists, you know. To study in depth an area that's been isolated awhile; they tell me the isthmus between Hansonia and the mainland disappeared fifteen thousand years ago. The local dromids, at least, never heard of humans before we arrived. The ouranids did get rumors, which may have influenced them a little, but surely not much."

"Dromids—ouranids—oh." Being Greek, she caught his meanings at once. "Fuxes and balloons, correct?"

Hugh frowned. "Please. Those are pretty cheap jokes, aren't they? I know you hear them a lot in town, but I think both races deserve more dignified names from us. They are intelligent, remember."

"I am sorry."

He squeezed a trifle. "No harm done, Chris. You're new. With a century needed for question and answer, between here and Earth—"

"Yes. I have wondered if it is really worth the cost, planting colonies beyond the Solar System just to send back scientific knowledge that slowly."

"You've got more recent information about that than I do."

"Well...the planetology, biology, chemistry, they were still giving new insights when I left, and this was good for everything from medicine to volcano control." The woman straightened. "Perhaps the next step is in your field, xenology? If we can come to understand a nonhuman mind—no, two, on this world—maybe three, if there really are two quite unlike sorts of ouranid as I have heard theorized—" She drew breath. "Well, then we might have a chance of understanding ourselves." He thought she was genuinely interested, not merely trying to please him, when she went on: "What is it you and your wife do? They mentioned to me in Enrique it is quite special."

"Experimental, anyway." Not to overdo things, he released her. "A complicated story. Wouldn't you rather take the grand tour of our metropolis?"

"Later I can by myself, if you must go back to work. But I am fascinated by what I have heard of your project. Reading the minds of aliens!"

"Hardly that." Seeing his opportunity, he indicated a bench outside a machine shed. "If you really would like to hear, sit down."

As they did, Piet Marais, botanist, emerged from his cabin. To Hugh's relief, he simply greeted them before hurrying off. Certain Hansonian plants did odd things at this time of day. Everyone else was still indoors, the cook and bull cook making breakfast, the rest washing and dressing for their next wakeful period.

"I suppose you are surprised," Hugh commenced. "Electronic neuranalysis techniques were in their infancy on Earth when your ship left. They took a spurt soon afterward, and of course the information reached us before you did. The use there had been on lower animals as well as humans, so it wasn't too hard for us—given a couple of geniuses in the Center—to adapt the equipment for both dromids and ouranids. Both those species have nervous systems too, after all, and the signals are electrical. Actually, it's been more difficult to develop the software, the programs, than the hardware. Jannika and I are working on that, collecting empirical data for the psychologists and semanticians and computer people to use.

"Uh, don't misunderstand, please. To *us*, this is nearly incidental. Mindscan— bad word, but we seem to be stuck with it—mindscan should eventually be a valuable tool in our real job, which is to learn how local natives live, what they think and feel, everything about them. However, at present it's very new, very limited, and very unpredictable."

Chrisoula tugged her chin. "Let me tell you what I imagine I know," she suggested, "then you tell me how wrong I am."

"Sure."

She grew downright pedantic: "Synapse patterns can be identified and recorded which correspond to motor impulses, sensory inputs, their processing—and at last, theoretically, to thoughts themselves. But the study is a matter of painfully accumulating data, interpreting them, and correlating the interpretations with verbal responses. Whatever results one gets, they can be stored in a computer program as an *n*-dimensional map off which readings can be made. More readings can be gotten by interpolation."

"Whe-ew!" the man exclaimed. "Go on."

"I am right this far? I did not expect to be."

"Well, naturally, you're trying to sketch in a few words what needs volumes of math and symbolic logic to describe halfway properly. Still, you're doing better than I could myself."

"I continue. Now recently there are systems which can make correspondences between different maps. They can transform the patterns that constitute thought in one mind into the thought-patterns of another. Also, direct transmission between nervous systems is possible. A pattern can be detected, passed through a computer for translation, and electromagnetically induced in a receiving brain. Does this not amount to telepathy?"

Hugh started to shake his head, but settled for: "M-m-m, of an extremely crude sort. Even two humans who think in the same language and know each other inside out, even they get only partial information—simple messages, burdened with distortion, low signal-to-noise ratio, and slow transmission. How much worse when you try with a different life form! The variations in speech alone, not to mention neurological structure, chemistry—"

"Yet you are attempting it, with some success, I hear."

"Well, we made a certain amount of progress on the mainland with both dromids and ouranids. But believe me, 'certain amount' is a gross overstatement."

"Next you are trying it on Hansonia, where the cultures must be entirely strange to you. In fact, the species of ouranid—Why? Do you not add needlessly to your difficulties?"

"Yes—that is, we do add countless problems, but it is not needless. You see, most cooperating natives have spent their whole lives around humans. Many of them are professional subjects of study: dromids for material pay, ouranids for psychological satisfaction, amusement, I suppose you could say. They're deracinated; they themselves often don't have any idea why their 'wild' kinfolk do something. We wanted to find out if mindscan can be developed into a tool for learning about more than neurology. For that, we needed beings who're relatively, uh, uncontaminated. Lord knows Nearside is full of virgin areas. But here Port Kato already was, set up for intensive study of a region that's both isolated and sharply defined. Jan and I decided we might as well include mindscan in our research program."

Hugh's glance drifted to the immensity of Argo and lingered. "As far as we're concerned," he said low, "it's incidental—one more way for us to try and find out why the dromids and ouranids here are at war."

"They kill each other elsewhere too, do they not?"

"Yes, in a variety of ways, for a larger variety of reasons, as nearly as we can determine. Let me remark for the record, I myself don't hold with the theory that information on this planet can be acquired by eating its possessor. For one thing, I can show you more areas than not where dromids and ouranids seem to coexist perfectly peacefully." Hugh shrugged. "Nations on Earth never were identical. Why should we expect Medea to be the same everywhere?"

"On Hansonia, however—you say war?"

"Best word I can think of. Oh, neither group has a government to issue a formal declaration. But the fact is that more and more, for the past couple of decades—as long as humans have been observing, if not longer—dromids on this island have been hellbent to kill ouranids. Wipe them out! The ouranids are pacifistic, but they do defend themselves, sometimes with active measures like ambushes." Hugh grimaced. "I've glimpsed several fights, and examined the results of a lot more. Not pleasant. If we in Port Kato could mediate—bring peace—well, I'd think that alone might justify man's presence on Medea."

While he sought to impress her with his kindliness, he was not hypocritical. A pragmatist, he had nevertheless wondered occasionally if humans had a right to be here. Long-range scientific study was impossible without a self-supporting colony, which in turn implied a minimum population, most of whose members were not scientists. He, for example, was the son of a miner and had spent his boyhood in the outback. True, settlement was not supposed to increase beyond its present level, and most of this huge moon was hostile enough to his breed that further growth did seem unlikely. But—if nothing else, simply by their presence, Earthlings had already done irreversible things to both native races.

"You cannot ask them why they fight?" Chrisoula wondered.

Hugh smiled wryly. "Oh, sure, we can ask. By now we've mastered local languages for everyday purposes. Except, how deep does our understanding go?

"Look, I'm the dromid specialist, she's the ouranid specialist, and we've both worked hard trying to win the friendship of specific individuals. It's worse for me, because dromids won't come into Port Kato as long as ouranids might show up anytime. They admit they'd be duty bound to try and kill the ouranids—and eat them, too, by the way; that's a major symbolic act. The dromids agree this would be a violation of our hospitality. Therefore I have to go meet them in their camps and dens. In spite of this handicap, she doesn't feel she's progressed any further than me. We're equally baffled."

"What do the autochthons say?"

"Well, either species admits they used to live together amicably…little or no direct contact, but with considerable interest in each other. Then, twenty or thirty years back, more and more dromids started failing to reproduce. Oftener and oftener, castoff segments don't come to term, they die. The leaders have decided the ouranids are at fault and must be exterminated."

"Why?"

"An article of faith. No rationale that I can untangle, though I've guessed at motivations, like the wish for a scapegoat. We've got pathologists hunting for the real cause, but imagine how long that might take. Meanwhile, the attacks and killings go on."

Chrisoula regarded the dusty ground. "Have the ouranids changed in any way? The dromids might then jump to a conclusion of *post hoc, propter hoc*."

"Huh?" When she had explained, Hugh laughed. "I'm not a cultivated type, I'm afraid," he said. "The rock rats and bush rangers I grew up amongst do respect learning—we wouldn't survive on Medea without learning—but they don't claim to have a lot of it themselves. I got interested in xenology because as a kid I acquired a dromid friend and followed her-him through the whole cycle, female to male to postsexual. It grabbed hold of my imagination—a life that exotic."

His attempt to turn the conversation into personal channels did not succeed. "What have the ouranids done?" she persisted.

"Oh...they've acquired a new—no, not a new religion. That implies a special compartment of life, doesn't it? And ouranids don't compartmentalize their lives. Call it a new Way, a new *Tao*. It involves eventually riding an east wind off across the ocean, to die in the Farside cold. Somehow, that's transcendental. Please don't ask me how, or why. Nor can I understand—or Jan—why the dromids consider this is such a terrible thing for the ouranids to do. I have some guesses, but they're only guesses. She jokes that they're born fanatics."

Chrisoula nodded. "Cultural abysses. Suppose a modern materialist with little empathy had a time machine, and went back to the Middle Ages on Earth, and tried to find out what drove a Crusade or Jihad. It would appear senseless to him. Doubtless he would conclude everybody concerned was crazy, and the sole possible way to peace was total victory of one side or the other. Which was not true, we know today."

The man realized that this woman thought a good deal like his wife. She continued: "Could it be that human influences have brought about these changes, perhaps indirectly?"

"It could," he admitted. "Ouranids travel widely, of course, so those on Hansonia may well have picked up, at second or third hand, stories about Paradise which originated with humans. I suppose it'd be natural to think Paradise lies in the direction of sunset. Not that anybody has ever tried to convert a native. But natives have occasionally inquired what our ideas are. And ouranids are compulsive mythmakers, who might seize on any concept. They're ecstatics, too. Even about death."

"While dromids are prone to develop militant new religions overnight, I have heard. On this island, then, a new one happens to have turned against the ouranids, no? Tragic—though not unlike persecutions on Earth, I expect."

"Anyhow, we can't help till we have a lot more knowledge. Jan and I are trying for that. Mostly, we follow the usual procedures, field studies, observations, interviews, et cetera. We're experimenting with mindscan as well. Tonight it gets our most thorough test yet."

Chrisoula sat upright, gripped. "What will you do?"

"We'll draw a blank, probably. You're a scientist yourself, you know how rare the real breakthroughs are. We're only slogging along."

When she remained silent, Hugh filled his lungs for talk. "To be exact," he proceeded, "Jan's been cultivating a 'wild' ouranid, I a 'wild' dromid. We've persuaded them to wear miniaturized mindscan transmitters, and have been working with them to develop our own capability. What we can receive and interpret isn't much. Our eyes and ears give us a lot more information. Still, this is special information. Supplementary.

"The actual layout? Oh, our native wears a button-sized unit glued onto the head, if you can talk about the head of an ouranid. A mercury cell gives power. The unit broadcasts a recognition signal on the radio band—microwatts, but ample to lock onto. Data transmission naturally requires plenty of bandwidth, so that's on an ultraviolet beam."

"What?" Chrisoula was startled. "Isn't that dangerous to the dromids? I was taught they, most animals, have to take shelter when a sun flares."

"This is safely weak, also because of energy limitations," Hugh replied. "Obviously, it's limited to line-of-sight and a few kilometers through air. At that, natives of either kind tell us they can spot the fluorescence of gas along the path. Not that they describe it in such terms!

"So Jan and I go out in our separate aircraft. We hover too high to be seen, activate the transmitters by a signal, and 'tune in' on our individual subjects through our amplifiers and computers. As I said, to date we've gotten extremely limited results; it's a mighty poor kind of telepathy. This night we're planning an intensive effort, because an important thing will be happening."

She didn't inquire immediately what that was, but asked instead: "Have you ever tried sending to a native, rather than receiving?"

"What? No, nobody has. For one thing, we don't want them to know they're being scanned. That would likely affect their behavior. For another thing, no Medeans have anything like a scientific culture. I doubt they could comprehend the idea."

"Really? With their high metabolic rate, I should guess they think faster than us."

"They seem to, though we can't measure that till we've improved mindscan to the point of decoding verbal thought. All we've identified thus far is sensory impressions. Come back in a hundred years and maybe someone can tell you."

The talk had gotten so academic that Hugh positively welcomed the diversion when an ouranid appeared. He recognized the individual in spite of her being larger than usual, her globe distended with hydrogen to a full four meters of diameter. This made her fur sparse across the skin, taking away its mother-of-pearl sheen. Just the same, she was a handsome sight as she passed the treetops, crosswind and then downward. Prehensile tendrils streaming below in variable configurations, to help pilot a jet-propelled swim through the air, she hardly deserved the name "flying jellyfish"—though he had seen pictures of Earthside Portuguese men-of-war and thought them beautiful. He could sympathize with Jannika's attraction to this race.

He rose. "Meet a local character," he invited Chrisoula. "She has a little English. However, don't expect to understand her pronunciation at once. Probably she's come to make a quick swap before she rejoins her group for the big affair tonight."

The woman got up. "Swap? Exchange?"

"Yeah. Niallah answers questions, tells legends, sings songs, demonstrates maneuvers, whatever we request. Afterward we have to play human music for her. Schönberg, usually; she dotes on Schönberg."

—Loping along a clifftop, Erakoum spied Sarhouth clearly against Mardudek. The moon was waxing toward solar fullness as it crossed that coal-glow. Its disc was dwarfed by the enormous body behind, was actually smaller to the eye than the spot which also passed in view, and its cold luminance had well-nigh been drowned earlier when it moved over one of the belts which changeably girded Mardudek. They grew bright after dark, those belts; thinkers like Yasari believed they cast back the light of the suns.

For an instant, Erakoum was captured by the image, spheres traveling through unbounded spaces in circles within circles. She hoped to become a thinker herself. But it could not be soon. She still had her second breeding to go through, her second segment to shed and guard; the young that it presently brought forth to help rear; and then she would be male, with begetting of her own to do—before that need faded out likewise and there was time for serenity.

She remembered in a stab of pain how her first birthing had been for naught. The segment staggered about weakly for a short while, until it lay down and died as so many were doing, so many. The Flyers had brought that curse. It had to be them, as the Prophet Illdamen preached. Their new way of faring west when they grew old, never to return, instead of sinking down and rotting back into the soil as Mardudek intended, surely angered the Red Watcher. Upon the People had been laid the task of avenging this sin against the natural order of things. Proof lay in the fact that females who slew and ate a Flyer shortly before mating always shed healthy segments which brought forth live offspring.

Erakoum swore that tonight she was going to be such a female.

She stopped for breath and to search the landscape. These precipices rimmed a fjord whose waters lay more placid than the sea beyond, brilliant under the radiance from the east. A dark patch bespoke a mass of floating weed. Might it be plants of the kind from which the Flyers budded in their abominable infancy? Erakoum could not tell at her distance. Sometimes valiant members of her race had ventured out on logs, trying to reach those beds and destroy them; but they had failed, and often drowned, in treacherous great waves.

Westward rose rugged, wooded hills where darkness laired. Athwart their shadows, sparks danced glittering golden, by the thousands—the millions, across the land. They were firemites. Through more than a hundred days and nights, they had been first eggs, then worms, deep down in forest mould. Now Sarhouth was passing across Mardudek in the exact path that mysteriously summoned them. They crept to the surface, spread wings which they had been growing, and went aloft, agleam, to mate.

Once it had meant no more to the People than a pretty sight. Then the need came into being, to kill Flyers…and Flyers gathered in hordes to feed on yonder swarms. Hovering low, careless in their glee, they became more vulnerable to surprise than they commonly were. Erakoum hefted an obsidian-headed javelin. She had five more lashed across her back. A number of the People had spent the day setting out nets and snares, but she considered that impractical; the Flyers were not ordinary winged quarry. Anyhow, she wanted to fling a spear, bring down a victim, sink fangs into its thin flesh, herself!

The night muttered around her. She drank odors of soil, growth, decay, nectar, blood, striving. Warmth from Mardudek streamed through a chill breeze to lave her pelt. Half-glimpsed flitting shapes, half-heard as they rustled the brush, were her fellows. They were not gathered into a single company, they coursed as each saw fit, but they kept more or less within earshot, and whoever first saw or winded a Flyer would signal it with a whistle.

Erakoum was farther separated from her nearest comrade than any of them were. The others feared that the light-beam reaching upward from the little shell on her head would give them away. She deemed it unlikely, as faint as the bluish gleam was. The human called Hugh paid her well in trade goods to wear the talisman whenever he asked and afterward discuss her experiences with him. For her part, she knew a darkling thrill at such times, akin to nothing else in the world, and knowledge came into her, as if through dreams but more real. These gains were worth a slight handicap on an occasional hunt…even tonight's hunt.

Moreover—There was something she had not told Hugh, because he had not told her earlier. It was among the things she learned without words from the gleam-shell. A certain Flyer also carried one, which also kept it in eldritch contact with a human.

The big grotesque creatures were frank about being neutral in the strike between People and Flyers. Erakoum did not hold that against them. This was not their home, and they could not be expected to care if it grew desolate. Yet she had shrewdly deduced that they would try to keep in its burrow their equal intimacy with members of both breeds.

If Hugh had been anxious for her to be soul-tied to him this night, doubtless another human wanted the same for a Flyer. It would be a special joy to her to bring that one down. Besides, looking as she fared for a pale ray among firemites and stars might lead her toward a whole pack of enemies. Rested, she began to trot inland.

Erakoum was hunting—

Jannika Rezek was forever homesick for a land where she had never lived.

Her parents had politically offended the government of the Danubian Federation. It informed them they need not enter a reindoctrination hospice if they would volunteer to represent their country in the next shipful of personnel to Medea. That was scarcely a choice. Nevertheless, her father told her afterward that his last thought, as he sank down into suspended animation, was of the irony that when he awakened, none of his judges would be alive and nobody would remember what his opinions had been, let alone care. As a matter of fact, he learned at his goal that there was no longer a Danubian Federation.

The rule remained in force that, except for crewfolk, no person went in the opposite direction. A trip was too expensive for a passenger to be carried who would land on Earth as a useless castaway out of past history. Husband and wife made the best they could of their exile. Both physicians, they were eagerly received in Armstrong and its agricultural hinterland. By the modest standards of Medea, they prospered, finally wining a rare privilege. The human population had now been legally stabilized. More would overcrowd the limited areas suitable for settlement, as well as wreaking havoc on environments which the colony existed to study. To balance reproductive failures, a few couples per generation were allowed three children. Jannika's folk were among these.

Thus everybody, herself perforce included, reckoned hers a happy childhood. It was a highly civilized one, too. In the molecules of reels kept at the Center was stored most of mankind's total culture. Industry was, at last, sufficiently developed that well-to-do families could have sets which retrieved the data in as full hologrammic and stereophonic detail as desired. Her parents took advantage of this to ease their nostalgia, never thinking what it might do to younger hearts. Jannika grew up among vivid ghosts: old towers in Prague, springtime in the Böhmerwald, Christmas in a village which centuries had touched only lightly, a concert hall where music rolled in glory across a festive-clad audience which outnumbered the dwellers in Armstrong, replications of events which once made Earth tremble, gongs, poetry, books, legends, fairy tales....She sometimes wondered if she had gone into xenology because the ouranids were light, bright, magical beings in a fairy tale.

Today, when Hugh led Chrisoula outside, she had stood for a moment staring after them. Abruptly the room pressed in as if to choke her. She had done what she could in the way of brightening it with drapes, pictures, keepsakes. At present, however, it was bestrewn with field gear; and she hated disorder. He cared naught.

The question rose afresh: How much did he care at all, any longer? They were in love when they married, yes, of course, but even then she recognized it was in high degree a marriage of convenience. Both were after appointments to an outpost station where they would maximize their chances of doing really significant, original research. Wedded couples were preferred, on the theory that they would be less distracted from their work than singletons. When they had their first babies, they were customarily transferred to a town.

She and Hugh quarreled about that. Social pressure—remarks, hints, embarrassed avoidance of the subject—was mounting on them to reproduce. Within population limits, it was desirable to keep the gene pool as large as possible. She was getting along in age, a bit, for motherhood. He was more than willing. But he took for granted that *she* would maintain the home, hold down the desk job, while *he* continued in the field...

She must not reprove him when he came back from his flirtatious little stroll. She lost her temper too often these days, grew outright shrewish, till he stormed from the hut or else grabbed the whiskey and started glugging. He was not a bad man—at the core, he was a good man, she amended hastily—thoughtless in many ways but well-meaning. At her time of life, she couldn't likely do any better.

Although—She felt the heat in her cheeks, made a gesture as if to fend off the memory, and failed. It was two days old.

Having learned from A'i'ach about the Shining Time, she wanted to gather specimens of the glitterbug larvae. Hitherto humans had merely known that the adult insectoids swarmed aloft at intervals of approximately a year. If that was important to the inhabitants of Hansonia, she ought to know more. Observe for herself, enlist the aid of biologists, ecologists, chemists—She asked Piet Marais where to go, and he offered to come along. "The idea should have occurred to me before," he said. "Living in humus, the worms must influence plant growth."

Moister soil was required than existed at Port Kato. They went several kilometers to a lake. The walking was easy, for dense foliage overhead inhibited underbrush. Softness muffled footfalls, trees formed high-arched naves, multiple rays of light passed through dusk and fragrances to fleck the ground or glance off small wings, a sound as of lyres rippled from an unseen throat.

"How delightful," Piet said after a while.

He was looking at her, not ahead. She became very conscious of his blond handsomeness. And his youth, she reminded herself, he was her junior by wellnigh a decade, though mature, considerate, educated, wholly a man. "Yes," she blurted. "I wish I could appreciate it as you do."

"It is not Earth," he discerned. She realized that her answer had been less noncommittal than intended.

"I wasn't pitying myself," she said fast. "Please don't think that. I do see beauty here, and fascination, and freedom, oh, yes, we're lucky on Medea." Attempting to laugh: "Why, on Earth, what would I have done for ouranids?"

"You love them, don't you?" he asked gravely. She nodded. He laid a hand on her bare arm. "You have a great deal of love in you, Jannika."

She made a confused effort to see herself through his eyes. Medium-sized, with a figure she knew was stunning; dark hair worn shoulder length, with gray streaks that she wished Hugh would insist were premature; high cheekbones, tilted nose, pointed chin, large brown eyes, ivory complexion. Still, though Piet was a bachelor, someone that attractive needn't be desperate, he could meet girls in town and keep up acquaintance by holocom. He shouldn't be this appreciative of her. She shouldn't respond. True, she'd had other men a few times, before and after she married. But never in Port Kato; too much likelihood of complications, and she'd been furious when Hugh got involved locally. Worse yet, she suspected Piet saw her as more than a possible partner in a frolic. That could break lives apart.

"Oh, look," she said, and disengaged from his touch in order to point at a cluster of seed pyramids. Meanwhile her mind came to the rescue. "I quite forgot, I meant to tell you, I got a call today from Professor al-Ghazi. We think we've found what makes the glitter bugs metamorphose and swarm."

"Eh?" He blinked. "I didn't realize anybody was working on that."

"Well, it was a, a notion that occurred to me after my special ouranid started me speculating about them. He, A'i'ach, I mean, he told me the time is not strictly seasonal—that is not necessary here in the tropics—but set by Jason—the moon," she added, because the name that humans had bestowed on the innermost of the larger satellites happened to resemble a word which humans had adopted, given by dromids in the Enrique area to an analog of the sirocco wind.

"He says the metamorphoses come during particular transits of Jason across Argo," she continued. "Roughly, every four hundredth. To be exact, the figure is every hundred and twenty-seven Medean days, plus or minus a trifle. The natives here are as keenly conscious of heavenly bodies as everywhere else. The ouranids make a festival of the swarming; they find glitterbugs delicious. Well, this gave me an idea, and I called the Center and requested an astronomical computation. It seems I was right."

"Astronomical cues, for a worm underground?" Marais exclaimed.

"Well, you doubtless recall how Jason excites electrical activity in the atmosphere of Argo, like Io with Jupiter—" the solar system, where Earth has her dwelling! "In this case, there's a beaming effect on one of the radio frequencies that are generated, a kind of natural maser. Therefore those waves only reach Medea when the two moons are on their line of nodes. And that is the exact period my friend was describing. The phase is right, too."

"But can the worms detect so weak a signal?"

"I think it is clear that they do. How, I cannot tell without help from specialists. Remember, though, Phrixus and Helle create little interference. Organisms can be fantastically sensitive. Did you know that it takes less than five photons to activate the visual purple in your eye? I suppose the waves from Argo penetrate the soil to a few centimeters' depth and trigger a chain of biochemical reactions. No doubt it is an evolutionary relic from a time when the orbits of Jason and Medea gave an exact match to the seasons. Perturbation does keep changing the movements of the moons, you know."

He was silent a while before he said: "I do know you are a most extraordinary person, Jannika."

She had regained enough equilibrium to control their talk until they reached the lake. There, for a moment, she felt herself shaken again.

A canebrake screened it from them till they had passed through, to halt on a beach carpeted with mosslike amber-hued turf. Untouched by man in its chalice of forest, the water lay scummy, bubbling, and odorous. The sight of soft colors and the smell of living things were not unpleasant; they were normal to Medea—yet how clear and silver-blue the Neusiedler See gleamed in Danubia. Breath hissed between her teeth.

"What's wrong?" Piet followed her gaze. "The dromids?"

A party of them had arrived to drink, some distance off. Jannika stared as if she had never seen their kind before.

Nearest was a young adult, presumably virgin, since she had six legs. From the slender, long-tailed body rose a two-armed centauroid torso, up to the oddly vulpine head, which would reach to Jannika's chest. Her pelt shimmered blue-black under the suns; Argo was hidden by trees.

Four-legged, a trio of mothers kept watch on the eight cubs they had between them. One set of young showed by their size that their parent would soon ovulate again, be impregnated by a mating, shortly thereafter shed her second segment, and attend it until it gave birth. Another member of this group was at that stage of life, walking on two legs, no longer a functional female but with the male gonads still undeveloped.

No male of breeding age was present. Such a creature was too driven, lustful, impatient, violent, for sociability. There were three postsexual beings, grizzled but strong, protective, their biped movements fast by human standards though laggard compared to the lightning fluidity of their companions.

All adults were armed with stone-age spears, hatchets, and daggers, plus the carnivore teeth in their jaws.

They were gone almost as soon as Jannika had seen them, not out of fear but because they were Medean animals whose chemistry and living went swifter than hers.

"The dromids," she got out.

Piet regarded her awhile before he said gently: "They pursue your dear ouranids. You tell me that will get worse than ever on the night when the glitter bugs rise. But you must not hate them. They are caught in a tragedy."

"Yes, the sterility problem, yes. Why should they drag the ouranids down with them?" She struck fist into palm. "Let's get to work, let's collect our samples and go home, can we, please?"

He was fully understanding.

—She cast the memory out and flung herself back into preparations for the night.

Hugh Brocket and his wife departed a while after sunset. Their flitters jetted off in a whisper, reached an intermediate altitude, and circled for a minute while the riders got bearings and exchanged radioed farewells. Observed from below, catching the last gleam of sunken Colchis on their flanks, they resembled a pair of teardrops.

"Good hunting, Jan."

"Ugh! Don't say that."

"Sorry," he apologized in a stiff tone, and cut out the sender. Sure, it had been tactless of him, but why must she be so goddamn touchy?

Never mind. He'd plenty to do. Erakoum had promised to be on Shipwreck Cliffs about this time, since her gang meant to proceed north along the coast from its camp before turning inland. Thereafter her location would be unpredictable. He must lock onto her transmitter soon. Jannika's craft dwindled in sight, bound on her own quest. Hugh set his inertial pilot and settled back in his safety harness to double-check his instruments. That was mechanical, since he knew quite well everything was in order. Most of his attention roamed free.

The canopy gave a titanic vista. Below, hills lay in dappled masses of shadow, here and there relieved by an argent thread that was a river or by the upheaving of precipices and scarps. The hemisphere-dividing Ring Ocean turned the eastern horizon to quicksilver. Westward in heaven, the double sun had left a Tyrian wake. Overhead reached a velvety dark, becoming more starry with each of his heartbeats. He saw a pair of moons, close enough to show discs lighted from two sides, rusty and white; he recognized more, which were mere bright points to his eyes, by their positions as they went on sentry-go among the constellations. Low above the sea smoldered Argo—no, shone, because its upper clouds were in full daylight, bands of brilliance splashed over sullen red. Jason was close to transit, with angular diameter exceeding twenty minutes of arc, and nevertheless Hugh had trouble finding it amidst that glare.

The shore came in view. He activated the detector and set his craft to hovering. An indicator light flashed green; he had his contact. He sent the vehicle aloft, a full three kilometers. Partly this was because he would be concentrating on encephalic input and wanted plenty of room for piloting error; partly it was to keep beyond sight or hearing of the natives, lest his presence affect their actions. Having taken station, he connected and secured the receiver helmet to his head—it didn't weigh much—and switched it on. Transmitted, amplified, transformed, relayed, reinduced, the events in Erakoum's nervous system merged with the events in his.

By no means did he acquire the dromid's full awareness. Conveyance and translation were far too primitive. He had spent his professional lifetime gaining sufficient fellow-feeling with the species that, after as much patience as both individuals could maintain over a span of years, he could barely begin to interpret the signals he gathered. The speed of native mental processes was less of a help—through repetition and reinforcement—than an added hindrance. As a rough analogy, imagine trying to follow a rapid and nearly inaudible conversation, missing many a word, in a language you do not know well. Actually, none of what Hugh perceived was verbal; it was sight, sound, a complex of senses, including those interior like balance and hunger, including dream-hints of senses that he did not think he possessed.

He saw the land go by, bush, branch, slope, stars and moons above shaggy ridges; he felt its varying contours and textures as feet went pacing; he heard its multitudinous low noises; he smelled richness; the impressions were endless, most of them vague and fleeting, the best of them strong enough to take him out of himself, draw him groundward toward oneness with the creature below.

Clearest, perhaps because his glands were stimulated thereby, was emotion, determination. Erakoum was out to get herself a Flyer.

It was going to be a long night, quite possibly a harrowing one. Hugh expected he'd need a dose or two of sleep surrogate. Humans had never gotten away from the ancient rhythms of Earth. Dromids catnapped; ouranids went—daydreamy? contemplative?

As often before, he wondered briefly what Jan's rapport with her native felt like. They would never be able to describe their sharings to each other.

Well into the hills, A'i'ach's Swarm found a grand harvest of starwings. The heights were less densely wooded than the lowlands, which was good, for the bright prey never went far up, and below a forest crown, the People were vulnerable to Beast attack. Here was a fair amount of open ground, turf-begrown and boulder-strewn, scattered through the shadowing timber. A narrow ravine crossed the largest of those glades, a gash abrim with blackness.

Like an endless shower of sparks, the starwings danced, dashed, dodged about, beyond counting, meant for naught save the ecstasy of their mating and of the People who fed upon them. Despite the wariness in him, A'i'ach could resist no more than anyone else. He did refrain from valving out gas in his haste to descend, as many did. That would make ascent slow. Instead, he contracted his globe and sank, letting it reexpand slightly as varying air densities demanded. Nor did he release gas to propel himself. Rhythmically pumping, his siphon worked together with the breezes to zigzag him about at low speed. There was no hurry. The starwings numbered more than the Swarm could eat. Plenty would go free to lay their eggs for the next crop.

Among the motes, A'i'ach inhaled his first swallow of them. The sweet hot flavor sang in his flesh. Thickly gathered around him, bobbing, spinning, rippling and flailing their corybantic tendrils, filling the sky with music, the People forgot caution. Love began. It was not purposeless, though without water to fall into, the pollinated seeds would not germinate. It united everyone. Life-dust drifted like smoke in the radiance of Ruii; the sight, smell, taste made feverish that joy which the starwing feast awakened. Again and again A'i'ach ejaculated. He went past his skin, he became a cell of a single divine being which was itself a tornado of love. Sometimes when he felt age upon him, he would drift westward across the sea, into the cold Beyond. There, yielding up the last warmth of his body, his spirit would take its reward, the Promise that forever and ever it would be what it was now in this brief night...

A howl smote. Shapes bounded from under trees, out into the open. A'i'ach saw a shaft pierce the globe next to his. Blood spurted, gas hissed forth, the shriveling form fell as a dead leaf falls. Tendrils still writhed when a Beast snatched it the last way down and fangs rent it asunder.

In the crowd and chaos, he could not know how many others died. The greatest number were escaping, rising above missile reach. Those who were armed began to drop their stones and ü boughs. It was not likely that any killed a Beast.

A'i'ach had relaxed the muscles in his globe and shot instantly upward. Safe, he might have joined the rest of the Swarm, to wander off in search of a place to renew festival. But rage and grief seethed too high. A far-off part of him wondered at that; the People did not take hard the death of a Person. This thing he wore, that somehow whispered mysteries—

And he carried a knife!

Recklessly spending gas, he swung about, downward. Most of the Beasts had vanished back into the woods. A few remained, devouring. He cruised at a height near the limits of prudence and peered after his chance. Since he could not drop like a rock, he must feint at one individual, then quickly jet at another, stab, rise, and attack again.

A wan beam of light struck toward him. It came from the head of a Beast which emerged from shadow, halted, and glared upward.

His will blazed forth in A'i'ach. Yonder was the monster which had his kind of bond to humans. If he had already gained a knife thereby, what might that being have gotten, what might it get, to wreak worse harm? If nothing else, killing it ought to shock its companions, make them think twice about their murderousness.

A'i'ach moved to battle. About him, the starwings happily danced and mated.

Jannika must search for an hour before she made her contact. An ouranid could not undertake to be at an exact spot at a given time. Hers had simply informed her, while she fastened the transmitter on him, that his group was currently in the neighborhood of Mount MacDonald. She flew there and cast about in ever-deepening darkness until her indicator shone green. Having established linkage, she rose to three kilometers and set the autopilot to make slow circles. From time to time, as her subject passed northeast, she moved the center of her path.

Otherwise she was engaged in trying to be her ouranid. It was impossible, of course, but from the effort she was learning what could never have come to her through spoken language. Answers to factual questions she would not have thought to ask. Folkways, beliefs, music, poetry, aerial ballet, which she could not have known for what they were, observing from outside. Lower down in her, dimmer, but more powerful—nothing she could write into a scientific report: a sense of delights, yearnings, wind, shiningness, perfumes, clouds, rain, immense distances, a sense of what it was to be a heaven-dweller. Not complete, no, a few wavery glimpses, hard to remember afterward; yet taking her out of herself into a new world agleam with wonder.

The thrill was redoubled tonight by A'i'ach's excitement. Her impressions of what he was experiencing had never been stronger or sharper. She floated on airstreams, life-scents and song possessed her, she was a drop in an ocean beneath Ruii the mighty, there was no home to hopelessly long for because everywhere was home.

The Swarm came at last upon a cloud of glitter bugs, and Jannika's cosmos went wild.

For a moment, half-terrified, she started to switch off her helmet. Reason checked her hand. What was happening was just an extreme of what she had partaken in before. Ouranids seldom took much nourishment at a single time; when they did, it had an intoxicating effect. She had also felt their sexuality; A'i'ach's maleness was too unearthly to disturb her, as his dromid's femaleness had disturbed Hugh when she mated and later shed her hindquarters. Tonight the ouranids held high revel.

She surrendered to it, crescendo after crescendo, oh, if she only had a man here, but no, that would be different, would blur the sacred splendor, the Promise, the Promise!

Then the Beasts arrived. Horror erupted. Somewhere a strange voice screamed for the avenging of her shattered bliss.

—As she trotted along a bare ridge, Erakoum had thought, with a leap of her pulse, that she spied afar a faint blue ray of light in the air. She could not be certain; through the brilliance cast by Mardudek, but she altered her course in hopes. When she had scrambled a long while among stones and thorns, the glimmer disappeared. It must have been a trick of the night, perhaps moonglow on rising mists. That conclusion did nothing to ease her temper. Everything about the Flyers was unlucky!

Because of this, she was behind the rest of the pack. Her first news of quarry came through their yells, "Hai-ay, hai-ay, hai-ay!" echoed around, and she snarled in bafflement. Surely she would arrive too late for a kill. Nonetheless she bounded in that direction. If the Flyers did not get a good wind, she could overtake them and follow along from cover to cover, unseen. Maybe they would not go further than she had strength for, before they chanced on a fresh upswelling of firemites and descended anew. Breath rasped in her gullet, the hillside struck at her feet with unseen rocks, but eagerness flung her on till she reached the place.

It was a glade, brightly lit though crisscrossed by shadows, cut in half by a small ravine, The firemites swirled about against the forest murk, like a glinting dust-cloud. Several females crouched on the turf and ripped at the remnants of their prey. The rest had departed, to trail the escaped Flyers as Erakoum planned.

She stopped at the edge of trees to pant, looked up, and froze. The mass of Flyers was slowly and chaotically streaming west, but a few lingered to cast down their pitiful weapons. From the top of one, dim light beamed aloft. She had found what she sought.

"Ee-hah!" she screamed, sprang forward, shook her javelin. "Come, evilworker, come and be slain! By your blood shall you give to my next brood the life you reaved from my first!"

There was no surprise, there was fate, when the eerie shape spiraled about and drew nearer. More would be settled this night than which of them was to survive. She, Erakoum, had been seized by a Power, had become an instrument of the Prophet.

Crouched, she cast her spear. The effort surged through her muscles. She saw it fly straight as the damnation it carried—but her foe swerved, it missed him by a fingerbreadth, and then all at once he was coming directly at her.

They never did that! What sheened in his seaweed grip?

Erakoum grabbed after a new javelin off her back. Each knot in the lashing was supposed to give way at a jerk, but this jammed, she must tug again, and meanwhile the enemy loomed ever more big. She recognized what he held, a human-made knife, sharp as a fresh obsidian blade and more thin and strong. She retreated. Her spear was now loose. No room for a throw. She thrust.

With crazy glee, she saw the head strike. The Flyer rolled aside before it could pierce, but blood and gas together foamed darkly from a slash across his paleness.

He spurted forward, was inside her guard. The knife smote and smote. Erakoum felt the stabs, but not yet the pain. She dropped her shaft, batted her arms, snapped jaws together. Teeth closed in flesh. Through her mouth and down her throat poured a rush of strength.

Abruptly the ground was no more beneath her hind feet. She fell over, clawed with forefeet and hands for a hold, lost it, and toppled. When she hit the side of the ravine, she rolled down across cruel snags. She had an instant's glimpse of sky above, stars and firemites, the Mardudek-lighted Flyer drifting by and bleeding. Then nothingness snatched her to itself.—

Folk at Port Kato asked what brought Jannika Rezek and Hugh Brocket home so early, so shaken. They evaded questions and hastened to their place. The door slammed behind them. A minute later, they blanked their windows.

For a time they stared at each other. The familiar room held no comfort. Illumination meant for human eyes was brass-harsh, air shut away from the forest was lifeless, faint noises from the settlement outside thickened the silence within.

He shook his head finally, blindly, and turned from her. "Erakoum gone," he mumbled. "How'm I ever going to understand that?"

"Are you sure?" she whispered.

"I...I felt her mind shut off...damn near like a blow to my own skull...but you were making such a fuss about your precious ouranid—"

"A'i'ach's *hurt*! His people know nothing of medicine. If you hadn't been raving till I decided I must talk you back with me before you crashed your flitter—"

Jannika broke off, swallowed hard, unclenched her fists, and became able to say: "Well, the harm is done and here we are. Shall we try to reason about it, try to find out what went wrong and how to stop another such horror, or not?"

"Yeah, of course." He went to the pantry. "You want a drink?" he called.

She hesitated. "Wine."

He fetched her a glassful. His right hand clutched a tumbler of straight whiskey, which he began on at once. "I felt Erakoum die," he said.

Jannika took a chair. "Yes, and I felt A'i'ach take wounds that may well prove mortal. Sit down, will you?"

He did, heavily, opposite her. She sipped from her glass, he gulped from his. Newcomers to Medea always said wine and distilled spirits there tasted more peculiar than the food. A poet had made that fact the takeoff point for a chilling verse about isolation. When it was sent to Earth as part of the news, the reply came after a century that nobody could imagine what the colonists saw in it.

Hugh hunched his shoulders. "Okay," he growled. "We should compare notes before we start forgetting, and maybe repeat tomorrow when we've had a chance to think." He reached across to their recorder and flicked it on. As he entered an identification phrase, his tone stayed dull.

"That is best for us too," Jannika reminded him. "Work, logical thought, those hold off the nightmares."

"Which this absolutely was—All right!" He regained a little vigor. "Let's try to reconstruct what did happen.

"The ouranids were out after glitterbugs and the dromids were out after ouranids. You and I witnessed an encounter. Naturally, we'd hoped we wouldn't—I suppose you prayed for that, hm?—but we knew there'd be hostilities in a lot of places. What shocked the wits out of us was when our personal natives got into a fight, with us in rapport."

Jannika bit her lip. "Worse that that," she said. "They were seeking it, those two. It was not a random encounter, it was a duel." She raised her eyes. "You never told Erakoum, any dromid, that we were linking with an ouranid too, did you?"

"No, certainly not. Nor did you tell your ouranid about my liaison. We both know better than to throw that kind of variable into a program like this."

"And the rest of the station personnel have vocabularies too limited, in either language. Very well. But I can tell you that A'i'ach knew. I was not aware he did until the fight began. Then it reached the forefront of his mind, it shouted at me, not in words but not to be mistaken about."

"Yeah, same thing for me with Erakoum, more or less."

"Let's admit what we don't want to, my dear. We have not simply been receiving from our natives. We have been transmitting. Feedback."

He lifted a helpless fist. "What the devil might convey a return message?"

"If nothing else, the radio beam that locks us onto our subjects. Induced modulation. We know from the example of the glitterbug larvae—and no doubt other cases you and I never heard of—how shall we know everything about a whole world? We know Medean organisms can be extremely radio-sensitive."

"M-m, yeah, the terrific speed of Medean animals, key molecules more labile than the corresponding compounds in us…Hey, wait! Neither Erakoum nor A'i'ach had more than a smattering of English. Certainly no Czech, which you've told me you usually think in. Besides, look what an effort we had to make before we could tune them in at all, in spite of everything learned on the mainland. They'd no reason to do the same, no idea of scientific method. They surely assumed it was only a whim or a piece of magic or something that made us want them to carry those objects around."

Jannika shrugged. "Perhaps when we are in rapport, we think more in their languages than we ourselves realize. And both kinds of Medeans think faster than humans, observe, learn. Anyway, I do not say their contact with us was as good as our contact with them. If nothing else, radio has much less bandwidth. I think probably what they picked up from us was subliminal."

"I guess you're right," Hugh sighed. "We'll have to sic the electronicians and neurologists into the problem, but I sure can't think of any better explanation than yours."

He leaned forward. The energy which now vibrated in his voice turned cold: "But let's try to see this thing in context, so we can maybe get a hint of what kind of information the natives have been receiving from us. Let's lay out once more why the Hansonian dromids and ouranids are at war. Basically, the dromids are dying off; and blame the ouranids. Could we, Port Kato, be at fault?"

"Why, hardly," Jannika said in astonishment. "You know what precautions we take."

Hugh smiled without mirth. "I'm thinking of psychological pollution."

"What? Impossible! Nowhere else on Medea—"

"Be quiet, will you?" he shouted. "I'm trying to bring back to my mind what I got from my friend that your friend killed."

She half-rose, white-faced, sat down again, and waited. The wine glass trembled in her fingers.

"You've always babbled about how kind and gentle and esthetic the ouranids are," he said, at her rather than to her. "You swoon over this beautiful new local faith they've acquired—the wind-borne flight to Farside, the death in dignity, the Nirvana, I forget what else. To hell with the grubby dromids. Dromids don't do anything but make tools and fires, hunt, care for their young, live in communities, create art and philosophy, same as humans. What's interesting to you in that?

"Well, let me tell you what I've told you before, dromids are believers too. If we could compare, I'd give long odds their faiths are stronger and more meaningful than the ouranids'. They keep trying to make sense of the world. Can't you sympathize the least bit?

"Okay, they have a tremendous respect for the fitness of things. When something goes seriously wrong—when a great crime or sin or shame happens—the whole world hurts. If the wrong isn't set right, everything will go bad. That's what they believe on Hansonia, and I don't know but what they've got hold of a truth.

"The lordly ouranids never paid much attention to the groundling dromids, but that was not symmetrical. The ouranids are as conspicuous as Argo, Colchis, any part of nature. In dromid eyes, they too have their ordained place and cycle.

"All at once the ouranids change. They don't give themselves back to the soil when they die, the way life is supposed to—no, they head west, over the ocean, toward that unknown place where the suns go down every evening. Can't you see how unnatural that might seem? As if a tree should walk or a corpse rise. And not an isolated incident; no, year after year after year.

"Psychosomatic abortion? How can I tell? What I can tell is that the dromids are shocked to the guts by this thing the ouranids are doing. No matter how ridiculous the thing is, it hurts them!"

She sprang to her feet. Her glass hit the floor. "Ridiculous?" she yelled. "That *Tao*, that vision? No, ridiculous, that's what your...your fuxes believe—except that it makes them attack innocent beings and, and eat them—I can't wait till those creatures are extinct!"

He had risen likewise. "You don't care about children dying, no, of course not," he answered. "What sense of motherhood have you got, for hell's sake? About like a balloon's. Drift free, scatter seed, forget it, it'll bud and break loose and the Swarm will adopt it, never mind anything except your pleasure."

"Why, you—Are you wishing you could be a mother?" she jeered.

His empty hand swung at her. She barely evaded the blow. Appalled, they stiffened where they stood.

He tried to speak, failed, and drank. After a full minute she said, quite low: "Hugh, our natives were getting messages from us. Not verbal. Unconscious. Through them—" she choked—"were you and I seeking to kill each other?"

He gaped until, in a single clumsy gesture, he set his own glass down and held out his arms to her. "Oh, no, oh, no," he stammered. She came to him.

Presently they went to bed. And then he could do nothing. The medicine cabinet held a remedy for that, but what followed might have happened between a couple of machines. At last she lay quietly crying and he went out to drink some more.

The wind awakened her. She lay for a time listening to it boom around the walls. Sleep drained out of her. She opened her eyes and looked at the clock. Its luminous dial said three hours had passed. She might as well get up. Maybe she could make Hugh feel better.

The main room was still lighted. He was asleep himself, sprawled in an armchair, a bottle beside it. How deep the lines were in his face.

How loud the wind was. Probably a storm front which the weather service had reported at sea had taken a quick, unexpected swing this way. Medean meteorology was not yet an exact science. Poor ouranids, their festival disrupted, they themselves blown about and scattered, even endangered. Normally they could ride out a gale, but a few might be carried to disaster hit by lightning or dashed against a cliff or hopelessly entangled in a tree. The sick and injured would suffer most.

A'i'ach.

Jannika squeezed her lids together and struggled to recall how badly wounded he was. But everything had been too confused and terrible; Hugh had diverted her attention; before long she had flitted out of transmission range. Besides, A'i'ach himself could hardly have ascertained his own condition at once. It might not be grave. Or it might. He could be dead by now, or dying, or doomed to die if he didn't get help.

She was responsible—perhaps not guilty, by a moralistic definition, but responsible.

Resolution crystallized. If the weather didn't preclude, she would go search for him.

Alone? Yes. Hugh would protect, delay her, perhaps actually restrain her by force. She recorded a few words to him, wondered if they were overly impersonal, decided against composing something more affectionate. Yes, she wanted a reconciliation and supposed he did, but she would not truckle. She redonned her field garb, added a jacket into whose pockets she stuffed some food bars, and departed.

The wind rushed bleak around her *whoo-oo-oo*, a torrent she must breast. Clouds scudded low and thick, tinged red where Argo shone between them. The giant planet seemed to fly among ragged veils. Dust whirled in the compound, gritty on her skin. Nobody else was outdoors.

At the hangar, she punched for the latest forecast. It looked bad but not, she thought, frightening. (And if she did crash, was that such an enormous loss, to herself or anyone else?) "I am going back to my study area," she told the mechanic. When he attempted to dissuade her, she pulled rank. She never liked that, but from the Danubian ghosts she had learned how. "No further discussion. Stand by to open the way and give me assistance if required. That is an order."

The little craft shivered and drummed on the ground. Takeoff took skill—with a foul moment when a gust nearly upset her but once aloft her vehicle flew sturdily. Risen above the cloud deck, she saw it heave like a sea, Argo a mountain rearing out of it, stars and companion moons flickery overhead. Northward bulked a darkness more deep and high, the front. The weather would really stiffen in the next few hours. If she wasn't back soon, she'd better stay put till it cleared.

The flight was quick to the battleground. When the inertial pilot had brought her there, she circled, put on her helmet, activated the system. Her pulse fluttered and her mouth had dried. "A'i'ach," she breathed, "be alive, please be alive."

The green light went on. At least his transmitter existed on the site. He? She must will herself toward rapport.

Weakness, pain, a racket of soughing leaves, tossing boughs—"A'i'ach, hang on, I'm coming down!"

A leap of gladness. Yes, he did perceive her.

Landing would be risky indeed. The aircraft had a vertical capability, excellent radar and sonar, a computer and effectors to handle most of the work. However, the clear space below was not large, it was cleft in twain, and while the surrounding forest was a fair windbreak, there would be vile drafts and eddies. "God, into Your hands I give myself," she said; and wondered as often before how Hugh endured his atheism.

Nevertheless, if she waited she would lose courage. Down!

Her descent was wilder still than she had expected. First the clouds were a maelstrom, then she was through them but into a raving blast, then she saw treetops grab at her. The vehicle rolled, pitched, yawed. Had she been an utter fool? She didn't truly want to leave this life…

She made it, and for minutes sat strengthless. When she stirred, she felt her entire body ache from tension. But A'i'ach's hurt was in her. Called by that need, she unharnessed and went forth.

The noise was immense in the black palisade of trees around her, their branches groaned, their crowns foamed; but down on the ground the air, though restless, was quieter, nearly warm. Unseen Argo reddened the clouds, which cast enough glow that she didn't need her flashlight. She found no trace of the slain ouranids. Well, they had no bones; the dromids must have eaten every scrap. What a ghastly supersition—Where was A'i'ach?

She found him after a search. He lay behind a spiny bush, in which he had woven his tendrils to secure himself. His body was deflated to the minimum, an empty sack; but his eyes gleamed, and he could speak, in the shrill, puffing language of his people, which she had come to know was melodious.

"May joy blow upon you. I never hoped for your advent. Welcome you are. Here it has been lonely." A shudder was in that last word. Ouranids could not long stand being parted from their Swarm. Some xenologists believed that with them consciousness was more collective than individual. Jannika rejected that idea, unless perhaps it applied to the different species found in parts of Nearside. A'i'ach had a soul of his own!

She knelt. "How are you?" She could not render his sounds any better than he could hers, but he had learned to interpret.

"It is not overly ill with me, now that you are nigh. I lost blood and gas, but those wounds have closed. Weak, I settled in a tree until the Beasts left. Meanwhile the wind rose. I thought best not to ride it in my state. Yet I could not stay in the tree, I would have been blown away. So I valved out the rest of my gas and crept to this shelter."

The speech held far more than such a bare statement. The denotation was laconic and stoical, the connotations not. A'i'ach would need at least a day to regenerate sufficient hydrogen for ascent—how long depended on how much food he could reach in his crippled condition—unless a carnivore found him first, which was quite likely. Jannika imagined what a flood of suffering, dread, and bravery would have come over her had she been wearing her helmet.

She gathered the flaccid form into her arms. It weighed little. It felt warm and silky. He cooperated as well as he was able. Just the same, part of him dragged on the ground, which must have been painful.

She must be rougher still, hauling on folds of skin, when she brought him inside the aircraft. It had scant room to spare; he was practically bundled into the rear section. Rather than apologizing when he moaned, or saying anything in particular, she sang to him. He didn't know the ancient Terrestrial words, but he liked the tunes and realized what she meant by them.

She had equipped her vehicle for basic medical help to natives, and had given it on past occasions. A'i'ach's injuries were not deep, because most of him was scarcely more than a bag; however, the bag had been torn in several places and, though it was self-sealing, flight would reopen it unless it got reinforcement. Applying local anesthetics and antibiotics—that much had been learned about Medean biochemistry—she stitched the gashes.

"There, you can rest," she said when, cramped, sweat-soaked, and shaky, she was done. "Later I will give you an injection of gas and you can rise immediately if you choose. I think, though, we would both be wisest to wait out the gale."

A human would have groaned: "It is *tight* in here."

"Yes, I know what you mean, but—A'i'ach, let me put my helmet on." She pointed. "That will join our spirits as they were joined before. It may take your mind off your discomfort. And at this short range, given our new knowledge—" A thrill went through her. "What may we not find out?"

"Good," he agreed. "We may enjoy unique experiences." The concept of discovery for its own sake was foreign to him…but his search for pleasures went far beyond hedonism.

Eager despite her weariness, she moved into her seat and reached for the apparatus. The radio receiver, always open to the standard carrier band, chose that moment to buzz.

Argo in the east glowered at the nearing, lightning-shot wall of storm in the north. Below, the clouds already present roiled in reds and darknesses. Wind wailed. Hugh's aircraft lurched and bucked. Despite a heater, chill seeped through the canopy, as if brought by the light of stars and moons.

"Jan, are you there?" he called. "Are you all right?"

Her voice was a swordstroke of deliverance. "Hugh? Is that you, darling?"

"Yes, sure, who the hell else did you expect? I woke up, played your message, and—Are you all right?"

"Quite safe. But I don't dare take off in this weather. And you mustn't try to land, that would be too dangerous by now. You shouldn't stay, either. Darling, *rostomily*, that you came!"

"Judas priest, sweetheart, how could I not? Tell me what's happened."

She explained. At the end, he nodded a head which still ached a bit from liquor in spite of a nedolor tablet. "Fine," he said. "You wait for calm air, pump up your friend, and come on home." An idea he had been nursing nudged him. "Uh, I wonder. Do you think he could go down into that gulch and recover Erakoum's unit? Those things are scarce, you know." He paused. "I suppose it'd be too much to ask him to throw a little soil over her."

Jannika's tone held pity. "I can do that."

"No, you can't. I got a clear impression from Erakoum as she was falling, before she cracked her skull apart or whatever she did. Nobody can climb down without a rope secured on top. It'd be impossible to return. Even with a rope, it'd be crazy dangerous. Her companions didn't attempt anything, did they?"

Reluctance: "I'll ask him. It may be asking a lot. Is the unit functional?"

"Hm, yes, I'd better check on that first. I'll report in a minute or three. Love you."

He did, he knew, no matter how often she enraged him. The idea that, somewhere in the abysses of his being, he might have wished her death, was not to be borne. He'd have followed her through a heavier tempest than this, merely to deny it.

Well, he could go home with a satisfied conscience and wait for her arrival, after which—what? The uncertainty made a hollowness in him.

His instrument flashed green. Okay, Erakoum's button was transmitting, therefore unharmed and worth salvaging. If only she herself—

He tensed. The breath rattled in his lungs. Did he *know* she was dead?

He lowered the helmet over his temples. His hands shook, giving him trouble in making the connections. He pressed the switch. He willed to perceive—

Pain twisted like white-hot wires, strength ebbed and ebbed, soft waves of nothingness flowed ever more often, but still Erakoum defied. The slit of sky that she could see, from where she lay unable to creep further, was full of wind....She shocked to complete awareness. Again she sensed Hugh's presence.

"Broken bones, feels like. Heavy blood loss. She'll die in a few more hours. Unless you give her first aid, Jan. Then she ought to last till we can fly her to Port Kato for complete attention."

"Oh, I can do sewing and bandaging and splinting, whatever, yes. And nedolor's an analgesic stimulant for dromids too, isn't it? And simply a drink of water could make the whole difference; she must be dehydrated. But how to reach her?"

"Your ouranid can lift her up, after you've inflated him."

"You can't be serious! A'i'ach's hurt, convalescent—and Erakoum tried to kill him!"

"That was mutual, right?"

"Well—"

"Jan, I'm not going to abandon her. She's down in a grave, who used to run free, and the touch of me she's getting is more to her than I could have imagined. I'll stay till she's rescued, or else I'll stay till she dies."

"No, Hugh, you mustn't. The storm."

"I'm not trying to blackmail you, dearest. In fact, I won't blame your ouranid much if he refuses. But I can't leave Erakoum. I just plain can't."

"I...I have learned something about you....I will try."

A'i'ach had not understood his Jannika. It was not believable that helping a Beast could help bring peace. That creature was what it was, a slaughterer. And yet, yet, once there had been no trouble with the Beasts, once they had been the animals which most interested and entertained the People. He himself remembered songs about their fleetness and their fires. In those lost days they had been called the Flame Dancers.

What made him yield to her plea was unclear in his spirit. She had probably saved his life, at hazard to her own, and this was an overpowering new thought to him. He wanted greatly to maintain his union with her, which enriched his world, and therefore hesitated to deny a request that seemed as urgent as hers. Through the union, she helmeted, he believed he felt what she did when she said, with water running from her eyes, "I want to heal what I have done—" and that kind of feeling was transcendent, like the Shining Time, and was what finally decided him.

She assisted him from the thing-which-bore-her and payed out a tube. Through the latter he drank gas, a wind-rush of renewed life. His injuries twinged when his globe expanded, but he could ignore that.

He needed her anchoring weight to get across the ground to the ravine. Fingers and tendrils intertwined, they nevertheless came near being carried away. Had he let himself swell to full size, he could have lifted her. Air harried and hooted, snatched at him, wanted to cast him among thorns—how horrible the ground was!

How much worse to descend below it. He throbbed to an emotion he scarcely recognized. Had she been in rapport, she could have told him that the English word for it was "terror." A human or a dromid who felt it in that degree would have recoiled from the drop. A'i'ach made it a force blowing him onward, because this too raised him out of himself.

At the edge, she threw her arms around him as far as they would go, laid her mouth to his pelt, and said, "Good luck, dear A'i'ach, dear brave A'i'ach, good luck, God keep you." Those were the noises she made in her language. He did not recognize the gesture either.

A cylinder she had given him to hold threw a strong beam of light. He saw the jagged slope tumble downward underneath him, and thought that if he was cast against that, he was done for. Then his spirit would have a fearful journey, with no body to shelter it, before it reached Beyond—if it did, if it was not shredded and scattered first. Quickly, before the churning airs could take full hold of him, he jetted across the brink. He contracted. He sank.

The dread as gloom and walls closed in was like no other carouse in his life. At its core, he felt incandescently aware. Yes, the human had brought him into strange skies.

Through the dankness he caught an odor more sharp. He steered that way. His flash picked out the Beast, sprawled on sharp talus, gasping and glaring. He used jets and siphon to position himself out of reach and said in what English he had, "I haff ch'um say-aff ee-you."

—From the depths of her deathplace, Erakoum looked up at the Flyer. She could barely make him out, a big pale moon behind a glare of light. Amazement heaved her out of a drowse. Had her enemy pursued her down here in his ill-wishing?

Good! She would die in battle, not the torment which ripped her. "Come on and fight," she called hoarsely. If she could sink teeth in him, get a last lick of his blood— The memory of that taste was like sweet lightning. During the time afterward which refused to end, she had thought she would be dead already if she had not swallowed those drops.

Their wonder-working had faded out. She stirred, seeking a defensive posture. Agony speared through her, followed by night.

When she roused, the Flyer still waited. Amidst a roaring in her ears, she heard, over and over, "I haff ch'um say-aff ee-you."

Human language? This was the being that the humans favored as they did her. It had to be, though the ray from its head was hidden by the ray from its tendrils. Could Hugh have been bound all the while to both?

Erakoum strove to form syllables never meant for her mouth and throat. "Ha-watt-tt you ha-wannit? Gho, no bea haiar, gho."

The Flyer made a response. She could no more follow that than he appeared to have followed hers. He must have come down to make sure of her, or simply to mock her while she died. Erakoum scrabbled weakly after a spear. She couldn't throw one, but—

From the unknownness wherein dwelt the soul of Hugh, she suddenly knew: He wants to save you.

Impossible. But...but there the Flyer was. Half-delirious, Erakoum could yet remember that Flyers were seldom that patient.

What else could befall but death? Nothing. She lay back on the rock shards. Let the Flyer be her doom or be her Mardudek. She had found the courage to surrender.

The shape hovered. Her hair sensed tiny gusts, and she thought dimly that this must be a difficult place for him too. Speech burst and skirled. He was trying to explain something, but she was too hurt and tired to listen. She folded her hands around her muzzle. Would he appreciate that gesture?

Maybe. Hesitant, he neared. She kept motionless. Even when his tendrils brushed her, she kept motionless.

They slipped across her body, got a purchase, tightened. Through the haze of pain, she saw him swelling. He meant to lift her—up to Hugh?

When he did, her knife wounds opened and she shrieked before she swooned.

Her next knowledge was of lying on turf under a hasty, red-lit sky. A human crouched above her, talking to a small box that replied in the voice of Hugh. Behind, the Flyer lay shrunken, clutching a bush. Storm brawled; the first stinging raindrops fell.

In the hidden way of hunters, she knew that she was dying. The human might staunch those cuts and stabs, but could not give back what was lost.

Memory—what she had heard tell, what she had briefly tasted herself—"Blood of the Flyer. It will save me. Blood of the Flyer, if he will give." She was not sure whether she spoke or dreamed it. She sank back into the darkness.

When she surfaced anew, the Flyer was beside her, embracing her against the wind. The human was carefully using a knife on a tendril. The Flyer brought the tendril in between Erakoum's fangs. As the rain's full violence began, she drank.—

A double sunrise was always lovely.

Jannika had delayed telling Hugh her news. She wanted to surprise him, preferably after his anxiety about his dromid was past. Well, it was; Erakoum would be hospitalized several days in Port Kato, which ought to be an interesting experience for all concerned, but she would get well. A'i'ach had already rejoined his Swarm.

When Hugh wakened from the sleep of exhaustion which followed his bedside vigil, Jannika proposed a dawn picnic, and was touched at how fast he agreed. They flitted to a place they knew on the sea cliffs, spread out their food, and sat down to watch.

At first Argo, the stars, and a pair of moons were the only lights. Slowly heaven brightened, the ocean shimmered silver beneath blue, Phrixus and Helle wheeled by the great planet. Wild songs went trilling through air drenched with an odor of roanflower, which is like violets.

"I got the word from the Center," she declared while she held his hand. "It's definite. The chemistry was soon unraveled, given the extra clue we had from the reviving effect of blood."

He turned about. "What?"

"Manganese deficiency," she said. "A trace element in Medean biology, but vital, especially to dromids and their reproduction—and evidently to something else in ouranids, since they concentrate it to a high degree. Hansonia turns out to be poorly supplied with it. Ouranids, going west to die, were removing a significant percentage from the ecology. The answer is simple. We need not try to change the ouranid belief. Temporarily, we can have a manganese supplement made up and offer it to the dromids. In the long run, we can mine the ore where it's plentiful and scatter it as a dust across the island. Your friends will live, Hugh."

He was quiet for a time. Then—he could surprise her, this son of an outback miner—he said: "That's terrific. The engineering solution. But the bitterness won't go away overnight. We won't see any quick happy ending. Maybe not you and me, either." He seized her to him. "Damnation, though, let's try!"

UNTITLED LIMERICK

An astronomer's swift limousine
went through a red light in Racine
  He was going so fast
  that the light which he passed,
through Doppler effect, showed as green.

Acknowledgments

The following people helped make this book possible.

Technical help was provided by Dave Grubbs and Alice Lewis.

Proofreading was done by David Anderson, Ann Broomhead, Jim Burton, David Cantor, Lis Carey, Anne Crimmins, Gay Ellen Dennett, Suford Lewis, Tony Lewis, Mark Olson, Priscilla Olson, Joe Ross, Jean Rossner, Sharon Sbarsky, and Tim Szczesuil.

A further round of proofing was then done by Suford Lewis, Jean Rossner and Sharon Sbarsky.

Dave Grubbs then did the final proofing of the book

Alice Lewis did her magic in producing the dust jacket.

Special thanks to Tom Easton for his introduction to the book and Karen Anderson who provided another nifty picture of Poul Anderson.

Rick Katze, editor
May 2010

Superlative SF Available from the NESFA Press

Call Me Joe (volume 1) by Poul Anderson $29

The Queen of Air and Darkness (volume 2) by Poul Anderson $29

Major Ingredients by Eric Frank Russell $29

Entities by Eric Frank Russell $29

Flights of Eagles by James Blish $29

Brothers in Arms by Lois McMaster Bujold $25

Robots and Magic by Lester Del Rey $29

The Mathematics of Magic
  by L. Sprague de Camp & Fletcher Pratt $26

The Masque of Mañana by Robert Sheckley $29

Magic Mirrors by John Bellairs $25

Transfinite: The Essential A. E. van Vogt $29

This Mortal Mountain (volume 3) by Roger Zelazny $29

Last Exit to Babylon (volume 4) by Roger Zelazny $29

Nine Black Doves (volume 5) by Roger Zelazny $29

The Road to Amber (volume 6) by Roger Zelazny $29

Details on these books and many others are available online at: www.nesfa. org/press/. Books may be ordered online or by writing to:

NESFA Press, PO Box 809, Framingham MA 01701

We accept checks (in US $), MasterCard, or Visa. Please add $4 P&H for one book, $8 for an order of two to five books, and $2/book for orders of six or more. For foreign orders, $12/book for one or two books, $36 for three to five books, and $6/book for 6 or more books. Please allow 3-4 weeks. for delivery. (Overseas, allow 2 months or more. Massachusetts residents please add 6.255% sales tax. Fax orders (Visa/MC only): (617) 776-3243.

NESFA Press

Post Office Box 809
Framingham, MA 01701
www.nesfa.org/press
2010